Balancing

on the

Wire

Balancing
on the
~~Wire~~
The Art of
Managing
Media

James Redmond and Robert Trager
University of Memphis • University of Colorado

coursewise
publishing
inc.

Boulder • Bellevue • Dubuque • Madison

Our mission at **coursewise** is to help students make connections—linking theory to practice and the classroom to the outside world. Learners are motivated to synthesize ideas when course materials are placed in a context they recognize. By providing gateways to contemporary and enduring issues, **coursewise** publications will expand students' awareness of and context for the course subject.

For more information on **coursewise** visit us at our web site: http://www.coursewise.com

coursewise publishing editorial staff

Thomas Doran, ceo/publisher: Journalism/Marketing/Speech
Edgar Laube, publisher: Geography/Political Science/Psychology/Sociology
Linda Meehan Avenarius, publisher: **courselinks**
Sue Pulvermacher-Alt, publisher: Education/Health/Gender Studies
Victoria Putman, publisher: Anthropology/Philosophy/Religion
Tom Romaniak, publisher: Business/Criminal Justice/Economics

coursewise publishing production staff

Victoria Putman, Production Manager
Lori Blosch, Permissions Coordinator
Mary Monner, Production Coordinator

Cover design and interior design by Scan Graphics
Cover art by Jeff Storm

The credits for this book appear on page 447 and are considered an extension of the copyright page.

Library of Congress Catalog Card Number: 98–071001

ISBN 0–395–93849X

Printed in the United States of America by **coursewise publishing, Inc.**
1379 Lodge Lane, Boulder, CO 80303

10 9 8 7 6 5 4 3 2 1

contents

foreword

This book is a product of more than two decades of experience in, and the study of, media organizations. It provides prospective and current media managers with considerable pertinent, useful information developed from rigorous academic research, court decisions, legislative actions, and our experience in the mass media, all presented in a readable and interesting way. We have included material from diverse disciplines that come together in the media manager's world, including ethics, law, marketing, mass communication theory, planning, psychology, and sociology. Our text is not meant to supplant further study in those areas, but to provide a foundation for you as a manager.

Media managers typically are people who have worked their way out of what they did very well, into what they never intended to do. There are many media managers who were so good at their former jobs—for example, reporter, news producer, agency or promotion department creative director—they literally were promoted out of them. This may happen to you. When it does, you enter a world for which much of your training and experience has not prepared you. Instead of driving yourself with your own internal, creative passions you have to motivate others, some of whom care little about their work beyond the hourly wage. And when you are a media manager, you find yourself dealing with bureaucratic processes and budgets. You also may manage people like you—dedicated media professionals who believe they know how to perform their jobs and would prefer not to have management interfere. But, now, you are management.

It is one thing to be a talented individual creating Pulitzer Prize- or Emmy award-winning journalism, and quite another to manage others to achieve that level of success. The media manager, like the conductor of a symphony orchestra, brings together many disparate personalities and instruments to become a cohesive team capable of superior achievement beyond what each individual can do alone. To be a successful media manager takes a great deal of knowledge and creativity. We hope this book provides some of that knowledge and helps you understand how to manage creatively in a media environment.

ACKNOWLEDGMENTS

The authors and **coursewise publishing** would like to thank the following individuals for their helpful input on the manuscript:

Professor Steven Helle, University of Illinois at Urbana–Champaign
Professor John Katich, University of Kansas
Professor Steven Anderson, Utah State Univeristy
Mary Rossa, freelance developmental editor

Their comments and suggestions are greatly appreciated.

INTRODUCTION

BALANCING ON THE WIRE: THE ART OF MANAGING MEDIA ORGANIZATIONS

Managing media organizations is exciting and personally rewarding. You can truly make a difference as a media manager, both to the people with whom you work, and to the public you and your media organization serve. But to manage media organizations effectively you need as many tools and as much knowledge as possible at your disposal. This text will give you a solid foundation on which to build your personal effectiveness and a sense of the real challenges of managing contemporary media. Here you will find a blend of material from the fields of psychology, sociology, business management, law, and journalism.

Media organizations are complex. The people in them are inherently challenging to manage. To succeed you need insight into human nature and a broad understanding of the dynamic contemporary media environment.

MANAGERIAL ART, SCIENCE, AND THE "WALLENDA FACTOR"

Media management combines the art and science of organizational and human dynamics. Although it may seem relatively simple on the surface, it is intriguing in its complexity and highly rewarding in its achievement. Effective media managers blend the power of personality and basic management skills within the complex, subjective arena of media product creation. Managerial techniques and principles that are often third-person distant concepts in textbooks are suddenly first-person experiences of the everyday world. The reality of managing others blends our analytical knowledge with the nuances of us as human beings. The management equation, then, encompasses cold facts and passionate emotions within ourselves and all those around us. To be an effective media manager you have to be intelligent about what you are doing while holding onto the passion for being a creative media person. Media organizations are special places full of special people, often with very special missions in society. Running such an organization is like managing no other.

Virtually any reasonably intelligent person can study the research, theories, and concepts of effective management. But applying those things in such a way that our artistic, creative employees buy into our managerial vision takes great care and understanding. Like any other art form, some of the managerial art is buried deep within our sense of self. It is driven by our view of the world around us and the way we engage with others. You can readily recall people others follow willingly or who, regardless of their official position in an organization, have the ability to get others to do things. The social skills that you began developing on childhood playgrounds are as important in moving your organization forward as your technical understanding of intricate organizational designs and hierarchical systems. Fundamentally, organizations are simply structures within which the human interrelationships evolve.

The roles of leader and manager are sometimes merged within a single person, but not always. Leaders can be good managers, and managers can be good leaders. But many of us really are one or the other, as will be discussed later in this text. Successful leaders generally view themselves very positively. They tend to have what has been called a "Wallenda factor," a metaphor for legendary high wire walker Karl Wallenda (Bennis & Nanus, 1985). He would walk on the thin strand high above the floor of an arena and never focus on the danger to such a degree that it would make him nervous and cause him to fall. He just walked across the wire. He focused on the success of what he was doing with total confidence. If there had been significant doubt in his mind, he would have started wobbling around and fallen. But instead Karl Wallenda concentrated on getting to where he wanted to go and went there. Confidence and a clear sense of direction are paramount.

As a media manager you need great confidence in yourself. And confidence is strengthened by knowledge, which this text will help provide. It is the straitjacket of the fear of failure that so often immobilizes us and that usually flows from ignorance and uncertainty. But high achievers tend to acquire the necessary knowledge and operational technique so that they have no reason to fear. Fear has no place in the mind of someone who knows what to do and how to do it. Such individuals are just like you. They want to be better at what they do, so they go after the knowledge, and then practice a great deal on the techniques necessary to accomplish their goal. That's true regardless of the vocation involved. Truly great athletes, artists, and leaders are not conceited about their talent, merely supremely confident of their abilities. They are confident because they continually hone those abilities through practice and self-analysis. A person who will not spend the time playing the scales cannot hope to play the piano very well. And so it goes for being a manager. Successful people usually have a powerful vision of where they want to go, or what they want to accomplish, and they work extremely hard to perfect themselves so they can do it. They take whatever natural talent or ability they have and then through hard work hone it to a superior level. Such exceptional people tend to manifest their focused, clear-eyed approach to most aspects of their lives, not just their job. As a Chinese restaurant fortune cookie revealed one day, "Your happiness is intertwined with your outlook on life."

LEAPING INTO THE "CHASM" OF MANAGEMENT

Media managers often are chosen from people who hold creative jobs, such as reporting, editing, and producing. These people often have little knowledge of, or preparation for, the business side of media organizations. So, though they may know the newsroom side of things, they are seriously deficient on the business side of media organizations. In effect, they learn by doing and, hopefully, by having the chance to observe other good managers on the way up and by having a strong mentor. But that means luck has a great deal to do with their effectiveness. Having good role models is one thing. Having bad ones is quite another. A recent national study found that 84.4 percent of one group of media managers had learned their jobs by observing others and then doing the job. In other words, they only learned how to do the job through experience, with little real advance knowledge. And nearly two-thirds of them indicated they had received neither college course work nor corporate seminar training in management (Redmond, 1993). Media managers tend to get promoted to a management role because they are good at something else. They write great copy because they love writing. They tend to work well individually and are self-directed. That's the nature of a writer's or reporter's work. But then, as an ironic penalty for their own success, we give them a little more money, a new title, and other creative people to oversee. The news division head for one of the nation's top television station chains described it this way:

> Someone is good as a journalist. He or she gets promoted, and then suddenly they make that leap off into the chasm of management. And probably without much preparation. Nowhere in their professional career are they confronted with this until the moment of truth when suddenly they're promoted. They're promoted 'cause they're real good, and then it's almost as if they're thrown off into an entirely alien universe. (Redmond, 1992)

But it's only an "alien universe" because they haven't prepared themselves, as you are doing in this course of study.

Increasingly complex business environments require decision makers to be able to balance the competing forces of economic goals, personal values, and the definitive values of the corporation by using techniques such as process models and systematic decision analysis (Kirrane, 1990). As resources decline, managers need to increase productivity for an organization to maintain the same level of performance as before the resource reduction. The job of management has been described as focusing on the identification of what makes organizations, groups, and individuals more effective (Gibson, Ivancevich, & Donnelly, 1997). However, a person who has developed skill at doing daily media production work, such as reporting, writing, editing, layout, design, or creating campaign concepts in an advertising or public relations agency, may not inherently possess the skills for the very different "job of management." One media manager said, in retrospect, nothing actually prepared him to be a manager. At first, he said, he felt out of place at department head meetings where "they were all talking Greek." Then, after several years as a newsroom manager his employees suggested he was too far removed from the day-to-day operation as he was increasingly involved in managerial responsibilities such as budgeting and strategic planning (Redmond, 1993).

Increasingly, in the climb up the corporate ladder, media managers need to expand their knowledge in a different direction from the focus of a production journalist. As a manager, daily tasks include budgeting and conveying the journalist's point of view to corporate executives who don't always understand the greater purpose of "informing the public," a philosophy to which many working journalists subscribe. As such, the media manager is a representative of the working journalist to the corporate world, and at the same time the representative of corporate back to the world of writers, photographers, and other creative professionals. Thus, the media manager has a foot in each of two worlds. When you do it well, it is a superbly rewarding experience at the center of a swirl of different viewpoints and concerns, weaving them together like a great tapestry. It's a boundary-spanning role where so much depends on everything you do. There is a great sense of responsibility, but of power and control, too. In a realistic sense you are the hub of a media organization wheel around which turn the organizational forces. A leading media organization consultant described the middle manager as being

> in charge of . . . supervising or oversighting [sic] all aspects of an organization that creates news products, a whole variety. . . . He must deal with labor negotiations; must deal with talent contracts; must deal with budgets, not just annual budgets but month in, month out budgets; must deal with logistics; must deal with special program production; must deal with innumerable personnel problems, and must deal with shaping the over-all marketing plan. (Redmond, 1992)

The result can be a tremendous sense of achievement and great personal reward for those who do it well. Growing as a manager is one of the ways you can expand your horizons. But that means growing in a different way than you would as a columnist, reporter, or photographer. Some media managers may strive to be managers to acquire the money, power, and prestige. The rewards of the job are centered in the sense of accomplishment in moving people and an organization in the direction you want them to go. It takes a lot of work in acquiring knowledge, as you are doing right now. And it takes a lot of work in then applying that knowledge to the vibrant human context that is a newspaper, television station, magazine, advertising or public relations agency, or any other creative media context. But when all that is done, few things will bring you as great a sense of accomplishment. For when a person engages with your media organization, in a very real sense they engage with you. Media management is a very personalized kind of management where you serve individual human beings (your audience or readers) things (your media product) that really matter to them (news, information, entertainment) and in the process make life more fulfilling.

THE MEDIA MANAGER'S PRESSURED WORLD

All media managers operate under a lot of pressure. This can be seen by looking at contemporary television news directors. They operate in a world with intense pressure to produce ratings success (Flander, 1986). The career field is notorious for substantial turnover (Stone, V., 1987, 1992, 1997a). The demands of the job include managing budgetary issues, implementing market research, selecting and motivating staffs in high-stress environments, supervising newscast content, and engaging in strategic thinking for a dynamically changing industry (Flander, 1986). The working environment is stressful due to the intensely competitive nature of television news. On top of that, the 1980s and 1990s featured significant changes in television station ownership and federal deregulation, which put even more pressure on newsroom managers. Corporate owners expanded news programming as a way to maintain a local identity in the fragmenting world of mass media, and to generate more profitable local advertising. At the same time, industrywide, there was a focus on cutting costs and maximizing productivity. Thus, contemporary television news directors are faced with trying to hold their audience share against increasing competition amid continuing pressure to trim budgets due to declining station revenues that focus owners and managers on the financial bottom line (Stone, V., 1987, 1997a).

Former University of Missouri journalism professor Vernon Stone conducted annual surveys of news directors during the 1980s and 1990s. Throughout the period, though some small adjustments occurred from year to year, a general picture emerged of people prone to short tenure at their stations. For most of the period the average television news director lasted a little more than two years at a station, worked 55 to 60 hours a week, had been at three or four different stations in his or her career, and spent more time working on managerial concerns than with journalism issues. In general, Stone's data show an upward trend in the average number of years in news and the number of years in management for news directors. Meantime, the length of time a news director, on average, remained at a given station dropped from 2.7 years in 1972, to 2.0 years in 1986, and then began increasing in 1992 and 1993 (Stone, V., 1986, 1987, 1992, 1997a) (see Fig. I.1).

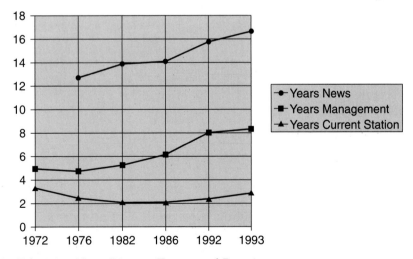

Figure I.1   Television News Director Tenure and Experience

The rise of women in the position of news director has been significant from 1972 to 1996. In 1972 only two women held news director positions of the 630 then available. But by 1996 just over 24 percent of television newsrooms were being run by women, 205 of 850 news director positions (Stone, V., 1997b). The dramatic change is shown in Figure I.2.

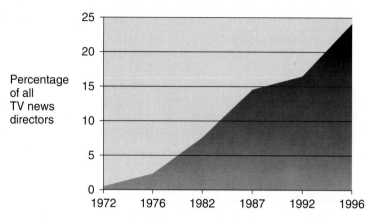

Figure I.2 Women as News Directors, 1972–1996
(Source: Vernon Stone, University of Missouri)

Interestingly, minorities have not fared as well in newsroom management. Stone's data for the first 4 years of the 1990s show news director positions held by minorities dropping slightly from 10 percent in 1990 to just under 8 percent in 1994. That compares to a sharp increase for women toward the end of the period (Stone, V., 1997c) (see Fig. I.3).

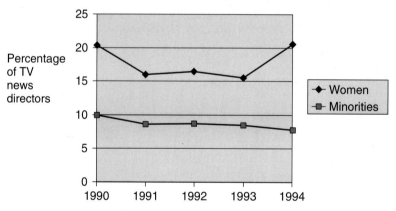

Figure I.3 Minority and Women News Directors, 1990–1994
(Source: Vernon Stone, University of Missouri)

Finally, overall television newsroom employment indicates a majority of positions filled by white men in 1996 (see Fig. I.4). White women composed 28 percent of the workforce, with minority women employed in 10 percent of the positions and minority men holding 8 percent (Stone, V., 1997c).

Stone's two decades of annual studies demonstrates that although news directors are seasoned news and management professionals, they have trouble with job stability

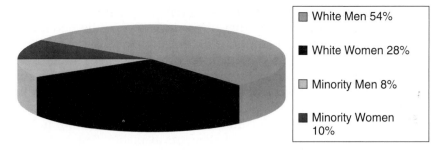

Figure I.4 Newsroom Employment, 1996
(Source: Vernon Stone, University of Missouri)

once they become department heads. The inherent stress of the job may be a factor. One way to escape stress is to quit and move on. Another factor appears to be the penchant for television station general managers to demand instant fixes to ratings problems, since ratings determine station revenues. Stone's news director data are industry means. Thus, significant numbers of news directors are at a station much less than two years or more than two years. A previous observation about the career field remains valid for hundreds of television news directors: "The life expectancy of a news director at a station is more like 18 months. Three years in the job is a career" (Vitale, 1987, p. 38).

Think for a moment, and see if you can name another job that offers as much immediate challenge and, when successful, any greater sense of accomplishment. That is precisely why so many news directors keep at their profession. It's tough, it's often unforgiving, and when you succeed despite the odds, the feeling of achievement is like few others.

THE HOMOGENIZATION OF THE AMERICAN MEDIA

As a media manager, one of the problems you will encounter is the pressure to use what works in one place as the solution to a problem in another. That is most evident, again, with television news partly because of the transitory nature of news directors. As they move from market to market they take with them their experiences of what works and what does not. Additionally, the pervasive television news consulting business promotes formulaic approaches involving market research studies to determine what viewers of a particular station want, and then providing the packaging to satisfy those wants.

Every segment of the media industry has consultants, and unless you, as a media manager, understand that their advice has to be weighed and situationally applied, they can do as much harm as good. Any successful news director, newspaper editor, or advertising or public relations professional will tell you that each community has unique aspects, different attitudes, and cultural differences that demand market-specific approaches. So, to be an effective media manager, you have to be aware that the contemporary trends are toward sameness, but the audience needs are still very community-specific. Consultants, who advise media clients across all regional and cultural areas of the world, may be as responsible as any other factor for the emphasis on entertainment and presentation factors in media content and the concurrent movement away from traditional news coverage in favor of more audience-friendly content determined by market studies. The result is a homogenization of viewers despite dissimilar communities in widely diverse geographic and cultural areas. Morgan (1986) found that, with respect to television consumption, "Across nine regions of the U.S. and a wide variety of dependent variables, heavy viewers were more concentrated and homogeneous, even with demographic controls taken into account" (p. 135).

Each media organization necessarily tailors its products to the technology that is fundamental to its corner of the industry. While newspapers and magazines focus on the printed word, audio media emphasize the importance of sound. In television, the visual element, the picture, dominates newscast content selection. Visual technology is what differentiates television news from other forms of journalistic endeavor. Thus, television news covers stories that lend themselves to being filmed or videotaped and provide "immediacy." What is considered worthy of coverage is tied inextricably to the technology of the medium delivering it (Gans, 1980, p. 158). Television newscast producers focus on the video elements available, first and foremost, and then fill in holes in the newscast with stories the anchors will read on camera. So what is included in a television newscast may or may not be "news" in the traditional sense, though it will almost always be visually stimulating. It is not uncommon to see car wreck footage leading newscasts in major markets, wrecks that are inconsequential for everyone but the few people actually involved. Yet there is usually little coverage of legislative action that affects everyone in the state. Car wrecks make good pictures, with the banged-up fenders and police lights blinking, but shots of the state senate chamber are inherently boring. And complicated issues are harder to explain, often requiring more time than the industry standard of 1 minute, 30 seconds for a "package" story from a reporter. Television favors the exciting and simplistic but discourages the visually dull and complex (Yardley, 1992).

Another contributing factor to a similarity among American media is the steady coalescence of media organizations and outlets into the hands of a very small ownership elite. Ben Bagdikian (1992) has studied this phenomenon extensively. A Pulitzer Prize—winning newspaper journalist, Bagdikian went on to a successful second career in university research and teaching as a professor at the Graduate School of Journalism at the University of California, Berkeley. Through four editions of his heavily researched analysis of media ownership and interlocking corporate board memberships, Bagdikian charted the steady coalescence of media ownership in the United States from 50 major corporations in 1983 to 20 in 1992.

> Although there are sometimes hundreds or even thousands of small firms sharing the market that remains, the power of these scattered smaller firms is negligible. They operate in a world shaped by the giants. For example, there are more than 3,000 publishers of books, but five produce most of the revenue. (Bagdikian, 1992, p. ix)

Ownership concentration, combined with the rise of expensive and elaborate mass media technologies, has encouraged the homogenization of American media. It is cheaper for a television station chain to buy a graphics package and news set design for all its stations at one time than for each station to buy those things individually. Simple economies of scale benefit the chain owner in media company just as in the drugstore business. Chains also tend to spread their management and content philosophies throughout their properties. What works in one unit of the company is often then transferred to another.

Homogenization of media occurs when there is a sameness in content and form across regions of the country and from town to town. Although individual story facts may be unique, the format, placement, visual treatment, and follow-up coverage tend to become predictable as accepted conventions are spread through the media professions and among media outlets. The result can be an interesting feeling when, for example, you are in a hotel room in Seattle watching a newscast that looks just like the one in Cleveland. Or you pick up the morning paper and, except for the publication name at the top, you could be in just about any other big American city.

THE DIFFICULT COMBINATION

The complex pressures media managers face as we enter the 21st century can be illustrated by looking at the news side of the business. Under the American model, media are supported, with few exceptions, through advertising. This uneasily blends the need to generate as large an audience as possible by entertaining people with a social responsibility to provide news and information to the public. As Liebling (1961/1981) so aptly put it, "The function of the press in society is to inform, but its role is to make money" (p. 6). For example, news is redefined as simply another form of commercial speech when marketing studies designed to increase audience shares for advertisers drive the journalistic content. Increasing audience, in contemporary American media, is not only about being able to communicate ideas to more people. It is also fundamentally about delivering those people, as a commodity, to the commercials and display advertisements imbedded within the journalism product. Without an audience, which ratings and newspaper circulation studies measure, the work of the journalist cannot be accomplished. Buildings, people, paper, ink, electricity, and all the technology it takes to produce modern media in their many forms are primarily funded by advertising.

The American concept of the mass media pursuing truth is today based on whatever truth will generate as large an audience as possible for the real main event, the advertisement. That often means a preference for highly visual, fast-paced, simplistic, positive, and easy-to-comprehend content over the complex and seriously analytical. It is a marriage of information and entertainment into what is increasingly referred to in television as "infotainment."

For example, because the firms that measure the performance of television stations announce well in advance when they will do their audience measurements, there is a built-in tendency to manipulate the outcome. Every year, the A. C. Nielsen company conducts television ratings in every market in the nation in the months of November, February, May, and July. These are called "sweeps." It is a game in which all the participants pledge themselves not to inflate the numbers artificially but then do just that in sometimes blatant and contrived ways. Stations win with higher advertising revenues. Advertising agencies win with higher commissions on higher rates. There are only two losers in this game: (1) the advertiser who buys audience exposures that may not exist, but are merely illusions based on promotional hype during the measurement period, and (2) the consumer to whom the cost of advertising is passed.

Emotionally charged stories are sometimes included as a kind of manufactured reality contrived to match market study analysis of the kinds of things the station audience wants to see (Blacklow, 1992). It is not uncommon for so-called hot-button series topics to be fashionable across the country in a given year, with stations in one market duplicating a series that seemed to raise viewer interest in another. Series topic lists are sometimes circulated among news directors. For example, in the fall of 1996 television stations in Memphis, Tennessee, were involved in the trend of featuring reporters in contrived docudramas coping with various high-risk situations. Those ranged from stories about dealing with muggers, with a reporter masquerading as a mugger, to escaping from burning buildings, to what to do if your car ends up in a lake filling up with water. Theoretically, the point of such "special reports," which set up the reporter as "our hero" in the minidrama, is to help the audience protect themselves from a danger they'll likely encounter. However, as Memphis *Commercial Appeal* television columnist Tom Walter pointed out, while an estimated 350 people drown in automobiles a year, getting caught in your car by rising waters is "not exactly an immediate danger to the rest of the country's approximately 260,000,000 people" (Walter, 1996, p. C1). But it was exciting footage of "our hero," the reporter, extricating himself from a car filling up with water in a lake.

Within the framework of media organizations, a sometimes wide gulf exists between those who do the work of journalism and those who manage them. For the business owners and senior managers the measure of success is the margin of profit. A successful media company is one whose profit expands and whose stock price escalates. Increasingly, newspapers, broadcast stations, public relations firms, advertising agencies, and other media enterprises are collected under the ever-expanding corporate umbrella.

But for the professionals working within the creative environments of those media organizations, particularly in the traditional "news" operations in both print and electronic media, there is often a greater sense of purpose serving as an undercurrent of motivation. The news media organization itself is seen as a kind of necessary evil by some journalists in their effort to convey the "truth" to the public. They see their role of journalist as one of greater purpose than other vocations—"a calling, not just a job" (Auletta, 1991, p. 559).

Managing such people in an industry with countervailing forces of profit, greed, public service, and pursuit of truth is a complex and challenging role. There is inherent tension among the professions engaged in media organization work. Each specialty has its perspective and its positive and negative contributions to the entire mosaic of the mass media experience. But they are all—newsroom journalists, advertising and public relations specialists, media conglomerate owners, and everyone in between—bound together in the conveyance of messages to an increasingly empowered audience who can instantly disappear with a click of the remote control or computer mouse, or simply by turning the page.

Clearly, to be an effective manager in a media organization you need as much knowledge as possible in several different areas. This text will provide, for the current or aspiring media manager, some of the keys to success. However, it only touches the surface of many management and media organization concepts to provide some basic tools. The literature is vast. Organizational management, as well as finance and accounting, are separate business school professions. Psychology and sociology are different academic disciplines. Indeed, news/editorial, television and radio news, public relations, and advertising are separate disciplines within the general journalism field. But with what is contained here you will have an increased awareness of the complexity of managing media organizations along with a research foundation upon which to build your own personal managerial development as you ascend to the challenge and fulfillment of becoming a superior media manager.

Media organizations are full of exceptional people in the midst of dynamic forces of change. In the American model of journalism the free press is contained within the constraints of advertising, which is the primary funding mechanism to exercise that freedom. In many respects Liebling's (1961/1981, p. 32) observation is true—"freedom of the press is guaranteed only to those who own one." There is a constant struggle between the need to generate a sizable audience and the need to serve a higher social purpose in a democracy based on the concept of an informed public. And a similar struggle occurs on the nonnews side to bring audiences quality entertainment programming.

The great broadcaster Edward R. Murrow described these tensions in a speech to the Radio-TV News Directors Association four decades ago. Although he specifically referred to broadcast news, his description of advertising-based mass media applies across the various media products in today's audience-fragmented world.

One of the basic troubles with radio and television news is that both instruments have grown up as an incompatible combination of show business, advertising and news. Each of the three is a rather bizarre and demanding profession. And when you get all three under one roof, the dust never settles. (Sperber, 1986, p. xvi)

section 1

THE MEDIA INDUSTRIES:
THEIR RISE AND
MANAGEMENT ENVIRONMENT

chapter 1

THE RISE OF THE AMERICAN MEDIA MODEL

EVOLUTION OF THE AMERICAN MODEL OF A FREE PRESS

An extensive discussion of the history of the free press is best left to a text of its own, but a brief overview of how we got to where we are is useful in understanding the reality of contemporary American journalism and media. It has been a journey of technological and philosophical change as the concept of a free press has evolved into what we know today. By understanding the past we can more fully comprehend the present and more intelligently approach the future. To successfully manage in American media it is important to understand the press culture, its undercurrents, and the historical context upon which any defense of the free press must rest.

As the American newspaper rose during the 17th, 18th, and 19th centuries it evolved from simple pamphlets to multiple-page subscription publications. The seeds of the American concept of a free press were planted in the rich earth of rebellion against centralized control of ideas in England during the mid-17th century. It was an evolution beginning with the Reformation, which started a century before, and firmly set into the U.S. Constitution a century and a half later (Emery & Emery, 1996).

The invention of the printing press had radically changed information flow throughout Europe, which was seen by governments in generally negative terms. A struggle ensued over the concept of how best to seek the truth. Where previously truth was handed down from the king or the church, the Reformation fostered heated debate about the most fundamental concepts of religion and government. During the English Civil War (1642–649) the Puritan Roundheads, led by Oliver Cromwell, struggled to defeat King Charles I and in the process relaxed many of the controls on freedom of expression (Grimm, 1965).

John Milton wrote his great argument for open public discourse, the *Areopagitica*, in 1644. He opposed the practice of the English government licensing the press and thereby practicing censorship. His ideas, based in tolerant Calvinism, centered on the belief that only when all ideas are on the table can truth be determined. For, if censorship keeps some ideas out of the debate, for whatever purpose, who can tell if that which is excluded is truth? In *Areopagitica* the great English poet eloquently placed free discourse above all other freedoms. "Give me the liberty to know, to utter, and to argue freely, according to conscience, above all liberties" (Harvey, 1967, p. 38). The practice of licensing printers in England began with Henry VIII. The point of licensing was to keep opposing views out of print. A subsequent struggle occurred throughout the 1600s and 1700s in Europe and later America to escape government censorship and reduce autocratic power. It was a period of expanding tolerance of diverse viewpoints and acceptance of Milton's sense of the inherent necessity to have all ideas included in any search for the truth.

In the nearly century and a half between Milton's argument and the writing of the U.S. Constitution, the idea of an inherent right of individuals to debate publicly any and all ideas attracted a wide following. At the same time, as the industrial revolution expanded, a rising tide of capitalism fostered a new, powerful class of large-scale merchants. The ability to advance diverse points of view, which shared power required in order to build alliances, resulted in the growth of a concept of government as responsive to the general public, not just to an aristocracy. Printing and reading became widespread, as did the importance of having a press through which to communicate with the larger, increasingly literate society (Morison & Commager, 1962).

The result was the First Amendment to the U.S. Constitution, which succinctly states, "Congress shall make no law respecting an establishment of religion, or prohibiting the free exercise thereof; or abridging the freedom of speech, or of the press; or the right of the people peaceably to assemble, and to petition the Government for a redress of grievances" ("The Bill of Rights," 1997). The First Amendment is, then, a later generation's rewriting of Milton's essential marketplace-of-ideas treatise that truth readily emerges from among all other ideas when all are permitted to be heard. The counterlogic was clear. When any idea is kept out of the marketplace of ideas, for whatever reason, who is to know whether that idea might be the truth? And if truth is not allowed into the marketplace, only falsehood prevails, not infrequently in the form of cultural mythologies.

This concept of ensuring a diversity of unfettered viewpoints and voices in the public debate, from which the public determines its sense of right, is a cornerstone of the Western model of journalism (Hachten, 1981). This marketplace-of-ideas view of deriving truth—articulated by Milton, later expanded by John Stuart Mill, and fundamental to Jefferson—was used by U.S. Supreme Court Justice Oliver Wendell Holmes in *Abrams v. United States* (1919). He argued that "the best test of truth is the power of the thought to get itself accepted in the competition of the market" (Francios, 1975, p. 18). In *Miller v. California* (1973) the court reaffirmed the marketplace-of-ideas principle in a landmark obscenity case. Chief Justice Warren Burger argued, in the majority opinion, that "the First Amendment protects works which, taken as a whole, have serious literary, artistic, political or scientific value, regardless of whether the government or a majority of the people approve of the ideas these works represent." He added, "The protection given speech and press was fashioned to assure unfettered interchange of *ideas* for the bringing about of political and social changes desired by the people" (p. 232, emphasis in original, quoting *Roth v. United States* [1957]).

Much of the debate over control of publication ends up in the difficult area of legal definition. Truth is imbedded in perception and, under the Miltonian concept, can best be seen when contrasted with falsehood. Good is obvious, the argument goes, when placed in contrast with the bad. Without the light of truth shining in the marketplace of ideas, the dark side of falsehood, which alone may not clearly be wrong, escapes detection. The problem of detecting falsehood is that it is often muddled, without clear and easily defined definitions that betray it. One must see it side by side with truth to appreciate its falsity. Indeed, Justice Stewart, in *Jacobellis v. Ohio* (1964) said that although specific definition of what is obscenity eluded him, "I know it when I see it" (Franklin & Anderson, 1990, p. 160).

The power of media to do what they will in the marketplace has generally been upheld by the courts with only very narrow constraints in specific circumstances, as discussed further in Chapter 14. That has occurred even though historical research has supported the contention that the framers of the Constitution didn't conceive of a mass media–centered marketplace culture with ideas as entertainment commodity, nor of a multimillion dollar pornography industry that would rise in the wake of the First Amendment. They were concerned with political speech—the right to openly criticize the government (formerly the king) and arguing the great issues of the day in a democratic forum. Simply put, "the Framers either did not appreciate, or appreciated but did not fear, the consequences of a free press" (Franklin & Anderson, 1990, p. 10).

MEDIA FACTORIES AND AUDIENCE AS COMMODITY

The American press quickly expanded in the 19th century from simple penny press offerings to huge daily newspapers with circulations of more than 100,000, featuring reporters in far-flung cities and battlefields. Before 1800, with some notable exceptions, most newspapers were side businesses of printers whose main effort was commercial printing of documents and books. After 1800 newspapers quickly evolved into stand-alone enterprises. They rapidly became multimillion-dollar-a-year businesses with huge staffs, business offices, and considerable political power. The industrial revolution provided innovative technology in typesetting and printing that made possible the large circulation dailies. Just as in other forms of mass production, media factories were created as part of the growth of the modern machine age. And with mass production the essential focus of the media factories shifted to serving wider audiences than merely the intellectual/political elite of former centuries. Urban newspapers with complex newsrooms, press systems, and distribution networks rose within the context of the modern city. Capitalism dominated with a fundamental emphasis on expanding sales while driving out competitors. Winning in the publishing business had been redefined from getting an idea affecting the social order published and debated to capturing an expanding circulation audience for advertising messages and driving the opposing newspaper out of business (see Fig. 1.1). Newspaper wars developed in major U.S. cities in the latter part of the 19th century, with a concurrent rise in the concept of a professional journalism culture that used the ideals of fairness and objectivity to build its credibility. That

---

- Newspaper factories emerge.
- Media becomes profit centered.
- Advertising increases importance.

Figure 1.1 Nineteenth-Century American Press

occurred despite the growing dominance of the business side of newspapering that ushered in the era of "yellow journalism," a period at the end of the 19th century that underscores how manipulative American newspapers had become. Their circulation-pumping, incendiary coverage of events leading up to the 1898 explosion of the U.S. battleship *Maine* in Havana harbor literally provided the spark that started the Spanish-American War (Emery & Emery, 1996).

Advertising and newspapers evolved together, and by the mid-1700s people were complaining about their tendency for overstatement to draw attention (Presbrey, 1929). From an owner's point of view, using newspapers to sell things for advertisers had become the real point of producing them, not the idealistic conveyance of the day's events. Content was determined increasingly by what would sell media usage. Efforts to control markets fostered a coalescing of the industry into a dwindling number of major corporations. Chains had been born in the media business, and throughout the 20th century they expanded their dominance on the mass media landscape in every form of audience engagement.

It is beneficial to consider, retrospectively, the evolution of broadcast news in order to add perspective to its contemporary situation. When commercial radio took hold of the nation in the 1920s, it did so providing entertainment programming. For example, in 1927 a content analysis of broadcasts originating in New York indicated music was the primary format of three-fourths of the programming. The next largest programming segment, with 15 percent of airtime, was religious or educational. Only a few programs were in the categories of drama, sports, or information (Lundberg, 1928). For the next two decades radio news expanded, particularly with World War II coverage, improved by the development of tape recorders. Broadcasting technological expansion grew in its impact on the selection of the most dramatic subjects that, at the same time, fit the particular medium. Edward R. Murrow, for example, rode along on a bomber in the 1943 air raid on Berlin to describe the event from a first-person perspective, with the sounds of the action giving listeners half the world away the sense of being there. Increasingly larger audiences, using first radio and then television, became witnesses, via broadcasting, to major events including national elections, wars, and scandals such as the McCarthy hearings in the 1950s (Emery & Emery, 1996).

The power of broadcasting to carry the sights and sounds of events to audiences, to give people in their homes and places of work a sense of participating in occurrences quite apart from their physical location, is a double-edged sword. Entertainment values influence the conceptualization of stories that "must fit the particular requirements of each news medium" (Gans, 1980, p. 157). From the inception of broadcasting it was music and entertainment that filled most of the airwaves, to such a degree factory schedules were shifted to accommodate employees' desires to listen to radio programs such as *Amos 'n' Andy* (Emery & Emery, 1996) (see Fig. 1.2).

Despite the great events that occurred from the 1920s to the 1950s, including World War II, the rise of the Cold War, and McCarthyism, the broadcast medium's

- Broadcasting was originally entertainment centered.
- Technology takes audience to distant events.
- News becomes a profit center.

Figure 1.2   Twentieth-Century Broadcasting Evolution

entertainment programming provided the greatest audience for television. In January 1953 the *I Love Lucy* show recorded the highest rating for any broadcast program in the United States to that time, with 72 percent of the 21 million homes with television (Emery & Emery, 1996). Rating (the percentage of all television households in a population tuned to a particular station) and share (the percentage of homes actually using television at a particular time, tuned to a particular station) have had a pervasive impact since the 1930s on broadcasting, because of the reliance of the medium on advertising revenues (Wimmer & Dominick, 1987).

By the 1970s television newscasts had become advertising revenue profit centers of stations with increasing entertainment programming values. News had evolved into slick packaged products that were designed as much to attract viewers to the program commercials as to inform the public of significant events or movements. The key advertising demographic group, 18- to 49-year-olds with substantial disposable income, became the barometer that measured the rise or fall of network programs, news anchors, even the types of stories covered based on widespread use of market research. Everything from basic content to the pro-produced evening news program opening sequences was fodder for focus group testing by various consultants and station researchers anxious to drive up ratings (Powers, R.,1977). As former *ABC Evening News* producer Av Westin described the then-existing state of broadcasting,

> . . . television is essentially an entertainment-advertising medium. Its "spin-off" is news. . . . So as soon as you get into a conflict of news as opposed to entertainment, the TV "publisher"—that is, the station manager—is going to try to find ways of increasing his circulation at the cost of the quality. He is not really dedicated to quality. (Powers, R. 1977, p. 52)

THE CHANGING MEDIA ORGANIZATION CONTEXT

All of a modern organization's parts have to be in concert to adapt to a constantly changing dynamic environment. The contemporary media context is just such a place, featuring continuous audience fragmentation among increasing numbers of media players, including broadcast and cable television, satellite direct broadcast services, specialty publishers large and small, and the plethora of growing Internet options, including audio and video services. There are, literally, so many places for advertisers to invest their money that no one media segment can expect to get a dominant piece of the pie. What's more, audiences are increasingly impatient, armed with technology that lets them avoid advertising messages while still getting the content they desire. VCR users zip through commercials on videotaped programs using fast-forward. Television audiences punch their handheld clickers to avoid commercials by channel hopping. And on the Internet the mouse click quickly moves one through web page options with many users hardly noticing the increasing number of banner advertisements. Because it has become pervasive, people have learned to ignore or avoid the advertising pitches, like so much clutter they must cut through, to get the content that is meaningful to them. Such an audience filtering context requires considerable innovation at all levels to maintain advertising effectiveness, which is crucial to paying for all that the audience enjoys. In the Western model, readers, listeners, viewers, Internet surfers, and the rest who enjoy all contemporary mass media offers for little direct, personal cost do so because advertising has paid for it. Typically, there are four ways to fund any mass media enterprise: (1) government, (2) subscription fees paid for by users, (3) advertising, or (4) some combination of any number of the previous options. By far, the dominant option in the United States has been advertising.

Increasing Media Ownership Concentration

Bagdikian (1992) has documented the American mass media collapse, during the latter part of the 20th century, into a continuously shrinking group of conglomerates controlling the newspaper, publishing, motion picture, television, radio, and recording industries worldwide. Media conglomerates are discussed later in this chapter in the section entitled "Media Conglomerate." When he published his first study in 1983, Bagdikian found that 50 corporations controlled a large majority of American mass media. By his fourth edition of *Media Monopoly* in 1992, that figure had dwindled to just 20 giant firms. In newspapers and magazines he found the most dramatic shift, from independently owned publications to conglomerate dominance of the publishing industry.

> At the end of World War II, for example, 80 percent of the daily newspapers in the United States were independently owned, but by 1989 the proportion was reversed, with 80 percent owned by corporate chains. In 1981 twenty corporations controlled most of the business of the country's 11,000 magazines, but only seven years later that number had shrunk to three corporations. (Bagdikian, 1992, p. 4)

Among factors affecting the concentration of mass media are the tax laws and increasing media options for consumers. The tax laws make it virtually impossible to shelter family wealth beyond the third generation. That has encouraged the old family-owned newspaper chains to become publicly held corporations. As stock is acquired by small and large investors, it makes the newspaper chain a monkey on the quarterly dividend string, where investors charge into a stock or sell it based on the quarterly profit projections. So, along with losing the original family entrepreneur's vision of what a newspaper is all about, after three generations the newspaper is usually transformed into just another business, in terms of its basic financial structure and vision (Bagdikian, 1992). Additionally, in corporate finance the last thing you want to do is declare a huge profit, because much of it will be taken away from you in the form of corporate taxes. So companies carefully project revenues and frequently buy things—equipment, more newspapers, other businesses—when they're having a good year or have built up substantial reserves. Expansion is a legitimate business expense and an excellent way to convert tax liability into corporate equity. Instead of giving the money to the government, a company uses it to buy something, which is an expenditure against revenues. Thus the system encourages companies continually to reinvest in themselves and get bigger (see Fig. 1.3).

By 1997 the largest U.S. newspaper chain, Gannett Company, Inc., owned 91 daily newspapers, smaller community newspapers in 40 states, 16 television stations, 5 radio stations, cable television systems in major markets, and numerous other businesses with some 37,200 employees and more than 14,000 stockholders worldwide. The company reported $4.4 billion in operating revenue in 1996 (Gannett, 1997). However, the

---

- Family ownership declines.
- New technology fosters more consumer options.
- Tax laws and business climate favor corporate expansion strategy.
- Conglomerates take over media industries.

Figure 1.3 Media Concentration

Thomson media empire based in Great Britain remained the largest media conglomerate with $7.225 billion in sales from its holdings. Those include 76 U.S. dailies, 9 Canadian dailies, a large book and magazine publishing division, and a technology services branch that includes more than 100 Internet support providers serving thousands of individuals engaging with the World Wide Web (Thomson, 1996).

The number of daily newspapers has also steadily declined. Some of that decline has been caused by the rise of chains. It is not uncommon for a chain to buy a competitor in a market just to close it down. Another factor is the increase in alternative media options for consumers. From 1980 to 1995 the number of daily newspapers in the United States dropped from 1,745 to 1,532. Aggregate circulation remained virtually constant, which reflects a substantial loss in readership when factored against the increase of population over the 15 years (Veronis, Suhler & Associates, 1996). But all media industries have been involved in a steady concentration of holdings in the hands of a relatively few major players. These vary from one segment of the media industries to another. In 1994 the top five cable television multisystem operators, or MSOs as they are known in the industry, controlled a little less than half of all U.S. cable television subscribers. But by the end of the following year, 1995, they owned systems providing cable service to more than two-thirds of the nation's cable customers. The two largest players were TCI, with nearly 12 million subscribers, and Time Warner Cable, with an estimated 11.5 million ("market share," 1996). It was estimated that only a few years would be necessary for the top five cable conglomerates to extend their control to 80 percent of the cable systems in the United States ("must-carry wars," 1996).

Deregulation of Electronic Media

During the 1980s the federal government began deregulating the electronic communications industries, which encouraged media companies to expand their holdings. The Reagan administration saw deregulation as a way to get bureaucratic red tape out of business. But the result of deregulation, particularly in broadcasting, was a dramatic change in more than half a century of policy and law.

The Radio Act of 1927 and the Communication Act of 1934, the foundation of broadcast regulation, set out the standard of "public interest, convenience, or necessity" for broadcast license holders. It was seen as a trade-off. Since broadcasters would use public property to make money, with exclusive rights to a limited number of frequencies, they had a social responsibility to provide some higher-purpose programming and community service (Head, Sterling, & Schofield, 1994). Until the deregulation period of the 1980s (see Fig. 1.4), radio and television stations, and any other service that used the public airwaves to transmit its signals, were held to that standard and required to show proof of their good efforts at each license renewal. This

- Redefined broadcasting "in the public interest."
- Trimmed ownership restrictions.
- Reduced financing requirements.
- Accelerated trend toward conglomerate mergers/acquisitions.

Figure 1.4 Deregulation of Electronic Media

regulatory approach was supported by an entire body of court cases, many decided by the U.S. Supreme Court, and is discussed in depth in Chapter 15.

When Reagan appointee Mark Fowler became chair of the Federal Communications Commission (FCC) he set about radically changing a half-century of policy and law. He changed the definition of "public interest, convenience, or necessity," from a concept of higher purpose to a more simple and pragmatic approach. "Television," Fowler said once, "is just another appliance. It's a toaster with pictures" (Nossiter, 1985, p. 402). In other words, the public's interest was redefined as whatever the public is interested in (Boyer, 1987). Marketplace business principles would determine electronic media courses of action, not federal requirements for specific categories of content.

The Fowler Commission dismantled the entire process of regulating licensees, including removal of the so-called antitrafficking rule in 1982, which had required an owner to hold a station for at least three years prior to selling it (Bates, 1988). The rule had prevented station owners from trading stations like shares of stock and forced them to keep stations viable, even if they were speculating with them. When the antitrafficking rule was dropped, it touched off a frenzy of station trading, with entrepreneurs backed by the new junk bond financing scheme in the stock market ("Changing hands," 1985; Rattner, 1986). Stations were bought with high-interest capital, sometimes by individuals and corporations with no previous broadcasting experience, as speculative investments.

The FCC also radically changed the number of stations a single company could own. Going into the 1980s the "rule of 7s" applied. That meant a given owner could have seven AM radio stations, seven FM radio stations, and seven television stations throughout the United States. In 1985 that was expanded to a "rule of 12s," 12 stations in each of the three categories, plus a caveat that no chain could own stations whose coverage exceeded 25 percent of the U. S. population ("FCC Grilled," 1985). The 1996 Telecommunications Act removed restrictions on the number of stations broadcasters could own nationally, allowing up to 8 radio stations in large markets that include 45 or more stations. In the case of television stations, owners are restricted from owning stations that reach more than 35 percent of the nation's television households. The result of the ownership regulations was a collapse of both the radio and television industries into huge companies owning dozens of stations each. In just the first 6 months of 1996, radio station trading amounted to $5.2 billion. By July the two biggest radio owners were Clear Channel with 102 stations and Westinghouse/CBS with 82 (Rathbun, 1996a). Just three months later Clear Channel had put together more station buys, pushing its broadcast empire to 121 radio stations and 11 television stations (Rathbun, 1996b). Mergers and acquisitions also hit a fever pitch on the television side of broadcasting. In terms of the largest number of stations, Sinclair Broadcast Group totaled 29 stations by mid-1996, with Paxson Communications a close second with 27. Based on the percentage of U.S. population reached, the largest single station group was Westinghouse/CBS with 31.53 percent of American homes (Jessell & Rathbun, 1996).

One of the reasons television did not consolidate to the extent radio did was that the duopoly rule was kept in effect, which limits each television owner to a single station in each market (Sandin & Jessell, 1996). But the head of one fast-rising company, David Sinclair of the Sinclair Broadcast Group, predicted the broadcast business would continue to consolidate into seven giant conglomerate owners. Duopoly and other ownership rules are discussed further in the electronic media law chapter later in this text.

As the concept of broadcasting changed there were concerns over whether the Miltonian marketplace-of-ideas concept is viable with relatively few ownership groups controlling the media industry. Former CBS News President Fred Friendly argued, "when there are more people who want to operate stations than there are stations to give out, you can't talk about an open marketplace. You can't talk about the rules of free enterprise in a closed marketplace" (Boyer, 1987, p. C15). However, because of the limits of the electronic spectrum, only so many broadcast stations can be licensed over the air. Thus, by virtue of the limited spectrum, broadcasting has always been, to one extent or another, a closed marketplace. The question is whether federal regulations or normal business forces prevalent elsewhere in American life should rule the broadcasting marketplace.

In the years following the Fowler chairmanship of the FCC, there was some discomfort about what had occurred, with hearings in Congress centering on issues of content regulation, particularly of children's programming. When Alfred Sikes became the commission chair in 1989, the former radio station owner said he did not agree with Fowler's view that television is just a kitchen appliance with pictures. "There is something special about the broadcasting business, in the public and legal sense, as well as in the more personal sense" ("FCC gains," 1989, p. 29). Shortly after Sikes left the FCC, he and former commissioner Nicholas Johnson appeared on the ABC Network "Nightline" program in June of 1993. They both questioned the direction broadcast regulation had taken in the previous decade and asserted that a trade-off in a higher public interest, convenience, or necessity standard is a fair exchange for using the public airwaves. To Johnson the trade is fair because a broadcaster is a public trustee of a community resource; for Sikes, stations and networks using the public airwaves have social obligations beyond merely the profit they can generate. However, determining exactly which programs fit such a social obligation is the rock everyone keeps tripping over on the regulatory road. Sikes cited the Home Shopping Network as an example of fulfilling the public interest, convenience, or necessity standard when you consider some people prefer to shop that way, and those confined to their homes have to ("The Battle," 1993).

Such an approach to a mass media, dominated by an increasingly smaller group of giant conglomerates with multimedia marketing schemes and cross-promotion of everything from motion pictures to cartoon characters, begs the question "When the pursuit of profit determines content based on marketing studies of what people want, can society really expect media to provide what it needs?" And is a mammoth entertainment empire—integrating conglomerate-owned theme parks, motion picture and television production, book publishing, and a retail chain of stores selling products reinforcing the corporate brand—any less a creator of a social mythology than were royal houses of Europe in former centuries? Can Milton's concept of a marketplace of ideas, where truth prevails because it is obvious when placed beside falsehood, function in a society where only profitable ideas are placed on the table for discussion? The answer, clearly, is no. Thus, as McQuail (1987) and others have argued, profit considerations of modern mass media vehicles—newspapers, radio, television, Internet web page availability, and other media forms—may be as much a form of censorship as overt government action.

MEDIA ORGANIZATIONAL STRUCTURES

Media organizations are generally organized in line with a basic, structural/functional approach that is hierarchical in nature. Like many other businesses, the organizational chart usually reflects a vertical, top-down flow of authority, though certainly the structure does not preclude information flowing from the bottom up. But the normally practiced reality is that information and orders come from above. People below tend to analyze the corporate game for themselves and adjust the degree to which they champion new ideas to what appears favored by senior management. That's only natural, since management controls job survival, promotion, and raises. The inherent problem is that the people doing a lot of the work are too often not the ones making the major decisions. If those in the trenches of the organization are reticent about being proactive in decision making, their productivity may be adversely affected because of nothing more than managerial ignorance.

In the business world much has been written about reorganization, downsizing, rightsizing, and other euphemisms for making sure everything is as efficient as possible. Recent major approaches have included participative management, Total Quality Management, reengineering, and kaizen theory (a Japanese-based concept fostering a collaborative work environment). Some of these will be discussed in more detail later. But the fundamental issue of all the varying approaches is motivating employees and managers to work together rather than as opposing units, within a context of trust and mutual support. That doesn't sound all that hard, but it is. Otherwise, best-sellers would not be published year after year that, regardless of their snappy titles and slogans, are aimed at that same, fundamental concept—working together rather than against one another.

Usually organizations are set up along the classical management approach of dividing jobs according to the grouping of functions. The classical management approach, based in the writings of such authors as Henri Fayol (1949) and Frederick Taylor (1947/1967) started with the division of labor and centered on daily processes. Typically, work is divided into special categories that comprise departments. Although departmentalization may help coordinate various organizational activities, it also naturally lends itself to sharply defined units with walls between them, both physical and psychological. So, in a media organization, you may have the editorial department doing one thing and the promotion department another. Or the creative people in an advertising agency may put together something that does not make a client happy because of poor communication among the account executive, the client, and the creative folks.

Formalized Structures

Large organizations commonly have formalized structures because of the need for extensive coordination among large groups of people often not working in the same geographic location. They feature clear lines of authority, rigidity in process-oriented repetitive tasks, and usually a high degree of supervision. Jobs are often set up to accomplish specific and limited functions that are critical to the flow of work. Like a huge set of gears, everything is ordered to ensure the many parts effectively mesh together. The assembly line is a classic example of a formal structure set up to maximize efficiency with tightly controlled work flow. Everything has to be done in a given order at a given time, with considerable job-specific skill required at numerous steps in production. In that sense there is little difference in basic function between an automobile assembly plant and a newspaper. Both are highly coordinated systems turning out thousands of copies of product on strict time schedules. The bigger an organization, the more formal and bureaucratic it tends to get. The measures of success in formal structures are frequently quantitative in nature because numerical measures of productivity are relatively easy to define and measure.

Informal Structures

Informal organizations are usually the reverse of their formal cousins in just about every way. They are normally smaller and more niche oriented. Rather than multiple departments and/or divisions, they tend more toward the informal boutique; a handful of people work together sharing the various duties and responsibilities as situations demand. Smaller advertising and public relations agencies are good examples. A half-dozen or so people work together more as a collective team than as an assembly line. People frequently have a lot of formal training and are almost like independent contractors, or trained specialists, inside the envelope of the organization. There is considerable autonomy, and the primary motivation for productivity is internally driven within the individual worker rather than by external influences such as formal work rules. In such informal structures personal pride in producing quality work is a key factor. The measures of success in such structures are often qualitative in nature, dependent upon the level of professionalism of the workers, and quite subjective. Informal structures seem to draw creative people to them because of the relative freedom to express themselves in work that is evaluated in more than simple numerical measures. For example, a "good" television commercial produced by an advertising agency is a creative work, the goodness of which is a question of perception. If something about it helps attract buyers for a product, it is successful. Another example is copy writing. Writer A turns out more copy than writer B, but it's generally dull. Writer B, on the other hand, has a lot of flair and creativity in her copy. Whereas a numerical standard of productivity would rate writer A as better, because of the higher volume, the quality of writer B's work is clearly superior. If you want to crank out a lot of copy, it is one thing. If you want to win the Nobel Prize in literature, it is another.

Media Organizations as Complex Blends

Mass media organizations are very different, in some ways, from ordinary business structures. They may seem on the surface to be similar, but deep inside they are not. That's because they are combinations of the formal and informal structures—a kind of split personality. They typically have very rigid assembly lines that turn out media product under tight deadlines with clearly defined work rules and/or standards. Yet the content of what is produced on the assembly line is highly professional in nature, with qualitative measures usually used to determine the worth of the work. Journalism is highly creative. Newsroom employees frequently "resist management control and are driven by forces of internal satisfaction and commitment to ideas" (McQuarrie, 1992, p. 234). For example, after the basic rules of grammar are met, what makes one writer's work explode off the page while another reporter is boring? Why is it that some photographers take pictures while others create intense portrayals of human emotion?

Media work is a combination of accepted technique and loosely defined art brought together to convey subjective emotion and meaning. Because of that, media professionals tend to see their work as their own, even though the copyright is owned by the newspaper. See Chapter 14 for a detailed discussion on the legal ramifications of current copyright law. Reporters in the newspaper business usually keep clipping files with all their byline stories. Television reporters keep their pieces on videotapes. Photographers have collections of their favorite images. And when you talk to them about their work it is always referred to as "my story" or "my photograph." They retain psychological possession of work that they see as a manifestation of themselves. It is as though the media organization is merely a conduit that pays the rent and allows them to indulge in self-expression as artists of a sort.

So media organizations are frequently a kind of hybrid, a blend if you will, of machine and professional organizations. Parts of them are relatively rigid and highly controlled, but other parts are very flexible, with the quality of work very much in the hands of the individual. They are among the most difficult kinds of organizations to manage because they blend such diverse attributes.

BASIC ORGANIZATIONAL DESIGNS OF TYPICAL MEDIA ORGANIZATIONS

Because individual organizations evolve in the business world and are affected by the people within them, many have unique characteristics. They often become cultures with distinct personalities that longtime employees frequently reflect. But all have basic organizational structures that generally provide a sense for organizational command and control. The following are typical designs prevalent in the media industry today. Traditionally, these are top-down corporate maps based on the classic model of structural/functional application. Specific placement of various departments, or even their names, vary from one company to another. But, generally, all of the attributes in each type of organization are common to firms within that industry segment.

Media Conglomerate

The media conglomerate is generally set up with a separate corporate management group including presidents and vice presidents of major divisions. Reporting to the management group are the various operating units and/or companies owned by the conglomerate. Figure 1.5 shows a multinational company with considerable holdings in the mass media industries, including television and radio, publishing, theme parks, retail stores, music recording, and motion pictures. Normally such huge organizations have a board of directors and a chief executive officer (CEO). They are assisted by experts in corporate finance who continually analyze existing holdings and prospective acquisitions to adjust the corporate profile as markets, products, and technologies ebb and flow.

As you can see, the finance, operations, and strategic planning division heads are grouped together under the CEO as a working group. Strategic planning can't do its job without reliable information from finance. The operations division head is closest to the daily activities of the field units and provides data to finance and strategic planning. Operations is also directly affected by decisions in strategic planning and in finance. Below that management tier, the separate divisions are usually quite independent. Although aware of each other within the corporate umbrella, they may have little to do with another division. On the other hand, some media companies have strong cultures that are pervasive throughout all aspects of the organization. Two contemporary media conglomerates with powerful corporate personalities are Gannett Company, Inc., a giant company with newspaper and other media holdings, and The Walt Disney Company, an entertainment empire that grew out of its founder's highly creative genius in creating motion picture cartoons.

Newspaper Organization

A traditional newspaper organization is shown in Figure 1.6. Daily Newspaper, Inc., has a publisher at the top who may report to a board of directors or a holding company. Holding companies are generally set up for no other purpose than to own other firms. They are companies in their own right but with no products other than their management expertise, for which they normally charge a fee to those companies they own. They, in effect, "hold" other corporations. Under the publisher, most papers split the revenue-generating functions and news coverage into two branches to maintain an ethical separation so that journalism is not unduly influenced by business considerations. The editor heads the news-editorial side, with a managing editor handling the organizational paperwork of schedules, travel budgets, and so on. The various section editors

24

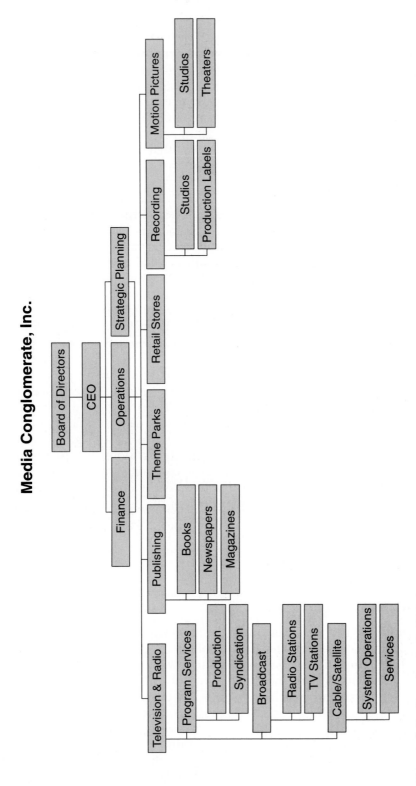

Figure 1.5 Conglomerate Structure

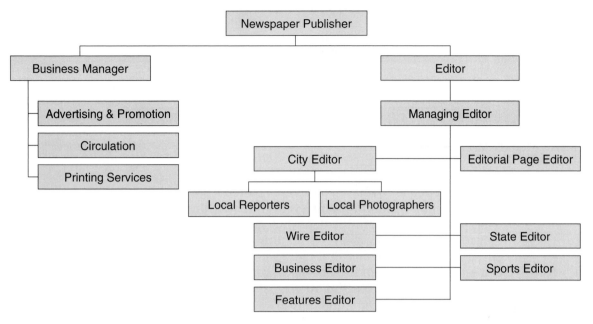

Daily Newspaper, Inc.

Figure 1.6 Typical Newspaper Organization

are usually below the managing editor. On some papers the city editor functions as an assistant editor in charge of all the other section heads. In other papers the managing editor also functions as the city editor. The advertising and promotion departments sell and market space in the paper, circulation handles subscription and street sales delivery, and printing services gets the paper printed. The organization usually reflects variances in a particular newspaper's market. For example, if a newspaper is located in a city with major-league baseball, football, basketball, and hockey, the sports editor may have a fairly large staff. On the other hand, in a city with lots of politics there may be a political editor. It all depends on local newspaper size and needs.

Broadcast Organization

Figures 1.7 to 1.10 show the way a broadcasting parent company is typically structured, along with a radio station and a television station owned by the corporation.

In Figure 1.7, Big Time Broadcasting, Inc., you can see the CEO has two assistants. One is for the broadcast technology of the corporation, the corporate chief engineer. The other is for legal matters, the corporate legal counsel. Typically these two specialists work directly for the CEO. Sometimes they are separate heads of company divisions, but they often are seen as technical advisers on major policy issues that cover the entire range of corporate operations and are, thus, attached to the CEO rather than another division head. Under them are the vice presidents, and in our design we have them linked together as a group with considerable overlap in responsibilities. For example, all the stations' managers report to the VP-stations, but each station uses some programming that the VP-programming can purchase from suppliers at lower-per-unit cost when buying for all the stations as a group. Additionally, the business managers of each

Big Time Broadcasting, Inc.

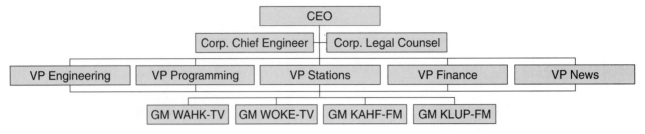

Figure 1.7 Multiple Station Corporate Parent

station will frequently have considerable interface with the VP-finance about fiscal matters at the station and corporate level. So the vice presidents are a kind of executive-level team with each vice president having responsibilities for certain areas involving individual stations. However, overall station management comes under the VP-stations.

Figure 1.8 shows a typical radio station management structure with the three general areas of station endeavors: sales, programming, and engineering. Each is usually operated separately from the others. Sales worries about selling the available time for commercials while programming focuses on the over-the-air operations, including quality and format of the on-air product. Engineering strictly handles the technical aspects of operating the machinery of broadcasting—transmitters, studios, control rooms, and so on—maintaining everything in working order and ensuring compliance with FCC technical standards.

Big Time Broadcasting's KLUP-FM

Figure 1.8 FM Radio Station Organization

Figure 1.9, the television station organization, is quite similar to radio, probably because most television stations evolved out of radio stations. Typically in television you have the additional roles of promotion director and news director at the department head level. In most local television stations, news is perceived as the single most influential department in maintaining station local identity in the midst of growing media options for consumers. It also usually has the largest staff of any department because of the complicated nature of producing several hours of live news programming every day. Some stations put the units that can transmit live reports from the scene of a news story—known as "live trucks"—under the news department, or they may have some studio production personnel involved with newscasts report to the news director. However, this organizational chart reflects a common arrangement.

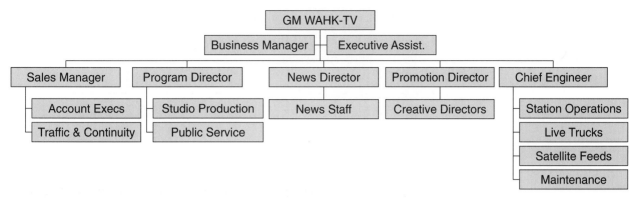

Figure 1.9 Local TV Station Organization

Figure 1.10 is a separate organization chart of a typical small-to-medium market television news department. Weather and sports are usually separate offices, or subdepartments, and put together their own coverage. Sometimes sports has specifically assigned producers, photographers, and video editors. However, frequently those are assigned out of the pool of people managed by the assignment desk and general newscast producing staff. As you can see, the assignment desk coordinates the reporter/photographer teams. The producers put the various newscasts together, including determining the order of stories and usually working with the assignment desk in developing coverage. Newscast anchors are typically managed separately by the news director, although they work closely with producers as scripts are written, edited, and prepared for reading on air by the anchors.

Figure 1.10 TV News Department

Advertising/Public Relations Agency Organization

Although advertising and public relations agencies are often separate organizations, it is very common for them to be combined as is shown in Figure 1.11. Many advertising professionals also provide public relations consultation for their clients, and public relations firms are often asked for help to integrate a company public image campaign into an advertising program.

Superior Advertising/Public Relations Agency

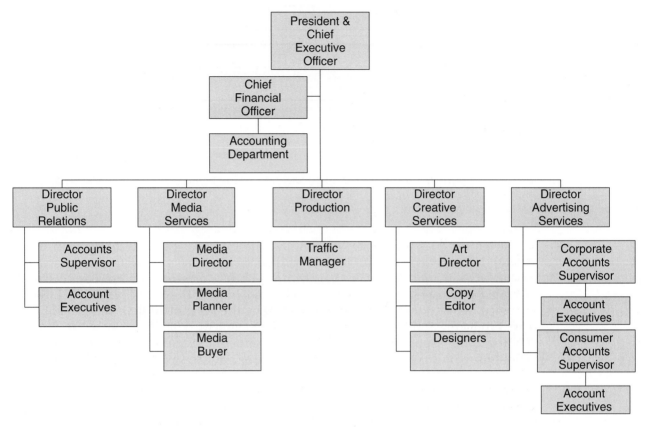

Figure 1.11 Advertising/Public Relations Agency Structure

As you can see, an agency is a combination of client services in producing advertisements, whether in print or electronic media, as well as making the purchases of the television, radio, or print advertising commercial time or space. While the account executives work directly with a client in either the public relations or advertising side of the agency, the various creative services are needed to support the client's needs. The importance of communication within the agency cannot be overemphasized. For if an account executive sells the client one thing, and the creative people in the agency deliver something else, the account is jeopardized.

Figure 1.12 illustrates an in-house public relations department of a major company. Most large corporations have some public relations professionals. The office may have limited responsibility advising the senior executives, or it may have numerous functions. Those may include preparing in-house newsletters, ongoing community outreach programs, crises management, and preparing materials such as the company annual report that go to stockholders and investment firms. Typically, public relations organizations are set up with a focus on the publics they will serve on behalf of the company. It is important in such an office to design the structure with one fundamental question in mind: "To whom are you talking?" As a spokesperson for a company the public relations department is the outreach of the firm. It must engage potential audiences in ways that are meaningful to them. As you can see in Figure 1.12,

Corporate Public Relations Department

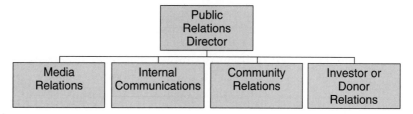

Figure 1.12 Corporate Public Relations Department

dealing with the news media is a specialty, as is internal communications, community relations, and investor or donor relations.

It's important to understand that all media structures represented here are merely average representations of typical organizations. Media companies often have particular characteristics that have evolved due to their unique personalities, resulting in slightly different names or titles for management personnel, and they may have some departments or tasks located in different places from those in another firm. But, generally, they all have the same key areas represented somewhere on their organizational chart.

One great danger in any organized structure is that it can become a prison from which it is hard to escape. It can become an excuse and/or cause for a lack of organizational flexibility. Media organizations may become highly bureaucratic and institutionalized after a few years, sometimes allowing form to dictate substance, or the lack of it. In a dynamic industry, static organizations are a quick trip to failure. So media managers have to guard against the tendency to get caught up in formalized procedures that are in place "because that's the way we do it," or "because we've always done it this way." The first question a media manager needs to ask when considering the way a place is organized is, "Why do we do it this way? Is there a better way to help us work together instead of being a house divided?" Structure sometimes defeats efforts to be team oriented and pits one department against another. Organizational procedures develop themselves into entangled bureaucracies, which then lock up an organization when the world shifts. Because it's hard to unlock entrenched old procedures or chains of authority and generate new ones, the organizational structure itself can contribute to an inability to respond to fast-changing situations. Dynamic environments require dynamic, flexible organizations. Many media organizations are not as flexible as they should be and can easily get caught behind sudden changes in the marketplace or in technology.

Matrix Organizations and Redesigning Newsrooms

One of the problems that large media organizations have is coordinating production across traditionally separate functions. For example, in a newspaper the printing plant frequently prints not only the newspaper itself but subcontracts for other large, specialized printing jobs to fill the time between newspaper editions. Likewise, some advertiser groups are extensively involved in the planning, development, and publication of special sections on things like real estate or car buying. Also, in large media organizations, which have several companies in different media industries, it frequently makes good business sense to place some functions at the corporate level that can service all of those products. If you are the owner of newspapers, television stations, advertising agencies, and theme parks, maximizing brand awareness across all product lines can have a very positive effect due to the economies of scale and brand exposure in a wide range of audience vehicles.

The matrix organization is a concept that rose out of the 1960s and 1970s and gained momentum with increasing federal deregulation of business into the 1980s. Although matrix organizations vary considerably from one firm to another, the fundamental design of them is simple. The major functions, which span all of the subunits involved, are handled at the senior corporate level as each product line connects as necessary with specific functional areas (Galbraith & Kanzanjian, 1986). In effect, the functional groups provide expertise to all the subunits. Because of the combination of product and functional organization within the matrix, one of the particular attributes of the model is a duality of authority. Essentially, two managers are involved in most aspects of work, the production manager and the functional area manager (Gibson, Ivancevich, & Donnelly, 1997). Despite what appears to be the complicated nature of involving two bosses, because of the ability to coordinate focused resources at the production and functional levels, matrix designs are particularly suited for organizations faced with three key issues: rapid change, uncertainty, and restricted resources (Lawrence, Kolodny, & Davis, 1977).

The first issue, rapid change, is particularly matrix oriented when it occurs in more than one area of the business. An example would be technological change with concurrent dynamic adjustments in customer or audience bases. That has been the recent experience of American television. The traditional networks, ABC, CBS, and NBC, lost one-third of their audience as competitors proliferated with advancing technology (Auletta, 1991). By November 1996 the total prime-time share of the traditional networks combined with three emerging broadcast competitors—Fox, United Paramount, and Warner Brothers—was 64 (Rice, 1996). Essentially, American television viewing went from almost exclusively over-the-air broadcasting to the proliferation of cable, satellite, and other newly emerging technology competitors in a mere decade of dramatic change.

The second key issue that fosters a matrix approach is a substantial degree of uncertainty that produces much information processing as both production and functional sides of the organization flex. In other words, lots of reports, studies, memos, and other information elements are moved around the organization as it attempts to cope with the uncertain conditions. An example of this attribute would be the sudden rise of the Internet as a mass media vehicle, which caused upheaval in the newspaper industry. Some newspaper companies raced to develop online editions while others had a "wait-and-see" attitude. They were concerned the Internet might be just another fad similar to the 1970s citizen's band radio craze.

The third issue present among those companies that have successfully implemented matrix organizations is the need to cope with serious financial and personnel restrictions while addressing an increasingly dynamic environment. In both of the two previous examples, newspapers and broadcast television, recent decades have seen significant audience erosion, which has forced increased cost consciousness right at the time when positioning for the future has meant redefining media companies, often an expensive proposition requiring a lot of market analysis and change of technology. Caught between the pressures of cutting costs but still investing money to reposition for the future, it makes a lot of sense to combine resources wherever possible.

Now, look at the basics of the matrix concept, spanning product lines with functional responsibilities. Consider marketing as a functional group. All product lines need to be properly marketed and that entails substantial market analysis, planning to intersect potential customers at their point of desire or need, and coordinating advertising, promotion, and other marketing concepts to support the product. Effective marketing is usually involved at several places in product evolution. Whereas a specific product line may well have a marketing office specific to its needs, at the corporate level considerably more resources can be shared as necessary because all of the subunits basically chip in to pay for it. Together they can afford a much higher level operation than could the individual units. An example would be market research. That can be an expensive undertaking, whether done inside a company or contracted out. If you have several product lines that need frequent and extensive research support, it may make sense to have a research department at the corporate level designing and implementing telephone, mail, or other research programs for each product line. At the corporate level it becomes a full-time endeavor, and the company can afford to hire top-quality researchers and operate large telephone banks doing research year-round. But at the individual product line level you may only need two weeks of telephone survey work done in a year. Additionally, some large functional groups contract with other companies to do their research during slack times, much like the printing plant mentioned earlier. Such integrated corporate efforts can be done under any structural design to some degree, but as you can see in Figures 1.13 and 1.14, the matrix organizational approach enhances the integration concept by creating a kind of umbrella of major functions across the top of the numerous product lines.

Figure 1.13 is an example of a large conglomerate matrix. The general areas of corporate finance, technology development, facilities and real estate, and marketing and promotion are shown as operating functions of the conglomerate holding company. The separate operating companies are set up along product lines. In this case all of the mass media companies have a need for technology expertise. Although each would probably have its own personnel for local concerns, you can see that the corporate

Product Lines	Holding Company Functions			
	Corporate Finance	Technology Development	Facilities & Real Estate	Marketing & Promotion
Newspaper Publishing Company				
Television Station Company				
Radio Station Company				
Internet Services Company				

Figure 1.13 Conglomerate Matrix Organization

Product Lines	Media Company Functions			
	Finance & Accounting	Technology Development	Facilities & Real Estate	Marketing & Promotion
Newspaper Publishing				
Internet Online Services				
Radio Station Company				
Internet Services Company				

Figure 1.14 Small Media Organization Matrix

technology division would be able to buy printing presses or television equipment cheaper due to the economies of scale. Consider this conglomerate as owning 40 daily newspapers. All of the papers are fairly mature operations and need new presses to reduce production costs and substantially improve product quality. The newest press in the entire company was installed in 1967. Do you think it would be cheaper per unit to buy one new press or to negotiate a deal to buy ten presses a year for the next four years? Obviously, the concept of economy of scale would help the conglomerate in buying ten presses a year. Such a large order would produce a quantity discount. The same is true of television equipment. If the television station company decides to buy new robotic studio cameras, it is likely a significant quantity discount would be available if 21 cameras were purchased, three each for seven stations, rather than only three cameras purchased by an individual station. Again, economy of scale is an important business factor that is one of the major elements priming the pump of corporate expansion. Bigger firms often get things cheaper because they are in a position to leverage suppliers when they go into the marketplace and buy in quantity.

Figure 1.14 represents a much smaller media organization matrix that was formerly a newspaper company. However, this organization realized that the new technology of the Internet, and the demand for online newspaper editions, requires separate product lines. Each of those still need to have extensive finance and accounting, technology development, facilities and real estate, and marketing and promotion support. Newspapers have learned quickly that effective online editions are not merely a regular newspaper put on a World Wide Web site. They must be reformatted and restructured to fit the medium. Also, the way in which computer users engage with online editions differs from the way we read newspapers. This requires the integration of journalists and computer technology experts at the production level, people who don't always appreciate one another's focus or values. Additionally, contract services, which formerly only concerned itself with keeping the newspaper presses producing revenue during the idle time between newspaper editions, now has additional responsibilities. It has set up a newspaper-owned Internet service provider, known in the computer industry as an ISP, to sell Internet access time to computer users. The ISP also provides World Wide Web home page design, storage, and operational support to the growing number of companies who want to develop those products. The former small-computer operation at the daily newspaper has suddenly grown into a new, rapidly expanding profit center with several dozen people designing new products such as online small-business services. All of this effort requires the same basic corporate functions inherent in all of the organization's various product lines. All this can be coordinated at the corporate level.

ECONOMIC REALITY AND AMERICAN BROADCASTING: A CASE STUDY

The economics of network television have dramatically changed, particularly for the three traditional broadcast networks and their affiliated stations. Understanding the rapid way the network environment was altered provides a valuable lesson in the dynamic nature of media and their audiences.

An Industry in the Midst of Radical Change

In the space of just 15 years the traditional broadcast networks—ABC, CBS, and NBC—lost a third of their audience (Auletta, 1991, p. 3). The cumulative profits of the so-called Big Three were chopped in half in just four years—from $800 million in 1984 to $400 million in 1988—as cable television and home video tape recorder use exploded in the mid-1980s (p. 3). In 1991 CBS and its subsidiaries reported a net loss of $85.8 million on net sales of $3.035 billion. Only intense cost accounting kept CBS from showing much worse losses, since the net sales for 1991 were 7 percent below net sales in 1990 ("CBS Announces," 1992). NBC ended 1991 with what Wall Street analysts termed a marginal loss (Mermigas, 1991a, p. 1).

The decade of the 1980s was a historic watershed for change in American electronic media. A climate of extraordinary change fostered major shifts in television audience, station financing, and federal regulation of the industry. The tradition of economic stability enjoyed by the networks disappeared. ABC, CBS, and NBC found themselves on the defensive against a plethora of competitive forces (Auletta, 1991). Profound change swept through the culture of television as the industry became more focused on "bottom-line management" (Blumler & Spicer, 1990, p. 91). That bottom line became increasingly important as stations and networks found themselves in a more fragmented marketplace. Between the mid-1970s and mid-1980s, viewers increased their television options by more than 400 percent, from an average of 7 channels to 33 (Auletta, 1991). Program quality suffered because of the emphasis on producing cheaper series with as much promotional potential as possible (Blumler & Spicer, 1990). Despite attempts to cope with declining audience, including layoffs and continuous cost cutting, the network financial problems continued. By 1991 investors could make more in a money market fund than by purchasing network stock (Mermigas, 1991a).

A major shift in television broadcast ownership has complicated the economic situation involving the networks and their affiliated stations. The traditional networks, ABC, NBC, and CBS, all changed owners from 1985 to 1986 (Auletta, 1991). Additionally, federal deregulation changed the limits on how long owners had to hold stations before reselling them (Bates, 1988) and the number of stations each broadcasting concern could have and encouraged increased minority ownership ("FCC Grilled," 1987). The changes set the stage for a surge in local television stations sold to new owners, which increased from a rate of 30 per year in 1982 to 82 in 1984 ("Changing Hands," 1985). Additionally, new Wall Street capital was available to finance stations through high-interest "junk bonds" (Rattner, 1986). Many broadcasting companies took advantage of the changing regulations and junk bond availability to increase their holdings. Media industry mergers and acquisitions in the five-year period of deregulation, from 1983 to 1988, amounted to $60 billion ("Staff," 1988).

In the wake of deregulation and the trend of high-leverage financing through junk bonds, a national recession continued deepening through the latter half of the 1980s, shrinking advertising revenues necessary to pay the high-interest financing. The price of network commercial time dropped by more than one-third by November 1990 (Zoglin, 1990). At the same time, ABC, CBS, and NBC combined drew the smallest number of viewers in their history (Tyrer & Granger, 1990). It took just 14 years for the networks to skid from a 92 combined share of evening television viewers to a 63 share (Auletta, 1991).

As the networks faltered, their affiliated stations across the country also saw revenues skid (Butcher, 1992), and they increasingly sought refuge in the world of syndicated programs to draw more viewers than those watching network programming. Syndicated programs are sold separately from network programming by independent syndicators. They frequently are programs not aired during evening prime time and may include former network series, game shows, talk shows, and other forms of entertainment. The networks also began reducing the compensation paid to affiliates for carrying network programming (Goldman, 1990). Stations found that dropping network shows to run other programs they independently purchased made economic sense on two fronts. They didn't have to pay the increasing network compensation for hours they programmed themselves, and they could sell all the commercial time available in the syndicated shows rather than sharing that with the network (Auletta, 1991). The result was a weakening of the network relationship.

The fundamental changes in network television broadcasting through the 1980s and continuing into the 1990s have been termed "an earthquake in slow motion" (Auletta, 1991, p. 4). In April 1991, CBS announced the elimination of another 400 jobs, the fourth in a wave of cuts made since Laurence A. Tisch took over the company in 1986 (Shales, 1991). It was estimated up to 140 of those jobs would be in CBS News, reducing the division to 1,067 from a pre-Tisch employment of 1,467. The cuts were made midway through the year, in the midst of forecasts the CBS Television Network would lose between $100 million and $300 million. Howard Stringer, president of CBS Broadcast Group indicated 1991 would be "only the second time in the last 40 years" that the television network side of the company has lost money. The first was 1990, when the network posted more than $200 million in losses, including a $55 million write-off of the Tisch-approved major-league baseball contract (Shales, 1991). As the networks have struggled to redefine themselves in the deregulated mass communication environment, so too have their affiliates. The combination of declining revenues and high-leverage financing, which many station chains utilized during deregulation for acquisition and merger activities, has contributed to bankruptcy for some owners (Bettelheim, 1992, p. 1C), and continuing efforts to restructure for others (Mermigas, 1991b).

The market forces in media company development have continued to feed the acquisition process. By 1996 the top ten newspaper companies had a combined circulation of more than 25.5 million readers through a combined ownership of 318 daily newspapers. Expansion makes good business sense in expanding corporate revenues, which benefits shareholders. Additionally, moving into a large conglomerate context tends to bring a more global focus to media companies no longer local or regional in nature (Middleton, 1996). Deregulation of the telephone, cable, and broadcast television industries was cited as a positive outcome of the 1996 year in Washington, D.C., by the U.S. Chamber of Commerce (Holzinger, 1996). Part of the expansion has been caused by the threat of new technologies. Existing media organizations have seen their market shares eroded as new ways of getting news, information, and entertainment have evolved. Sullivan Broadcasting argued that the FCC should further relax its duopoly rule, which limits the number of stations an individual owner may have in a market. Duopoly is discussed further in Chapter 15. Sullivan based its argument for a single owner to control up to 50 percent of the stations in a market, providing that only one was a VHF television station, on the increasing competition from Direct Broadcast Satellite (DBS) and wireless cable (McDonnell, 1996).

Another way media companies are trying to enhance their competitive posture is to blend complementary businesses. For example, in 1996 the Walt Disney Company bought Capital Cities/ABC for $19 billion. Disney spokesman Ken Green said, "Walt Disney Company is a provider of content and programming and Capital Cities is in the distribution business. These are complementary businesses" (Middleton, 1996, p. E-1). Time Warner Inc. and Turner Broadcasting System merged in 1996, though the Federal Trade Commission required some restructuring for the combined broadcasting, cable, and publications empire to avoid future antitrust litigation ("The Federal Trade Commission," 1997). Additionally, the $3.7 billion merger of Westinghouse/CBS's radio operations with Infinity Broadcasting Corporation created a 79 station giant with an estimated $1 billion in annual advertising revenues and featuring some of the leading names in the on-air side of radio: Howard Stern, Charles Osgood, and Don Imus. In 1997 Westinghouse/ CBS also purchased The Nashville Network and Country Music Television from Gaylord Entertainment Company to increase its cable presence. The two cable networks reached a combined 108 million homes at the time of the Westinghouse/CBS acquisition (Burgi, 1997). A former executive vice president of NBC radio and small-market radio station owner, Robert Sherman, observed that such large ownership groups serve advertisers more effectively. They don't have to spend so much money within a market to compete among themselves for the same advertising dollars and can be most cost-effective in combining operations such as accounting. That can mean more money for research and program development to increase their audience. Sherman argued, "If you have enhanced value for the advertisers, then you will have more goods sold" (Colford, 1997, p. B48).

The Effect on Television News

Since the 1970s there has been increasing importance placed by television station managers on the ability of newscasts to generate viewers. News is a "major profit center" in most television stations (Stone, V.,1990, p. 16). That is underscored by the amount of self-promotion stations engage in to attract viewers to carefully researched and constructed newscasts. When Ron Powers published his highly critical book on the television news industry in 1977, he reported that one network-owned and -operated station was already spending $1.4 million per year to promote its own newscasts (Powers, R.,1977, p. 13). The visual elements distinguish television news from other journalism products and are the fundamental technological determinants of content (Gans, 1980, p. 158). It is a medium with a troika of extremely powerful influences on what is covered and how: the pressure to provide ratings and thereby income to the station; emphasis on visually powerful stories; and promotability during the four critical audience measuring periods a year known as "sweeps" (O'Brien, 1991).

It is one thing to talk about journalism from a third-person perspective, separated from the art and craft of the practice of it. But journalism is a kind of "calling" where the overarching principles of informing the public tend to create a heavier burden for those who do it for a living. News managers find themselves trying to serve two masters. There is the business side of generating circulation or ratings, and thus profit. And there is the journalism side of covering what needs to be covered, not always something the audience desires. In the contemporary media environment of fast-paced change, news managers find themselves facing powerful, countervailing forces swirling around them. They are besieged.

> I think that the most important thing, to survive, is that you're willing to embrace change. . . . Especially in broadcasting where change is constantly happening and what you need to do is realize that the way you do it today, and the way you accomplish it, is not the way you're going to do it tomorrow. (Medium-market news director)
>
> This is a profession where you're as good as the last thing you did. You're not as good as the best thing you did. A lawyer who successfully argues a case before the Supreme Court always has that. A doctor who performs a difficult surgery for the first time, or did some kind of finding, always has that. A reporter's as good as his last story. A news director's as good as his last rating book, or budget report, a monthly budget report. And it's easy to say that that stuff can be overlooked. But, let's face it. We're in a tough business here. If my ratings go down I don't expect to get fired the next book. But if there's a serious loss and I'm not showing that I'm making moves to change that, the fact that I've got four Emmys at home doesn't mean anything. It doesn't mean a darn thing. (Major-market news director)
>
> We're in the news *business*. It's the same as the newspaper *business*. If your circulation is up and your ad revenue is up and your readership is up, then you're a success. But demographic rating and share is what we're about. It always has been about that. It's even more about that now because the profit margins are big, but not as big as they used to be.
>
> I was at ABC when Capital Cities took over. And within the first several weeks they were there, in my newsroom, in our television station alone, 55 people were laid off. So, I spent a very short amount of time in my career in a rich, fat and happy kind of environment. (Top-ten market news director)

The rise of the Western model of media industries has been concurrent with quickly changing technology, considerable freedom of expression, and capitalistic free enterprise all put into a kind of philosophical blender and spun around. A constant tug-of-war goes on between the principles of journalism, grounded in the Miltonian concept of the marketplace of ideas, and the profit-oriented financial foundation of the Western economic system. Great things can be and have been accomplished when the power of ideas and the power of money come together in positive ways, but not so great things occur as well. At the center of this hurricane is the contemporary news manager who has to keep the various forces at play in balance. Short-term greed can severely impair the journalistic credibility of a news organization, and though immediate ratings improvement may occur, long-term erosion is set in motion. Failure to maintain the marketability of journalistic products for a changing, and sometimes fickle, audience can do the same.

> The management of my budget is one of the key things that I'm rated on. But, conversely, quality newscasts are the other thing. And those things don't really go hand in hand. I think you have to put a quality product on the air first. And I'd rather explain why I'm over budget doing good newscasts than explain why the budget looks good but our newscasts are junk. It's a constant struggle. (Major-market news director)

CHAPTER SUMMARY

The rise of the American media model has produced dramatic change in both the basic form of media companies and the way they engage with their audiences. Where once small, individually owned print shops dominated American media there are now multinational corporations. Technology has evolved from the hand-operated printing press and transportation that took weeks to carry a message across one ocean, to almost instantaneous transmission of satellite and Internet communication worldwide.

Media have increased in complexity and size, with large conglomerates now dominating the industry with complex organizational structures and intricate financial reporting to track revenues, expenditures, and profits. Advertising has come to dominate all media forms. Market research has become an everyday tool not only in the basic design of media products but also the daily content of newspapers and newscasts.

As technology and media structures have changed, so too has the competitive environment. Several times over the last 250 years media forms have become dominant, only to be supplanted later by something new and innovative that lured audiences away from the older form. Newspapers dominated the 19th century. Cinema, radio, and television dominated the 20th century. As we move into the 21st century the Internet and new forms of communication are providing individual audience members increasing control over what media they engage with at any given time. Innovation continues to expand media alternatives as the American media landscape is continuously altered, and the manager's challenges never end.

STUDY QUESTIONS

1. Discuss the concept of the "marketplace of ideas" and how it has evolved from 1644 to today.

2. In the Western model of mass media, advertising plays a significant role. How is that affected by the positive and negative implications of this vehicle for underwriting a "free press"?

3. What is the difference between typical media organizational structure and the "matrix" approach? If you've worked in a mass media organization, what kind of media organization structure have you personally experienced?

4. Discuss the rise of late 20th-century technology and the concept of audience fragmentation—its realities and implications.

chapter 2

MANAGING IN A MEDIA ENVIRONMENT

The media environment is particularly challenging for managers. Although media organizations are like other kinds of human collectives, there are things that separate them from the kinds of organizational models common in business management training programs. However, the basic package of contemporary media management responsibilities includes the same general management areas identified by Henri Fayol in the early part of the 20th century and discussed in detail later in this chapter. Those are planning, organizing, commanding, coordinating, and controlling,

The concepts of management have been considerably refined over the years by numerous organizational management theorists, ranging from the classicist school, which was generally process oriented, to contemporary scholars focused on human dynamics. But throughout the 20th century the development of management theory has been based on one fundamental assumption. More knowledge in the specific practices of a given type of production, combined with understanding the psychosocial forces at work among the workers engaged in that production, can be combined to maximize efficiency and product quality. In other words, if you have a handle on the process, and an understanding of the people involved, you can make things work better.

The human relations school of organizational management was articulated by Douglas McGregor (1960). It perceives the person engaged in organizational work, rather than the mechanical processes, as the real key to productivity. Thus, people have more effect on outcomes than the actual pattern of work itself. Contemporary media organizations, which employ substantial numbers of well-educated, professionally oriented employees with considerable judgment responsibility, depend on the quality of individually controlled work. Although they are factories, in the sense of turning out product every day on a fixed schedule, the product itself depends on the subjective nature of creativity within the individual worker. In such a context it is crucial to have a managing and leading style that can marshal each person's creativity to achieve the highest quality possible while still meeting unrelenting deadlines.

Media companies are different from many other businesses, but there are a lot of similarities, too. One is that any organization has to have a sense of where it is going, along with someone to help get it there. Like a ship at sea, all the technology in the world is useless without a firm hand on the tiller and a captain who has a good sense of direction. So what kind of person is best suited to be at the tiller? Warren Bennis and Burt Nanus (1985) found striking similarities among 90 successful business executives. Those similarities were used to formulate four attributes common to those most effective in leading others (see Fig. 2.1).

Effective managers have

- A vision of where to go.
- The ability to communicate the vision to others.
- A talent for building trust in others.
- The ability to positively manage themselves.

Figure 2.1   Effective Manager Attributes

The first one is having a vision of where the organization needs to go. Second, successful managers must be able to communicate that vision internally to those in the organization to convince them it can be achieved. Third, effective managers must have the ability to build trust among subordinates who buy into the vision of the senior manager. And, fourth, effective managers know how to manage themselves. They generally are positive in outlook with a kind of tempered confidence. They resist impulsiveness as they assume risks along the road to their vision of the future. That means they have an idea, can get others to buy into it, develop confidence among others, and, while convinced of the rightness of their course, are not foolhardy, too impulsive, or conceited about themselves to the degree that it impairs their judgment. They have to keep themselves in order, first and foremost. There are quirky personalities who succeed, with a lot of flash and penchant for teetering on the edge of disaster. But the reality is that most long-term successful leaders and managers have their own act together before they try to get others to do anything.

A number of writers of popular business literature have used scholarly theory to produce best-sellers read widely among business practitioners seeking ways to improve their performance. The most successful of those include William Ouchi's *Theory Z*, published in 1981, an analysis of the cultural differences of Japanese and American companies; Tom Peters and Robert Waterman's *In Search of Excellence*, published in 1982; and Kenneth Blanchard's *The One Minute Manager*, coauthored with Spencer Johnson in 1982. But such widely read guidebooks on how to manage have not provided complete answers to the problem of both working within the structure of an organizational bureaucracy and, at the same time, leading it into the future. Perhaps that's because the future is just that, an unknown void into which we steadily move, which is an evolutionary experience producing new contexts, problems, and solutions.

But constants exist that seem to transcend time and space in organizational dynamics. Peter Drucker (1988a), for example, has underscored that management is an act of structure. As mentioned earlier, managers usually have to concern themselves with the basics of planning, organizing, commanding, coordinating, and controlling. However, Abraham Zaleznik (1989) contrasts such structure-oriented management philosophy with his concept of visionary leadership. It requires more than just putting a given person into a managerial position. The *position* of manager is not what makes the difference. It is the manager's *vision* that guides an organization and its people into the future. To be effective, any manager has to have, coupled with the ability to think in future terms, the power and personality dynamics to implement the vision within the context of the organizational bureaucracy. Structure by itself is just that, a framework. Present within it must be someone with the sense, and interpersonal skill, to make it do something.

In the rest of this chapter you will find more explanation about some of the theorists mentioned so far and further discussion on the aspects of media organizations that make them particularly challenging to manage.

CLASSICAL INDUSTRIAL MANAGEMENT APPROACH

Classical industrial management theory evolved from the simple concept of pushing more "widgets" out of the factory faster. Charles Babbage, a mathematician at the dawn of the industrial revolution in the early 19th century, was interested in worker efficiency and set the stage for the concept of the division of labor (Lavine & Wackman, 1988). In the early part of the 20th century, the study of organizations and how to make them more efficient flourished. Within the classical school of management two writers stand out: Henri Fayol and Frederick Taylor.

Fayol's Functions of Management

Henri Fayol (1949) had a career in the French coal mining industry. He spent most of his life as a manager, and in the last couple of decades of his life, he tried to unpack management to help other people do it better. His focus was on trying to provide a set of managerial skills necessary and applicable across the organizational landscape. He developed a basic package of 14 principles for effective management. They are the foundation upon which the study of modern management is based.

Fayol's structural/functional approach to organizations presupposes that the fundamental concern is to arrange the daily work process. Like the coal mines from which he came, Fayol is concerned with how to get as much work done within the complexity of bureaucracy as possible through careful command and control of the organization. He was one of the first to list key areas of management competence necessary to succeed. His five basic areas of management responsibility include: planning, organizing, commanding, coordinating, and controlling (Fayol, 1949). Within those general areas, his 14 principles provide a kind of checklist of managerial responsibilities, beginning with the proper division of the labor to be accomplished into appropriate departments and teams. The framework of Fayol's principles is shown in Figure 2.2. Note that although most are specific, quantitatively focused, the 14th principle is *espirit de corps*. Fayol recognized that without a positive spirit within an organization, it is in trouble from the start—that a key part of effective management is managing the attitude of people toward their work.

1. **Division of labor**—Specialization of tasks based on individual expertise.
2. **Authority**—Managers direct activity with clearly defined hierarchy.
3. **Discipline**—Duality of roles; employees obey management that provides responsible leadership.
4. **Unity of command**—Each worker has one boss with no conflicting lines of authority.
5. **Unity of direction**—Everyone involved in a particular activity has the same plan and objectives.
6. **Subordination of individual interests**—The goals of the firm are dominant.
7. **Remuneration that is meaningful**—Pay, in its many forms, is a key motivator.
8. **Centralization**—Amount depending on the needs of the specific organization.
9. **Scalar chain of communication**—Vertically through management hierarchy, but with lateral information flows so long as superiors are kept informed.
10. **Order**—Everything from materials to social relations need to be kept in appropriate order.
11. **Equity**—An overriding sense of fairness in the organization.
12. **Stability in personnel**—Some change is inevitable, but too much costs too much. Successful businesses tend to have stable management over time.
13. **Initiative**—Everyone should have opportunities to show initiative and contribute.
14. ***Espirit de Corps***—Positive morale directly affects productivity and is a fundamental managerial responsibility.

Figure 2.2 Fayol's Fourteen Principles

Taylor's Scientific Management

Frederick Taylor (1947/1967) studied pre–World War I steel mill workers and developed the theory of "scientific management." His focus was the efficient use of the human being as a work unit interfacing with the technical equipment provided to maximize assembly line output. He measured the size of shovels and the amount of coal shoveled by individual workers. He then determined the size of each worker's shovel and the load for that person to function at optimum efficiency throughout the day. Different-sized people required different-sized shovels and moved different amounts of material. But if each could work optimally, productivity would be at a maximum. To make workers push themselves harder, Taylor developed the concept of incentive pay. Workers who shoveled more coal than their daily quota got a few more dollars. Over the years Taylor's concept of incentive pay has been developed into a high art in some companies, with complex formulas for profit sharing, stock incentives, and other kinds of bonuses when the company has a particularly good year. Taylor's imprint on contemporary management clearly remains.

Although he has often been viewed negatively, because of his penchant for efficiency, Taylor's work, when you read it and not just the criticisms of it, reflects a man who believed that the most efficient worker was the happiest. So even the often criticized mechanical classicist, Taylor, was driven by humanistic considerations. To him, the more productive a person was, the happier the person was. And the happier a worker was because of being particularly good at a job, the more both the worker and the employer benefited from the worker's increased productivity, assuming Taylor's incentive pay concept was present.

The critical flaw in Taylor's approach was the focus on financial reward as the primary motivator. His utilitarian approach did not encompass the concept of financially secure workers driven by deeper psychological considerations in the pursuit of happiness far beyond basic survival issues manifested in a weekly paycheck. The way people interface with their work is very different when they are just trying to keep food on the table to survive, compared with when their physical needs are more than satisfied and they begin thinking about whether they are "happy" in their jobs. Happiness and contentment rest upon the quickly shifting sands of a person's immediate context. And so the concept of knowledge framed by a growing understanding of employees' psychosocial perspectives threads its way through decades of management research. Considering all of that, it is clear that increasing productivity can be very complex. Considerable pay disparity is a negative motivator across employee types who often perceive the amount of remuneration they receive as an indicator of their worth. As a manager, you may not be able to do much about pay disparity, but you need to be aware of its corrosive effect. A little time and effort showing personal appreciation for the work lesser-paid individuals do can go a long way in making them feel they matter to you and the media organization.

GROWTH OF HUMAN RELATIONS MANAGEMENT CONCEPTS

McGregor's Theory X and Y

Douglas McGregor published his Theory X and Y typology in 1960, two opposing managerial attitudes toward the workplace. It is most effective to see these two extremes as opposite ends of a management philosophy continuum (see Fig. 2.3).

Theory X	Theory Y
• People don't really want to work and try to avoid doing it.	• Work is a natural part of living that people do not inherently dislike.
• Managers have to control and coerce workers, using negative reinforcement (punishment), to get them to do their jobs.	• Employees want to achieve goals to which they're committed.
• Workers have little desire for responsibility and prefer to be directed rather than be self-directed.	• People commit to goals they see as producing personal reward.
	• Workers both seek and accept responsibility when given a chance.
	• Workers can be innovative in providing organizational solutions.
	• Frequently, workers' intelligence is not used fully.

Figure 2.3 Theory X and Y Management Presumptions

Theory X is an authoritarian command-and-control approach. It assumes that most people really don't want to work and thus must be "coerced, controlled, directed, threatened with punishment to get them to put forth adequate effort toward the achievement of organizational objectives" (McGregor, 1960, p. 33–43). Management and employees are seen as opposing factions with considerable tension.

This approach is still very much a part of the managerial subconscious, reflected in the tendency of many managers to be solitary decision makers and order givers who depend on the power of their official title to get employees to respond. It may be that when a person is put "in charge" there is a natural tendency to order others around and expect obedience. After all, you are "in charge." When managers are held directly responsible for the performance of subordinates, it only serves to make them more paranoid about the way things are done. Firing a manager because a subordinate makes a mistake is clearly questionable, since the subordinate committed the error and should be held accountable. However, in many organizations being a manager means being the person held accountable. This is sometimes manifested in "workaholics" who think they have to do everything themselves to ensure it's done right. When "it's your responsibility" you tend to be very personally involved and hesitate to delegate.

In media organizations where the quality of the product is primarily in the hands of the people doing the creative work, this is a fast track to failure. A typical response to authoritarian managers is to do only what they order, and only the way they order it done. The employee withdraws personal ownership of the work and adopts the attitude of, "push button, pick up check." Suddenly the manager is being asked to make all manner of small decisions and cannot concentrate on the larger questions. Nothing moves without his or her say-so. When authoritarians are present, it is common to see a lot of positive reinforcement of them by subordinates who play a political game of pleasing the boss, even though they may doubt the wisdom of what's being done. Since authoritarians frequently perceive questioning, proposing alternatives, or criticism of their suggestions as signs of disloyalty, people adopt a self-preservation approach. Then the "Emperor's new clothes" syndrome will likely set in, where no matter how ridiculous the authoritarian looks, his or her subordinates will keep smiling and saying how great things are. "Yes" people are often the kind within the inner circle of such a personality who reinforce the flaws of the authoritarian and do not counterbalance his or her weaknesses with strengths of their own. If the authoritarian is also very good at his or her job, the organization works. But when the person is mediocre or worse, job performance declines rapidly.

McGregor contrasted his Theory X typology with what he labeled the Theory Y approach. It assumes that people are not negatively predisposed to the work environment at all. In fact, they are the reverse. Given the opportunity, they expand their knowledge and not only accept responsibility but actively seek expanding their role and position in the organization. Fundamental to Theory Y is the concept of personalizing organizational goals. In other words, people in a Theory Y company have the sense that if they work hard to achieve corporate goals, they will be rewarded individually and as a group. Effort on the personal level has a direct relationship to improved organizational performance. That improved performance then makes possible greater individual rewards for those involved. In effect, one hand washes the other, as the individual and organization are seen as complementary rather than as opposing forces. This is the essence of contemporary team building and participation of employees as vested interests in positive organizational performance. If the employee understands how he or she benefits from organizational success, there is a personal vested interest that is a powerful motivator.

Whereas Theory X sees the employee as, basically, another machine on the assembly line to be manipulated, Theory Y recognizes the effect of that employee perceiving a personal vested interest in the success of the company. It is important to understand that McGregor's X and Y typology represents opposite extremes on a continuum of management. Most organizations are somewhere between the two, with some elements of each. For example, a newspaper may have an editor with a strong personality who exercises firm control of the newsroom. That person may have a clear vision of where he or she wants the paper to go and, as long as everyone stays within the framework of that vision, enormous flexibility and tolerance for creative license is provided. Writers can write the way they want to, and reporters have great personal responsibility for working their beats. As long as you don't cross the editor in the areas that are important to that person, it's a Theory Y operation. But when you end up with silly factual errors, for example, the yelling starts.

Such managerial style is fairly common when you have people engaged in a profession, such as journalism, that they perceive as a higher calling with greater social responsibilities than ordinary work. Often it is evidence of intense caring and pride in what is being done. The key is to balance the managerial equation within such a work environment that has as much passion as pragmatism. There has to be enough X to satisfy the need to command an organization, counterbalanced with enough Y to spur on its creativity and build strong employee cultures focused on achieving organizational goals. Achieving this balance is anything but easy.

The Rise of Participative Management

The second half of the 20th century saw a major shift of American business and industry away from autocratic management centered on command and control to participative management styles (Brown, 1992). It is not incidental that this occurred concurrently with a significant rise in the education level of American workers and a shift from an economy based on manufacturing to one increasingly driven by service industries (Van Auken, 1992). But the involvement of more than just the leaders in decision making is not a 20th-century phenomenon. Consensus of those being led has always been part of the human experience. Group consultation in important matters is reflected in the writings of St. Benedict in A.D. 529 (Vroom & Jago, 1988). Even the great conqueror of the ancient world, Alexander the Great, found that a disciplined army sometimes has a mind of its own. His dramatic campaign, which spread Macedonian control from Greece through the Middle East and Persia to India, ended when his army refused to go farther. Contrary to the desire of one of the greatest military leaders in history, the soldiers said no (Langer, 1972).

Although collective decision making, in various forms, has always been part of the human experience going back to tribal cultures, a precise definition is in order for us to consider it as a managerial technique rather than a sociological phenomenon driven by particular circumstances. If you are going to implement the concept of participative management as a daily process, you have to know exactly what you are talking about. This management style is not simply discussions around a campfire that build into a confrontation with the general. It is not just exchanging ideas about which way to move the small hunter-gatherer band in search of food. It is, in the contemporary business sense, a philosophy of operation that extends contribution of ideas and responsibility for action "to the lowest level appropriate to the decision being made" (Plunkett & Fournier, 1991).

Participative management's roots are in the 1930s with the experiments conducted by Elton Mayo at the Hawthorne plant of Western Electric Company. Basically, Mayo found that when he increased the amount of light on the assembly line, productivity increased. And when he turned down the light, productivity increased. At first that seemed odd. But Mayo found that what was really causing the increased motivation on the assembly line was the sense employees had that someone was paying attention to them. What mattered was not whether the light was turned up or down, but rather that someone cared enough to do something with it at all. The seeds had been sown for paying greater attention to employees, a practice that had been proven to increase productivity. Employees were participants in the achievement of corporate objectives, no longer simply work units.

Mayo's work contributed to the human relations approach to management, in which it is understood that people need to feel important to an organization; that motivation is often increased by personal recognition and being included, rather than simply being paid in rudimentary financial rewards (Mayo, 1946). More than money drives employees. Other researchers contributed to further understanding of the dynamics of the workplace until participative management was finally defined as a concept by Likert (1961). Likert found that groups of workers who were particularly productive generally had looser supervision, had a sense of responsibility in their jobs, and had bosses who were more people-oriented than focused on daily production. The idea of employees personally involved in the design and implementation of their own work really caught on in American business during the 1970s and 1980s (Schmidt & Finnigan, 1992). That fostered the rise of such concepts as self-managed work teams and other measures to widen the span of control in organizations, making them less hierarchically dependent (Odiorne, 1991).

The basic approach to participative management includes several elements, which are shown in Figures 2.4 and 2.5.

Most organizations apply these elements situationally. In other words, some aspects of work lend themselves to participative approaches, and others do not. There aren't many organizations that are driven completely by teams with few central authority figures. As will be discussed later, the context of the work to be done is the best indicator of the approach to be used. But based on Rensis Likert's (1961) research, and that which has been done since, it is clear than many employees respond to increased responsibility. And often the people engaged in the day-to-day work are the best ones to decide how to do it. When provided an opportunity to participate in the management of themselves, individuals often feel a sense of ownership in the decisions that are made and then work harder to make sure they are effective. That alone may be the heart and soul of participative management.

- Loose supervision of work with considerable employee self-direction.
- Wide use of teams to solve problems, often across departmental boundaries.
- Wide involvement of employees at all levels on an equal basis.
- Team leaders encourage free expression without management interference.

Figure 2.4 Key Aspects of Participative Management

All of the following are normally most effective with fewer than a dozen members.
• Task forces work on long-term issues.
  — Often span organizational division.
  — Usually appointed with unit representatives.
  — Address a wide range of concerns.
  — Usually have specific time span in which to accomplish work.
• Teams usually focus on a specific problem or issue.
  — Within a department or division.
  — Usually have appointed members, but sometimes include volunteers.
• Quality circles focus on quality issues.
  — Usually transcend organizational lines.
  — Typically are dominated by volunteers, though some appointees are common.
  — Focus on production and product issues.
  — Often set up with open-ended time frame as an ongoing work group.

Figure 2.5 Task Forces, Teams, Quality Circles

Key aspects of participative management include the following:

♦ Work groups are loosely supervised, and details of task accomplishment are left up to them.

♦ Teams are set up to address specific projects. Those projects may be general in nature, crossing departmental boundaries, or more narrowly defined.

♦ Organization membership criteria are relatively free, which encourages people at all levels to become involved as equals on the team. This fosters more open dialogue and encourages individual ideas and varying perspectives.

♦ A team leader is often designated to help facilitate discussions and keep the team on the agenda. However, it is crucial that team members feel free to express themselves without managerial repercussions. Otherwise dialogue is severely restricted. It is best to have team leaders who are not members of management. If the team is comprised of managers, a peer of the majority should be the leader.

There are differences between teams and other participative groups, such as quality circles or task forces. All of these are most effective when membership is limited to fewer than a dozen people (Lacy, Sohn, & Wicks, 1993). That's basically because larger groups become unwieldy, and discussion among large collections of people gets protracted and hard to keep focused on the issue(s) at hand. Task forces are usually focused on long-term major issues. They normally are appointed with representatives from departments or divisions. You might have a task force set up to work on what kind of new press to buy for a newspaper, for example, or to investigate how to approach setting up a media organization entry into the World Wide Web. Generally, teams are focused on a specific problem or issue within a division or department that needs to be resolved in a relatively short time. People may be appointed by management, or elected by work groups, or asked to volunteer. Quality circles, which focus on quality issues, usually are set up on the departmental or divisional level. They are very common in production environments, usually staffed by volunteers, and seek to involve workers to ensure quality is maintained.

Ouchi's Theory Z

Theory Z was published by William Ouchi in 1981. It has a simple underlying principle that can be quite complex to integrate into the fabric of an organization: "Involved workers are the key to increased productivity" (p. 4).

In the 1970s Japan had become a major economic force in the world. Following World War II, in which Japan's industrial sector was decimated, American business dominated. But just 25 years after the end of the war the foreign trade balance had shifted dramatically in Japan's favor, particularly in automobiles and electronics. There was a lot of concern about whether American competitiveness had lessened, as the foreign trade balance continued to shift in favor of the Japanese. Ouchi studied the managerial practices of Japan at a time when Japanese firms were surging ahead of the rest of the world in quality and productivity. Dramatic cultural differences in the two nations are manifested in their approaches to everything, including corporate life.

Individualism is a cherished American concept manifested in the mythic Western cowboy alone against the odds. In American culture, people try to stand out against the herd, not blend in. Asserting one's individualism is almost a national pastime. American corporate executives have a tendency to jump from firm to firm every few years with little real corporate loyalty. Five years at one company is a considerable length of time. To get ahead, you move to a better position in another firm. Climbing the corporate hierarchy is more difficult within an organization than by accepting promotions from other firms and hopping from one company to another as higher status positions are offered. American résumés tend to be lengthy regarding the number of companies for which one has worked. When problems are found by managers, it is common to seek expertise from outside the organization, hiring external consultants or bringing in a new manager to fix things rather than seeking solutions within. American organizations typically have significant corporate political games with quickly shifting loyalties among middle managers. It is not uncommon to have people do things to make someone else look bad who is perceived to be a rival on the corporate ladder. After all, in a relatively short time you, or the other person, will be gone anyway, off to another company and another game.

By contrast the Japanese management style has embraced a concept of "lifetime employment." The Japanese have greater social regimentation beginning in their school system and working all the way up into the corporate world. Once hired by a company a person finds it more than just a workplace. It provides extensive social relationships along with the job. The corporation and employees form unique, long-term cultures of complementary values where one tends to mirror the other. Because they live in a dense population and have a deeply ingrained culture, Japanese people are accustomed to group identity, group activities, and diminished individualism. Japanese employees work their way up through the maze of corporate offices, with years of experience in various departments and offices, by building long-term alliances and intricate social connections within the organization. Comparatively little corporate political game playing occurs, because Japanese employees know they have to work with the same people next year and the year after. If a worker does something against someone, that person will be there to get even next year or in five years. So the system breeds a climate of cooperative consensus, which is rewarded with an attitude of mutual loyalty, dedication, and permanence. Traditionally, a key attribute of Japanese firms has been the concept of lifetime employment. The firm a person went to work for out of school was, in all probability, the firm from which he or she would retire.

There are signs the Japanese management style is changing to a more pragmatic style. Recent economic changes in Japan have increased the corporate focus on profits and worker productivity. Leading Japanese firms are reassessing such traditional practices as pay based on seniority, and lifetime employment, which are being criticized as having a potential for limiting efficiency and productivity (Terazono, 1996). Another factor is increasing globalization, which has caused Japanese firms to shift manufacturing overseas where other cultures do not always hold the same values as are prevalent in Japan. The strong emphasis on managerial consensus is being criticized by some as slowing down response in rapidly changing environments (Makiuchi, 1996). However, as the debate in Japan continues on how to redefine managerial philosophy, a focus remains on maintaining mutually respectful relationships. As one commentator emphasized, "the focus should not be solely on returns" (Asami, 1997, p. 5).

Whereas Japanese companies generally continue to offer lifetime employment, slow advancement, close control of information, and consensus decision making, American firms are generally characterized by short-term employment, specialized career paths, rapid advancement, and top-down decision making. Given the fact that Japanese companies came to dominate the economic landscape by the late 1970s, Ouchi set out to determine whether some of their management methods might be transferable, to one degree or another, to American firms. He found a number of the best-run companies in the United States had found ways to blend many of the attributes found in both cultures, particularly the ability to retain the American need for individual achievement but with a greater sense of organizational community. Those American firms he called Type Z organizations and used them as a model for other firms trying to increase their competitiveness.

The following key ten characteristics help define Type Z organizations (see Fig. 2.6 for a summarized version of these points):

1. Longer-term employment. Although contemporary American firms don't subscribe to "lifetime" employment, Type Z organizations do feature more stable employment, with a high value on experienced workers.

2. Relatively slow evaluation and promotion. Type Z companies are more measured in their analysis of employees and see promotion as a process of growth, not a short-term reward.

3. Cross-departmental career paths that provide experience in a wide range of company operations so managers have a wider sense of the entire organization as they climb the corporate ladder.

4. Extensive use of modern management tools (accounting, information, planning, etc.), not as controls but as monitoring devices. Budgets, strategic plans, and other business components change as the environment changes. Type Z companies are quick to make adjustments in whatever is necessary.

5. Attention to "fit" and "suitability" of decisions. A Type Z company makes sure it has as many facts as possible but still uses intuitive sense and feelings about itself and its market to reach final decisions. There is a sense of doing the "right" thing for the company in the long run.

1. Longer-term employment.
2. Relatively slow advancement.
3. Management experience in different departments.
4. Careful monitoring of activity with maximum flexibility.
5. Attention to appropriateness or "fit" of decisions and activities of the organization in terms of synchronizing with the corporate personality.
6. Emphasis on participative decision making and consensus.
7. Wholistic attitude with a sense of family.
8. Self-directed employees with emphasis on positive motivation.
9. Emphasis on teams and other ways to include employees at all levels of the organization.
10. Strong communication flow throughout the organization with positive efforts to keep everyone informed of what's going on.

Figure 2.6 Type Z Organization Characteristics

6. An emphasis on participative decision making and consensus. That doesn't mean Type Z firms do not have decision makers. The ultimate decision usually rests in the hands of one individual, but with considerable input and consultation from many others whose concerns are usually addressed during the decision process.

7. Holistic attitude toward all members of the corporate culture. Relationships tend to be broader and less formal. There is more of a sense of family.

8. A high degree of self-direction by employees, who are then more committed, motivated, and loyal.

9. Heavy emphasis on teams, quality circles, and other techniques to directly involve employees in the decision process at every level.

10. Extensive communication through the organization, with open information flow creating an atmosphere of trust through honesty.

In Ouchi's view one of the major negatives in the American system is the tendency for corporate political game playing to develop because long-term relationships are rare. In Japanese organizations corporate politics are discouraged by the fact workers have to get along over long periods of career development. Because of the deeper personal relationships and long-term associations inherent within them, Type Z organizations depend heavily on participative decision making. Everyone in a given department or office works to reach agreement on how to deal with a problem. Theoretically that promotes creativity and more effective implementation of decisions.

In Type Z auto plants, for example, when something stops the assembly line, the workers literally swarm around the problem to resolve it quickly with as many ideas as they can muster as quickly as they can. Fundamentally, the keystone to participative management is the quality of the people participating. They all have to be highly knowledgeable and positively engaged in the corporate culture or participative management can break down very quickly. And they have to want to participate. Some people enjoy pitching in to decide things. Others just want to be told what they need to do. Others want to command, to tell others what to do as a central authority figure. Clearly, who is on the participative management team is the most important issue to resolve before anything further can be accomplished.

Ouchi's Theory Z was the beginning of substantial literature focusing on how to integrate Japanese management methods into the American production model. Masaaki Imai (1986) included many of the same concepts in his kaizen theory. The Japanese word *kaizen* means continuous, positive improvement. That change can only be harnessed in positive terms if all members of the organization see their role as fostering continuous quality improvement. The kaizen approach attempts to create a corporate culture that perceives every aspect of human endeavor—daily work, home, and social life—as deserving of steady improvement. It is implemented, similarly to Type Z organizational efforts, with inclusion of organizational members in teams, quality circles, and encouraging the rise of informal leaders among work groups. Thus, employees develop a sense of pride and self-direction by contributing to the setting of goals and participation in decisions and resource allocation. A presumption of kaizen theory is that the work environment is made more stimulating and gratifying (Imai, 1986).

For media organizations the concept of continuous efforts to improve and include knowledgeable employees in that effort clearly is fertile ground for this approach. Media organization employees tend to be highly creative and see their work as having great importance. So including them as team members in how work is designed and directed clearly attempts to capitalize on their desire to have some level of control over that work. In effect, participative management attempts to make them partners in the organizational effort. James Grunig (1992) argues this is particularly an advisable approach to foster excellence in public relations agencies and offices. In public relations the goal is to provide positive internal and external communication to benefit the organization. In effect, the public relations professional is in the middle, as a kind of translator between an organization and its various publics, be they customers, media, or internal personnel reading a corporate newsletter. So the highest possible quality, with constant effort at improving that communication effort, is in the best interests of everyone.

Japanese management concepts, such as kaizen theory, are grounded in the Japanese culture, which focuses on collaborative approaches to systematic problem solving. The difficulty, when jumping to another culture that may be more independence oriented, is that when people are predisposed to doing things alone, they may resist teaming. That means integration of collaboration may take more time than assumed at the beginning. In effect you are changing people's habits and presumptions of social interaction when you alter work relationships. That is not to say such change is not advisable. Just that when you begin doing it, you need to understand changing culture is sometimes a more difficult thing than it appears on the surface and can be much more time consuming than first presumed. You don't just, one day, order everyone to do it.

What is important to understand when considering any of the various theoretical approaches to management is that all have pluses and minuses. For example, although longer-time employment and deeply ingrained culture are benefits in relieving employees of the sense of being at risk, they also create entrenched bureaucracy that tends to control everything by seniority. That in turn can make an organization very slow to adapt to anything new. And people who are aggressive, imaginative, and creative can get frustrated very quickly in a culture that requires time-consuming consensus building and group or committee meetings on virtually every level. Leader personalities, particularly, are stymied in such an environment. Additionally, such organizations sometimes foster mediocrity with people who have little sense of being at risk and whose vested interest is in the status quo. By contrast, the traditional American cultural approach has a penchant for trying instant solutions to complex problems. Because people move quickly and need to make themselves stand out, high risk is a featured position, which produces extremes of great rewards or catastrophic failure. American firms are notoriously short-sighted, with a quarter-to-quarter paranoia fed by the system of financial reports and stock market analysis that generally uses quarters of the year to track corporate financial health. Everything in American business culture is focused on the immediate, with much less sense of long-term strategy and future thinking. It's faster and more dynamic, but it is also subject to the latest trend or quick fix.

One downside to participative management, whether in the culture-steeped approach of Japanese organizations, or in its many altered forms, is that it takes a lot of time. It can be very frustrating when everyone has to have a say in something and a deadline is approaching. Collaborative decision making sounds like a good idea, except to the newspaper columnist or editorial cartoonist who wants to be independent and not influenced by some kind of committee definition of issues and points of view. Some media jobs are definitely collaborative, others are intensely independent, and still others are intricate blends of the two. Because of that, making participative management a part of contemporary media organizations can be tricky. Deadlines are unyielding and create the need for individual decision makers who move quickly. There is often no time for a meeting to decide which headline to use or whether to drop the television news live remote from the first segment of the newscast to the third because the microwave truck is having trouble getting the signal in with two minutes until air. In the pressure of daily news production the philosophical side of participative management seems almost ludicrous. People are in jobs that require speed, critical evaluation, and snap decisions throughout the day.

Another problem can be what Irving Janis (1973) first identified as "groupthink." The term describes members of a group reaching a decision, or taking an action, that none of them would individually. Janis studied the Kennedy administration and the way in which some cabinet decisions were reached. The group dynamics resulted in individuals rationalizing their positions to sustain group cohesiveness by reinforcing their collective sense of self-righteousness, unity, and conformity to the president's wishes. Janis found that reduced critical thinking and overruled any outright challenging of basic assumptions that some members held covertly. Thus, group loyalty had a tendency to distort reality and warp the collective view of the appropriate action necessary for a particular circumstance.

Clearly crisis management at the presidential level may be different, in terms of the stakes, than in a media organization newsroom. However, subconscious desires to get ahead with one's career clearly affect how vociferously a reporter or staff writer argues with an editor or executive producer. There is an old adage, "You can't buck City Hall," and in organizational dynamics that sense of holding your views and positions in check is an everyday factor. Indeed, one of the biggest problems for contemporary managers and leaders is getting honest opinions from their subordinates instead of having those people tell their bosses what they think they want to hear. A fact of corporate life is that you tend to get farther ahead by agreeing with the boss than by arguing with him or her.

One of the selling points of participative management is that power is shared. The theory is that when employees feel they have a greater effect on decisions, they have a vested interest in making the right decisions. But the problem of groupthink—encouraged by a desire to achieve popularity and status among one's peers—may result in a dependence on consensus decision making that produces bad results. It can turn decision making into such a laborious and politicalized process that the organization ties itself up.

But that does not mean participative management can't work in media organizations. What it really emphasizes is a key point of any management approach. Everything depends on the environment and must be tailored to what that environment demands. The environments of daily newspapers, magazines, cable television systems, public relations and advertising agencies, and electronic newsrooms are very different. All have things that are individually centered and things that are not. All have some periods of crises when decisions are rapid-fire, and other times when ideas can be mulled over for a while. Why not tailor the management style to fit the needs of the organization? Can we not have organizations that flex with situations and use the most effective approach at the time? In fact, that seems to be happening more as increasingly enlightened managers evolve in media organizations. What seems to occur in typical media companies is that long-term strategic decisions, which lend themselves to careful study, lengthy debate, and consensus building, fit the participative management concept and are best handled that way. But in day-to-day tasks requiring quick decisions, individuals are provided the necessary authority, and a tighter, almost autocratic command-and-control system is used when necessary to make sure the deadline is met. It is not uncommon to hear a producer or an editor say, "OK, I see your point, but right now we've got to get this on-air (or in the first edition) so we're going to do _____. We'll talk about your concerns later!" In other words, there is a lot of participative decision making in some things, and none in others where individual authority rules out of necessity. So the honest, and very simple, answer to the question of "Where should you have participative management and where should you avoid it in a media company?" is, it depends. What that, then, means is that you, as a manager, have to know your organization, your people, and the work to be done. It is an intricate equation.

TQM and Contemporary Team Approaches

Total Quality Management, or TQM as it is commonly referred to, is a culture of performance attitude. You try to create within the organization a sensitivity toward both the employees within and the people without. All are customers in various ways. Everyone is a customer of everyone else. For example, the printing department is a customer of news editorial in that the galleys and art have to get produced in time for the plates to be made and the presses to run on time. On the other hand, news-editorial is a customer of the printing plant because if the printers don't do a good job getting the ink on the paper, the end product looks bad and hurts the effort of news-editorial. You mutually reinforce and serve and focus on one another, meeting one another's needs in as excellent a manner as possible.

Total Quality Management evolved in this atmosphere of employee participation. It began as a 1940s concept called *statistical quality control*. The philosophy embracing quality as a fundamental corporate goal was expanded by W. Edwards Deming and Joseph Juran in resurrecting Japanese industry during the 1950s. In the fertile ground of post–World War II Japan, whose industries had been decimated by the war, they developed TQM (Marash, 1993). It is not a simple formula, but a transformation of the corporate culture. The TQM concept requires that everyone be considered a customer. Customers fall into two basic categories, internal and external. The external customers do business with the organization. They can be suppliers, buyers, or anyone else who engages from outside the organization itself. All internal people of the organization are perceived as internal customers. Everyone inside is a customer of everyone else: person to person, department to department, division to division. For example, if a secretary calls an executive with a question, the executive should treat the secretary as a customer and strive to provide the highest quality response possible. The method is not hierarchically driven but is centered on providing excellent service to every person every time. Along with the customer service focus, everyone in the organization, from the highest-ranking executive to the janitor, has a responsibility for continuous improvement of quality, so the approach is not a static form but rather a dynamic, ongoing experience (Desai, 1993). TQM is not meant to be just another snappy slogan for management to charge up the troops, but a pervasive and complete attitude adjustment throughout the organization. It is a philosophy of continually improving at every level (Brocka & Brocka, 1992).

When TQM begins at a small or large company, usually a committee is set up to implement it and may be called the "quality committee," "quality council," "steering committee," or some other appropriate designation. Employees from all levels should be represented on the committee. Additionally, self-directed work teams are set up from people in specific work process areas or other normal divisions within the firm. Teams pick their own leaders, who should not be regular managers in most cases. What is important is to generate personal ownership and involvement in team efforts by all employees. Teams don't work when they are management driven because people tend to try to please the boss rather than campaign for their own, possibly different, ideas. The only additional person involved, who usually is not a regular team member, may be what's called a *facilitator*. That person is sort of a neutral observer who must keep the team focused on the issue at hand. Effective TQM implementation requires that all employees in the company have opportunities to be on teams and contribute to the improvement effort. What you are doing in TQM is giving employees a feeling of empowerment in making the organization better while at the same time establishing a sense of ownership in the organization. Employees are personally involved, then, and the organization is no longer just a place they spend time to collect a paycheck. It becomes a part of themselves with deeper, personalized meaning (Wellins, Byham, & Wilson, 1991).

Soin (1992) argues that the benefits of TQM include higher productivity, lower prices, higher market share, higher profits, and more customer satisfaction, which then breed stronger customer loyalty with increased repeat purchases. Three attributes of TQM distinguish it from other theories of organizational management: (1) It has to be integrated into the culture companywide to be truly effective; (2) steady improvement is emphasized, based on facts, with continuous effort to reduce variability of products or services; and (3) performance is improved by turning the company into an efficient organization focused on satisfying customer requirements (Schmidt & Finnigan, 1992). The fundamental driving force behind TQM is that it has been shown to increase corporate profitability. An organization's customers determine who has the highest quality for the best price in their decision to purchase what the organization has to offer, or go elsewhere. Thus, quality is, fundamentally, tied directly to making money. It is a very pragmatic issue, not a philosophical state of mind. Quality has a tangible purpose, to increase market share (Tunks, 1992). For media companies the customer's perception of price may not be in only monetary terms. One kind of price is spending the time to engage with a medium. Another is to what degree the time required is personally convenient. CNN Headline News rose as a television force because it provides half-hour newscasts continuously. Viewers can tune in at their convenience rather than waiting for traditional newscasts broadcast at the network's convenience.

It is useful at this point to consider the essential ingredients of the 14 points Deming sees as necessary for transforming organizations into quality-based corporate cultures. They are shown in Figure 2.7. As you read down the list, consider how dramatic a change these points can bring to organizations that may be steeped in their own processes and procedures spun of their own bureaucracy. Without constant attention toward satisfying customer wants and needs through the highest quality possible, it is not uncommon for organizations to become encumbered by their own mythologies of the marketplace, which don't always mesh with how the customers really view things.

1. Constant attention to improving product and service as key to competitiveness.
2. Take on leadership role with new proactive managerial philosophy.
3. Stop using inspection to control quality. Build it in from the ground up.
4. Don't just buy from the lowest bidder. Use single suppliers, relationships, and trust.
5. Consistently improve the system of production and service to decrease costs.
6. Use on-the-job training to increase employee skill and efficiency.
7. Encourage leadership. Supervision is more than just keeping things going.
8. Eliminate fear in the organization so everyone can work positively.
9. Drop barriers between departments; work across boundaries to solve problems.
10. Eliminate sloganeering and numerically driven production targets. They make adversaries out of employees, causing declines in overall quality and productivity.
11. Stop factory quotas and management by objective. Lead people to work better.
12. Instill pride of workmanship and pride in personal quality achievement.
13. Aggressively pursue a program of education and self-improvement.
14. Involve everyone in transforming the company to a quality-based organization.

Figure 2.7 Essential Ingredients of Deming's Fourteen Points

The original work by Deming and Juran in Japan set off a revolution of sorts in management analysis and design, which resulted in the growth of considerable research focused on quality as the centerpiece of organizational activity. There are, literally, hundreds of books and articles on the subject, many attempting to reframe the concepts into simpler sets of organizational criteria. Chris Hakes (1991), for example, sets out six basic concepts necessary to implement a TQM program. They are shown in Figure 2.8.

With a strong orientation to customer satisfaction, a never-ending drive toward improvement, and the other four aspects of Hakes' list, which are focused on the managerial effort to minimize cost and maximize productivity, the organization is quicker to respond to marketplace changes. Quality is defined from the customer's perspective. As the customer's needs adjust, so does the organization. Theoretically that means the organization is much more responsive to its main reason for being, the customer. It is less prone to be caught up within its own corporate illusions, which sometimes result

1. Customer satisfaction.
2. Never-ending improvement.
3. Control of business processes.
4. Upstream preventative maintenance.
5. Ongoing preventative action.
6. Leadership and teamwork.

Figure 2.8 Hakes's Concepts for Implementing TQM

in products placed in the marketplace that fail immediately because no one really wanted them. The needs of the customer, regardless of any established work patterns in the company or any preferences of management for product design, must be the central aim of any quality program (Barrier, 1992).

Quality-oriented organizations usually feature teams working across departmental boundaries. Those teams are usually set up to address specific problems or tasks, or sometimes as permanent working groups to facilitate information flow across the breadth of the organization. Particularly in large, complicated corporate structures, it is very easy for the proverbial right hand not to know what the left hand is doing. This is especially important in companies, such as media organizations, that span more than one customer market or product. For example, a daily newspaper or evening newscast has many roles with many different kinds of customers. Some engage with the media product to get specific information or to meet their general surveillance needs so they have a sense of being an informed person. Many newspaper subscribers take the paper so they can get the weekly grocery ads. Other customers use the media organization as a communication tool. Politicians create photo opportunities to get themselves covered as news events. Advertisers buy space or time to reach potential customers. Still other media organization customers use media for amusement or to get their mind off their immediate concerns.

Although we may think of a newspaper, or a television broadcast as one thing, it clearly is really many different things to many different kinds of customers. Therefore, various areas of concern need to be addressed in the planning, production, and distribution of the media product (Lacy, Sohn, & Wicks, 1993). Teamwork within an organization is crucial to its success. When different departments function like isolates, decisions can be made that impair the efforts of other departments. If the promotion department of a newspaper launches a major campaign to surge circulation, but doesn't let the printing department know what's being done and how much of an increase in the newspaper run is anticipated, they may not have enough paper and ink to satisfy the increased customer demand. The result can be catastrophic. When customers can't get products they've been convinced they need, they tend to get irritated. That can create a negative image in the marketplace that endures for a long time. Only through teamwork and free-flowing communication within a media organization can its many aspects be orchestrated effectively to maintain harmony.

Media Organizations: Combinations of Machine and Professional Models

Media organizations are among the most challenging to manage because they really are a combination of two fundamental types of organizations that are very different. They are assembly lines with strict deadlines and involved processes that must be done in order, with speed, and are repetitive. Everything happens at a certain time, like a set of gears fitting together. You set the speed and everybody works with it. It develops its own inertia and it moves right along. Media organizations are a lot like auto assembly plants in some ways. But they are also work environments where employees have a lot of creative control of their work; are highly educated and use their mental abilities to do their work, which is full of judgment calls; and tend to see their work as a higher calling. They tend to do the job because of reasons beyond just a paycheck. It is an extension of self. Media employees tend to think of the product as their personal property even though the media organization owns the copyright. Particularly the news-editorial types see themselves as independent professionals working within the general framework of the media organization. They are not so much employees, as providing their professional talents for a fee.

So you have factory workers who are really not factory workers, laboring under tight production line schedules, but who see their work as more than a mere production. It is a managerial environment unlike most others. You have to think about that when you try to manage these people. They behave differently. You can't just tell them, "Do this," or, "Do that," because though they may do it, they may not do it as well as they can. The quality of their work depends on them more than in just about any other job. They can write a story that is OK, or they can write the same story so it jumps off the page. The difference between *acceptable* and *exceptional* is within themselves.

In media organizations you end up with a lot of the traditional industrial organization elements of factories, tossed into a blender with workers who see themselves as professionals similar to doctors and lawyers. And you end up with a soup that is context driven. Sometimes, because of the demands of the organization, you have a lot of screaming and shouting and order giving. It looks like an authoritarian model if you walk into the middle of it. Other times you have a very collegial, easygoing, democratic, kind of meet-and-discuss-and-we-all-agree attitude. It all depends on the time and situation and the pressure. Media organizations appear to be a blend of two configurations that Henry Mintzberg (1989) characterized as the "machine" and "professional."

Inherent in the machine organization is a closely controlled system designed to maintain efficiency of routine processes. Producing news product on a daily or hourly basis requires continuity of formats and deadlines oriented to a rigid production schedule that is very machinelike. Five attributes (listed next and summarized briefly in Fig. 2.9) are commonly found in machine organizations:

1. Substantial specialization of jobs, generally defined by strict procedure, which leaves little margin for performance up to the individual.

2. Fairly rigid command and control with formal decision-making policies.

3. Job grouping where similar skills are brought together and define departments.

4. Numerous subordinates in a narrowly defined specialty area for each supervisor, also called a narrow span of control.

5. A tendency toward substantial and frequent supervision. (Walton, 1981)

- Substantial job specialization.
- Rigid command and control.
- Skill-driven job grouping.
- Narrow span of control with numerous workers for each supervisor.
- Substantial supervision.

Figure 2.9 Machine Organization Attributes

Obviously in such an organization individualism and creativity are dampened, if for no other reason than there is relatively close control and supervision in which work is forced to fit the demands of efficiency. Such organizations, typically, rely on what worked before and have problems with flexibility.

Professional organizations are quite different. The individual, not the organizational system, drives them. The professional person is generally provided a great deal of latitude to analyze and do the work that is often very much a reflection of the person. Professionals perceive themselves as independent experts working within the organizational structure and resist control of their work by others. They, typically, are most concerned with the quality of their labor, not the quantity. Professional organizations often include the following (also see Fig. 2.10):

1. A wide range of job latitude defined as general responsibilities. The individual has significant control over what is done and how it is accomplished.

2. Loose command and control with considerable informality in the work environment, which encourages collective, consensual decision making.

3. Departments or divisions broadly designed with wider-ranging areas of individual responsibilities set up as multifaceted teams.

4. Limited managerial supervision generally approached as a coordinating activity more than a controlling one.

5. A sense of professional ethic defining the work as higher-order activity with greater social purpose.

- Wide job latitude.
- Loose command and control.
- Broadly defined departments/divisions.
- More limited direct supervision. Management more coordinating than controlling.
- Sense of "professional" ethic with work as a higher level activity of greater social purpose.

Figure 2.10 Professional Organization Attributes

The professional organization relies on coordination for the standardization of skills. Those are usually developed in formal training environments, often outside of the organization itself. An example would be a partnership of medical doctors. The physicians learned standard skills in medical school, but in their practice they exercise considerable latitude in judgment based on individual patient needs. Professionals typically have considerable control over their own work (Mintzberg, 1989).

Regardless of the structural design of organizations, Mintzberg argues impersonal bureaucracy will result without a focus on distinctly human attributes within the organizational equation. Because of that it is important in Mintzberg's view for organizations to remain focused on their core missions, with extensive understanding of the people they serve, being attentive to the motivation needs of those they employ and maintaining a culture that encourages knowledge, competitiveness, and a sense of social purpose.

That is an extremely complicated challenge encompassing a multifaceted interrelationship of organization and individual with myriad interdependencies. Media managers frequently find themselves caught between opposing forces: their professional ethic and sense of higher purpose, and the product line they are serving. Particularly when experiencing increased pressure from expanding competition, preserving market share can mean doing on the organizational level that which you might not do on the professional. Is it possible for people to be committed to both and maintain a kind of balance in themselves so they don't feel like they are selling out their ideals with what they do to generate market share? What appears to be the key is dynamic leadership at the top of the organization that makes clear its commitment and general goals to everyone. A sense of unifying purpose is critical to avoid falling into organizational ambiguity where multiple layers of authority sometimes send confusing signals to employees, who then focus on self-preservation (Fink, 1992).

People want to know what's going on so they seek information. If it isn't there, rumors are easily triggered. They also maintain a surveillance of their job level environment, including the way they anticipate managers to operate and how they perceive their own relative independence (Stogdill, 1950). Thus, the environment within which a business operates must be matched to the internal organizational structure and style for maximum effectiveness (Belasco, 1989). That can obviously mean a blending of management and leadership typologies, depending on the unique requirements of the organization at the time.

MEDIA ORGANIZATION ENVIRONMENTS ARE FLUID AND DYNAMIC

In media organizations you have a rapidly changing, dynamic atmosphere where people within the organization frequently see themselves more as independent contractors than employees. They see the organization as merely a conduit for *their* work. But the people who run the organization are always trying to bring everyone together and consider "the paper" or "the newscast," for example, as a team product. Therefore, you have a built-in clash of values. What's more, in the media world, reporters, photographers, and columnists rise in stature as their individuality is exerted to make them stand out. So they are part of a team while not being part of the team, while they are separating themselves from everyone else. It makes it even more difficult to be an effective manager in such a context.

To have effective bonding of people in such a dynamic environment you have to get members of the organization to relate to one another, to build trust and confidence, and to have the ability to reach group decisions while they work independently and make crucial decisions on their own. The rise of myriad media competitors, particularly in the second half of the 20th century, has required traditional media organizations to adjust dramatically the way they do things. We have moved from a culture where the daily newspaper was, for most Americans, the only regular news and information vehicle, to an environment where the wider landscape of newspapers, magazines, radio stations, television stations, cable television, the Internet, and interactive media all cut up the audience pie into ever-smaller pieces. It is increasingly difficult to generate a substantial audience share and with it significant advertising revenues. It is a time that requires maximum flexibility and a willingness to be innovative in the midst of severe budgetary restraints to maintain profit margins.

Media management texts frequently emphasize the fiscal side of companies in the traditional "business" context of generating profit by concentrating on strategic planning and financial manipulation in what is termed the *management science* perspective (Lavine & Wackman, 1988, p. 85). Media management case study problems often approach the predicament of trying to preserve existing profit margins despite declining market shares by using "economy in operation and higher revenues" as the goal of management (Coleman, 1978, p. 38). But it has become increasingly apparent that simply cutting costs and driving employees harder are only temporary solutions to a much deeper problem among media organizations undergoing fundamental market changes in a complex modern society.

Abraham Zaleznik (1989) argues that an organization sacrifices its competitiveness when it is focused on profit margins and stock prices. That short-term myopia can seriously damage long-term goals and dampen innovation. Cutting costs and driving employees harder are only temporary, short-term measures that may exacerbate a much deeper problem (Hawkins, 1990). The supposed "cure" for an organization's bottom-line problem may actually be worse than the profit decline disease; by eliminating necessary workers, eroding morale, and severely stressing the corporate climate, the organization's product quality and long-term competitive capability are reduced (Powers, A. 1990).

The media business's focus on fiscal matters, and the parallel concentration of print and electronic media outlets in the hands of a limited number of giant corporations, is well documented by Ben Bagdikian (1992). Such conditions can result in formulaic approaches to disparate audiences. Some major newspaper chains force the adoption of corporate formulas, both in newspaper makeup and tenor of papers they take over, but that can backfire, as it did on Gannett in Little Rock, Arkansas. The emphasis on profit resulted in a rapid rotation of editors who redefined the product each time the position changed (Kwitny, 1990).

Often an editor is faced with making both journalistic and marketing decisions, choosing between opposing values. Large chains often make sure the favored choice will be the decision likely to increase immediate profit by tying editor's pay to the profit performance of the newspaper, putting the editor in a vise between profit and journalistic quality. As one Knight-Ridder editor described it, "Suppose you meet all your precise goals-a new section, better sports coverage, whatever—and the newspaper has a 10 percent shortfall on its profit goals. You can kiss your bonus goodbye" (Kwitny, 1990, p. 28).

Maintaining Flexibility in Changing Social and Technological Contexts

Clearly, today's media manager cannot hope to succeed the same way a person in a similar position would have in 1950. The whole world has changed, and it seems to be squaring in speed of change as technology rapidly advances. In 1993 the first Mosaic browser was developed for use on the Internet ("History of the Internet," 1996). Two years later, what had been an arcane system mostly used by government researchers and academics had become the Information Superhighway with an estimated 14 million users. The number of individual and business web pages grew from 1,700 to 60,000 in just the 1994–96 period ("What's the Internet," 1996), with one estimate of a new person joining the Internet every 30 seconds (Simons, 1996). In just three years, the number of online newspapers exploded, growing from one, the *San Jose Mercury News,* to 789 with pages on the World Wide Web (Noth, 1996). One study indicated regular newspapers would lose up to 14 percent of their customers to online news servers (Levins, 1996). To compete, many traditional newspapers are developing online versions that are not simply reproductions of their printed product.

Electronic newspapers merge digital technology with traditional information in a whole new format. Electronic news is confined to a computer monitor where indexes to sections and stories have to be graphically designed to look simple but provide complex and extensive information as the user wishes to engage with it. You can't just put the regular print newspaper story online. It's a different product that requires different graphic displays, headlines, and jumps to related articles that can be manipulated with a computer mouse. It's text, but with the graphics and sound of television and radio. Electronic newspapers, to be competitive, have to utilize audience interactive capability, generate visual excitement, and provide information databases while enabling personal customization of users. All of that means some papers have added a "new media staff," including journalists and Internet technology experts, to translate raw material into the new media form, sometimes within their own separate newsroom (McAdams, 1995).

This is not confined to newspapers, of course. Because the Internet combines text and video and audio capabilities, all forms of mass media are being affected to one degree or another. One of the best examples of how much of an audience can be drawn to World Wide Web sites is the rise of CNN Interactive, the cable news channel's Internet offering. CNN Interactive began with a single staff member in 1994. Two years later there were more than 100 employees and 10,000 individual pages created on three major web sites under the CNN Interactive umbrella. By midsummer 1996 CNN Interactive was receiving 40 million accesses, or "hits" as they are referred to in the Internet industry, each week ("Internet Access: CNN and PointCast," 1996). On the local station level, KPIX-TV in San Francisco put a "CityCam" option on its new Internet site in November 1995. By mid-February 1996 it had been accessed 1.4 million times. Competitor KRON-TV launched its web site in January of 1996, receiving 160,000 hits on the first weekend. Within a month the station was averaging 300,000 hits a week (Carman, 1996).

Internet media organization sites are not just promotional vehicles. The World Wide Web is increasingly being viewed as an entirely new market whose audience is former users of more traditional media. Advertising revenue on the Internet was estimated to top $312 million in 1996 (Eckhouse, 1996). The majority of people "surfing" the web are in the 25- to 34-year-old demographic group, more than half of whom have incomes in excess of $50,000 per year (Petrozello, 1996).

Responses to Change Agents

The rise of the Internet, like the rise of radio and television before it, means significant change in how audiences engage with new media and with old. Whenever a significant change agent, in the form of radically new technology, is introduced into an environment, change occurs as old organizations attempt to cope, and preserve existing market shares. There are four basic approaches for organizations to cope with substantial change: structuralist, strategic choice, collective action, and natural selection (LeNoir, 1987). The one selected and its effectiveness depend on the corporate culture's attitude toward whatever is altering the operating environment, and its inherent ability to adapt. Figure 2.11 presents a summary of the following approaches:

1. Structuralists see the organization as operating within the context of greater forces than itself, which require it to adjust to those forces. The media organization, then, is reactive to external factors that have considerable impact on the choices available.

2. The strategic choice view perceives management as having considerable impact on organizational effectiveness through the choice of niches toward which the organization is directed. The environment is considered a precondition that management strategy analyzes to determine where to direct its efforts based on the best chance of success. The environment is not so much manipulated, as simply picked apart to find the best potential place for the organization to focus its energies.

3. In collective action a change agent is perceived as dramatically altering the operating environment. The organization and environment must then mutually redefine one another according to the context presented by the change agent. Organizations are not seen as independent elements but intertwined with their environment. So the organization and environment redefine one another, a collective mutually interdependence.

4. The natural selection concept is just Darwinism revisited, with an organization either being appropriate to its environment and surviving, or not appropriate and dying. Sometimes dying organizations go out fast, and sometimes they struggle on for a long time against the changing environment, which ultimately consumes them because the demand for adaptation simply outruns their ability to adapt.

- **Structuralist**—Organization structure is adjusted to fit whatever changes require change, generally in a reactive mode.
- **Strategic choice**—Management chooses where to compete based on what the environment provides. Choices are made in which direction to move proactively.
- **Collective action**—Organization and environment mutually redefine themselves in response to a change agent and are collectively interdependent.
- **Natural selection**—Organizations are either appropriate to their environment or not. When the environment changes they may no longer fit and die off regardless of their efforts to respond.

Figure 2.11 Responses to Change

In the contemporary media organization environment managers have to be, above all else, flexible. The more knowledgeable they are, with the key managerial skills discussed elsewhere in this text, the more likely they are to succeed in the difficult job of maintaining current media creation and production while envisioning how to adapt to a very rapidly changing world. For managing media organizations, in the contemporary sense, is not just maintaining the status quo, but actively participating in reinventing news and information in many varied forms.

The inherent tension of the journalism work culture has increased because of expanding competition across American media. In the face of declining profits, traditional markets are being fragmented. Media businesses, ranging from major daily newspapers and traditional television networks to Internet services, are trying to limit costs while concurrently increasing productivity. In the last 20 years particularly, American mass media have undergone the same acquisition game that has permeated most other business sectors. Owners have bought and sold firms in widely diverse geographic, economic, and cultural areas as the media have coalesced into ever-larger firms tending to use formula approaches throughout their chains (Bagdikian, 1992). Frequently a new owner brings a style of management and leadership with him or her and "plugs it in" to the new environment with little absorption of the existing corporate culture (Lagerkvist, 1988). As media companies have merged, such corporate culture shock has become relatively common. For example, mergers expanded in the 1980s in the American television industry because of deregulation, which spurred station sales and corporate takeovers ("Two Years," 1986). Such radical change in company ownership and management often produces upheaval, alienation of employees, radically different market approaches, sometimes success and sometimes failure (Lagerkvist, 1988).

The management problem is the perception that companies, often diverse in myriad aspects, are just cogs in huge conglomerate wheels. One critical factor in the rise of the industrial revolution was the interchangeable part. But media companies are not mere machines easily intermingled with banks, insurance companies, jet engine firms, and meatpacking plants. Yet, recent conglomerate acquisitions put media companies in the hands of those who made their fortunes and developed their corporate values in just those industries. Although certain business fundamentals are similar, the cultures of the businesses are frequently disparate. And for media organizations the balance sheet often depends on sociocultural elements that may be beyond the vision of the insurance executive who suddenly controls a broadcast network. Newspapers and television stations and their markets cannot simply be interchanged without major adjustments, despite the well-documented trend in homogenization of mass media in the United States (Morgan, 1986). Media companies may have homogenized much of themselves and their products, but the fact that audiences continue to fragment seems proof those audiences are anything but homogeneous (Sherman, 1987). In one sense a less diverse media is trying to tie itself to an increasingly diverse audience.

Like any other organizational manager, you must be open to new ideas but guarded about promises of quick solutions. You always must keep the unique aspects of your industry in the front of your mind, since what may be described as successful in one business context could spell doom in another. As you continue to evolve in your quest of management knowledge you will find that there are many different approaches to doing it better, often using trendy terms of the moment. Indeed, many popular nonfiction books on management, or management-related issues such as selling more effectively, grace the shelves of every bookstore in America. Micklethwait and Wooldridge (1996) chart the rise of management consulting and the sometimes schizophrenic reaction that organizations have exhibited as they attempted to adopt the latest trend. The result can be a very confused organization, with so many games being played no one is really sure of what rules to follow.

What might be called the velocity of management fadism increased exponentially just about everywhere. The more companies panicked the more they flitted from technique to technique in search of salvation. Of the 27 fads highlighted by Richard Pascale in Managing on the Edge *in 1990, two-thirds were spawned during the 1980s. Since then the process has only speeded up.*

And, from the management industry's viewpoint, the beauty of the system is that none of the formulas work—or, at least, they do not work as completely as the anguished or greedy buyers hope. The result is enormous profits for the gurus but confusion for their clients. "In the past 18 months," one Midwestern equipment manufacturer told Pascale, "we have heard that profit is more important than revenue, quality is more important than profit, that people are more important than profit, that big customers are more important than our small customers, and that growth is the key to our success. No wonder our performance is inconsistent." (Micklethwait & Wooldridge, 1996, p. 60)

Recent years have seen emphasis on versions of Japanese-style management, excellence, reengineering, cookbook types of management pointers you can supposedly memorize to be a better manager, and many others. But when you really boil all of these various approaches down to the essential element that distinguishes the good manager from the less able, it is one of the oldest and simplest principles of human dynamics. When you manage others as you would like them to manage you, the problems very often take care of themselves. For in so doing you create stronger relationships that foster loyalty, dedication, and personal involvement, elevating work beyond the mere mechanics of doing it. It is then no longer defined merely in terms of hours spent and wages earned, but in terms of people working together as social beings to achieve something that is mutually satisfying. Treat other people as you would have them treat you. That very simple, and very effective, approach can make all the difference. 🏠

STUDY QUESTIONS

1. Discuss the differences between the "classical" and the "human relations" approach to management.

2. Is it possible for a classicist to also be a humanist, and vice versa?

3. What's the difference between Theory X, Theory Y, and Theory Z?

4. How could TQM be used in a media organization? Or, if it cannot, why?

5. What are the differences between "machine" and "professional" organizations and the implications for media organizations?

section 2

INDIVIDUALITY IN THE ORGANIZATIONAL CONTEXT

chapter 3

HUMAN INFLUENCES ON MEDIA ORGANIZATIONS

The study of media organizations and the people within them involves a number of different areas. It includes wide-ranging concerns of those who are directly involved in mass media businesses and academic theorists working to understand those entities better. An enormous body of research exists in broad and often interrelated areas of organizational study, including adaptation, behavior, decline, effectiveness, and general management. Other disciplines also contribute to our understanding of organizations as human collectives, including communication, psychology, and sociology. Finally, all of this occurs in a media organization within the context of creative disciplines that bring to bear their own cultures, ethics, and perspectives of information and entertainment production. Clearly, a vast amount of knowledge is available far beyond the limits of one book. What is reviewed here is relevant to the general focus of this text: to provide a substantive foundation for you as a student of media organization management and to encourage you to seek more understanding of management techniques and processes throughout your career. Think of this, then, as a starting point, a foundation. It is humanly impossible to know everything. But it is possible to have a good, general overview of major areas of concern and know where to go to find what you need to resolve your future challenges.

INDIVIDUALITY IN THE ORGANIZATIONAL CONTEXT

Organizations are complicated entities, regardless of the simplicity of their surface structures. Human nuances and individual perceptions of reality ebb and flow within the interactions of the social beings of which groups are composed. Media organizations are even more so, because of the combination of mechanistic and professional aspects to the activity, as discussed in previous chapters, as well as the inherent difficulty of managing creative people.

The difficulty of dealing with collections of people begins with the first word or glance. For we are symbolic beings who interpret meaning in sometimes highly variable ways. Each person's perspective of the world is personally derived from the context of individual experience. We interpret what we see, hear, and feel. It is filtered through our values, experiences, opinions, and beliefs. Reality, then, is not necessarily the same from one person to the next (Carey, 1989). Two people can watch the same movie together and come away with different feelings, one in tears, the other ambivalent to the emotional message of the film. As we drive along the highway, a particular song on the radio may trigger a memory or emotion within us, to such a degree that later we don't remember driving that section of road, our mind off in a different place and time. Yet another person might not notice that particular song at all. As humans we filter everything that comes our way to construct a very personalized reality. That's why it is so difficult to communicate. The meaning of something depends on the complicated nature of our minds and emotions, which are washed by our individual life experiences.

Perceptions of Reality

We all look at things individually. As human beings we have some things in common but other things that separate us. We have different backgrounds, grow up in different parts of the country, have different kinds of parents, different friends, different successes and failures. "Every man is in certain respects like all other men, like some other men, like no other man" (Kluckhohn & Murray, 1948, p. 35). In other words we have some things in common with many people, other things only in common with a more narrowly defined group, and some things are unique to each of us. If you consider that idea in a sports context, it may make more sense to you. Millions of people call themselves sports fans. However, within that broad category of interest there are numerous sports and teams that vary in both performance and personality. For example, the National Football League includes the Atlanta Falcons, Dallas Cowboys, Green Bay Packers, New Orleans Saints, and Oakland Raiders. All have distinct team personalities and different ownership and organizational cultures, and all attract different fans nationwide.

Each of us, then, has a unique sense of reality within the broader context of those commonalties that bind us together into our various groups, whether those are religious, recreational, work related, or something else. We are symbolic beings who tend to see things emotionally as we turn them around within our minds, which are laden with memories, patterns of learned behavior, our core beliefs and values. In essence we each are washed by our personal sea of emotions, hopes, fears, illusions, and disillusions that contribute to our fantasies and our dreams. Because meaning is so internalized we frequently have an inaccurate understanding of how others feel, as well as our own capabilities.

It is important to understand the profound nature of the different ways people look at the same things, whether physically or philosophically. Burke (1966) described the individual filtering mechanisms as "terministic screens":

> When I speak of "terministic screens," I have particularly in mind some photographs I once saw. They were *different photographs* of the *same* objects, the difference being that they were made with different color filters. Here something so "factual" as a photograph revealed notable distinctions in texture, and even in form, depending on which color filter was used for the documentary description of the event being recorded. (p. 45, emphasis in original)

The concept of photographic filters is an effective one in understanding the nuances of meaning. Consider another example, also visually oriented. In the sport of alpine skiing, goggles or sunglasses are used to keep the wind out of your eyes and reduce the harshness of the sun on the snow. But when it's a heavily overcast day skiers don't use dark lenses. Instead they usually use yellow lenses in their goggles to increase the contrast of the soft, cloud-diffused light. Looking down a slope with no special lens at all, on a heavily overcast day, the ski run will appear to be smooth with no bumps or swails. On the other hand, a yellow lens reveals many bumps, ruts, and terrain undulations—a slope that is anything but smooth. If you skied down the slope without a yellow lens, you'd get bounced around a lot by all the bumps and ruts you couldn't see, and you'd probably fall. But with a yellow lens the amount of contrast in the available light would be greatly increased and you'd see all the nuances of the slope, so you could adjust your skiing to compensate for them.

Whether perceiving a reality through special colored lenses, photographic filters, or our internal values, those terministic screens through which a person views the world and relates to it can be very difficult to define.

> Even if any given terminology is a *reflection* of reality, by its very nature as a terminology it must be a *selection* of reality; and to this extent it must also function as a *deflection* of reality. (Burke, 1966, p. 45, emphasis in original)

Thus, a person's values and experiences frame a kind of selective process. Whatever conflicts is often discarded, while that which supports those values and previous experiences is absorbed and reinforces. That means our basic view of things is hard to change. Or, as songwriter Paul Simon described it in his song "The Boxer," "A man hears what he wants to hear and disregards the rest" (Simon, 1972).

Reality, in this way, is a personally experienced social construction caught up in our emotions, not a simple and finite thing of concrete facts. Indeed, a given set of facts may trigger radically different meaning in two people. Content analysis research has demonstrated that viewers don't always get the same meaning from television programs that producers intend. Indeed, they don't always perceive exactly the same meaning while watching the same program together. For example, how people see the social and sexual roles of television dramatic characters "may depend upon the way they perceive themselves" (Anderson, 1988, p. 35). As already discussed, meaning and perceived reality are subjective, dependent upon human interpretation centered among individual values and experiences that are highly variable from one person to the next.

In modern media, we often experience emotionally that which we don't actually physically experience. Watching television we see events half the world away and develop feelings about them. All forms of media help us create our own mental images of reality for which we do not have any physical connection. When you read a particularly exciting novel, the words on the page may seem to disappear and you might experience a kind of motion picture of the mind of the characters and story. In effect, your mind manufactures a set of mental images that visualize the text. When they make a Hollywood movie of the book, some scenes and characters just don't seem right to you, because of the unique mental images you created earlier when you read the novel.

Walter Lippman observed that, "the only feeling that anyone can have about an event he does not experience is the feeling aroused by his mental image of that event" (Lippman, 1922, p. 13). When those mental "pictures in our heads," as Lippman described them, are fed by modern video technology, which has the ability to create realistic digital imagery of things that do not exist, the whole concept of meaning is increasingly complicated. Watching television we have impressions of countries we haven't visited and long-distance experiences of events we haven't physically attended. All are distorted to some degree by both what the camera has shown and how we personally interpreted the pictures transmitted to us. We feel we have been where we have never been at all; a part of things we have never truly touched. We have become creatures of a reality that is manufactured within our minds with the help of myriad cultural and communication influences, including the multifaceted modern mass media. To cope with all this, human beings fall back on their basic outlook on life, which, as discussed earlier, is a product of individualized experiences and personal values.

Cassirer (1944) suggests that our individual interpretive differences flow from the way each of us perceives the world. As the Greek stoic philosopher Epictetus explained, "What disturbs and alarms man are not the things but his opinions and fancies about the things" (Cassirer, 1944, p. 25). We see ourselves at the center with everything swirling around us, like the eye of a massive knowledge and information hurricane. Because of that, our personally experienced reality is a presumed "normal" standard against which we measure everything else. When something conflicts with our core beliefs, our initial tendency is to doubt it and defend those core beliefs. It is difficult for most people to admit readily when they are, or might be, wrong since that disrupts the feeling of personal centeredness as well as our basic ego.

It takes a very mature and confident person to resist the defending impulse and consider another point of view. That is particularly true when you are caught in an error. The first impulse is to blame it on anything but yourself. So accepting responsibility and saying, "I messed up, I'm sorry" is not the most common approach. Interestingly, people who can say something like that when they are wrong, or have made an obvious error, quickly disarm those who call them into question. If the boss says, "What's this all about?" And you say, "I messed up, I'm sorry," the confrontation is usually quickly deflated. Most bosses don't keep chewing on a person who has admitted an error and is trying to fix it. The admission of error tends to stop the finger-pointing game and move all parties toward resolving the situation. Making excuses, on the other hand, puts everyone into a confrontational posture, defending positions. A simple error can mushroom quickly into a major confrontation because of excuses and refusal to be held accountable.

Think about being in the boss's shoes. What are you going to say to a person who admits he or she made a mistake? Probably, "Don't do it again," and then you would be off to work on the next problem. But if the person to whom you are talking hems and haws around with one excuse after another, you'd probably get increasingly irritated. And your trust of the other person would be undermined, particularly if you knew the person was at fault. Everyone makes mistakes. What is important is to learn from them so they are not repeated. Accepting responsibility for your actions is a major conflict resolution strategy, as well as a trust-building approach that can foster increasing stature within the organization.

Selective Influence Theory

Selective influence theory takes the position that when human beings engage with meaning, they sift out that with which they have less fundamental agreement. In other words, they select those things they allow to affect them and deny access to those things with which they have significant disagreement. The following are three basic approaches (also see Fig. 3.1) a person may use in this process of engaging the communication environment:

1. Selective attention is used to "screen out vast amounts of information" in which the person has limited interest so attention can be paid to that which is of interest.

> - **Selective attention.** We filter out "clutter" to concentrate on what matters to us.
> - **Selective perception.** We perceive meaning based on what we have learned (socially and intellectually).
> - **Selective action.** We choose on what to act, ignore, or just hold for future use.

Figure 3.1 Selective Influences

2. Selective perception is imbedded in the cognitive differences of "interests, beliefs, prior knowledge, attitudes, needs and values," so that "individuals will perceive—that is, attribute meaning to—virtually any complex stimulus differently than will people with different cognitive structures."

3. Selective action comes into play in the way individuals choose to react differentially to particular communicative stimuli. It is a fundamental problem in the organizational communication area because group activity is substantially affected by differentiated meanings members attach to messages that flow within the organization. (DeFleur & Ball-Rokeach, 1989, pp. 195–197)

We learn things climbing up the ladder of life. The problem is that a lot of that makes us rigid and inflexible in our thinking, because we base everything on what worked before. When something comes up, we naturally compare that, consciously or unconsciously, with what we have experienced before. That means we tend to look at new problems and new solutions within the context of old problems and old solutions. Consider that for a minute. Because something worked a certain way five years ago, you tend to think something today will work that way, too. We tend to fall back on our previous knowledge and experience base. If the new issue is similar to the former one, within the same environment, that is one thing. But if what is occurring is unlike anything in our prior experience or the environment has substantially changed, we have a serious problem. Old solutions used to deal with new problems, or new environments, may mean failure. A mass media example of this is the concept of audience flow.

In the limited competitive environment of network television in the 1960s and early 1970s there were only three major networks available to Americans. And most communities had, in addition, only one independent station and one Public Broadcasting System outlet. So for most people there were just five television choices, and only three of them—the traditional networks, ABC, CBS, and NBC—offered popular, first-run series during prime-time viewing. Cable television was not widely available and satellites had not yet become available. At that time, the network that had the hottest television program at the beginning of prime time tended to keep its large share of viewers through the evening. Prime time has historically been defined as beginning at 8 p.m. on the East and West Coasts, 7 p.m. in the Central and Rocky Mountain time zones. The remote control had not yet become common, so changing channels also meant the viewer had to get up and walk across the room to the television set to change channels manually.

Audience flowed from the strong lead-in program and tended to remain for shows that might not have been as highly rated on their own. Ratings particularly benefited from viewers too lazy to get up and walk across the room to turn to another channel. The key to programming then was to have a strong audience draw at the beginning of prime time, and maybe another toward the end of prime time, with shows of lesser strength sandwiched between. Networks tried to grab a big share of the audience early and then it would carry over through the rest of the evening. They created audience flow with a kind of intricate game of program chess with other network opponents. Usually the network with the strongest program at the beginning of prime time carried that evening.

By the 1990s that all had changed. Networks could no longer count on a strong show at the beginning of prime time carrying the evening. Most communities now had the five original broadcast signals available, plus additional UHF (channels 14 and higher) and cable services. The average American television household had a potential of at least 40 channels. The remote control had become commonplace and with it a phenomenon of channel hopping, where many viewers churn through numerous channels with little patience. The television viewing environment now featured people quickly changing channels when commercial breaks began, or when they became momentarily bored as the action slowed down. In just a decade and a half the concept of audience flow radically changed. The audience had become more active than passive. There was still some residual effect from one strong ratings draw to the next program, but much less than before. However, television executives who learned their business in the 1960s and 1970s kept trying to manipulate blocks of viewers the way they'd learned to do in a very different, limited-viewer-choice context. The competitive environment had been significantly altered but these broadcasters, now many of them station managers, kept trying to solve their eroding audience problem with the solutions that had worked in a different competitive environment. It was dinosaur thinking.

In 1976, before technology revolutionized the amount of television offered American consumers and created the remote control device, on a typical evening 92 percent of homes using television were tuned to one of the three major networks, ABC, CBS, or NBC. By 1984 that had dropped to 75 percent, and by the early 1990s it had skidded to 62 percent. In the space of just 15 years the three major networks lost one-third of their audience share (Auletta, 1991, p. 27). This erosion of the major networks is discussed further in the chapter on media organization decline. However, for the purposes of this discussion you can see that when the environment radically changed, due to the rise of new technology, the old solutions simply failed. The audience no longer simply flowed from one show to another because there were few options among traditional broadcasters, most of those rather similar anyway. Now the audience was hopping all over the place, with dozens of new programming options siphoning off small pieces of the viewing audience. Television was in the process of fragmenting into a niche product much as radio and magazines had done before. The reality of the marketplace was quickly changing, but the perceptions of it among broadcast television executives evolved much more slowly. The old solutions to the new problems only increased their share erosion. They fell back on what they knew from their earlier experience but it didn't work. The new, viewer-empowered environment wasn't like the old passive viewer one. No longer could the President of the United States request time from the three major networks to talk to the nation and be seen by virtually everyone. Now such a request would mean talking to only slightly more than half of American households. The mass audience had been demassified!

All three of the selective influence options listed earlier probably affected broadcast executives to one degree or another. Selective attention came into play as they screened out the early signs of major change coming to their operating environment. Basically, they ignored them. After all, they were huge and wealthy, and the new competitors were small entrepreneurs for the most part. Selective perception added to the problem as the traditional networks relied on their "beliefs, prior knowledge, needs and values," which were steeped in the tradition of network broadcasting itself (DeFleur & Ball-Rokeach, 1989, p. 197). Their world was centered in a limited competitive environment where three major players basically cut the national television audience into large chunks, which guaranteed all three a substantial profit. They believed they were giving Americans what they wanted and had huge audience shares to prove it. What they didn't understand was that the only reason so many people watched them was because little real choice existed. Finally, selective action was applied as the major networks initially took no action at all against the new competitors, instead continuing to focus on each other. They chose simply to ignore such innovative programming services as Home Box Office and Ted Turner's first superstation. After all, the networks frequently ran movies during prime time—although with so many commercials inserted, substantial parts of the motion pictures had to be edited out to make them fit into the prime-time window. And old network programs were already being rerun by local broadcasters in non-prime-time day parts.

So why would any significant number of prime-time viewers pay money for a movie service like HBO when the networks aired movies without additional viewer charges? And why would anyone watch old series reruns on a cable channel programmed by a superstation when they could watch the new series on the networks? The emerging alternatives to the traditional networks were seen as upstart, inconsequential, niche-oriented services that were no real threat. Those networks kept doing what they'd always done, and with which they had been imminently successful. Of course, time proved that none of the individual niche services attained the same total audience as any one of the former dominant networks. But with an ever-expanding number of niche offerings, the total niche market share grew to almost 40 percent of prime time by 1990 (Auletta, 1991). The trend continued with the audience share for basic cable continuing to expand into the 1996/97 season (Rice, 1996). The end of the Fall 1996 sweeps period saw a historic low for the traditional broadcast networks, as their combined share of the national audience fell to 49 percent of homes using television (Grahnke, 1996).

Blending Individual and Organizational Values

When people enter a work environment, they begin to acquire organizational knowledge through which their perceptions of coworkers and management are mediated. Organizationally accepted behaviors, ranging from the prevalent style of dress (informal, formal, etc.) to the way people act around superiors and subordinates, are among the first things we learn when we begin a new job. Because work environments are generally social in nature we begin to make acquaintances and learn from them the organizational knowledge that is part of group membership. Our individual selective perception, discussed earlier, comes into play immediately as our predisposition for certain types of people tends to influence our attitude toward others. In other words, like children on a playground, we quickly build alliances and friendships and make sometimes unconscious decisions about whom to trust and not to trust.

These are all based, initially, on very superficial knowledge and sometimes change dramatically after we've been in an organization for a while. Sometimes the person who seemed so nice and helpful at the outset, we learn later, is a political game-playing manipulator. Or the person who seemed cold and aloof really is a warm and friendly mentor after the social ice has been broken. The negotiation of our meaning within the organization we enter begins with the first step, and never stops evolving. We know our organization, and it knows us, in continuously adjusting ways. Those are sometimes through small nuances but other times due to large events of repositioning and redefining ourselves and the organizational power we acquire over time.

It is vitally important that the values of the organization and those of its members be fairly similar. Otherwise, frustrating conflicts inevitably occur because the sense of what is right or wrong conflicts. For example, in serious journalism organizations there is a sense of higher purpose in the job. Very often people working in such organizations see being a journalist as having special responsibilities. They are often extremely concerned about ethical issues affecting telling the truth and not distorting reality. That conflicts with the other mission of any media organization business, trying to attract an audience.

When promotion people or advertising sales personnel get involved in news coverage decisions, you have the worst possible situation. Although most contemporary media organizations have one mechanism or another to balance interests, there is inherent conflict. When journalists feel the promotion people are deciding what series to produce for a television rating book or what special sections of the newspaper to develop for marketing purposes, their core values are besieged. Serious journalists may feel abandoned by their organization, which they see as "selling out" to profit motives. To cope, they turn away from the promotion schemes and do only what they must to keep from being fired. Their frustration may escalate, along with a sense of their organization being journalistically "unethical," to the point where they become seriously depressed. A sense of betrayal can set in, and, over time, such high-minded journalists can suffer a kind of burnout, not from the amount of work or daily deadlines, but from the constant clash of values and conscience.

Finding an organization that fits our values is one of the most critical aspects of maximizing happiness and productivity. But it is also often quite difficult. That's because when we get hired, it is based on first impressions on both sides. The deeper understanding of ourselves and those with whom we work, which we learn over time, is sometimes quite different. What seems like a positive, collegial place at first may be revealed later as a snake pit full of petty squabbling and factions. The problem is the lack of organizational knowledge going in, something only time can develop. In contemporary organizations the prospective manager and subordinate too often have only superficial knowledge of each other. The résumé is on the table (written by an intelligent person who is trying to get the job and has tailored it accordingly) and the conversation is usually cordial and businesslike, with each person trying to put forth his or her best behavior. An employment interview is, in many respects, a first date. And illusions on both sides can lead to uncomfortable consequences later. In companies where the hiring process goes through a human resources department, the technical fit of job qualifications to tasks required may be more effectively managed, but quantitative tests and job tasks don't tell you much about the level of comfort the personalities have with one another. That's why the personal interview is such a crucial part of the employment process.

In the rest of this chapter we will discuss several areas crucial to putting the proverbial "square pegs in square holes and round pegs in round holes"—in other words, reducing the chances misfits will happen that are to no one's benefit.

MOTIVATIONAL FIT IN MEDIA ORGANIZATIONS

Theoretical Concepts of Motivation

Throughout the 20th century, behavior management theories have extended beyond the fundamental considerations of speeding up assembly lines into creative influences, team management, and psychosocial forces that affect organizational member attitudes (Mayo, 1946). The complexity of human interaction with the environment has been the focus of considerable research on motivation and organizational efficiency dependent upon the individual members who make up the collective known as an organization. Various content theorists, such as Maslow (1954/1970), Herzberg, Mausner, and Synderman (1959), and Alderfer (1972), have attempted to reconcile the external world to internal motivational considerations within the individual.

Maslow's Hierarchy of Needs

Maslow (1954/1970) perceived organizational members driven by a layered hierarchy of needs (see Fig. 3.2). To move up to each successive level, the needs of the previous level must be met. Maslow's initial layer of needs includes the essential physiological requirements of food and shelter, the foundation of physical survival. Once those needs are met, concerns of the second level can be considered—the need for safety and security from external threats. When the needs of the first and second level are met, only then does Maslow see the human being as focusing on the happiness factors such as developing friendships, love relationships, and building up a sense of affiliation by being concerned with social interaction. At that point the individual becomes concerned with self-esteem and gaining esteem from others. The final motivational pinnacle in Maslow's hierarchy is self-actualization where, with the previous levels' needs satisfied, a person experiences a need to reach full potential through maximum use of skills and abilities (pp. 35–59).

Self-actualization—A sense of self-fulfillment, deeper meaning in life's accomplishments; a sense of "happiness."

Esteem—Positive regard of self and by others.

Belonging—Friendship, love, social affiliation.

Security—Feel safe, free from external threats.

Physiological—Food, drink, shelter, basic survival needs.

Figure 3.2   Maslow's Hierarchy of Needs

In effect, one cannot be concerned with anything except rudimentary survival, until survival is ensured. Then, when you have enough to eat, your concerns expand into the more abstract areas of love, social interchange, and thinking about whether you are "happy." Conversely, when a person's survival is threatened (i.e., "You'll be fired if you don't . . ."), all else becomes secondary to that fundamental issue. It is clear that to have people take chances by exercising personal judgment or championing new ideas, they cannot be worried about losing their jobs, that is, on the survival level of the motivational hierarchy.

The development of motivation schema centered on the individual as moving up through various levels of psychological focus—from elementary survival to defining meaning in life with abstract concepts such as love, friendship, and a sense of doing something worthwhile—has cultural roots deep in the Judeo-Christian tradition of human values existing on a higher plane than mere animal survival. Without the sense of greater purpose to our lives, "we begin to lose our humanity as soon as we begin to lose the emphasis that what we do makes a difference" (Schaeffer, 1976, p. 364). Within this philosophical context the individual becomes an empowered agent, "a human organism to which beliefs and desires can be ascribed on the basis of the Principle of Humanity." Individual agents then form "collectives in order to pursue their objectives" that at "the most developed and formalized are *organizations*" (Callinicos, 1988, p. 134, emphasis in original). As part of an organization, an individual agent's wants are tied to "the objective environment on which his or her opportunities for realizing those wants depend" (p. 122). Thus, "the main concern is with humans as doers, rather than as just another species with a fixed essence waiting to be defined, or as mere observers" (Dancy, Moravcsik, & Taylor, 1988, p. 2).

Herzberg's Motivation/Hygiene Theory

Herzberg developed his concept of people reacting to two sets of forces in *The Motivation to Work* (Herzberg et al., 1959) and *Work and the Nature of Man* (1966). His "motivation-hygiene theory" is based on the premise that "man has two sets of needs: his need as an animal to avoid pain, and his need as a human to grow psychologically" (Herzberg, 1966, p. 91). The individual is seen as positioned between two diverse sets of forces. The hygiene factors are "dissatisfiers," which describe the "relationship to the context or environment" (p. 94) in which a person performs a job. Herzberg included them within the category of dissatisfiers because his research found they were "rarely involved in events that led to positive job attitudes" (p. 93). They include "company policy and administration, supervision, salary, interpersonal relationships and working conditions" (p. 94). The "satisfiers" category of motivators, according to Herzberg, includes "strong determiners of job satisfaction—achievement, recognition, work itself, responsibility and advancement—the last three being of greater importance for lasting change of attitudes" (p. 92).

Thus, on the one hand are the extrinsic conditions of the working environment—the job context—juxtaposed with the intrinsic factors within a person that provide greater personal meaning from working in one place rather than another—the personalized job content (see Fig. 3.3). The extrinsic conditions include the surface rewards for having a position, the tangible things like pay, working conditions, and specific job status. The intrinsic factors are the intangibles that may include having a sense of responsibility, achievement, recognition, and the chance for advancement and status growth within the social collective of an organization. The combination of extrinsic and intrinsic factors bubble around in each of us in a kind of motivation stew, individually spiced by our personalities and values.

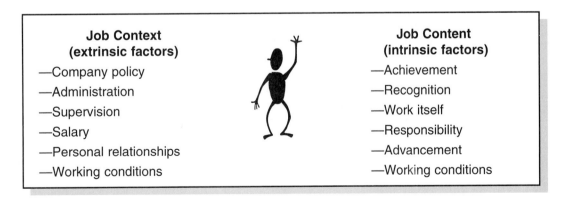

Figure 3.3 Herzberg's Motivation-Hygiene Theory

Herzberg's motivation-hygiene theory does not argue that a person cannot be motivated with either extrinsic or intrinsic factors only. Rather, it is the basis for considering the human being as more complex, wherein the personalized meaning of work is tied to much more than the external rate of pay. True job satisfaction results from tying the extrinsic and intrinsic motivators of an individual together, which, ideally, then results in extraordinary performance (Gibson, Ivancevich, & Donnelly, 1997).

Alderfer's ERG Theory

Alderfer framed the essential motivational ingredients in a similar human needs hierarchy called the ERG theory (for Existence, Relatedness, and Growth). In this view, pay and working conditions are included with food and water as basic existence requirements. After those existence issues, a person becomes concerned about "relatedness," or having meaningful relationships with other individuals. Alderfer's "growth" needs, the third area of concern, are based on a person's desire for helping create things and having a sense of being productive (see Fig. 3.4).

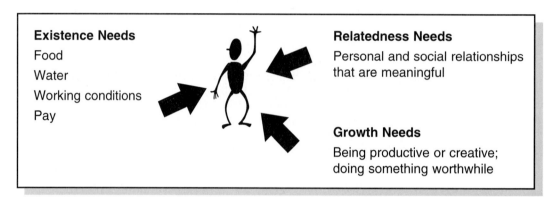

Figure 3.4 Alderfer's ERG Theory

In Alderfer's words, "Growth needs impel a person to make creative or productive effects on himself and the environment" (Alderfer, 1972, p. 11). In ERG theory the three ingredients work together, balancing one another to maintain a kind of equilibrium. If a person cannot fulfill one area, he or she adjusts the others to compensate. In effect we justify the unfulfilled area by placing more importance in the others. So people who receive low pay may see their jobs as being more important, or focus on the potential they have for future development. For example, a strong sense of organizational belonging may be used as the rationale to remain in a lesser job than you'd really prefer. You like the people, the general working conditions, and what you do while you're at your job. So you figure that's worth something and you stay, even though you might be able to make more money somewhere else. Having nice people around you, and a job you basically like, has value. Some people, such as junior attorneys in law firms, toil long hours for reduced immediate reward because of the chance of being promoted to the greatly increased status and money of full partnership. Early career sacrifice is perceived as necessary for later career status and reward.

Bandura's Social Cognitive Theory

Maslow (1954/1970), Herzberg et al. (1959), and Alderfer (1972) provided the foundation upon which an interactionist perception of psychological complexity has evolved. Bandura (1986) proposes a "social cognitive theory" in which the human being is seen as the junction of complex knowledge, perception, and desire strands, which are all affected by the particular environment at hand.

> In the social cognitive view people are neither driven by inner forces nor automatically shaped and controlled by external stimuli. Rather, human functioning is explained in terms of a model of triadic reciprocality in which behavior, cognitive and other personal factors, and environmental events all operate as interacting determinants of each other. (Bandura, 1986, p. 18)

Bandura's "triadic reciprocality," is the view that the way we act (behavior), our knowledge acquisition (cognitive) processes and other personal factors, and the environment within which all of this occurs fold together interactively to create individualized meaning (see Fig. 3.5). Our personality and our way of engaging with the world around us cannot be separated into neat categories presumed to be mutually exclusive and unaffected by the others. All are contributors to, and products of, one another.

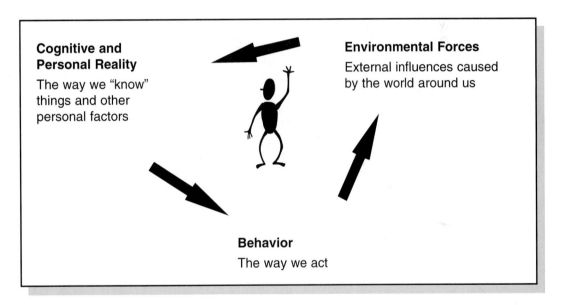

Figure 3.5   Bandura's Triadic Reciprocality Theory

Because the way each of us combines the three elements in triadic reciprocality is highly individualized, a given motivational factor inserted into a group of people may produce results that vary considerably. Any particular action or reaction is caused by a number of factors coming into play within an individual. Because we are all unique composites of a myriad of individual qualities, including our backgrounds, experiences, and interpretive understanding of the world around us, the same externally induced factor may contribute to significantly different reactions from one person to the next.

This explains what we so often see in the world around us. Someone says something one person perceives as a minor comment, which to another person in the same group is a major issue. From a management point of view, this just squares the difficulty.

Whatever you say or do will be perceived in varying degrees and tone of meaning from one person to the next. So great care must be taken in not only *what* you attempt to communicate, but *how* you communicate it. Little nuances often have dramatic effect on the received meaning.

Several things come into play in Bandura's social cognitive theory. A "self-regulatory capability" allows individuals to govern much of their behavior by "internal standards and self-evaluative reactions to their own actions" (Bandura, 1986, p. 20). Additionally, there is a "self-reflective capability" that "is the capability for reflective self-consciousness," wherein people "think about their own thought processes" (p. 21). We are also "enactive learners" where our observations of what goes on, and the experiences we build up over time, exert strong influence on our decision making. When people have an outcome they particularly desire, they tend to use their organization or group experience to decide what action to take to attain it.

Along with the intellectual knowledge necessary to do a given job, the individual develops sophisticated social learning in which "correlated experiences create expectations that regulate action" (Bandura, 1986, p. 188). What has gone before can, thereby, set up a decision-making process that is based on experiences of the past rather than the realities of the present. So what was successful yesterday we presume will be successful tomorrow. And what did not produce great results yesterday is presumed to be a quick path to failure today. The natural reaction, then, is a kind of defensive behavior prohibiting innovation because we are, in effect, trapped by the experiences of the past. The boundaries are presumed to be static, not fluid. We are, in a very real sense, prisoners of our experience and resistant to flirting with presumed danger even though the new environment may not contain the risk that was there before. "This is because protective avoidance prevents individuals from learning that what they perceive to be dangerous is actually quite safe" (p. 189).

As the perceptions of threats, rewards, expected outcomes, and social learning come together in the human dynamic, we carefully watch for signals that predict the outcomes we desire. When we see those signals, we are positively reinforced that we're on track. But when we don't get those signals, or we get signals we don't expect, fear may escalate as we worry about how things will turn out. Sometimes that can mean artificial crises and stress within us as we spin ourselves into fretting over something that exists mostly in the swirling clouds of our minds and emotions. In general we pay close attention to those things that reinforce our thinking and disregard, or downplay, that which refutes it (Bandura, 1986, p. 205).

Within the social cognitive theory frame, motivation has two broad divisions, biological and cognitive. Like Maslow (1954/1970), Herzberg et al. (1959), and Alderfer (1972), Bandura (1986) sees the human being as driven on the biological level by the need to fulfill essential survival and human interrelationship requirements (food, sex, basic social interaction). On the cognitive level, however, Bandura argues that rationality and thought provide "guides and motivators of behavior," instigated by "forethought," or the expectation of certain outcomes grounded in previous observational, enactive, or social learning experiences (p. 233). Rather than a Maslow-like hierarchy of needs in which each higher level depends on the previous level's needs being satisfied, in social cognitive theory biological motivators do not necessarily have to be satisfied prior to cognitive motivators coming into play. Indeed, it is possible for the biological and cognitive to be at work concurrently and together shape the overall perception of the individual's world and the response to what it brings his or her way. The psychology of an individual is a mixture of the cognitive and behavioral influences that, together, define a personality (pp. 521–522).

Job Fit and Job Enlargement

Early work in management theory centered on delineating processes and procedures of organized industrial activity. It was generally from a top-down managerial perspective aimed at increasing worker efficiency. The "mechanistic model" evolved partly as a way to increase employee involvement in work. It was believed that a more efficient worker would be happier due to higher pay and greater personal satisfaction at being better at the job. But it was too narrow a view focused on how to maximize the efficiency of each person as a work unit. People are much more complicated than machines. As social beings they require more to achieve peak efficiency than superior machine design and premium pay. The rise of the human relations approach in motivation theory asserted that positively oriented workers did better work. Particularly in jobs where workers have some direct control over the quality of what they do—for example, writing, photography, layout, publication design—attitude is a fundamental factor in productivity.

Since the World War II period the concept of the individual motivational interface with the collective of organization has been the focus of numerous research efforts to define and understand better the interrelationship (Campion & McClelland, 1991). Caldwell and O'Reilly (1990) found that a technique of sorting specific job requirements and personal characteristics, and then using those attributes to match the worker and job, was effective across a range of jobs and management levels. The concept of fitting together individual and organization attributes to enhance performance has been the focus of numerous studies in recent decades (e.g., Downey, Hellriegel, & Slocum, 1975; O'Reilly, 1977; Karasek, 1979; Lopez, Kesselman, & Lopez, 1981; Diener, Larsen, & Emmons, 1984; Schneider, 1987; Chatman, 1989).

But it is one thing to use various matching criteria to select new organizational members for particular positions, and quite another to use such criteria in managing existing personnel as they are moved around the organization, and through managerial upheavals, over time. Caldwell and O'Reilly (1990) conclude that these person-job fit efforts are best used to ascertain training needs for an individual who has already been hired, or to decide what specific duties might be assigned to a given person. It is an issue to consider after more fundamental concerns in the hiring process such as basic personality and values, and how those interface with the organizational culture. For if a person does not mesh with the collective of social beings already in place, there is little chance for a long-term positive relationship. Person-job fitting, then, is not so much an initial personnel hiring mechanism as a refining activity to help realign human resources once they are in place. Initially, the hiring needs to be concerned with how the values and personality of the individual fit the organizational culture. Tasks are more easily adjusted. But the fundamental values, perceptions, and behavior patterns of people are not. Yet, we often, in organizations, hire based on task requirements and do not spend enough time considering personality and values fit.

Consider a simple example of this type of hiring criteria. If a person can type a certain number of words a minute, we presume a level of secretarial skill. But the job of secretary often includes wide-ranging talents of diplomacy and persuasion far beyond mere word processing. Nevertheless, many organizations continue to require typing tests as a primary requirement for a job that now includes virtually no typing. Most contemporary secretaries need expertise with sophisticated computer word-processing programs. And with spell checkers, keeping typing errors to a minimum during the entry of copy is an irrelevant issue.

Perhaps the reason we are so quantitatively oriented and dependent on job descriptions, which describe "duties" rather than philosophies, is that it's easier. We tick off the list of requirements and make a decision, instead of taking the time to find the "right" person in the broader sense. And we set ourselves up to compromise both the organization and the new member in the process. No one wins in such a situation, though both may lose a little. The result may be more frequent turnovers than necessary, with significant expense in searching, hiring, and retraining the next person. Too often we look around us and see jobs and duties, rather than organizational cultures and social beings moving within them.

The person-job fit approach is one of the latest in a complex stream of diversified refinements of the humanistic approach that flow through a continuum of interactionism in organizational behavior. Within this area is the concept of "job enlargement," which traces its motivational psychology roots to Herzberg's work, mentioned earlier. In job enlargement, work is expanded through such techniques as adding variety to tasks, giving people a sense of greater responsibility and autonomy, and increasing our sense of meaning in what we do. In other words, attempting to expand intrinsic motivators and, thus, job *meaning* for the individual. Philosophically job enlargement is meant to be a way to make people feel more important while tapping more of his or her potential. In the pragmatic reality of daily organizational life, it is frequently just a way to increase the load of some workers so others can be fired. Of course, that is usually referred to by euphemisms that sound much more humane. But firing is firing even when you play semantic games with terms like "downsizing," "reengineering," or "departmental reorganization." When the jobs of those who remain are loaded up with additional duties due to cutbacks, you have a motivational backfire. Rather than positively motivating people who see themselves as having more opportunity to do what they do best, workers are overloaded and frustrated. That can lead to a subtle withdrawal of service, which will be discussed later in this text in the section on organizational justice, as the organization literally bogs down under the weight of too much work for too few people.

In their study of the costs and benefits of positive job enlargement, Campion and McClelland (1991) examined more than 20 field studies reported in the organizational behavior literature. They found: "In most interventions guided by motivational approaches, the results were positive" (p. 187). But a caveat remains here; as in most efforts to manipulate workers into being more productive, there are trade-offs:

> Enlarged jobs had better motivational and worse mechanistic design. They had the predicted benefits of more employee satisfaction, less mental underload, greater chances of catching errors, and better customer service, and the predicted costs of higher training requirements, higher basic skills, and higher compensable factors. (p. 194)

People were more satisfied, but it took more to train those who then had higher levels of skill development, and they had to be paid more. It sounds like one of those "darned if you do, darned if you don't" scenarios. Enlarged jobs were better for the people and for the companies who implemented them, but they were not a cheap road to success. It takes time for the benefits of more satisfied workers who do a better job to overtake the higher initial costs involved. Therefore, adopting job enlargement as an organizational strategy is not a quick fix for mundane profits. It is most successful as a long-term strategy that involves trying to improve quality for both workers and customers.

Like much of management theory, whether job enlargement works positively depends on the situation. Not all people in an organization want more responsibility or bigger jobs. Individuals often react differently from the way managers anticipate when efforts to adopt job enlargement begin, making performance forecasting difficult. Part of that is because people inherently resist change and fear the unknown. When management tries to do something, some organizational members may suspect ulterior motives unless trust relationships are strong. As in so much of management, attitude is at the heart of success or failure ("Job Redesign," 1973/1987).

Efforts to enlarge jobs have been shown to produce positive results in specific situations where personal attributes closely fit functional requirements (Campion & McClelland, 1991). Thus, when you attempt to enlarge a person's job, you have to be careful to add things they can do well. It is a complicated matter to blend individuals into mutually compatible frameworks of organizational culture and norms (Caldwell & O'Reilly, 1990). Among eight key attributes that Peters and Waterman (1982) emphasized in their much-quoted work, *In Search of Excellence,* are "productivity through people" and "hands-on, value driven" approaches (pp. 14–15). Management style must include a personally involved approach that keeps at the forefront the essential values of the company; that is, what it stands for besides the simplistic pursuit of profit. Peters and Waterman used the example of the McDonald's hamburger chain's emphasis on "Q.S.C. and V. (Quality, Service, Cleanliness, and Value)" as evidence that if the underlying philosophy of a business is strong, the profits will come, but if the emphasis is only on profit, success is temporary (pp. 14–15). Fitting the person into the organization to foster maximum performance, then, takes much more than just matching job skills to job requirements. It becomes a question of attitude and value matching to fit a new member effectively into a concept of the organization as an extension of self and vice versa. For, in the fully developed organizational culture sense, the people reflect the organization and the organization reflects them (Mackenzie, 1991).

PRACTICAL APPLICATION OF THEORETICAL CONCEPTS

Management efforts are most conducive to improving productivity when they fit the needs of each person to their job requirements, and where individual and organizational attitudes are mutually reinforcing. Individual productivity has been demonstrated to increase as organizational and personal values and goals become more closely aligned. Positively motivated people who perceive a sense of self in the organization are increasingly vested in the organization's success. They become what Drucker (1988b) termed "stakeholders."

The challenge of being successful for an extended period of time requires a strategic view that defines organizational measures of success in more than rudimentary, short-term profit terms. Fixation on quarterly profit statements may hinder a longer-term, strategic approach. It takes time to develop strong organizations and the fiercely competitive products that evolve from such environments. Like the farmer, the effective manager must understand when to plant the new crop, have the right amount of patience as time provides the space to grow, and then carefully nurture the seedlings of excellence as they mature. None of this ever happens during ideal conditions, of course, but we are continually tested by the winds and drought and unforeseen problems. Patience, indeed, is a managerial virtue that takes considerable discipline in the face of performance demands. You can make superficial changes rapidly, but fundamental organizational change does not come so quickly.

As you work as a media organization manager, some challenges are more daunting than others. Motivating others is one of the toughest. The laboratory of life is sometimes very different from the cold analysis of textbooks and theoretical constructs. That's because you, as well as the person you're dealing with, are caught up in the context of the moment. Emotions, stress, hopes, and fears all spin around in your head as you struggle with a given situation. In other words, you are sitting there reading this textbook in a quiet place thinking about the abstract material. But when you have to apply it someday, it will be in an atmosphere of tension as a crisis erupts.

With that managerial reality in mind, here are some basic things to remember (see Fig. 3.6 for a summary of these points):

1. Put a sign on your desk or wall, where you can see it when things get a little crazy and you wonder if you're working with lunatics. That sign should have nothing more on it than the following formula originally proposed by Davies (1963/1978). When you've long forgotten the abstract psychology of some of the authors discussed in this text, Davies' formula will keep you focused on how to deal with people.

$$B = f(SO)$$

It means that behavior is a function of the situation and the organism. Too often we focus on behavior without looking for the cause. If we understand the situation and the organism, behavior becomes relatively easy to predict. And it can become relatively easy to change. Just change the situation or the organism. Put the right people in the right situations and you'll have the behavior you want. But put the right people in the wrong situations and you have a mess on your hands.

As a manager you must not be lured into responding to reactions but must focus on causes. Behavior is a symptom of something going on elsewhere that produces that behavior. What you are interested in is changing behavior. So get to the root causes of it and a solution will be at hand. But if you do not treat the causes, efforts to change the behavior can end in frustration. Remember, behavior is a function of the situation and the organism—$B = f(SO)$.

2. Your subordinates are not you. In other words, what you think makes perfect sense, from your perspective, may have nothing to do with how the people you are managing see things. Don't assume your values, goals, or dreams are shared by others.

---

1. B = f(SO).
2. Your subordinates are *not* you.
3. Be aware of what motivates *others*.
4. Media people have a sense of *"calling."*
5. Extrinsic = external comfort—*symbols* of worth.
   Intrinsic = internal comfort—*feeling* of worth.
6. Coach them from their perspective. Help them find the solutions to their problems.
7. Put square pegs in square holes; round pegs in round holes.
8. Treat others as you'd want to be treated, particularly if termination is unavoidable.

Figure 3.6 Basic Keys to Motivating Subordinates

3. You have to be aware of what motivates others and whether the rewards you are providing are things they value.

   a. It is not uncommon for managers to give symbols of achievement to subordinates that the employees don't care about at all. For example, if a person in your office really likes antique cars, a day off to go to the local antique car exposition may mean a lot more than a cheap plaque from the local trophy shop engraved with "Employee of the Month." Rewards, at any level, must be relative to the person receiving them or they are a waste of time and effort.

   b. You have to know yourself and your people as individuals. If you don't want to take the time to do that, you're not a manager, just someone who occupies the office. Some people will respond positively to you if you bring in donuts some morning. Others are cynical about such efforts. Because a person doesn't attend office social functions doesn't mean he or she is not a team player. Some very effective organizational members stay away from socializing with coworkers because all they talk about is work. Different people have different needs. Try to help them have a good fit from *their* perspective.

4. People in media organizations typically have a higher need for self-actualization. Many media professionals engage in the work because of a sense of "calling" and see it as having higher purpose than just the pay. Because of that, there is a need to feel respected, important, and central to the job. When that occurs, the individual has a great sense of stature, power, and control even if much of that is a personal illusion.

   a. The media organization needs its creative people to perform well. But when creative personalities don't feel appreciated, they can become adept at doing only what's required. In other words, they don't do so poorly that you can fire them, but they don't really do great work either. There's a lot of difference between writing an acceptable news story and crafting a great one.

   b. When media professionals are overcontrolled or overedited or feel threatened, their work can quickly become pedestrian. A major metropolitan newspaper adopted a process of suspending people for infractions large and small. There were a lot of errors in the paper and something had to be done. But the solution just exacerbated the problem. The paper still had a lot of errors. And one night when major tornadoes were in the region, featured on CNN and in plenty of time to change the front page, nothing was altered. The morning edition had little mention of the storms, which had flattened a shopping center in one town within the regional area of interest, damaged a number of houses in another community, and shut down a freeway in the middle of the state for several hours. In an atmosphere of second guessing and frequent suspensions, would you risk changing the whole front page with fragmentary information about the tornadoes coming in? Or would you play it safe? You can almost hear people in the newsroom saying, "I'm not going to risk getting a suspension for dumping the story about the police department reorganization we worked on all day."

   c. People won't take risks, or champion ideas they may have, if they think they'll go nowhere or get them into trouble. When you increase the sense of risk for your subordinates, you are heading down a very dismal road.

5. When you start thinking about subordinate needs, and get bogged down in the language of "extrinsic" versus "intrinsic," unpack it this way.

   a. Extrinsic motivators are outside of yourself—paying the rent, having a nice car, being able to afford a decent lifestyle. They are the symbols with which we surround ourselves that say all the work is worth it.

   b. Intrinsic motivators are our deeper emotions—dreams, sense of purpose, and greater meaning. When people have a lot of creature comforts, but still say they're not happy, it's the intrinsic things that are missing. Journalists are often driven more by the intrinsic. Many feel their work is special, of greater importance to the society than other vocations. It is "important" that they are there. Media professionals are usually creative, well educated, and have a sense of calling about their work. Superficial rewards are not as effective in motivating such people. Giving them raises or punishments has limited effect on their work. Media people cling to ownership of their creative work and see their employer as a conduit necessary to get their material out to the audience (whom they really see themselves serving). So you need to tell them when a particularly good story is turned in, and spend time consciously noticing the extra things they do. They are cynical enough so you can't tell them something's good when it's not. But when the manager notices little things (often perceived by employees as "caring"), the whole quality of work gets notched up a bit. Being noticed and having an impact is what being a media person is all about.

6. When you want to increase the quality of work, you have to come at it from the organizational member's perspective. They won't necessarily do it "for the paper," or "for the network." Coaching is usually the best approach.

   a. In counseling such a person, the better approach is to ask questions that generate a positive, self-criticism approach. "Do you think you've reached your potential as a great reporter?" If they say no, the follow-up is, "What can we do to help that happen?" Or "Your work is solid, but I have the feeling there's a lot more creativity in there itching to get out. What can we do to prove you're the best writer around here?" A coaching approach, that recognizes their ability but makes it clear you know they aren't using all of it, is much more effective than ordering them to write with more passion. With creative people, you have to get them to do it because of their own pride and need for accomplishing that journalistic higher calling.

   b. It is not uncommon to have the following kind of interchange with a media subordinate.

      Editor—"How are things going?"

      Reporter —"Oh, OK."

      1. They make up things, sometimes because admitting the truth is perceived as a kind of failure, the "I should be able to handle this," pride problem.

      Editor—"Well, I've noticed the stuff you're doing just doesn't seem to have that old pop. Are you sure everything's OK? Is there something I need to know about, or that I can change for you?"

2. Such an approach says, in effect, "Hey, we're partners here and if it's something I'm doing as a manager I'm willing to fix it." You are creating empathy and reflecting genuine concern. Often, when you do that, problems or concerns you didn't even know about come spilling out.

c. The best way to talk to a person you suspect is having problems, is to use what are called "open-ended questions." Those are questions that don't betray what you think but ask for the other person's view. Here are some examples.

1. How would you describe what's going on here?

2. What would you like to do with this story?

3. If you were in my shoes, what would you do about this?

4. From your perspective, what can be done to improve things?

When you ask people for their point of view, they often will give it to you. But when you state your opinion right off the top, they'll tend to give you the answers you want to hear. You already know what you think. You need to get them to tell you what *they* think.

7. Put square pegs in square holes, and round pegs in round holes. In many media organizations people end up in jobs they don't particularly like and aren't particularly good at. Part of that is the career ladder, promoting people out of what they want to do into a position that pays better and has more status, but is not as fulfilling or as much fun.

a. Don't put people in positions where they'll probably fail.

b. Ask them what they like to do, or hate to do, and try to make it fit. It's absurd to have a person answering phones who hates the phone.

c. When you walk into a new management role, don't take existing staffing positions for granted. People often end up doing one thing or another because of the personality preferences of the previous manager. The "in" people are often where they are more because of social comfort with the previous boss than their actual skill. Keep a loose outlook, and don't be afraid to move people around. If you sense that has to be done, ask everyone involved what they really like to do, or what they might prefer. Seek their input. Often, when you ask people what they think or prefer, they'll tell you. By soliciting their opinion you are empowering them to tell you. Also, because they're involved in the decision process they'll have a stake in making any changes succeed.

d. Finally, when all efforts have been made and you can't effectively manage a problem person, you should consider removing him or her. But that is always a last resort. Sometimes people force you to let them go because of their intransigence. Sometimes they're just burned out and need a change but don't have the courage to do it themselves. Never fire someone out of anger, or without sleeping on it. And never presume a person should be fired for what appears on the surface to be good cause. Getting back to Davies' formula discussed earlier, you have to consider the situation and the organism fully to accurately conclude behavior cannot be changed. ***B = f(SO)***

When you have to fire someone, it shocks the whole organization. People identify and empathize with the person let go. If you have to do it, do it out of sight of others and with a way for the person to get out privately. Just because your relationship failed doesn't mean you have to have the security guard escort them from their office carrying a box of their personal effects in the middle of the afternoon. Treat them as you would like to be treated in such a difficult circumstance. The worst subordinate you've ever met may well become the strongest asset you've ever had. But it takes both an intelligent manager who understands the psychological complexity of others, and a willingness on the part of the subordinate to change.

CHAPTER SUMMARY

Understanding the psychology of the workplace may be the most important part of being a media manager. That's because it is a people-intensive business that relies on the creativity of organizational members for the quality of its products.

The people who work for you need to be in the right positions. When the individual and the job fit, productivity is generally higher. When you have people in the wrong jobs for their personality or skill level, the organization bogs down. A person who hates editing won't make a very good editor. A person who is shy and uncomfortable talking on the phone won't make a very effective receptionist. But they won't always tell you what they really want to do. People have a habit of telling the boss what they think he or she wants to hear, not what needs to be said. When people are in the jobs that fit them, they generally have greater confidence and a more positive attitude. And when people are positively motivated, they usually produce higher-quality work.

By understanding the way people perceive reality, sift information, and selectively engage with the influences of their world, you can better achieve a blend of your organization's goals and those of the individuals upon whom you, as a manager, rely. You become a facilitator for optimum performance by bringing together organizational and personal values and goals so one compliments the other. Organizational commitment is increased with a greater focus on the pursuit of excellence.

Being a media manager is a difficult job. People aren't machines. They aren't always predictable. But by taking the time to try to understand another person's perspective, you expand your own understanding of the world around you and how it works. You are more effective in your relationships with them and in making them stakeholders in your mutual success.

STUDY QUESTIONS

1. What are the implications, for you as a media manager, of this chapter's discussion of perceptions of reality and Burke's concept of "terministic screens"?

2. What is selective influence theory all about?

3. This chapter considers some of the major approaches to motivation. Summarize and explain what those imply for you as a media manager.

4. From a media management point of view, discuss the pluses and minuses of job fit and job enlargement. What should you consider before enlarging a person's job?

5. Given what you have studied thus far, what aspect of your personal approach to managing others do you think you might need to adjust to be an effective media organization manager?

chapter 4

EQUITY, EXPECTANCY, AND CLIMATE FACTORS

THEORETICAL CONSTRUCTS

The work environment is a complex arena. Our interaction is a dynamic balancing act involving a sense of fairness, an expectation of the course of events, and the atmosphere of the organization in which the calms and storms are fed by human emotions. Key concepts in this chapter will help you broaden your perspective of the way a media manager can help frame the conditions to maximize productivity while keeping conflict to a minimum.

Equity and Expectancy Theory

How people perceive the fairness of their world, and what they expect it to provide, are major determinants of what they do and how they do it. We all make adjustments in our daily lives, our personal relationships, and our careers that depend on how we think things will turn out. We try to do what we think will move matters toward a positive outcome, and avoid what we think will probably fail. We learn to anticipate various types of consequences from actions that are taken. This area of organizational dynamics is particularly intriguing for effective managers. By anticipating our subordinates' sense of fairness and expectation, we can set in motion opportunities for both personal and organizational growth. Ingersoll (1896/1980) once said, "In nature there are neither rewards nor punishments—there are consequences" (p. 615). Everything is a consequence of something else. Understanding that, it is clear that to affect what consequences occur we need to look for causes. Equity and expectancy are causal factors for many consequences in the media organization world.

Equity Theory

Equity theory in organizational dynamics was originally advanced by Adams (1963) (see Fig. 4.1). The basic assumption is that workers compare their tasks and rewards with the tasks and rewards of the workers around them. They then develop perceptions based on that comparison of whether they are fairly treated. You see people do that all the time. They are very cognizant of what other people are paid, what their benefits are, whether they get choice assignments, all manner of the context of work. They determine whether things are equitable.

- Workers compare their tasks and rewards with the tasks and rewards of those around them and develop a perception of whether they are fairly treated.
- When individuals do not believe there is equity, they move to restore the balance by whatever means are necessary.
  —Changing the way tasks are done.
  —Making suggestions for improvement.
  —Creating the illusion of productivity.
  —Withdrawing (physically or psychologically) into minimalism.

Figure 4.1   Equity Theory

When people do not believe things are equitable, there is an imbalance. What do they do? They move to restore the balance. They adjust the weight of things they can control. In the work environment there are lots of ways to do that. Those may include altering outcomes, or adjustment of work, either objectively or psychologically (Harder, 1991). Employees can change the way they do tasks, whether they suggest new ideas, how much real effort they put in as opposed to appearing to work, and many other subtle things that go into the performance equation. They look around and say, "Well, that person makes more than I do and they don't do anything, so I guess that's what management wants." This attitude becomes an organizational disease if it grows, particularly when fed by a poor performer who is accorded special treatment. It can become a part of the organizational culture wherein the group attitude toward work is minimization. As one broadcast engineer once said, "Push button, pick up check!" Indeed, in some organizations, where management is not enlightened, keeping your mouth shut and focusing on the mechanics of your job is the way to survive.

Problems of employee-perceived inequity often rise from a lack of knowledge. People may know just enough of what's going on to get it wrong. Work environments are ripe places for rumors to flourish, particularly in organizations that permit "star" systems or where managers play favorites. Frequently the stars (or favorites) are viewed by others as getting unjustified special treatment, higher pay, or other perks based on their actual productivity. Alienation sets in.

What is true in athletics is true in the newsroom. The great quarterback cannot hope to complete a pass without linemen who block. But the quarterback gets most of the money and glory, and the linemen get dirty and tired. Stars are often paid well to put spectators in the seats, or viewers in front of television sets, or publications in the hands of readers. Media organization stars may include news anchors, newspaper columnists, specialist reporters, or other people who are highly promotable as audience draws. Research has demonstrated that many people who watch newscasts develop "a personal relationship—an empathy—with the anchors and reporters who are there in their living rooms every day" (Cremer, Keirstead, & Yoakam, 1996, p. 82). Additionally, advertising research has demonstrated the power of celebrity in developing pseudosocial interactions with viewers who identify with television personalities (Basil, 1996). Thus, the anchor has a great effect on ratings. Television news operations spend a lot of time, effort, and market research expense in selecting and promoting their anchors. The anchor is then paid a great deal more than the TelePrompTer operator (often a starting position with the station's production crew) who has no audience recognition. It should also be noted that the anchor's job is a much higher risk position. If the ratings slide, the anchor is replaced but the TelePrompTer operator doesn't have to worry about the ratings. Team players in both the athletic and organizational arenas may understand the substantial reward disparity, but it still may irritate him or her. And the reality of both the football team and the newsroom is that the overall level of excellence is determined by the competence of a team's worst player, not the public status of its highest rewarded individual. Unless the TelePrompTer operator does the job correctly, the highest paid anchor in the world will be ineffective.

The way organizations justify the inequity of various roles is to perceive some positions as requiring more "talent" than others. That becomes a justification for inequity in pay and working conditions, even though every member of the team is important to its success. An anchor may be paid $180,000 a year and only required to be at work 4 hours a day. But the producer, who is really the power behind the newscast deciding what is included and in what order, may be paid $30,000 a year and required to work 10 to 12 hours a day. It should be noted that not all anchors are so lazy, nor are they all prima donnas. But the television news industry has a penchant for tolerating such behavior, which inevitably has a profoundly negative effect on the entire organization. It is not uncommon for the work culture to justify such inequity of roles, pay, and performance demands as an unchangeable reality of a unique business. That has been done for decades in the Hollywood film industry, where the name performers are more highly valued in terms of money and prestige because they sell tickets at theaters.

The effects of the star system can be reduced if the person who is the star is a decent sort; pleasant to the other members of the team, and someone whose expertise is respected. However, when the star is egoistic and treats others as "lesser persons," those "lesser persons" will find ways to rectify the situation. That can mean a newscast director rolls tapes a little late, just enough so the anchor sits there for a second or two looking uncomfortable. Or a camera operator intentionally moves the camera a little to the left so flares appear in the TelePrompTer glass from the lights on the news set, causing stumbles. Suddenly the newscast just doesn't seem right, though it's hard, watching on the television set at home, to pin down the reason. Clearly, when pay is enormously unequal, the personality of the star is instrumental in the performance of all involved in what the star does. The social dynamics of a newsroom sometimes are not unlike those of an elementary school playground. In both places, if you don't treat others right, they'll get even one way or another.

Equity problems also arise from the inherent conflict in the nature of media work. On the one hand, it is a factory kind of endeavor with tight production schedules and time constraints. On the other, it requires well-educated and creative people who tend to pursue excellence in their self-expression. As media organizations get larger, they tend to be more control oriented because of the coordination problems involved in complicated enterprises. But control and coordination are not easy companions of artistic creativity.

Gaziano and Coulson (1980) studied newsroom management styles and found that the more a media organization is centralized within a large corporate bureaucracy, the more it tends to breed job dissatisfaction. Why? Because of diminished autonomy among those who cherish independence. Large media organizations have intricate production bureaucracies necessary to turn out their products on tight, demanding schedules. They can easily develop a kind of fast-food atmosphere that breeds dissatisfaction. To meet the tight production requirements there are frequent deadlines with regimented coordination of assignments. Stories are edited or rewritten entirely, positions in the newspaper or newscast are shifted around, and other adjustments made due to the technical demands of the production line. It is not uncommon for reporters in any media form to feel their work is incomplete as it is rushed to meet the deadline. The work environment is inherently frustrating for people who see what they produce as a reflection of themselves. Their dissatisfaction is manifested in many ways. One of the most common is that media workers get upset at what they see as unfair or as compromising their artistic integrity. They then withdraw their best performance, sometimes unconsciously. It's as much a part of the equity question as the issue of pay discussed earlier, and it can produce the same kind of effort to compensate for perceived inequality—employees not working as hard as they could or some other retributive approach.

Expectancy Theory

Tied into the issue of equity is expectancy theory, originally advanced by Vroom (1964). From our knowledge and experiences, we expect things to happen based on what we do. In other words, a certain type of behavior is expected to produce a predictable outcome. If you rob a bank, you can expect to go to prison. If you study hard, you expect to earn a good grade. Expectancy has a big effect on us when coupled with rewards we desire. If you really want a good grade in this class, you expect to have to study harder than if you just try to slip through (see Fig. 4.2).

Expectancy theory assumes two outcome paths motivate us:

1. The probability that effort produces desired performance.
2. The probability that performance produces a desired outcome.

Figure 4.2   Expectancy Theory

The attractiveness of desired outcomes has a direct influence on the amount of work exerted to achieve them. The more attractive the outcome, the harder you'll be willing to work. Correspondingly, when the value of what you are trying to achieve is diminished for some reason, you reduce the amount of work and drive to attain it. Sometimes, based on the balance of things we have to accomplish, we internally reduce the value of something. For example, if you are taking a heavy academic load, you might decide to study only hard enough to make a C in a general subjects course, so you can spend more time working for a higher grade in your major. You decide that the course in your major is more important and the general education course is less important. People balance the values and expected rewards all the time, continually adjusting their performance based on the anticipated results of their work.

When people operate from an expectancy perspective, they have linear logic that says, "If I work harder, I will do a better job. If I do a better job, I will be rewarded." If they think they are working harder and doing a better job, but they are not rewarded, it becomes an equity imbalance. We all shift various incentives that occur in the work environment to balance our perceived inequities. Many inequities, large and small, exist, and a lot of incentives come to bear in the complexity of the human social environment. For example, job autonomy is an incentive. Pay is an incentive, as is freedom to do your work without interference. Having a collegial atmosphere with pleasant coworkers is an incentive. Those and many other things are important reasons people work hard initially to earn them, and then to keep them.

Equity/Expectancy Interaction

An analysis of professional baseball players involved in the 1977 to 1980 free agency dispute found that individuals sift their various incentive options to balance any inequity they perceive in the amount of work required for the value they expect it should produce (Harder, 1991). When the rewards are significantly less than they expected, they decrease their performance. They do the job acceptably, but not extraordinarily. That's because although the current situation may not be to their liking, they don't want to quit for any number of reasons other than the pay rate. So they stop working as hard. They sometimes may say something like, "Forty hours of work for forty hours of pay," meaning the company isn't paying for extra effort, so they won't give any. If they think their long-term situation will be hurt, they do something else to restore their sense of equity, or they accept that the situation can't be fixed and they quit.

Other equity/expectancy conflicts can produce very serious actions and consequences. Consider a real-life example from the sport of figure skating. Going into the 1994 Winter Olympics, Tonya Harding believed Nancy Kerrigan had to be removed from competition in order for Harding to win a medal. The logic went something like this. "I can't win because they like her. Therefore, through some unfair means she has to be prevented from competing, and I will win." Harding had a fellow conspirator ambush Nancy Kerrigan at the end of a practice session, hitting her knee with a blunt instrument in hopes of seriously injuring her so she couldn't skate. But they failed. In the 1994 Olympics Harding turned in a dismal performance, and Kerrigan won the silver medal. A police investigation into the assault on Kerrigan resulted in Harding and her four fellow conspirators being found guilty. The four males, including Harding's ex-husband, were given prison sentences. Harding was sentenced to three years' probation, fined $160,000, and ordered to do 500 hours of community service. Harding was also stripped of her national title and banned for life by the United States Figure Skating Association following the 1994 Winter Olympics ("Gillooly Sentenced," 1994; Fishbein, 1996).

This example underscores that sometimes people get caught up in their perceptions and will take very strong approaches to restore equity. What's important for you to consider as a media manager is whether anything in your area of responsibility may be fostering the feeling of inequity among coworkers that will then trigger negative consequences. Additionally, it is vital that you talk with your subordinates so you will have a sense of their perceptions. Equity, like beauty, is in the eye of the beholder. If one of your subordinates thinks he or she is being treated, or rewarded, unfairly when compared with others, that is a fact to that person. You may know it's not true, since you have access to the personnel records and the confidential payroll numbers. But your subordinate is going by what he or she sees, and to that person it is the truth.

An important aspect to restoring equity and keeping expectancies realistic is using different rewards for different people. Your media organization may have areas you can't really change (e.g., the anchor-TelePrompTer operator pay disparity mentioned earlier). Then you look for other things the person you're dealing with may value that you can add to their equity scales. As you know from our earlier chapter on motivation, the effectiveness of rewards depends on the person. One individual may seek only more money, but another person may be positively affected by getting compensatory time for extra hours they put in. Focus on the personalized environment within which people toil. Make it apparent you care about them, and they'll feel more important as a team player. Put human dynamics to work for you in resolving the problems that inequity causes. It's amazing how a small thing, such as remembering the TelePrompTer operator's name and saying "thanks," can change a person's attitude.

Organizational Justice

What we've just sketched out in equity and expectancy theory is related to another area called organizational justice (Moorman, 1991). It is a two-part concept. One element, distributive justice, focuses on the fairness of the benefits employees receive and how they are distributed among those doing the work. The other element is procedural justice, the perception of whether the process and/or guidelines used to determine those benefits are fair (see Fig. 4.3).

- Two sides of the organizational justice equation affect employee attitudes:
  —Distributive justice = fairness of benefits employees receive for work performed;
  —Procedural justice = fairness of the process and guidelines used to determine those benefits.
- There is a causal relationship between employees' perception of the justness of an organization and their organizational citizenship behaviors.

Figure 4.3 Organizational Justice

The underlying assumption in organizational justice is that "if employees believe they are treated fairly they will be more likely to hold positive attitudes about their work, their work outcomes, and their supervisors" (Moorman, 1991, p. 845). Moorman's research involved two medium-sized production firms in the midwestern United States. He found a causal relationship between employee perceptions of organizational justice and the behavior they exhibit as organizational members. Those organizational citizenship behaviors were outlined by Organ (1988) as including such things as altruism, courtesy, sportsmanship, conscientiousness, and civic virtue.

Thus, if a manager wants to encourage subordinates to be more active as organizational citizens, effort should be put into expanding their sense of fairness regarding the organization in general, and the manager in particular. If an organization is perceived by employees as being a "just" place, they tend to behave more positively toward it (Moorman, 1991). Recall our discussion in Chapter 3 regarding Davies' (1963/1978) formula for understanding behavior, $B = f(SO)$. Behavior is a function of the situation and the organism. When you want to affect behavior, you have to adjust the interaction of the situation and the organism, to produce the behavior desired. Behavior is the symptom; the situation and the organism relationship are the underlying causes. To fix things, as a media organization manager, you have to go after the causes.

Organizational Hologram Theory

This theory by Mackenzie (1991) holds that organizational effectiveness is higher when the organizational culture and individual values and norms are enfolded within one another. In other words, the employee and the organization blend so effectively they are virtually reflections of each other. That does not mean forcing people into a mold that they may or may not fit. Rather, it argues strongly for ensuring a fit exists between an organization and the people within it. If an individual does not hold the same values that the organization espouses, internal value conflict creates tension that detracts from organizational effectiveness (see Fig. 4.4).

- The more individual and organizational culture, norms, and fundamental values are "enfolded" within one another, the more effective the organization.
- The employee and organization are blended so effectively they mirror one another.
- Organizations are complex, interdependent systems of resources and people that must work in concert to adapt to dynamic environments.

Figure 4.4 Organizational Hologram Theory

The evolution of the humanistic approach in management theory—for example, McGregor's Theory Y and Ouchi's Theory Z as discussed earlier in this text—set the stage for greater emphasis on person-job fit (Caldwell & O'Reilly, 1990). Other branches of organizational behavior and employee motivational development such as job enlargement and job enrichment further amplify the concept of building stronger, deeper bonds between organization and employee (Campion & McClelland, 1991). Upon this growing river of humanistic research, grounded in the underlying Miltonian/Judeo-Christian belief that the individual is inherently important, rides the concept of the organizational hologram.

Mackenzie argues the key to the future is deep in the past, in the success of ancient, long-lasting organizations such as the Roman Empire, which were able to function without even the rudiments of modern organizations:

> Pity poor Julius Caesar who had the responsibility of governing the Roman Empire. He had no telephones. He had neither Xerox nor access to a printing press. Most of his "employees" could neither read nor write. He had no computers and no telecommunications. His couriers could not hop a TWA flight from Rome to Jerusalem. There were no automobiles, trains, steamships, or trucks. His "employees" did not all speak the same language. He was beset by internal enemies. The Roman empire was under assault on three continents and a few islands such as Britain and Sicily. He did not have a cadre of certified public accountants, tax attorneys and management scientists to guide his decision making. In fact, Julius Caesar had few of the tools we now take for granted as being necessary to run a large organization. (Mackenzie, 1991, p. 3)

The way the Romans did it was relatively simple. Steeped in Roman values, traditions, and organizational methods, regional administrators knew intuitively what to do and how to react to problems in a precisely Roman way:

> Everywhere these Romans went, they created little Romes. They had the same system for administration, laws, military, culture and even architecture. Every Roman outpost became a little Rome. In this sense the parts resembled the whole in terms of how they operated. (p. 17)

Thus, Mackenzie argues that organizational effectiveness can benefit by a highly refined "fit" of individual and organizational culture, norms, and values within all organizational activity. When there is such pervasive mutually compatible fit, potential friction is reduced because the organization and its members have a much deeper relationship with one another than merely hours worked for pay received.

At first blush the concept seems to take on an Orwellian cast, but the concept is not meant to be an argument for uniformity and compliance in organizational behavior. Organizational hologram theory is grounded in humanistic school elements with extensive relatedness across organizational and individual boundaries. The foundation of Mackenzie's theory is that productivity is fundamentally enhanced when an optimum fit occurs between personal and organizational values. The model includes 12 organizational approaches necessary to achieve that optimal fit. They are listed here (and in Fig. 4.5) so you can see the holistic philosophy of inclusion they embody:

1. Establishing and maintaining clear strategic direction.
2. Defining and updating the organizational logic.
3. Ensuring best decision making.
4. Adapting to ensure position clarity.
5. Ensuring systematic planning that is workable, involved, and understood.
6. Integrating associate selection, development, and flow with the strategic direction.

- Establishing and maintaining clear strategic direction.
- Defining and updating organizational logic.
- Ensuring best decision making.
- Adapting to ensure position clarity.
- Ensuring systematic planning that is workable, involved and understood.
- Integrating associate selection, development and flow with the strategic direction.

- Nurturing and rewarding, opportunistic and innovative problem solving.
- Ensuring health problem solving throughout the organization.
- Setting tough and realistic performance standards.
- Operating equitable and effective rewards systems
- Ensuring compatibility of interests.
- Encouraging and rewarding ethical behavior for all associates.

Figure 4.5 Processes Fostering Hologram Organizations
(Source: Mackenzie, 1991, p. 387)

7. Nurturing and rewarding, opportunistic and innovative problem solving.

8. Ensuring healthy problem solving throughout the organization.

9. Setting tough and realistic performance standards.

10. Operating equitable and effective rewards systems.

11. Ensuring compatibility of interests.

12. Encouraging and rewarding ethical behavior for all associates.
    (Mackenzie, 1991, p. 387)

When all of these things are at work, they produce six characteristics of organizations (also see Fig. 4.6) that have maximum adaptability and effectiveness within dynamic operating environments:

1. Clarity of direction

2. Clarity of structures

3. Clarity of measurement

4. Successful goal achievement

5. Results oriented problem solving

6. All organization members are both assets and resources. (Mackenzie, 1991, p. 19)

1. Clarity of direction.
2. Clarity of structures.
3. Clarity of measurement.
4. Successful goal achievement.
5. Results oriented problem solving.
6. All organization members are both assets and resources.

Figure 4.6 Highly Adaptable Organizational Characteristics
(Source: Mackenzie, 1991, p. 19)

These characteristics must be "enfolded" into the essential values of an organization and adopted by its members. When that happens, the corporate culture is, to the highest degree possible, a product of the values of its organizational members. Conversely, the organizational members mirror the organizational values. One side is an exact copy of the other, a "hologram."

ORGANIZATIONAL CLIMATE AND CULTURE

There is much more at work within any organization than shows on the organizational chart. We often think of an organization in quantitative terms—its organizational chart, number of employees, and various other accounting measures of assets and liabilities. But all organizations are fundamentally qualitative collections of social beings driven by hopes and fears, dreams and ordinary personal problems. They may be quantitatively described and designed, but their effectiveness depends as much on the qualitative feeling they and their organizational members share. Two concepts—organizational climate and organizational culture—need to be understood at this point. Each contributes to the definition of the other, and both elements are always at work within every organization.

Organizational Climate

Organizational climate is a complex area with a substantial literature available to anyone who wants to delve into it further. It has been defined by Poole (1985) as, "collective beliefs, expectations, and values regarding communication, and is generated in interaction around organizational practices via a continuous process of structuration" (p. 107). For purposes of this discussion think of it as the atmosphere of a company (see Fig. 4.7). This organizational weather system swirls through every corner of an organization "continually interacting and evolving with organizational processes, structured around common organizational practices" (Falcione, Sussman, & Herden, 1987, p. 203). It can have a profound effect on organizational performance because it, "serves as a frame of reference for member activity and therefore shapes members' expectancies, attitudes, and behaviors; through these effects it influences organizational outcomes such as performance, satisfaction, and morale" (p. 96).

- Climate is the beliefs, expectations, and values within the organizational collective that serve as a frame of reference for member activity.
- Climate is the atmosphere or the feeling that permeates an organization.
- Climate is fundamental to the nuances of organizational personality that permeate its physical processes and structure.

Figure 4.7 Organizational Climate

Climate is affected by the ups and downs of daily events that cause organizational members to think about any aspect of their relationships with each other and management. When business is down, an organizational climate will typically be a little more tense than when things are rolling along positively. When serious challenges occur in the marketplace, or threats of corporate takeovers emerge, there are effects on organizational members' attitudes that then alter their feeling for the organization and one another. Just as regular weather can have a strong effect on our attitudes—sunny days make us feel good, dreary days contribute to our feeling down—organizational climate is a prime factor in our attitude toward work. We like to be in sunny places more than drizzly ones. We prefer to be around people who are happy rather than those who are in a funk. Organizations take on these human characteristics. After all they are nothing more than collections of human beings—and can be quite distinct in their overarching moods.

Organizational Culture

While climate is the atmosphere within an organization, culture is better thought of as the framework that includes rituals, practices, and behavior patterns that set an organization apart. Schein (1985) has defined organizational culture as

> the pattern of basic assumptions that a given group has invented, discovered, or developed in learning to cope with its problems of external adaptation and internal integration, which have worked well enough to be considered valid and, therefore, to be taught to new members as the correct way to perceive, think, and feel in relation to those problems. (p. 9)

As such, culture is an acquired knowledge base that evolves within the organization as it resolves problems and adapts to its environment. In effect, things that have worked well enough in the past to be considered valid are taught to new organizational members as the correct way to perceive, think, and feel (see Fig. 4.8). Those may include relatively simple overt manifestations such as a dress code, or more pervasive and aggressive blending of personal and organizational values. Strong cultures reinforce a powerful sense of belonging.

- Organizational culture is the physical reality of human rituals, practices, and patterns of behavior that develop over time.
- Organizational culture is the pattern of basic assumptions a given group has invented, discovered, or developed
  —in learning to cope with problems of external adaptation and internal integration,
  —that have worked well enough to be considered valid and, therefore,
  —have been taught to new members as the correct way to perceive, think, and feel in relation to those problems.

Figure 4.8 Organizational Culture

People take pride in attaining organizational member status and adopt encouraged behaviors. Those outside such a culture may be cynical about it, particularly if it is very effective. A contemporary example of a strong media organization culture is a giant newspaper chain that has branched into other media as well. Gannett has, as a company, a distinct personality. Cynical outsiders sometimes refer to members of the culture as "Gannettoids." Gannett newspapers and other products share Gannett values, mythology, and corporate-reinforced approaches to work and daily life. Another example of a strong organizational culture is the auto parts chain AutoZone. Its retail outlet employees wear uniforms, and the company has uniform days when everyone at corporate headquarters also wear their AutoZone shirts. Such team emphasis may make employees feel positive as part of something big and successful. Others, who are more independent minded, may resist such collectivity. A self-selection process is always at work in organizational dynamics, wherein people remove themselves from organizations where they don't feel comfortable and gravitate toward cultures that fit them. In so doing, they tend to reinforce that with which they feel a strong sense of association, and it reinforces them.

Effects of Climate and Culture on Performance

The ability of managers to communicate has been linked to organizational performance (Penly, Alexander, Jernigan, & Henwood, 1991, pp. 57–76). Of particular importance is the effectiveness of both oral and written messages in accurately conveying meaning within the context of organizational climate and individual message filtering. Some companies have been particularly adept at instituting climate conditions where the vested interests of all parties are based on clear communication and positive performance, blended with organizational goals and individual values. Moskal (1990) studied Honda's automobile plant in Marysville, Ohio. The plant was designed to incorporate participative management teams set up to make everyone feel like a kind of minimanager with personal responsibility and authority for product quality. All employees were called "associates" and voted on wide-ranging issues from overtime schedules to quality circle production targets. The plant had extensive "Voluntary Involvement Programs," which were tied to a bonus points system. Moskal (1990) found that one cardboard box recycling idea cut costs more than $2 million. The organizational climate fostered individual improvement through extensive optional training programs with a focus on the importance of the individual. "When you ask for their help, it makes people feel that they count. Morale goes up, and quality goes up," one midlevel associate explained. "As soon as quality problems are found, we get immediate feedback on what might be wrong. Five or six associates swarm around the problem area and solve the problem on the spot, usually within minutes" (Moskal, 1990, p. 54).

Moskal (1990) determined that the hierarchical structures of companies vary considerably. For example, Donnelly Corporation, a manufacturer of window products, began participative management in 1951 but four decades later still had a detailed set of personnel regulations in a 100-page handbook. Despite the detail of the regulations, the work teams of 20 to 25 people at Donnelly were still able to set their own goals and work together to change things to help achieve those goals. Donnelly worked to expand trust and openness within supportive and cooperative relationships. By doing that, employees increased their sense of ownership that the company reinforced through a bonus plan, paid quarterly, based on the overall corporate return on investment. If the minimum return on investment wasn't met, each employee's bonus fund was charged and that had to be paid back before further bonuses were earned. The employees shared in the profits, and the responsibility to maintain them. This concept is a shared benefit/risk approach meant to connect the individual worker with the company's overall health.

Much of the difficulty for management, particularly new management that has just entered an existing organization with a strong culture, is understanding the nuances that make up a considerable part of the shared experience. Those are often things not contained in mission statements, or spreadsheets, or the memo file. They are the fabric of cultural experience. One business consultant described it as "the unwritten story." That's because often the information most needed for organizational members to communicate and function effectively is not written down anywhere. It's learned behavior unique to the organization. "It is stored in the minds and feelings of employees—ourselves, or those who work for us" (Gunneson, 1991, p. 135). Because such critical information is within the employees, managing them positively so they will want to contribute their knowledge and expertise is clearly a critical management responsibility. In autocratic organizational cultures, or those in serious turmoil with high risks, that knowledge may not be forthcoming, and organizational effectiveness is impaired.

Organizations as Complex, Living Systems

Some organizations approach changes in the environment defensively, resisting making internal adjustments in the way they do things, while others seem to seek adaptive strategies readily. What makes the difference is the propensity of the particular corporate culture to depart from tradition in order "to replace existing methods with more productive ones" (Kanter, 1988, p. 406). But that is often a very complex problem due to traditional ways of doing things, large and small. Grove (1988) termed "organizational inertia" that which is generated "when the day-to-day protocols and procedures of a company get in the way of employees trying to do their jobs." Grove asserts such inertia is more prevalent over time, that "the older and bigger an organization, the more inertia it will tend to have" (p. 418). In Schneider's (1983, p. 41) view, "it is clear that organizations, unless they are pushed, will tend toward stability or slow decay."

Organizations that initiate efforts to change the way they are managed fundamentally are embarking on a long and difficult process. For example, one of the oldest media businesses in the western United States launched a concerted effort to change its management style in the late 1980s because of intense competition in one of the few markets with competing daily newspapers left in the nation. Research confirmed that senior managers saw the way employees were managed as pivotal in an environment where newspaper production technology had been equalized among competitors (Redmond, 1991a). Additionally, the study confirmed the long-term nature of making such a fundamental change in the corporate culture. Indeed, after several years of effort, senior managers indicated the process was still in the infant stage and predicted no specific time frame or calendar target for reaching the style-shift goal. A major metropolitan daily newspaper in existence since the mid-1800s is steeped in traditions that compound the complexity of its inertia, as one former editor emphasized:

> A newspaper is a culture and within a newspaper are many subcultures. . . . There is the subculture of the editorial office which ought to be ultimately the subculture of the editor himself, but there is an interrelationship on some newspapers between the editor's office and the publisher's office, and there's another subculture downstairs. And then you have the subculture of the marketing department. (Redmond, 1991a, p. 36)

Organizations are made up of individuals who form subcultures of departments or offices. Within the human dynamic of organizations there is a continual trade-off of power and responsibility in a balancing act of individual and organizational self-interests. Both the organization and the individual are "agents" in a relationship. The individual agent acquiesces to organizational demands for which benefits are derived. The organization agent acquiesces to individual demands for which benefits are likewise derived. The "Causal Theory of Action" provides a context of understanding the power of the psychology at work in the relationship. Within the theory, "to act is to be caused to behave by mental states of one's own—mental states that make the behavior reasonable in the circumstances" (Schachter, 1983, p. 10). It is important to understand that "to act" may include the conscious decision not to do something, as well as to do it. "Even an agent who remains stock still may yet be 'performing an action,' and a welter of activity may amount to the 'action' of failing to do something else" (p. 13). Thus, an agent may be actively engaged in doing nothing in an organization.

The "mental states" impacting behavior of organizational members include perceptions of reality an agent develops in the workplace where two distinct channels of communication are influential. Formal channels of communication are those built into the organizational hierarchy. Informal channels are created when coworkers take part in off-the-record conversations or engage in general organizational gossip. The informal channels are pervasive, interwoven with the social interchanges of work groups (Schachter, 1983). "No matter how elaborately the formal systems are planned, employees always find opportunities for sharing information through unauthorized channels—even through those that are expressly forbidden" (p. 13).

Mackenzie sees organizations as "complex living systems of interdependent processes, resources and people" (p. 51) that must work in concert, to adapt to a constantly changing, dynamic environment. Those organizations that can achieve a high level of internal compatibility have a competitive edge because they eliminate much of what stymies organizations with weaker cultures. When traditional bureaucratic layering of position and power permeate an organization, there is both rigidity in adjustment to change and a kind of myopia of management based on past practices, which hinders adaptation. That, then, results in managers relying on past experience to make future decisions. But often the current conditions of the marketplace are not the same, so the decisions are flawed.

An example of this occurred as Cap Cities was finalizing its takeover of the ABC network in late 1985. The top executives at Cap Cities grew impatient with then-ABC president Fred Pierce, a career employee of the network. At the time, audience fragmentation, due to cable and other television alternatives to the broadcast networks, was just beginning. But while Cap Cities executives grew increasingly wary of the way ABC was spending money, the network president continued justifying his actions by concentrating on the bright spots in the network efforts and ignoring the accelerating overall financial erosion. Cap Cities chair Tom Murphy, and chief operating officer Dan Burke finally decided to replace Pierce. The symptom was continuing financial erosion of the network, but the underlying cause of Pierce's increasing ineffectiveness was summed up by Burke, who said, "Fred was a hostage to his experience." It was discovered later that Pierce had even put a psychic on the ABC payroll to advise him on programming the network (Auletta, 1991, p. 114).

> Executives struggle to make sense out of what is happening to their organizations using a lens crafted in a different time, a time of slower change and less interdependence. Too many are trying to apply ideas from another era to the resolution of modern problems. (Mackenzie, 1991, p. 7)

Much of the difficulty of being a "hostage" to your experience comes when those around you don't serve the vital role of pointing out dangerous assumptions, new issues, or other things that may run contrary to the manager's predisposition. The position and power hierarchies within organizations contribute to the problem as people trying to curry favor hesitate to take issue with a manager. You have the proverbial "emperor's new clothes" syndrome, where the emperor looks ridiculous but no one will tell him because, after all, he's the emperor. Mackenzie seeks to avoid this corporate politics trap by envisioning in his model a stronger voice of each organizational member. By more careful fitting of the organization and its members, each has a higher vested interest in the other. That means subordinates are empowered to a greater degree and will more readily become involved proactively in the decision-making process.

> Any organization facing a dynamically complex milieu must proactively engage and motivate all Associates and units in the formulation, interpretation and implementation of the strategic direction, as appropriate to each situation, in order to become and remain efficiently adaptable. (Mackenzie, 1991, p. 70)

The Reality of the Workplace

The blending of equity, expectancy, organizational justice, climate, and culture perspectives may produce positive or negative results. In normal work environments people withdraw the level of service when their expected rewards, either extrinsic or intrinsic, are not realized. In other words, as discussed previously, if they don't get the rewards they think they should get for what they do, they do less. They usually choose the avenue of decreased performance to the extent that it doesn't affect future rewards. They do the least they can without its being noticed. That can be a significant reduction in productivity in creative environments. Media employees are not as closely supervised as on a factory assembly line, and the speed of their work is important. In the creation of a new advertising layout, getting out a public relations project, or writing news copy, a slight slowing down of each daily task can have dramatic consequences in overall productivity.

A new manager, brought in to "fix" a place that's having some trouble, is usually in a hurry and doesn't like to hear senior employees say, "that won't work here." It is not uncommon for such a person to fail to learn even rudimentary aspects of the new organization climate/culture complex. Often the new manager brings in a few key lieutenants. Those in the organization who jump on the bandwagon are seen as team players and those who are more hesitant as obstacles to success. Some folks are perceived to be "on the bus and others aren't," as one media manager put it. The problem with that sort of approach is you create serious division within the organization, particularly if what you do is contrary to the prevailing organizational culture mythology. Favoritism can flourish in such an environment. Certain people go for drinks after work, or socialize, with certain other people. If the boss likes a drink after work, and a regular group tends to gather around him or her repeatedly for that activity, the situation is acute. An "in" group develops, and everyone else in the department sees themselves as members of the "out" group, excluded from the inner circle.

In any work setting, but particularly in those that have become highly politicized with divisions of employees into groups of varying management favor, the stage is set for a serious loss of productivity. Those trying to impress the boss have a tendency to tell him or her what that manager wants to hear. So there is a lot of reinforcement, warranted or not, that the manager's ideas and decisions are the right ones. The manager ends up surrounded by yes men and women who hope to realize personal gain through their relationship with the boss. But the out people typically perceive danger in extending themselves. Knowing the history of high managerial turnover, organizational members may play a waiting game until another management change occurs. And, of course, while they wait a year or two, they *appear* to be working hard at everything they are really doing minimally. After all, they are not an in person. They see themselves on a kind of survival level, trying to hang on until either the situation changes to include them, or there's another management change. They are reduced to doing their jobs only to the degree necessary so their competency cannot be questioned. But they are not spurred on to excellent performance. They are, in effect, in a holding pattern, turning circles in the air going nowhere as fast as they can.

In some jobs slowing down means nothing more than "doing it by the book." During the Reagan administration there was a conflict with the nation's air traffic controllers. They managed to impair aircraft traffic flow seriously, particularly in the nation's busiest flight corridors and airports, by doing everything exactly according to regulations, no longer bending the rules slightly to squeeze more flights into a given amount of airspace. They ultimately went beyond the slowdown to a full-blown strike, though legally barred from doing so, and were fired by President Reagan in 1981 (Thanepohn, 1991).

You must pay attention to people's feelings and try to avoid being seen as unfair, arbitrary, or capricious. You have to keep political games out of the work environment, and you must treat everyone equally. You can't have the in group—out group business going on where there is even the appearance of favorites. Employees and managers do form alliances and perceptions of some people as helping and others as standing in the way of progress. So the sociopolitical nature of the work environment is always present. That can be exacerbated in industries where you have frequent management turnover and a demand by senior managers for quick fixes (e.g., American media industries dependent upon ratings and circulation studies that determine advertising rates that produce corporate revenues).

The Malicious Compliance Syndrome

Consider an example of organizational behavior as a real-life illustration to begin our discussion of the serious problem of malicious compliance. One disgruntled employee in a public relations agency takes a pen from the office supply cabinet every day and throws it away partly used. That is about 225 pens a year (the number of regular work-days). Now, if ten employees are involved in this get-even exercise, an additional 2,250 pens are consumed by the organization in a year. It doesn't take long for such activity to affect the operating budget dramatically.

Well-meaning managers can trigger such responses when they, through their actions, say, "I don't trust you and I think you're taking advantage of the company." Consider this scenario. Media organization executives decide employees are spending too much time playing games on their computers. The organization's computer systems manager is sent around to all the offices and deletes the games from the computer hard drives. This is a case of treating a symptom instead of the cause and, in the process, angering workers. The cause may be too little work to do and too much idle time. Or it is entirely possible the employees who play games on their computers also come in early and leave late and really are dedicated. They may be merely relieving a little tension and amusing themselves for a few moments while they actually maintain a high level of productivity. By removing the games from computers, do you think the employees are encouraged to work harder for the company? Would you be?

The appropriate managerial response would be to look at the amount of work being done and the patterns of processing it. Adjusting work flow is a better solution. Some employees may play games because they are waiting for someone else to complete part of a project. Others may use the games for a little recreation during their lunch hours when they eat at their desks or for a short break. In those cases, removing the games from their computers will make those employees angry that they were being branded as lacking productivity when their surplus time is either caused by poor work flow (waiting on another person) or is really their own (their lunch hour or coffee break). The normal result of such a managerial approach described here is a further reduction in productivity and increased alienation of workers who develop an "us versus them" mentality toward their employer. In addition, a kind of game begins in which people move their office furniture around so others can't see what they're doing on their computers. If they're inventive, they hide new games in files on the computer where the games can't easily be found. As a manager, you must fight the tendency to jump to conclusions and really work at getting at the underlying reality of what is going on. Assume that nothing is what it seems, and you will avoid the trap of treating symptoms rather than causes.

When an individual attempts to decrease the effectiveness of an organization by doing a job in a way that appears to comply with directives and goals but in fact has negative effects, the result is a kind of malicious compliance. It can have pervasive effects on an organization because of its subtle, camouflaged nature. For example, intentionally overlooking or downplaying something to reduce a media organization's competitiveness, such as not telling an assignment desk in a newsroom about a phoned-in news tip or producing a potentially extraordinary story in such a way as to render it mundane. As Schneider (1983) stated, "Where an organization is going is not where someone says it is going but where its internal behavioral processes actually take it" (p. 34) (see Fig. 4.9).

- Doing work that appears to comply with directives and organizational goals but that really harms effectiveness.
  - —Pretending to work hard, when real productivity and creativity is reduced.
  - —Doing only what the job description says with no circumstantial adaptation.
- Media organization manifestations may include:
  - —Intentionally overlooking or downplaying something to reduce effectiveness.
  - —Doing work that could be extraordinary in a mundane but acceptable way.

Figure 4.9 Malicious Compliance Syndrome

When you are trying to move people forward in an organization, you will encounter malicious compliance. It's important you recognize it, so you can keep it from getting out of hand. Malicious compliance is when people do their job to the worst of their abilities, but only to the degree they won't get caught. Usually it is a conscious effort, but sometimes it can be an unconscious reaction to negative feelings that build up toward management. It is very common when existing employees feel threatened by a new manager. When senior management introduces you as the person "we've brought in to fix this place," the trigger for malicious compliance has been pulled, because in saying that, existing subordinates have been told they are in need of "fixing." They naturally assume changes are coming. We inherently resist change because of a natural fear of the unknown. So you, as the new manager "brought in to fix" the place, are feared and not trusted from the outset. What existing employees want is to keep their jobs and survive. But fixing may mean they won't. So they have a vested interest in your failure to "fix" the place.

Perception Is Truth

It is very important to understand that belief is what frames "truth." In other words, if people *believe* something, it is true *to them*. That means rumors containing false information that are spread gain credibility as they are passed from one person to another. They take on a life of their own. Once widespread, they are very difficult to reverse, because they become part of the "received truth," acquired from others whom the person trusts. Another thing happens in organizations that worsens the rumor problem. When information is restricted, the work culture creates its own information. Sometimes management has very good reasons for not disclosing things to the general employee populace. But unless it is critical, for competitive or legal reasons, that something remain confidential, all that restricting information flow does is feed the rumor mill. When people don't know what's going on, they worry and develop scenarios of what they think is probably happening. Then they pass those around, and in the process the illusions gain credibility as they spread.

Pretending to Work While Slowing Down or Removing Service

When anyone has a vested interest in your failure, he or she will actively help you fail. Such individuals do their jobs, but not as well as they should, or could. There is an illusion of competence. People move around fast and seem to be working very hard diving into the problems at hand. But much of the activity is just action for the sake of action, with nothing serious being accomplished. In any work environment, people can do what they are supposed to, or they can do what they are supposed to as well as they can. There is a big difference, particularly in qualitative work such as that in which media employees engage. Removing service is not always overt. It can be subconscious. For example, copy editors don't make all the corrections. They start missing things they shouldn't. Photographers don't shoot wonderful videotape that comes alive, just ordinary pictures. You look at the tape and everything is there, but it doesn't have any creative fire. When malicious compliance is at work in an organization, things are mundane despite the surface illusion of great energy being put into them. As managers try to improve things, they sometimes react, out of frustration, by giving orders that come back to haunt them. For example, because advertising copy is not as good as it should be, the agency manager orders that "no copy will leave the agency without the director of creative services personally approving the copy." All responsibility has been removed from the people who are actually causing the problem and dumped on a middle manager who doesn't need the extra work. The director of creative services ends up swamped while the real culprits, the staff members who haven't been held accountable for their mundane writing, escape accountability.

When people in a work environment *believe* something, they react to it. The concepts of organizational justice, equity theory, and expectancy theory come into play in that reaction, both positively and negatively. When perceptions of justice and equity are violated, serious negative consequences can be set in motion for the organization. Individuals may exert whatever power is available to adjust expectancies to balance the scales of justice and equalize inputs with outcomes. In simple terms, people get even in whatever way(s) they find available. Employees may steal company property (pens, pencils, notebooks), spend company funds with little care to minimize costs they control (staying in more expensive hotel rooms when less expensive ones are available), run up their expense account rather than treating the company's money as their own, and withdraw service in whatever way they can without getting fired. In short, the company becomes an enemy to be taken advantage of, rather than a partner with whom one excels. And this happens, in some cases, over nothing but rumors fed by the lack of accurate information flow and the subsequent illusions that arise in its place.

Conditions That Foster Malicious Compliance

Malicious compliance flourishes in environments where employees don't trust management or where there tends to be a high managerial turnover. Consider the situation in television news. The average television news director in the United States has a life span at a given station of about two and a half years (Stone, V., 1987, 1992). When first hired, to prove they are aggressively working to improve things, news directors typically change things senior managers will immediately notice. Those things may include changing the newscast set, perhaps adding an anchor or two, and maybe redesigning the look of the newscast graphics. The new manager spends a lot of time going around marking his or her territory in the most obvious ways to senior management. That gives senior management the illusion of change, when what has been altered may only be superficial to the serious problems hidden within the fabric of the work culture. The serious problems in fact-gathering, reporting, and internal processes that determine the underlying quality of work are left until later. Unfortunately, time usually runs out and later never comes, as another news director begins the process all over again.

One reason the serious problems are left until last is that they are difficult to resolve and usually take a lot of time. Another reason is that many news directors don't know how to even detect them. A national study of television news directors found that most had neither college-level management training or corporate management seminars. More than four-fifths indicated they learned the job of news director by observing others, and then doing it themselves (Redmond, 1993).

Television news is an "instant fix" business. Senior managers give a news director the first year, because they're working with the previous news director's budget and personnel. But in the second year, they are expected to have the station back on track to expanding ratings and profits. The person who doesn't like a news director, or who feels threatened by a new one, has to wait only about 18 months or so before the manager's power starts being taken away and the machinery put into motion to get rid of her.

For the employee who is at odds with the news director—perhaps an anchor who has been reassigned or a reporter who was getting all the top assignments but has now been reassigned to the education beat—it's just a waiting game. These people, sometimes very influential leaders among their newsroom coworkers, have a vested interest in the news director's failure. So they help it along any way they can. Such subordinate resistance creates a climate of mediocre performance and feeds the rumor mill, which increases anxiety among everyone else. "A lot of changes around here," someone may say one day at lunch, "and I understand there may be some layoffs." All of a sudden it's a mess, and when the rumors get up to the general manager, the impression is that the news director doesn't have control. Once the seeds of doubt have been sown, it's only a question of time. Additional factors fostering malicious compliance include all those mentioned earlier in the sections on equity theory, expectancy theory, organizational justice, and the reality of the workplace. Foremost among those are star systems in media organizations, significant pay and work differentials among coworkers, and social alignments of office politics that produce in and out groups (see Fig. 4.10).

These do not necessarily occur in any particular order. One or more will probably be at work within any media or organization.

- Lack of employee trust in management.
- High managerial turnover that increases a "survival" attitude among existing employees.
- Quick- or "instant"-fix approaches that often treat superficial symptoms but do not alleviate underlying causes.
- Inequity of pay, benefits, or status that creates "in" and "out" groups among employees.
- Lack of information flow that encourages rumors.
- Other conditions that increase employee vested interest in managerial failure.

Figure 4.10 Conditions Fostering Malicious Compliance Syndrome

CHAPTER SUMMARY

Where an organization is going is not where someone says it is going, but where its internal behavioral processes take it. You can have all kinds of great slogans in organizations, but if those slogans don't mirror real attitude within the organization, they are meaningless words on the wall. Basically, effectiveness is higher when an organization and the individuals within it are mutually synchronous with maximum compatibility. That doesn't mean there are no conflicts or diverse opinions. But the overall direction is the same, and there is an overriding sense of unity of purpose.

Organizations, as we have discussed, are complex, living systems that are the personification of the people who compose them. Those people create the climate and culture, and together they are all part of the organizational personality that can transcend time and substantive change. Bureaucracy itself breeds layering of position and power where structure and rigidity can dominate. Thus, the larger an organization, the more difficult it is to preserve entrepreneurial spirit and

dynamic flexibility. What works in small groups may or may not be effective in large groups. Although value matching between the organization and its members may reduce the inherent value friction, it is far from a perfect solution. For media organizations are composed of creative people who inherently resist conformity and pursue independence.

As a media manager, then, you must stay flexible and pay a great deal attention to the human dynamics at work in your organization. When you do that, you can see problems coming early, and go after the causes rather than treating symptoms. You can watch for inequitable situations, poor information flows that contribute to distorted perceptions and rumors, and increase your awareness of the expectancies your subordinates bring with them to the work environment. Then managing media organizations takes on a dynamic sense, where you orchestrate a kind of symphony of human endeavor instead of a cacophony of organizational chaos.

STUDY QUESTIONS

1. Discuss equity and expectancy theory in terms of their effect on media workers.

2. What is organizational justice and how does it apply to the work environment?

3. Explain the difference between organizational climate and culture. Are they easy or difficult to change?

4. Consider anywhere you have been employed, whether a media organization or some other enterprise. Was malicious compliance a factor?

chapter 5

MEDIA ORGANIZATION EFFECTIVENESS

Assessing organizational effectiveness has proven to be complex, driven by diverse perspectives (Gibson, Ivancevich, & Donnelly, 1997). Using formulaic approaches to effectiveness, or attempting to use universal categorical criteria, doesn't always work well across different organizations because the meaning of what is effective is highly variable from one place to the next (Au, 1996). Does effective mean being the advertising agency with the largest number of clients, or, perhaps, the agency with the largest margin of profit? Those are two different measures of effectiveness. Effectiveness, like good looks, means different things to different people. In one survey of the organizational effectiveness literature it was found that authors took different approaches and came to conclusions based on different indicators of effectiveness (Cameron & Whetten, 1983).

The effectiveness question is an absorbing one. You can approach it from an overview perspective, considering effectiveness in the macro sense of the "greater" organizational goals. Or you can become absorbed in the intricacies of microanalysis. For example, some researchers have produced wide-ranging sets of up to 25 variables in some 17 models as test matrices (Zammuto, 1982) while others argue effectiveness is inextricably tied to a fundamental approach toward improving quality (Elmuti & AlDiab, 1995).

SITUATION-SPECIFIC NATURE OF EFFECTIVENESS

The fundamental problem is deciding what effectiveness is and whose values should be the criteria for determining it. Is it management's perspective, the employee culture's, the customer's evaluation, or perhaps the attitude of federal regulators toward a company in one of the media industries subject to oversight by such agencies as the Federal Communications Commission (FCC) and Federal Trade Commission (FTC)? Each of these groups, and many others that may interact with a media organization, has a different perspective and, therefore, a different assessment. Because of that, the range of organizational constituents affects how its effectiveness is judged (Martin & Kettner, 1997).

Systems theory considers the need to balance such multiple constituencies within and without an organization (Zammuto, 1984). The organization, then, is always in somewhat of a state of flux as problems in one area are recognized and resolved, and then concern arises in another area. Toward the end of the fiscal year, staying within budget may become a critical issue and, therefore, override everything else. In media organizations, during the time when field data are collected for circulation and ratings reports, controlling budget items such as overtime are of lesser importance than providing product with the most positive effect on surging market shares.

Effectiveness, then, has many masters within an organization, and they change places on the ladder of power from time to time. Altogether they provide a sum total of the system's effectiveness, and, like other team endeavors, organizations typically rise or fall on the basis of their weakest elements.

Particularly in media organizations, where the span of activity ranges from basic business considerations to effects on society and the ideals of a free press bound up within the First Amendment, there is a danger of adopting too narrow a view of effectiveness. That is particularly true as media coalesce into ever-larger conglomerates, as discussed elsewhere in this text. Remote ownership and investor-driven concerns may produce a narrow, profit-margin view of a medium as merely another retail product. On the other hand, higher-purpose perspectives focusing only on the ideals of journalism can also be a narrow view. In the context of contemporary American media, successful organizations have to be successful businesses that make the money necessary to pay their bills, but they also serve greater public interests as integral threads of the social fabric. A newspaper has to make a profit, and practice good journalism satisfying audience wants and needs, to be considered effective by its diverse constituencies of investors, advertisers, and readers. For the media manager, then, the challenge is developing a mutually reinforcing blend of effectiveness measures.

Occasionally a news organization, based on good journalistic practice, may need to report information that major advertisers dislike. The businesses may reduce or eliminate their advertising in the newspaper or newscast that runs a series of stories the advertisers consider negative. But advertisers cannot be permitted to dictate news coverage or the media organization becomes a sham, relinquishing its greater responsibility to the public, which is based on developing a trust relationship with an audience expecting truthful reporting. Attempts to influence the media began as soon as there were media. And all media organizations daily face the difficult task of balancing interests that are not always compatible. Clearly the question of effectiveness depends on the specific situation and the various constituencies to be served—shareholders, employees, customers, society—which means effectiveness is bound up within the organizational culture (Denison & Mishra, 1995).

People engage with media on a wide range of levels. The media have audiences, with varying perspectives, needs, and wants that are served in different ways. The media are a continuum through our political, economic, and cultural life. A television station provides entertainment to help us escape, and news to keep us informed. A radio station—a daily companion for many—plays music we like to hear at home, as we drive around, or while we work in our offices.

Consider the daily newspaper. It is a business and so has the aforementioned basic categories of shareholders, employees, and customers. But the customer concept fragments into important uses and gratifications. When a customer buys a paper, what is really purchased is a multiplicity of products wrapped up in one. A newspaper provides the daily news and information we need to meet our current events surveillance needs. It also contains grocery ads and coupons to satisfy our need to better manage our household budgets. Classified ads help us buy and sell items. Finally the newspaper may serve as packing material around our fragile possessions when we get ready to move. During World War II many Americans even used newspapers folded a special way to line household garbage cans, instead of regular paper sacks, as part of the effort to conserve materials for the war effort. The city council member, insurance executive, teacher, laborer, homemaker, and student all have different ways they use the daily newspaper, and assessments of its worth is based on how it fulfills their individual wants and needs. Effectiveness, then, is a reflection of attitudes and relationships (Ryan, Schmit, & Johnson, 1996).

Myriad variables of organizational effectiveness assessment exist both internally and externally in all organizations (see Fig. 5.1). Internal corporate considerations may range from employee social interaction and office politics to the labor atmosphere and the frequency of personnel turnover. External forces with which a specific corporate culture must engage may include vigorously changing competition, audience/customer perceptions, public attitudes toward the organization in times of crises (for a media company being the publication or station "of record" to whom people turn when something big happens), and government agency regulation of a given business sector. The various constituencies engaged with an organization look through the prism of reality from their unique perspectives, forming perceptions of the organization by the way it affects them individually (Judge, 1994). For example, if a daily newspaper drops the grocery ad section for one week, people looking for the latest political news may not notice, but those trying to manage their household budgets would. So any attempt to analyze how good an organization is has to come at the question from each of the perspectives that organization serves (Campbell, 1996).

- **Internal:**
    - —Employee social interaction (e.g., team atmosphere or formal hierarchy).
    - —Office politics.
    - —Labor atmosphere and turnover of personnel.
- **External:**
    - —Changing competitive situation.
    - —Audience/customer perceptions.
    - —Public attitude during crises (e.g., to whom do people turn for news and information when something big happens . . . the media outlet of record).
    - —Attitude of regulators (where applicable, e.g., FCC, FTC).

Figure 5.1 Variables of Effectiveness

In the attempt to understand better the complexity of environmental factors and organizational response to them, organizational theorists have generally approached the problem of analyzing organizational effectiveness from one of four perspectives: structural, strategic choice, collective action, or natural selection (LeNoir, 1987).

1. Structuralists see the organization as operating within the context of greater forces than itself, which requires it to adjust to those forces. The organization, then, is reactive to external factors that have considerable impact on the choices available.

2. The strategic choice view posits management as influencing organizational effectiveness through the choice of niches toward which the organization is directed. The environment is considered a precondition that management strategy analyzes to determine where to direct its efforts based on the best chance of success. The environment is not so much manipulated as simply picked apart to find the best potential place for the organization to focus its energies.

3. The collective action perspective considers the process of change as a revolutionary one in which organization and environment mutually redefine each other. Here, organizations are seen not as independent elements opposed to the environment but as intertwined within it. They rise within an environmental context, are part of its very definition, affect the way it changes over time, and in their adjustment to change further redefine that context.

4. The natural selection concept is fundamental Darwinism, an organization being either appropriate to the environment and surviving, or inappropriate and dying, regardless of any attempt to fight for survival. Within this view organizations have a limited capability to adapt to a changing environment (LeNoir, 1987). To use a Darwinian example, dinosaurs were doomed to extinction when their environment shifted, and there was nothing within the scope of their adaptive capabilities they could do to survive in the newly changed world.

Maximizing productivity and adaptability is more likely to occur in organizations where there is a merging of organizational attributes with those of organizational members, blending organizational goals and individual values. There is no magic formula for organizational effectiveness since the environment is fluid and dynamic. Likewise there is considerable variability among successful organizations, from hierarchical structure to shop-floor management style, that creates individualized organizational cultures. Those organizational cultures that develop their own traditions resist change. Effectively managing people in the context of organizations requires specific skills ranging from verbal communication to motivation to managing conflict (Wilson, Boni, & Hogg, 1997).

THE FRAMEWORK OF COMPETITION

In any competitive situation, the game is dynamic. As your opponent makes a move, you counter. That means that you are continually adapting, looking for a way to gain an advantage. The ancient Chinese philosopher Sun Tzu saw the ability to adapt as a fundamental principle in *The Art of War,* originally written in about 100 B.C. Media organization competitive environments are battlegrounds in many respects, where survival depends on your ability to meet the competition and defeat it. But adapting does not simply mean changing. It means changing the right way. Or, as Sun Tzu put it, "not clinging to fixed methods, but changing appropriately according to events, acting as is suitable" (Tzu, 100 B.C./1988, p. 125).

Over time any organization must adapt to large and small changes. How that is accomplished determines its ability to maintain the status quo, grow, or decline. It is the underlying concern of such best-selling works as *Theory Z* (Ouchi, 1981) and *In Search of Excellence* (Peters & Waterman, 1982). Those two often-quoted texts, the former a comparison of the Japanese corporate culture to that of the United States and the latter a profile of the firms the authors determined as "America's best-run companies," focus on how to manage more effectively in a vigorously changing business environment. Substantive changes were occurring at the time they were published, both in financial and social conditions—for example, the rise of "junk bond" leveraging as a corporate finance strategy, shifts in international business threatening American economic dominance, and increasing female presence in the white-collar workforce, to name a few. Turbulence is always present as the organizational equation evolves. It is important to understand that nothing will be the same tomorrow as it is today, and adapting to change is a continuous process, whether in large or small increments. The world is never static but, like the tide, is always moving in ebbs and flows.

The Competition Environment

Five environmental conditions provide the framework of competition (see Fig. 5.2). Those include existing competitors in the marketplace, new competitors that join the fray, substitute products, buyer power in making the decision whether to purchase a product, and supplier power in providing goods and services upon which an organization depends (Porter, 1985).

Five environmental conditions affecting all media organizations include:

1. Existing competitors in the marketplace.
2. New competitors entering the marketplace.
3. Substitute products.
4. Buyer power affecting media product purchasing.
5. Supplier power affecting raw materials necessary for media organization product creation.

Figure 5.2 Environment of Competition

Rivalry Among Existing Competitors

When competitors become established in a market, they tend to divide it up into portions that may remain relatively stable. Although each may seek to dominate a market, there are often, in media companies, distinct nuances that differentiate each newspaper, television station, radio station, advertising agency, and public relations agency. It is not uncommon for competitors to go through a natural process of individualizing products and approaches that distinguish themselves from one another. Each has a personality that attracts some customers and alienates others.

In Denver, Colorado, a fiercely competitive environment exists between two daily newspapers founded in the 19th century. It is one of the few remaining markets with competing dailies. In the case of *The Denver Post* and the *Rocky Mountain News,* the rivalry has produced two very different publications covering essentially the same body of news and information.

The Denver Post continues to publish what is called a "broadsheet." That is the large-format newspaper most common in America. It has separate sections, each folded twice, once with the left and right halves brought together, and then again with the bottom and top halves folded. When you read a broadsheet, you need room. You first open up the section vertically, and then spread the pages out before you, covering most of a normal-sized desk or kitchen table. A broadsheet has a lot of space for information, but the negative of the fold is the space it takes up. It's challenging to read on a bus, or at breakfast.

The *Rocky Mountain News* publishes what is called a "tabloid" format. Don't get confused about that term at this point. Although we recognize tabloid, in colloquial language, as a disparaging term commonly applied to supermarket gossip and entertainment publications, it is technically a type of fold. The paper is usually about one-third smaller than a broadsheet and only folded in half from left to right. The sections are usually distinguished only by section headlines within the main paper, not as separately folded portions. The advantage of the tabloid fold is that it's easy to read just about anywhere—on a bus, at the breakfast table, sitting in a crowded doctor's office. You don't have to spread it out to see everything. The disadvantage is that each page of a tabloid holds a lot less news and information than a typical broadsheet. That problem is solved by making a fatter paper with more pages.

In the early 1980s the *Rocky Mountain News* took over as the number one daily newspaper in Colorado's capital. The paper continued to grow significantly, until the Denver market circulation split was in the 60/40 range with the *Rocky Mountain News* dominating. *The Denver Post* struggled for several years just barely above the point of no return in what is known as the circulation spiral (Lacy, Sohn, & Wicks, 1993). This is a downward spiral of a newspaper toward business failure because of combined advertising and circulation decline. In two-newspaper markets the largest paper tends to be more successful attracting advertisers because of its greater number of subscribers and lower cost-per-thousand reader impressions for advertising space. Even though an advertisement may cost more in total dollars to place in the larger paper, a lot more people see it, so the advertisement is actually cheaper in terms of the number of potential customers it will reach. Additionally, major advertisers only have to buy a few major media players among newspapers, radio, and television in a market to cover virtually everyone in that market. So the biggest media organizations get a disproportionate amount of the advertising dollars spent in the market (Bagdikian, 1992).

When a large newspaper has 60 percent of the market in circulation, it is likely to have up to three-quarters of the newspaper advertising dollars spent in that market. So the weaker paper loses both in papers sold and in advertising sold. The combination of economic factors makes it extremely difficult for competing papers to survive once they drop below 40 percent of a market's total circulation. Declining advertising revenues for the weaker paper combine with its problem of lower circulation, and the two compound one another as it spirals downward (Lacy et al., 1993).

We are not always aware of how fast our markets change. Considering the number of people who enter or leave a given market area within five years it is quite possible to have a 30 to 40 percent shift in audience. That is a large number of people coming in from other places who may have different ideas of what they like. And they are media customers who have not developed brand loyalty to any local media organizations. In highly competitive environments, strategically positioning a media product for new arrivals in a market may produce significant growth in market share over a five-year period. Existing reader, viewer, and listener habits are hard to break. But new arrivals have not developed those habits and tend to sample local media products more readily.

Sidebar 5.1 Front Page Ducks

Shortly after the *Rocky Mountain News* claimed first place in the Denver market, the circulation manager, asked to describe the single biggest factor in the paper's success, answered simply, "the fold!" In a faster-paced society, with substantial suburban commuting, the tabloid is easier to manipulate on buses, at lunch counters, and anywhere else. But other broadsheets have continued to be successful, so something else had to be affecting newspaper sales. Asked what was the second most important factor in his paper becoming the largest Denver daily he said, "Ducks!" and held up a copy of the paper with a picture of ducks swimming in a local park late on the front page. Ducks? What would they have to do with pumping up circulation in an intense newspaper war with huge staffs and substantial resources on both sides?

Then came a short course in the marketing of newspapers. The *Rocky Mountain News* had recently changed its approach to the front page, intentionally printing a large, positive, color photograph covering most of the page whenever possible. The newspaper's research, the circulation manager said, had found that the typical "hard news" coverage, with photos of car wrecks, shooting scenes, and other negative visuals, made people uncomfortable. So, unless a major negative story was in the news that necessitated front page photo coverage, the newspaper tried to keep the image softer and more positive in tone. That appeared to help increase vending machine sales too, because impulse buyers were more prone to pick up a paper with positive images than negative ones. This marketing approach does not mean the *Rocky Mountain News* shies away from hard news coverage. It simply means that when deciding what to use for the front page photograph, something positive is preferred unless the enormity of another event requires photo coverage on the front page. And even then, it is possible to remain positive. In a flood, for example, rather than destroyed houses, a photo of people picking up the pieces of their lives and starting over might be used with a headline such as "We'll build again!"

Entry of New Competitors

When another newspaper, television station, advertising agency, or public relations firm arrives, the pool of existing players in the market is increased. It usually is an uphill battle for the new entrant because brand loyalties have been built up by the veterans. Except in extraordinary circumstances, most new entrants into a market have either to offer radically different products to differentiate themselves or wait for existing competitors to make a mistake that will send some of their customers shopping for a new alternative.

During the wait for the strong to grow weak, a new entrant can focus on share-point-by-share-point growth to build internal confidence as small, incremental successes build up. And it is far less daunting than attempting to become the dominant player overnight. While senior management may have lofty expectations of dominating the market long term, it is very frustrating for media workers to see little progress day to day. So, particularly on the departmental level, it is wise to adopt what is called the "small-wins" strategy concentrating on small, positive steps toward the desired end (Whetten & Cameron, 1995). That means setting goals that are achievable for the near term. Even though accomplishments may seem minor, they are still accomplishments and can have a positive effect on motivation. The trick in "small-wins" strategy is focusing everyone on the next small step of the climb and, in effect, putting the whole mountain looming ahead out of your mind.

Innovation is the friend of those with nothing to lose, climbing up from the bottom. They tend to be more open to innovative ideas, encourage individual creativity, and frequently take pride in a kind of "spoiler" role. When the small agency in town suddenly grabs a significant client from the premier agency, it's like a small-town basketball team winning the state championship. On the other hand, it is not uncommon for large, dominant media companies to develop a kind of arrogance and reliance on past practices that sets up their eventual decline because they resist innovation.

Threat of New Technologies

New technology can have a major impact on a marketplace. In media a prime example is the evolution of radio. Prior to radio Americans were entertained by going to the theater. At first it was for weekly vaudeville shows, variety programs that might feature jugglers, singers, comedians, magicians, and other individual acts. When motion pictures came along, they only partially displaced vaudeville, since you still had to go to a theater to see a movie, and vaudeville still had the edge in spontaneity. But then came radio. It was the first mass medium that allowed the audience to determine the content with which an individual would engage. That was particularly true when large numbers of stations with various programming became widely available. As the late comic George Burns, who transcended vaudeville, motion pictures, radio, and television put it,

> It's impossible to explain the impact that radio had on the world to anyone who didn't live through that time. Before radio, the only way to see a performer was to see a performer. And maybe most important, before radio there was no such thing as a commercial.
>
> Radio made everybody who owned one a theater manager. They could listen to whatever they wanted to. For a lot of performers, the beginning of radio meant the end of their careers. (Burns, 1988, p. 84)

When new technology disrupts a marketplace, it is common for existing competitors to retrench and drive even harder at the old technology and the formulas for success that worked in the previous environment. But their efforts are almost always doomed to failure because the new technological innovation has forever altered the playing field. They often recognize a new competitor exists but downplay its importance. They resist accepting that the environment itself has shifted significantly.

In the 20th century, vaudeville disappeared, silent movie stars quickly faded when sound came along, and radio rose to become the dominant home entertainment medium with situation comedies and other dramas. When television began to dominate the home entertainment scene, radio became primarily a music machine, with most stations featuring sharply defined formats of rock, country, rap, and other program niches in the music world. Then talk radio evolved for those interested in hearing, and participating in, discussions of various types. What had been a mass medium became a niche medium. When radio grew to be a major mass medium, it was predicted that newspapers were dead. But they survived and evolved into altered forms. The same has been true for radio, motion pictures, and broadcast television. Each was the primary mass medium of its heyday until a new technology evolved. Then the older technology settled into a more-specialized role while continuing to survive as a significant media form (Emery & Emery, 1996).

As we head into the 21st century, the Internet has exploded since the first Mosaic browser was introduced by student researchers at the National Center for Supercomputing Applications in Illinois in 1993 (Borzillo, 1995). Exponential growth of Internet use followed, altering what had been the arcane domain of researchers and military users for the previous two decades. From 1994 to 1996 the number of individual and business web pages grew from 1,700 to 60,000, with an estimated 14 million users tapping into the system of interconnected computers ("What's the Internet?," 1996). By 1996 a new person somewhere in the world was signing onto the Internet for the first time "every 30 seconds" as the exponential growth in computer use continued to expand unabated (Simons, 1996, p. 59). The pressure on the Internet system became so intense that data flow was restricted as several major computer outages affected some of the nation's largest services, including America Online ("Company News," 1997).

As millions of people began to spend time browsing the various Internet offerings in an activity commonly known as "surfing the net," the old media forms began moving into the technology. Radio and television stations launched web sites as quickly as they could, with more than 1,500 of them by 1996 (Redmond, 1997). Online newspaper editions became commonplace, with hundreds of Internet newspapers worldwide, just two years after the first Mosaic browser provided the graphical interface necessary for average people to get much out of Internet communications ("Newspapers Roll with the Punches," 1996). Clearly, lessons had been learned during the earlier audience fragmentation experiences. Existing media increasingly saw their world as dynamic and moved to more quickly adapt than ever before. Part of that was fueled by the extraordinary statistics of the new competitor.

During 1995 the number of online service users grew by a robust 25 percent. But in just the first half of 1996, the use literally exploded with an estimated 115 percent increase over the previous year ("On-line Services," 1996). With online newspaper editions, radio web sites featuring streaming audio services for home computer users half the world away, and television sites, such as CNN's, with news video available to home computer screens, existing mass media had clearly learned about adaptation and were aggressively pursuing it in an increasingly dynamic media marketplace.

Consumer Resistance to Change

Human beings are creatures of habit. Changing those habits usually takes some kind of external impetus or, in the case of media companies, some change in the product that causes audience members to go sample a competitor's product. That can come in the form of disrupted programming schedules, favorite personalities being replaced, or any other disruption in what the client/customer/reader/viewer expects. That's why media managers are very careful about changing main anchor talent in television stations, maintaining continuity of columnists used every week on the newspaper editorial page, and carefully researching short lists of familiar songs—called "play lists" and usually including only about two dozen titles in a station's respective format—to be played regularly on radio outlets.

It is important to note that changes the audience perceives need to be implemented carefully. In any product, whether a soft drink, newspaper, newscast, or radio station play list, the quantitative data from surveys do not always reveal the passion with which people cling to that about which they care. So change has to be undertaken very carefully, with sensitivity toward those without whom no media organization can

Sidebar 5.2 The Coca-Cola® Controversy

A classic example of how careful you have to be about changing products in a market place is what happened to Coca Cola® in the early 1980s.

The company decided to replace its old formula with a new one. Expensive advertising and public relations campaigns were developed to persuade consumers to shift to the "new" coke. The problem was, there was a backlash against changing a tradition. The original Coca Cola® recipe had been used for 99 years, an icon of sorts for generations of American youth. Coke lovers quickly mounted a popular campaign against the new formula. They claimed it tasted more like Pepsi and if they wanted to drink Pepsi, they would. Coca Cola® executives had indicated the original Coke formula

would be retired as packaging plants converted to the new formula. But with runs on the remaining old Coke supplies, and a barrage of criticism in radio talk shows, newspaper columns, television news stories, and seemingly everywhere else, they recanted (Coit, 1986).

In July, 1985, just three months after they announced the new soft drink formula, Coca Cola® announced it would keep the original recipe available under the label "Coca Cola® Classic." Newspaper columnist John Coit observed that the company executives "really believed the market research, which is useless when you're talking about a product that has become a personal habit and holds great attachment in the popular culture" (Coit, 1986, p. 85).

---

exist, its audience. The media business is really about connecting with people and creating media products relevant to their wants and needs (Stepp, 1996).

Bargaining Power of Suppliers

This area is, perhaps, the least complex of the elements of the framework of competition. In media organizations generally the supplies for creating the media product come from a relatively few firms doing business with everyone. So, except for economies of scale benefiting the large-volume purchaser, the basic costs of raw materials are much the same for each player in a market. For example, in the radio business there are two clearance houses for commercial music rights, ASCAP and BMI. Stations pay those two organizations fees based on market size. The same is true for the Associated Press wire service.

The newspaper business has only a few suppliers of newsprint, the raw paper stock on which newspapers are printed. The yearly average price per ton for newsprint went from $466 to $658 in 1995, a one-year jump in cost of 41.2 percent (Veronis, Suhler & Associates, 1996). Such a dramatic increase in basic materials cost can seriously affect the financial bottom line.

A simple truth exists in any business endeavor. There are really only two basic ways to increase profits: (1) increase sales and (2) reduce costs. When faced with a substantial increase in the cost of supplies, passing that along to customers in the form of a dramatic price increase is almost certain to affect sales negatively. But as a media manager you can be creative within those two areas to serve your dual responsibilities to your owners and your customers. It is one of the great challenges of balancing on the high wire of media management.

Sidebar 5.3 Raising Prices Is No Easy Solution

A newspaper cannot increase advertising or subscription rates by such a substantial amount without a serious loss in the number of advertisers and readers. However, if you were a media manager facing this situation, you could adjust your product mix to offset part of the increased raw materials cost. For example, a newspaper may expand its revenue-producing advertising space to increase revenues by cutting the column inches reserved for news coverage. It can also reduce the total number of pages in the paper, thus cutting the amount of newsprint necessary for each edition. A few pages in each edition, hardly noticeable in a large daily, could add up to several tons of newsprint saved each year. Of course, any changes would have to be carefully considered in terms of how they would affect customer perception of the product. Decreasing the space reserved for news could reduce the essential reason many readers subscribe to a paper. Or reducing the space for grocery advertisements could produce the same result. Managing the product mix of a medium is a delicate balancing task and should not be done in a cavalier manner.

Enhancing Competitive Position

Within the context of the five fundamental operating environment forces discussed previously an organization has three strategic approaches to take in enhancing its competitive position: (1) cost leadership, (2) differentiating from competitors, or (3) developing a niche within a product area (Porter, 1985) (see Fig. 5.3).

Three strategic approaches to improve competitiveness:

1. Cost leadership—pricing below the competition.
2. Differentiation from other competitors—making yourself different in order to stand out from others.
3. Niche within a product area—deliberately narrowing your target market by increasing specificity of product appeal to a more sharply defined market segment.

Figure 5.3 Strategies for Marketplace Competition

Cost Leadership

Cost leadership means minimizing costs at all levels of the organization and pricing below the competition. Everyone wants to buy things for the best price, so you sell at that price counting on higher volume to make up for the reduced profit margin. It is the concept adopted by many national chains where economies of scale help reduce individual item costs. Large chains can often buy products much cheaper than small, individual businesses. Because of quantity discounts, it is possible for very large concerns to sell items at retail for less than small businesses must pay wholesalers for the same items.

In media organizations, undercutting the competition can be achieved in lower client and customer fees (trimming commissions, dropping advertising rates, etc.), rates charged to consumers (e.g., cutting the price of the Sunday newspaper), or any other way that will give you a pricing edge. Often the price reduction can be made up through increased sales, which then produce higher advertising revenues. At this point, keep in mind that price need not be monetary in nature. It can also be the convenience, or lack thereof, of engaging with a media product, or any other value context for the buyer.

Differentiating from Competitors

The second approach to enhance competitive position is to adopt a strategy of "differentiation." Here the organization intentionally sets out to be unlike other competitors, to create something that is unique. When successful, this separates one organization's products from all others because of the "difference." When talk radio began growing into a major format, it was a strategy of differentiation. Most radio stations played music most of the time with, perhaps, some news in the morning and evening. Cutting out all music means saving thousands of dollars annually in rights that no longer have to be paid to ASCAP and BMI. All you need for a talk radio station is a not very complicated setup for answering phones, and a host to whom listeners want to talk. Because no music rights fees have to be paid, the basic operating cost requires a much smaller audience to make a profit. An entire industry grew out of this concept and became a significant force in AM radio. When FM began stereo broadcasting in the 1960s, it quickly supplanted AM as the primary radio band because of the better sound quality. AM stations were left with a poorer audio quality, despite the fact their signals go farther. But in talk, signal quality isn't as critical, and you don't need stereo. Talk radio, as a strategy of differentiation in many markets, gave AM radio stations a viable product, particularly among older listener demographics accustomed to using the AM dial (Head, Sterling, & Schofield, 1994).

Developing a Niche

The third option is for the organization to limit itself intentionally to a narrow market or product area. In this case, you purposefully shrink your concept of what you will do to focus on a particular aspect of an overall business or industry. The magazine industry has evolved, in the last half-century, from generalized products in the news and entertainment category, to an almost completely niche environment (Stengel, 1997). In any supermarket magazine rack you can see niching at work. Virtually every publication is positioned to attract very tightly defined customers, whether they are bodybuilders, automobile hobbyists, home gardeners, computer enthusiasts, or any one of a plethora of other special-interest segments. Magazines have survived in the multimedia world because of niching (Bull, 1997). The fundamental concept in niching is to serve a very "narrow target market more effectively and efficiently than competitors who are competing more broadly" (Porter, 1985, p. 38).

One of the most important things in niching is to maintain a continuity of the perception your audience and/or customers hold of you (Brooks, 1992). The very concept of niching is to define your media organization personality more tightly. Image is crucial in the marketing of any media product, but particularly so in the case of niche products (Weinstein, 1994). If you have a magazine targeted for pickup truck users, an article on the latest sports cars is clearly out of place. Expectancy is a key part of audience engagement. We tune into certain programs, or read certain publications, because we expect them to deliver what has been promoted and/or what we have become accustomed to receiving from them. The same is true for corporate public relations. As part of the overall strategic marketing plan, public relations must reinforce the image the company is attempting to convey, not throw up confusing signals.

Danger of Indecisiveness

When an organization does not, or cannot, make critical adjustments in the way it approaches the market, by becoming the overall cost leader, differentiating from its competitors, or adopting an effective niche focus, it becomes particularly vulnerable. "A firm that engages in each generic strategy but fails to achieve any of them is 'stuck in the middle.' It possesses no competitive advantage" (Porter, 1985, p. 16). It then drifts, either unwillingly or unable to move in any one of the three general directions necessary to adapt to the new environment. The winds of change, if they happen to be blowing positively, may carry it along for a while. But without decisive management an organization is merely flotsam floating on the current, rather than a swift and well-trimmed craft sailing through contrary waves. It is not uncommon for such organizations to maneuver as they formerly did, using the tactics of the past. But when the environmental conditions have changed, that can prove to be disastrous. Basically, the dynamically changing environment leaves behind a statically bound-up firm continuing to base decisions on conditions that no longer exist and/or practices that are not relevant in the contemporary suitation.

It is, therefore, vital that you have extensive and reliable market research and continuously study the nuances of the competitive arena within which you operate. Media organization marketing is discussed further in Chapter 8. Additionally, it is important that you perceive everything that consumes audience time as a competitor. Many media organizations perceive as competitors only those doing the same thing. In other words, newspapers may consider other newspapers competitors, but not radio and television stations. Radio stations typically consider other radio stations as competitors, but not the newspaper. But in the contemporary media marketplace, with a plethora of organizations all trying to get slices of the same advertising pie, the reality is that everyone is a competitor for advertising share with everyone else. That also reinforces the need to be in a well-defined niche you can strongly defend from other competitors.

Profit Centers and Maximizing Resources

A common approach to business is to set up each division or department as a cost center, also called a profit center, to track expenses and revenues down at the smallest manageable unit level. On the surface it makes sense to have the parts department and the retailing department budget their respective expenses against their revenue with each assigned a profit margin goal. Theoretically, weaker units of a company become clearly evident with such cost centering as each division is run as though it is not interdependent with the others (Mager, 1989; Mellman, 1995; Merchant, 1989).

Although it may be handy to divide up an organization into units for various internal purposes, the reality is the whole organization succeeds or fails together. Like the human body, the arms are not independent of the trunk, nor is the head separable from the heart. Each part has different but interrelated functions that occur in concert with the others. Ultimately, media organizations sell a product to an audience, whether that is a public relations program, an advertising campaign, a newspaper, or an electronic media program. The audience engages with the medium as a single entity. "I read *The*

New York Times," someone may say, meaning a single paper that is put together by thousands of workers and many different units of a large conglomerate. And the perishable nature of media products complicates the situation. Media companies do not, in most cases, build up inventory in warehouses. The media business is an immediate kind of endeavor, whether it is trying to take advantage of the latest trend in music, film, television programming, or advertising design and placement. It is predominantly a here-and-now activity.

Profit center philosophy encourages organizational units to think and function independently, but that can cause serious problems in the complexity of media operations. One is a kind of unit-level myopia that is so focused on the internal, departmental-level concerns that the wider organizational needs are not appropriately addressed. Maximizing resources requires coordination spanning managerial units. For example, the promotion department at a newspaper is supposed to do things to drive up circulation, while the printing department is supposed to use paper and ink efficiently, buying supplies as cheaply as possible. If the promotion department puts together a major public relations and advertising blitz that surges circulation, but the printing department isn't included in the planning, the whole project could fail. The printing department has to know how much paper and ink will be needed every day the newspaper is printed. Significantly changing the number of pages in the paper requires more paper and ink. A complicating factor is the way newspapers control their raw materials costs. Many use what is called "just-in-time" inventory management. That means having the truck with newsprint back up to the loading dock the day you would run out of paper. That way, you don't have to pay any long-term warehousing costs for paper and ink supplies. A new truckload is always scheduled to arrive just in time.

Thus, you can see that any major promotion to increase the consumption of paper and ink has to be coordinated throughout the entire paper. Advertising has to be sold, pages have to be laid out with additional news copy or promotional materials, paper and ink have to be ordered well ahead of time, and finance may have to arrange for the money to execute the whole effort, since revenues may not come in until after the product is in the marketplace or at least in production.

Sometimes media organizations add products by using existing resources. Many television stations produce more than one newscast each day with, essentially, the same staff. There is, of course, a law of diminishing returns when the workload is expanded. But it is often possible to add considerable product in media organizations with a limited number of additional people. Anchors, for example, can read more than one newscast, but it is so draining to produce newscasts that an additional producer may need to be hired. From a business standpoint, as long as the additional newscast generates more revenue than the new producer costs to hire, it would be a success.

On the other hand, you can often repackage product into different forms that extend the value of existing material into another venue. One example would be the growing cable television news market. Some major market cable news organizations have been successful with local news channels offering their own news, or recycled newscasts from local broadcasters (Walker, 1996). Some stations have been very effective in using existing broadcast newsrooms simply to repackage their coverage for additional cable newscasts, or to work out cooperative arrangements as product suppliers for cable channels (Thistle, 1994). CNN, for example, provides local broadcasters the option of inserting a segment of their news into the half-hour cycles of Headline News aired on local cable systems (Walter, 1997). Some broadcast organizations have changed their election coverage to integrate viewing options with cable services or public broadcasting outlets. Instead of doing an entire evening of election watch coverage on the main television station, preempting regular programming, short updates are provided on the hour and half-hour (Brown, 1991; "Technology Could Alter," 1993). Viewers who prefer their regular entertainment programming are not alienated while broadcasters only interrupt normal programming for brief updates on major election trends. Concurrently, on a PBS station or cable channel, the station provides traditional, continuous election returns all evening long to serve those interested in political coverage in depth. By combining efforts, local broadcasters and cable outlets can thus serve diverse audience interests (Feder, 1996; Jicha, 1996; Saunders, 1996).

It is also common for media companies to sell access to their facilities used only part of the time for their own production needs. Television and radio stations frequently sell studio time to clients for the creation of advertisements. Many publishers generate revenue by selling the use of their printing facilities to commercial printing clients during the long periods when their primary product, a newspaper, is not being run on the presses (Rosenberg, 1995).

Everything a media organization does needs to complement its primary role. It is very easy, in profit/cost center approaches, to be taken in by the illusion that a media company is a wide-ranging entity of separate elements. But all media companies have a core personality that is recognized by the primary product audience. It is that personality that defines it, regardless of the internal divisions, units, departments, or products. Thus, maximizing resources has be done in such a way that nothing interferes with that public image and function.

One of the most important assets that a public relations firm, advertising agency, newspaper, or electronic media company has is the intangible value of its reputation among its customers or audience, its "goodwill" (Lacy, Sohn, & Wicks, 1993). The

Sidebar 5.4 The Profit Center of Image

Companies have two kinds of assets. The most obvious are the tangible assets, physically defined things such as the manufacturing plant, equipment, hardware—the kinds of things for which value can be fixed with relative ease. Then there are the intangible assets that have no physical existence but are still of significant value.

Foremost among the intangible assets is the "goodwill" a media company can generate for itself in its market. The attitude of others toward a media company is critical to its success, for that goodwill directly affects the demand for the media firm's products. People generally don't purchase newspapers from a publishing company they detest or watch newscasts presented by people they dislike from stations toward which they feel hostile. Indeed, considerable media organization market research and self-promotion is focused on increasing audience/customer goodwill toward the media organization.

So, goodwill is a profit center, in some ways more important than all others. In the media business, the reputation of the media organization, and concurrent public attitude toward it, are fundamental aspects of its financial worth (Lacy, et al., 1993). Indeed, in financial accounting intangible assets including goodwill, exclusive market franchises, patents, and other factors enhancing a company's value beyond that of its physical possessions can even be amortized, or depreciated, over a period not to exceed 40 years (Merrill Lynch, 1997).

perception of a media company within its market is the foundation of its value. It is what separates one media organization from another and creates the bond with audiences. Fundamentally, printing plants are all the same, television towers are all the same, videotape machines are all the same. But the context of how your audience perceives you and the intangible side of you as a personality in the marketplace is the single most important profit center. Therefore, any change in product positioning or mix needs to be carefully considered and analyzed since it can have long-term consequences.

PERSPECTIVES OF EFFECTIVENESS

When you talk about how effective a media organization is, you are venturing into turbulent waters. It seems simple, just one word, *effectiveness*. But it is a very complicated concept. There are many ways of defining effectiveness and many different perspectives of the organization that have to be considered.

Most media organizations are evaluated continuously and simultaneously by their management, employees within the organization, those using the organization's media products, and any regulatory agencies that have oversight rights/responsibilities over a particular media sector (see Fig. 5.4). Clearly, the perspective of each of those categories of evaluators will be very different.

- Management
- Employees
- Consumers
- Regulatory agencies

Those in each group view the organization from a vested interest point of view. Thus, whereas management may focus on return on investment, employees may be more concerned about working conditions. The standards used for evaluation, and the results, may vary considerably.

Figure 5.4 Perspectives of Effectiveness

Management Perspectives

Management, because it works for the owners and shareholders of the media organization, usually looks at things in business investment terms. Business economic indicators such as return on equity, current assets, inventories, and long-term debt are used in financial analysis and also by investors to gauge the health of a firm. Those indicators, among others, are also used by stock analysts and are reflected in the fluctuations of the company's stock price (Merrill Lynch, 1997). That means the price of a share of company stock on the stock exchange is a critical issue for the company. Shareholders are part owners who buy stock in anticipation of a positive return on their investment.

In large companies with stock trading on one of the major exchanges, owners and senior managers typically have substantial stock holdings. When the company does well, the stock goes up. And when the stock goes up they are paid twice, once with their normal compensation, and second through increased personal wealth as their corporate shares gain in value. Thus, senior managers are very interested in how the company performs in the stock market, because it is their measure of organizational effectiveness.

Managers are usually provided performance goals and, sometimes, substantial financial incentives for meeting them. So profit margins are at the forefront of their concern. When management looks at the media organization, it is seeking a rate of return. In a different age, before large conglomerate and chain ownership came to dominate the media industries, the individual owner/entrepreneur often lived in the same town as the media outlet he or she owned. It was a reflection of that person and as such often had a wider concept of success steeped in serious community involvement and service.

Ben Franklin lived in Philadelphia, owned a print shop, and worked there. When a newspaper publisher or the owner of a radio station has coffee at a restaurant with longtime associates, and they chat about how good or bad the paper or station was the day before in terms of its contribution to the community, there is a pride of involvement factor. A positive view of the owner's media organization, by that owner's friends and neighbors within the community, is a kind of effectiveness feedback. But when local owners are displaced, companies may become, to the corporate psyche, abstract sets of numbers on profit and loss statements. As remote entities they are not an everyday part of the corporate managers' lives. Thus, little sense of a media organization as a reflection of community values and personality may exist (Bagdikian, 1992). Although some powerful media organizations do have strong ethics of publishing newspapers and conducting professional journalism oriented to their respective markets, the fundamental measure of success with displaced ownership is usually the profit margin, not the media organization as a community citizen. Either perspective can be positive or negative, depending on the personalities involved. As a media manager you must be very aware of the measure of success senior management is using to determine the worth of your efforts.

Employee Cultures

Employees look at the world from their personal perspective and they develop strong cultures over time. In media organizations those cultures provide unwritten codes of conduct and standards of performance that are passed on to new members by the old. If you get a job at *The New York Times,* you enter a fully developed culture that for a century has considered itself the newspaper in America. Working for Scripps-Howard, Gannett, NBC, or CNN means becoming part of an ongoing mythology of personality each organization develops within itself that defines it and into which new members are enculturated. Like a rite of passage, a person is taught the various mysteries of the craft of organizational behavior from more senior employees and becomes part of the culture. And that culture may have very different perceptions of the point of the effort than its senior managers (Hirschhorn, 1991).

An example of this is provided in Chapter 9, Sidebar 9.1, p. 222. Two local employees are talking about a speech just given by the company's chairman. The executive has focused on company stock performance without addressing serious maintanance problems frustrating a broadcast technician. The chairman and the technician were looking at the prism of corporate effectiveness from two different angles and seeing very different spectrums of color. While the chairman saw profit, the technician saw tightfisted management that was making it more difficult for him to do his job. He didn't have a particularly positive view of organizational effectiveness, contrary to the chairman's view. Indeed the production workers at the media organization unit had little to do with corporate hierarchy, only seeing the chairman of the board every few years. He was usually in corporate headquarters in another city; a different geographical and philosophical place from them.

How the employee culture perceives the organization is instrumental to its success. Much of media organization production work is qualitative in nature; that is, not ruled by counting numbers in various ways but with "human interpretation at the core" in which meaning flows from the "thoughts and sentiments of the observed" (Stempel & Westley, 1989, p. 360). Developing advertising concepts, layouts and commercials, devising public relations strategies to enhance corporate images, and writing news stories is creative work that is subjective in nature. To many media workers it is insulting to render their creative effort into what they consider to be mere stock price quotes. What ignites fire and passion in a senior executive of a multinational company may well extinguish it in an idealistic media worker who believes what he or she does is of "greater importance" for the benefit of American society.

In media industries, workers create product that is qualitatively judged throughout the production cycle in every area of the organization except management, where the quantitative evaluation takes over. That creates a built-in culture clash between the business side of media organizations and their creative side. While senior media managers may see themselves as being in business to make a profit, many of their employees want to make a difference. They tend to be more highly educated, independent minded, and perceive their job as serving the society as a whole. They seek creative autonomy in the workplace so they can do their jobs as they see fit (Gaziano & Coulson, 1988). There is, then, an inherent clash of values within many media organizations between the selling side of the business and the "serving the public" sense of those who do the production work.

Media Organization Consumer Views

The perspective of the consumer is the key to any business, because without a consumer of the product there is no business. We don't always think of those who engage with media organization products as consumers, or customers, but that's what they are. In advertising and public relations agencies, the term is usually "client," while in newspaper it's "reader," "subscriber" or "advertiser." Radio customers are "listeners," and television consumers are "viewers." But regardless of the semantics, those are the people who use that which a media organization produces and in the process pay for its existence directly or indirectly. For the advertising agency, a satisfied client means repeat business and that client spreading the word about the superior product the agency provides. The same is true for public relations work. Satisfied clients tend to recommend an agency or firm to their friends. Being good at what you do, and then using that ability to satisfy a client with products that work, is the key to success.

In news-oriented media organizations there is a sense of higher purpose, mentioned earlier, of serving the society by providing important information for critical decision making. That may be political information to help the electorate decide who will govern and otherwise fulfilling the surveillance needs of Americans wanting to understand their world better. Journalists often see their work as providing essential information of daily life and therefore as more "important" than other jobs. Indeed, media products fulfill a wide range of people's wants and needs. The grocery advertisements of any newspaper may be more important to some than whatever is said on the editorial page. The comics add a little humor to the day, and sports provides the latest on our favorite athletic diversion. In radio the morning traffic report is significant for millions of Americans weaving their way through rush hour. On television the weather is one of the most important elements for viewer selection of a particular newscast (Lin, 1992).

Because we tend to see the world from our place in the scheme of things, successful media managers must consciously put themselves into the customer's position. If you are an advertising agency executive and you are trying to provide a service to a furniture store, you need to ask yourself, "What would I expect of me if I owned that store?" The same is true for those engaged in news/editorial work. If you are an editor on a major newspaper, to be really successful, you need to look at the paper from the perspective of the average reader. What would you, as an ordinary subscriber, expect to get from your paper every day?

Many media professionals, be they creative agency people or those who work in a newsroom, develop a kind of cultural myopia, or tunnel vision. They look at the world through a very narrow window. People in the news industries watch their competitors, all the wire services, CNN, and many other sources every day. If you are an editor you read, on a daily basis, your own publication and numerous others such as *The New York Times, The Wall Street Journal,* and *USA Today.* You also may read weekly news magazines such as *Time, Newsweek,* and *The Economist.* Journalists are immersed in news coverage to an extreme degree far beyond those they serve. And that can warp their perspective relative to their customers. Other people don't spend all their time keeping up with current events. They check with a couple of sources each day (usually scanning the daily paper in the morning, and watching a TV newscast at night) and spend the rest of the time working at their jobs and managing their family. News, to most people, is a brief encounter, though to you as a media professional it may be a daylong continuum. As you decide what should go in your publication you have to remember that what is getting old for you, because you've read about it or seen it all day, may still be fresh and new for a person who has been cooped up in an office all day without an hourly Associated Press news summary available. Additionally, news professionals often socialize with other news workers. In some respects, then, journalists are a culture apart from mainstream America deciding what that mainstream wants and needs to know. To be accurate in representing that mainstream you have to go wading in the waters from time to time. It can take considerable effort to do that when you work odd shifts and have a demanding schedule that makes being involved in community organizations difficult.

Regulatory View

The perspective of regulators, if you are in a regulated sector of media organization work, is important to stay in business. Depending on what your media organization does, you may need to be familiar with FCC or FTC rulings, as well as general media legal issues discussed later in this text. Broadcasters, for example, have to comply with very specific requirements to retain their licenses from the FCC. In advertising agency work, you have to be aware of the laws and regulations regarding product representation. In media organizations, knowledge of news gathering and reporter shield laws, and other legal matters including copyright, appropriation, libel, slander, trespass, and freedom of information requests, is very important. Also of concern are general business functions such as administration of personnel and financial reporting.

Generally in the United States, the legal/regulatory system applicable to the mass media is relatively clear. But you must be informed about the issues in your particular discipline. Legal trouble can cripple a media organization, though sometimes in controversial matters it is unavoidable. See Chapters 13, 14, 15, and 16 for more on legal issues affecting media organizations. Many media firms have law firms retained to provide legal advice as events require. You should become familiar with any legal resources at your disposal, and, as a media manager, you should consult lawyers at the first sign of a potential legal problem.

GOAL-BASED MANAGEMENT

One of the oldest techniques used by organizations in the pursuit of effectiveness is the concept of goal-based management. It has become endemic to American business culture. Almost everywhere you go there are goals to be negotiated, set, and met in a process known as "management by objectives." It is as though no one would know how to work without having goals set for them they must attain (Gibson, et al., 1997). We all tend to work against some goal-based measure, whether it is in our goal to graduate by a certain time or in our job performance evaluation process.

It is not uncommon to set goals at the beginning of a period of evaluation, perhaps a year. Then at the end of the period of evaluation, management determines if the goals are met. Formal planning documents may be prepared in which a person describes what he or she expects to accomplish the next year. Then, when the year is over, the evaluation report must indicate that what was planned was accomplished. If yes, you win; if no, you lose. Using a goal-based approach to management has advantages and disadvantages, both of which a manager must be aware.

Advantages

Goal setting has three major advantages, when done properly. First, it provides clear priorities and targets for both the manager and the subordinate against which progress may be easily checked. Second, goals provide a relatively simple measure of success with little room for debate. Third, using specific goals removes ambiguity in the performance evaluation process. Thus, both the manager and employee have a clear idea of what needs to be accomplished. Goal-based management also, theoretically, removes political considerations and personality differences from the evaluation process so the work a person does is the measure of success, not the social nuances of the workplace. But, as will be discussed later, the reverse may occur.

There are large and small goals affecting many aspects of our lives. They range from personal goals such as getting enough sleep at night and losing some weight to loftier objectives such as obtaining a master's degree to enhance our competitiveness in the job market, or becoming the chief executive officer of a corporation. We set many kinds of goals in many ways on many levels.

Goals can positively influence achievement if they include three key elements: (1) specificity, (2) consistency, and (3) suitable challenge (Locke & Latham, 1990; Whetten & Cameron, 1995) (see Fig. 5.5).

When done properly, goal setting incorporates all of the following:

1. Specific, concise, and clear measures of success.
2. Consistent productivity benchmarks.
3. Suitable challenge appropriate to the person and the task.

Figure 5.5 Advantages of Goal Setting

Specificity

Goals have to be clear, concise, and without any confusion. They cannot, to be effective, be overarching and so general they cannot be easily and quickly measured. For example, if you decide to "lose some weight" you have an ineffective goal. That's not specific enough to be a clear measure of success or failure. But the vow to "lose four pounds by March 15th" is specific and easy to stay focused upon. In an office environment, setting a goal for the receptionist of "doing a better job answering the phones" is too ambiguous and encompasses everything from the sound of the voice to whether the phone rings twice or a dozen times before it is picked up. What is a "better job of answering the phones"? In goal management you need to define exactly what you mean in specific detail. An appropriate goal for the receptionist might be "to answer the phone by the end of the second ring on every call" or "be positive and cheerful" when answering.

Consistency

Unless you are very careful, you can create mutually contradicting goals, the accomplishment of one being inconsistent with the accomplishment of another. If one goal for an account executive is to "provide detailed customer follow-up for every client," but a second goal is to "develop 30 percent more new clients," you have a problem. The first goal requires considerable time and effort in continually checking back with clients and taking extra time with even their more trivial concerns. And the second also requires a great deal of time to network, prepare presentations, and make calls on prospects. Inconsistent goals only produce frustration and, in the worst case, a sense of hopelessness in which the person gives up even trying to attain them.

Suitable Challenge

Goals offer challenges. But they have to be attainable. It is absurd to set for yourself the goal of winning the 100-yard dash in the Olympics unless you are a very accomplished and talented track athlete. When a goal is absurd in its difficulty, it is discounted as ridiculous and simply ignored. Employees faced with that situation simply wait for the inevitable failure. Although challenging goals are necessary to get our maximum level of performance, we have to perceive them as within our grasp. If they seem attainable, we usually rise to the challenge and go after them. But if they are so hard they seem impossible, or nearly impossible, our own self-esteem requires we discount them and they become demotivating. Goal-setting theorists emphasize that subordinate participation in setting goals contributes significantly to their attainment, since the subordinate then has a personal stake in achieving the goal that is set (Locke & Latham, 1984).

Disadvantages

Though goal setting is a pervasive activity, it is not without serious criticism. It can be an isolating mechanism, where employees perceive themselves as contestants pitted against each other rather than as team members. That is particularly true when goals are individually set apart from group, unit, or department goals (see Fig. 5.6).

Goal setting, when not properly done, can have serious negative consequences for the organization and its members.

1. It can erode cohesiveness, producing internal conflict when one group's or individual's goals conflict with another's.
2. It is hard to manage and prone to game playing, which may increase office politics.
3. It presumes stability despite often rapidly changing conditions. Once set, goals have a habit of becoming inflexible.
4. It can be a crutch for poor day-to-day management that focuses only on the goals, not the daily processes involved.

Figure 5.6   Disadvantages of Goal Setting

Goal Setting Can Erode Organizational Cohesiveness

Some researchers have been critical of the goal-based approach, particularly where management independently sets them often by assigning different goals to separate profit centers within the organization (Zammuto, 1982). Such an approach does not create a stakeholder relationship between the goal and the person who is supposed to attain it. It becomes another edict handed down the corporate ladder, not something employees buy into.

Goal Setting Is Complex and Difficult to Manage

Although on the surface goal setting seems like a relatively simple activity, when done well, it is the reverse. It can be time-consuming and hard to sustain, may work well for relatively simple jobs but not for complex jobs, encourages game playing with the way goals are set and their difficulty, and can become an obsession causing neglect of job responsibilities (Gibson, et al., 1997). Assigned goals may create internal conflict. An example would be pressure on a printing department of a newspaper to limit inventory by tying bonuses and promotions to maintaining a just-in-time delivery of newsprint and ink—which cuts storage costs—while pressuring the promotion department to surge circulation through special promotions. Without coordinating the goals of both departments, demand for newspapers could exceed the supply of newsprint and ink. Advertisers promised additional circulation would have to be compensated for the shortfall. If the special promotion was something that created a sudden increase in reader demand—for example, a collector's issue of sports coverage of a bowl game win—there could be negative consequences in overall public image.

Goal Setting Presumes Stability

Basing evaluations on goals tends to make organizations more static while their environments may be increasingly dynamic (Zammuto, 1982). Goals set six months ago may not be right today because of how things have changed in the interim. But the tendency in goal-based systems is for the goals to, in effect, take over everything since they are the benchmark of success. Once they are set, they become the point of work, rather than the quality of the work itself. Part of the art in goal setting is in knowing when to change or adjust goals along the way. Sales targets set in January may be irrelevant in September if some extraordinary economic development occurs.

A Management Crutch

Goal setting may generate such a focus on the goal, at the level of being a corporate culture fixation, that management fails to pay appropriate attention to the daily work processes necessary to accomplish the task at hand. An attitude may evolve wherein the attainment of the goal is all that matters, and people assigned that goal do whatever is necessary to reach it, including bending company rules or violating the law. Management, in such goal-paranoiac situations, may literally cease to be little more than a task accomplishment monitor, not so much management as a goal referee. Yet management's real job is to put the right people in the right circumstances to achieve maximum performance. If a goal is set, but the wrong people are involved in the work (e.g., don't have the right job skills), or the work process is not efficient or properly designed to accomplish the goal, failure is probable despite the best efforts of the workers involved. Goal setting and achievement can become a crutch for poor management that fails to understand that the daily processes necessary to goals is what matters. Goals merely provide benchmarks to keep you on track toward maximum organizational development. Goal attainment, or failure, is only symptomatic of what is going on deeper in the organization. Goals are indicators of the effectiveness of an activity, but they are not the activity itself.

Implementing Goal Setting

Despite the controversy over setting goals, you will have to deal with them. As stated earlier, they are a pervasive part of American management. Fundamentally, goals must include the following to be effective: (1) relevance to the individual, (2) reliability as a measure over time, (3) discrimination between good and poor performers, and (4) practical application for the organization (Gibson et al., 1997).

An additional, fifth, factor is crucial to managing a goal-oriented organization toward optimum performance. You should set very specific, relatively short-term goals rather than broad, long-term ones. Or at the very least, divide up long-term goals into shorter time-frame elements. People respond positively to what's known as a "small-wins" strategy (Whetten & Cameron, 1995). Cutting some large task into small, manageable pieces helps prevent frustration and gives people the sense things are moving along. It's also easier to focus on something in the immediate future, rather than a year or more away. You are better off setting monthly goals than yearly goals or at least dividing the yearly goals into single month increments. They are more immediate, the feedback is faster, and you can more easily adjust incremental goals to fit changing situations. Thus, the criteria used to set goals must be flexible when the course of events requires them to be adjusted, for example, in the rapidly changing world of media organizations.

Since goal achievement is the measure of success for individuals for whom goals are assigned, once goals are in place people are very hesitant to abandon them, or even to bring to the attention of superiors the growing difficulty of achieving them as a situation changes. If not meeting a goal is perceived as a kind of failure, asking for a goal to be changed may also be perceived as a sign of inadequacy, even though the situation has changed. Clearly, the small-wins approach may help avoid the lofty isolation of large, long-term goals and bring them down to earth where people work with them on a daily basis, adjusting as necessary.

Goal setting is an art. It takes time and effort to work with employees to set challenging, but achievable goals. They need to be periodically reassessed and adjusted if necessary. Employees have to be a partner in creating their goals because that gives them a vested interest in their accomplishment, and because their work processes are involved. You may not be aware of some aspect of an individual's work that could directly affect a goal you arbitrarily set.

A major problem in goal setting is that it's a game in many organizations, managers and subordinates manipulating the process for personal reasons. That may include a manager setting artificially easier goals for those he or she likes, and harder goals for those he or she dislikes, or employees trying to set easy goals rather than more difficult/challenging ones to guarantee accomplishment.

Commitment vs. Compliance of Employees

Considerable research has documented the relationship between individuals within an organization and the impact of their commitment on the achievement of organizational goals, while the debate continues about how to formulate an empirically predictive model. Generally two areas of the relationship from the employee perspective come into play. First is the emotional attachment an employee develops to the organization based on how individual and organizational goals fit together. The second is the pragmatism of the employment relationship, the exchange relationship between worker and organization (Huselid & Day, 1991). Turnover within an organization is affected by the relationship of the individuals' commitment to the organization and the level of job involvement (Blau & Boal, 1989; Mathieu & Kohler, 1990). That means, in general,

> employees who exhibit both high organizational commitment and high job involvement (institutional stars) should be the least likely to leave the organization. Employees with low levels of organizational commitment and job involvement (apathetics) would be the most likely to leave the organization voluntarily. (Huselid & Day, 1991, p. 380)

The way in which organizational members are evaluated is critical in their growth as "institutional stars," being considered "apathetics," or sifted somewhere between those performance dichotomies. It is, therefore, a keystone in the arch of management's formal power.

Performance Review

Although theoretically meant to be a pragmatic measure of the way an individual is doing his or her job, performance evaluation can easily become enmeshed in organizational politics. The performance rating area is a widely diffused, subjective one that is far from perfection. Researchers evaluated causal models of supervisory performance ratings and found them lacking because they did not incorporate large enough variable schema, particularly personal relationship and personality factors between those being rated and those doing the rating. Numerical rating scales are the most common way of determining job performance, but a person's temperament influences it (Borman, White, Pulakos, & Oppler, 1991).

Figures 5.7 and 5.8 provide an interesting comparison of two models of factors involved in performance ratings. Figure 5.7 is Hunter's (1983) four-category model. Figure 5.8 is the expansion of that model by Borman et al. (1991) to include eight areas of influence. The researchers determined that "dependability had a direct (albeit modest) effect on job knowledge," which "illustrates the role of personality in knowledge

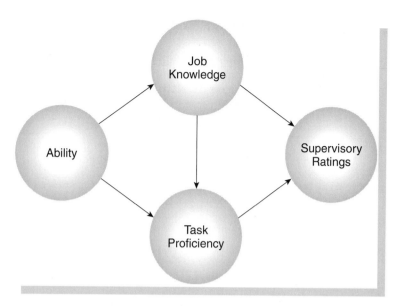

Figure 5.7 Hunter's Causal Model of Performance
(Source: Hunter, 1983)

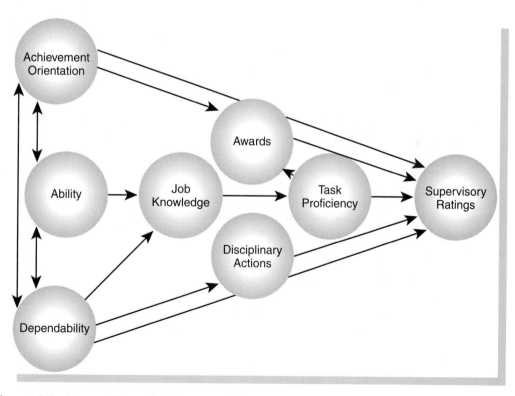

Figure 5.8 Borman Expanded Rating Model
(Source: Borman et al., 1991)

acquisition" (p. 871). Additionally, while their study confirmed Hunter's finding "that the major impact of ability was on the acquisition of job knowledge which, in turn, had a major impact on task proficiency" (p. 867), it reinforced that analysis of empirically derived categorical data such as tests of cognitive ability and technical proficiency were substantially influenced by attitudinal factors such as ratee problem behavior and perceptions of dependability. Thus, despite attempts to keep personal dynamics out of the rating process,

> there is a long way to go toward understanding the factors that affect performance ratings. More variables must be included in future model development and testing. Rater-ratee relationship variables might prove especially fruitful. For example, the amount of trust and support demonstrated by the rater toward the ratee, the degree of liking shown by the rater for a ratee, and the frequency of ratee complaints or problems brought up by the ratee deserve attention. (Borman et al., 1991, p. 871)

As in goal setting, discussed earlier in this chapter, performance evaluation is easily influenced by the way people get along. Standards may be set higher or lower, or evaluations reflect a more critical or forgiving attitude depending on how well the supervisor and subordinate work together. In most large organizations, performance evaluation is bureaucratically controlled to minimize such problems; however, there is no way of escaping the reality that it is often a power and influence game.

Some organizations, for example, require planning documents to be filled out at the beginning of each year indicating what you intend to accomplish. Then, at the end of the year when your performance is evaluated, the game is to make sure you have accomplished what you said you would. The flaw in this system is obvious. No one who is very smart puts anything on the annual planning document that isn't guaranteed to occur. Or the language is intentionally vague. Throughout the year there is inherent rigidity fostered by the planning document. Since success depends on achieving what was included, there's no point in achieving more or something different. And changing criteria midstream is usually difficult. So the organization, through such a formal evaluation system, loses flexibility as it dampens any innovative or creative ideas.

There is a major advantage to annual performance review systems that is probably the real reason so many of them exist. When people have to be disciplined or fired, the evaluation system provides evidence. A pattern of poor performance can be established that can be effective in countering the argument action was taken for personal reasons. A manager may provide a bad performance review of an employee and give the employee 30 days to improve his or her performance. At the end of the 30 days, another review of the work may produce a much stronger warning letter indicating that if significant improvement does not occur within the next 30 days, the person could face termination. Finally, after the final 30-day period, the person is terminated. It takes three months to fire a person in such a way, but it is a relatively common procedure as organizations attempt to avoid lawsuits over their handling of personnel. However, lawsuits do result from terminations, and some of those have affected the attitude toward performance reviews. They cannot, for example, be so loosely defined they are clearly value judgments by a manager without any scientifically derived criteria for what job performance should be. You can't just give all of the people with dark hair better ratings because you like brunettes, unless hair color is directly related to the position. The performance standard has to be pertinent to the job, uniformly applied across all employees doing that job, distinguish between different levels of performance, and it has to be practical (Gibson et al., 1997). See Chapter 16 for a further discussion of some of the legal issues in personnel management.

MBWA—Management by Walking Around

In a media organization there are creative people with whom a trust relationship must be built. They are often wary of new managers, and it takes time to break down the natural defense mechanisms. The best way to do that is to understand the people in the organization fully, and they you. One of the most effective approaches is to be highly visible and connect with them personally. The phrase that is used for that is "management by walking around," or MBWA (Peters & Waterman, 1982). Some management consultants believe up to half a manager's time should be spent doing that; wandering around seeing what is going on, appearing unexpectedly in the middle of the work process. Too many managers become prisoners of their offices (Taylor, 1994).

As in all things involving management, there's a right way and a wrong way to practice MBWA. You can't go off on your rounds of the organization at the same time every day, or you'll see the same few people and the same work processes at the same point. You have to vary your interactions consciously (Hopkins-Doerr, 1989). One week do your office work in the morning, and MBWA in the afternoon. The next week, reverse them. Use the regular staff coffeepot on the other side of the newsroom, rather than your own in your office. That gets you out among those working at frequent, unscheduled times ("The CEO on the Move," 1994). Too often when people become managers they are given an office and are then trapped in it by the various organizational clutter that comes with being responsible for weekly reports to those higher up the management chain. But you have to get out from behind your desk into the daily life of those you manage (Todd, 1995). You need to be part of the ongoing atmosphere in order to design more effective ways of accomplishing the work (Zahniser, 1994).

It is imperative that when you move among your subordinates you know a little bit about them. For example, if you walk up to a person and ask "How's the family?" to begin a little dialog, and that person is single, you may be perceived as a manipulator. It is vital that managers know their subordinates. You should, as a matter of course, review their résumés and have some formal and informal conversations with them about their backgrounds, training, career goals, and so on. Then, when you are managing by walking around, you will be able to talk to the people who work for you intelligently and engage with them on their level with a more personalized approach.

Additionally, as mentioned, it is advisable for you to walk around at different times. If you always come out of your office at the same time of the day, you become predictable. When people know you'll be around at a certain time, they'll be ready for you. But what you want is to observe what goes on normally, without any orchestration for your benefit. You should manage your MBWA program by scheduling time for it on your calendar. Some managers block half of each day for office work, and half for being out in the media organization working with their people. If you do that, be sure to rotate the morning and afternoon schedules weekly. Another way to manage your MBWA time is to pen in an hour or two on your calendar every day, at various times, and then schedule other appointments around that MBWA time. It doesn't really matter what technique you use, as long as you are connecting with the people you supervise at various times during the entire workday and are somewhat unpredictable. Your subordinates are as important as any other people who need to have contact with you. So manage time with them just as you manage it for everything else. Put it on your calendar. If you don't, you will fall into the trap of seeing empty time on your calendar and filling it up with other appointments. Management time is valuable. There is so much to do with so many demands from those who want a piece of your time, including your boss, your customers or audience members, community organizations, and everyone else. When you don't schedule MWBA time with those you are supposed to supervise, you will tend to take the time away from those people who are most important to your success. That can be a fast road to failure.

CHAPTER SUMMARY

Assessing organizational effectiveness is a complex process, dependent upon the variety of perspectives available. It is "situation specific" and involves inherently problematical issues such as conflicting goals within the organization and the interaction of the organization with the dynamics of the environment within which it functions. The organizational environment is fluid, multifaceted both internally and externally, requiring constant adaptive adjustments among multiple constituencies (Zammuto, 1984; Judge, 1994).

Because of the fluid nature of the organizational environment, with its continuous fluctuations, both internally and externally, the fundamental question for any organization is how to remain effective when everything is in a constant state of change. If an organization does not adapt to change, it clearly cannot remain effective over time. The equation of effectiveness is squared in its difficulty because, as Schneider (1987, p. 34) observed, "where an organization is going is not where some say it is going but where its internal behavioral processes actually take it!" (emphasis in original). Employees grow attached to organizations with mutually reinforcing values and attitudes.

As discussed earlier in this text, it is therefore important for both the employee and the employer to have a good fit in basic values as well as in specific job skill. When fundamental values contradict, relationship failure is usually the result. But when you are in a culture where there is a good fit, the social nuances are reinforcing and work is enjoyable to a higher degree of satisfaction (Smith & Barclay, 1997). Symbiotic relationships evolve extending the concept of pay from a mere exchange relationship of money to a broader context of belonging and mutual appreciation.

To attain maximum media organization effectiveness, you will face a serious challenge to your managerial abilities. An organization has many masters, each of whom may judge it and them differently. Researchers have made numerous attempts over the years to define specific performance criteria, including goal-setting strategies (e.g., Barnard, 1938; Hannan & Freeman, 1977; Hitt & Middlemist, 1979; Judge, 1994; Mahoney & Weitzel, 1969; Price, 1972; Steers, 1975). But the research has not produced a set of surefire elements, or a fail-safe formula, that can be applied across organizations to evaluate them. So, organizational effectiveness is still part art and part science, dependent upon whose perspective is used in the first place. For example, the motto of *The New York Times* is "All the news that's fit to print." That may be true for a person living in New York reading that paper. But for a person living in Billings, Montana, *The Billings Gazette* may have more of the news that is fit to print relative to life in Yellowstone County.

While other kinds of endeavors have only shareholders to please, the media organization manager's world is much more complex. Media organization effectiveness is judged in four essential areas:

1. You must be perceived as effective by the shareholders/owners. So you must generate a profit, or meet the profit plan senior management sets for you. Put in its simplest terms, if a newspaper doesn't make any money, there won't be a newspaper tomorrow. Paper, ink, staff salaries, and all the rest of the things it takes to run such an enterprise take money.

2. Once you keep the lights on, you need to provide a challenging and positive working environment for your employees. Motivational theory has provided strong evidence that people who are positive about their work do better work. And, as discussed elsewhere in this text, media employees tend to be intrinsically driven more by their deeper, philosophical commitment and creativity than simply by hourly wages.

3. Media organization effectiveness is judged by those external to it on the basis of its products. The highest quality possible is always an essential media organization goal since the relationship with the customer/listener/reader/viewer is the point of the activity that drives all other concerns.

4. Media organizations in American society are culturally presumed to have a higher purpose of contributing to the society. A free and democratic society is knowledge based, and, as such, all media forms theoretically contribute to expansion of understanding and the social conscience. Media has a "special" role bound up in the mythology of government and cultural forms.

Thus, as a media manager you have to keep an eye on the budget, provide leadership and team building for your subordinates, do everything you can to have the highest quality media product possible under the circumstances, and understand that between the lines of the First Amendment where the rights are written in ink is the meaning of implied responsibility to serve the best interests of society.

When you engage in goal setting, make sure you create a partnership with your subordinates so the goals are mutually defined and agreed. Additionally,

1. Goals must be challenging but attainable.

2. Goals must be fair and free of any office politics or preferential treatment.

3. All subordinate goals should be relatively short term but specifically geared toward achieving the long-term organizational goals.

4. Make it clear to your subordinates that goals can be revised, and you are available any time to reconsider them.

5. Frequently monitor progress toward goal attainment and determine whether you need to alert your superiors to any problems.

Finally, to be an effective manager you must connect with the people you manage. Management By Walking Around is a key to this challenge. Unless you are out among those you are supposed to supervise you cannot hope to know what is going on. Too many managers become isolates within their offices, removed from the daily work of the media organization. It's an easy trap to fall into with constant budget pressures, information, and demands generated by your own superiors, along with the sea of paper that all bureaucracies generate. But management is a people business. Schedule your MBWA time and let nothing stand in the way of a few hours a day with those upon whom your career rests, those you manage. They are the key to effectiveness.

STUDY QUESTIONS

1. Select any organization of which you are a part. It can be a media organization, a club, a school, a department, a social organization such as a fraternity or sorority, or any other formal group.

   A. Audit your organization's effectiveness from the perspective of the following. Think for a moment to identify those who fit into the following perspectives of effectiveness.

      1) What is management's perspective—the owner/shareholder, or next higher organization level's view?

      2) What is the organizational member perspective—the people within the group at the local level?

      3) What is the external consumer view—the perception of non-members who consume its products?

      4) What is the regulatory perspective—the way those who govern it feel about the organization? This should be an official authority—a local governing board, activity council, university administrator, and so on—responsible to some degree for organizational activity.

   B. Interview a sample of three to five people from each of the preceding perspective groups. Ask the following questions of each person interviewed.

      1) What are the most positive things about the organization?

      2) What are the most negative things about the organization?

      3) What would you change about the organization?

   C. Draw four columns on a sheet of paper. Label them at the top, from left to right, as "management," "member," "external consumer," and "regulator." Halfway down the paper, draw a horizontal line, labeling the top half "positives" and the bottom half "negatives." See the sample layout that follows. Put a few words or a phrase from each of your respondents where appropriate. You do not need an entry in every column and category, only those where your respondents indicated an opinion.

	Management	Member	Consumer	Regulator
Positives				
Negatives				

You now have a cross-tabulation of the major positive and negative perceptions of your organization from four different points of view relative to each person's place inside or outside the organization. How do they compare?

2. Based on your audit, design a strategy to enhance the positive attitudes toward your organization and decrease the negatives.

3. Goal setting takes some thought and practice. Do the following from your personal perspective.
   A. Set up several goals you would like to achieve for the next year (12 months from today).
   B. Work backward from where you want to end up, and set up a series of monthly goals to get you there.
   C. Consider the enormity of the long-term goal when you consider it alone, and the difference of breaking it into short-term, doable pieces (a small-wins strategic approach). Does it make sense to set smaller hurdles to cross day to day than creating a mountain of challenge down the road? If your goal is to be a great newspaper editor or network anchor, you may get very frustrated in the 20 to 30 years it takes you to get there. But working each day to do a better story than the last is satisfying along the way. Do not focus so hard on tomorrow that you do not get the most out of today.

section 3

MEDIA MANAGER SKILLS DEVELOPMENT

chapter 6

COMMUNICATION AND POWER

Individuals effectively performing the many roles required of a manager must have considerable interpersonal skills in two critical areas: the ability to communicate with other organizational members, and the exercise of power. This chapter focuses on the basics of organizational communication, the essential concepts of power, and their use in the organization. The goal is to give you a foundation in these two complex areas and to point you toward the considerable research into both these topics. Additionally, this chapter introduces important concepts relating to the following chapter on leadership, for the abilities to communicate and to exercise power are critical elements in any effort to get others to do something a manager or leader desires.

COMMUNICATION FLOWS

Although we often think of communication in the formal sense of bureaucratic forms, letters, memos, and meetings, it is much more than that. Indeed, communication is a continuous, pervasive activity permeating an organization as information is exchanged through myriad channels. Management sends information down into the organization. Feedback comes back up the formal chain of command. Information and feedback are also exchanged laterally across organizational divisions and units. Organizational members communicate with one another, officially and unofficially. All of this occurs through such diverse channels as memos, electronic mail, notes, and ordinary conversation. It all generates a kind of mulligan stew of organizational communication with all the various ingredients blending into the final organizational flavor.

The communication process, on the surface, is fairly simple. Lasswell's (1948) classic model defines it as follows: Who says what, in which channel, to whom, with what effect? However, complexity swirls within those five brief, interrelated questions, for the process of communication is the transference of one of the most intricate of all human concepts—meaning. The elements of communication include the *message* itself, the *sender,* the *encoding* of meaning by that sender, the *channel* through which the message

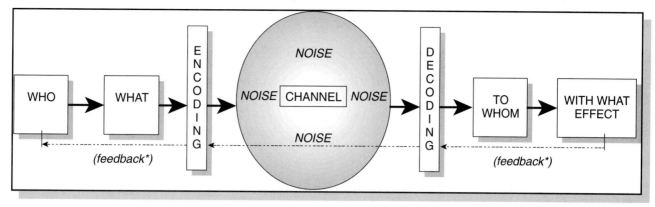

Feedback reverses message direction through coding and channel noise. Feedback is usually affected as much by distortion as the original message since it often returns by the same original message route. However, feedback may take an alternative route. For example, a formal message passed down through normal channels could produce a direct, personal confrontation (feedback) between an employee and the president of the corporation.

Figure 6.1 Fundamental Communication Model

is transferred to the receiver with often-attendant "noise" affecting its transmission, the *receiver,* the *decoding* by the receiver of meaning that gets through the noise, and any *feedback* that then flows back to the sender. See Figure 6.1 for a fundamental model of the communication process. Consider that at each step, the original meaning to be conveyed is altered to some degree by the process.

The effects of the communication are subject to the inherent difficulties of encoding and decoding meaning. This is directly influenced by symbolic interactionism as organizational members come to understand the predominant language and behavior patterns they use to interpret what they send and receive. A context of shared meaning evolves that members use to interpret the messages they send and receive within the organizational context, and into which new organizational members have to be assimilated (Krone, Jablin, & Putnam, 1987). That shared meaning typically blends the various organizational myths, official statements of purpose and vision, and informal organizational personality into a meaning interpretation screen. So in one organization a statement might be treated as a passing remark, while in another the same statement could trigger a major reaction reverberating from the top to the bottom of the organizational hierarchy (Huber & Daft, 1987).

Much of the effort to improve the way organizations function rests, like an upside-down pyramid, on the essential human process of communication. It is through communication, in its many forms, that meaning is conveyed, misconstrued, distorted, or even blocked. It seems so simple: Send a message to another person. But depending on the nuances of sender and receiver, and the noise in the channel that can distort message transmission, what is understood isn't always what was intended. Indeed, in one way of looking at organizations, they are

> a complex of meaning centers, interpretation centers, power centers, decision centers, and—most of all—communication centers, with interchange of messages among these centers overshadowed by the multiply understood relations among centers to which the messages contribute and within which they are interpreted. (McPhee & Tompkins, 1985, p. 11)

Such a view may seem daunting. But in the real world of daily organizational life it is possible to communicate more effectively if, as a media manager, you are more aware of some of the basic communicative forms and understand how they affect everything you try to accomplish. For the purposes of this discussion, all forms of communication are expected to occur in an organization from body language and informal conversation, through e-mail, formal memos, official directives, and letters. Indeed, the communication environment of organizations is media rich, with multiple channels available for construction of a system of meaning sharing that minimizes discord and encourages appropriate action for the organizational situation (Huber & Daft, 1987).

Sidebar 6.1 The Message Game

When you were in grade school you may have played a classroom communication game demonstrating how information changes as it is passed from one person to the next. The teacher whispers something to the first student. It is then passed around the class one person at a time. The last student to receive the message dictates it to the teacher who writes it on the blackboard. Then the original message whispered to the first student is compared with the final message passed back to the teacher. Usually, the final message is considerably different from the original.

Each person in a message chain tends to adjust the language of the message, the emphasis on certain words, or some other aspect. All of that affects meaning. The same thing happens in organizations.

It is important to understand that the "organization" can be a single office, a department, or the entire company—any collection of people. Indeed, different communicative climates occur within the subunits of larger organizations. The newsroom may have a different flow of information among its members than does the advertising department or publisher's office. And another information exchange pattern may exist across departmental lines. How organizational communication works depends on both the organization and the personalities of the people functioning within it. You may have, in your organization, a policy of open communication stipulated on the mission statement, but a reality of restrictive, formal communication with subsequent extensive rumor information exchange. As in many other areas of human endeavor, what people say they do and what they really do are sometimes quite different. Saying you want your subordinates to tell you how they really feel is meaningless unless you do, indeed, listen and take to heart what they say. Otherwise, you will quickly be perceived as an insincere manipulator.

Vertical Communication

The most obvious form of communication within an organization generally follows the official organizational structure "for decision support, management information, work evaluation and compensation, and financial control" of divisions, departments, and work groups—the established system (McPhee, 1985, p. 149). Vertical communication may be either formal or informal. It typically travels up and down the chain of command and is the primary vehicle for command and control. The degree of formality is often a reflection of the people involved. Some managers prefer more of a conversational approach to their subordinates and so may just pick up the telephone and call someone or walk down the hall to have a conversation. Others are less comfortable with such personalized interaction and prefer to send more formal memos, letters, or notes to maintain a kind of distance from their subordinates.

In general terms, the social dynamics of vertical organizational communication connect an individual to those one layer above and one layer below him or her in the official hierarchy. In many organizations, sending a message to a person higher than your immediate supervisor requires permission, or at least notifying the supervisor. Many people take a very dim view of others "jumping over their heads." That is a defensive attitude manifested in the sense of risk many organizational players have. Obviously, organizational politics influence the communication process. There are nine communication strategies that organizational members use to gain or use influence. They include reasoning, coalition building, altruism (appealing to one's sense of good-will and caring for others), ingratiating, bargaining, asserting, invoking higher authority, threatening or initiating sanctions, and circumventing (Frost, 1987).

Depending on the particular situation, an individual may construct different personae to achieve a desired end. For example, in front of the general manager a department head may demonstrate an outward appearance of controlling everything, with close attention to budgetary considerations and posturing authority. But in a different setting, for example, working with a star reporter, the same individual may become an empathetic coach focused on uncovering the facts of a story regardless of the overtime it takes. People in organizations are performers who adopt various roles or characters relative to what they see as necessary to achieve their goals as they interact with one another (Trujillo, 1983).

An estimated two-thirds of the time a manager spends communicating is vertically, either with superiors or subordinates. And as information works its way up and down the vertical information channel, it is edited, with senior managers often relying on executive summaries from subordinates who decide what those above them really need to know. This filtering process obviously has considerable potential for distortion and manipulation. It is a kind of noise in the communication channel that alters messages and therefore their meaning (Blair, Roberts, & McKechnie, 1985). Considerable filtering can occur as packages of information are tailored to the perceived needs of the message recipients. A climate of mutual reliance develops wherein the nine information influence strategies mentioned earlier come into play as "messages establish functional relationships through which individuals manage and coordinate their activities as they strive to accomplish personal, group, or organizational goals" (Stohl & Redding, 1987, p. 460). Everyone tends to manipulate, to one degree or another, information and the channels through which it passes to achieve their desired ends.

Lateral Communication

Communication across divisions, departments, and work groups, irrespective of the vertical command-and-control structure of an organization, provides considerable information exchange, often informally. When people join an organization—and that can mean new hires or those who are transferred from different divisions, departments, or groups—they go through a socialization process by which the organization's culture is transferred to them. That culture includes the "shared norms . . . reminiscences, stories, rites, and rituals that provide the members with unique symbolic common ground" (Bormann, 1983, p. 100). Commonly, such new organizational members seek inclusion,

Sidebar 6.2 Communication Strategies

The following communication strategies are used by people to communicate and influence one another. The choice of the initial strategy used depends on a person's initial assessment of what will work best. Usually if the first attempted strategy isn't effective, most people quickly move to another or even blend strategies where necessary to achieve their desired end. The nine basic strategies are numbered only to provide easy reference and are in order from the most cooperative to those which are more authoritative.

1. **Reasoning**—This is the use of logic to support an argument. Usually reasoning applies the selective use of data to support the person's point of view, influencing the other individual(s) with factual information rather playing to the emotional senses.

2. **Coalition building**—This is a strength in numbers approach wherein a person attempts to get others to join in a group effort to influence an outcome. Rather than advocating a position individually, the support of others in the organization is solicited to demonstrate wider appeal, and therefore increased validity.

3. **Altruism**—This is the "greater good" approach, often reflected in appeals to a person's sense of goodwill or *esprit de corps.* Emphasis within organizations on teams, on doing something for the good of the organization, or, for a particular person, on the sense of belonging or affection is grounded in this strategy of engendering benevolence.

4. **Ingratiating**—Flattery and other personally oriented approaches to creating goodwill are used to positively influence another. This approach is personal impression centered, attempting to get compliance by virtue of the decision maker's positive regard toward the communicator.

5. **Bargaining**—This is the exchange relationship of trading favors, benefits, or future influence for support or a positive decision. "If you do this for me today, I'll do that for you tomorrow."

6. **Asserting**—This is typically used by a person in power, or someone who has a particular strength position and is able to force his or her will on another. It is usually direct, forceful, and demanding in an authoritarian way. Asserting, in most organizations, typically follows some effort at reasoning or bargaining where a person in power finally grows weary of the influence game and simply says, "We're going to do it this way!"

7. **Invoking higher authority**—This technique is used when a person is representing people higher in the organizational power structure or has been able to convince others he or she has the ear of senior management. Invoking higher authority may be a factual use of real, delegated, power, or it may be nothing more than an individual throwing out the name of a senior executive to make others think he or she has such delegated power.

8. **Threatening or initiating sanctions**—This is the application of the reward and punishment system present in an organization to coerce others to accept whatever is being argued or demanded. It is the exercise of overt power and frequently follows other less direct influence strategies. This is often thought of as a top-down strategy. However, people at all levels usually have ways of causing problems, ranging from quitting to simply slowing down the work process.

9. **Circumventing**—This is simply trying to go around the person, decision, or situation. It may include deception or merely ignoring a policy, order, or procedure to achieve the desired end. Rather than trying to convince others to change, you simply go around them. (Frost, 1987).

to be part of the social fabric into which they've entered. So individuals are predisposed to accepting the organizational values and operational concepts as they seek to identify with the new group they've joined. Indeed, team management approaches attempt to capitalize on this predisposition to build personal identity, which makes building group identity easier (Tompkins & Cheney, 1983).

Together, the organization and its members create a climate of communication that is a combination of what members expect and do. Their expectations and their actions continuously interact with organizational processes and practices (Falcione, Sussman, & Herden, 1987). This blend creates a communication flow that is not mere information exchange but contributes to the deeper social structure within the organizational framework as people interact and make sense of what goes on (Smircich & Calas, 1987). Organizational members also maintain a surveillance of others to interpret what things mean in the organizational context, determine the organizationally appropriate action, and then adjust their own conduct (Conrad, 1985).

There is considerable variance from one kind of organization to another in the way communication relationships evolve. Some industries foster much more rank-ordered information exchange patterns than others. Highly technical organizations featuring extensive and intricate coordination may require more rigidity in their communication networks. Other types of organizations provide more flexibility and energy in their communication flows, transcending the vertical rank and order of the formal organization. The way communication takes place is directly influenced by the kinds of information needs, type of work, and sociology of organizational members. What's more, they are actively adjusting and changing as the environment flexes and people create, maintain, redesign, and terminate their various internal and external communication relationships (Monge & Eisenberg, 1987).

The Rumor Mill

The rumor mill, also commonly referred to as the "grapevine" and office "gossip," transcends vertical and lateral communication. It is an omnipresent fact of daily organizational life. People communicate to seek out information and to give it to others. Having information is a kind of expert power, and so the person who supposedly knows what's going on gains in stature among his or her peers. A rumor is an unsubstantiated idea or notion that circulates informally in or around an organization (Rosnow, 1980). The rumor mill has both positive and negative aspects (see Fig. 6.2).

On the positive side, work-related gossip is part of the way individuals build closer relationships with their peers, exchanging information of much and little importance as they assimilate organizational culture, including organizational mythology and rites to expand their organizational identity. The informality of the rumor mill means it transcends formal communication channels. Formal communication channels tend to be slow, harder to use (e.g., circulating memos to verify something rather than just passing the word around the cafeteria at lunch), and unsatisfactory in meeting the information needs of organizational members (Euske & Roberts, 1987).

Research has demonstrated that at least three-quarters of what travels through the rumor mill is accurate (Watson, 1982). Because it so often proves true, the grapevine is frequently considered more trustworthy than official communication from management. Management communication may be presumed to have an agenda of getting employees to work harder or more productively, while the rumor mill may be presumed to exist only to meet the information needs of employees that formal communication channels do not satisfy.

Positives	Negatives
• Speed of distribution.	• No control of content. All information is in the mill, true or false.
• Generally it is reliable (75% of rumors are true).	• False information gains credibility as it is passed around, becoming an "accepted truth."
• Information channel crosses organizational structural.	• People and organization can be damaged by false or inappropriate information.
• Information sharing helps build personal interrelationships and mutual team reliance through information inclusion.	• Organizational cohesiveness can be eroded by personality cliques fed by informal gossip cells.

Figure 6.2 Rumor Mill Pluses and Minuses

Typically, rumors travel person to person, disregarding organizational dividing lines. They jump from one office, department, or division to another as quickly as a person can pick up the telephone or walk down the hall. Along with a rapid rate of distribution, distortion of the information does occur, but usually as a result of people filtering the information they receive before passing it on (Stohl & Redding, 1987). Part of the reason that rumor mills have been found to be so accurate in the information distributed may be that a person's stature among peers as having expert information power is directly related to the veracity of what he or she says. In other words, if you generally put out information that proves to be true, you will be perceived as increasingly reliable.

Sometimes the rumor mill can be used by managers. For example, let's say you're thinking about changing the shifts around to a monthly rotation schedule so no one is stuck permanently on nights or weekends. By getting a rumor circulating that management is thinking about taking such an action, the employees will start thinking about it. Some may give you personal feedback by coming into your office to voice their feelings about what they've heard. If you are planning to discuss such a policy change at the next staff meeting, a trial balloon in the rumor mill a week before might result in staff members having thought it through, so you could get some valuable feedback at the meeting.

The rumor mill has some serious negatives. First, everything goes into the grapevine, principally because there is nothing to control content but the curiosity of those engaged with it. Factual information is mixed in with hopes, fears, opinions, and outright falsehoods reported as truth. Second, if three-quarters of the information passed through rumor mills is correct, that means a quarter of it is false. One out of every four messages passed through the grapevine is not true. The third big negative is that damage done by false rumors can build up before management knows what is going on. Reversing that damage can consume considerable time and effort and is not always successful. Assertions of opinion, after being passed through a few people, easily become statements of presumed "fact," and once information is accepted as fact it is very hard to correct. In effect, rumors take on a kind of permanent quality and strengthen over time. Finally, rumors can be very damaging to individuals, who are often the subject of rumors. For example, if a rumor is started to the effect that a person in the office is a spy for senior management, that individual may be ostracized by others who fear the connection. The subject of the false rumor becomes a social isolate. Or, in the case of interpersonal relationships, a rumor of a manager and a subordinate having an affair can have a deleterious effect on both people, both inside and outside of the organization. Because rumors are a form of gossip, and gossip is inevitably personal in nature, it has a corrosive effect on people cast in a negative light.

So what can you as a manager do about rumors? First, you need to think about why they exist. The bottom line is that people want to know what's going on, and when they don't get the information they want, or it is ambiguous, they tend to make up things. Rumors are ways to explain that which has not been explained another way. They are coping mechanisms for uncertainty, anxiety, and confusion (Stohl & Redding, 1987). When media organizations are under considerable stress, for example being threatened by the success of a competitor causing declining market share, rumors may fire up about the newspaper, television or radio station, or agency being sold. Television news anchors are often subjected to rumors about whether they will be dumped if ratings growth stops or trends down. Knowing the rumor mill exists means management has an excellent conduit for information it wants to convey to employees quickly. The issue is what message you want to introduce to that particular information channel and who should be used as the conduit. One of the things you, as a manager, need to do is have an awareness for who talks to whom and with what frequency. In any organization there are people who are "in the know." Connect with them and you are connected to the rumor mill.

It is important for you to be able to monitor the rumor mill and use it if necessary. Obviously, from the positives and negatives outlined previously, it is in management's best interest to know what false or misleading information needs to be corrected as soon as possible. And because the rumor mill is usually accurate, fast, and accepted by organizational members as valid, it can be a valuable information tool. The trick is how to counter the negatives while taking advantage of the positives. Indeed, the most effective way for a manager to deal with the rumor mill is to provide plenty of information to subordinates (Mishra, 1990). When people know what's going on, they are less likely to make it up. And when they don't feel the need to spend considerable time engaging with the rumor mill, it is logical to assume their time will be spent more productively doing the media organization's work.

Communication and Conflict

All organizations have some degree of conflict. Unless it is managed well, the friction between individuals or units in the organization may not only slow down employee productivity but also cripple an organization (Gibson, Ivancevich, & Donnelly, 1997). It is the worker's perception of organizational membership that is the key, and that is directly affected by the way information is exchanged.

Everything that occurs in the organizational environment is individually interpreted by its members relative to their personal hopes, fears, values, and aspirations. Thus, a seemingly innocuous comment by a manager may trigger deep-seated fear in a subordinate that severely impairs that person's productivity. Understanding those with whom you communicate is crucial, because otherwise you may not frame messages the right way. Individuals analyze what they see around them. Based on the information they have, or are provided, they make value judgments about the organization, their place in it, and their relationships with other members. At the same time, most people in organizations try to get along socially. Despite those occasions when people come in direct conflict with one another, generally they attempt to minimize social friction among themselves.

The result is usually a kind of work collegiality allowing individual organizational members to maintain a kind of neutrality. They try not to offend others overtly by their actions, while they avoid getting too close personally (Trujillo, 1983). Work relationships are often cordial, even friendly, while maintaining a certain amount of social distance to keep the work relationships in a "professional" context. Indeed, it may be advisable for media organization members to make sure they do that. Because of the shift nature of much of media work, there can be a tendency for night shift journalists to socialize together in their free time, which is when most other people are working. The danger is there is no escape from the concerns of work, no real time away from job-related issues, as off-work conversations inevitably become work centered. When you spend your free time around those with whom you share your work time, there is obviously a narrowing of focus toward commonalties.

Conflict Is Not All Bad

The view of conflict has changed throughout the development of management theory to the current concept of its being a positive force if kept at a moderate level. That way employees retain conviction and are willing to champion causes and take risks, but not to the degree they rebelliously disrupt the organization and render it dysfunctional (Bergman & Volkema, 1989). The goal in managing conflict is for companies to "develop strong cultures to gain the commitment not the compliance of employees" (Tjosvold, 1989, p. 3). But management often has an illusion of how conflict is perceived. Perspective is relative to the position of the person doing the evaluating. Thus, the first step in improving communication is to seek out and understand the viewpoint of those being managed. You should not expect to affect positively those you do not understand. You cannot look down from the top of an organization and see it as do those looking up from the bottom. The superior manager works hard at doing all he or she can to see the world from the perspective of those being managed.

Some major roadblocks to motivation are bound up in the communication process. Those include inconsistency in policy and decision making, management decisions that are seen by employees as thoughtless, management that is distant or unclear, a lack of a sense of teamwork, the lack of recognition at the individual level, and the lack of opportunity to grow (Persico, 1990). You can see that all those things are directly dependent upon the way information is communicated in the organization. They are all subject to individual interpretation. What is one person's "thoughtless management decision" may be a well-considered matter to another, depending on the information each person has available on which to base his or her judgment and position in the organization. There is a positive relationship between employee satisfaction and productivity (Hultman, 1988). That may be negatively affected when managers do not communicate effectively.

Communication also has a "symbiotic relationship with conflict" (Putnam, 1989, p. 67). The way the communication process takes place can eliminate conflict issues, hold them neutral, or exacerbate them. How you say, write, or otherwise communicate a point of view is often as important as what is actually contained in the message. As Carey (1989) emphasized, "communication is a symbolic process whereby reality is produced, maintained, repaired, and transformed" (p. 23). It is conveyed through both our body language and linguistic utterances. It is highly abstract and inherently complex.

Communication is the process of transferring meaning from one person to another. But what one individual sends isn't necessarily what another person receives, regardless of channel noise. We are symbolic creatures and communication is an abstract activity. People sense things differently. Often what the sender thought he or she sent is not what the receiver understands from the message. If you think for a moment, you'll quickly recall some instance when you misunderstood what someone else meant, or another person misunderstood you. Because we are emotion-laden human beings, our personal experience and attitude color our interpretations. Indeed, the seemingly simple effort to have an ordered transmission of meaning is anything but simple.

In the simplest communication a message goes from a sender, through a channel, to a receiver. Within that channel, noise affects the message clarity. That noise can be technologically induced, such as static on the radio or a corrupted computer file with missing sections and strange characters appearing here and there on the screen. Or the noise may be emotionally induced. For example, if an employee is under a lot of financial stress, he or she may be paranoid about possibly losing his or her job. The person's anxiety is increased, and productivity may suffer. Such an individual may read a lot more into a terse comment than was really there. So message clarity is affected by both physical and emotional noise. Also, regardless of channel noise, message interpretation by both sender and receiver complicates the communication process.

Media Manager Communication Roles

The media manager serves a multiplicity of communicative roles. He or she monitors the various information channels available, disseminates the information to others, and serves as a spokesperson for various factions within the organization, and often externally as the organizational representative to those outside (Trujillo, 1983). Whatever is communicated, or not communicated, by a media manager has an effect. "People want to know what the problem is, why they are being asked to do certain things, how they relate to the larger picture" (Gardner, 1988, p. 224). And when they are not given messages that are clear to them, the rumor mill often turns out fabrications. Those fictions can quickly take on organizational legitimacy, gaining validity among organizational members as they are passed from one person to the next. As discussed earlier, one of the best ways to keep rumors under control is fostering communication flow. Conversely, one of the surest ways to cause rumors to spread is for management to restrict information. When organizational members are curious about something they perceive as either important or confusing, the grapevine often provides the answers, since "in general, rumors are grounded in a combination of uncertainty and anxiety" (Stohl & Redding, 1987, p. 481).

Part of the communicative difficulty for media managers, particularly for middle managers at the department head level, is that the job is a boundary-spanning one, serving both the managers above and subordinates below. So effective managers must learn how to stand, metaphorically, with one foot in the newsroom and one in the publisher's office. It is an odd feeling, to be part of two distinctly different sides of a media organization and not really feel completely part of either. But that is the reality for many media managers. And, as such, they "must learn early to cross boundaries and to know many worlds" (Gardner, 1988, p. 225). In effect, midlevel managers (e.g., department heads and first-line supervisors) walk a high wire of trust that, unless balanced upon with great care, can cause them to slip into extremely negative consequences; "zealous subordinates, trying to interpret vague statements from the top, frequently take strong action in the wrong direction" (Kanter, 1988, p. 410). This is just one example of *balancing on the wire.*

MEDIA ORGANIZATION POWER DISTRIBUTION

One of the most interesting dynamics in human relationships is that of power. In its simplest form, power is that quality enabling one person to get another to do something. Powerful people are those who can get others to do what they want them to do in a wide range of ways, from direct coercion to the loosest form of collective consensual decision making. Some powerful individuals are commanding and charismatic, while others are barely noticeable to anyone outside the group. For purposes of this discussion, power is considered to be everywhere, touching everything in sometimes discreet ways. So what is the difference between power and control? One of the most succinct definitions of the interrelationship of power, control, and organizational members is provided by Tompkins and Cheney (1985):

> We define the noun *power* as an ability or capacity to achieve some goal even against the resistance of others; we define the verb *control* as the exercise or act of achieving a goal; we define the direct object of control as those members who can provide services essential to organizational goal attainment. Organizational power then is the ability or capacity of a person or persons to control the contributions of others toward a goal. (p. 180, emphasis in original)

Although you may have thought of power as a thing held by those in charge, it is also held by those who are not. Power comes in many forms in human relations (Cobb, 1986). Within the organizational framework, power and communication are closely interrelated. The exercise of power uses communication channels to convey meaning to organizational members. At the same time, the power structures create, validate, and shift the communication channels to suit their needs. Both are omnipresent in various forms and levels throughout the organization (Frost, 1987).

The possession, control, and use of power are much more than ordering people around. Power is complicated in that it comes in many forms and degrees. Everyone has some kind of power, even if it is the power not to do something and, in the process of withholding one's effort, having a direct effect on what happens. When another's power is resisted, that is a use of power on the part of those no longer accepting another's attempt to influence them. Rebellion is an exercise of power, whether it is to overthrow a government, oust management at a shareholders' meeting, or reduce the quality of work and do a job only "by the book."

Types of Power

Researchers have investigated organizational power and have broken it down into various categorizations (Pfeffer, 1992; Kanter, 1979; Kotter, 1977). Power is produced by a mixture of factors. They include at least the following factors, but others as well: the person's ability to do a job; attractiveness to others, which may include physical looks as well as social interaction skill; an individual's work ethic through which respect is earned for diligence and dedication; the person's formal role or title.

In the literature of power, there are many different approaches to analyzing power. One separates an individual's personal power from the position power relative to his or her official rank. Personal power may include an individual's expertise, personality, work ethic, and how he or she fits into the work culture. Position power, on the other hand, includes factors relative to the person's official place in the organization, with its attendant factors of centrality, criticality, flexibility, visibility, and relevance, further defined in Figure 6.3 (Whetten & Cameron, 1995). As you consider these, think about the range of people who may have all these qualities.

Centrality—The person is the hub of information, at the center of things and around whom the organization seems to turn. If it happens, this person knows about it and is sought out by others.

Criticality—The person is critical to the daily accomplishment of organizational activity. The person who controls office supplies is critical to the person who needs some. Power is not only vested in those at the policy level.

Flexibility—The range of options a person has for accomplishing daily work; if an individual has significant discretion in the way things are done, he or she has flexibility in work flow and, thus, power over it.

Visibility—Others in the organization see the person as having influence over them and the accomplishment of tasks.

Relevance—The individual is relevant to organizational priorities, daily work processes, and organizational success.

Figure 6.3 Position Power Factors
(Source: Whetten & Cameron, 1995, pp. 307–315)

Clearly, a secretary may be one of the most powerful people in an organization. The secretary is often central to the action, is so critical to daily work flow that things don't get done when she or he is sick, has daily contact with most organizational members (high visibility), and is perceived as instrumental in getting things accomplished (the person to whom others go for everything from pens and paper to appointments with the boss). Rank and role are very different ways to analyze and understand power. It is one thing for a chief executive officer to order something by virtue of that person's hierarchical position and quite another for a computer systems engineer to shut down an entire company because she finds a problem on the main file server. Both have power, but very different kinds. Some power is based on legal authority of duly elected or appointed leaders, and some is rooted in knowledge or relationships. The application of power can be direct or indirect but always requires an agent to apply it to accomplish something. Power agents come in all sizes, forms, and job descriptions. A manager may be a power agent and so, too, may be the janitor. What matters is what happens when that power is used.

The literature on power provides numerous discussions of categorizations of power and ways of understanding it. One of the most useful continues to be the seminal typology devised by French and Raven (1959). It transcends both personality and position and can be used in virtually any human collective to understand better why things happen the way they do. As you consider the five types of power that are applied in most situations, to varying degrees, consider how each may be used formally or informally. They include: legitimate power, reward power, coercive power, expert power, and referent power (see Fig. 6.4).

Legitimate power—Officially acquired through title or formal role.

Reward power—The ability to provide something beneficial to another. Often tied to legitimate power, but not always.

Coercive power—The ability to affect another negatively; like reward power, it may or may not be controlled by formal managers.

Expert power—The power of knowledge over those who do not know as much and therefore must defer to the expert's point of view.

Referent power—Centered in an individual's attractiveness to others. When people are so liked that others seek out their opinions and accept their views, they have considerable social power.

Figure 6.4 French and Raven Typology of Power
(Source: French & Raven, 1959)

Legitimate Power

Legitimate power is that accorded by title or official role of an individual. A king has legitimate power by virtue of being king. So, too, does the President of the United States have substantial legitimate power to fill many government jobs, command the armed forces, and conduct the official business of the nation's highest elected office. In a media organization, the editor of a newspaper has substantial legitimate power over both the daily production of the paper and its long-term philosophical approach, and an individual beat reporter has legitimate power vested in the specific responsibilities that person is assigned. Legitimate power is usually defined hierarchically, that is, by the organization chain of command, with each person's legitimate power subservient to his or her immediate superior. That's really what a chain of command is, an official list of who reports to whom and, thereby, who has power over whom.

An individual may have legitimate power over another person or group of people, but that does not ensure subordinates will do everything possible to support their superior. Numerous governments have been toppled by less well equipped and trained revolutionaries. As dictators, generals, and charismatic leaders have experienced, it is one thing to have the power to order something to be done and quite another to get subordinates to carry out the order with passion, conviction, and a drive to perfection. Thus, legitimate power only goes so far.

Reward Power

The power to reward is usually vested in the person holding legitimate power. The boss gives raises and promotions based on his or her perception of subordinate achievement. However, it is a separate kind of power that is frequently delegated. A committee of peers may have the power to reward a promotion, raise, or work certification. In union organizations there is a power to reward in the granting of a journeyman's card, which then opens up opportunities for the person beyond what an apprentice may anticipate. In media organizations the power to reward may be held by individuals below the department head level who handle the job tasking of others such as a city desk editor, assignment manager, or chief photographer. On an even more personalized level, people who work well together often use their power to reward by providing superior work to those they personally prefer. A reporter who is well liked by a photographer may get higher-quality pictures than the photographer might shoot for a person he or she dislikes. We reward those we respect and/or like with our greater cooperation and effort. The power to reward, which at first blush seems a managerial power, is often bound up within the dynamics of ordinary personal relationships.

Coercive Power

Coercive power is the power to punish and usually includes such things as not promoting, administering suspensions or demotions, or firing. However, it can also include personal attacks, ostracisim, or other subtle forms of negative consequences. Whenever an act of retribution is taken, it is exercising the power to punish. When parents ground a teenager for doing something the parents don't like, they are exercising the power to punish. When a person convicted of a capital crime is executed, the ultimate power to punish is being exercised. But between those ends of the coercive power continuum are many degrees and types of coercive power at the organizational and personal levels. In media organizations a person can be changed to a less appealing beat, or a story can be broken down into a form where the reporter isn't identified. Having your name on a story as a byline is a kind of reward, while not getting a byline may be a way of saying "your work just isn't up to par these days." Sometimes people fall from grace in an organization, and coercive power is used to motivate them to quit. It's less risky, in terms of legal complications, if a person quits and less expensive in terms of severance pay or other expenses incurred by layoffs or outright firing. So a strong reporter who has been labeled as a troublemaker may get reassigned to pedestrian stories while others get the choice assignments. If you've been the star state house reporter and suddenly find yourself writing filler material, you may be experiencing someone else's power to punish. However, there are legal consequences for some coercive power actions. See Chapter 16, "Contract and Employment Law," for more discussion of this area. It is also advisable to consult corporate personnel managers and an attorney prior to using coercive power.

Expert Power

This is one of the most interesting forms of power, for it is not based on holding a certain position in the organization or having a title. People who know their jobs especially well, who have developed exceptional skill at something upon which the organization relies, have expert power. As technology advanced, the production of a mass media product became the realm of specialists. In the Middle Ages, before the invention of the printing press, monks hand copied books. It was very tedious, took years of sitting with pen and ink, and required exquisite handwriting skill. Books cost, literally, a small fortune and were individual works of art. After the printing press was invented, other special skills became important as the age of scribes passed. Before the invention of the offset press, linotype operators held considerable expert power when newspaper copy had to be keyed into a machine that then created lines of type from molten lead (Emery & Emery, 1996). A century ago, no one had heard of a computer, but today most large media organizations have computer specialists to keep all the file servers, terminals, and sophisticated programming functioning. In contemporary media organizations the computer specialist can cause a lot of problems if he or she suddenly announces, "We have a hard drive problem. We'll have to shut down the system." That is a form of expert power, which can be wielded by the expert in both legitimate and illegitimate ways.

Expert power, though, is usually much more subtle in its application. People who really know how to do things within an organization become well recognized by organizational members and their opinions are sought out when something happens. These "experts" are listened to, and their opinions often hold considerable sway in the prevailing attitude of the work culture. When a radio station engineer says it would be inadvisable to try to get an audio signal out of some remote location, expert power is at play. What is important to keep in mind for you as a media manager is that experts come in many forms and in many contexts in a media organization. It is important to know who the experts are, in terms of technology and in terms of organizational culture. They are the people to whom others look for advice and counsel because they are perceived to be more knowledgeable and, therefore, are more credible. Having those individuals on your side can really help you, while strong opposition from them can doom your efforts.

Referent Power

This final category of power is often connected to expert power but is, nonetheless, separate. It is the power of personality and style. Some individuals acquire followers due to their ability to form positive personal relationships. Their attitude, behavioral style, or any number of other things separately or in combination may make them particularly appealing to their coworkers. Often those with this form of power have been around for a while and have some amount of expert power, too. Regardless, others use them as a reference when there are questions, new developments, or other issues large or small. Their power is centered in personal magnetism, in their being liked. They are often charismatic figures who have some quality about them that causes others to follow. Referent power is discussed further in the next chapter on leadership regarding charismatic leaders.

Acquiring Power

In media organizations there are normally two power structures at work concurrently. One is the formalized power structure that is obvious to everyone through official titles and positions in the organizational structure. It is the vertical chain of command, or authority line, that flows from the top of the organization down to the bottom. The power that is exercised in this formal, vertical, and official power line is based on each person's position relative to those above and below, and the compliance of subordinates. It is rank centered. One dictionary definition of authority is "the power or right to give commands, enforce obedience, take action, or make final decisions" (*Webster's*, 1994, p. 92). A second, informal power structure, which may not disperse power along the official authority lines, exists in all organizations. It is the informal, organizational culture distribution of power in which personality, job knowledge, and other factors influence to what degree others follow someone's lead in matters large and small. This "shadow" power distribution system may have a substantial effect on organizational performance (Frost, 1987).

It is one thing to consider power distribution in a typical factory production line setting where individual workers have little control over the quality of a specific task, just the speed of it. It is quite another issue in an organization where product quality is more in the hands of the individual worker. In other words, there's a big difference between the power a stamping machine operator has—the control of the machine speed and, therefore, the *quantity* of work—and the power a creative media industry worker has over the *quality* of individual writing or photography. In the latter case, considerable variability is possible depending on worker attitude, because of the creative nature of the end product. A gifted writer has the power to be truly creative or to turn out merely satisfactory copy. Therefore, the successful media manager must have a deeper understanding of the dynamics of power, both formal and informal, and the way in which his or her organization blends official, personal, and creative power within the motivational framework.

Power and motivation, discussed in Chapters 3 and 6, are intertwined. A powerful person motivates others to do something. Very different kinds of people, with very different kinds of behavior, can be powerful. How power is applied has as much to do with the personality involved as anything else. A charismatic individual may be flamboyant and obvious in applying personal power to generate recognition as well as goal achievement. But a more reserved individual may accomplish as much, or more, through careful persuasion, building teams, being sensitive to others, and sharing rewards while avoiding overt, public recognition. Power is a product of organizational resource control, the sociology of relationships, and the dynamics of organizational politics. Because of its complexity and pervasiveness, power eludes simplistic models that work across organizations (Kanter, 1987). Although some aspects of power are common, it is situationally produced. It is multifaceted with manifestations that are obvious to everyone. But at the same time,

> power is a more subtle phenomenon, its origins and impact being embedded in the symbols and systems that evolve out of contests and struggles among organizational actors. Such contests are in many cases preserved and renewed through the perpetuation of earlier power relations, hidden beneath the surface of current organizational functioning. (Frost, 1987, p. 505)

Clearly, from the previous discussion, the five basic types of power are acquired in different ways and in different degrees. They can also be held in various combinations by single individuals. For example, for a person to hold expert power he or she must first become an expert at something and then be recognized as such. That takes time. Likewise, referent power, which is centered on one's personal relationships and charismatic effect on peers, is time-consuming to acquire. On the other hand, most managers have legitimate power the moment the staff is told they have been named to the position. If a manager is a recognized organizational expert at something, has considerable personal attraction among organizational members, and is favored as a managerial resource by senior executives, he or she has blended three mutually enhancing power bases.

Increasing one's power in the formal structural sense can be less complex and time-consuming than building informal power. However, in highly technical organizations, or those steeped in tradition, the informal "shadow" power structure can be very strong in a kind of counterbalance of management's authority. The very definition of power, as discussed earlier, rests on the ability to get others to do something. The official authority hierarchy of an organization typically provides the manager with responsibility for allocating resources and support, and controlling official information flow. Those are important influence factors on subordinates. But the subordinates have strong influence in the third element of power, the willingness to engage in the work (Kanter, 1979). They control that, to a substantial degree in media organizations, where the quality of the work is much more in the province of the individual.

If, for whatever reason, workers do not cooperate with the supervisor's effort to manage them, organizational effectiveness is reduced. Particularly where there is a relatively rapid turnover of managers, the informal power structure based on expertise and personal relationships among organizational members provides continuity. In some cases it may carry out the daily work despite attempts by managers to change things. Managers may be seen as "just passing through" and therefore only of temporary concern while the work culture endures as members become increasingly reliant on each other for survival. In the last analysis there is a kind of codependency between the formal and informal power structures.

Building Formal Power

Formal managerial power in organizations is defined by being able, by virtue of position, to acquire resources, make decisions, and get or control information (Gibson et al., 1997). So acquiring formal managerial power is based on being recognized as a person worth promoting, or hiring, for a management position. Qualifications and experience certainly do matter in management promotions, but how you are perceived in terms of being a committed organizational member is crucial. Organizations become highly politicized, with corporate game playing a part of daily life. Mintzberg (1983) identified several types of political games that go on inside organizations, including those centered on building bases of power, coalition building, getting a more powerful manager to be your sponsor, and the game of defeating rivals. What is important to understand is that the games go on continually and that doing a good job is not enough. For your career to move forward, you have to be adept at social relationships, building alliances, and building trust among those above and below you in the hierarchy. Additionally, you need to be aware that managing news workers is more difficult, because they tend to be more dependent on their sense of control, autonomy, and relations with coworkers than are other professions (Pollard, 1995). Also, power has an infectious quality in that it expands as people become aware it exists. Thus, if coworkers perceive someone as having power, they will tend to defer to that person's point of view. The applied reality of an individual's power rests on the perception others have of it (Macher, 1986).

Building Personal Informal Power

Building personal informal power requires you to be perceived by others as trustworthy and expert. People in the work environment place great value on those who know what they are doing and can be counted upon. How you get along is as important as what you do. Media organizations, because they generally have well-educated workers engaged in creative efforts, are relationship oriented. Team approaches are common, and the very concept of team fosters mutual interdependence. Thus, expert power and referent power are what have to be developed to become an informal person of power. That means knowing the job better than anyone else and at the same time having strong social skills in relating to others so they look to you for leadership.

To be a truly successful media manager, you need to become powerful in all five areas of the French and Raven typology: legitimate, reward, coercive, expert, and referent. Effective managers are people who want to be in charge but who often use their power in more of a coaching approach to subordinates (Whetten & Cameron, 1995). After all, the job of the manager is not to do, but to get others to do. That means working with subordinates to bring out the best in them by giving them the resources they need, encouraging when necessary, disciplining when necessary, and understanding the world from their perspective. Such individuals reach the pinnacle of organizational power. The problem is there is no simple formula. It is something gained from experience and being aware of others and the organizational personality. It requires all five of the types of power discussed in this chapter, used where appropriate. It is very much a situationally determined part of the great challenge of being a media manager.

Power Seekers

Power seekers commonly are aggressive personalities who want to be where the action is. They are prestige oriented, concerned about job titles, particular automobiles, and memberships in social status organizations that reflect the power they are accumulating. And they typically circulate among several groups or more, with a keen eye on those that add to their power and prestige, which increases their sphere of influence (McClelland, 1975) (see Fig. 6.5).

- Aggressive, competitive-oriented personality.
- A preference for being where the action is.
- Prestige oriented (concerned about titles, possessions that reflect their status).
- Active in joining multiple groups, which increases their sphere of influence.

Figure 6.5 Power Seeker Profile
(Source: McClelland, 1975)

Powerful people typically have a greater sense of autonomy and are prone to exercising greater freedom in decision making. They are more self-confident and are eager to forge ahead. Such individuals often seek out opportunities to champion their ideas and, because of their sense of powerfulness, are willing to take what others would perceive as risks. Tightly structured bureaucracies with substantial hierarchies and sometimes entrenched traditions—large metropolitan daily newspapers, for example—do not always encourage such personalities trying to exercise the power they either feel they have or desire.

The Application of Power

The use of power is an important challenge after acquiring it. Considerable judgment has to be used when exercising power. It is situationally determined. To get the maximum performance out of individuals requires more than ordering them to do something. Although you, as a manager, may have the formal attributes of legitimate, reward, and coercive power over others, to get maximum performance it may not be wise to use those types of power. That may require your informal personal power attributes of expertise and referent power (charisma). Remember the point of the exercise: to get others to do things exceptionally well. When you order people to do something, they may do it, but often only minimally, just enough to stay out of trouble, in effect withholding their true expertise as a form of their exercise of power.

In the fast-changing, dynamic world of American business, people often find themselves in a position of trying to preserve self while being concerned about those who are working for them. Relationships constantly adjust. Changes in the business context may cause alterations in the functional relationships of an organization that affect the balance of power among those who depend on one another (Kanter, 1988). In other words, as the situation changes, so do the power relationships. Power, or the lack of it, are not static conditions but tend to expand themselves. That is,

> power is likely to bring more power, in ascending cycles, and powerlessness to generate powerlessness, in a descending cycle. The powerful have "credibility" behind their actions, so they have the capacity to get things done. . . . The coping mechanisms of low power are also those most likely to provoke resistance and further restriction of power. (Kanter, 1987, p. 308)

When organizations become large and multilayered, there are a lot of vested interests in maintaining the status quo. The less powerful, who tend to acquiesce to the prevailing attitudes and ideas, may be perceived as more reliable in bureaucratic organizations as the culture rewards those who go along with the system. They may be more reticent to try things and may prefer a structured environment with close supervision, rule-bound behavior, and narrow areas of responsibility (Argyris, 1964). The difference in how the powerful and less powerful engage with the work environment can have a profound effect. Interestingly, when the degree of supervision is relaxed to the point where even the less powerful have a greater sense of autonomy, their sense of power may grow with a concurrent experience of greater job satisfaction (Worthy, 1950). In effect, expanding the trust relationship, allowing people to feel they are more responsible for their actions, can produce higher-quality work. Based on what is known about psychological motivation, such individuals no longer attempt to be minimalists at their jobs, hiding within the safety of bureaucratic process and structure, but gain in confidence and raise the quality of their work despite the bureaucracy.

Bringing about such a change in the way people approach their work in an organizational context is not necessarily all that difficult. The basic ingredient is relieving their fear of risk, usually with small changes in how they are managed. By giving subordinates a greater sense of trust and empowerment, in effect providing them positive self-esteem incentives as organizational members, you may dramatically improve the quality of their general attitude and the quality of their work because their fear of survival is eased.

> Small changes in behavior aided by positive incentives can cause lasting personal changes when they inaugurate individuals into new social relationships. The incentive and modeling influences within this new social reality expand and sustain the new patterns of behavior. (Bandura, 1986, p. 260)

ORCHESTRATING COMMUNICATION AND POWER

Clearly, much of what goes on in an organization occurs without management's direct control. As we have discussed so far in this chapter, organizational members define much of the communication activity and content, as well as significant amounts of the power relationships within an organization. Management, despite the impression that many people seem to have, is not as much a command-and-control role as a coordinating one. The truly effective manager is aware of the personalities within the organization and the perceptions and value systems at work among members of the organizational culture and applies that knowledge to get things done with a minimum of resistance (Whetten & Cameron, 1995).

Consider the metaphor of a symphony orchestra. Various string, woodwind, horn, and percussion instruments are used to play different parts of a symphony. The individual musicians are highly trained experts whose technical skill on their respective instruments usually exceeds that of the orchestra conductor. But the conductor is the specialist in blending all the others into mutually compatible sounds that together are more powerful than any are separately. So, too, the manager of an organization is a highly knowledgeable individual who brings together sometimes very diverse people and units to achieve what they could not alone. Managing, like conducting, is the art of pulling together all the diversity at hand to fashion a cohesive and superbly effective unit of mutually compatible entities.

Organizational life is a dynamic experience. As the environment adjusts, the organization flexes with it. That is particularly true in the highly competitive media arena where technological innovation is a continuous process of creating new media competitors and forms. The balance of organizational power constantly adjusts among people who depend on one another across functions. That makes team management particularly important. Coordination is crucial and cannot happen without good communication flow and the use of power to orchestrate the necessary actions and reactions.

Obstacles to Communication

There are obstacles to communication that are tied in with individual values and perceptions (see Fig. 6.6). They can reduce communication effectiveness in a number of ways, from slight distortion to complete blocking of intended meaning. First, each individual's values and experiences provide different receiver contexts. Everything else remaining constant, what two different people understand can vary significantly. Then people tend to screen out information based on their own wants, needs, fears, or expectations. We all practice selective listening, selective perception, and selective action based on what something means to us individually. See Chapter 3 of this text, "Human Influences on Media Organizations," for a review of the perceptions of reality, selective influence theory, and the way in which individual and organizational values contribute to human interaction.

The abstract nature of human communication means that some groups have specialized language, acronyms, or other reference mechanisms used to interpret

1. **Individual screening of information**—Tending to avoid that which conflicts with our predisposition toward something through selective listening, selective perception, and selective action.

2. **Organizational hierarchy**—You can't always get to the person with whom you need to communicate.

3. **Specialized language/symbolism of the organization**—Makes understanding difficult for new members or outsiders.

4. **Time constraints**—Haste interferes with message clarity and may add to confusion through misunderstanding.

5. **Information/data overload**—Too much information flow creates clutter that has to be sifted to get to that which is relevant.

Figure 6.6 Obstacles to Organizational Communication

organizational meaning. There are influences in how we communicate based on the relative status of those sending us messages, the stress of any time constraints involved, and the sheer volume of messages that innundate us, ranging from simple conversation to extensive reports and data analysis. Through all of this, considerable filtering occurs as we make many decisions every day to get through the clutter of information overload. An information-rich society has the advantage of having a lot of information. But that also means we are deluged with information, not all of it necessary or relevant to the immediate task at hand.

One of the continuing challenges to being a manager is clearing the obstacles to communication. The interrelationship of communication and power means that as communication diminishes, power is eroded. Before you can exert power, you have to be able to communicate what you want to those who must necessarily respond to its application in order to achieve your goals.

Engage with All Communication Networks

One of the first things any successful manager must do is engage with all communication networks, including the rumor mill, to understand what messages are flowing, and where. There is no way you can decide what information to distribute unless you know what information is already in the communication channels. That means auditing the various channels as best you can to understand what is already there or has gone before. That is easier in formal communication, where you can review the previous memos, letters, and other data sources kept on file. But it gets complicated when you attempt to engage with the informal communication patterns, including the rumor mill discussed earlier in this chapter. Because information communication generally takes place person to person, you need to have a trust relationship with someone in the network to have access. That means taking the time to build your alliances and then asking them to let you know what rumors are being circulated. Some organizations have even set up special mailboxes for employees to drop off anonymous notes regarding rumors to which management could respond (Danziger, 1988).

Encourage Information Flow

As a manager, you control a lot of the information that flows to those you supervise. A good policy is to provide as much information as you possibly can, which makes people feel better about being included and also counters the rumor mill. When you decide to restrict information, make sure it is for competitive reasons. For example, if you are working hard to land a particular client for your advertising agency, you may need to keep the name of that client restricted to just a few people. But the fact you are aggressively pursuing future business would be a positive piece of information to increase employee excitement about the firm moving ahead and possibly expanding. On the other hand, if you don't tell anyone anything about trying to develop business, a rumor could start that the firm is in trouble, that nothing is going on. That would increase anxiety and encourage your best employees who can quickly find other employment to do so.

Monitoring the Message Stream

Managers need to pay attention to what happens when information is put out to organizational members. How they react, what they say, and the attendant office gossip that is created around the initial message are forms of feedback. Feedback is nothing more than response from the receiver of a message. It tells you if the message was understood the way you intended and gives you an indication if further communication is necessary. Too often, in vertical communication only limited feedback flows back up the hierarchy. People may be hesitant to tell the boss something they think will be perceived negatively. They'll say everything is fine, when in fact they are furious. Attributable feedback up the organizational hierarchy typically comes from people who do not feel at risk for doing so. If you don't feel in danger of being fired, there is a higher probability you will open up and give honest opinions about organizational concerns. However, if you are concerned your superior may be irritated at what you have to say, and it could result in your being reprimanded or fired, you will probably keep your opinions to yourself.

As a manager it is important that you do everything you can to keep the emotional restrictions on feedback to you at a minimum. You need honest people telling you what's going on, not just massaging your managerial ego by telling you what you want to hear. Some managers are very good at interpersonal relations and are able to get their subordinates to open up to them. Others may accomplish the same thing by encouraging anonymous mail from subordinates, or some other technique for encouraging honesty rather than political correctness. Political correctness in organizational management is a serious social disease that produces a surface illusion of pleasant agreement, which may mask a strong undertow of discord. You want to know what your subordinates are thinking, not merely their political posturing. Organizational information flows adjust to fit the needs and perceptions of organizational members, so it is paramount you encourage honest, forthright information exchange focused on optimizing organizational performance (Mishra, 1990; Stohl & Redding, 1987).

One of the most important management skills is listening. If you don't listen, you can't hear what others are trying to tell you, directly or indirectly. And you have to actively solicit subordinates to communication with you. That means asking the right questions so you can get the answers you need. Many people are hesitant to initiate communication with a boss. That is not only because the boss has considerable power over a subordinate's future but also because of concern for the way other employees will react. Many work environments have an atmosphere of division between management and workers, a kind of us versus them mentality. Approaching managers, or appearing to be friendly to them, can be perceived as trying to curry favor from the opposition.

As a manager you will have to initiate much of the communication that takes place with subordinates, particularly early on in the relationship when they are still making up their minds about you. So how do you get people who don't know you very well to tell you what you really need to know? First, reduce their sense of risk by allaying their fears about their job security. Representing yourself as a caring, coaching kind of manager will go a long way toward easing fears about you. But along with being empathetic toward your subordinates, you have to ask the right questions.

Close-Ended Questions

When you are after facts that are not products of value judgments, direct questions are best. "Where were you born?" is an example. Another would be, "How much did we spend on overtime last month?" No emotional, value-laden interpretation of reality should cloud the answer. You're seeking plain, unadorned information, often of a quantitative nature that is specific and easy to define. Close-ended questions are relatively simple and matter-of-fact with the information preferred by the questioner readily apparent (Hsia, 1988).

Open-Ended Questions

Much of what a manager in a media organization has to do deals with human relations and the way creative people interpret the actions of others and the company. In those value-laden situations, you need to get people to tell you what they're thinking, and that is not usually simple, nor necessarily matter-of-fact.

One of the most effective ways is to use what are called open-ended questions (see Fig. 6.7). That means the questions do not specify an answer nor betray the values or preferences of the person asking them. So the respondent is free to answer any way he or she wants to. With open-ended questions there are no right or wrong answers, but rather complete respondent freedom to frame the context and meaning of the answer (Hsia, 1988). Usually, open-ended questions are fairly general in nature, though they may be focused on a certain area of interest. Typically they seek qualitative respondent meaning, not straightforward quantitative data.

- Do not indicate questioner's preference for an answer or opinion.

- Respondent is free to answer any way he or she wants to.

- No right or wrong answers. The respondent provides the meaning while the questioner maintains complete neutrality. You are after the respondent's view, not merely reinforcement for what the questioner prefers.

- Questions usually seek qualitative meaning, a person's perspective on something, not straight-forward, quantitative data.

Figure 6.7   Open-ended Questions

The following examples illustrate effective open-ended questions. Note how you cannot tell where the questioner stands on the subject and how sometimes the question actively elicits the person's personal view, in effect granting the right to provide personal perspective.

1. In your view, what should our policy be regarding community journalism?

2. How would you describe the situation?

3. What do you think the ideal job would be?

4. From your perspective, what can we do to solve the problem?

5. If you were the publisher, what would be the first thing you'd do to resolve this?

Once you get information flowing from the respondent's perspective, more direct follow-up questions may be necessary to expand the information. For example, if you initially ask a person, "What do you think is the problem here?" the answer might be, "Senior management!" Then you have to follow up with something like, "What do you mean by that?" or "Well, what specifically do they do that irritates you?" You have to be very careful in using open-ended questions to make sure they are just that, open-ended without betraying any opinion on your part. Once the person being asked the questions has a feeling for what you want to hear, you'll usually get it. But you don't need an echo of yourself, you need their honest perspective.

Now, to reinforce the neutral nature of open-ended questions, consider the following pairings of the previous five examples of open-ended questions, with a close-ended way of rephrasing. Assume you are an employee of the person asking the questions. Answer each separately. Then consider how the close-ended version signals the boss's preference and you, wanting to have your career advance and get that raise next month, respond.

1. In your view, what should our policy be regarding community journalism?

   Close-ended version: Community journalism is just a marketing ploy, don't you think?

2. How would you describe the situation?

   Close-ended version: What a bunch of idiots. Can you believe they blew that?

3. What do you think the ideal job would be?

   Close-ended version: I want to put you in charge of editing. It'd be a great opportunity for you, don't you agree?

4. From your perspective, what can we do to solve the problem?

   Close-ended version: It's clear to me the reporters are just lazy. Let's rotate the beats. Do you want Smith on society or criminal courts?

5. If you were the publisher, what would be the first thing you'd do to resolve this?

   Close-ended version: I'm going to subcontract subscriber distribution to the Post Office to get rid of our regular carriers. Good idea for a daily newspaper, don't you think?

When you're first working with this technique, you may want to write out a very direct question you'd like to ask someone and then rewrite it in an open-ended format so your opinion is not revealed. If you ask "How are things going for you?" you have signaled you really want the other person's perspective. But if you say "Things are going fine, aren't they?" you are really demanding the other person agree with you or find themselves in the middle of an argument. "What do you think this means?" solicits their opinion with no telegraphing of preferences. "How would you describe what's going on?" also encourages them to provide their interpretation freely. Those are two very different questions from "Don't you think this is dumb?" or "It looks to me like creative services is just playing games with the numbers, don't you agree?" If you ask "What's your spin on this?" you will probably get a very different answer than if you say "I think this is just ridiculous. What's your spin on it?"

If you, as a manager, let your sentiments show, you'll tend to hear a lot of agreement as your subordinates jump on the boss's bandwagon to raises and career development. That's not good for you or the organization. You need honest, and forthright points of view from subordinates you trust and who trust you. You need their unfettered expertise and their full contribution, not merely their politically correct manipulation of you. Otherwise you are just reinforcing mediocrity.

You must be clear in the messages you send and send them through multiple channels. The more people hear a message in the various networks with which they are engaged, the more likely they will be to believe it. That's particularly true when what is sent down through the formal channels is reinforced by information flowing through the informal networks. And you have to encourage honest, forthright information flowing back to you through the trust relationships you build and techniques such as open-ended questions that encourage people to give their honest perspective.

Building "Stakeholder" Relationships

One of the most effective ways to increase the sense of power employees have is to help them increase the perception of themselves as "stakeholders" in the success of the organization. Peter Drucker (1988b) coined the term to describe organizational members who are, in effect, psychological part owners. They see the success of the organization, and the success of themselves, tied together. When that occurs, a cause/effect relationship is developed that benefits both. But a critical element to stakeholder development is building trust, which contributes to the sense of increased power. In order for employees to buy into the organization as mutually beneficial partners, they have to have a sense of commitment from both management and their peers. But that is particularly difficult when the operational environment is under stress. When there are rumors of layoffs, or the euphemisms "downsizing" and "rightsizing," or the competitive environment is substantially intensified, the sense of being at risk grows. The very time when you need more trust and mutual reliability within an organization to respond to serious challenge is when it is harder to generate because of the external threat to organizational success (Weick, 1988). Somehow the various "stakeholders"—members of the organization from top to bottom—"have to be brought into the management process" (Drucker, 1988b, p. 11). When employees don't have confidence in themselves or trust management, they

> frequently perform below potential to avoid exposure, and they resist change because of a fear of performing poorly. Lack of confidence leads to avoidance values as people seek to protect their self-esteem, and on-the-job performance inevitably drops. (Hultman, 1988, p. 36)

Whenever there is a major change in the corporate climate of a company, perhaps caused by new ownership or a senior management change, typically managers and other power holders adjust their relationships to fit the new situation. The normal flexing of power relationships takes on a whole new dimension as realignment occurs throughout the organization. People seek out those they feel they can trust to help them survive the discontinuity of change. In colloquial terms, when the chips are down you want to know who you can count on. As the stress of uncertainty increases it logically follows that those with referent power, mentioned earlier, become more important due to the higher degree of trust and reliance others place in them (Kanter, 1987).

COMMUNICATION STRATEGIES FOR MANAGERS

We all implement different strategies in our efforts to communicate and, through that communication, exercise power to one degree or another. Managers need to understand the various communication approaches people employ so they can respond accordingly. Nine different strategies have been identified that are used on both the individual and organizational levels. In practice they are usually blended into various combinations to fit the situation. Because we are symbolic beings with a lot of experience communicating with one another, we aren't always conscious of the technique we use at a given time but naturally apply it based on the feedback we are receiving from whomever we are attempting to communicate to and influence. The nine communication strategies are:

reason, coalition building, ingratiating, bargaining, assertiveness, invoking higher authority, sanctions, altruism, and circumventing (Frost, 1987). See Figure 6.8 for more on the differences among the strategies.

1. **Reason**—The use of factual information to support one's argument.

2. **Coalition building**—Getting other people in the organization to join in support of one's point of view.

3. **Ingratiating**—Attempting to generate goodwill toward the communicator through good impressions, using flattery, or otherwise gaining the favor of someone higher in rank and/or power.

4. **Bargaining**—Exchanging benefits and/or favors to get the desired result. This is often connected to coalition building.

5. **Assertiveness**—Applying whatever power, or the impression of it, that is necessary to get what's desired.

6. **Invoking higher authority**—Using higher-ranking allies, or the impression they are available if necessary, to pressure others into going along.

7. **Sanctions**—The threat of something to cause acceptance.

8. **Altruism**—Appealing to personal relationships or loyalty, such as asking someone to "do this for me," or "do this for the good of the organization."

9. **Circumventing**—Going around the real issue to achieve indirectly the desired result by other means.

Figure 6.8 Communication Strategies
(Source: Frost, 1987, p. 522)

The order of the strategies is meaningful in that generally within organizational contexts individuals proceed down through the strategies from reason toward circumventing until they get the results they want. So, if reasoning works, there's no need to shift to coalition building. However, as individuals move to each successive step they typically begin blending attributes of the different strategies. For example, reasoning may not convince your boss of the wisdom of what you want, but it may help build a coalition of support among others, and together you may try to bargain with the boss in an ingratiating way, at first, and then using the strength of numbers more assertively later.

The effective use of the communication strategies is crucial for a manager. Communication is involved in nearly everything a manager does, to one degree or another. One analysis of 402 managers identified by their peers and supervisors as highly effective resulted in a top ten list of the areas where managers should focus their skill-building efforts. Of the top ten, four were directly tied to the managers' communicative ability: "verbal communication . . . recognizing, defining, and solving problems . . . motivating and influencing others . . . setting goals and articulating a vision" (Whetten & Cameron, 1995, p. 8). Together the management skill areas involving communication comprise 40 percent of the top ten list.

The second key communication focus for you as a manager is information sifting. Managers get an enormous amount of communications. A half-century ago managers had to deal with interpersonal communication, the telephone, letters, and memos.

Today, a manager has all of that, as well as faxes and the growing use of electronic mail. What's more, beepers and cellular telephones, while enabling us to stay in touch, also make it more difficult to escape all of those trying to get us to do things or effectively screen out what we don't want to receive.

One study found that electronic mail, voice mail, faxes, and the burgeoning Internet may actually be decreasing efficiency and frustrating workers because of the information overload. The new communication innovations haven't replaced old forms, but added to them. Seven out of ten workers indicated they are overwhelmed with all the communications, "creating a corporate world where many executives and managers feel crushed by the volume of communications bombarding them" (Woodward, 1997, p. B-5).

Clearly, sifting the truly important communications from the rest is an essential management skill. The question to ask yourself is, "Do I personally have to be concerned with this?" If the answer is no, it's junk communications and should be discarded just as you throw out the mass of junk mail that clutters up your mailbox every day. Elsewhere in this text we have repeatedly stressed the importance of empowering your employees as a motivational device. Empowering them to take care of their jobs, make decisions, and handle all communications that do not absolutely have to involve you increases their sense of importance, transfers decision making down to the lowest possible level, and relieves you of a lot of communications pressure. The result is more time for you to think about what needs to be managed, rather than simply trying to cope with the multitude of things others could be doing. Along with managing the workload of others, you have to manage your own.

CHAPTER SUMMARY

Each of us has different experiences and knowledge that provide the foundation of our future development. The effective manager understands that some management skills are not as well developed as others and works to improve himself or herself. Being a manager is a process of constant growing, learning, and maturing through experience and self-examination. And once you learn something new, repetition and practice are necessary—a kind of mileage-building process—to make the new or improved skill an inherent part of our expanded self. Particularly when you are under stress, what is called a "dominant response pattern" will emerge. That means you rely on behavior patterns that are entrenched in your perception of the world and have proven effective in the past. So, despite an intellectual analysis of a new situation, people tend to fall back on the solutions that worked before (Straw, Sandelands, & Dutton, 1981; Whetten & Cameron, 1995). The result can be catastrophic in dynamically changing environments.

Clearly, managers benefit from engaging in developmental programs to expand skills and response options. The quality of a group's work is a product of the individual efforts of those within it. Thus,

individual performance contributes to group performance, which in turn contributes to organizational performance. In truly effective organizations, however, management helps create a positive synergy, that is, a whole that is greater than the sum of its parts. (Gibson, Ivancevich, & Donnelly, 1994, p. 18)

One solution to problems involving poor communication, interpersonal tension, lack of trust, and general misunderstanding is for managers to increase their understanding of how people vary in personal values, learning styles, and response toward change (Whetten & Cameron, 1995).

Although the concepts of communication and power have been discussed separately to help you understand their various attributes and influences, the reality of daily life in organizational settings is that they are always connected. All communication relating to organizational processes, relationships, and information, whether formal or informal, fact based, or part of the rumor mill, in some way contributes to the decision-making process. Thus, communication, power, and the resulting decision making that occurs continuously on all levels of an organization, are intertwined and inseparable (Tompkins & Cheney, 1983). If you understand the essentials of how organizational members share information (communicate), and how they influence one another to achieve their respective ends (power), the path to success should be readily apparent.

As a manager you are going to have to make decisions or contribute to them. To do so you will have to work within the organization's communication and power relationships. As much as three-quarters of your time as a manager will be spent in some form of communication activity (Culnan & Markus, 1987). At the very core of an organization "messages establish functional relationships through which individuals manage and coordinate their activities as they strive to accomplish personal, group, or organizational goals" (Stohl & Redding, 1987, p. 460). In other words, the most important thing you do as a manager is communicate. All other things relate to it and/or depend on it, including the amount of power you have interpersonally and organizationally.

Consider the following guidelines to help you more effectively engage with others, as a member and/or a manager, in the fascinating and complex environment of media organizations.

♦ Build up your organizational power with both superiors and subordinates by expanding your job expertise, your personal relationships, and the perception others have of you as a hard worker and a team player.
♦ Increase your visibility in the organization by staying close to the center of things, being part of critical decision making, and accepting or volunteering for assignments closely tied to meeting organizational goals.
♦ In communicating with others, make sure what you really mean is what they understand. When you communicate a message, actively solicit feedback to make sure what others understand is what you intended, and follow up as necessary to clarify and keep track of progress.
♦ Manage the flow of information around you, formal and informal. Knowledge is power for a manager, especially the knowledge of what others believe about organizational concerns. At the same time, a great deal of contemporary communication is clutter that only gets in your way. Sift the meaningful from the irrelevant.
♦ Continuously seek feedback from both subordinates and superiors. All you do affects, is interpreted by, and causes reactions by others.
♦ Empower others. Give subordinates the power to do the work, including the pertinent communicating, and encourage them to exercise it. The real power of management is minimizing its role as organizational members achieve maximum performance with limited supervision. As others draw power from you, they become allies to support your efforts. In other words, you expand your own power, by helping others be more powerful.
♦ Think before you act. Impulsiveness is the great enemy of successful people. Bad decisions tend to flow out of a lack of information, while good decisions tend to rise from a more complete knowledge base.
♦ Be very careful with attitude problems. They are usually caused by power conflicts or communication failures. Do not treat the symptom (the attitude) but look for the underlying disease causing that symptom. But you cannot ignore attitude problems. When someone is not performing, allowing it to continue sets a lower standard and will infect the rest of the organization.
  ♦ First try to help the person improve in a coaching and empathetic manner.
  ♦ If that doesn't work, be more direct and authoritative.
  ♦ Finally, if you cannot turn the individual around, help the rest of the organization by removing him or her. Termination should be a last resort. But, inevitably, in your management career you will find yourself at that juncture with someone.
  ♦ Make sure, if you fire someone, it is unavoidable for the long-term health of the organization.
  🏚

1. Consider the fundamental communication model. Prepare three examples you have experienced where the message that was sent was not what the receiver understood. What was the problem in each case (noise in the channel, misinterpretation by the receiver, lack of clarity by the sender, etc.)?

2. What's the difference between vertical and lateral communication? Which one do you think has the most influence on how media organizational workers exchange information and why?

3. List three negative and three positive aspects of the rumor mill. If you were aware of a rumor about you that was untrue, and personally damaging, how would you handle it?

4. List the five types of power originally defined by French and Raven. Write them down the left side of a piece of notebook paper. Then draw a line down the middle of the remaining space. Label one column "Professional" and the other "Personal."

   a) Now, consider the power you have in both your professional and personal lives and describe that power in two or three sentences for each power type.

   b) Are they different? Does a person have different kinds of power blends in different situations?

   c) What is your weakest "professional" power category, and what should you do to increase it?

   d) What is your weakest "personal" power category, and what should you do to increase it?

5. Make a list of five close-ended questions you'd like to ask in class about this chapter's material.

6. Rewrite each of the questions in number five above into open-ended questions. In your next class discussion, ask some of those open-ended questions of your classmates or your teacher to see if they work.

7. On a piece of notebook paper, write the nine communication strategies down the left side so they are equally spaced on the paper. Across from each strategy write a couple of sentences about a real-life situation you have experienced where that strategy was used.

chapter 7

LEADERSHIP

Leadership is a complex part of human relationships. Leaders emerge and disappear, each historically both a product and cause of his or her individual circumstances. Separating a leader from the context of that individual's rise to preeminence is an impossible task because, like all of us, leaders are products of their experience (Bennis, 1994). If you are a leader, in the true sense of the word, you have a vision of the future and an obsessive nature about achieving it, despite the often countervailing influences of those around you.

> A leader is, by definition, an innovator. He does things other people haven't done or don't do. He does things in advance of other people. He makes new things. He makes old things new. Having learned from the past, he lives in the present, with one eye on the future. And each leader puts it all together in a different way. (Bennis, 1994, p. 143)

Leaders, by virtue of the aspects of their personalities and the context within which they emerge to the front of their followers, are separated from the rest of us to one degree or another. Many leaders have a kind of unintended but unavoidable distance from most of those they lead. Typically, only a few close confidants make up the leader's inner circle. Leading can be a lonely experience. It is not uncommon for a leader to distrust others and develop a siege mentality. Leaders, typically, stand out among others in social groups. They tend not to be compromisers, but drive toward their personal vision dragging everyone else along.

Leaders have always been part of the human experience. They have been credited with larger than life heroic achievement or abysmal failure. Unique figures at critical times have fashioned great political powers, found cures for the ravages of disease, provided civilization with myths and moral lessons, and created corporate entities more powerful than half the world's nations. Leaders are typically remembered in a military/governmental context because historians have tended to evaluate societies based on their political organizations. In ancient times the rulers employed most of the scribes and financially supported the artisans of society. Those people from whose work we draw our inferences about a bygone culture usually wrote about, painted, or sculpted their benefactors. So there is considerable information about the military conquests of Caesar but little about whoever ran his equivalent of an accounting department. Yet that chief accountant may well have been an effective leader. There are leaders, to one extent or another, in every type of human activity.

Through the ages people have been trying to figure out what makes leaders tick. The main reason is the hope that by better understanding leadership we can develop more effective future leaders through proper training and education. Many lists of leader attributes have been made in the attempt to better understand the phenomenon. In the latter part of the 20th century alone, several thousand books and articles have been published on leadership examining the range of leader traits, personal behaviors, situational development, motivational connections, and other theoretical aspects of how one individual comes to lead others (Muczyk & Reimann, 1989). But always, leadership has defied efforts to quantify it. After centuries of effort there is still no fail-safe formula to produce leaders.

The diverse nature of leaders' personalities combines with the course of events to sometimes foster astronomical success or abysmal failure. Leadership is interwoven with the circumstances in which it occurs. Some leaders are recognized as more successful than others because of what they ultimately achieved. But leadership is a journey of taking followers from where the leader finds them to somewhere else. So a leader's effectiveness is better viewed as a process of changes from what prevailed when he or she began to what is ultimately achieved. The leader is one ingredient in the complexity of human endeavor, albeit a critical one. A dynamic leader can move a society from the chaos of revolution, to empire building, and back again. And a superior leader can be overshadowed, or fall, at the hands of a lesser one due to the combination of circumstances at work in a specific time and place.

In the corporate world, because of unique circumstances one person may end up controlling a majority of shares of stock and become the head of a giant company. An individual whose expertise is trading stock and making speculative investments suddenly may direct the creative activities of a media empire with many subdivisions and product lines. Such a person may be an astute financier, but not necessarily a leader with vision to move a media company forward. Meanwhile, a leader personality, who might be much more effective heading such an organization, might never acquire the economic power to take command. In the contemporary media world, financial manipulation may be more of a determinant of who is in control than knowledge of an industry and its peculiarities, or real talent for leading (Auletta, 1991).

When leaders do rise, they sometimes fail not because of their leadership abilities, but because of altered circumstances and environmental changes either they do not anticipate or could not have predicted. One of the greatest military leaders was Napoleon, who ended his life a prisoner on a lonely island. From the depths of the French Revolution he twice rose to dominate Europe. But it was the coolness of the rain, fate determined by weather in a time lacking sophisticated forecasting, that stopped Napoleon at Waterloo. The day before the battle it slowed the French advance and then turned the battlefield muddy, making maneuvering more difficult. The timing of the French battle plan was thrown off, and the potency of their artillery negated. If Waterloo had taken place on dry ground, permitting a more timely attack with more effective cannon fire, the outcome may well have been reversed. The grandeur of the French emperor and his superior military machine were humbled by something beyond his or Wellington's tactics. It was the leaden clouds and hours of pouring rain that turned the tide of battle against the general considered by some the most effective commander since Alexander the Great (Seward, 1986).

A glance at the history of media organizations in America reveals a cycle of great media empires rising and then fading as their environments changed. Horace Greeley was a dynamic figure who created the New York *Tribune* in 1841 and was considered the greatest newspaper editor of his time. After several mergers and ownership changes, the New York *Herald-Tribune* died in 1966. But does that mean Greeley, as a leader, failed because what he created could not endure? Hardly. For most of its 125 years the paper was a major influence on American culture in sometimes dramatic ways. And the environment of newspapering in 1841 was very different from that when the *Herald-Tribune* folded in 1966 (Emery & Emery, 1996).

How does a visionary like Bill Gates of Microsoft rise to multibillionaire heights dominating the worldwide computer industry? By having the right technology and the right business circumstances come together at the right time with his personae, and then maintaining innovation. Leadership succeeds partly through what the ancient Greeks called the "Fates" bringing together all the critical elements. But successful leaders also have a talent for making the most of their timing and circumstance to move their vision forward. "Learning to lead is, on one level, learning to manage change. . . . Unless the leader continues to evolve, to adapt and adjust to external change, the organization will sooner or later stall" (Bennis, 1994, p. 145).

Considering the personalities of the individuals just mentioned, you can see few common traits among them. Bill Gates is a spectacled man you'd hardly notice at a social gathering if no one called attention to him, a typical computer engineer without a particularly striking appearance. Napoleon, by contrast, was short, very dominating, with considerable bravado in the classic image of a military genius. And Horace Greeley, a legendary figure in American newspapers?

> He walked with a shambling, uncertain gait, as though he were feeling his way in the dark. His usual garb was a light-gray "duster," or gown, which he had purchased from an immigrant for $3 and wore winter and summer over his ill-fitting, nondescript suits. His guileless, baby-blue eyes were set in a moonlike face fringed with wispy whiskers sprouting out of his collar like reeds around a mossy stone. A high-pitched whiny voice added nothing to this unimpressive ensemble. Yet this was the man who was to capture the loyalties of newspaper readers, as few editors have in the history of American journalism. (Emery & Emery, 1996, p. 107)

One of the difficulties in understanding leaders from a different time is that we are not part of their context. To really understand Horace Greeley, you have to understand Horace Greeley's era. Consider another man of that age thought to be one of the greatest of American presidents, Abraham Lincoln. Could such a homely, unpretentious person who wrote perhaps his greatest speech, the Gettysburg Address, by hand even be considered a serious candidate in our age of mass-mediated politics featuring speech writers, press secretaries, "spin doctors," and cosmetically correct candidates? It is undeniable that "leadership is not only a function of the leader but also of the complex interaction of the leader, followers, and the historical moment in which they are operating" (Kets de Vries, 1989, p. 190).

THE CONCEPT OF "LEADING"

The English language has included the term "leading" in its lexicon since about 1300. It is the art of persuasion and influence beyond normal lines of authority. It has been defined as the way in which the activities of a group are influenced toward maximum goal achievement in a given situation. Leadership is persuading others to aggressively pursue the leader's goals. What's more, effective leaders are able to get followers to accept the leader's goals as their own (Koontz & O'Donnell, 1978; Locke & Kirkpatrick, 1991; Schachter, 1983; Stogdill, 1950). They are, to put it simply, infectious personalities who transfer their vision and passion to others.

Three keys are necessary to exercise leadership (see Fig. 7.1). First, it requires the ability to relate to other people. Leaders have to be able to create a relationship with, and among, their followers that inspires those followers to achieve what they could not without the leader. Second, leading is a proactive process of moving people from one circumstance to another. The very concept of leading means actively doing something. You cannot be a leader and only observe passively. Third, leaders use whatever is necessary to get others to help them achieve their vision. They use the formal authority they have, provide personal examples, set goals for followers, provide rewards and punishments, change the organization, and redefine the roles of its members and teams (Locke & Kirkpatrick, 1991). Their focus is their vision and they simply refuse to let anything stand in the way.

Exercising leadership requires the following:

- The ability to relate to other people.
- Taking an active role.
- Doing whatever is necessary to accomplish the vision.

Figure 7.1 Exercising Leadership

Some theorists view leadership as highly flexible depending on the situation in which the organization and leader find themselves (Yukl, 1989). Important factors influencing the leadership equation include how quickly the organization environment changes, how large the organization is, what kind of authority the leader actually has, the impact of new technology, the organizational culture, and other key elements that significantly shape the organizational operating context (Yukl, 1989). Although the ascent of a given leader is tied to his or her time and circumstance, it is driven by the leader's personality. So, in understanding leaders, the appropriate place to begin is with them as individuals.

LEADERSHIP TRAIT IDENTIFICATION

Fundamental to any leader's effectiveness is power over others. Power is the basic energy needed to initiate and sustain action. For a leader that means along with a vision of the future there has to be "the *capacity to translate intention into reality and sustain it*" (Bennis & Nanus, 1985, p. 17, emphasis in original). That capacity is not usually restricted to a person's official power but, in leaders, is a blend of all the power types discussed in Chapter 6, "Communication and Power."

The power issue is intriguing. Although we may think of power as an obvious manifestation of leadership, it is sometimes quite subtle. Some leaders are powerful personalities, but others are more subdued, less charismatic. The less obvious leaders get things done through relationships and connections without calling a lot of attention to themselves. Such a person, in effect, leads from within, rather than being a revolutionary upsetting the status quo (Kiechell, 1989). Such leaders may not be described as charismatic by any sort of rhetorical stretch, but they nevertheless managed to inspire an enviable trust and loyalty in their co-workers. And through their abilities to get people on their side, they were able to effect necessary changes in the culture of their organizations and make real their guiding visions. (Bennis, 1994, p. 155)

There are several models, lists really, of what various researchers have found common among those who have become recognized leaders. Not all leaders possess all of the traits, but leaders tend to share most of them. However, the way the traits are mixed within individual leader personalities varies considerably. As you consider the following sets of leader traits, consider how they may be similar, and whether the traits are finite elements, or conceptual frameworks, of a personality.

Bennis and Nanus Leader Traits

Bennis and Nanus (1985) analyzed 90 recognized business leaders. They identified four common strategies effective leaders use to achieve their objectives. Their leader behavior patterns, shown in Figure 7.2, are pervasive. They extend through every aspect of leader behavior within the organizational context.

- Strategy I: attention through vision.
- Strategy II: meaning through communication.
- Strategy III: trust through positioning.
- Strategy IV: the deployment of self through (1) positive self-regard and (2) the Wallenda factor.

Figure 7.2 Bennis and Nanus Leader Traits
(Source: Bennis & Nanus, 1985, pp. 26–58)

"Strategy I: attention through vision" is the ability to see beyond today, to have a vision of tomorrow. "Strategy II: meaning through communication" enables the leader to get that vision, that dream of what can be, across to his or her subordinates so they, too, are infected by it, convinced of its achievability. It is the leader's talent for managing meaning in an organization, orchestrating it to play his or her symphony of change. "Strategy III: trust through positioning" is "the glue that maintains organizational integrity." To be a leader means to have followers trust you enough to accept your vision and work hard to achieve it. "Leaders who are trusted make themselves known, make their positions clear," and in so doing those leaders "are reliable and tirelessly persistent." The researchers' "Strategy IV: the deployment of self through (1) positive self-regard and (2) the Wallenda factor" is the ability of the leader to manage herself or himself. Among the leaders they analyzed, Bennis and Nanus did not find conceit—the exaggerated opinion of one's self, or excessive vanity. But all did have a high level of confidence that enabled them to walk the high wire of vision and risk taking, like that of famous high-wire walker Karl Wallenda, without focusing on the danger to such a degree it contributed to their fall. Effective, long-term leaders, then, have supreme confidence in themselves, ignoring the possibility of failure, but without the damaging conceit that warps perceptions among some charismatic leaders who often rise quickly, but just as rapidly plummet into failure (Bennis & Nanus, 1985, pp. 26–58).

A realistic confidence in self, coupled with a clear vision of the future, allows effective leaders to empower subordinates, a key to motivation.

> Most employees welcome leadership that provides them the opportunity to express themselves, develop their competencies so that they can get better jobs, and play on a winning team.
>
> People at work want bosses to use power, but they want it used productively, to create power for them also. . . . People at work eventually resent a leader who manipulates, motivating by seduction, false promises, misleading use of the transferential relationship, and unreal visions of opportunity. Productive motivation results when we want to do what is *needed by the organization*. (Maccoby, 1988, p. 77, emphasis in original)

Effective leaders, then, have key abilities to relate to their subordinates while keeping themselves in balance. "The management of self is critical. Without it leaders may do more harm than good" (Bennis & Nanus, 1985, p. 57).

Kotter's Leader Traits

A number of theorists on leadership assert that effective leaders see the world differently than do their subordinates. That's what really separates them. The basic perception of meaning, as events are observed, is altered by the way a person engages with his or her situation and whether he or she is absorbed in the daily processes or looks beyond at the conceptual level.

Kotter (1988) sees managing as really learning to use a set of specific tools and techniques that are products of analysis and testing and are believed to work across a range of organizational applications. The tools of management are the fundamentals of planning, budgeting, organizing, staffing, and controlling. But those management tools can tie up an organization, over time, with increasing bureaucracy, reduced innovation, and more control than necessary. But part of a visionary leader's role is to counter that tendency. Otherwise an organization can become a product of the systems that are supposed to help run it—the proverbial tail wagging the dog.

The leader uses four elements of leadership, according to Kotter (1988), to counterbalance the traditional management tools so they don't bog the organization down with bureaucratic minutia (see Fig. 7.3). The elements of leadership include: a vision, a strategy for achieving that vision, a resource network, and motivated people to follow the leader. The leader, then, keeps the focus on where he or she wants to take the organization despite itself.

- A **vision** of what should be, a vision that takes into account the legitimate interests of all the people involved.

- A **strategy** for achieving that vision, a strategy that recognizes all the broadly relevant environmental forces and organizational factors.

- A **cooperative network of resources,** a coalition powerful enough to implement that strategy.

- A **highly motivated group** of key people in that network, a group committed to making that vision a reality.

Figure 7.3 Kotter's Leader Traits
(Source: Kotter, 1988, p. 19)

Taylor and Rosenbach Leader Traits

Another attempt at defining a universal set of leader criteria is conceptual in nature. The Taylor and Rosenbach leader behaviors shown in Figure 7.4 are complex qualitative concepts at the core of an individual's personality: vision, communicating, inspiring, creativity, commitment, and loyalty. They are fundamental to the leader's way of approaching the world. A leader personality, in the Taylor and Rosenbach view, has a "vision" of where the organization needs to go. The leader must also be effective in "communicating" that vision to others while "inspiring" them to achieve it. As the effort moves forward the leader provides considerable creativity to solve problems along the way. Finally, the effective leader has a very strong sense of "loyalty" to those who become part of the effort to achieve the leader's vision (Taylor & Rosenbach, 1989).

- **Visioning**—A distinguishing characteristic of leaders is their vision of the future. They typically are obsessed by it.

- **Communicating**—Effective leaders are usually exceptional communicators to get others to adopt their vision.

- **Inspiring**—Leaders typically have a talent for exciting others about their ideas.

- **Creativity**—Leaders are often very creative in developing strategies to put their ideas, or crusade, into action by others. They are intensely goal focused and find ways to accomplish goals despite barriers.

- **Commitment**—Leaders are fully committed to the task.

- **Loyalty**—Leaders are people persons who usually place loyalty at the top of the values they cherish in others and exhibit themselves.

Figure 7.4 Taylor and Rosenbach Leader Traits
(Source: Taylor & Rosenbach, 1989)

Kets de Vries Leader Traits

Kets de Vries (1989) provides another comparative framework for us to consider leadership and the complex, philosophical ways leaders engage with the world (see Fig. 7.5). This model of leader behaviors begins with the concept of visioning, calling it "the dream." Seven other qualities of leadership follow "the dream" and underscore the complicated nature of leadership. The effective leader manages the meaning of his or her dream as it is communicated to followers. The leader must also be adept at building networks of alliances. In other words, he or she must be a good organizational political player who quickly sees patterns of behavior in people and in the circumstances of the situation. The Kets de Vries model also presumes the leader is a competent person with considerable knowledge about the enterprise, yet willing to empower others, sharing authority. Leaders are viewed as tough people with a lot of hardiness and perseverance. And they are vigorous individuals who push for things to get done.

- **The Dream**—Effective leaders are propelled by a vision. They have a view of the future that becomes highly compelling to others.

- **Management of Meaning**—Leaders need to articulate their dreams and make these attractive to their followers. . . . Effective leaders are masters in the manipulation of meaning.

- **Network Building**—Those who rise to the top are very skilled in influencing, controlling, and manipulating their followers. . . .Effective leaders are very sensitive to other people and listen and understand others' points of view.

- **Pattern Recognition**—Effective leaders are masters of sense making, of bringing order to the chaos that tends to surround them. They can sort relevant from irrelevant information.

- **Empowerment**—Effective leaders communicate high performance expectations to their followers and show confidence in their ability to meet those expectations. By making their followers feel significant, they manage to motivate them.

- **Competence**—Leaders need to be familiar with the substance of the matter. They have to know what they are taking about. If they don't, they quickly lose credibility.

- **Hardiness and Perseverance**—Effective leaders know how to manage stress. They possess a positive and stable self-image. They firmly believe that they can control what affects their life.

- **Enactment**—Effective leaders are . . . proactive . . . [with] a great ability to initiate and sustain interaction with others . . . [and a] high need for achievement.

Figure 7.5 Kets de Vries Leader Traits
(Source: Kets de Vries, 1989, pp. 192–209)

Kirkpatrick and Locke Leader Traits

Our final comparative list of leader attributes was identified by Kirkpatrick and Locke (1991). As in the previously discussed sets of attributes, they provide characteristics that are wide-ranging. Consider their list, shown in Figure 7.6. How, using this set of criteria, can we differentiate between leaders and followers? How does the "drive" in a leader personality differ from that in an ordinary person?

Clearly, the Kirkpatrick and Locke list is a value-laden, cultural-context-dependent set of attributes. Some very effective leaders have not had, as judged through the prism of history, what would be considered particularly notable honesty and integrity, or cognitive ability. Perhaps the most glaring example is Adolf Hitler. He was certainly a powerful leader. But did he have honesty and integrity? Was his cognitive ability beyond that of his followers? Or was Hitler the product of a unique set of circumstances set in motion by the end of World War I who rose to prominence for a number of reasons not explained by this particular set of leader attributes?

- **Drive**—achievement, ambition, energy, tenacity, initiative.

- **Leadership motivation** (personalized vs. socialized).

- **Honesty and integrity.**

- **Self-confidence** (including emotional stability).

- **Cognitive ability.**

- **Knowledge of the business.**

- **Other traits** (weaker support): charisma, creativity/originality, flexibility.

Figure 7.6 Kirkpatrick and Locke Leader Traits
(Source: Kirkpatrick & Locke, 1991, p. 49)

As you can see, defining any set of universal leader criteria is a challenge. If you went around your classroom, or office, or any other collection of people, you could find some level of most of these concepts in each person. But how many of those people would you really consider to be a leader?

Comparison of Trait Models

It is particularly interesting, in our effort to understand leadership better, to compare the major typologies of leader behaviors. Figure 7.7 shows the key attributes identified by the five previous leadership attribute lists. Within each of the lists, the original order has been retained. Vertical spacing was adjusted in the comparison to align the obviously similar areas to help you identify common attributes.

The categorizations are strikingly similar. Semantic differences in the choice of attribute labels appear to be more of a variable than the fundamental leadership characteristics each research effort identified.

As you can see in the comparison of various leader attribute lists, they have a lot in common and tend to be philosophical in approach. The first four of the six leader behaviors identified by Taylor and Rosenbach (vision, communicating, inspiring, creativity, commitment, loyalty) are complex, abstract, and ambiguous because of their broad definitions. So, too, is the Kets de Vries list one of conceptual elements. The ability to have "the dream," to manage the meaning others will attach to it, and to engage in what Kets de Vries identified as "pattern recognition" are very complex concepts. Bennis and Nanus, in their four strategies, likewise use vastly complicated notions to distinguish leaders as people with a "vision of tomorrow," who convey their "meaning through communication," developing "trust through positioning," and with skill in the "deployment of self."

Each of the different researcher leader attribute lists vary slightly, but they all include conceptually driven attributes of the internal prism of individual personality. As such, they are highly variable from one person to the next, which, perhaps, explains why leaders are also very different and hard to identify ahead of time.

Traits/Behaviors of Leader Personalities*				
Bennis & Nanus (1985)	Kotter (1988)	Taylor & Rosenbach (1989)	Kets de Vries (1989)	Kirkpatrick & Locke (1991)
Vision	Vision	Vision	The Dream	
Communication		Communicating	Management of meaning	
Trust through positioning	Organizational strategy	Inspiring		
		Creativity		
Deployment of self		Commitment		Drive Leadership motivation Honesty and integrity Self-confidence Cognitive ability
	Networking		Network building	Knowledge of the business
			Pattern recognition	
	Motivated subordinates	Loyalty	Empowerment	
			Competence	
			Hardiness and perseverance	
			Enactment	Other (charisma, creativity/ originality, flexibility)

*To avoid confusion, research lists were kept in the same order, using only vertical spacing to align the obvious similar areas. The categorizations are strikingly similar.

Figure 7.7 Leader Trait Comparison

ORGANIZATIONAL DYNAMICS AND LEADERSHIP

The complicated nature of human relations within the organizational setting provides a highly fluid state of affairs requiring constant adjustments. Keeping any organization focused is a challenge that begins with the exercise of authority.

Controlling Approaches

Whenever you have a number of people working together, there is an issue of command and control. The way organizations maintain control usually depends on the person in charge, though organizational cultures develop a predisposition to a particular way of accomplishing it. Five basic control approaches are used in organizational life. They set the tone of authority, while the individuals using that authority usually have considerable freedom in how they tailor their personal relationships to fit their specific needs.

First, we will consider the five basic control approaches in organizations. They include: authoritarian, bureaucratic, democratic, charismatic, and laissez-faire (Procaccini, 1986). It's important to note here that these are overall concepts within which organizational relationships are usually defined.

- ◆ **Authoritarian**—This is a directed style of command and control in which organizational members are told what to do. Typically, organizational communication flows from the top down. Orders are given and work is done to accomplish it in the manner demanded. People who favor this approach prefer to tell others what to do, or in the case of subordinates, prefer to be told what to do. Authoritarian organizations can be very efficient and effective. They depend on a hierarchy of those who want to give orders and provide direction, with a culture of subordinates who prefer having little say in what's done. Clear objectives and tightly defined processes are typical of authoritarian environments.

- ◆ **Bureaucratic**—This style tends to use established processes and procedures as the justification for much of what is accomplished. In such organizations the process of doing things almost seems to be the reason to exist, rather than what actually needs to be done. Often there are extensive, written manuals for even the most mundane of tasks and everything has a "standard operating procedure." Organizations with this approach tend to be process centered and very slow to change.

- ◆ **Democratic**—This style perceives everyone as having a vested interest in the outcome of organizational activity. It is presumed that when individuals participate in decision making, the decisions are better, though that, of course, really depends on whether those involved know what they're doing. This style actively solicits the involvement of organizational members in decision making and has considerable allure where organizational members are committed, skilled, and desire a high level of decision participation. The democratic approach spreads out supervisory responsibility. Those in positions of authority still do exercise considerable influence, but usually with a lot of diplomacy.

- ◆ **Charismatic**—This style is one of the most obvious to people outside the organization. It is the power of personality. The leader's personal attractiveness provides the energy to marshal others to the leader's vision and then expand their sense of loyalty. The emotional attachment of the followers to the leader is the key to this style. Many extraordinary figures of history were charismatic leaders, which is much of the reason they are remembered. They stood out from their contemporaries.

- ◆ **Laissez-faire**—The laissez-faire style of organizational control is basically a hands-off approach. Subordinates are expected to, and left to, do what needs to be done. The name, in French, literally means to let people do as they please. For this style to be effective a powerful culture of subordinates must exist, people who inherently understand what to do, and then do it with little direction. True leader personalities may rarely adopt this approach. (Procaccini, 1986)

Think of the five control approaches previously discussed as acting as a sort of organizational umbrella. Under any given preferred organizational controlling style the individual managers and leaders use personal relationships to get things done. The personal relationship level is where a person's way of analyzing the world, and their preference for encouraging others to adopt their position or point of view, really comes out. For example, some people are most comfortable simply telling others what they want done; others may prefer a less direct, guiding approach.

When leaders begin to exercise their will, they normally use one of four key approaches to those around them to accomplish their goals: "structuring," "coaching," "participating," and "delegating" (Payne, 1988). The leader personality is the key in choosing the method to get others to do what the leader wants done.

- **Structuring** focuses on the organizational mechanisms and work flows. A person who prefers this approach generally looks for structural problems in an organization as the first step in making it more effective. It is organizational design centered, in that the first problem to solve is making sure the structure provides the right form for the people within it to accomplish their tasks.

- **Coaching** is centered on encouraging followers to perform at a higher level, which then elevates the organization as a whole. Coaches typically have considerable expert power and like to work with subordinates to increase their skill. The coaching approach presumes that when people aren't performing as well as they should, it is a lack of understanding, motivation, or expertise that is the problem. Given the right encouragement and knowledge, people will achieve more. Because journalists tend to have a strong sense of purpose and ownership in their work, the coaching approach may be the most effective in media organizations.

- **Participating** leaders seek to bring more people into the leadership level, sharing power. This approach may be most common among leaders who do not have much of a need for recognition. Such leaders may prefer to stay in the background. What is important to a participating leader is the end result, not public acclaim. Participating leadership means involving others in the act of leading, so taking this approach may be a sign the leader has strong self-esteem and great confidence in subordinates.

- **Delegating** means giving various responsibilities to others so the leader can concentrate on what he or she does best. This is also a participating approach, but generally delegating leaders are astute at recognizing their personal strengths and weaknesses and then surrounding themselves with people who balance the leader's abilities. In other words, if a delegating leader is not good with budgets and other financial considerations, or doesn't want to take the time to do certain things, he or she will find someone who is and delegate that responsibility to them.

Leaders come in all shapes, sizes, and personality types, so these are certainly not exclusive categories. Any given leader may combine parts of those necessary to achieve his or her goals, for example, in one case be structuring, in another coaching. But usually a leader has a predisposition toward one of the four categories, trying it first and then moving to another approach if necessary.

A common flaw in leaders is the failure to assess accurately their weaknesses and then find people to compensate for those limitations. As leaders rise in power, they sometimes develop illusions of themselves as more expert in a wider range of areas than they are. And if their subordinates fear them, there is a tendency for no one to take the risk of bringing to the leader's attention his or her inadequacy. For example, a person who is a powerful orator and political firebrand may, once ascended to the seat of power, think he or she should decide complex military tactics despite a lack of expertise in that area—Hitler. On the other hand, a delegating leader in a similar circumstance would find the best general available to run the military side of things, concentrating on the political issues and influencing public opinion—Churchill. Of the four basic types of leader behavior approaches, delegating appears to be the most effective in the long term. But it requires a leader who is very good at recognizing his or her personal strengths and weaknesses and doesn't let ego get in the way of achieving his or her vision of the future.

From the previous discussion of organizational control approaches and individual leader behavior styles you can see that the two need to be complementary for the organization to be as effective as possible. Organizational members learn preferred ways of doing things as they spend time in the culture. If a leader suddenly does something that doesn't fit what the organizational culture anticipates, it's confusing. For example, it might seem strange, in an autocratically controlled organization, to have someone suddenly using a participating or coaching leader approach. The organizational culture would be predisposed to top-down direction and control, but suddenly subordinates would be asked for their input with a leader encouraging them to develop their skills and expand their involvement. It just wouldn't fit. Clearly, conflicting personal and organizational approaches may leave subordinates confused, or at least unsure of themselves (Payne, 1988).

When leadership is changed, it may be necessary to change styles on the organizational level, the leader behavior level, or both. The predisposition of an individual toward a given approach defines his/her comfort and effectiveness with that approach. An autocrat will have great difficulty making a democratic style effective. Likewise, a laissez-faire individual who comes into a completely different kind of organizational culture may not be able to lead it effectively. Finally, a person who is a recognized expert at compromise may not have the necessary power of personality to lead an organization that has been previously centered on a charismatic force.

People in organizations develop expectancies based on what they've experienced before. When everything changes, they don't always know how to adjust to the new environment. That's why new management, or leadership, that is brought in from outside an organization may cause substantial upheaval, anxiety among organizational members, and is not always able to succeed.

Participative Leadership and Style Change

The participatory approach is, fundamentally, an act of sharing power down to the lowest possible level (Kanter, 1987). It puts heavy emphasis on the collective. Typically there is an avoidance of direct confrontation with compromise used to reduce conflict. This produces a negotiated compliance so "there are no losers" (Zaleznik, 1989, p. 24). But that also means that there are no winners, either. No one gets what he or she really wanted, just pieces of it. For a leader with a passionate vision of the future, ending up in compromise is frustrating.

The result can be more power held within the organization as a whole and less for the person at the top. When that happens, the organization can seemingly drive itself to wherever the compromises take it. "Managerial goals are passive, deeply embedded in the structure of the organization, in contrast to entrepreneurial or individual leadership goals that actively shape ideas and tastes" (Zaleznik, 1989, p. 24). Thus, the style an organization embraces has a direct bearing on its potential for leaders to grow within it. It's become popular for management to emphasize team approaches. But they may not provide the most conducive atmosphere for true leaders to evolve in an organization. Team-centered requirements for negotiated positions, coalition building, and consensus decision making clearly conflict with a leader's sense of vision and focused energy. On the other hand, organizations with such an approach may be less subject to the whims of a leader and may be positioned to survive difficult technological and other transitions. Not all leaders are good. While participatory style organizations do not provide a rich environment for great leaders to evolve, they do help resist bad leaders.

As our earlier leader trait discussion indicated, research has supported the view that leaders are typically focused individuals who know exactly where they want to take the organization. Because of that, they have considerable drive. They are impatient when things get in the way, or when they consider the process of change as being too slow. They know what they want to do, so why waste time doing it?

One way effective leaders accomplish their vision is by getting subordinates to "buy in" to their approach. They often create an atmosphere of organizational members as guided partners. This is particularly useful if there is a higher need for followers to feel included. In one study of journalists' preferred management styles, researchers found that media workers widely supported the participative, democratic approach to controlling their work. But using such an approach poses considerable difficulty in getting the job accomplished (Gaziano & Coulson, 1988).

Part of the problem in a media company is that it is usually a combination of machine and professional organizations. It has an assembly line with unrelenting schedules for product manufacture, but at the same time the media workers are very much in control of the quality of their effort with a professional ethic and control over their creativity. That's because the intense deadline pressure of a daily newspaper, for example, leaves little time for consensus building and participatory decision making. Many media organizations demand maximum creativity from writers, editors, artists, creative directors, and photographers, but on the tight schedule of an assembly line. So a participatory management style, though preferred by organizational members, may cause an inherent conflict with the necessary efficiency required to run the organization day to day. It may be, in media organizations, that participatory management can only work on some levels, with more authoritative command and control on others (Gaziano & Coulson, 1988).

Organizations have a kind of power of their own that creates an inherent resistance to change. The levels of formalization, information systems development, control systems, and internal hierarchy all impact how an organization reacts to change (Friedman, 1985, p. 38). In contemporary, complex media organizations maximum effectiveness appears to depend on how well the roles of manager and leader are blended at the top, linking dichotomous elements of each. In an ideal world the visionary leader may be out front spreading his or her vision and igniting competitive passions, but still working within the nuances of internal interrelationships as a strong consensus-building manager creating a sense of team. That is extremely difficult, because team approaches can be a serious impediment to leader personalities. Teams function through compromise and consensus. Yet "individuals are the only source of ideas and energy," and individualism is suppressed in team cultures (Zaleznik, 1989, p. 6).

In today's world you have to understand the organizational bureaucracy well enough to use it as a tool in achieving your vision. In other words, the leader personality has to be enough of a team player to use the system to accomplish highly individualized goals. In complex systems, which most media organizations are, leaders are much more than merely infectious personalities to which others respond.

> The leader, as social architect, must be part artist, part designer, part master craftsman, facing the challenge of aligning the elements of the social architecture so that, like an ideal building, it becomes a creative synthesis uniquely suited to realizing the guiding vision of the leader. (Bennis & Nanus, 1985, p. 139)

Bureaucracy as a Limiting Force

The inherent danger of team management is the tendency toward "the culture of teams based on conformity" (Hirschhorn, 1991, p. 8). The division of work groups within an organization can extend beyond to the social world. Bosses run with bosses, and production line workers run with production line workers. It's that simple. There is a kind of class distinction based on work environment hierarchy. People often try to maneuver their way into a social world of those above them, as a way of raising their profile and being seen as a person with potential. Although any industry is susceptible to this tendency, the classic example of this tendency is the American automobile industry in the middle part of the 20th century:

> People who wanted to be promoted had to be male, live in fashionable suburbs of Detroit, join the right golf clubs, and commit their wives to social activity within the company. General Motors was their world. The upwardly mobile manager who joined the culture felt privileged and powerful to be on the inside. (Hirschhorn, 1991, pp. 8–9)

The problem in complicated media organizations is generating a sense of team, but without the downside of a culture of conformity that dampens innovation and ingenuity. You need to get people to pull together to achieve the media organization's goals, but not at the expense of creativity. On the one hand, you need a level of group bonding to get the members of the team to relate to one another, build trust and confidence, and have the ability to reach decision consensus. On the other hand, media organization members have to be empowered, indeed encouraged, to think independently to fashion new ideas, concepts, approaches, and initiatives. In the qualitative nature of media creative work, you need their minds as much as their hands.

Boundary Spanning

Boundary spanning is what happens as departments and division interface with one another. Something or someone has to provide the connection across organizational walls, or boundaries. In a typical media organization, boundary spanning is usually part of the role of the department head where that person is both a member of the department and a constituent of the upper management group. You have to represent the department to senior management, and senior management to the department. The middle manager is, literally, caught in the middle representing the viewpoints of each to the other (Gardner, 1988).

Boundary spanning poses enormous difficulties. To each side you are both a member and representative of another group. You serve both the management above to whom you report and those below whom you supervise. Each person's behavior is based on the way meaning is constructed, based on what we individually observe and experience. Working the boundary means you have to function as an interpreter of meanings across diverse groups with sometimes strikingly different perspectives. That is a particularly difficult perceptive challenge (Rentsch, 1990). For example, a person who has developed a successful career working within the confines of a newsroom, immersed in the values of the journalism culture, will tend to look at the world differently than a person who has always worked on the business side of a media organization and has a Masters of Business Administration (MBA). Perceptions, loyalties, and responsibilities to one group may conflict to varying degrees with perceptions, loyalties, and responsibilities to the other.

In the case of media organizations, for example, different departments may define the quality of their work in radically different ways. News personnel may see themselves as serving the public *through* the media organization, not really serving the newspaper or TV station. The corporation may be perceived as a kind of necessary evil, there to pay the salary but often in the way of better public service through its marketing plans, cost accounting, and other business considerations.

Within such an environment the boundary spanner is often caught between the conflicts of leading and managing. A department head may put in a lot of effort to convey to subordinates his or her vision of how to improve. That usually includes a lot of personal dynamics to orchestrate the departmental members in the direction the leader wants to go. But then when the department head works with senior management, included as a member of the management "team," the visionary leader of a department becomes a group participant on the staff of a higher-ranking leader. That requires more of a manager type working within a bureaucracy, building alliances and consensus, being what senior management desires, a "team player."

The Context of Leadership

The environment within which a business operates must be matched to the internal organizational structure and style for maximum effectiveness (Belasco, 1989). That can obviously mean a blending for management and leadership types, depending on the unique requirements of the organization at the time.

> Leadership is not performed in a vacuum. Rather it is situational. It is not only the leader's needs and behaviors that count. There are two other important factors, which together with the leader's preferred style, form the three essential ingredients for every supervisory act: the follower and the task at hand. (Procaccini, 1986, p. 36)

One of the keys to leading any organization is "mastering the context" within which the leader finds himself or herself (Bennis, 1994, p. 34).

Despite the evolution of more democratic management styles, the authoritarian model grounded in what McGregor (1960) originally defined as "Theory X" behavior still appears to be common. That approach may, in fact, be necessary in certain types of businesses, including some media companies (Sherman, 1987). That is for a number of reasons, principal among them the serious time constraints in media organizations.

Because media managers tend to ascend the career ladder from newsrooms and other production environments where time is short and decision making necessarily rapid, their behavior, despite a job that is more strategic in nature, may be similar. There is a tendency toward authoritarianism in media organizations, as much because of the environment within which media managers evolve, as anything else. But creativity may suffer significantly, and the media organization products become mundane because of such overt command-and-control tendencies. For a further discussion of the evolution of management styles and workplace psychology see Chapter 2, "Managing in a Media Environment," and Chapter 3, "Human Influences on Media Organizations."

Staff writers who are dealt with in an authoritarian way by an editor in individual story structuring may be understandably hesitant to volunteer suggestions for a different layout of the paper. In effect, the reality of the work environment for story editing spills over to other types of relationships. With authoritarianism, risk taking is dampened at all levels. The threat of the authoritarian is, expressed openly or not, "do it my way, or you'll be fired!" That means employees tend to operate at the psychological survival level of performance, rather than progressing toward the goal of self-actualization in the work environment (Maslow, 1970). A shrinking away from risk taking and the championing of new ideas then occurs as competitiveness decreases, often with concurrent drops in market share and revenue. Typically what follows is more intensive management effort aimed at improving cost accounting and productivity. That, then, can have the effect of squaring the problem instead of correcting it.

Regardless of an individual's particular style preference, successful leaders are usually focused on both the results they want to achieve, and the people on whom they rely to get those results. They tend to be skillful in manipulating different styles to get their people to accomplish their goals. In the last analysis, "leader effectiveness depends upon the interaction among the leader, follower, boss, associates, organization, job demands, and time constraints . . . a change in one may create a change in the others" (Hersey, 1984, p. 43). But always the true leader makes whatever adjustments are necessary in the situation at hand to accomplish his or her vision. It is that vision that drives them, and all else is adjustable to accomplish it.

Leadership is situationally derived and implemented. No one way of doing things applies to every case. Creative organizations, such as media companies, foster highly politicized environments where the personal relationships of creative participants have as much, or more, effect on how the work is done than the formal management structure. Such qualitative, subjective work—perceiving one story as "good," but another as less well written—is not measured in quantitative, assembly line production rates. It requires more emphasis on people skills and an understanding that employee motivation goes much deeper than pay and benefits. Additionally, newsroom employees have been characterized as individuals who resist management control and are driven by forces of internal satisfaction and commitment to ideas.

As American media organizations have become more profit oriented, with increasing competitors fragmenting all media markets, the challenge for corporate managers to interface effectively with newsroom workers has increased, requiring more sophistication in the leader and manager roles. For the media, the challenge is not managing "hands," but rather managing minds. Media organization workers typically have higher levels of education and professional attitudes, believing they are members of a "calling" that demands independence with a higher level of trust and power over their work.

DIFFERENCES BETWEEN MANAGERS AND LEADERS

In the 1977 *Harvard Business Review* one of the foremost theorists about leadership, Abraham Zaleznik, published an essay that touched off a major debate in American management circles. It was republished by the *Harvard Business Review* nine years later, and his thesis continues to fuel debate about leading and managing. In "Managers and Leaders: Are They Different?" Zaleznik focused on the key problem that has plagued modern business since its inception. Managers can be trained to analyze spreadsheets. Technocrats can be taught to design intricate systems to process things. But generating the spark of ignition for the human side of organizations is an entirely different matter. Although managers and leaders have similarities in how they approach things, there are some fundamental, critical differences in their styles. The view of managers and leaders as being elements of a kind of split personality has continued to fuel the debate over leadership in modern organizations (Zaleznik, 1977/1986).

There is a difference between leading and managing people but one that is not always clear. That's because what sets them apart are not clear divisions but rather more diffused transition zones where one blends into the other. Both leaders and managers may work hard, but the leader is driven by a long-term vision of the future beyond the manager's focus on the current situation. Leaders "master the context" within which they function while managers "surrender to it," performing the requisite tasks. "The manager does things right, the leader does the right thing" (Bennis, 1994, pp. 44–45). Additionally, the manager often has to translate the leader's power down to lower levels with authority and conviction, in effect serving as a kind of surrogate leader. In such cases it is usually the leader's power that is being exercised, through the manager. But without the leader there would not be as much effort to comply, if, indeed, there was any. The classic example is Alexander the Great. Before him, the Greeks were, generally, confined to their own country. When he was alive, they conquered much of the known world, his generals commanding, and the Greek armies performing, in his name. But when he died, the empire disintegrated, lacking the authority of Alexander the Great to bind together his organization.

Without a leader at the top, an organization is not as effective as it could be. Likewise, without managers who buy into a leader's vision, that vision cannot be achieved. Managers create much of a powerful leader's connection to the bottom rungs of the organizational ladder as the vision is communicated to organizational members. Indeed, in some ways, "in a successful organization every leader works and every worker leads" (Murphy, 1996, p. 3). In small organizations, the leader may be well known to everyone on a personal basis. But in very large organizations, that is not possible, requiring the flow of leadership power through surrogates at different levels.

> The key function of a *leader* is to establish the basic vision (purpose, mission, overarching goal, or agenda) of the organization. . . . The key function of a *manager* is to implement the vision. The manager and subordinates act in ways that constitute the means to achieving the stated end. (Locke & Kirkpatrick, 1991, p. 4, emphasis in original)

Separating Managers and Leaders

Being a leader means exercising power over other people. With that power come many risks. One of those risks for a media organization is that leaders tend to be mavericks rather than conformers. But the bureaucracy of the corporate environment encourages conformity rather than independence among those individuals trying to work their way to the top. A conservative attitude in concert with the existing corporate inertia develops as an organization tends to breed conformist managers. That, in turn, tends to generate a corporate malaise rather than encourage risk taking and innovation. Playing it safe becomes a career strategy, as opposed to seeking out higher risk, change making, leadership opportunities (Zaleznik, 1977/1986).

A vast difference exists between running a media organization day to day and guiding its long-term future course. The former—managing—requires knowledge of processes such as finance, planning, organization, and the other functions Fayol (1949) originally defined and various management texts have built upon. The latter—leading—requires vision to guide an organization and its people into the future, along with the power and personality dynamics to implement that vision within the context of the organizational bureaucracy. There are clear, and dramatic, differences in the typologies of manager and leader. Managers orchestrate organizational processes; leaders ignite the passions in people. Zaleznik (1989) emphasized that

> managers are practical people. Typically they are hard working, intelligent, analytical, and tolerant of others. Because they hold few convictions with passion, except perhaps for the need to extract order out of potential chaos, they exhibit a high degree of fair-mindedness in dealing with people.
>
> Leaders are more dramatic in style and unpredictable in behavior. They seem to overcome the conflict between order and chaos with an authority legitimized by personal magnetism and a commitment to their own undertakings and destinies. (Zaleznik, 1989, p. 23)

Some theorists argue that the emphasis on managerial skill development may have contributed to a decline in leadership growth. The rise of business school popularity, with an emphasis on MBA approaches may have contributed to a culture of management standardization, rather than encouraging the visionary individual creativity that fosters true leadership development. Part of the problem appears to be the psychosis of quarter-to-quarter profit reporting that plagues American business. Quarterly profit statements can have a dramatic effect on the price of a company's stock, and therefore the net worth of its major shareholders (owners and often senior executives). In such a climate, things may be done to boost profits today that impair growth and development tomorrow. There are significant differences between production line managerial skills to maximize productivity and profits in the short term and the intuitive social interaction nuances of personality-driven magnetism that leaders typically possess to implement their long-term vision.

> Most administrative and interpersonal skills are learnable, so these cannot form any unique set of talents. Conceptual abilities, however, are developed fairly early in life and, although they can be modified a little, no one has as yet figured out how to improve them dramatically.
>
> Teaching good judgment, or the ability to break set, or the ability to pick key problems, or the courage to make unpopular decisions is not something that can be reduced to simple formulas. Such abilities are terribly complex, and require dealing with ambiguity as a matter of course. (Lombardo, 1989, pp. 26–27)

Leader Training

As discussed earlier, much development of leadership theory has centered on the attempt to identify traits leaders have but followers may not. The underlying belief driving this approach is that leadership is not an artistic talent but can be learned as a pragmatic skill. Some theorists argue that "everyone has the capacity for leadership," even though "not everyone will become a leader" (Bennis, 1994, p. 8). One leadership training approach even redefines leader functions as workplace processes, arguing that "anyone can learn to be a "workleader" by studying the areas in which the individual is weak (Murphy, 1996).

But the difference between the traditionally defined managerial skills—planning, organizing, commanding, coordinating, and controlling—and a more holistic style of leadership thinking—balanced upon achievement, self-actualization, and humanistic encouragement—is dramatic (Lafferty, 1990). The differences in the managing and leading approaches are fundamental issues at the core of human relations. "Managers pay attention to how things get done, and leaders pay attention to what things mean to people" (Zaleznik, 1989, p. 28).

There are also substantial, qualitative variances among human personalities that affect who steps to the front. Any individual may have leadership potential; the real issue is who takes advantage of it. Leading involves aspects of the human personality that are particularly difficult to transfer to another person. The initiation of action is a breakwater that divides the leader from the led. That involves knowing when to act. But "what can't be taught in leadership is good judgment" (Terry, 1993, p. 3). The implication of such an axiomatic difference of perspective fuels the debate about whether leaders can, in fact, be trained, or whether the ambiguities of leadership make it a talent with which one is born and education can only further refine.

Earlier in this chapter you were provided several different sets of leader attributes that some of the influential contemporary researchers have developed. Rather than a list of quantitative skills that can be taught to people, all of them provide philosophical concepts that tend to be centered at the core of one's personality. Obviously, then, attempting to train leaders has to be concept centered. It is more than the acquisition of particular skills. That is not to say effective leadership training is beyond our reach. Indeed, for centuries humanity has attempted just that in the training of military, governmental, and other individuals to lead others. But despite such efforts to teach people to lead, it only happens when those being taught have a talent for the role. Leadership, in the last analysis, is grounded in the individual's personality and the way others respond to that personality.

> For all the studies, case histories, and experiments, we still know relatively little about the cause and effect of successful leadership. The issues are complex; human personalities, social change, technological innovations, and dynamic organizational environments are linked in strange ways. No two settings, no two individuals combine the same mix of attributes. The result is that we have been unable to isolate leadership as a unitary phenomenon. (Taylor & Rosenbach, 1989, p. xi)

The realm of personal experience includes nuances that fashion perceptions and are difficult to categorize or replicate. Training leaders is closely parallel to teaching music. There is an element of science and instructable skill in the mechanics of reading the notes and playing the scales, but an element of art remains that separates the mere mechanical musician from the true artist.

Despite the efforts of many researchers, leadership remains an elusive quality that some people have while others do not (Muczyk & Reimann, 1989). You can't take "Leadership 101" and be a leader, because leadership is more than a set of applied skills. That does not mean you should give up any effort to become an effective leader. You may have the talent. But you need to assess realistically whether your personality coincides with the inherent characteristics of leaders. For example, if you are not the kind of person who thinks a long way out, dreaming about what you want to accomplish in five years or so, you may not possess the visioning quality typical of exceptional leaders. It is one thing to have a dream of an ideal job you'd like, but quite another to have the focus and drive to reach that level of career achievement, regardless of what it takes to get there. Many dreams are derailed by the complexity of daily life, including the desire for a social life, marriage, and family. Some careers require everything else be put second.

True leaders, in the classic sense, appear to be rare. But in studying leadership all managers can expand their own individual abilities to deal with a leader persona more effectively when one comes along. The preponderance of evidence supports the view that people may be trained to do certain tasks more effectively. Leading, however, involves talent that is part of one's personality, directly affected by the particular circumstances, and involving some degree of luck and intuition (Bennis & Nanus, 1985). Thus, "it is one thing to understand leadership; it is quite another to live it" (Terry, 1993, p. 6).

THE SUCCESSION PROBLEM

The process of changing leaders, and managers too, can produce a great deal of personal anxiety, upheaval, and conflict. It is often a time of high emotion for the person being replaced, the candidates to fill the position, and everyone affected by the change. Particularly in the case of popular leader figures, it can be traumatic, similar to coping with the death of someone we care about. The experience of leadership change reinforces mortality. It requires the difficult act of letting go (particularly difficult for entrepreneurial founder-leaders who created the organization they are leaving) and substantial realignment of subtle power networking with the organization. That can produce a negative attitude by the outgoing leader toward the heir apparent when the realization sets in that loyalties are shifting to the new person. Informal social networks, as well as more systematized patterns of influence, undergo considerable adjustment and redefinition (Kets de Vries, 1989).

Leadership of a complex organization is a process that brings together formal and informal influences, which may be obvious or imbedded below the visible surface (Barnes, 1986). In some cases the person moving out of power may consciously or subconsciously use both formal and informal organizational influence to subvert the new leader. The reason may be an effort to ensure the legacy of the old leader's successful tenure at the top. A fear exists that what was built up over the years will be changed. Thus, there is a powerful motivation within the outgoing leader, which may be conscious or subconscious, to subvert the succession effort. If the next in line fails, or at least is noticeably less effective, the prior leader gains status. In some organizations, previous leaders attain an almost mythological status because their successors are seen as less effective.

Succession may be something a leader plans carefully with a lot of intellectual concern paid to making sure the new leader succeeds. The organization that has been created will continue to grow. But emotionally the soon-to-retire leader begins to feel a sense of loss and may harbor the hope the organization won't be quite as good when he or she leaves. Intellectually you want to make sure everything works after you leave. But emotionally you really hope it doesn't. If you worked all your life to climb the career ladder to the publisher's office, leaving it for retirement life when no one cares if you show up for work can be a serious shock to your self-esteem. Because of the internal, and often subconscious, resistance of leaders to let go, many organizations have marginal, if any, succession plans. The sitting leader would have to be involved in creating them.

Occasionally a leader will informally chat about "one of these days we've got to talk about who to get ready to take over for me." But that is not serious planning and preparation for the ascent of the new leader. Frequently the person chosen to be the new leader is a person no one in the organization might have identified as such more than a few months before the change. When future leadership is not clear well ahead of time, once the new leader is identified organizational politics consume an enormous amount of energy as everyone jockeys for position. That is particularly true when the new leader is from outside the organization without established relationships and knowledge of the organizational political situation. A time- and energy-consuming game of realignment of influence may go on for months until new relationships and alliances have been formed.

Bigger and older organizations are more likely to have succession planning mechanisms in place. Succession systems vary widely, often including informal approaches where superiors personally groom key subordinates. Formal training programs, mentoring, and various special projects and committee assignments are also used to broaden individuals identified as having the potential to move up the organizational hierarchy (Kotter, 1988). In newer, fast-track industries, succession planning is frequently limited. That's because in youthful organizations the problem is attracting and retaining new employees. Typically such companies don't have a long enough history to have had a generation of managers and employees reach retirement longevity (Friedman, 1985). Older, more stable organizations often have strong cultures with the ability to develop future leaders from within, thus avoiding the kind of upheaval that new, outside leadership inevitably brings. In such organizations there is often an

> importance of being able to hire from within; for having grown up in an organization one knows how to get things done in it. As a rule, when the best person for a job is only to be found outside, it is a sign that the system for executive development has gone awry. (Friedman, 1985, p. 115)

The effort to expand those identified as potential future leaders is often dovetailed with overall management development programs. One analysis of leader development found four areas essential to effective leadership evolution: "personal growth experiences, conceptual development, feedback, and skill building. Each integrates and builds upon the others" (Conger, 1992, p. 180). Although some organizations choose to hire individuals from outside with experience as leaders or managers, rather than develop their own from within, two problems are inherent in that approach. First, it is sometimes difficult to transfer experience in one organizational culture to another. Second, there is a question of whether the experience at the previous position is really closely related to that required of the new job. Was the previous position mostly confined to overseeing day-to-day operations with little involvement in media organization strategy? Or was the individual included as a key management staff member developing budget, personnel, and long-term vision? If the person was a strategic thinker in the previous position but hired at the new company to be a day-to-day operational manager, there could be problems.

The advantage of promoting from within—presumably leaders, managers, and corporate culture all fit well together—has a definite downside. It encourages organizational inbreeding and in the process may fail to keep the company at the front of industry innovation. New ideas are not brought in by new organizational members. Rather, past practices become entrenched in the organization. That is a serious problem when there is a high percentage of inside directors (members of the board of directors who also work within the company). They may tend to be influenced by organizational politics as they take part in promoting executives (Friedman, 1985).

It doesn't take a complicated system of succession planning to minimize problems with the inevitable leadership change. There should be a system of identifying potential leaders, as well as integration across divisions, so potentially innovative candidates are not bureaucratically screened out. Gaining experience throughout diverse operational units should be encouraged. That helps build expert power. And it is important to have incentives that reward managers for moving those with the best potential up the succession ladder.

One problem in many organizations is that once an effective manager is in place there's a hesitancy to move that person to a new job. For example, if a television news director is highly successful—has turned around a mediocre department so it is challenging the dominant station in the market—the last thing the station general manager wants to do is move that news director to another job. The tendency is to "play it safe" and keep effective people where they are. Obviously that means if you do a good job, you are *hurting* your chances of moving ahead. The same thing happens with superior reporters who, because they can do much more work than someone else, get more work to do. But for its long-term health the organization needs a way to provide changing opportunities so employees can broaden their experience and demonstrate their abilities as fully as possible. It's a cliché, but it's true: People need to grow (McElwain, 1991).

A CONTEMPORARY MEDIA STYLE SYNCHRONIZATION MODEL

We have emphasized throughout this chapter that leading and managing are related, but different, concepts. While the manager typically works within the organizational structure, attempting to use the bureaucracy to achieve immediate, pragmatic goals, the leader is usually concerned with a wider strategic view, which includes developing a vision of the future and then moving the organization toward that vision.

Whether leader or manager, the person at the top of an organization will have a personal style of relationship development and control. It is most effective when synchronized to the style toward which the organizational culture is predisposed. When new leaders and managers come into an organization and impose a different style, there can be considerable difficulty, particularly if that style is radically different from what the organizational culture anticipates.

To be effective, a contemporary media organization leader has to be much more than an entrepreneurial business executive with a vision, or just another MBA armed with reams of statistics, flowcharts, and graphs. First and foremost, that person has to be a proficient communicator who understands employee motivation, as well as marketing techniques such as product placement. With the exception of special kinds of media organization production situations, in place of autocratic managers must come altruistic leaders with the vision to bring the other caring, complex human beings in an organization together.

In effect, media organizations are usually combinations of dichotomous organizational designs: the machine organization and the professional organization. Machine organizations have standardized processes with a dominant need for routine efficiency with quantitative measures of success in production schedules and manufacturing timing—for example, a newspaper printing facility. Professional organizations, by contrast, encourage independence and creativity with a loosely defined structure emphasizing the quality of work more in the control of the individual—such as writing and reporting. So the media organization has to operate like a mechanistic factory, on the one hand, and like a creative think tank on the other. It is one of the most difficult of leadership challenges.

As we head into the 21st century, the human side of the organizational equation has become the focus of virtually every sector of organizational involvement (Williams, 1986). The creative talent, the ingenious person who sees what others do not see, is critical as technology expands and the marketplace continues to go through repeated major adjustments. Because of the give-and-take relationship of leadership, the more a leader encourages his or her followers to increase their self-esteem, the more bound those followers become to that leader (Curtin, 1988). In effect, it is a hand-in-glove situation where the more one improves, the more the other does, like a kind of perpetual motion machine. But to make it run smoothly requires a politically sensitive leadership style that includes coalition building, continual bargaining and persuasion, as well as some degree of coercion (Isherwood, 1985). There are distinct parallels to other aspects of life from which our models of how to conduct human relationships are often drawn. The work environment is not an isolated place. Rather, it is a reflection of the manager's and the employee's emotions, ideals, dreams, and perceptions of reality—the individual's cultural context. In the last analysis, organizations, leaders, and followers are just people who respond to one another on an individual basis.

The theoretical model shown in Figure 7.8 is an effort to reflect the dynamic relationship of leadership controlling style on the personal and organizational levels. The personal leadership style is represented by the circle. You can see that around the circle are the different personal approaches typical of leaders, including coercive, demanding, commanding, directive, suggestive, and guiding. The organizational culture's predisposition toward Theory X (authoritarian), Theory Y (libertarian), or Theory Z (participative) command and control is represented by the triangle. (See Chapter 2, "Managing in a Media Environment," for a full discussion of these concepts.) The model is shown in alignment, with the expected leadership personal style—the circle—over the relative organizational control theory—the triangle. You can see that when the organizational culture prefers a participative style—the right side of the triangle between Theory Y and Theory Z—the personal style of the leader (represented by the circle) needs to range from suggestive to guiding. But in the lower left corner of the triangle, a Theory X organization, which tends toward authoritarian leadership, would be better served by a leader who is demanding and/or commanding. The circle represents the cyclical nature of style, evolving from one type to another. The same is true of the triangle of organizational culture predisposition. Around the circle, and along the sides of the triangle, the styles gradually shift from one type to another. The model, then, includes the full range of variability of both organizational culture command-and-control preference and individual leader styles.

In the reality of daily organizational life, organizations and leaders commonly mix elements of the styles shown in our model, with a general tendency toward a type of behavior. A person may be generally participative in nature, but with an occasional tendency to be authoritarian. So that person would be on the left side of Theory Z, with a more coercive personal approach, but still somewhat guiding. With that in mind our model is a dynamic one. In real life, the circle—the leader—and triangle—the organization—are continually flexing with one another, adjusting as the business and cultural conditions require and creating some tension in the organizational climate represented by the column.

The problem is when the leader and organization get seriously out of alignment. Consider how a person's leadership/managing style would create a kind of organizational "twist" against the organizational culture's predisposition for influence and control if the leader's style didn't fit the organization's. You can see how a leader who is "guiding" (at the top right of the leader circle) may work well with a Theory Z participative organizational culture, where it is aligned on the model. But if that person were brought into a Theory X organization where a commanding style was expected, there would be a serious conflict with a lot of tension caused by the lack of fit.

All leaders depend on situational conditions and their subordinates' ability to make the right decisions or take the right action. Leaders apply varying levels of power and authority depending on their subordinates' ability to carry the leader's vision forward. Thus, the culture of leadership is one of intuition, innuendo, anticipation, and expectation throughout all players in the decision/action orbit. Leadership ceases to be effective when the expectations/needs of subordinates oppose those of the leader. The resulting conflict between the way the leader prefers to exercise command and control, and the way the organizational culture expects to be led, can severely impair efficiency and productivity. Each resists the other.

Strong organizational cultures compensate for the lack of effective leadership by spreading authority out through subordinate power, increasing bureaucratization,

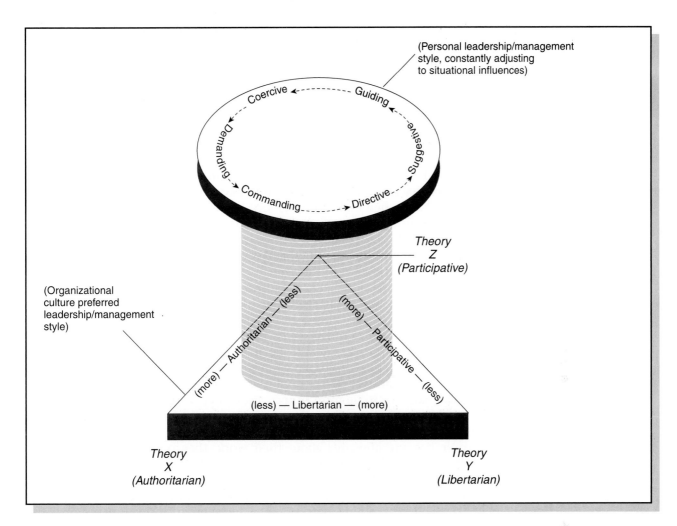

Figure 7.8 Leader-Organizational Synchronization Model

and using other self-adjusting mechanisms (Howell, 1990). For maximum effectiveness the leader's circle of personal command-and-control style must be fairly close to the organization's or one will counter the other with a resulting loss of harmony. In the extreme case noted earlier, where the guiding leader ends up trying to run a culture that is predisposed to an authoritarian person, there is inherent tension rather than a comfortable fit. This tension will foster a basic conflict in perception and approach that may absorb considerable organizational and individual energy, increasing the potential for failure. In effect, the organization and leader fight between themselves.

MAINTAINING LIFE BALANCE

One of the most difficult things for any leader or manager to achieve is life balance. This area of managing oneself appears in the list of leader traits by Bennis and Nanus (1985) as "deployment of self." As we've discussed, leaders are focused on their vision of the future, and they often exhibit obsessive behaviors in pursuit of that vision. Any cursory glance at history reveals leaders who eventually succumbed to their own obsessions as their personal lives fell apart.

It is not uncommon for a person to be swept up by a career and see it as an end in itself. In contemporary American culture a strong work ethic and dedication to the job are much admired attributes. But our culture also has serious problems with divorce as well as alcoholism and other substance abuse. Personal lives are as challenging to manage as are our professional lives.

In your career in media organizations you will encounter many people who get caught up in the greater purpose of journalism, or career climbing, to the extent they become one-dimensional. The media organization career is demanding, and in many jobs there is a 24-hour-a-day nature to the work. You can easily fall into the trap of going in early and leaving late until your work is all that defines you. In newsrooms there is always another story to write, a few more calls to make, and other odds and ends of the daily process of producing news and information. Likewise, because media writing is a creative endeavor, it is not uncommon for journalists to cling to control with a misimpression no one else can do the job as well as they can. In such an environment, "workaholics" are common who give their families, and their own peace of mind, short shrift as they drive themselves to excellence in their job at the sacrifice of everything else.

Can you achieve success as a media organization leader or manager, or employee for that matter, without the cost of losing everything else? Is it possible to manage yourself as successfully as you manage others? The answer to both questions is yes! But just as managing the media organization takes constant attention, so too does managing yourself. Along with empowering others to do their jobs, you must actively empower yourself to maintain your life balance. That means being involved in things that are not work related. It doesn't matter if it is a hobby, a social organization unconnected to media organization work, or some form of recreation such as running, playing softball, golf, or anything else. You need to have time away from the concerns of work, and you need to get enough rest.

When people become obsessive about their work, they often fail to get enough sleep, or they don't sleep well when they are trying to rest. At the same time they tend to cut back on their extracurricular activities, becoming one-dimensional. They work, and sleep poorly, and then work again. Eventually their energy is eroded, their decisions become flawed partly due to fatigue, both physical and mental, and failure becomes the ultimate price. That failure can be at work, at home, or both.

One of the best ways to keep your life in balance is to understand it in the metaphor of the equilateral triangle. As you can see in Figure 7.9 an equilateral triangle has equal length sides and equal angles. If each side has eight units, you can see that they add up to 24, the hours in the day. Think of the baseline as eight hours of work. You need a job to provide the living for everything else. The left side of the triangle is your hours of sleep. The right side is the hours you spend getting ready in the morning, commuting, relaxing with your family, or pursuing your outside interests and hobbies. So along with eight hours of work and eight hours of sleep, in a balanced life you have eight hours for rest, relaxation, and refreshing your perspective on what life, career, and those around you are all about.

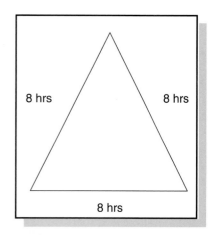

Figure 7.9 Triangle of a Balanced Life

Now, when you work longer hours, the time has to come from somewhere. Typically, we steal it from both sleep and our relaxation and personal time. We sacrifice going to our child's play, or being involved in the Parent-Teachers Association (PTA), or riding a bike in the tranquillity of the evening to reinvigorate our mind and body. We rationalize this as necessary to "get ahead," to further our career so we can keep getting promoted and make more money. Work becomes both a reason and an excuse for not doing everything else we know we really should. But later in life children don't remember why we weren't there, just that we weren't. They don't frame life's quality in monetary terms, but in hugs and time spent with others who care about them. And when you leave a company, no one will remember or care about the extra hours you sacrificed for the organization. You'll just be gone, and someone else will be in your former place.

Figure 7.10 shows what happens to our triangle metaphor of life balance when you work a ten-hour day. You can see that the top of the triangle is lower, as the figure—and the person it represents—moves toward a more one-dimensional plane. That is readily apparent in Figure 7.11 when the work hours go up to 12, and there are only 12 other hours left to split between sleeping and everything else outside of work. If you still sleep eight hours, you only have four left for everything else including getting up, showering, commuting to and from work, having dinner, and relaxing in the evening. Or you may cut your sleep to six hours, leaving six for everything outside of work. But there's not enough time, with a 12-hour workday, to get enough sleep and have much time to yourself.

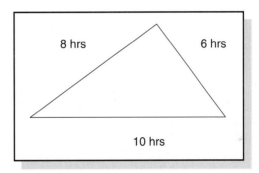

Figure 7.10   Ten-Hour Workday Triangle

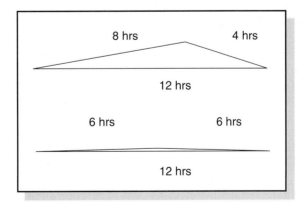

Figure 7.11   Twelve-Hour Workday Triangles

In Figures 7.12 and 7.13 you can see what happens when a person goes to an even longer workday. There is no way the lines on the other sides of the triangle can connect, since the baseline of work exceeds the total length of what's left. That gap, where the sides of the triangle of life no longer connect, is where serious dysfunction occurs: alcoholism, psychological problems such as deep depression, dissolution of personal relationships ending in divorce or destroyed friendships, and many other personal problems.

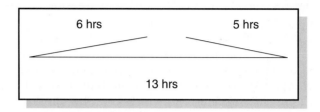

Figure 7.12 Thirteen-Hour Workday Triangle

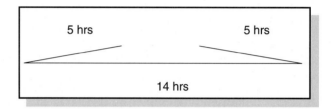

Figure 7.13 Fourteen-Hour Workday Triangle

One of the failures of modern organizations is that they do not always manage their people with life balance in mind. On the surface, it is better for the organization to drive its members to work longer hours than necessary and become obsessive in their work. With salaried people the organization is then paying for eight hours a day but actually getting many more hours free from organizational members. But deep, long-term costs are involved. Flawed decisions and wrecked lives eventually have to be corrected, sometimes at great cost to the organization as well as to the individual. And when the person in such a situation leaves the organization, either through resignation, termination, or retirement, he or she loses a sense of his or her identity. When all you do is work, work is all you have. And when it is gone, you've lost what defines you as a person. Both for your organization and for you as a leader or manager it is advantageous over the long term to keep yourself and those around you in balance. Indeed, "deployment of self" is, perhaps, the most important leader and manager responsibility for the long-term health of both the leader and the organization.

Leading and managing are related, but different, concepts. While the manager works within the organizational structure, attempting to use the bureaucracy to achieve goals, the leader is concerned with a wider strategic view, which includes developing a vision of the future and then moving the organization toward that vision. Locke and Kirkpatrick (1991) argue that visioning is fundamental to the very concept of leadership:

> *The vision should be the primary guiding force of all organizational activity. A leader's key function is to develop that vision. After translating it into a precise and succinct vision statement, the leader must convince followers that working to implement the vision is in their best interests and must provide them with a strategic plan for that implementation. (p. 61)*

Management is more task oriented, utilizing the existing tools at hand, while leadership is the fashioning of new tools through development of fundamental orientations in the macro level relationships with organizational members.

Much of the impact of either leaders or managers rests on their ability to use power and communicate their ideas, as discussed in Chapter 6, "Communication and Power." Trust is crucial in developing the relationships with subordinates that will develop them into "stakeholders" and help them to see their futures as vested in that of the organization, as well as the organization's achievements as their own.

When considering the leadership-follower-corporate need equation, one must be careful to keep in mind the fundamental reality that "leadership is not by itself good or desirable. Leadership is a means to an end. Leadership to *what* end is thus the crucial question (Drucker, 1989, p. 109). What may serve one kind of business well, with a particular corporate culture, may be ineffective in another set of circumstances. To be effective, the leader must have the ability to blend the bureaucracy with his or her vision and mobilize the organizational members to drive toward that vision. Both leaders and managers have preferred styles of control, which are most effective when synchronized to the style toward which the corporate culture is most predisposed.

> *In environments where competition is limited by regulation or a cozy oligopoly . . . leadership sometimes seems not to make much difference one way or another. Factors that economists and sociologists call "structural" are often the key. But in an intensely competitive environment, where the capacity to identify and implement intelligent change and to motivate superior performance is central to corporate results,*

> *the capacity of management to provide leadership takes on new meaning. (Kotter, 1988, p. 14)*

An example is the change in broadcast television, from highly regulated to virtually nonregulated in terms of ownership, during the final two decades of the 20th century. Based on the environmental change factor, it may be arguable that the decline in broadcast television shares during that period was exacerbated by corporations and networks failing to adjust to a new environment. The business of broadcast television rapidly changed. But the industry had evolved into heavily managed bureaucracies lacking the leadership vision necessary to cope with the change. In other words, they continued to operate as they always had, in terms of basic programming and content decision making, though the world in which they function shifted dramatically over a relatively short period. Their failure to adjust adequately to new technological competitors, and a new business context due to deregulation, contributed to their decline. They lacked dynamic, visionary leadership.

It is the overall operating environment that must be evaluated when considering how an organization should be managed and/or led. It is arguable that, in leadership, context is everything. Although many advocates support the participative style over a more authoritarian approach, it "simply may not work in some situations. Leadership is a two-way street, so a democratic style will be effective only if followers are both willing and able to participate actively in the decision-making process" (Muczyk & Reimann, 1989, p. 90). Leadership is situationally derived and implemented. No one way of doing things applies to every case (Hersey, 1984).

Organizations faced with rapid technological change that depend on talented people to do the work—media organizations—also tend to be highly politicized environments driven more by the human relationships than the formal management structure (Lavine & Wackman, 1988). News and information is produced through interpretive and perceptual skills translated into written or video form. It is not easily directed, since so much of the quality of what is produced depends on the attitude of the people who apply their talent to the task. That requires what is called "transformative leadership." It emphasizes the leader's ability to relate to others, understand their different values, and blend them within the organization, to transform their artistic creativity into marketable product (Ogilvy, 1987). News workers may, to themselves, serve the public interest with the perception they are helping people deal with the forces of the modern world. But what they do has to fit within the context of an organization that uses it to generate circulation or ratings and sell advertising.

The economic consideration of maintaining profits, despite continuing audience share decline, has increased the tension in American media between the business owners and their editorial employees. Research on news organizations has found a relationship between the behavior of leaders and the job satisfaction of organizational members. Newsroom employees have been characterized as people who are driven by an internal need for meaningful work and commitment with a sense of higher purpose (McQuarrie, 1992). Among such people a more democratic management approach has been found to be more effective since journalists often engage in their profession as much for the intrinsic motivations as the extrinsic (Powers & Lacy, 1992). They tend to be highly creative people who value a sense of belonging to a special group with positive social relations among coworkers, substantial control over their work, and considerable autonomy in what they do (Pollard, 1995). Money is of less importance to them than nonfinancial rewards such as doing meaningful work and contributing to the good of society (Lavine & Wackman, 1988, p. 188). It has been likened to a "calling," rather than simply a job (Auletta, 1991, p. 559). Thus, mass communication and society are intricately interwoven from the concept of a free press to the perception of special meaning many contemporary journalists attach to their profession.

One of the problems in mass media organizations is that they are distinctly different from the fundamental business model from which prevailing management theory has evolved (specifically the assembly line industrial plants examined by Taylor (1947/1967), and Mayo (1953). There the challenge is "managing hands," whereas, in the information company, the task is "managing minds" (Ogilvy, 1987). Media organization workers in both print and electronic journalism on the national and local levels have been found to be overwhelmingly college educated (Gans, 1980; Gaziano & Coulson, 1988; Smith & Becker, 1989). Additionally, total annual enrollment in the more than 400 university programs emphasizing journalism and mass communication education exceeds 140,000 students (Kosicki & Becker, 1996). Considering journalists' high level of education, and the research that shows the need for journalists to have a sense of purpose in what they do, more of a coaching approach to management appears more likely to increase journalists' competitiveness.

Because media organization workers tend to be highly educated, with intrinsic drives pushing them to excel in their chosen profession, it is particularly important for a manager or leader to ensure some balance exists in the lives of everyone involved in creating media product. Obsessive tendencies that result in extra hours at work over extended periods of time may lead to flawed decision making and perceptions as the individual becomes one-dimensional. Such immersion in the work environment, at the exclusion of normal social connectivity may also contribute to a narrower perspective than the audience the media organization is trying to reach. In other words, media employees may report to an audience of which they are not part. Ultimately the individual who does not maintain balance in his or her life is setting up eventual failure through flawed decision making and a one-dimensional perspective.

In the intricacies of the relationship of leader and follower, as much as in any other human endeavor, Weber's assertion that "man is an animal suspended in webs of significance he himself has spun" rings true (Carey, 1989, p. 56). Interwoven relationships, dependencies, and influences combine in extremely fragile ways to form webs of failure or success, each unique but still similar to those hanging around it. In the last analysis a manager can be a leader, and a leader can be a manager. But a leader isn't necessarily a manager, nor is a manager a leader just because he or she has the title of Chief Executive Officer. In a sense leadership and management are like a series of interlocking rings that *may* overlap, but don't always complement one another.

It is logical to expect performance benefits to come from increased training in the identified attributes of leadership. However, exposing those in management positions to concepts such as visioning, and the psychology of human relations, does not mean those managers will become visionaries or great motivators. More effective management may occur as those managers assemble additional tools to do their jobs, but they may not necessarily become leaders in the process. For, as Zaleznik (1989) underscores,

before a leader can change how other people think and feel, he must go through a personal transformation in which he is tested and changed. This psychological transformation produces objectivity and clear-sightedness that enable such leaders to remember and use the past. It is for this reason that teaching leadership is especially difficult. Although it may be easy to generalize the qualities leaders should have, it is more difficult to stimulate in the student the transforming experience that makes leadership in practice transcend the ordinary. (p. 241)

In this chapter we have tried to provide you with a better understanding of leading and managing. Truly extraordinary leaders are rare combinations of managerial skill and innate talent for getting people to do their will. You may be a leader personality, or a manager personality. It takes both kinds to take a media organization from the ordinary to the extraordinary.

With your expanded knowledge of managing and leading, you know guiding others is a great challenge. Success depends on your adopting a basic approach to your daily life that puts the complexity of the organization and its members into a manageable set of principles. You must master four essential things to be an excellent media organization manager or leader, regardless of your personality. They are the CORE of all that has been discussed in this chapter.

♦ **Context**—What is the entire organizational situation including its history and contemporary framework?

♦ **Organizational dynamic**—What are the internal systems, procedures, and processes at work in your organization and how do they respond to change?

♦ **Relationships**—Who are the players, inside the organization and outside it, influencing the course of events. Who has the power, formally and informally, and how can it be marshaled to achieve your goals?

♦ **Environment**—What's going on in the organizational niche causing change, and what can you do to help your organization adapt to it?

The easiest way to remember the list is as an acronym. The first letter of each of the elements of our list is CORE. The CORE of leading and managing a media organization is in fully understanding the four elements and using them to achieve your goals. It's really fairly simple. In any given situation you must ask four questions based on the CORE concept:

1. What's the organization situation and how did we get here (the organizational **C**ontext)?

2. How's this really organization work (**O**rganizational dynamic)?

3. Who's really got the power (**R**elationships)?

4. What external factors affect the organization (the **E**nvironmental pressure requiring adaptation)?

One of the foremost challenges in managing or leading is in cutting away the clutter of daily events to find out the causes of what's going on and, therefore, what needs to be done. Focusing on the CORE will help you do that and increase your personal and professional effectiveness.

STUDY QUESTIONS

1. Considering the various leadership trait comparisons provided in this chapter, prepare a list of the top five most important leadership characteristics you think are necessary to be a true leader in a contemporary media organization. List them in order from most important to less important. Compare your list to those of your classmates.

2. What is the "Wallenda factor" and why is it so important in the personality of leaders?

3. There are five basic controlling approaches used by leaders. What are they? Describe the positive and negative aspects of each.

4. To be effective, all leaders must have people around them to help them achieve their goals. If you were to be your media organization's leader, what kind of people would you select to be around you?

5. What is "life balance" and how do you see it applying to you?

6. Take a piece of paper and draw a triangle that accurately represents the hours of your typical day with sides for work, sleep, and everything else. Are you out of balance? What is the danger of being seriously out of balance for an extended length of time?

chapter 8

MARKETING THE MEDIA ORGANIZATION

BY RICK FISCHER, PH.D. (UNIVERSITY OF MEMPHIS)

RELATIONSHIPS AND TRANSACTIONS

Think about why your media organization exists. Are you looking for long-term growth and profit? Do you want to be around for another ten years or more? Great! But there are media organization owners who buy and sell properties to make a quick buck or to gain some financial advantage at tax time. They are not interested in operating the business long term. The business itself is the unit of exchange.

This chapter is not about buying and selling media organizations. Instead, it is geared to those who want to operate and grow a business. That requires attending to transactions and relationships. We'll look at media factors, how we position our product or service, and some of the marketing research tools available to managers. This chapter will consider the separate needs of print media, electronic media, and media counselors. Finally, we'll consider some marketing issues associated with media organizations.

DEVELOPING THE MARKETING MIX

Marketing operates on at least two levels. The first involves creating a demand for your organization's products or services. The second level involves creating media products and services people will buy. Both are important for the media organization and require regular attention. And both levels require an understanding of the marketing mix. At a fairly high level of abstraction all media organizations must consider their product or service, the price, who will use the product, distribution channels, and the competition. And so this first section is about the fundamental activity of *transactions*.

Product or Service

The media generally view themselves in three ways: in the *context* in which they operate, through the *content* that fills their respective forms, and as *audience-providing mechanisms* for others. And, on the surface, media enterprises sound simple enough. You sell newspapers, a newsletter, a magazine, books, radio or television programming, Internet content, advertising services, or expertise in public relations. But that's just a start. It's only one way managers of print and electronic media organizations may think about their products. With the exception of advertising and public relations, in general terms media managers and workers identify primarily with their media form, the context of what they do.

But we could just as well emphasize content. Take the classified section of a typical newspaper, for example. Classified ads—content—have traditionally been the domain of newspapers. Then some radio stations began running classified ads over the air. Newsletters run classifieds as a service to their readers, either for free or at a nominal charge. Electronic bulletin boards and the Internet now carry what we traditionally thought of as classified ads. Here, the unifying concept is *content*. The medium is merely the distribution channel. Sidebar 8.1 explains how the Arizona Republic extends the value of its regular material for those with access to the World Wide Web.

Still, a third component must be considered. Media managers provide access to audiences. They sell column inches, pages, and time to people who want to bring a message to a particular audience. This is an extraordinarily competitive side of the business. Rate sheets are only the beginning point for the bargaining process. See Picard (1989) for a more complete discussion of the economics of media and markets.

Sidebar 8.1 Arizona Republic Web Site

Phoenix, Arizona, newspapers get a lot of mileage from their regular content. Their Web page (http://www.azcentral.com) goes well beyond mere self-promotion and a summary of the day's top stories. You can search this site for a home, look for a new car, check out community services like schools and hospitals, link up with a kindred soul in the personals, decide on a movie, or plan a day trip to other Arizona towns. The data are dynamic and change regularly.

The home search options let you select your price range (anywhere from $50,000 to $500,000), your preferred location within the Phoenix area, and the number of bedrooms. If you like, you can look at a map of greater Phoenix and select the school you want to be near. Once you select a home that fits your needs you can click on the built-in mortgage calculator to determine the monthly payment (principal and interest). You can then fill in the principal, interest rate, years financed, and how often you intend to make payments (monthly or every two weeks) to compute the annual income you will need to get a loan on the home. The final arrangements for financing may vary, but the mortgage estimator feature is handy for comparison real estate shopping and a good example of providing useful content.

So, understanding our product or service is no trivial matter. How we perceive ourselves, and the point of what we do, guides all of our business decision making at the highest levels.

Price

There are a few people for whom price is not a consideration, but most of us want the most product for the least money. At least that's what we say. But that's an impossible criterion because we would be trying to optimize (value) and minimize (cost) at the same time. It can't be done. The answer is a whole range of values where the cost curve and value curve intersect. The best we can do is optimize value for some fixed price, or minimize cost for some standard of quality (see Fig. 8.1).

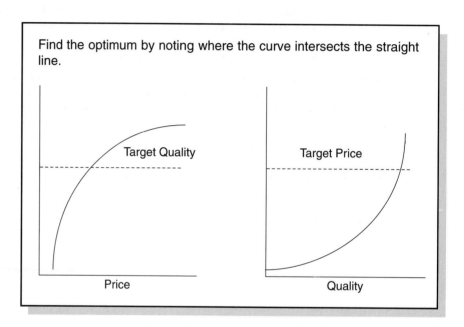

Figure 8.1 Optimizing for Quality or Price

So how do we arrive at a fair price? Those who study the mathematics of management can pick the points where we will sell the most product and where we will make the most profit (Thierauf & Grosse, 1970). Sometimes these points are the same, but more often they are not. See Sidebar 8.2 for an example of a new magazine start-up.

In this example we believe we will sell the most product when we charge $ .50. But, we won't make any money at that price. We see that our dollar sales are highest when we sell our magazine for $1.25. Finally, after figuring in fixed and variable costs, we see that our profits are highest when we sell our magazine for $1.50. So what's the best price? Part of that depends on your psychology and how important it is for you to be a major player in terms of size. Some people define winning as being the largest media organization in their market. Others prefer the greatest return on investment in raw dollar terms. The two are not necessarily synonymous. A second-place player can make more money than number one, because of the costs of being first. Winning depends on how you define your goals!

Sidebar 8.2 New Magazine Start-up

Suppose you are a publisher and want to start a new regional magazine. A lot is involved here. There are computer programs to help analyze such a situation, and cost accountants are trained to do involved analysis. But work through this example so you can see how various factors relate and how what may seem to be the best plan isn't necessarily the most profitable.

First, you need to figure out what a realistic expectation of circulation is, based on various cover prices, and concurrently determine the most profitable number of magazines to produce based on production and distribution costs. Profitability is complex and involves numerous factors. Sometimes the biggest volume of units distributed does not generate the most bottom-line profit for the media organization. One way to determine price is to approach the decision as an optimization problem. First, we need to generate an estimate of demand for each price we are considering. Our marketing vice president gives us her best forecast.

Forecast	Proposed selling price	Estimated demand— the first year
A	$ .50	100,000
B	1.00	75,000
C	1.50	50,000
D	2.00	25,000

The marketing VP believes the demand will be linear and could be plotted (see Fig. 8.2).

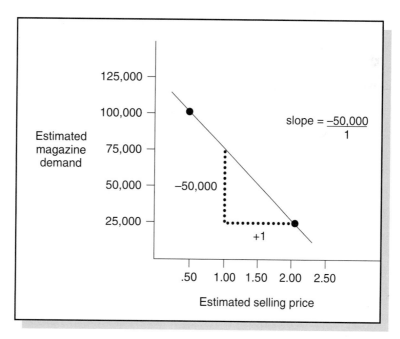

Figure 8.2 Demand-Price Slope

Continued

That linear relationship could be expressed as the general formula $(y = a + bx)$, where a is the point where the forecast line intersects the y axis (125,000 in this case), b represents the slope of the line, and x represents the selling price. The marketing VP estimates the demand will go down 50,000 copies if we increase the price by $1, so the price/demand slope is −50,000. Once we have determined the price/demand relationship, plotting it allows us to quickly determine the demand for any price for our product. So the graphing approach is very effective in analyzing various production and pricing strategies.

$$y = a + bx$$
$$y = 125,000 - 50,000x$$

Our production manager figures that our basic annual production costs for the first year will be $25,000, setting up and operating the production system and staff. On top of that, it will cost us another $.50 per copy to actually run the magazine on the presses. In reality the unit costs would decrease after we had recovered our editorial and prepress costs, but for the purposes of this example assume that the breakeven point is somewhere beyond 125,000 units. Since we are a business, we are interested in profits, not just magazines sold. We want to know how many units we have to sell to cover our costs, and then how much circulation has to increase beyond that point for a reasonable rate of return. The first step is to work up our estimates of total costs and total sales. The total cost equals the fixed cost plus the product of the variable cost and the demand.

The Total Cost formula is:

$$C_t = C_f + (C_v)(y)$$

where:

C_t = total costs
C_f = fixed costs or $25,000
C_v = variable costs, $ .50 for each unit produced
y = demand

Thus,

$$C_t = 25,000 - .50 \, (125,000 - 50,000x)$$
$$C_t = 25,000 - 62,500 - 25,000x$$
$$C_t = 87,500 - 25,000x$$

The Total Sales equation is:

S_t = Total Demand × Selling Price per Unit
If $D_t = y$ (remember, $y = 125,000 - 50,000x$)
and x = Selling Price per Unit
then $S_t = (125,000 - 50,000x) \times$
$S_t = 125,000x - 50,000x^2$

Now let's plot total sales for the prices above $.50—our cost per copy. You can use the total sales formula or locate the equivalent demand on the graph.

Selling Price	×	Units Sold	=	Total Sales Revenue
$ .50		100,000		$ 50,000
.75		87,500		65,625
1.00		75,000		75,000
1.25		62,500		**78,125**
1.50		50,000		75,000
1.75		37,500		65,625
2.00		25,000		50,000
2.25		12,500		28,125
2.50		0		0

Continued

We sell the most papers when we only charge $ .50. But at $1.25 we make the most money. And neither of these takes into consideration our fixed costs and variable costs. We can include those in the Profit formula.

We now have all the information we need to work the Profit equation. Here is the combined equation that starts with the 125,000 copies at the point where the demand slope intersects the y axis (the Total Costs term), and then works down the slope.

Profit = Total Sales – Total Costs

$P = (125{,}000x – 50{,}000x^2) –$
  $(87{,}500 – 25{,}000x)$

$P = 125{,}000x – 50{,}000x^2 – 87{,}500 +$
  $25{,}000x$

combine like terms:

$P = 150{,}000x – 50{,}000x^2 – 87{,}500$

rearrange the terms:

$P = –50{,}000x^2 + 150{,}000x – 87{,}500$

Take the first derivative to find the selling price, which will maximize our profits:

$\dfrac{dP}{dx} = (2) –50{,}000x^{2-1} + (1)150{,}000x^{1-1} = 0$

(the term 87,500 drops out)

$\dfrac{dP}{dx} = (2) –50{,}000x^1 + (1)150{,}000x^0 = 0$

simplify the equation:

$\dfrac{dP}{dx} = (2) –50{,}000x^1 + (1)150{,}000 = 0$

$\dfrac{dP}{dx} = –100{,}000x + 150{,}000 = 0$

solve for x:

$–100{,}000x = –150{,}000$

$x = \dfrac{–150{,}000}{–100{,}000}$

$x = \$1.50$

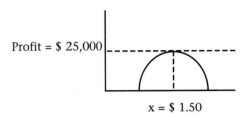

Profit = $ 25,000

x = $ 1.50

You can follow this example to find the selling price that maximizes your profit. Software programs like Mathcad can solve the equations for you. You may also want to consult your local university's math department or business school. As a media manager you need to have some knowledge of what's involved. But you also should consult a trained accountant for sophisticated analysis beyond your ability. In two areas, particularly, good managers readily seek the counsel of experts; law and accounting.

Picard (1989) asserts that supply and demand rarely enter into the pricing decision for print media products. Price is pegged arbitrarily. For the media markets he studied, demand did *not* vary predictably with changes in price (as assumed in our example). But the contemporary market for media products is in turmoil. The advertiser today has many more media options to get his or her client's message to a target audience. That means that the media consumer also has more options to get news, information, and entertainment. The bottom line: Know your industry. Use the optimization formulas as a guide and exercise good judgment.

Before we leave this topic we need to consider one more factor—we'll call it psychic cost. It's a consumer variable. It's the idea that things like time and convenience are factored in when consumers consider value (Lavine & Wackman, 1988).

Would the busy manager rather read an academic journal or a breezy newsletter to stay up on what's happening in the business? If the goal were reading for enjoyment, would you rather have *The Complete Works of Shakespeare* on a digital CD-ROM or as a series of books? If you needed to look up information about the U.S. presidents, would you rather have an encyclopedia on a digital CD with a hypertext search engine or in 26 bound volumes plus annual supplements? All things being equal, people will choose the medium involving the least psychic cost. In other words, what do you want it for, and does the media form you choose really suit your need? Bound encyclopedias on a shelf may look nice in the library, but do you ever use them? And if you bought a CD-ROM version of that encyclopedia, would you ever use it on your computer? If it is important for you to have the bound volumes there, so you have a kind of home library, that value may be a key in determining your psychic cost/benefit ratio.

Distribution

Be careful. Technology is upsetting a lot of the assumptions about how content can be distributed. You can get radio programs and read newspaper stories over the World Wide Web. You can get coupons online (at http://www.valpak.com) and print as many as you need. You listen to local television news simulcast on your car radio as you drive home from work. We've moved from television with an antenna, to cable, to direct broadcast satellites. Magazines, newswires, and newsletter articles are available through databases like NEXIS. Revenues from books on cassette were $1.5 billion in 1995 and estimated to continue to grow (Veronis & Suhler, 1996). Dick Estelle will read a book to you for free on a public radio station. Soon you'll be able to download (for a fee) the latest audio release from your favorite recording artist. And a Dutch company is experimenting with a technology that would allow you to download a video to your VCR. You will be able to view it twice before it deactivates. You will need a special electronic digital delivery (EDD) VCR, but the potential for alternate delivery systems is certainly there.

What this means is that the distribution decision is a lot more complicated than it used to be. Traditionally, newspapers had two options: use local carriers or send it through the mail. There are even entrepreneurs who are willing to go head to head with the U.S. Postal Service (Barr, 1991). Today, many local daily papers use adult carriers to deliver the printed edition and also provide telephone dial-in services for sports scores, current stock prices, and other information over the phone. The traditional newspaper is being repackaged for users who have increasing options for media engagement, including availability over the World Wide Web of the Internet. We already can deliver a customized product, giving the consumer only stories on a particular topic or industry, weather information from a preselected part of the country, tailored astrology readings, and sports scores only from our favorite teams.

Houghton Mifflin is one of many book publishers that offer custom publishing. Build a custom book from chapters you like from among any of their publications. Just call a toll-free number.

Advertising and public relations people can choose from the mail, couriers, fax, e-mail, media distribution services like PR Newswire or Business Wire for print materials, and CDs, videocassettes, and satellites for video products.

Competition

Managers have to consider what the competition *is doing* as well as what the competition *might do*. That moves us from a deterministic world to a probabilistic one. You can no longer think in terms of the "given" conditions of today but must consider the probable scenario that will develop in the future. In strategic thinking that means you must have a wider view. You look not only at the probability that the competition will select a likely strategy, but you also have to consider the odds of that strategy being successful. It is one thing to attempt a course of action, but quite another to succeed with it. Your competition may adopt an unwise strategy and fail, working to your advantage. Because the competition initiates an action does not mean you should immediately jump on the bandwagon. It is very easy to get swept up in trendy developments. But strategic thinking means weighing all the options and deciding on the right course of action for your media organization based on your circumstances. Sometimes you need to move with the competition, and other times allow your competitors to move independently. Deciding what course to adopt requires as much knowledge as possible and a lot of judgment. It is a combination of skill and art.

Someone will make money on the Internet, but most people are still trying to discover how. Is there something to be gained by getting in early even though we will likely lose money in the short term? Some companies are betting heavily that the future of the Internet lies in the family television. Yet a Dataquest Inc. poll of 7,000 households reveals that consumers aren't interested. Ninety-three percent of those responding indicated that they were not interested in buying an Internet-enabled television set or a setup box (*Investor's Business Daily*, 1996). Will consumers change their minds, or should this be an area we should stay away from?

Let's consider media programming. Radio stations can change formats overnight. Is it better to fight for dominance as the number three country station in a large market or change to an easy listening format where there is no competition (at the moment)? That can only be answered by knowing the size of your listener market, knowing your advertisers' (and potential advertisers') preferences, comparing the costs of producing both formats, *and* factoring in what the competition might do if you change.

ANALYZING MEDIA COST FACTORS

As we saw earlier, one of the key variables in pricing media products is cost of production. Production costs vary from medium to medium. Media managers often think about competition only in terms of their own medium. But that's shortsighted. Advertisers have many choices. To make that point, consider costs across media from the Memphis, Tennessee, market, including newspaper, electronic media, and billboard.

Print Media Costs

The Memphis daily newspaper, *The Commercial Appeal,* does not charge to produce a simple ad for its own paper. A simple ad includes layout, type, clip art, and minor enlargements or reductions of photos. However, if original art or color separations for a color photograph are required, expect a production charge. Depending on the work involved, the additional costs could range from $50 to $300 per ad.

Let's say you want to run that same ad in another paper. *The Commercial Appeal* will charge for extra copies of the final layout. The costs for additional veloxes (camera-ready copies of the ad) are $13 for the first velox and $7 for each additional velox.

On the other hand, the weekly *Memphis Business Journal* does charge for production work. The average cost is approximately $25, but the cost depends on the size of the ad. If you take your ad layout from *The Commercial Appeal* to the *Memphis Business Journal,* there would be no additional charge to use it beyond buying space in the *Journal.*

Electronic Media Costs

Television spots require writing the script, selecting talent, shooting, and editing. Most television stations will produce a spot if it runs on that station. For an additional charge, the stations typically will allow you to run the spot on other stations. But production costs can be substantial. For example, the typical cost for a television station to produce a spot includes:

Shooting	$130–$225 per hour
Editing	$175–$200 per hour
Script writing	no additional charge
Talent	no additional charge or up to $1,000 per spot

Where you shoot the commercial will affect the cost. Location shoots often cost more than simply using the television station's production studio. Other cost factors may include the use of TelePrompTer or multiple camera angles or location setups. The cost of editing usually depends on the time of day that the editing takes place. Typically, daytime hours are busier and therefore more expensive than nighttime hours.

The talent cost depends on the going rate of the person you use. A voice-over announcement, where copy is spoken but no one appears on camera, typically will cost less than on-camera talent. The voice-over fee may be included in the overall production cost. And production houses and television stations with staff announcers usually provide the voice as part of the basic production charge. However, if you choose a popular television personality or other well-known individual to appear on camera, you will pay more depending on the person's popularity.

A good rule of thumb for the total cost for a 30-second local television spot is to estimate two to three hours of shooting time and two to three hours of editing time with approximately six scenes. If you want to use the spot on other stations, you will have to pay $25 to $45 for additional videotapes.

Finally, the cost of producing the commercial, or spot, is only part of the total expenditure. Once it's finished you have to purchase the time to air it. Obviously it will cost more to air the spot for 26 weeks than for 13 weeks. However, longer advertising contracts usually provide a quantity discount so the individual spot price may be less for the 26-week run, even though the total cost of the campaign is more.

For radio, you will need studio recording time, script writing, and talent. The following are typical radio production charges:

Studio time	$35–$45 per hour
Script writing	$35–$50 per script
Talent	no additional charge or up to $60 per person

To use the announcement on another station, plan on an additional $4 to $10 per reel of tape. But be aware that if you use one radio station's familiar voice on your commercial, that station's archrival in the market may require a different voice to be used. The actual production of a 60-second radio spot will take one to two hours of studio time.

Radio and television use sound, and frequently the client will want to use a popular song. No problem as long as you follow proper legal procedures and pay any required rights fees. It's important to note here that some artists refuse to allow their work to be used for commercials. You cannot just use a recording you like. Copyright and appropriation are discussed in detail in the legal section later in this text. If you are going to use music, the first step is to contact the publisher of the song. See Sidebar 8.3 for ways to obtain permission.

Sidebar 8.3 How to Obtain Permission to Use a Piece of Music

Contact the Publisher Directly

The publisher's name is usually located on the label of a cassette or compact disk. Locate the publisher's address and phone number in the *Recording Industry Sourcebook,* available from Whitehurst & Clark, Inc. at (800) 233–9604. In addition to lists of publishers, this book also contains many other music industry contacts such as music attorneys, artists and booking agents, recording studios, and music libraries. Software is also available that contains the *Sourcebook* plus a music industry database.

Use a Publisher's Representative

If you do not know the name of the publisher or choose not to deal with the publisher directly, you can contact The Harry Fox Agency, the American Society of Composers, Authors and Publishers (ASCAP), Broadcast Music Incorporated (BMI), or SESAC.

The Harry Fox Agency was established by the National Music Publishers' Association, Inc. to serve as an information source, clearinghouse, and monitoring service for licensing musical copyrights. The agency represents more than 16,000 American music publishers and licenses a large percentage of the uses of music in the United States on records, tapes, compact discs, and imported records. If the agency represents the publisher, it will clear the use of the song with the publisher. Be prepared to provide details about how you intend to use the song, such as, markets where it will air, length of time it will run, and type of media used. The agency will give you a quote for the rights, called synchronization rights, to use the song in your radio or television spot. If you agree, the agency issues the license, collects and distributes the royalties, and helps to monitor use of the song by the advertiser. You must contact the record company for master recording rights. These are the record company's rights to record the song. If you intend to rerecord the piece, you will only need the publisher's rights, not the master recording rights from the record company.

ASCAP, BMI, and SESAC are performing rights organizations. Any of these three organizations can tell you if they represent the publisher of the song you are interested in.

ASCAP, BMI, and SESAC issue licenses to users, mainly television and radio stations, of publicly performed, nondramatic music for a fee and then pay performing rights royalties to the publishers and songwriters of the performed works. For example, if a song is represented by BMI, then a radio or television station must be licensed by BMI before the station can play the song. The same holds true for ASCAP and SESAC.

Although BMI and ASCAP do not give permission to use a song, both organizations can help you locate the publisher. You then contact the publisher for permission, or synchronization rights, to use the song. You will have to contact the record company for recording rights. The cost for these rights will vary depending on the type of media in which the song will be used, how long it will air, and in which markets it will air. If SESAC represents the song, SESAC can issue a mechanical license, which gives you permission to use the song.

Continued

Music industry contacts:

Harry Fox Agency
711 Third Avenue
New York, NY 10017
(212) 370–5330
http://nmpa.org/hfa

BMI—New York
320 West 57th Street
New York, NY 10019
(212) 586–2000
FAX (212) 245–8986
E-Mail: newyork@bmi.com

BMI—Los Angeles
8730 Sunset Boulevard, Third Floor West
Los Angeles, CA 90069
(310) 659–9109
FAX (310) 657–6947
E-Mail: losangeles@bmi.com

BMI—Nashville
10 Music Square East
Nashville, TN 37203
(615) 401–2000
FAX (615) 401–2707
E-Mail: nashville@bmi.com

BMI—London
79 Harley House
Marylebone Road
London NW1 5HN, England
Phone 011–44–171–935–8517
FAX 011–44–171–487–5091
E-Mail: london@bmi.com
http://bmi.com

ASCAP—Nashville
Two Music Square West
Nashville, TN 37203
(615) 742–5000
FAX (615) 742–5020

ASCAP—New York
One Lincoln Plaza
New York, NY 10023
(212) 621–6000
FAX (212) 724–9064

ASCAP—Chicago
1608 West Belmont, Suite 200
Chicago, IL 60657
(773) 472–1157
FAX (773) 472–1158

ASCAP—Los Angeles
7920 Sunset Boulevard, Suite 300
Los Angeles, CA 90046
(213) 883–1000
FAX (213) 883–1049

ASCAP—London
#8 Cork Street
London W1X 1PB
Great Britain
Phone: 011–44–171–439–0909
FAX: 011–44–171–434–0073

ASCAP—Puerto Rico
Office 505
First Federal Savings Condo
1519 Ponce De Leon Avenue
Santurce, PR 00910
(809) 725–1688
FAX (809) 721–1190
http://www.ascap.com
E-mail: info@ascap.com

SESAC—Nashville
55 Music Square East
Nashville, TN 37203
826–9996

SESAC—New York
421 West 54th Street
New York, NY 10019
(212) 586–3450

SESAC—London
20 Watford Road
Radlett Harts
WD7 8LE
Phone: 011–44–192–385–7792
Fax: 011–44–192–385–8052
http://www.sesac.com

One way to keep the costs down is to use library music. Library music is produced by companies that sell the rights to use the music along with the music itself. You can find library music at recording studios. For example, if you record your radio spot at a sound studio, you can look through the studio's music library for a track of music that fits your needs. The tracks are organized by categories, such as jazz, up tempo, or easy listening. The studio will charge you by the hour for studio time, which often includes use of their library music. The studio pays a monthly fee to the companies that provide the royalty-free music. If you want to take the library music out of the studio to use somewhere else, then you will typically have to pay for each track of music that you want. One Memphis, Tennessee, sound studio charges $75 per hour for studio time and $50 for each track you take outside of their studio. Frequently it is more cost-effective to have the studio do the music and narration mix all at once.

What happens when you write your own jingle or song? You can use it as you please, since it's yours. However, it's wise to register the copyright of anything you create of commercial value to prevent others from using it in an unauthorized manner. See Chapter 14 for more about copyright.

Community service and charitable organizations can run public service announcements (PSAs) rather than a paid television or radio spot. U.S. radio and television stations do not charge for airtime to run PSAs. Submit copy for the PSA to the radio station, and a disk jockey will voice it, often live on the air. Some radio stations require preproduced PSAs. Television stations often produce PSAs for free, including the studio time and special electronic graphics that would cost a commercial client a considerable amount of money.

Billboard Costs

A 14' × 48' billboard will typically cost between $1,000 and $5,000 per month, depending on the market in which it's displayed and the particular location. This size is typical of the boards along an interstate highway. The cost usually includes both production and running the board. The cost also depends on whether it is a permanent board or a rotary board. Permanent boards stay in one location for the duration of the contract, usually six months or one year. Rotary boards rotate locations. For example, a rotary board on a six-month contract may spend two months in each of three locations.

PRODUCT POSITIONING

At this point let's assume that we have a product that people will want. We'll also assume that our research tells us that sufficient potential demand exists to make this launch a financial success. We are now ready to consider positioning, or the *relationship* our organization has with the customer.

Since the term "positioning" was first introduced in 1981 (Ries & Trout), it has been used in a number of ways—each emphasizing a different relationship between the media organization, the product, and the consumer.

The first use of the term emphasizes *the media organization itself.* Marketers attempt to capture in a phrase how their media organization is different from other similar media organizations. Broadcast stations, for example, usually add a positioning statement just after their station name. It is not uncommon for stations to purchase such positioning statements as part of their news formatting packages from national consultants and suppliers. So as you travel around the country you see and hear familiar promotional material, with a local, region, or state name added where appropriate. Examples from the Memphis market include:

Action News 5: *Coverage you can count on every day*
Channel 3: *Where local news comes first*
News 24: *Your Mid-South news leader*

Another use of the term emphasizes *product*. We have time, space, a product, or a service to sell, so we need to find people who will buy it. In this case the commodity is the starting point as we look for ways to distinguish our product from our competitor's product or service. Positioning in this case is a strategy to move product. Our product presumably satisfies certain consumer needs better than others. People will buy our product if we position it properly to attract their attention.

Both of these uses conceptualize positioning as something the organization does *to* others or *for* others. If we help people structure their thinking about our product, then they will understand how that product is differentiated from other similar products. Understanding that difference is supposed to lead consumers to *buy our* products. But the process is much more complex (Schultz, Tannenbaum, & Lauterborn, 1995).

A third use of the term starts with the *media consumer* and works backward. In this approach the marketer asks "how do consumers *perceive* my organization or product?" Positioning in this case is synonymous with perception or framing. It can form one side of an analysis that asks two questions:

1. How do we view ourselves?
2. How do others view us?

The answers can be used in a communication campaign to reorient (or position) the media organization and its products. Or the organization might want to align itself or its products more closely with the perceptions consumers already hold about our organization and its products.

When researchers investigate consumer perceptions, they usually are guided by a set of assumptions that help them make sense of their findings. These assumptions are rooted in presumed relationships between media preferences and consumer demographics, psychographics, and a fairly new area relating to an organization's social responsibility ("New attempt," 1997).

Demographics

The term "demographics" brings together a number of consumer dimensions like age, gender, income, education, religion, occupational status, and zip code. Others include social class and cultural background, although these are much harder to operationalize and measure (Scott & O'Hair, 1989). When we cluster people along one or more of these dimensions, we may find that there are meaningful similarities regarding their media use and preferences. Perhaps the best example is used by media salespeople when selling ads. "Our listeners are women between the age of 25 and 34"—the group many advertisers favor. Also, they will add average income, education, and whatever other information potential advertisers might find important. In this approach the media organization is using its audience's demographics to sell advertisers on reaching those demographic groups. But the marketer who wants to use media to sell productions may come at the problem from a different perspective. If we ask, "What media products do women between the ages of 25 and 34 prefer?" the answer may lead to a change in our products or product mix. In the first point of view we are trying to match a given product to a demographic group. In the second perspective we are trying to tailor a product to existing preferences of those within the demographic group. As a media organization manager you need to be aware of the difference in trying to meet people where you think they are, as opposed to trying to meet them where they want to be. The reality is that media consumers typically use multiple media sources to satisfy a range of wants and needs. You can find tables of preferences by different consumer groupings listed in Simmons Market Research Bureau reports that are very helpful in trying to design and position media organization products.

Observing cluster similarities is a purely descriptive exercise. Media managers understand that not every woman between 25 and 34 prefers adult contemporary radio programming, but they will be right more times than not if they presume she does. There is no attempt here to explain *why* groups hold the preferences they do. And managers need to recognize that media preferences, like other consumer behavior, will likely change over time.

Acorn by CACI uses demographic data—census, Bureau of Labor Statistics, and proprietary information—to classify U.S. neighborhoods into one of 40 clusters or market segments. These segments are sorted on 61 demographic characteristics that predict consumer behavior. Terms like "Successful Achievers" and "Baby Boomers with Children" describe segments in terms of lifestyle, socioeconomic status, type of home, and where people in these social clusters live.

Psychographics

One attempt to improve our ability to predict consumer behavior is through the use of psychographics. The approach was developed in the early 1970s and clusters people by attitudes, values, and lifestyles. Researchers collect information on consumers and try to develop models that predict their response to messages. All the models discussed here are proprietary and data associated with those models are sold to organizations to use in their marketing programs.

SRI International of Menlo Park, California, owns the Values and Lifestyles (VALS2) marketing system. This model started with product use and income to create eight general categories (Heath, 1996). The original VALS typology combined Maslow's (1954) hierarchy of needs with Riesman, Glazer, and Denny's (1950) idea of social character to create nine discrete types in four categories (Kahle, Beatty, & Homer, 1986). Because motivations and needs are fairly constant within groups, individuals within those groups are thought to react in similar ways to messages. That means that marketers can construct messages for individuals based on group membership. Under development is iVALS, a system that focuses on the Internet and its users (Heath, 1996).

PRIZM is Claritas' system for segmenting people into any one of 62 clusters with names like "Blue Blood Estates" and "Inner Cities." This system provides descriptions of people at the neighborhood level. They factor in such things as auto registration data, magazine subscriptions, and product use information. Users can combine demographics with media, product, and lifestyle preferences to identify current customers and locate new ones.

Claritas sells custom and off-the-shelf information, as well as software for marketers and telemarketers. Those using the online Claritas Connect system can access the information any time, day or night, and the data can be imported into GIS-compatible mapping programs.

Claritas acquired Strategic Mapping in 1996, giving them two products of interest to marketers. ClusterPLUS is a geodemographic segmentation system that uses census data and lifestyle information to create 60 clusters of consumers with similar characteristics. ClusterPLUS will tell you which media these groups use and what leisure activities they prefer. MarketQuest is an integrated marketing system that provides powerful integrated analysis for site selection, target marketing, trade area analysis, media selection, and customer profiling. Claritas is a subsidiary of VNU Marketing Information Services of New York.

Equifax National Decision System's MicroVision combines a number of factors to profile segments of the U.S. population. These include census data, socioeconomics, housing characteristics, lifestyle segments, consumer purchase behavior, media use, and consumer attitudes.

Customer (household) profiles are broken down into nine groups and 50 segments. For example, the *group* called "mainstream families" consists of nine segments: home sweet home, family ties, country home families, stars and stripes, white picket fence, traditional times, settled in, buy American, and rustic homesteaders. Each market *segment* consists of households that share similar interests, needs, purchase patterns, and financial resources. MicroVision identifies segment members at the zip+four level, allowing marketers to plot the location of customers and potential customers (MicroVision, 1995).

Finally, the annual *Yankelovich MONITOR®* reports consumer media habits, attitudes, values, beliefs, lifestyles, and behaviors in the United States. There is also an edition for Canada. Yankelovich Partners, Inc. conducts one-on-one interviews with 4,000 Americans (age 16 and over) and reports its findings in specialized publications. They also produce the *Pop Monitor*—measuring the overall celebrity power of 1,000 personalities—*Hispanic Monitor, African-American Monitor, Asian-American Monitor, Green Action Monitor, Youth Monitor,* and *Young Adult Monitor.* Yankelovich offers several other more targeted products and services, including custom research (Yankelovich Partners, 1997).

So what do we do with all this information? We can use it in at least three ways.

First, we can use it to find new customers. If we know that people in a certain part of the city prefer our product, then it might be useful to target people with similar characteristics. "Clusters" provide us with a way of identifying characteristics that can lead us to places where we will find more people like them. Sometimes we know who our customers are—we just need to locate or find more of them. These systems help us do that.

Second, clusters tell us things about our customers that we can use in other parts of our marketing efforts. By knowing their preferences and lifestyle we can adapt our products and services to their special needs. For example, newspapers found that they needed a procedure to stop daily delivery while people were away from home or customers would simply stop daily subscriptions.

Third, media organizations that sell advertising space can use the information to help their advertisers reach the people in whom they are most interested. By providing maps of real customers rather than a sheet of demographic data on listeners, viewers, or readers, the ad salespeople can provide better service to their customers.

Media Social Responsibility Influences

Allied with consumer values is the expectation by some in the public that media organizations have a social responsibility to give back to the community ("New Attempt," 1997). If this is widely believed and accepted as a core value among a media organization's target market, the media organization may want to reassess its own values and decide whether changes might be required. In this sense, the media organization aligns itself with the expectations of its consumers.

Of course, it is better if media organization owners adopt community values because they hold those values themselves. Then all they need to do is express acceptance of their target market values through their actions and words. On the other hand, for a media organization to attempt to align itself with community values to which it does not fundamentally subscribe is not advisable. People are very perceptive, and in the marketplace, illusions often result in customer retribution and business failure. If your organization's values are substantially different from those of your market, you are looking at a long-term question of reorienting your organizational culture, not a relatively short-term marketing strategy.

SPECIFIC MEDIA MARKET RESEARCH DATA

This section will look at how organizations use commercial services to track customers and how they are using some general techniques in unusual ways. We will look at newspaper circulation studies, tracking techniques for electronic media, how databases are changing the marketer's thinking, and, finally, how basic research can help fill in the gaps.

Electronic Media Ratings

Arbitron measures the listening habits of radio audiences in more than 260 local markets and tracks consumer behavior, media, and product sales in more than 100 markets.

Listeners in the top 94 markets are measured four times a year in 12-week increments. The other 169 markets are measured two times a year, with Arbitron upgrading the 55 smallest markets to twice-a-year measurement in 1998. Previously the smallest markets had only been measured once a year. Arbitron generates a representative sample based on the key demographic characteristics of the market. From this theoretical sampling frame, households are selected at random to participate for one week of the 12-week rating period. Each member of the household over the age of 12 records his or her listening activities in a personal diary for seven days. Individuals note the station selected, the times the radio was on, and whether the station is on the AM or FM band. Participants are expected to record listening in the home, the car, at work, and in "other" places. Hispanic households receive their diaries and supporting material written in English and Spanish. Each participating person receives a cash premium along with their diary (Arbitron, 1997).

At the end of the week, families return the diaries to the Arbitron collection center in Columbia, Maryland. Data from approximately 1 million diaries are used each year to compile station reports. The sample size for each market depends on the population in the metropolitan area. For example, in Arbitron's Spring 1996 ratings book, the sample sizes range from 452 people in Casper, Wyoming, with a metro area of 52,200 to a sample size of 23,567 in the New York City metro area, with a population of 14,114,400.

In addition to written reports, stations can purchase Maximi$er software to customize survey areas, day parts, demographics, and time periods to target their marketing. Advertisers and agencies use Media Professional software to obtain the same output.

Arbitron's NewMedia service provides qualitative and quantitative information to help marketers evaluate the new electronic media, for example, interactive television, online services, local cable, and direct broadcast satellite (Arbitron, 1997).

Nielsen Media Research Company is the foremost ratings research firm in television, along with products in other areas (A. C. Nielsen, 1997). The television Nielsens are a measure of viewer preference for television programming and are produced by the Nielsen Media Research Company. Although they are criticized by many, media executives have not been able to agree on a better measurement tool. Nielsen uses two methods to sample television viewers, the "people meter" and the "diary."

The people meter is placed in 5,000 randomly selected households for the national television ratings of network programming. Nielsen also offers "overnight" ratings in the top markets and is expanding that service as stations in more markets become willing to pay the additional costs. The so-called Nielsen households receive small gifts in exchange for their participation, whether people meter households or diary households, and can remain part of the sample for up to two years.

With meters, family members and their guests log in by pressing a button assigned to that person on a small control box, or check in with a handheld remote device. The people meter records the time and length of viewing. Since age, sex, and so on are already known for family members, the information can be combined with program information to produce a profile of a show's audience. Data are passed nightly by phone lines to a collecting point, aggregated, and available to report the next day. To account for the possibility of people leaving the room without logging out, an infrared scanner now sweeps the room at regular intervals and records whether it senses the body heat of viewers (Jawitz, 1996). Still awaiting development is a means to determine whether the people in the room are *attending* to the program rather than sleeping, reading, chatting with each other, or any of the other many things people do in rooms while the television is on.

A separate black box monitors whether the set is on, the channel selected, and the program actually being aired. Since a special identification number is encoded with each program and episode, Nielsen Research can easily determine what program was selected. Every set in the household is monitored with equipment that can determine whether the set was running cable, satellite, a tape through the VCR, or even a video game.

Nielsen continues to use the diary method of sampling in most television markets in the country. In this method homeowners are asked to participate and provided a small token for their participation, as in people meter households. However, with the diary method, the television viewer has to manually log all of the programs watched during the rating period. Nielsen provides the diaries, and the logging is a simple process of checking off programs and time of day. Viewing is recorded in diaries to the nearest quarter hour. Sweeps are collected during the same four times a year as with meters—February, May, July, and November. When diaries are used, it takes about three weeks for the data to be processed and results provided to Nielsen's station customers.

The third tool Nielsen uses is a check of the other methods. Nielsen Research calls thousands of households at random and asks whether the set is on, and if so, what program is selected and who is watching. That information can then be compared with both the people meter and diary information. Meters tell when the set is on, not always who's in front of it. Diaries, on the other hand, tend to get ignored some days, with viewers going back and checking what they think they watched the day before. The telephone cross-check is an attempt to compensate for the respective methodological flaws.

In addition to tracking regular programming and viewers, Nielsen Research also tracks when and where these programs are aired. Nielsen plans to develop systems to monitor the Internet.

Other organizations rate the size of television program audiences, but Nielsen Media Research remains the most widely used and reported.

Print Media Circulation Studies

Just as radio has its Arbitron ratings and television has its Nielsens, newspapers, magazines, and business publications have their Audit Bureau of Circulations. Since ad rates are based in part on the number of copies distributed, it is important for advertisers to be able to directly compare competing media. The Audit Bureau looks at paid circulation by market area and reports the number of copies in circulation and the percentage of coverage for that area. That means an advertiser can compare circulation figures on 1,500 daily and weekly newspapers, and more than 1,000 other periodicals. The Audit Bureau's database permits comparison by county, zip code, designated market area (DMA), or metropolitan statistical area (MSA) (Audit Bureau of Circulations, 1997).

The Audit Bureau collects publishers' reports every six months and conducts an on-site audit annually. Weekly papers and dailies with paid circulation less than 15,000 are audited every two years. Audit Reports for newspapers and other periodicals are issued annually. Only members have access to publishers' filings and audited reports. The Audit Bureau of Circulations recently began auditing "hits" on the Internet.

And although the Audit Bureau provides uniform data across print media, at least one critic believes that the report underrepresents the number of people who actually read a paper. Lawrence Beaupre, 1995 Associated Press Managing Editors (APME) president, told conferees at the APME convention in Indianapolis that "newspapers today are held hostage by a creature of their own creation, the Audit Bureau of Circulation, which clings to the primitive philosophy of one sale/one reader to measure newspaper reach" (Beaupre, 1995). What he is getting at is that newspapers are "passed along" and read by more than one person. If this phenomenon were taken into account, then newspaper reach would appear more favorable vis-à-vis electronic media and direct mail.

Reports Across Media

Information Resources' BehaviorScan attempts to tie consumer behavior and media use in a way that isolates such factors as the effects of advertising, coupons, promotions, price, and shelf location. It uses panels of more than 3,000 representative households that agree to have their purchases monitored. At the same time, sales data are collected from all the grocery, drug, and mass merchandiser stores in the market. With Targetable TV, Information Resources has the ability to direct different commercials to selected households, thereby setting up experimental conditions within a market. The company does the same with newspaper routes and direct mail appeals (BehaviorScan, 1994; IRI, 1997).

One service that spans media sources in the top 59 markets is Scarborough Research. It samples data from 140,000 consumers from around the country using telephone and mail surveys. The largest sample comes from the New York City area, and no sample has fewer than 1,650 consumers. Both qualitative and quantitative information are gathered on media use and shopping preferences. Scarborough is a joint venture of VNU Business Information Services and Arbitron (Scarborough, 1997).

RetailDirect is another Arbitron service that surveys television, radio, and cable audiences to determine how media consumers actually use the media. Measurements include purchasing behavior. The service covers 39 medium or small markets not served by Scarborough Research.

Claritas introduced the PRN Convergence Database in 1996. It looks at behavior and attitudes toward the telecommunication, multimedia, and cable industries. It includes data on product switching, brand loyalty, and awareness of competing products. Data are accessed through PRIZM.

See Sidebar 8.4 for a listing of the major media marketing sources discussed in this chapter.

Sidebar 8.4 How to Contact Marketing Support Organizations

Customer Identification Services

Acorn

CACI Marketing Systems
1100 N. Glebe Road
Arlington, VA 22201
(800) 292–2224
(703) 841–2904

ClusterPLUS

Claritas Corp.
1525 Wilson Blvd., Suite 1000
Arlington, VA 22209
(703) 812–2700
(800) 284–4868
http://www.claritas.com/

MicroVision

Equifax National Decision Systems
5375 Mira Sorrento Place, Suite 400
San Diego, CA 92121
(800) 866–6520
(619) 622–0800
http://www.ends.com/

PRIZM

Claritas Corp.
1525 Wilson Blvd., Suite 1000
Arlington, VA 22209
(703) 812–2700
(800) 284–4868
http://www.claritas.com/

VALS2

SRI International
333 Ravenswood Avenue
Menlo Park, CA 94025
(415) 326–6200
http://future.sri.com

Yankelovich Monitor

Yankelovich Partners
101 Merritt, No. 7
Norwalk, CT 06851
(203) 846–0100
http://www.yankelovich.com/

Media and Purchase Monitoring Services

A. C. Nielsen

299 Park Avenue
New York, NY 10171
(212) 708–6949
http://www.nielsenmedia.com/

Arbitron

142 West 57th Street
New York, NY 10019
(212) 887–1300
http://www.arbitron.com/

Audit Bureau of Circulations

900 N. Meacham Road
Schaumburg, IL 60173–4968
(847) 605–0909
http://www.accessabc.com/
http://www.accessabs.com/

BehaviorScan

Information Resources Inc. (IRI)
150 N. Clinton Street
Chicago, IL 60661
(312) 726–1221
http://www.infores.com/

Scantrack

Nielsen Media Research
299 Park Avenue, 22nd Floor
New York, NY 10171
(212) 708–7500
http://www.nielsenmedia.com/

Focus Groups and Surveys

The measurement systems covered so far in this section are largely quantitative, that is, the results are expressed as numbers. These are typically expressed as ratings points, share of audience, percentage of some category—even who buys what. But numbers do not tell us anything about *why* people tune in or tune out, choose one product or another. To get at this kind of information we have to talk to media consumers either one-on-one or in small groups.

Focus group research involves asking groups of 8 to 12 individuals questions about their media or purchasing habits. Focus groups also are used to pretest new shows or ads, and fine-tune products, packaging, and messages. Whatever the purpose, the results are very much dependent on the moderator and the kinds of individuals selected to participate (Greenbaum, 1987).

Executives from the organization sponsoring the research typically watch from behind a one-way mirror and have access to the videotaped proceedings. This serves as a check on the report submitted by the moderator.

Media organizations also can commission or conduct their own surveys to learn more about how the public perceives their organization and products. These can take the form of local phone, mail, or face-to-face surveys, or can involve buying space in a national survey. Major media organizations like New York Times Company and CBS conduct their own national polls.

CHAPTER SUMMARY

Some consider media marketing, particularly in print journalism, a step back from responsible journalism. Underwood (1993) argues that the marketing orientation leads to briefs and capsule news, packaged information, entertainment news, visually appealing formats, upbeat stories, and news-you-can-use features. This "reader-driven" or "customer-driven" approach, he says, has pushed many committed and creative journalists out of the newsroom. Further, it could lead to a lost sense of the journalistic mission, a lost spirit of community service, a loss of good writing, and the loss of the commitment to enterprise reporting.

Underwood (1993) observes that many reader surveys were taken in the 1970s and 1980s. Taken together, readers said they wanted *more of everything*. They wanted more *good* news, news that was easy to digest, features,

more hard news, facts about health care, science, and technology. And publishers obliged. They changed their products, and the number of readers continued to decline. Underwood blames part of this problem on the people doing the research, especially academics. He says they ask the wrong questions, use samples that are too small, and take the editor's word for life in the newsroom. According to Underwood, we are sacrificing substance to make our products look pretty.

But must we? It should be possible to do both, and *that* is the challenge for media managers. It requires sensitivity, judgment, an awareness of your medium, and, finally, your operating environment. It requires particular attention to transactions and relationships. They are, fundamentally, what the mass media, in all of their forms, are about (Peppers & Rogers, 1993).

1. Describe your own organization's products and services. Compare your products and services with those of your competition in terms of price, quality, and distribution. What information do you need to complete this analysis? How would you get this information? What will you do with the results?

2. How do you think your production costs compare with those of your competition? What does that mean for the way you market your products?

3. Who are your customers? Describe them in terms of demographics, psychographics and location. Where would you find more customers with those characteristics? How could they be persuaded to try your product or service?

4. How do your *customers* perceive your products and services? How do you know? How do *you* perceive these same products and services? Is there any difference? What are the implications of this analysis?

5. Investigate one of the marketing services discussed in this chapter and report your findings. How could you use that service to improve your marketing program?

6. Do you believe it is possible to know and predict consumer behavior? What are some of the problems in knowing and predicting behavior?

7. Consider your organization and its products and services. Develop a list of products and services you already offer. Opposite each item list the group or groups that wants or needs this product or service.

8. Now consider other products or services your organization could produce that people on the list from #7 above might be willing to purchase. Are there other groups that have needs that your organization could meet?

chapter 9

MEDIA ORGANIZATION FINANCE

Money is the fundamental issue in mass media organizations operating in capitalist economies. It takes money to run media companies, which are generally for-profit businesses. Even in the case of publicly supported media operations such as the Public Broadcasting Service (PBS), money has to be raised—revenues generated—and then spent through a financial management process. Every media organization has to provide some kind of a return—be that in monetary, cultural, or philosophical terms—to those who support it.

The existence of a media organization may be to fulfill a public service mission, provide bottom-line profit to a corporate owner, or some combination of these to satisfy the vision of those who own and/or control it. Although some media organizations, for tax purposes, are technically defined as "nonprofit," they still have to take money in and allocate it to cover expenses. So the basic principles of financial accounting and budgeting are pervasive in all media forms. You cannot create a great epic film, buy printer's ink for a newspaper, pay for the electricity to send a signal up to the top of a broadcast tower or satellite, or create effective advertising or public relations campaigns without money.

This chapter is not meant to make you an expert in corporate finance. Financial management, while adhering to some basic principles, tends to be tailored to unique organizational requirements. Specific budget design and implementation varies considerably. But the essential principles are fairly consistent across organizations, and no media manager can survive very long without the ability to manage a budget.

CORPORATE FINANCIAL REPORTING

Basically, financial management is a simple concept. You keep track of what comes in, and what goes out, just as you do with your personal funds. Managing the money just gets a little more complicated when you move up the corporate ladder because there are more sources of revenue and expenditures. One essential principle holds true in personal and corporate finance. Don't spend more than you have. If you bring in more money than you spend, you have a profit, which on the personal level you may put in a savings account. If you spend more than you receive you have a deficit. Checks bounce for corporations just like they do for individuals. And bad credit hurts both. Operating for very long with what is called "negative cash flow" will result in one of two forms of bankruptcy: (1) Chapter 7, liquidation of an entity by selling off all its assets or

(2) Chapter 11 reorganization, which keeps creditors at bay while financial affairs can be reorganized to continue operations. Chapter 7 bankruptcy is the death of an organization, while filing for chapter 11 is an attempt to save it. But you don't want to have to do either.

Accounting is a profession that requires considerable expertise. Although media managers have to deal with budgets and financial matters, it is advisable to seek assistance from qualified accountants whenever money matters get complicated. Most media firms have accounting departments whose job it is to help department and division managers deal with financial issues. Use those accounting professionals as much as possible. Hiring an accountant or bookkeeper in your department may be wise, if it can free you up to focus on other issues facing your media organization.

Department managers can easily get trapped by budget processes in which they are not expert and that eat up valuable time that could be put to other uses. You need to have a fundamental understanding of your budget and cash flow so you can work with the financial professionals. This chapter will cover some key fundamentals to help you succeed in the media organization money game.

Different kinds of organizations have different requirements for financial reporting. Privately held companies (individual or family owned with no publicly traded stock) are not required to reveal much of their financial condition, but government regulations for regular corporations are much more stringent. This chapter will focus on financial documents and processes for publicly traded companies since they are the most complex, and you will likely work in such a company. Public companies also have the most extensive reporting requirements placed upon them by federal and state governments, as well as any exchanges that trade the company stock (Scholl, 1991).

Annual Reports

The annual report of a company profiles the previous year's activities and usually includes an overview of management's perspective on the future. It typically has the following sections.

1. Letter to Shareholders—This sometimes lengthy discussion provides management's spin on how the company is doing financially and its general business strategy. A vision statement, or philosophy of business, is often either included as a titled subsection or simply integrated in the text to explain management's strategic view. The letter to shareholders is normally published over the chief executive officer's (CEO) or corporate president's signature.

2. Business Activity Review—This section of the annual report focuses on the latest developments in corporate enterprises. Trends in the particular business sector(s) in which the company is engaged are included, as well as its corporate objectives relative to its competitive environment. Typically, this section focuses on the contemporary situation and the company's approach to the immediate future.

3. Financial Review—This is the numbers section. Corporate performance is shown in mathematical terms of dollars and cents. Typically, along with numerous spreadsheet summaries of assets, liabilities, revenues, costs, profits, and losses, which include audited financial profiles of corporate endeavors, the section contains a narrative analysis of what the numbers mean to shareholders. In this section you will find the key financial statements: balance sheet, income and shareholder equity statements, analysis of cash flow, and any graphic

representations of numerical data management uses to emphasize specific areas. The financial review section usually includes a report from an independent auditor who has examined the company's books to ensure they accurately reflect the economic health of the corporation.

(Merrill Lynch, 1997)

Annual reports, and their quarterly report cousins, are important tools that investors and stock analysts use in deciding whether to buy or sell shares in a firm. So annual and quarterly reports have a significant effect on a company's stock value and the net worth of major stockholders. Those major stockholders frequently include senior managers who typically will be given stock, or options to buy company stock, as part of their compensation package. They have a vested interest in cutting costs and maximizing profits. See Sidebar 9.1 for an illustration.

The Balance Sheet

This spreadsheet shows the assets and liabilities of the company. It's called a balance sheet because all of the assets have to add up to the same number as all of the liabilities. In accepted financial analysis, all assets are counterbalanced by liabilities or shareholder's equity.

At first that may seem strange, since you might think a company isn't making any money if what it owes (liabilities) is the same as what it owns and took in (assets). But the value of a firm includes everything it has, including intangibles such as reputation in the marketplace, as well as the value of the shares of stock being held by investors. A prestigious newspaper's reputation has a direct effect on its advertising and subscription revenues. For example, people sometimes subscribe to, or advertise in, the *Wall Street Journal* just because of its stature—its reputation—as a national financially focused publication. And a stockholder's portion of the ownership of the company—her equity—has a value although she isn't selling the stock, but holding it. The balance sheet takes into account the intangibles and the tangibles and produces a picture of the economic health of the business. It is a "snapshot" in time, usually reflecting the condition of the company at the end of the last day of the fiscal year (Merrill Lynch, 1997, p. 1).

See Figure 9.1 for an example of a typical company. This model of a balance sheet, provided by Merrill Lynch, Pierce, Fenner & Smith, is used across all business types, though there will be variability based on unique aspects of particular industries or firms.

As you examine Figure 9.1, consider the following definitions of the key areas. First, the Asset side of the balance sheet.

◆ Current Assets—These are things the company owns that can be converted into cash within one year of the balance sheet statement date. Current Assets usually include cash on hand, or in checking accounts, marketable securities—such as treasury bills or other financial instruments in which the company has invested some of its liquid capital—money due from customers (also called accounts receivable), any inventories on hand, and most prepaid expenses. These are often referred to as "liquid assets" because they can be liquidated quickly.

◆ Property, Plant, and Equipment—This is also commonly titled Fixed Assets. It includes the land owned by a company, the building it has, and other equipment such as a printing press, cameras, furniture, and vehicles. Everything except land can be depreciated. You can see that in the changes in the values for everything but land in the two years represented in Figure 9.1.

Sidebar 9.1 The President's Visit

A fictional media company sent its president around to the different business subsidiaries annually to inspect the diverse operating units and get together with employees. The annual visits were part personal inspection and part public relations by the head of the company to help give workers some positive motivation.

One fall afternoon the employees of one television station subsidiary were assembled in the main studio for a reception, where the president met them and shook many hands, then gave a speech. The crowd included some 300 people, ranging from news anchors to maintenance engineers who worked on keeping the technical equipment working.

In his speech, the president said he was very proud of how the station had done the previous year, cutting costs and increasing net profit. The whole media conglomerate had surged ahead in earnings, and for the first time the company's stock had gone over $50 a share. Previously, its high on the New York Stock Exchange had hovered around $40 to $45 a share.

As the speech droned on for more than a half-hour, many in the crowd grew restless. The station had serious problems with equipment breaking down because it was beyond its life expectancy. Some in the room felt the station was losing its competitiveness because budgets were continually being tightened, and the parent company wasn't, in their view, reinvesting the necessary funds to enable the station to keep up with its home market competitors. Others just didn't connect with what was being said, caught up in the more immediate problems of their daily jobs. But everyone in the room remained, superficially, attentive to the president as he kept talking about return on investment, stockholder equity, and other financial concepts most of them knew little about.

When the meeting was over, and the requisite applause for the president had died down, the employees began filing out of the room. The technical people were muttering to themselves about wasting time listening to a speech they didn't see as addressing any of their problems. One engaged in a brief conversation about the speech with the station's business reporter as they were walking out of the room together.

Engineer: "What was that all about? Why should I care about how much the stock went up? We can't even keep the videotape machines running!"

Reporter: "Well, if you owned a million shares of stock in the company and it was selling for one dollar a share how much money would you have?"

Engineer: "A million dollars."

Reporter: "And if the share price went up to two dollars in a year, how much would you have?"

Engineer: "Two million."

Reporter: "Well, last year the company stock was at $40 a share, and this year it's at $50. The president owns about 10 million shares. That means he made $100 million for no other reason than the stock price went up."

After a brief pause, with a sly smile, the reporter continued.

"Why do you think the price of the company's stock went up?"

Engineer: "Beats me."

Reporter: "Because costs were down, which helped pump profits up above where they've been. Investors like profit growth. The stock market people think we're a better-run company because we made more profit. They don't know the place is practically falling apart. And they don't really care, as long as their shares keep increasing in value and the dividends are paid."

The engineer had just learned a fundamental lesson in the economics of publicly held companies.

Consolidated Balance Sheet

(Dollars in Thousands, Except Per-Share Amounts)

Assets	As of December 31, This year[1]	Last year
Current Assets:		
Cash & cash equivalents	$19,500	$15,000
	51,000	
Accounts receivable—net of allowance for doubtful accounts	156,000	145,000
Inventories at the lower end of cost or market	180,000	185,000
Prepaid expenses & other current assets	4,000	3,000
Total Current Assets	**405,800**	**380,000**
Property, Plant, & Equipment:		
Land	30,000	30,000
Buildings	125,000	118,500
Machinery	200,000	171,100
Leasehold improvements	15,000	15,000
Furniture, fixtures, etc.	15,000	12,000
Total property, plant, & equipment	385,000	346,600
Less: accumulated depreciation	125,000	97,000
Net Property, Plant, & Equipment	**260,000**	**249,600**
Other Assets		
Intangibles (goodwill, patents)—net of accumulated amortization	1,950	2,000
Investment securities, at cost	300	—
Total Other Assets	**2,250**	**2,000**
Total Assets	**$668,050**	**$631,600**

Liabilities & Shareholders' Equity	As of December 31, This year	Last year
Liabilities:		
Current Liabilities:		
Accounts payable	$60,000	$57,000
Notes payable	51,000	61,000
Accrued expenses	30,000	36,000
Income taxes payable	17,000	15,000
Other liabilities	12,000	12,000
Current portion of long-term debt	6,000	—
Total Current Liabilities	**176,000**	**181,000**
Long-term Liabilities		
Deferred income taxes	16,000	9,000
9.12% debentures payable 2010	130,000	130,000
Other long-term debt	—	6,000
Total Liabilities	**322,000**	**326,000**
Shareholders' Equity:		
Preferred stock, 5.83 cumulative, $100 par value; authorized, issued and outstanding: 60,000 shares	6,000	6,000
Common stock, $5.00 par value, authorized: 20,000,000 shares; issues and outstanding: 19×9 – 15,000,000 shares, 19×8 – 14,500,000 shares	75,000	72,500
Additional paid-in capital	20,000	13,500
Retained earnings	249,000	219,600
Foreign currency translation adjustment (net of taxes)	1,000	(1,000)
Unrealized gain on available-for-sale securities (net of taxes)	50	—
Less: Treasury stock at cost (19×9 & 19×8 – 1,000 shares)	(5,000)	(5,000)
Total Shareholders' Equity	**346,050**	**305,600**
Total Liabilities & Shareholders' Equity	**$668,050**	**$631,600**

[1]Year is normally indicated numerically.

Figure 9.1 Corporate Balance Sheet (Source: Merrill Lynch, 1997, pp. 4–5)

- Other Assets—This is where the value of intangibles such as the reputation of a company are shown. Other Assets is also a catchall category for items that don't fit elsewhere. An example would be investment securities that cannot be sold quickly (within one year), as required by those listed under Current Assets. Another example would be a new patent a firm has been granted, but which the company has not been able to begin using.

(Merrill Lynch, 1997)

On the liability side of the balance sheet the following general categories will summarize what the company owes.

- Current Liabilities—This is the flip side of the current asset category. Current liabilities are those that have to be paid within one year. Typically that includes accounts payable to suppliers, any interest due for money the company has borrowed, salaries, and taxes.

- Long-term Liabilities—This is where any deferred taxes are shown, as well as long-term interest commitments, mortgages, and any reserve fund the company might have set up to deal with unexpected contingencies. Earmarked reserves would have to be shown here, rather than in Current Assets, because the money would be specifically designated for something and not available (not liquid) for other purposes.

- Shareholders' Equity—This is where the company's stock profile is shown. When a company authorizes stock to be sold, it specifies the maximum number of shares. But not all of that will necessarily be sold. So the authorized number of shares is often different from that which is issued and outstanding. Here you can see how many shares are outstanding, what nominal value the company has assigned to its various stock categories (par value), and something called "retained earnings." That's money the company reinvests in itself rather than paying out to stockholders in the form of dividends. Treasury stock is a term applied to shares the company has bought back and can sell to investors or cancel. It does not have any voting rights, nor are dividends paid on treasury stock.

(Merrill Lynch, 1997)

The main value of the balance sheet is that it shows, in a succinct format, everything a company owns offset by what it owes (Scholl, 1991). When analyzing a company, comparing balance sheets over a period of years is an excellent way to see how the shape of the firm is changing. And when looking at different companies within the same industry, balance sheets can be excellent tools to analyze the different players in a competitive market.

The Corporate Income Statement

Although the balance sheet provides a profile of the company, including its assets, liabilities, and details of its ownership equity (amounts of stock outstanding), it is a static report indicating the status of the company on just one day, typically the last day of the year. With the balance sheet you can usually ascertain the basic financial condition of a firm, but not much detail of the flow of money (Livingstone, 1992). That comes from the income statement.

This is the report watched more closely by business analysts, stockholders, or those who might buy stock in the company, and it is monitored by corporate executives as they work to enhance profit. The income statement reflects the dynamic relationship, over time, of the various aspects of managing the money of the company (Scholl, 1991). See Figure 9.2 for an example of this key document provided by Merrill Lynch, Pierce, Fenner & Smith.

Consolidated Income Statement
(Dollars in Thousands, Except Per-Share Amounts)

	As of December 31,	
	This Year*	**Last year**
Net sales	$765,050	$725,000
Cost of sales	535,000	517,000
Gross margin	230,050	208,000
Operating expenses:		
Depreciation & amortization	28,050	25,000
Selling, general & administrative expenses	96,804	109,500
Operating income	105,196	73,500
Other income (expense):		
Dividends & interest income	5,250	10,000
Interest expense	(16,250)	(16,750)
Income before income taxes & extraordinary loss	94,196	66,750
Income taxes	41,446	26,250
Income before extraordinary loss	52,750	40,500
Extraordinary item: loss on earthquake destruction (net of income tax benefit of $750)	(5,000)	—
Net income	**$47,750**	**$40,500**
Earnings per common share		
Before extraordinary loss	$3.55	$2.77
Extraordinary loss	(.34)	—
Net income per common share	**$3.21**	**$2.77**

*Year is normally indicated numerically.

Figure 9.2 Corporate Income Statement
(Source: Merrill Lynch, 1997, p. 27)

If net sales increase, you will likely see concurrent increases in the related items such as the cost of sales, and direct selling, general, and administrative expenses. If the firm does a better job of investing any short-term, liquid cash in interest-bearing accounts or other financial instruments, its dividends and interest income would increase. By carefully taking advantage of the tax laws it might be possible to reduce income taxes. Buying new equipment, improving physical facilities, or acquiring a new business subsidiary—another broadcast station, newspaper, or other enterprise—are all ways of converting tax liability dollars into reinvestment capital, which would potentially enhance the long-term value of the company. Money spent on expanding the business may reduce its yearly profit, and thus its tax liability, while increasing the total value of the company.

In some media companies you can see this effort to convert tax liability to corporate equity by analyzing quarterly reports. Throughout the first 3 quarters of the year, if money is flowing in, senior managers may consider an acquisition due to the firm's ability to pay for the new subsidiary based on improved cash flows. Then in the fourth quarter they may consummate the purchase of a new property. At the end of the year, such a company would appear not to make a substantial profit. But the acquisition activity would have converted potential taxes into company growth.

Media giant Tele-Communications, Inc., known commonly as TCI, has grown into one of the largest cable companies in the world. Yet, "TCI rarely shows earnings, pays no income taxes, no dividends and plows its near $7 billion in revenues into operations, acquisitions and debt service" (Keating, 1997, p. H1). It is a media giant that has reinvested its money in continual acquisitions to expand while avoiding profits (Hofmeister, 1997; Loomis & Kupfer, 1997). However, such strategy can only go on so long before a company's stock is negatively affected. Investors look at profits as a key indicator of corporate health. And after time, stockholders want to see dividends come their way (Keating, 1997).

It is important to understand, when using income statements, that their value comes when you look at a company's activity over time—that is, in comparing successive years of income statements. A dynamic picture of the firm will then be forthcoming, while a single year's statement only provides the numbers for a single 12-month period. At first glance, some of the items may seem confusing; others are fairly easy to understand.

For example, near the top of Figure 9.2 you can see the notation "cost of sales," and then four items lower there is another category that includes "selling" expenses. The cost of sales usually means any production costs involved in creating products. In an industrial company, this includes money paid for raw materials, labor used in direct manufacturing activities, and any overhead costs directly attributable to the manufacturing process itself. In other words, cost of sales means the cost of making the product so it can be sold. But those costs are not the same as the marketing expenses in taking the product to potential customers, including commissions and/or salaries paid to the sales force. Typically, such costs are included with the administrative overhead, since they are all apart from the actual manufacturing costs but integral to getting products in the hands of customers. The selling, general, and administrative expenses usually include "sales agents' salaries and commissions; advertising and promotion; travel and entertainment; executives' salaries, office payroll; and office expenses" (Merrill Lynch, 1997, p. 28).

In a media company, where advertising space—in a newspaper—or time—in an electronic medium—is the product sold, there may be very small product creation costs of sales. The raw material is not something purchased from outside at great expense, and there isn't any manufacturing cost to make it into something the customer can use. Many advertisers provide their own layouts and commercials. On the other hand, an advertising agency, advertising production house, or public relations firm may have a greater cost of sales because of the time and materials invested in creating products for agency clients. Those products are then provided to newspapers and electronic media to be used within the advertising space or time.

Highly leveraged financing is a common technique used by media companies to expand rapidly by acquiring other properties or firms. Corporate bonds may be sold by the firm through investment banking concerns, which require considerable interest payments to bondholders (Merrill Lynch, 1997). Bonds are traded like stock but are essentially loans to a company with specific annual interest paid to bondholders. Or the media firm may have loans from financial institutions that require interest payments.

By looking at the interest expense of a company, you can get a good idea of how leveraged—deeply in debt—it is. What's more, if a manager can figure out a way to reduce the interest expense, net profit can be substantially increased. That's why you so often hear about "restructuring" or "refinancing" a company's debt. For example, if interest rates were higher five years ago, when the company first issued its corporate bonds, it might have had to guarantee an interest rate of 10 percent to sell those bonds. But if today's market is much lower, with interest rates in the 5 percent range, it might make sense to issue new bonds to pay off the old ones and reduce the overall interest expense, even with the cost of setting up the new bond issue including broker commissions (Lahart, 1991).

A highly leveraged company is "betting on the come," which means it believes that its ability to increase future revenues or trim expenses, will generate enough money to pay the large interest expense. If that does not happen, the majority stockholders may suffer a reduction in their stock value, as investors shy away from a company in trouble. It is not uncommon for such businesses, built like a financial house of cards on little more than promises and aggressive salesmanship, to get into trouble. During the 1980s, following the rise of so-called junk bond financing, numerous companies found themselves in such situations (Bettelheim, 1992; Brown, 1986; Knox, 1990; Mermigas, 1991b; Rohatyn, 1988; Staver, 1987).

When that happens, the usual way of resolving the problem is to sell the company to another owner. When a new owner takes over, that owner has incurred interest expenses to make the purchase. Typically, the new subsidiary that has just been purchased is required to pay those expenses. Simply put, the new owner tries to cut expenses and pump up revenue so the acquisition pays for itself. The extreme type of this activity, where the debt will be substantial compared with a company's assets, is called a "leveraged buyout," or LBO. Usually LBOs require the parent company to restructure or refinance in some way to survive in the long term (Livingstone, 1992).

An example may help make this process clear. If it cost 5 percent interest to borrow the money to purchase a newspaper, that newspaper would have to produce 5 percent more revenue to cover the payments and still generate the same amount of profit as before the sale. When someone buys a media organization, he or she typically expects to make money from the acquisition, not pump money into it. Often, new owners anticipate more efficiency on their part than on the previous owner's and instigate changes to increase revenue. But, fundamentally, any company can increase its net income in only two ways: cutting expenses or selling more product. Many companies try to do both at the same time. But in highly competitive environments it is not always possible to raise prices or quickly surge sales. That can mean the only alternative, to recover the acquisition interest expense and still have the same profit margin as prior to the sale, is to cut staff and other expenses. When that occurs, there is a very good chance the organization's competitiveness will be reduced. A snowball effect can then occur, where steps taken to respond to a problem only worsen it.

The all too common senior management order to "cut the fat out" may sound like an easy solution. But not all media organizations have a lot of fat, and that which exists is not always where managers think it is. For example, a new owner decides to cut one of three maintenance engineers working at a local television station, based on a survey of staff size in similar stations around the country. But if the station equipment is older than average, it might require more maintenance. Reducing maintenance could result in more breakdowns and errors while airing commercials. That would then mean those commercials would have to be made up, irritating advertising customers and reducing the available inventory of commercial positions that could be sold.

The bottom line is that a media manager can get into trouble very fast by trying to manipulate the bottom line without fully understanding the complexities, and individual situation, of a media operation. The income statement provides important numbers used in managing a firm. But what is crucial is understanding what is going on behind those numbers.

Key Business Ratios

Before we get into the specifics of financial statements included in the annual report you need to understand how to look at the numbers. Business professionals use some key indicators to analyze the health of their companies, or those they are thinking about investing in or trying to acquire. Although numerous ratios are used for various purposes in financial analysis, there are just a few that are most commonly used, which provide the media manager a quick way of sizing up how the company is doing.

Current Ratio

The current ratio is an easy way to get a sense of how strong a company is. It is simply a comparison of what the company owns to what it owes based on the normal business cycle, usually one year. All you have to do is divide the total cash and other assets that can be converted to cash—within the "current" term—by the liabilities that must be paid within the "current" term. As a general rule of thumb, two dollars in assets should back every dollar in liabilities. That does vary by the type of industry. For example, some manufacturing companies have to maintain large, and very expensive, inventories with their attendant holding costs. When the ratio moves closer to a dollar of assets for every dollar of liabilities, the company has less "backing" for what it owes with what it owns. When that happens, its bond rating may drop, requiring higher interest payments to investors should the firm attempt to sell more bonds to finance an acquisition or some other endeavor (Merrill Lynch, 1997).

The following example shows how the formula works, with numerical data taken from Figure 9.1, "Corporate Balance Sheet."

$$\frac{\text{Current assets}}{\text{Current liabilities}} = \frac{405,800}{176,000} = \frac{2.31}{1}$$

(Merrill Lynch, 1997)

Quick Ratio, or "Acid Test"

This very common financial tool provides an indicator of the responsiveness the company has to sudden, unexpected occurrences. If the firm has something happen that requires a lot of money right away, how much could it quickly get in the bank to cover expenses?

Any cash on hand would, of course, be available. But usually a company has other things that can rapidly be converted to cash. For media companies, there usually aren't substantial inventories stored up, as is the case in some industrial manufacturing concerns. Available commercial space or airtime, not yet purchased by advertisers, is a type of inventory that has value. But it doesn't cost the company anything if it sits there as would be the case for a steel manufacturer with 400 tons of sheet metal in a warehouse.

However, inventory in the form of newsprint rolls in storage ready for press runs might constitute an inventory that could not be readily turned into cash. And the company may have prepaid some of its expenses. That money would not be available, since it's already been spent. In the following computations the numbers are being drawn from Figure 9.1.

To get the quick ratio, or make the "acid test" of a media firm's liquidity, you first subtract any inventories and prepaid expenses from the current assets to determine the "quick" assets—assets that can be quickly used as cash. Note that in accounting, items to be subtracted, or that are negative, are enclosed within parentheses.

Current assets	405,800
Less: Inventories	(180,000)
Less: Prepaid expenses	(4,000)
Quick assets	221,800

(Merrill Lynch, 1997)

Once you have the quick assets, all you have to do is divide those by the current liabilities. As in the current ratio, this shows how much support the company has for what it owes, but in terms of just the short term (a year or less, the normal business cycle).

$$\frac{\text{Quick assets}}{\text{Current liabilities}} = \frac{221,000}{176,000} = \frac{1.26}{1}$$

(Merrill Lynch, 1997)

Net Profit

Businesses exist to make money. The proverbial "bottom line" is how much you make after all is said and done. That is the net profit and is normally expressed as a percentage. In financial circles, within any given industry, business analysts typically deal with percentages because the numbers from one company to another vary considerably. For example, if one company makes $1 million in profit, and another generates $500,000, the second company may actually be the more profitable. It depends on the relative expenses and sales volume of each company. The biggest company with the largest gross dollar flow isn't necessarily the best run or most profitable. The only way to compare firms regardless of gross dollar size and unique budgetary conditions is to deal in percentages.

Net profit is simply how much money is left over from sales, after all the costs have been taken out. Usually, in corporate financial reports where very large numbers are being used, there will be a notation that those numbers are in thousands. So the last three zeros are not shown. That is the case in Figure 9.2. If you look at that figure, you can see that net sales this year are $765,050,000. And after all the costs shown on the income statement are taken out, you have net income of $47,750,000. That's a lot of money, but what kind of profit margin is it? The net profit ratio is found by simply dividing the net income by the net sales, as in the following example.

$$\frac{\text{Net income}}{\text{Net Sales}} = \frac{\$47,750,000}{\$765,050,000} = 6.2\%$$

(Merrill Lynch, 1997, p. 31)

Obviously, the higher the net profit, the better a business is for those who own it. Typically, general businesses make in the neighborhood of 5 to 8 percent net profit a year. However, many media companies perform much better than that, frequently exceeding double-digit net profit margins (Bagdikian, 1992).

Earnings per Share

Many investors in media companies are stockholders who purchase shares through the stock market. Additionally, most media company senior executives have stock paid to them as part of their compensation, or receive options to buy company stock at a fixed price—typically below the market cost.

The emotion of the stock market, whether the "bulls" are charging and running up the indexes of stock market value or the "bears" are fueling a stock market downturn, has a lot to do with how a company's stock performs. A combination of emotional and pragmatic factors continually influence stock prices. While fear and greed are the two strongest emotional factors, earnings per share is one of the strongest pragmatic indicators used by investors to make decisions whether to buy or sell a particular company's stock. Market performance is often influenced more by the earnings per share than by other indicators of corporate health such as dividend payout.

There are two classes of stock, preferred and common. Preferred stock is a higher class of company ownership. It normally costs more when initially issued, includes preferential dividends, higher value at liquidation, and may include predetermined conversion factors to other securities issued by the company. Common stock normally includes no predetermined dividend schedule and ranks lower than preferred. It is a simple ownership, or share, of the company with no other privileges and usually doesn't receive a dividend unless company managers choose to pay one. Common stock is the most widely traded type of stock and usually costs considerably less, per share, than preferred (Merrill Lynch, 1997).

The earnings-per-share formula makes it very easy to understand what corporate performance means, because it reduces it to a per-share basis. Earnings per share is a key measure for investors considering whether to buy or sell a company's stock. It is an easy way to compare different stocks and, therefore, different companies. It tells, in dollars and cents, how much money a company earned for each share of stock it has issued. Theoretically, a company with strong earnings per share is building strength that will benefit investors with higher dividends and possible future stock splits that will, in turn, increase the number of shares an investor owns (Kluge, 1991; Livingstone, 1992).

Earnings per share is determined in two steps. First, the amount of money paid to satisfy required preferred stock dividends (shown in Fig. 9.1) is calculated and subtracted from the net income (shown in Fig. 9.2). If you look at Figure 9.1, you will see that there are 60,000 shares of preferred stock outstanding, with a dividend of $5.83. That means $349,800 must be paid in preferred dividends first. Then the remainder of the net income is divided by the average number of outstanding shares of common stock to get the earnings per share for common. Thus, using the relevant numbers from Figure 9.1:

Step #1

Net income	$47,750,000
–Preferred dividend	349,800
Net income for common	47,400,200

Step #2

$$\frac{\text{Net income for common}}{^1\text{Average \# shares of common}} = \frac{\$47,400,200}{14,750,000} = \$3.21$$

(Merrill Lynch, 1997, p. 33)

The $3.21 is shown at the bottom of the corporate annual income statement, in our example at the bottom of Figure 9.2. Obviously, if the company can figure out a way to reduce its operating expenses for the next year, or increase sales without significant increases in operating expenses, the earnings per share would rise. That would tend to attract more investors seeking to buy the stock. When there are more buyers than sellers in the stock market, the price goes up. So all of the corporate executives who own company stock have a vested interest in doing whatever is necessary to make the earnings per share number rise.

For this reason, it is not uncommon for companies to have a very short-term management focus with ownership emphasis on the next quarterly report. That is the Achilles' heel of the American business system. Short-term, quarter-to-quarter emphasis on earnings performance may overshadow the long-term strategic effort to grow a business. Sometimes it is necessary, for long-term growth, to do things that reduce short-term profit. But the economic deck is stacked against the strategic approach in an economic system focused on the next quarterly report due in three months or sooner.

MEDIA ORGANIZATION BUDGETING

All media organizations have budgets, and usually the budget process is a long, drawn-out affair. That's because, at every level, people argue over finite resources. The media organization only has so much, based on what it takes in from customers, and that has to be cut up among the divisions and/or operating units, which in turn cut up what they are allocated among subsidiary units and departments. It is a continuing process of coming up with plans and projections, and then defending those over and over again. Indeed, many department-level managers find that the budget is the most time-consuming activity they have, which often diverts their attention from other concerns. And when media workers rise from the production side, as creative workers, into management, they often find themselves in a very different world that is focused on money, not the creative products that have consumed them up to that point (Van Deusen, 1995).

Budgeting in Media Organizations

There are two basic ways of coming up with a budget: "zero-based" budgeting or the more common "incremental" budget process.

In zero-based budgets, the manager starts off with nothing, no reliance on previous budgets or presumptions. The point of zero-based budgeting is to start fresh, just as though you were opening up a brand-new business or department where you consider all that has to be done and what it will take to accomplish it. There are no preset parameters dictated by corporate accountants. The approach encourages more free thinking about necessary resources to accomplish the organization's goals, and how to allocate them (Van Deusen, 1995). Particularly in media companies where there is a prior history of serious problems, either in dismal market performance or with strong political

---

[1]The company has had different amounts of common outstanding for the past and current year. So the two are averaged together to give a best estimate of the real number of shares currently owned.

influences at work, zero-based budgeting is a way to get out from under the mantle of the past. "The slate is wiped clean, and the manager builds an ideal budget without worrying about what happened in prior years" (Lavine & Wackman, 1988, p. 171).

Zero-based budgeting, despite its intriguing philosophical draw in releasing managers from past practices—which may include many flawed assumptions and misconceptions—is not the most common. Part of the reason is that it is difficult and time-consuming. You have to start from scratch, ignoring everything, including the way you set up your allocation categories. What's more, you have to be highly creative and good with money. Not all managers have the interest, talent, energy, or time to accomplish effective zero-based budgeting. Although occasionally it may be fruitful for a media company to do zero-based budgeting to encourage rethinking financial management, it isn't very workable year in and year out for most managers.

The more common approach to developing a budget is simply to take the previous one and make adjustments to factor in whatever increases or decreases corporate accounting has indicated are necessary based on anticipated revenue and expenses for the year (Van Deusen, 1995). From one year to the next, changes in the basic structure of an incremental budget are minor, with managers generally confined to adjusting the amounts of money within the specific categories. In this type of budgeting the manager inherits what has gone before, learns to work with its peculiarities, and has a more limited role in controlling the budget's overall character. In this "incremental" approach, as conditions change, a media company may make adjustments but the basic resource allocation plan—the budget—remains mostly intact.

Because most businesses, media operations included, use the incremental approach to budgeting, discussed earlier, the current year's estimated budget is usually based on a percentage increase, or decrease, assigned by senior management. When a television station, newspaper, or agency is owned by another company, the owner usually requires what is called a "profit plan" for the subsidiary managers. That means they are assigned a specific amount of money to generate for the parent company each year, and which the parent company counts on as revenue for its budgeting.

Normally, the profit plan is a specific dollar amount based on what the parent company thinks the economy will do. It is often set during negotiations with local managers. When the parent company uses national estimates of economic growth, there can be problems. The United States—and for international companies, the world—is a vast area with different regions, economic factors, and trends. A drought in an agricultural market may mean a recession in one part of the country, while the overall gross national product (GNP) continues to climb.

If a parent company in New York, using national economic forecasts, sets the profit plan for a station in Texas to be 7 percent, and Texas suffers a recession, what do you think happens? Either the parent company admits its mistake and reallocates funds from other units to cover the regional downturn, or it forces the Texas property to cut its budget and possibly lay off staff. In large conglomerates, where the profit center approach is common, the latter is often the choice. Each subsidiary is operated as a profit center and must exist within its own revenues and expenses, though with the additional requirement to produce "management fees" for the parent company.

Budgets come in layers. That is, at each level of management there is a budget. Typically, budgets at the higher levels are general in nature but at the lower level are in detail down to the penny of office supplies. Often such budgets resemble income statements, with each level's revenues and expenses shown. Obviously, if you are going to manage your expenditures effectively, you have to have an idea of how much money you have to work with.

The examples in this section include two- or three-year totals with the oldest budget on the far right, and the most recent in the left column nearest the category headings. This is a typical budget layout and is designed to help show trends. The manager wants to know where things stand "right now," so the most recent numbers are typically adjacent to the category headings in the first column of numbers to the right of category names.

Differences Among Media Budgets

Media organizations come in many forms, with highly variable ways of defining themselves and tracking their money. The following sections discuss the basic forms of newspaper, television station, and news department budgets. As a media manager, wherever you end up working, you will have to spend some time with the business manager or chief accountant for some training in the particulars of that organization's way of tracking its money. Basic accounting conventions will be used, but beyond that budgets are tailored to the unique demands of the individual media organizations using them.

Newspaper Budget

Newspapers are in the print business, so what they do is driven by paper and ink. Figure 9.3 is a basic newspaper budget for a small paper generating just over $2 million in total revenues. The numbers may or may not be relatively close to a budget you have seen before. What is important to note, as you look over this budget, and the other media organization budgets included in this chapter, is the way budgeting requires detailed separation of expense categories.

As you can see, after revenues, the newspaper has extensive expenses divided up into what it pays its people—compensation—allocates for the basic supplies of its publishing business—paper, ink, offset plates and chemicals—and then the general operating costs for everything from computer research to wire services. Look at the detail of these numbers. How would you, as a manager, cut the current year's budget by 20 percent if the company was hit by an expensive lawsuit judgment? What's more, the cuts you impose cannot adversely affect the quality of the newspaper product in the eyes of consumers.

A media manager is often judged on how he or she controls the budget. Staying within the budget is always important, but if you can accomplish everything and have a budget surplus, senior management will really be impressed. Your career will advance, because more profit will be generated. You'd like that next raise, and maybe another promotion. So, your mind begins to work like a manager's, questioning why you're spending what you're spending. Do we really need to spend $5,200 on stringers—people outside the station who are paid on a per-story basis—to help with news coverage? Why are our office supplies running $1,550 a year? Are people just unnecessarily throwing away paper and pens? Look at travel and entertainment. Couldn't we cut a chunk out of that $18,000? Why do we need all that travel, when newspaper reporters work mostly on the telephone? And how many people do we have to entertain, anyway?

When those times come along where you need to throw out the budget and do what's necessary for the long-term credibility of your media organization—disaster coverage, for example—you must be prepared to argue not only the journalistic merits of what you want to do, but how it will benefit the organization over time as credibility is increased and the company's intangible asset of reputation as the "news source of record" is enhanced in the market. Unless there is a compelling reason literally to throw

Sample Newspaper Operating Budget

Category	Current year (estimated)	Last year (actual)
Revenue		
Advertising		
Classified	265,900	252,605
Legal notices	143,700	136,515
Local	993,900	944,205
National	137,400	130,530
Circulation	84,000	79,800
Commercial printing	412,300	391,685
Total revenues	**2,037,200**	**1,935,340**
Expenses		
Compensation		
Advertising	110,300	107,785
Circulation & mailroom	61,900	58,805
News editorial	197,000	187,150
Printing	127,000	120,650
Production & layout	85,000	80,750
	581,200	555,140
Printing supplies/inventories		
Inks	60,000	57,000
Newsprint	600,000	570,000
Plates & chemicals	74,000	70,300
	734,000	697,300
General operating costs		
Computer research	10,500	9,975
Computer systems	43,000	40,850
Contract services	63,400	60,230
Depreciation	54,400	51,680
Leases	37,300	35,435
Office supplies	1,550	1,473
Physical plant, utilities, & maintenance	62,500	59,375
Postage	13,000	12,350
Stringers	5,200	4,940
Taxes	61,000	57,950
Telephone	9,900	9,405
Training	5,500	5,225
Transportation	145,000	137,750
Travel & entertainment	18,000	17,100
Wire services	11,000	10,450
	541,250	514,188
Total expenses	**1,856,450**	**1,766,628**
Pretax net income	**180,750**	**168,712**

Note: Budget includes a 5 percent increase for the current year. Figures are hypothetical. This budget is an illustration for instructional purposes only.

Figure 9.3 Media Organization Two-Year Newspaper Budget
(Sources: Newsom, 1981; Sohn, Ogan, & Polich, 1986; Willis, 1988)

out the budget—and that often means senior management's profit plan, which means trouble with the parent company—it is not going to happen.

Sample Television Station Budget

Figure 9.4 shows what a general television station budget might look like for a relatively small operation. You will note that under income, the numbers for the commissions category are deducted before the net revenue is computed. While the commissions might have gone under the operating expenses, they are a direct cost of the actual advertising sales, and this station deducts them within the income area to get the net revenue figure—the money actually available to cover station expenses. Within the confines of accepted accounting practices, different media operations will have different ways of setting their categories, and even what they choose to categorize. So, in your career, you will see many ways of laying out budgets. As long as you understand the fundamentals, you will be able to find your way around them. The basic concept is always the same: income – expenses = profit or loss.

In the case of the station in Figure 9.4, the annual budget has grown at a 5 percent annual rate, with the exception of the new Internet ISP/Web site revenues. The station got into the Internet business by accident. It decided to put up a station World Wide Web page. After going through that expense, it found a ready local market for connections to the Internet, and began offering dial-up connections as an Internet Service Provider at $19.95 per month. The business literally exploded, as you can see, from only $14,843 in revenues two years ago to an estimated revenue projection of $357,424 in the current year. The only increased cost to the station has been adding ten new inbound phone lines and modems for dial-up customers during the three-year period. Just $10,000 was spent in the previous year, and $18,000 will be spent in the current year for this expansion. The enormous growth of Internet ISP/Web site revenues—18.7 percent last year, and an estimated 30 percent this year—has turned this once promotional idea into a very profitable enterprise for the station. Costs are running only 7.8 percent of revenues. It's almost all profit!

Clearly, this station manager is exceeding whatever profit plan was set for her by the ownership group. However, senior management will undoubtedly revise their assessment of the local operation and begin factoring in higher expectations for revenue generation in future years. One of the inherent problems in business is that success fuels higher expectations. Perhaps the station manager will succeed in convincing her corporate bosses that the large growth rate for Internet service will begin topping off due to more competitors in the market and, eventually, satisfaction of the demand for new Internet connections.

Sample Television News Operating Budget

Figure 9.5 represents another television news operation's budget. In this case, the station has not been able to develop a new business subsidiary but is simply running the news department as a news and information operation in the traditional sense.

As you look over the budget, consider the different categories that have to be included by the news director to keep track of department money. All department-level managers have two categories of expenditures in their budgets, fixed and discretionary. Fixed expenses are those you can't really change, and discretionary expenses are within the individual manager's power to alter.

Often, some of the largest categories in a budget are fixed in nature. For example, payroll often has fairly limited flexibility. Anchors are typically under contract.

Sample three year budget for a local television station

Income	Current year (estimated)	Last year	Two years ago
Advertising sales			
Local	$3,274,300	$3,110,585	$2,955,056
National	1,065,334	1,012,067	961,464
Commissions	(646,896)	(614,551)	(583,824)
Commercial production	643,150	610,992	580,443
Internet ISP/Web site	357,424	104,139	14,843
Net revenues	4,693,312	4,223,232	3,927,982
Operating expenses			
Administrative expenses	551,487	523,912	497,717
Engineering	147,600	140,220	133,209
Facilities maintenance	37,300	35,435	33,663
News	371,400	350,130	329,773
Internet facilities & operations	18,000	10,000	0
Production	145,225	137,964	131,066
Programming	797,841	757,949	720,052
Promotion	127,971	121,572	115,494
Total operating expenses	2,196,824 / 2,496,488	2,077,182 / 2,146,050	1,960,974 / 1,967,008
Nonoperating expenses			
Corporate management fee	325,000	308,750	293,313
Depreciation	480,500	456,475	433,651
Interest	750,300	712,785	677,146
Total Nonoperating expenses	1,555,800	1,478,010	1,404,110
Profit before taxes	**940,688**	**668,040**	**562,898**

Note: The company is growing at 5 percent annually with the exception of the new Internet ISP/Web site revenues, which have climbed dramatically. All figures are hypothetical. This budget is an illustration for instructional purposes only.

Figure 9.4 Local Television Station Three-Year Budget
(Sources: Lavine & Wackman, 1988; Van Deusen, 1995)

News Department Two-Year Budget		
Category	**Current year (estimated)**	**Last year (actual)**
Payroll		
Salaries	$450,000	427,500
Overtime	14,000	13,300
Stringers/freelance	60,000	57,000
Temporary help	10,000	9,500
	534,000	507,300
Operating supplies (expendable)		
Cellular telephone	10,000	9,500
General office	8,500	8,075
Photography/video tape	16,800	15,960
Satellite time	95,000	90,250
Travel & entertainment	18,000	17,100
Emergency contingency fund	20,000	19,000
	168,300	159,885
General equipment		
Acquisition	200,000	190,000
Maintenance	45,000	42,750
	245,000	232,750
Contract services		
Syndicated feed	39,000	37,050
Wire services	8,000	7,600
Computer research services	12,000	11,400
	59,000	56,050
Vehicles		
Leases (5 news vehicles)	27,000	25,650
Vehicle maintenance & fuel	11,300	10,735
	38,300	36,385
Total	**1,044,600**	**992,370**

Note: This budget includes a five percent increase for the current year over the previous year. All figures are hypothetical. This budget is an illustration for instructional purposes only.

Figure 9.5 Television News Department Two-Year Budget

Although there may be turnover in the department, the jobs still need to be done. So, while hiring, firing, and quitting is going on over time, the expenses for staff are stable from a budget point of view.

The individual manager does have control of the overtime her department spends, as well as the money that has been budgeted for stringers and other freelance people hired on an individual need basis for short-term work. These are what are called "discretionary" budget items, because the individual manager has discretion over how and when they are spent. Managing discretionary money is often the key to success for a department-level media manager. For that reason, and because discretionary funds exist in some form in all media operations, they are discussed further in the following section.

Discretionary Funds

All media managers, regardless of the specific type of media business, will have some discretionary funds to manage. To show how important it is to track discretionary funds closely, consider this. Overtime, in many media operations, is often considered to be "extra" money even though it is really meant for the extraordinary things that come along outside normal day-to-day needs. It can be quickly used up by the people who assign coverage. City editors and assignment managers tend to be focused on the here and now of news developments and, when they are short on staff to cover a story, see the overtime budget sitting there like a pot of available money. It will quickly disappear, nibbled away by such day-to-day needs as covering a school board meeting here, a court arraignment there, or the Friday night sports when extra people are needed to cover all the high school games. If the department-level manager doesn't watch overtime closely, that pool of money can quickly disappear. Then comes the tornado, or railroad tank car explosion, or other disaster for which overtime is really meant. But the money is gone.

Most businesses of any size have quarterly budget reports that help managers track the flow of money during the year. Figure 9.6 is an example of what such a report might look like. Because a quarterly budget report provides a quick way to compare actual and budgeted expenditures for the quarter and year to date, it is particularly handy in tracking overspending in some categories, and surpluses in others. As you can see, this report is for the third quarter of the year.

Look at the columns for year to date. Because this is a third-quarter budget these numbers also reflect the previous two quarters' activity. At this point, with three months to go in the year, you can see that some categories are way over budget while others are under budget. The biggest problems in this example are the expenses directly connected with increased coverage costs for a local tornado in May and brush fires in September. Overtime, stringers/freelance, satellite time, travel and entertainment, and vehicle maintenance and fuel are way beyond what was planned.

This news manager has been very careful with acquisition of new equipment and temporary help and still has the department's emergency contingency fund available. So the bottom line for the department budget is a cushion of $23,904, or 3.05 percent under budget despite the unexpected news coverage expenses. The moral of this example in budgeting is that money that doesn't have to be spent right away shouldn't be. Particularly in media organizations functioning in dynamic environments, maintaining any possible flexibility within a budget is a positive management approach.

In news operations, quarterly reports can be too infrequent to be useful, especially when there is a lot of news coverage going on. For that reason effective managers often keep track of their discretionary funds on a monthly basis so the expenditures don't get away from them between the quarterly reports. The accounting department of any media organization can set up a monthly budget allocation spreadsheet for you, if they don't provide it as a matter of course, similar to the one in Figure 9.7.

In this case, the news department's overtime budget has been divided up monthly with columns showing the actual expenses and what's left. You can see how this helps a media manager keep track of how fast overtime is being consumed in the heat of the news battle. If you look at Figure 9.7, you will note some very large overtime costs for April, May, and September. During April there were county elections in a particularly intensive campaign. Then in May, a tornado destroyed a housing subdivision. The summer was fairly normal, but then due to a particularly dry year, brush fires erupted in September. By October (the current month) the overtime budget is already in the red by $421.78. Obviously the station manager and news director are going to have to work out

News Department Quarterly Budget Report (Rounded to nearest dollar)

Category	3rd Quarter				Year to Date			
	Budget	Actual	$ surplus/(shortfall)	$ surplus/(shortfall)	Budget	Actual	$ surplus/(shortfall)	$ surplus/(shortfall)
Payroll								
Salaries	$112,500	112,500	0	0	$337,500	$337,500	0	0
Overtime	3,500	4,978	(1,478)	(42.23)	10,500	14,421	(3,921)	(37.34)
Stringers/freelance	15,000	31,000	(16,000)	(106.67)	45,000	57000	(12,000)	(26.67)
Temporary help	2,500	0	2,500	100.00	7,500	1250	6,250	83.33
	133,500	**148,478**	**(14,978)**	**(11.22%)**	**400,500**	**410,171**	**(9,671)**	**(2.41)**
Operating supplies (expendable)								
Cellular telephone	2,500	2,200	100	4.00	7,500	8700	(1,200)	(16.00)
General office	2,125	1,987	138	6.49	6,375	5985	390	6.12
Photography/video tape	4,200	3,300	900	21.42	12,600	13700	(1,100)	(8.73)
Satellite time	23,750	31,425	(7,675)	(32.32)	71,250	93000	(21,750)	(30.53)
Travel & entertainment	4,500	6,250	(1,750)	(38.89)	13,500	18415	(4,915)	(36.40)
Emergency contingency fund	5,000	0	5,000	100.00	15,000	0	15,000	100.00
	42,075	**45,162**	**(3,087)**	**(7.34)**	**126,225**	**139,800**	**(13,575)**	**(10.75)**
General equipment								
Acquisition	50,000	37,400	12,600	25.20	150,000	91700	58,300	38.87
Maintenance	11,250	11,250	0	100.00	33,750	41725	(7,975)	(23.62)
	61,250	**48,650**	**12,600**	**20.57**	**183,750**	**133,425**	**50,325**	**27.39**
Contract services								
Syndicated feed	9,750	9,750	0	0	29,250	29250	0	0
Wire services	2,000	2,000	0	0	6,000	6000	0	0
Computer research services	3,000	3,000	0	0	9,000	9000	0	0
	14,750	**14,750**	**0**	**0**	**44,250**	**44,250**	**0**	**0**
Vehicles								
Leases (5 news vehicles)	6,750	6,750	0	100.00	20,250	20250	0	100.00
Vehicle maintenance & fuel	2,825	6,150	(3,325)	(117.70)	8,475	11650	(3,175)	(37.46)
	9,575	**12,900**	**(3,325)**	**(34.73)**	**28,725**	**31900**	**(3175)**	**(11.05)**
Total	**261,150**	**269,940**	**8,790**	**(3.37)**	**783,450**	**759,546**	**23,904**	**3.05**

Note: This budget includes a 5 percent increase for the current year over the previous year. All figures are hypothetical. This budget is an illustration for instructional purposes only.

Figure 9.6 Quarterly Budget Report (Source: Van Deusen, 1995)

239

News Department Overtime Budget—Current Year
Total for Year—$14,000

Month	Budget	Actual	Planned Balance	Actual Balance
	14,000.00		14,000.00	14,000.00
January	1,166.66	434.80	12,833.34	13,565.20
February	1,166.66	0	11,666.68	13,565.20
March	1,166.66	247.65	10,500.02	13,317.55
April	1,166.66	3,487.42	9,333.36	9,830.13
May	1,166.66	4,851.75	8,166.70	4,978.38
June	1,166.66	421.78	7,000.04	4,556.60
July	1,166.66	68.90	5,833.38	4,487.70
August	1,166.66	1,141.45	4,666.72	3,346.25
September	1,166.66	3,768.03	3,500.06	(421.78)
October	1,166.66		2,333.40	
November	1,166.66		1,166.74	
December	1,166.66		.08	
Total	**100%**	**14421.48**		**(421.78)**
% of Total	**100%**	**103%**		**(3%)**

Note: Major events which consumed overtime budget include: (1) April—county elections; (2) May—South Meridian tornado; (3) September—Brush fires.

Figure 9.7 Monthly Overtime Budget

some way to move money from other accounts, or the news director will have to trim internal department expenses to make up the difference.

Sometimes things just pile up, and the budget has to be thrown out when big disasters strike that must be covered, no matter what. But typically, year in and year out, news budgets are predictable. News managers are expected to live within their budgets and justify any serious deviation from them.

FORECASTING: THE ART OF BUDGETING FOR MEDIA ORGANIZATIONS

Although media managers have to live within budgets once they are set, they also are instrumental in deciding what future budgets will look like. Budgeting is a continuous activity in most organizations where today's reality is used to anticipate what will happen tomorrow. This year's budget, in most cases, is the model that is used for setting up tomorrow's—the incremental approach. It requires intensive, and ongoing, analysis and planning.

Formal organizational planning is discussed in detail in Chapter 10 and should be used where possible in the budget process. Typically, a business unit will have a budget team, which may include all department heads, to negotiate the budget. But each department, in turn, should have its own budget team to ensure that key organizational players are involved so nothing that should be included is missed.

Estimating Revenue

In many organizations, the first budget step is "guesstimating" what will happen to revenues in the next year. That term, *guesstimating,* is probably the most accurate way to describe the process. For though all of the possible data on future trends can be assembled and considered, the future always has an element of the unknown that changes the most carefully laid plans. Predicting the future is guessing what will happen on the best possible estimate of future conditions. Every time a significant downturn occurs in the stock market, a "crash" if it's a big loss in the trading indexes or a "correction" if less so, people are caught off guard. The morning-after analysis always sounds so logical you may wonder why so many people failed to see it coming. Hindsight, as the saying goes, is always 20–20.

Typically, a media organization spends considerable time developing its future revenues and profit estimates. Once that is accomplished, departmental budgets are normally done to fit within the expected revenue stream. Businesses, ideally, want to spend this year's money on this year's expenses for tax reasons. The costs of doing business are, in general, deductible. So whatever expenses can be put against current cash flow reduces the amount of profit on which taxes are computed. It would be easier if you spent money you already had. But that is never the case because of the tax issue. Rather than generating this year's revenue and then spending it next year—spending money after you have it—money is spent as it is coming in. For that reason, it is very important that revenue estimates be as accurate as possible.

This is usually done through a combination of three factors: (1) the general economic indicators available locally and nationally, (2) the objectives the media organization has set for its competitive position in the market, and (3) estimates of the advertising or other media revenue potential in the market. Sidebar 9.2 provides an example of how this process works.

Once the revenue targets are set, and the anticipated costs necessary to raise that revenue are deducted, the sales department is given its "budget" of anticipated sales to satisfy the revenue projection. Each sales executive is, in turn, given an advertising sales target. Typically, managers do all they can to make sure the incremental increases in market share and sales targets are realistic. But often they are handed down from displaced owners operating the subsidiary from distant headquarters.

Regardless of how much input local managers have, any percentage increase or decrease in revenue projections is easily translated into all budget categories through the incremental method of budgeting, discussed earlier. For example, if corporate decides local market revenue will grow at 7 percent next year, an entire station's budget may be factored up by that amount.

Clearly, the danger is making a mistake in the "guesstimate." When revenues are forecast to be one thing, but turn out to be lower, and budgets have been factored with the erroneous figures and money spent in them, serious repercussions can result. Those can be dramatic cutbacks in resources and/or personnel in the last quarter of the year as attempts are made to recover the losses, or some other way of cost recovery to maintain the profit plan.

Designing a Budget

When you set out to design a budget plan for the next year, the first thing you should do is divide the expenditures into fixed and variable categories. Fixed expenses are, essentially, those things that don't change much over time, or that you can't really

Our radio station is one of eight in the market. We have a 10 percent share of the local radio audience. Last year radio advertising in our market totaled $1,000,000. That logically means our 10 percent share of the audience should have generated $100,000 for the station (10% of $1,000,000 = $100,000).

Next year all indicators are the economy should grow by about 15 percent. Several new companies are moving into town, and retailing looks very healthy with increased payroll dollars already beginning to flow. With a 15 percent projected growth in the economy we figure the total radio advertising spending in our market should also increase by 15 percent next year, or an additional $150,000 (15% of $1,000,000 = $150,000). The total radio advertising market will then be $1,150,000 ($1,000,000 + $150,000 = $1,150,000). If our share remains 10 percent, our station advertising revenue should be $115,000 (10% of $1,150,000 = $115,000).

But we feel there is a real chance to improve our market share to 15 percent by shifting from an "oldies" format of music to "light rock." We anticipate it will cost an additional $10,000 in promotional expenses and new music acquisition to implement the new format and establish it among listeners. If we succeed, we will benefit two ways. We can expect more advertising revenue because the dollars being spent on radio advertising in the market will increase. And if we increase our audience share to 15 percent, we'll have a larger part of the advertising revenue pie.

A 15 percent share of an advertising revenue market of $1,150,000 would be $172,500. That would be $72,500 more than we took in last year. We will have to spend $10,000 on the new format, but even with that cost deducted, we still end up with an increase of $62,500 over the advertising revenue the station took in last year. That would be a 62.5 percent increase (the increase of $62,500 is 62.5 percent of the previous year's $100,000). With that kind of growth in station advertising revenue, the owners should be extremely happy.

We now set up our budget, allocating $5,000 to the promotion effort, and $5,000 for music.

---

change significantly. Variable expenses are those budget items that do change from time to time, or that management has the ability to control more directly (Willis, 1988).

In some cases, what would be a variable expense can become a fixed expense. For example, in the comparison of fixed and variable expenses that follows, you will note that payroll is a variable expense. However, if long-term contracts exist for some staff members, typically news anchors in television or columnists in newspapers, those particular items might be considered fixed. Once you know what fixed budget items you have, those should be incrementally increased by whatever inflation rate is currently causing the general economy to rise. Plugging in simple inflation factors is usually a close estimate for fixed costs.

With variable costs, you have to take a lot of time and do your research. There are internal political factors at work in any company, as well as external market realities. You need to be an expert in both. First, you have to understand your company, its politics, and its managerial processes. Second, you need to have a clear idea who your audience and/or customers are and what their tendencies may be. Market research is a critical element in profiling target audiences, both in demographic and psychographic characteristics, and then designing media organization products to take advantage of

Fixed Expenses	**Variable Expenses**
1. Contract services (wire services, syndicated features or news feeds, etc.)	1. Departmental supplies
2. Depreciation on plant and equipment	2. Fuel and maintenance of vehicles
3. Interest on loans	3. Graphics and art supplies or production
4. Leased equipment (including staff vehicles)	4. Newsprint and ink
5. Office and production equipment	5. Payroll
6. Office furniture	6. Photocopying
7. Office supplies (general)	7. Promotion expenses
8. Postage and shipping	8. Telephone (regular, cellular, long distance)
9. Property taxes	9. Training and development
10. Rent or mortgages	10. Travel
11. Utilities	11. Videotape and audiotape

whatever conditions prevail. Third, you have to understand the workings of your own department and the personalities within it (Van Deusen, 1995).

Designing an effective budget means involving other people in the process. No media manager can do it alone. And it is not just accounting help that is needed. You need to discuss budget needs with everyone directly affected. That means you need to discuss office supplies with the secretary, videotape or photographic supplies with the chief photographer, computer equipment needs with the information systems manager, weather forecasting graphics options and costs with the meteorologists. You want your budget to be efficient but workable. When you design a budget, if you miss something you generally have to live without it for a year.

Along with bringing your departmental team into the budgeting process to help make accurate cost estimates, you need to anticipate any special events that might increase expenses. News organizations have to spend more money during election years to cover campaigns and elections. If you live in a hurricane-prone part of the country, it's always wise to check on what kind of storm season the National Hurricane Center predicts for the next year. In 1997 the El Niño Pacific Ocean current warming cycle appeared to be setting up a particularly harsh winter for the western part of the United States, with higher than normal potential for devastating storms in California. With such trend development a prudent news manager would anticipate more costs in over-time might be necessary for disaster coverage if the scientists' predictions proved to be true (Graham, 1997).

Effective budget forecasting is part art and part science. It is a best-effort plan, in financial terms, of what is to be done. It is not just a dream of what we'd like, but a pragmatic, carefully drawn-out plan for what we expect to be done. It has to be specific. It has to have clearly defined goals that will be achieved if the conditions our analytical tools predict occur. And it has to support the vision of senior management both in terms of where the organization needs to go, and the profit plan that has been implemented for the unit within which you work (Van Deusen, 1995).

You do your homework, closely examine all trends, market research, and, anything you can get your hands on that will give you an idea of what might lay ahead. Then you set a budget within the parameters your boss gives you and do the best you can to live within it. But remember that to be effective, a budget has to be current and have some flexibility built into it. Notice the category called "emergency contingency fund" in Figure 9.6. If you look closely at the flow of expenses for the news department you can see that having that extra pot of money for special emergencies is what saves this manager from going in the red.

Finally, when you are managing a budget and you see it getting out of kilter, alert your boss as early as possible. Not staying within your budget is considered a sin in management, but a greater sin is not telling anyone when problems arise. All managers who have touched a budget have had their own struggles with items missed, or incorrectly factored, or suddenly finding that subordinates have spent all the overtime just when a hurricane is about to hit. Honesty with your senior manager is always the best policy when the budget goes awry, and as early as possible.

CHAPTER SUMMARY

Keeping track of the money is something many media managers initially find difficult. That may be because of their basic orientation to creative media work, or perhaps a lack of basic training. It is not uncommon for media managers to be elevated from the ranks of journalism production—reporters, copy editors, or news producers—and suddenly find themselves facing spreadsheets they don't understand. But when you become a manager, you are expected to be a budget person.

Part of the problem is that the traditional model of business places great importance on budgeting. Many managers want budget control because that's where much of the organizational power rests. The other problem is that senior managers often judge a junior manager as much by how he or she keeps track of the money as any real leadership provided to the highly creative people in media work.

Consider the following comments made by television news directors when asked about the challenges of their jobs. They describe a transition from creating information to having money and how the budget came to dominate their professional lives once they ascended into the managerial world.

[On attending the first department head meetings]

They were all talking Greek! (Redmond, 1993, p. 10)

[On learning to do a budget]

I came on the job and was handed the budget that the old news director had put together and tried to figure it out myself. . . . My budget experience has been primarily self-taught. . . . It was frustrating. It was real frustrating. Because I thought I understood certain things and then I'd find out I didn't, really. And I'd kind of go back to square one . . . I still don't completely understand some things that I think I should, although I have a pretty good working knowledge. . . . I mean it's really hit and miss, still. I put together a realistic budget and then it got cut.

And then when it gets back from New York we'll see if it resembles anything. (Redmond, 1993, p. 246)

[On the personalized importance of money management]

It wasn't until I went through my second layoff—and had to lay off some of the people that I liked the best—[that I decided] I was going to make good decisions and I wasn't going to play favorites. . . . I realized that I had a real obligation to make sure that I understood how the newsroom functioned. What role it played in the financing of the station and how healthy we were. . . . To save money when I could. Because, in the long run what I was doing is keeping myself and my employees in a job. (Redmond, 1993, p. 257–258)

[On the inherent difficulty of news budgeting]

It's the news business. Things change. You can't really predict. I'm asked to budget sufficiently and effectively for the next year. I have no clue what's going to happen tomorrow. You know, I don't really know what's going to happen day-to-day, and they're asking me to predict what's going to happen for the next year, and budget for it. For instance, probably a quarter of our budget over-runs for this year came in May. Because, we hit the ratings period, we had our first execution in California, the LA riots, earthquakes. I mean, all of a sudden that one month all this news hit. We had, you know, six months of news in one month. (Redmond, 1993, p. 261)

There is no such thing as a simple solution to a complex problem, for anything a manager does usually reverberates throughout the organization. Flexibility is critical in effective financial management, because of the dynamic nature of media organizations. The operating environment is continually adjusting and so, too, must the media organization. Because of that, media managers have to understand basic financial concepts and budget effectively.

Because contemporary business practices focus on the quarterly earnings report, which in turn can have major implications for everything a company does from its investment strategy to those considering investing in it, there is an inherent danger of being too shortsighted. Although media managers must pay attention to quarterly business trends, it is paramount that they keep focused on their strategy for the long term. It is very easy to become captivated by the monthly budget and not move the media organization forward.

The media manager has an important role bridging the gap between the creative forces engaged in developing media product, and the pragmatic forces of business management. It's important for a media manager to understand both of these sometimes opposing points of view, and be able to serve as an intermediary between them. A media organization is a business that has to remain solvent and turn a profit to keep going. But it also has to have the ability to touch peoples' lives in deeper ways than merely as a handoff for advertising. An effective media manager is a boundary-spanner between those who are focused on money and those who are focused on social meaning. Media organization strategy has to include a blend of quality media products, which serve the intended audiences, at a competitive price to attract market share. This relationship of quality, service, and price is an intricate balance that requires intelligent budget planning and implementation so the media product is of the highest quality, with a minimum cost of production, and fits within what the audience and other media customers (e.g. advertisers) consider worthwhile.

BUDGETING EXERCISE

The best way to understand media organization budgeting is for you to put it into personal terms. Running a company is really not that much different from running your own personal financial affairs. The numbers may be larger, and there may be different labels on the corporate and personal budget, but the basic principle is the same.

In any budget the real trick is to make sure you don't overlook anything. Budgets are detail plans for what you will do with your money, so all categories of expenses need to be included. Otherwise, the thing you overlooked is the thing that puts you in the red.

Figure 9.8 shows a personal budget planner for you to use in setting up your personal finances. Put in all of your various sources of income, making sure to show the after-tax amount you really have to spend, also known as "disposable income" in economic parlance, in line 6. Then, enter all of the things on which you spend money. You need to account for every expenditure, including your lunch money, fees, books, tuition, gasoline for your car, and so on. If you need more room to calculate all the little details of your spending, use another sheet of paper and add them up for a total in each category. There are expense categories for basic living, education, your insurance policies, entertainment, and any credit card or other payments.

Add up all your expenses and subtract those from your net income. If you have a shortfall, meaning you are spending more than you are taking in, you need to cut some of your expenses or you'll get in serious trouble very soon. If you have a surplus, what are you doing with it? Is it being invested in a savings account, mutual fund, or some other instrument to expand your net worth or provide extra money when something unexpected happens—for example, your car transmission goes out, or you get a speeding ticket causing your automobile insurance to jump $100 a month?

If you can manage your own financial affairs in detail, and account for every penny you take in and spend, you can manage a media organization departmental budget.

Personal Budget Planner

	Item total	Section total
1. **Gross Income**		
2. Federal withholding		
3. State withholding		
4. Social Security		
5. Other deductions (group medical, etc.)		
6. **Net income**	*Enter section total →*	
7. **Expenses**		
8. Rent or mortgage		
9. Car payment(s)		
10. Commuting expenses		
11. Utilities & energy		
12. Electricity		
13. Telephone		
14. Natural gas		
15. Gasoline		
16. Oil		
17. Other		
18. Groceries		
19. **Subtotal basic living expense**	*Enter section total →*	
20. **Education expenses**		
21. Tuition & fees		
22. Books & lab charges		
23. Other add-on college fees		
24. Other		
25. **Subtotal education expense**	*Enter section total →*	
26. **Insurance**		
27. Homeowner's		
28. Medical (if not payroll deduction)		
29. Life		
30. Car		
31. Other		
32. **Subtotal insurance costs**	*Enter section total →*	
33. **Entertainment**		
34. Dining out		
35. Movies		

Figure 9.8   Personal Budget Planner

Personal Budget Planner—(Continued)	Item total	Section total
36. Music		
37. Books		
38. Vacations		
39. Other		
40. Subtotal entertainment	*Enter section total →*	
41. Credit cards & debts not noted above		
42. Credit card (MC, Visa, etc.)		
43. Other card		
44. Other card		
45. Gasoline card		
46. Other card		
47. Other card		
48. Other		
49. Subtotal credit payments	*Enter section total →*	
50. Total expenses *(lines 19, 25, 32, 40, 49)*		
51. Enter net income here *(line 6)*		
52. Enter total expenses here *(line 50)*		–
53. Surplus or (shortfall)		

Figure 9.8 Continued

STUDY QUESTIONS

1. What is a balance sheet, and what does it tell us?

2. Media companies have, as a primary asset, their reputation which is often a major factor influencing their position in a market. Where do you show, on a balance sheet, the estimated value of that reputation or image?

3. When you look at a company's income statement, what do you look for?

4. What does it mean when a company is "highly leveraged," and how is that leverage satisfied?

5. How is net profit determined?

6. How do you determine earnings per share, and why is it so important to senior executives of large media companies?

7. What is the difference between "zero-based" and "incremental" budgeting? Which one is more common and why?

chapter 10

PLANNING AND DECISION MAKING

BY RICK FISCHER, PH.D.(UNIVERSITY OF MEMPHIS) WITH GERHARD BÜTSCHI, PH.D. (INTERNATIONAL PUBLIC RELATIONS CONSULTANT)

INTRODUCTION

Organizational life is inherently complex. It involves many people with diverse perspectives within a swirl of ideas, goals, and visions of the future. Just as you would not set out on a simple trip to another city without checking on the directions, neither will a well-managed organization go anywhere without a plan. Sometimes the plan is simple and easy to understand. Other times it can be complex and hard to develop. To carry our trip metaphor a step further, it is one thing to go to the next city but quite another to visit all the capitals of the world in a yearlong adventure. The first takes only a cursory plan. The second takes a very detailed one involving airline flights, mail forwarding services, a scheme for making sure your supply of funds will be available from faraway places with hard-to-say names, and many other details.

Earlier we considered some of the things that go into organizational planning and decision making. Those include goal setting and developing a shared vision among organizational members. Planning is the activity used to move an organization through goal achievement and eventual realization of its long-term vision. But to develop a plan, you have to understand the way an organization arrives at decisions, since that process is fundamental to acceptance of whatever your plan will ultimately provide.

This chapter provides an overview of the decision-making process and then introduces a new concept in detailed planning, the Bütschi model. Swiss business professor and consultant Gerhard Bütschi developed his eight-step approach to planning as a comprehensive approach to include all contingencies. His plan has been specifically adapted for communicators.

THE DECISION PROCESS

The first thing to understand is that different kinds of decisions require different approaches. One of the problems in developing any universal model for decision making is that it is a behavior-centered activity dependent upon the human variables at work in an organization. Each person, and each group of people we call an organization, has a personality that deals with some things better than others. So effective decision making, from the outset, has to have flexibility to adjust to the forces at work in the organization. On the surface, decision making appears fairly straightforward and simple: Set some goals or objectives, develop some alternative ways to meet the goals, evaluate those alternatives, choose the best one, and implement that choice. But each of those steps can be complex, with potential organizational failure when wrong choices are made.

Routine and Nonsystematic Decisions

One way of understanding decision making is to recognize that not all decisions are the same. Therefore, the approach to resolving them has to be adjusted to situational demands.

Routine decisions are often tied to a repetitive pattern of behavior or accepted practice that is procedure oriented. They are the kinds of things that happen over and over again, that usually involve some level of coordination among organizational members or units, and that are required by organizational processes. They are also called programmed decisions, originally identified by Simon (1960).

Typically, routine decisions are grounded in cause-and-effect relationships that are bound together in the organizational bureaucracy by accepted rules and procedures. A good media organization example of routine decision making is editing copy for a newspaper. We have rules of grammar that are accepted conventions of how we write. Routine copy editor decisions about how to adjust a story are based on those conventions. Additionally, to resolve disputes, *The Associated Press Stylebook* is used in most newsrooms as a reference. Though the U.S. Postal Service has changed all of the abbreviations for states to two letter designations with capitals and no periods—for example, CA, NY, MT, IL—the newspaper industry continues to use the AP abbreviations, which range from two to five letters with periods—Calif., N.Y., Mont., Ill. (Goldstein, 1996). Tradition clearly drives the continuing use of the AP style, since fewer characters would produce cost and space savings.

Many kinds of decisions fall into the "routine" category, but generally these involve things that happen frequently enough that standard procedures have been developed to deal with them. Typically they include budgeting and accounting, hiring and firing, and the organization's reward system for pay raises and other benefits—the kinds of decisions based on routine procedures.

Nonsystematic decisions are the opposite of routine decisions. They are decisions required by some spontaneous or new development for which established procedures have not been devised. They may be very carefully considered but are not products of an existing bureaucratic process or routine. They tend to be caused by new developments that require organizations to change. For example, the rise of the Internet has prompted many media organizations to rethink the way they publish, and many have launched World Wide Web sites to attract consumers to their products. Newspapers publishing on the Web have to consider the technology of the computer in designing ways for readers to navigate that are different from merely reading a traditional physical newspaper at the breakfast table. Search engines have been incorporated into many media Web sites, as they grow into expanded databases.

Changes in a media market due to new competitors or products, the determination to build a new media organization facility and all the decisions about how to design it, and even reorganization of a company call for nonsystematic but carefully considered decisions, because the old, standard way of deciding either does not exist or is no longer relevant due to environmental changes. Such decisions require innovative thinking because there is no previous pattern to follow. They are problems for which solutions have not been programmed into the organizational bureaucracy (Simon, 1960).

During any media manager's day, numerous decisions will probably need to be made in both the routine and nonsystematic category. The routine decisions take considerable organizational or job specific knowledge since they are steeped in past practices and coordination. So effectiveness as a decision maker in the routine category requires a process focus. Nonsystematic decisions, on the other hand, require just the opposite, an open mind able to understand the scope of something that has not previously been encountered and then to think creatively to resolve the issue.

The Decision-Making Approach

Let's start at a very simple level. To make a decision is to choose from among alternatives. To make a good decision a person needs to be able to identify reasonable options and to rank those options against criteria. The criteria embody the essential elements of what we want as an outcome or goal.

For years, decision researchers were concerned that decisions would be less than optimum unless all available options were explored. But finding *all* available options was unrealistic (March, 1978). We could never be sure *all* options were found; and besides, finding all options would be very time-consuming. To understand the differences in decision outcomes, researchers began to study the separate parts of the decision process. Some looked at the nature of the problem (Demorest, 1986; Harrison, 1975; Reitman, 1965). Others looked at the characteristics of the problem solver (Keen, 1973; McKenney & Keen, 1974; Tan & Lo, 1991). Still others focused on the problem-solving process (Abelson & Levi, 1985; Reitman, 1965). At the highest level of abstraction, researchers consider the social and cultural factors that define the decision environment (Pitz & Sachs, 1984; Weeks & Whimster, 1985).

But the harried media manager requires information that is, rather than increasingly abstract, concrete and usable in the day-to-day pressures of running a media company. Beach (1996) provides a practical guide to the decision-making process that begins with the essential element of every organization, the individual.

How We Make Decisions

When a person sets out to make a decision, he or she usually does it in three steps. First, the individual develops (sometimes subconsciously) a list of options. Second, options that really aren't practical or acceptable are eliminated from the list. Then in the third step the person chooses the best option from among those remaining. On the surface it's a relatively simple process of elimination, but as part of that process each of us makes complex value judgments regarding the choices based on our knowledge and the situation at hand. Past experience typically guides the entire decision process as we rely on what worked before to work again (Beach, 1996).

Once a problem has been identified, we attempt to solve it by engaging the decision-making process. As managers understand the scope of the situation by gathering information, they usually concurrently develop lists and sift information to get at the essential issues. In these early phases they already begin to see possible courses of action. This is the search phase of problem solving (Hey, 1982). Typically, we search our experiences and look for similar situations to the one we are facing. We then move to solutions we have heard or read about. People consult whatever sources of information they have at hand. Those can include colleagues, trade publications, books, their own experience—just about anything that can shed light on the subject at hand. For example, if you are working to win an advertising or public relations contract for your agency, you might look at the entries that won last year—the Addies or Clios in advertising and the Silver Anvil awards in public relations. Newspaper organizations put a lot of pride in winning Pulitzer Prizes, and in television an Emmy is considered a major recognition of superior organizational performance.

As we collect information we drop certain options for one reason or another. Some people search until they find a selection that looks like it will work, then they quit. This phase sometimes is done without a lot of thought. We apply intuition and judgment to make our choices based on how we think those options will turn out (Shacklee & Fischoff, 1982). But such seat-of-the-pants strategies overlook the fact that we typically use biased strategies for storing and retrieving outcome information (Einhorn, 1980). The problem is to overcome our reliance on our past practices and experience so our judgments are not based on our emotions. Although our knowledge of causal relationships will never be perfect, we can be more accurate if we apply a systematic approach to analyzing situations *before* we begin eliminating options.

Six basic strategies typically are used by decision makers to choose among alternatives (Klein, 1983):

1. The **linear additive strategy.** Here the decision maker evaluates each alternative on all important attributes and selects the one with the best overall evaluation.

2. The **conjunctive approach** eliminates all alternatives that fail to meet preset minimum cutoffs for certain criteria.

3. The decision maker may **"eliminate by aspects."** That means to choose an option because it has desired characteristics rather than by comparing it with other alternatives.

4. The **disjunctive strategy** is where the decision maker chooses the alternative that stands out because of any one attribute. There is no sense here of option complexity. A single desired quality causes the choice.

5. The **lexicographic approach.** Here the decision maker chooses the alternative with the best value on the most important attribute, as in the disjunctive approach, but also considers the next most important attribute to resolve any decision tie among options.

6. **Compensatory cutoff.** This approach is characterized by the analysis of just a few attributes of potential options and then a fairly quick decision to drop those that don't initially measure up.

Making Better Decisions

Obviously, based on the previous discussion, you can bog yourself down thinking about the complexity of decision making. In the day-to-day world of a media manager you don't sit around thinking about whether you are using a "linear additive strategy," a "conjunctive approach," or perhaps a "lexicographic" concept in working out what to do. It's useful to understand the different approaches, but you need something you can use effectively, and usually fairly quickly, within the context of each day's problems.

We are human beings who, given a situation, make many intellectual and intuitive decisions as we work through our problems, sometimes as a kind of stream of consciousness dialog with ourselves. So, to help you be more effective as a media manager, we suggest using the relatively simple but effective approach to general decision making advocated by Beach (1996). The three essential steps mentioned earlier in the chapter are:

1. Develop a list of options.

2. Screen out unacceptable options.

3. Choose from among the remaining options.

To use this approach, there is an important assumption that you know what you want to get out of the decision process. A goal has to be clear for you to develop a set of options for attaining it, to screen out unacceptable alternatives (how can you tell what's unacceptable unless you have an idea where you need to go?), and then to choose the best of the remaining options. In many situations decision makers using Beach's model will have a good idea of what they want as an output (goal) and what criteria they will use to choose the best option. But those goals and decision criteria can easily get muddled unless we write out the specifics of what we want to do (Klein, 1983).

Some organizations do that in a very detailed, process-oriented fashion, while others encourage less rigid, collective problem solving. The following is an example of a simple model of decision making. First, the objective is described with its important attributes defined using the format in Figure 10.1. Then alternatives that can be used to accomplish the goal are listed and evaluated using the format in Figure 10.2. Anyone who uses a list of goals, alternatives, and the process of elimination does this to one degree or another, though often informally. By being more formal, thinking tends to become more detailed and analytical. In group work, or when developing scenarios for upper management to consider, such detail is crucial. All possibilities must be considered, with potential positive and negative consequences weighed, before any action is recommended. It should be emphasized this is a very simple model that can be expanded in detail as necessary.

Putting Basic Decision Making to Work

It helps to understand the decision-making process when you see it in action. So we are going to follow a public relations executive as she decides how to diversify her client list.

Problem: What business sectors should we consider to attract new clients? Goal: Select one or two business sectors with high potential for success.

Since we don't want to introduce bias while compiling our options list, it's a good idea to identify up front what constitutes an unacceptable option and what criteria we expect to use when making our selections. Sometimes you won't set any restrictions on

```
┌─────────────────────────────────────────────────────────┐
│                      Decision Table                       │
│                                                           │
│  For each of the following, use only one sentence or a series of bullets. │
│  **Goal description:**                                    │
│    • *What do I specifically need to do?*                 │
│                                                           │
│                                                           │
│                                                           │
│    • *Why is this important (positive & negative consequences)?* │
│                                                           │
│                                                           │
│                                                           │
│  **Goal attributes:**                                     │
│    • *What do I absolutely have to accomplish with this?* │
│                                                           │
│                                                           │
│                                                           │
│    • *What do I want if I can get it (but not absolutely required)?* │
│                                                           │
│                                                           │
│                                                           │
│    • *What resources are available to do it?*             │
│                                                           │
│                                                           │
│                                                           │
│    • *What environmental factors affect the goal?*        │
│                                                           │
│                                                           │
└─────────────────────────────────────────────────────────┘
```

Figure 10.1 Sample Decision Table

Alternatives Analysis

1. List possible alternatives to accomplish the previously defined goal and attributes.

2. Estimate the positive and negative effects on the organization. Use 100 as the highest score for each category. Subtract the negative score from the positive to compute the net effect of the alternative. Reorder your list of approaches based on the highest net score.

Approach	% Pos.	% Neg.	Net Score

Figure 10.2 Sample Decision Table Alternative Analysis

the choices—they all will be acceptable. Now, that doesn't mean they all are weighted the same on some value scale, but at least you won't toss them out without considering other attributes. Some agencies might refuse to work with tobacco companies or represent companies with holdings in certain countries. If you hold strong values like these, state them *before* you begin your search for options. Selections at this level are absolute. If they fail your screening criteria, they will not be considered as an option. So in our example we will stipulate two reasons for rejection.

Basis for Rejection: 1. Tobacco company
2. Industry where we already have a client in a market

All other business sectors can be considered. You'll notice that public relations agencies try not to represent competing clients in the same market, so this is made explicit as a basis for not considering a sector.

Now we are ready to identify the selection criteria. We might list such things as industry growth potential, ease of entry (our learning curve), cost of entry (competition in that area), fit with our staff's strengths, accessibility (how easy it is to provide counseling services), and so forth. We probably should create a cell for how attractive this area is to us and our organization—we'll call this "attractiveness to our agency." Now we can weigh how important each is to our agency, from 1 to 10—where 10 is high and 1 is low. All of this is done *before* we list or examine options. If we were to lay these out on a spreadsheet, it might look like Figure 10.3.

Criteria	wt	*Option I* Gaming	score	wt score	*Option 2* Computer Software	score	wt score
Industry growth potential	10	(comments)	9	90			
Ease of entry							
Cost of entry							
Fit							
Accessibility							
Attractiveness to our agency							
Totals							

Figure 10.3 Linear Decision Matrix

We now begin our search for options—business sectors that do not involve tobacco and where we currently have no clients. Each is listed under a separate option at the top of the sheet. Now rate each option (from 1 to 10, where 10 is high) in terms of each criterion. For example, if one of the options was gaming and you believed the industry growth potential was high, you might give it a score of 9. Multiply the weight (10) times the score for industry growth (9) to get 90. Continue for each of the criteria. The sum of the weights times score values will give you a total. Enter the total at the bottom of the column. Compare totals to see which is the highest. Sometimes decision makers are surprised that an option they thought would score high didn't. Generally, this happens when we omit criteria that should have been included in the original list. If it is an oversight, add it to the criteria list and assign it a weight. Now, recompute the scores for all the options.

This approach to decision making is said to be linear. It moves through discrete steps. It is public in the sense that you made all your values explicit. Others might disagree with your selection of criteria, their weights, and how you scored the alternatives, but at least we know where the disagreement is. It is particularly useful when others accept the criteria, weights, and scores. Now, unless you made a math error, your narrowed list of choices should be reasonable.

Decisions Under Uncertainty

In the agency example we could assign values (or scores) because the information was largely knowable. Decisions become a lot harder when we have to deal with unknown events—for example, How will the economy perform over the next five years? What will our competition do? What is the likelihood of a new technology changing our business? What will government regulators do?

These questions affect all of our decision options but often affect *individual* options in different ways. There's no magic here. Successful managers use judgment based on research and intuition. Many successful managers will tell you they were plain lucky.

Here's how you can be a little more rigorous in making decisions under uncertainty. Take your top options—the ones with the best scores derived from your linear decision matrix. Run them through a decision tree. You can do this on paper (Thierauf & Grosse, 1970) or use software specifically designed for this purpose (Burnstein, 1995). The hard part is assessing the probability of the unknown event and assessing the profits (or loss) under the various conditions.

Figure 10.4 shows a decision tree for a decision that could be affected by government regulation. Let's say that we see the potential of making nearly $500,000 over five years if we move into representing gaming interests. Our assumption at the moment is that government regulations will not change substantially. If we begin working for computer software companies we see a potential of almost $350,000. Either could change if the government chooses to alter regulations. How do we factor this into our decision?

As a decision maker you would multiply the likely income from each possibility by the probability of occurrence—as you see it. Then you would add up the individual payoffs to see the overall payoff from that decision (e.g., payoffs from gaming). In this example, we see that in spite of the possibility of some very low returns if the gambling industry is regulated in ways that are unfavorable to the industry, the overall payoff from this option is favorable. We could do this for each area we are considering (e.g., the economy, effects of competition, and so on).

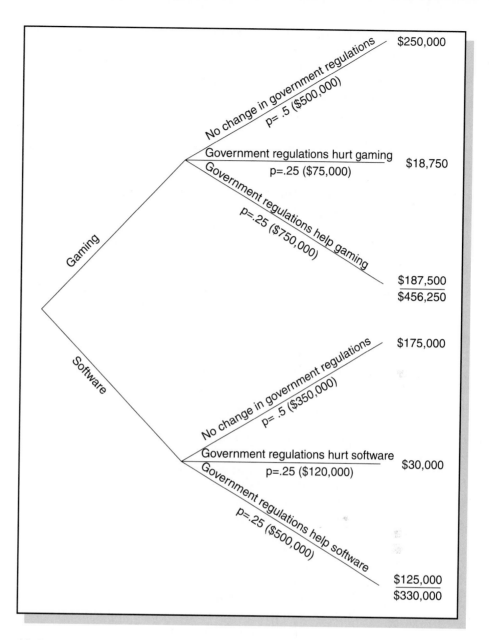

Figure 10.4 Decision Tree for Examining the Effect of a Change in Government Regulations on the Gambling and Computer Software Industries

Decision Making in Teams

One of the things we know about group decisions is that they tend to be supported by those participating in the decision. And when the group has the support of other workers, the decision typically is accepted across the organization. So why don't managers make more decisions this way? In a word: control.

When a manager gives a group a problem to solve, the manager has to be prepared to accept the group's recommendations. While the manager may believe he or she retains the ultimate responsibility for making the decision and the group serves only to make suggestions, the role of the manager and ad hoc groups are frequently misunderstood. Group members complain, "Why did we go through all that trouble if our recommendations weren't going to be taken seriously." Or, "I guess we were supposed to know which option he (or she) favored. Well, we didn't."

Along with clarifying roles, the linear approach (described earlier) can help problem-solving groups. The problem and goals are stated clearly and agreed upon in advance. In one approach the group selects and negotiates criteria as a group, develops a list of options, and assigns weights. In another approach the manager can give the group explicit instructions about organizational values, including criteria for rejection and how much the organization values certain criteria. If the manager would communicate values in this way, there would be fewer problems between managers and groups when it comes to decisions. This is consistent with the recent work on organizational culture and decision making (Weatherly & Beach, 1996).

One last point about decisions and decision making: Decision makers have to find and use information as they evaluate options. Information is often distributed unequally among group members. Team members may be suspicious of information with which they are unfamiliar. So "truth" tends to be negotiated. Status differences among team members can complicate this negotiation process. Then, we'll add the organizational context, for example, who is assigned to the team, real or perceived rewards for participation, and any existing relationships that may shade intragroup interactions. Your judgment and support will be required.

THE PLANNING PROCESS

Chung (1987) locates planning at the first step of a four-step management process (see Fig. 10.5). At the organizational level a plan determines the type of organizational structure you will need, the individual positions within that structure, and how much autonomy individuals should have in carrying out their tasks. This is called organizing. At the next two steps we operate the organization. Managers influence, that is, communicate with, lead, coordinate, and create conditions where workers can thrive. Finally, managers exercise controls by establishing standards for performance and providing feedback along with rewards and sanctions.

In this conception the plan drives the rest of the system. It works this way even in a start-up organization. Note in Figure 10.5 the feedback loop tying controlling with planning. When we fail to meet a goal or even exceed a goal, it's "back to the drawing board" or back to the plan for appropriate adjustments. That's the way it would look if you were starting a *new* organization.

It is much more common for managers to find themselves promoted or dropped into an ongoing planning cycle with an organizational structure that is already established, with a staff that has reached some accommodation about who does what (rarely agreeing with published job descriptions), and someone has already been telling them whether what they've been doing is good enough or not. You are typically not expected to plan; you are expected to "influence" and keep the organization going. And that may be all you will do for the first couple of months to a year. But at some point, the manager must take what he or she has learned about how the organization operates, look at the controls and outcomes, and go back to planning.

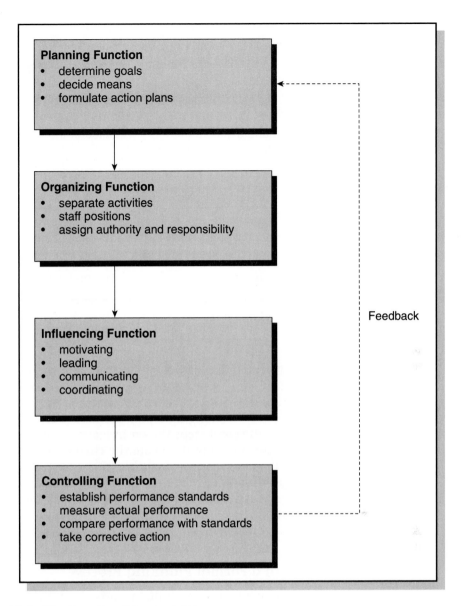

Figure 10.5 The Four-Step Managerial Process

METAPLANNING—THE BÜTSCHI MODEL

Swiss scholar and public relations practitioner Gerhard Bütschi has conceptualized a process for communication planners that he calls metaplanning—or planning to plan. Communication planners, like other planners, can benefit from a structure that guides their work. In contemporary media companies, where huge amounts of money are often at stake, it is crucial that every move be carefully considered. This section will look at an eight-step procedure that can help communicators as they prepare short-, medium-, and long-range plans. Figure 10.6 is an outline of the eight-step Bütschi model for metaplanning.

Step 1: Establish a formal planning process.

Step 2: Assess the existing communication planning function.

Step 3: Develop the features of the main variables of the communication planning concept.

Step 4: Assess and evaluate the main variables of the draft version of the communication planning concept.

Step 5: Refine the communication planning concept.

Step 6: Assess and evaluate the refined version of the communication planning concept.

Step 7: Document the elements and contents of the communication planning concept (write or revise the communication manual or planning handbook).

Step 8: Adopt and implement the newly developed communication planning concept.

Figure 10.6   The Bütschi Model for Communication Planning: An Eight-Step Process

The Bütschi model is designed to fit any planning need, large or small. In some cases it doesn't take much time at all to work through the model. In other situations it is a lengthy process that takes considerable time and effort. It is entirely possible, in relatively small projects—working up a plan for next week's staff party, for example—for you to simply take the eight steps shown in Figure 10.6 and use them as a checklist for what you should consider. But if you are the chief executive officer of a major newspaper chain, the eight steps must be carried out in great detail, involving hundreds of people with, perhaps, thousands of things with which to be concerned.

The following discussion will unpack the details of the Bütschi model so that if you are ever confronted with a major project, you will have a planning tool to help you achieve maximum effectiveness.

Step 1: Establish a Formal Planning Process

All communications planning is influenced by how the organization approaches the task, and how it is set up to undertake the planning process. Three elements are of immediate concern in any effort to plan: (1) a group set up within the organization to work on the plan—called the "planning group," (2) the methods you use to create the plan, (3) the plan taxonomy—the classifications used to categorize the relationships between the planning group and flow of information. This foundation of the planning structure is one of the most important stages, because it creates the basic boundaries of the planning process (Bechmann, 1981; Bütschi, 1997; Grünig, 1990; Hentze & Brose, 1985; Kühn, 1985; Pfohl, 1981).

The first category, the planning organization, is really the plan management tier. It includes the formal planning function itself, planning responsibilities, plan review authority, planning time schedules, and the plan revision cycle. The second category, planning methods, is the action arm for the formal planning process. It includes planning information resources, methods, tools, and evaluation techniques to be used. The third category is, in effect, the management structure and relationship design of the planning effort, often called the plan taxonomy. It includes variables such as the distinction between planning levels, plan horizons, hierarchies, and interrelationships.

Together the basic categories of the organization's planning infrastructure influence the formulation of communication objectives, strategies, and tactics. They may be stated formally or exist as a part of the informal operating procedures. They can be revised from time to time or accepted as "the way we do business around here." In most organizations, setting up the planning structure is the first big hurdle. When its design is set, and the process is accepted within the organization as formal and enduring, we have a "planning concept." It is the road map for our planning effort that determines when and in what sequence communication planning will take place, and the length of time a plan will be valid.

Managers should consider adopting a planning concept when they sense inefficiencies in their planning, implementation, and evaluation activities (Kühn, 1985). But the human element often causes inefficiencies. Those may be caused by a lack of staff planning skills, motivational problems resulting from a poorly structured planning process, or the lack of good planning coordination or synchronization (Grünig, 1990). When you try to move a planning effort forward, it's important to recognize it is a dynamic process. You may need to develop or revise your planning concept if the number of planning activities increases significantly, the general organizational planning process is modified, or the communication function itself has to be reshaped because of significant changes in the overall organizational design—as after a merger or acquisition.

Step 2: Assess the Existing Planning Process

Your project team will need to collect and analyze all pertinent planning documents and materials. These include planning handbooks, guidelines, procedures and principles, time schedules, plan evaluation techniques, charts, and checklists. The team should organize these materials so that they relate directly to the communication planning concept. Basically, you need to find out everything you can about how previous planning has been done, how the organizational structure deals with the planning function, and what resources are available to design, implement, and evaluate plans. Figure 10.7 is a checklist your team can use to set up its planning effort.

As you can see, the first thing you need to do to plan is get all the information you can about how the process has, or has not, been done before, and what you have to work with in terms of available resources and organizational structure. Once you have done your research, you can systematically sort and categorize all the information you have. If something you need is missing, you may have already found the problem area in previous planning efforts. Missing information may indicate weak areas that need attention (Kühn, 1985).

Step 3: Develop Main Plan Features

A planning concept has to fit each organization's goals, structure, and planning needs. That means no single procedure can be used for all situations. Each organization's decision makers must define the features they need included in their planning concept, and set up an internal structure to get it done (Kühn, 1985). However, several aspects of the planning process generally come into play in any plan development. They are the framework for an ideal concept of communication planning (Bütschi, 1997). Those ten basic variables are shown in Figure 10.8, page 263.

1. Find out everything you can about the various groups or classifications within your communication planning concept—gather documents, talk to people, and so on.
   - How is planning done and what's included (e.g., marketing communication, public relations, sponsorships, corporate contributions)?
   - How many planning levels are there, and what are the time frames for each?
   - In what order are things done? Long-range first, then middle, and finally short? Or is planning done from short-term to long?
   - Are there any current plans? Those may include a mission statement, communication guidelines, long-term communication strategy, resource allocation, communication budgets, and emergency communication guidelines.
   - How are existing plans structured?
   - What do they contain?
   - Can plans be worked on concurrently, or do they have to be done sequentially for some reason?
2. How is the organizational bureaucracy set up to deal with planning?
   - Who has the overall planning responsibility?
   - Who is responsible for the specifics of developing, implementing, revising, and evaluating the plan?
   - What are the anticipated plan revision cycles?
   - Are there any anticipated circumstances that would trigger an early revision effort?
   - How are the different levels of management involved?
3. Find out everything you can about the methods used to develop previous plans in the organization.
   - What planning resources (e.g., online databases, feedback mechanisms) are there to help develop plans?
   - What planning methods have been used, or can be used, in this effort?
   - What planning tools are available (e.g., charts, checklists, software)?
   - When and how are planning results evaluated?

Figure 10.7 Planning Effort Checklist

It is vital that all parts of the planning effort be compatible, and consistent. How to achieve that requires some effort in making sure each of the subissues of Step 3 in the Bütschi planning model, shown in Figure 10.8, are accomplished effectively. Attention to detail is very important, since a small oversight at this stage can set up a major failure later. Consider the aspects of planning that need to be included in Step 3 of the planning model shown in Sidebar 10.1, page 264. You can see planning is detailed work. That's because when something that seems incidental at the planning stage is overlooked, it can become a major flaw contributing to organizational failure later.

Step 4: Evaluate the Initial Plan Concept Draft

After the detail work in Step 3 has been accomplished, it is important for the planning team to step back and consider the ramifications of what has been done so far (in Sidebar 10.1, items 3.1 through 3.10). Each element of communication planning concept has to

3.1	Determine the planning levels.
3.2	Set the planning horizons.
3.3	Outline the communication planning area.
3.4	Define the subplanning areas.
3.5	Design the planning level hierarchy.
3.6	Sort the communication plans by planning cycle.
3.7	Categorize communication plans by type of event.
3.8	Set the planning flow (top-down, bottom-up, or a combination).
3.9	Specify the planning authority.
3.10	Create the plan revision cycles.

Figure 10.8 Developing the Features of the Main Variables of a Communication Planning Concept (Step 3)

be consistent and compatible with the others. Any inconsistency or incompatibility has to be resolved. Conflicts will usually be apparent if two approaches are used concurrently. They are checklists, really, to get you to focus on the essential questions that have to be asked at this important, foundation-building stage of plan development. First, each element developed in Step 3 of the planning concept needs to be double-checked. Answer the questions in Sidebar 10.2, page 266, to test the validity of each factor. Then use the criteria in Sidebar 10.3, page 267, to determine (1) how the first 10 elements of the communication planning concept interact with each other and (2) whether the rules and guidelines of the planning concept improve the quality of the planning process (Bütschi, 1997; Kühn, 1985).

Step 5: Refine the Planning Concept

Up to this point you have been focusing on the concepts of planning design. Once you are confident all the key aspects of your organization's planning needs have been included in that design, you move from conceptualization to implementation. In other words, at this point you begin making things actually happen. In any significant endeavor, you need to have some thinking time and some doing time. In the practical application of the concepts you have included in your plan are the pragmatic considerations of making the plan part of daily organizational processes. They are listed in Figure 10.9, page 269, and discussed in Sidebar 10.3, page 267. Take a few moments to consider the way the planning elements and issues encourage attention to detail. It is the detail of an organizational plan that often provides its power. Planning is an attempt to ensure the best possible approach to the future. Without considerable detail a plan is little more than a wish list. But with substantial detail it can be a key to success.

Step 6: Reevaluate and Finalize the Planning Conceptions

As you have undoubtedly noticed by now, the Bütschi model of planning features continuous checking and rechecking to ensure nothing is left to chance. In this step, the

Sidebar 10.1 Planning Model Step 3 Issues

3.1 Determine the Planning Levels

In the context of planning, levels refer to the plan contents and the length of time each plan is in effect. In general, period-oriented communication plans fall into one of the following categories: short-range (also called dispositional or tactical), middle-range (or operational), and long-range (or strategic) planning level. An organization may choose to have just one planning level if it operates in a fast-changing environment where communication plans cannot be developed for time periods longer than 12 months.

Two planning levels are useful when the organization operates under a one-year plan and uses mission statements or long-term communication guidelines that have indefinite validity. Three planning levels are preferred when a two-year advertising and public relations campaign or a three-year resource allocation budget is being prepared along with one-year dispositional plans and long-term communication guidelines. The three-level approach appears to be the standard in large U.S. corporations.

3.2 Set the Planning Horizons

This step requires that you establish the length of time each communication plan will be in effect. Short-range plans usually are valid for one year (normally a calendar year). Middle-range plans are typically set at from three to five years. Long-range plans generally run from five to ten years. Communication guidelines, principles, and planning procedures that are of indefinite validity are called long-range strategic communication plans.

3.3 Outline the Communication Planning Area

Outlining the communication planning area requires a clear definition of the scope of the communication function. You will need to decide what belongs to the communications unit and what will be handled elsewhere in the company (e.g., marketing or personnel). Here are some of the functions typically associated with communication: product advertising, direct marketing, sales promotion, point-of-purchase activities, merchandising, public relations (internal and external), corporate sponsorships, exhibits, special events, institutional advertising, producing TV programs and videos, strategic philanthropy, and fund raising. There may be others.

3.4 Define the Subplanning Areas

It is a burdensome task to prepare communication plans for each communication function. Therefore, you may want to partition the communication planning area into several subunits, thus creating several subplanning areas—for example, marketing communication, internal relations, external relations, sponsorships and corporate contributions, and communication services (corporate exhibitions, corporate events, and TV programs and videos). Each subplanning unit can also be partitioned, thus creating a number of sub-subplanning areas (e.g., partitioning the external relations subplanning area into investor relations, government relations, customer relations, distributor relations, supplier relations, community relations, interest group relations, trade relations, media relations, etc.).

3.5 Design the Planning Level Hierarchy

By planning level hierarchy we mean whether we begin with short-range plans and work to progressively longer-range plans, or vice versa. Large U.S. corporations tend to start with long-range plans. Typically they set their planning goals for the next five years, and then step back to shorter time frames and design intermediate goals and programs to achieve the long-term plan.

3.6 Sort the Communication Plans by Planning Cycle

At some point you will have to determine the types of communication plans you will adopt and their structures and contents. This step focuses on determining and then assigning plans to one of three categories: long-range, middle-range, and short-range.

- ♦ Long-range communication plans—for example, mission statements, communication guidelines, long-range public relations strategy

- ♦ Middle-range communication plans—middle-range resource allocation plans, middle-range public relations strategy, multiyear communication campaigns

- ♦ Short-range communication plans—one-year plans for advertising, sales promotion, public relations, sponsorships, yearly communication budgets, and so forth

3.7 Categorize Communication Plans by Type of Event

Planners typically consider predictable events (e.g., communication plan for the annual shareholder meeting) as well as contingency events (e.g., emergency communication plan). Identify each in this section.

3.8 Set the Planning Flow (Top-Down, Bottom-Up, or a Combination)

The planning philosophy of a corporation will determine whether your plan will start at a low level of the organization and then move up the hierarchy for review, or senior management prepares planning guidelines and passes them down. The first procedure is called the bottom-up planning procedure; the latter is known as the top-down planning procedure. Some organizations use a combination of the bottom-up and top-down planning procedures. The combination approach has the advantage of feedback going both ways as the planning process evolves.

3.9 Specify the Planning Authority

There are four alternatives for planning authority. They are:

a) Centralized communication planning. Members of a centralized staff are assigned to develop communication plans.

b) Decentralized communication planning. Line management exercises the communication planning authority.

c) Collective communication planning. The task of developing communication plans is collectively shared by members of a planning commission or a project team.

d) External communication planning. The task of developing communication plans is contracted to an outside consulting firm.

3.10 Create the Plan Revision Cycles

A fast-changing environment or market situation may force you to revise the contents of your plans before they are completed. Frequently planners set up a standard revision procedure to ensure plans are revised periodically in case events require adjustments. A one-year communication plan, for example, could be reviewed every six months or quarterly. The length of an ordinary revision cycle depends on your particular industry and how fast things change. In media organizations, because of the rapid evolution of technology and competitors for audience in the marketplace, you may need to revise your plans quarterly or even more frequently. For example, typically a network television program is scheduled for 13 weeks of show production. However, it is common for programs to be canceled before the end of the initial 13-week run because they don't generate enough audience.

Sidebar 10.2 Planning Model Step 4 Variables Assessment

♦ Planning levels (Step 3.1). Does the determined choice (one, two, or three planning levels) allow the planners to master the complexity of the communication planning tasks? Would another choice be better?

♦ The planning horizons (Step 3.2). Do the time horizons take the particular situation (environment, markets, industry) of the organization into account? Do the planning periods allow the planners to act proactively rather than react to external developments?

♦ Communication planning area (Step 3.3). Is the communication planning area clearly defined? Does the chosen solution integrate communication across the organization?

♦ Subplanning areas (Step 3.4). Is there a clear distinction between, for example, marketing communication, public relations, sales promotion, and advertising? Does the chosen solution lead to an efficient planning process?

♦ Planning level hierarchy (Step 3.5). Is the chosen solution consistent with the planning philosophy of the organization? Are we correct in our assumption about why we do short-term plans first or last?

♦ Communication planning cycle (Step 3.6). Is the proposed planning cycle compatible with the organization's personnel and financial resources? Do we have the resources to prepare the plans? Could we reduce the number of communication plans to be more efficient?

♦ Event-oriented communication plans (Step 3.7). Do we have the resources to produce special plans? Could we reduce the number of event-oriented communication plans to achieve leaner

planning? Would the costs be acceptable, especially for contingency planning?

♦ The planning procedure (Step 3.8). Is the chosen planning procedure (e.g., top-down or bottom-up) consistent with the company's overall planning philosophy? How does the chosen planning procedure influence the planner's motivation and sense of responsibility?

♦ Planning authority (Step 3.9). To what degree does the chosen solution involve line management in the communication planning process? Does the solution clearly define the planning responsibilities?

♦ Plan revision cycles (Step 3.10). Is there a plan revision cycle for each communication plan? How do the determined plan revision cycles take into account the personnel and financial resources of the organization?

♦ Consistency and compatibility check. Is each point in Step 3 consistent and compatible with the others?

♦ Planning quality. Do the principles, guidelines, and procedures of the first 10 variables of the planning concept improve the quality of communication planning?

♦ Planning efficiency. Does the proposed engagement of personnel and financial resources lead to an efficient communication planning process?

♦ Planning skills. Do the proposed planning procedures comply with the planning skills of the planners?

♦ Company management procedures. Are the proposed planning principles and guidelines in compliance with the organization's operating procedures?

Sidebar 10.3 Planning Model Step 5 Issues

5.1 Determine Final Communication Plan Structures and Contents

As a cross-check, to make sure you haven't overlooked anything, you should reevaluate your planning concept and its various elements to make sure all of the following main sections have been included.

1. Overview
2. Mission
3. Environmental assessment
4. Strategic issues
5. Objectives
6. Strategies
7. Communication measures
8. Time schedule
9. Budget
10. Plan evaluation

When a plan is near completion, a missing link will generally be obvious by its absence as you move through the cross-check in order. Be careful to do it item by item. Planning is very detailed work, and it is easy to miss something when you look at things generally, rather than examining one specific issue at a time (Bütschi, 1997).

5.2 Ascertain the Information Resources (Planning Input) to Be Used in the Planning Process

Successful planning relies on the availability and fast accessibility of planning data and information. This is where the team will specify how staff can access and retrieve the information you'll need for your plan. It will specify how and by whom the information resources are collected and stored. Your planners should consider the following information resources as they develop their communication plan: company brochures, annual reports, company publications, mail and telephone analysis, press releases, speeches, memos, letters, newspapers, magazines, newsletters, competitor publications, books, encyclopedias, yearbooks, library research, judicial rulings, polls and surveys, videos, photographs, online databases (e.g. LEXIS-NEXIS, NewsNet, Investext, Dialog, Dow Jones News/Retrieval, Data Times, Burrelle's Broadcast Database, Internet resources), target audience monitoring, issue management, and advisory panels.

5.3 Specify the Planning Methods to Be Used in the Planning Process

Planning methods are selected early to ensure efficient communication planning. You can choose from among: heuristic step-by-step procedures for the construction of advertising or public relations campaigns, creative techniques (e.g., brainstorming, brainwriting, method 635, discussion 66, synectics), and methods to compare the projected impact of communication instruments (e.g., expected-value analysis, what-if-not-funded scenario, shadow pricing, and cost-benefit analysis) (McElreath, 1993).

5.4 Assemble the Planning Tools to Be Used in the Planning Process

Planning tools are used to standardize and help develop communication plans. They include such items as: planning forms, checklists, planning techniques, and software. Planning forms are widely used to help planners organize and structure the contents of their plans. Checklists also represent a widely used planning tool (e.g., to prepare and organize press conferences or annual shareholders meetings). Planning techniques are used to solve complex planning problems.

Continued

Planning techniques (many are available on software for the PC) include: Critical Path Method (CPM), Program Evaluation and Review Technique (PERT), Metra Potential Method (MPM), project management software (Microsoft Project, TimeLine].

5.5 Finalize the Plan Evaluation Methods

A communication planning concept prescribes when and how to evaluate the impact and the results of communication efforts. To be credible within the organization, communicators need to measure those items specified in their communication objectives. These include direct measures of behavior or changes in opinion and/or knowledge. Lesser measures include measures of output and measures of intermediate effect (Bissland, 1990). One method that is particularly adaptable to public communication is called the control construct technique (Fischer, 1995).

5.6 Set the Time and Duration of Routine Communication Plan Revisions

An earlier step (3.10) prompted the planners to consider the plan revision cycles. Based on these decisions, the team now can specify the dates and duration of routine elements of the plan.

5.7 Provide for Extraordinary (Unforeseen) Communication Plan Revisions

Determining the extraordinary or unforeseen communication plan revisions implies listing the criteria and conditions that, if fulfilled, will lead to a plan revision. Volatile markets or a change of consumer behavior (e.g., consumer complaints exceeding a certain number or decreasing sales due to a consumer

boycott) may require that you revise your plan.

5.8 Designate Simultaneous and Sequential Plan Development Procedures

Simultaneous and sequential plan development procedures have to be determined at each planning level in order to shorten the planning process. Whether two communication plans can be developed simultaneously or in sequence depends on the interrelationships among the plans. If elements of one plan are needed as an input for the development of another plan, then these two plans have to be developed sequentially (one after the other). If no interrelationships can be found between two communication plans, then the planners can proceed simultaneously with the construction of those plans. The planning process can be shortened if communication plans can be developed simultaneously.

5.9 Prescribe the Planning Time Schedule

The communication planning concept should include guidelines of how to initiate, implement, and control the development of communication plans. Specify those guidelines at the outset so that each planner has enough time to plan. This step should produce a complete planning time schedule (planning calendar), showing a starting and an end date for each communication plan.

5.10 Allocate Planning Responsibilities

In this step we determine who is going to be responsible for the development, authorization, execution, revision, and evaluation of each communication plan. These responsibilities should be listed in the communication planning document.

5.1 Determine final communication plan structures and contents.

5.2 Ascertain the information resources (planning input) to be used in the planning process.

5.3 Specify the planning methods to be used in the planning process.

5.4 Assemble the planning tools to be used in the planning process.

5.5 Finalize the plan evaluation methods.

5.6 Set the time and duration of routine communication plan revisions.

5.7 Provide for extraordinary (unforeseen) communication plan revisions.

5.8 Designate simultaneous and sequential plan development procedures.

5.9 Prescribe the planning time schedule.

5.10 Allocate the planning responsibilities.

Figure 10.9 Step 5, Application of Final Communication Planning Elements

planning team reevaluates their previous work in Step 5 and tests each variable independently. Then the team will take a more global perspective and evaluate all features of the planning concept against each other. The team determines the most efficient features of the planning principles and guidelines. Those, then, lead to effective, coherent, and integrated communication with all organizational constituencies. Too many planning principles and guidelines will lead to a bureaucratic mess and will cause the planners to lose heart. Too few planning principles and guidelines will lead to suboptimal communication results (uncoordinated, chaotic planning—lacking cohesiveness, disintegrated communication). The following criteria should ensure the evaluation of the refined version of a communication planning concept (Bütschi, 1997; Kühn 1985). See Sidebar 10.4 for the two major elements of this step in the Bütschi model, and their specific issues.

Step 7: Document the Communication Planning Concept

The new communication planning principles, guidelines, and procedures should be documented and available to all who need them. This standard operating procedure for the organization's planning function should include the following information (Grünig, 1990):

1. Table of contents

2. Communication philosophy, principles, and guidelines

3. Parameters of the organization's general planning concept

4. Planning area and subplanning areas of the communication function

5. Tabulation and listing of all planning responsibilities

6. Plan taxonomy (list of all period- and event-oriented communication plans for each subplanning area)

Sidebar 10.4 Planning Model Step 6 Issues

6.1 Assess and Improve Each Variable of the Refined Version of a Communication Planning Concept

♦ Determine the communication plan structures and contents (Step 5.1). Are the structures and contents of the proposed communication plans detailed enough? Do the plan structures and contents lead to overplanning? Are they adequate?

♦ Determine the information resources (planning input) to be used in the planning process (Step 5.2). Are all the necessary information resources (planning input) available at the beginning of each planning process? If not, what should be available to the planners? Is the information easy to access? Do all planners have access to the information they need?

♦ Determine the planning methods to be used in the planning process (Step 5.3). Do the planners achieve a better planning result with the chosen planning methods? Do the planners have to undergo special training to use these planning methods? Are the planning methods proven?

♦ Determine the planning tools to be used in the planning process (Step 5.4). Do the planners achieve a better result with the chosen planning tools? Do the planners have the skills to use these planning techniques? Do the planning forms they designed lead to too much bureaucracy?

♦ Determine the plan evaluation methods (Step 5.5). Does every communication plan require that the communication results will be measured? Are sufficient personnel and financial resources available to measure results?

♦ Determine the time and duration of routine communication plan revisions (Step 5.6). Does the time schedule allocate enough time for each communication plan revision? Do plan revisions include the results of the communication plan evaluation?

♦ Determine extraordinary (unforeseen) communication plan revisions (Step 5.7). Was it possible to formulate criteria and conditions for communication plan revision?

♦ Determine simultaneous and sequential plan development procedures (Step 5.8). Could all plan interrelationships that lead to sequential plan development be detected? Could an efficient development sequence be determined?

♦ Determine the planning time line (Step 5.9). Is each step of the planning process clearly defined? Is the planning time line sufficiently detailed? Are the planning procedures efficient?

♦ Determine the planning responsibilities (Step 5.10). Could all planning tasks be assigned to one person or to a planning unit? How do the planning responsibilities affect employee motivation?

6.2 Assess and Improve the Impact and Interaction of All Variables of a Communication Planning Concept

♦ Consistency and compatibility check. Does the communication planning concept consist of a contradiction-free set of planning principles, guidelines, and procedures?

♦ Planning quality. Do the principles, guidelines, and procedure of all elements of the planning concept improve the quality of communication planning?

♦ Quantity and practicability of the communication planning principles, guidelines, and procedures. Are the number of planning concept elements optimal? Will the implementation be simple and practical?

♦ Contents of the communication planning concept. Are the planning principles, guidelines, and procedures worthy of being included in a communication planning concept, or do they just represent "busy work"?

♦ Planning efficiency. Is our use of people and money efficient?

♦ Validity of the communication planning concept elements. Do all communication planning concept elements have indefinite validity, or are some planning principles, guidelines, and procedures only valid for a limited time period?

♦ Organizational planning vs. communication planning. Are the chosen communication planning principles, guidelines, and procedures compliant with the general procedures of the organization?

♦ Acceptance of the communication planning concept. Does the communication planning concept represent a widely accepted management tool?

7. Planning procedures and time schedules (including operational communication principles and guidelines)

8. Distribution list for the planning handbook

Step 8: Adopt and Implement the Communication Planning Concept

After the new communication planning concept has been approved by management, a plan has to be developed and implemented that will ensure the introduction and adoption of the new communication planning procedures in the daily operations. Communications staff will need to learn the new planning procedures, methods, and tools. It may be necessary to provide training for your staff, particularly as personnel changes bring in new members who did not take part in the initial planning concept design.

The contents of the communication planning concept should be updated regularly. As indicated in Step 3.10 of the Bütschi planning model (see Fig. 10.8, p. 263), revision cycles should be included in the plan. Those dates should be included in the final plan to ensure periodic efforts are made to update the communication planning principles, guidelines, and procedures. Time and events in dynamic environments quickly age any plan and render some of its initial vision out of date. Maintaining currency is crucial to maximizing planning effectiveness.

Note: The Bütschi Planning Model is useful for planning for contingencies across a wide variety of potential uses. Communication planning software based on these eight points is available from Gerhard Bütschi. Contact him at: Bütschi Consulting, St. Alban-Vorstadt 92, 4052 Basel, Switzerland. Phone: +41 61 278 99 40. Fax +41 61 278 99 45. E-mail: gbuetschi@compuserve.com.

Planning and decision making can seem like the dull side of media management. That's because they usually involve a lot of detail work to make sure nothing is overlooked. The best-laid plans are often derailed by a small thing no one noticed.

Routine decisions are made on a daily or even hourly basis in media organizations. Some decisions are matter-of-fact and repetitive. Other decisions are complex, requiring a lot of analysis and involving many people. The planning process ranges from the very simple to the incredibly complex, depending on what needs to be accomplished.

This chapter has provided different approaches to planning and decision making. They range from a straightforward tabulated technique for evaluating alternatives to the in-depth Bütschi model of metaplanning. What is important to understand is that planning is the foundation for effective decision making. No matter what approach you use, it must be carried out with great attention to detail to ensure that nothing is overlooked. For no decision is any better than the planning that goes into it. If you forget to fill your gas tank before you head out on a long trip, you won't get very far. And if you don't check the directions, you may take a wrong turn and never end up at your destination.

Life is a constant swirl of small details that come together to determine every outcome. As a media manager your outcomes will be a direct result of the care you take in planning and decision making. Your attention to detail and care will separate you quickly from those who don't take the time literally to dot every *i* and cross every *t*.

1. Describe your organization's planning concept. What planning elements already exist within your organization? Is the process you use top-down, bottom-up, or some combination of these approaches?

2. What advantages do you see from using a team to develop your planning concept? Are there any disadvantages (or costs) to using a team? What are the alternatives to using a planning team? Which is most appropriate for your organization?

3. Why do planners suggest that you specify what you will measure in the communication plan?

4. Use Figure 10.3 to work through a problem of interest to you. It could be something as simple as: Where should we go on our vacation? How do you think your boss would react if you included a decision matrix (like the one in Fig. 10.3) along with your recommended courses of action?

5. Think of two problems that lend themselves to using a decision tree. Try laying out the options in the form of a tree. What would you need to know before you could fill in the detail of the tree?

6. What has been your experience when you've tried to make decisions in a group? What could have improved the process? What could have improved the result or output? Would these work with other teams and with other problems?

section 4

THE BUSINESS SIDE OF MEDIA MANAGEMENT

chapter 11

Audience Theory and the Concept of "Demassification"

Considerable theoretical research over much of the 20th century has focused on the relationship of mass media to audience. The body of literature is vast, including diverse perspectives in numerous aspects of mass media in society (e.g., Blumler, 1979; Carey, 1989; DeFleur & Ball-Rokeach, 1989; Lasswell, 1948; McQuail, 1994; Schramm, 1949). This chapter is by no means meant to be a full discussion of the field, but rather to provide the media manager a basic understanding of the concept of mass audience and how it is changing. Clearly, if you are to effectively manage a media organization engaging with an audience, it is paramount you understand how that audience relates to your organization and its communication efforts.

Historical Perspective

As you consider the rise of mass media, keep in mind the historical period being discussed. When we consider the past, we need to put it into a frame of reference of that time. In other words, you can't evaluate mass media development without considering the social and media reality of the period being studied. From our information-rich perspective, the communication environment at the beginning of the mass media age in the early 1800s is almost inconceivable. There were only pamphleteering, local handbill circulation, and a few newspapers, most of which were relatively small and localized. Most information was passed person to person, or through speeches to, by our standards, very small audiences. After all, there were no microphones or speaker systems to boost a speaker's voice. There was no television, no radio, no electric lights, and no real mass media. It is worth noting, to keep our historical perspective, that as late as 1815 communication was so poor that the Battle of New Orleans—in which 2,036 British were killed or wounded with only 8 American dead and 13 wounded—was actually fought two weeks after the war ended with the signing of the Treaty of Ghent in England. News traveled so slowly, American and British generals didn't know they should have put down their weapons before the first shot of the battle was fired (Schlesinger, 1983).

Also, in the American model there has always been the concept of journalism apart from, and critical of, political leadership. It is theoretically an adversarial relationship with roots deep in the free speech movement of 16th-century England (McQuail, 1994). The press was an effective tool for opposition to the British leading up to, and during, the Revolutionary War. Afterward it became the only business specifically protected by a clause of the Constitution, the First Amendment.

Throughout the first half of the 19th century the concept of the newspaper as conveyor of fact, apart from the government, gained momentum despite frequent press excesses of hyperbole and outright fictional accounts. The newspaper was no longer just a side publication of the village printer, but a mass advertising vehicle, a big business with the largest circulation possible as the goal. In 1833 advertising covered the entire back page of the *New York Sun* and was quickly growing as a major revenue source for the so-called penny papers trying to expand. They were called "penny" papers because they sold on the street for 1 cent, a penny. By 1849 the advertising business had its first agent, Volney B. Palmer. The American Civil War pumped up circulation even more as news from the front was eagerly consumed, and the role of the press as observer of great events was firmly established. When Custer made his ill-fated attack on a camp of Native Americans along the Little Big Horn River in South Central Montana in June 1876, a reporter died with him (Emery & Emery, 1996).

THE RISE OF MASS MEDIA

Mass communication as we know it was made possible by the industrial revolution in the late 18th and early 19th centuries. Coupled with the rise of literacy, the shift from an agrarian-based economy to an urban-centered one created large numbers of potential media customers in central locations. The conditions were ripe for an evolution to the modern, large-circulation newspaper. At the same time, industrial technology was making fast and inexpensive reproduction possible. It is one thing to have a lot of people in an urban center providing a potential market for a newspaper. It is quite another to produce and distribute hundreds of thousands of copies to those people on a daily basis. Steam provided the necessary industrial energy source for the early, large-capacity, flatbed presses of the 1830s. Higher-volume machines with movable type attached to large, revolving cylinders quickly followed. By the mid-1850s some presses could generate 20,000 impressions an hour. The pace of innovation has continued as mass media evolve hand-in-hand with technology (Emery & Emery, 1996).

As media gained the capacity for high-volume publishing and distribution, the view of the audience changed. No longer was an individual printer publishing materials in a relatively small community where there was a good chance the reader and printer knew each other personally. Instead, a large collection of displaced media consumers, with no physical attachment to one another other than the common media products they used, came into being: the concept of a "mass audience." An expanding "reading public" was "delocalized" and diversified in socioeconomic attributes (McQuail, 1994). It was a new sociological phenomenon: people with no personal relationship with one another, but considered a group in the sociological sense as consumers of media product. This concept of a mass audience for media products, combined with an already developing commercialization of magazines, created a new way to take the retail store to the individual. Mass advertising was born.

RESEARCH ON MASS COMMUNICATION

In the early 20th century researchers began delving into the relationship between mass media and their audiences. Along with the established newspaper and magazine industry, new media technology was rapidly expanding in the forms of motion pictures and radio. Since individuals no longer had to be physically present to experience some event, but could do so vicariously to one degree or another through a mass medium, questions arose about the effects mass media messages had on audience members. As media consumers engaged with public debates and events through the window of a mass medium, and had a sense of experiencing things with which they actually had no physical connection, concern arose about a media-constructed reality apart from the physically experienced one. Could the media create distortions of reality, or even complete illusions that, by virtue of its technology, would be perceived as true? And if so, could such distortions or illusions be used to further one ideology over another?

The first great concern about media "power" centered on its use for political purposes in the spread of propaganda. Propaganda is defined as "any systematic, widespread dissemination or promotion of particular ideas, doctrines, practices, and so on to further one's own cause or to damage an opposing one" (*Webster's,* 1994, p. 1078). It was used in World War I as an effective mass media tool by both sides. Every type of available mass medium was used, from handbills and posters to newspapers, motion pictures, and radio broadcasts. It was effective principally because there were limited mass media sources.

During the World War I period the opposing governments either directly controlled, or powerfully influenced, virtually all mass media that could reach their populations. The new mass media forms of motion pictures and radio were exciting innovations. People were clamoring to experience them. With only one point of view dominating such media, mass communication was an effective public perception tool. The "magic bullet" or "hypodermic needle" theory of direct and powerful influence of the media gained acceptance in this unique environment. The assumption was that if you put a message through the mass media, it was received and accepted by the audience. And the experience of the World War I period seemed to justify that view (DeFleur & Ball-Rokeach, 1989).

In the two decades between World War I and World War II mass media technology dramatically expanded in both political and commercial applications. Mass media research also expanded to include the disciplines of political science, sociology, and psychology (Tan, 1985). President Franklin D. Roosevelt used his "fireside chats" beginning in 1933 as part of the effort to raise national spirits in the Great Depression. He is recognized as the first American politician to understand the one-on-one nature of broadcasting communication. His informal, warm conversations connected with audience members listening to his ideas for solving the national crisis. Sitting by his fire in the White House, he chatted informally with millions of Americans as though he'd dropped by for a cup of coffee after dinner. It was interpersonal communication on the scale of millions. The president talked like an old, close friend as each person listened individually to him in their home on the radio (Halberstam, 1979).

Network radio, while effective for Roosevelt, was primarily an entertainment medium with music, comedy, and dramatic programs broadcast every evening. In October of 1938, supporters of the idea that mass media could powerfully influence society got some of their strongest evidence. It came in the form of the broadcast of "War of the Worlds," a radio drama on *The Mercury Theater.* Orson Welles created a play within a play, with frequent interruptions by fictitious news bulletins about an invasion of the earth by Martians. The longer the program went, the more frequent the "news bulletins" from various locations until the invasion play became the main drama. Despite the program having been clearly labeled as drama, mixing in supposed "news" bulletins that sounded authentic turned the program into one of the most controversial broadcasting hoaxes. There was panic among some listeners when they believed what they heard (Head, Sterling, & Schofield, 1994).

Although the "War of the Worlds" hoax may seem humorous to the contemporary mind, you have to consider the time. In 1938 the United States was still climbing out of the Great Depression, where many had experienced breadlines and being swept up by a course of events they could not control. It had only been two decades since the Russian Revolution and the end of World War I. Totalitarianism was on the rise in both communist and fascist regimes. The coming war in Europe was more obvious every day. There were frequent news reports about rising tensions and newsreel footage in the movie theaters of goose-stepping soldiers and fanatical politicians. Emotions were high and anything seemed possible. Against this backdrop, "War of the Worlds" was all too plausible.

Within two years the world was at war again, and mass communication was used to support national interests. When World War II began, the U.S. government asked the radio industry to cooperate in conservation, civil defense, public morale, and war bond campaigns. Singer Kate Smith provided more evidence of the powerful influence mass media can have in a series of special broadcasts to sell war bonds. At the time, the population of the United States was a little more than 132 million people (U.S. Census Bureau, 1997a). Ms. Smith's broadcasts were influential in more than $100 million in bonds being sold in what remains one of the most successful mass media persuasive efforts (Gross, 1995; Merton, 1946).

Powerful and Limited Effects Models of Mass Media

During the tumultuous 1940s and 1950s, which included World War II, the Korean War, and the dawn of the Cold War, two mass communication theoretical streams gained prominence. The first is the powerful effects view in which the audience is considered as generally passive, something that can be manipulated by mass media. Research on propaganda studies, the influence of radio, and the effectiveness of motion pictures as a training and opinion change device supported the powerful effects position. Research also identified important aspects of the communicator, medium, message, and audience that contributed to changes in audience attitude. It was determined, for example, that a key factor in singer Kate Smith's influence during the war bond drive, mentioned earlier, was her high credibility as a sincere and trustworthy communicator. In one 18-hour program alone she received pledges of $39 million at a time when 80 percent of American families earned less than $5,000 per year (Hovland, Janis, & Kelley, 1953; Hovland, Lumsdaine, & Sheffield, 1949).

The second main theoretical stream holds that mass media produce only limited effects on society. The foundation for limited effects was laid by Lazarsfeld, Berelson, and Gaudet when they published *The People's Choice* (1944). The researchers analyzed the way mass media influenced voting and argued that mass media served primarily as reinforcement of existing attitudes. In the limited effects model of mass communication, audience members are understood to filter messages coming their way, altering the intended meaning through selective attention, selective perception, and selective recall. Media messages conflicting with the person's perception or value system may be ignored, while those supporting existing beliefs may be used to reinforce them (DeFleur

& Ball-Rokeach, 1989). The limited effects theory was later supported by Klapper (1960) and numerous other researchers. More recent work on schemata theory, which focuses on the way people cognitively store and recall information, has provided more evidence of limited media effects as people filter news media messages and "read between the lines" with considerable skepticism (Fredin & Tabaczynski, 1993, p. 811).

In the latter third of the 20th century, a reframed powerful effects model with a different twist gained popularity among theorists. The early powerful effects researchers concerned themselves with trying to prove mass media could produce predictable changes in specific attitudes. It was a direct cause-and-effect approach. Contemporary powerful effects researchers have, instead, concerned themselves with how the mass media, as a pervasive part of everyday life, changes culture in sometimes subtle but fundamental ways. It is a wider, macro philosophical view of media interaction as an instrument of social transformation, rather than a perception of media as change agents for specific behavior—the micro effects perspective (Tan, 1985). For example, in a study of news media coverage of the 1991 Persian Gulf War it was found that individual use of all channels of news media expanded as Americans depended on the media for knowledge of the conflict and its progress. There was increased dependency on the media due to the intense nature of the social conflict involving U.S. military forces and the desire of audience members to know what was going on (Pan, Ostman, Moy, & Reynolds, 1994).

Expanding Theory Development

Research has produced a number of additional theories that fall under one of the two dominant philosophies—powerful or limited—of the effect of mass media on society. One was initially called the "two-step flow" theory, but it has since evolved into a multistep concept of the stages of information exchange. It is concerned with how opinion leaders who tend to use the media more may influence others who are not so active as media consumers. People who are well informed pass mass-mediated information on to those who are not, and, in the process, mass-mediated message influence is multiplied (Katz & Lazarsfeld, 1955).

Another theoretical approach presumes that what the media include in their messages governs public issue concerns. If the newspaper covers a story, the audience will be concerned about it. This agenda setting theory perceives the media as instrumental in defining the "important" issues in public discourse. However, while issue prominence may be affected by media coverage, individuals tend to form their own meaning about such issues. In other words, the newspaper may set the agenda of public discourse by what it publishes for readers to consume, but it cannot, in the process, control what people think regarding the issues it covers (McQuail, 1994). It can tell people what to think *about* (setting the agenda for public discourse), but not *what* to think regarding those issues.

Selective influences research, mentioned earlier as a part of the limited effects perspective, focuses on the way people filter media. Individual selectivity determines choice of media, the perception of the meaning from it, and what action, if any, the individual takes because of media messages. Basically, according to this approach, people use the media selectively to reinforce existing attitudes and discount information that conflicts with their beliefs. That can also produce a backfiring against a mass-mediated message when audiences do the reverse of what the message sender intended (DeFleur & Ball-Rokeach, 1989).

Throughout the development of mass media research, social scientists have tried to determine why audiences use the media at all. The "uses and gratifications" stream is concerned with how the mass media meet audience members' wants and needs. Audience is perceived as active, selective, and demanding in its use of the media (Tan, 1985). Uses and gratifications research has identified substantial reasons people spend their time with media. Those include: getting information for various uses; as a source of personal identity reinforcement and behavior modeling; to provide social integration and interaction; and for entertainment purposes such as escape, relaxation, time filling, and emotional release (McQuail, 1994). Uses and gratifications theory is the driving force behind advertising-supported media in their effort to expand the loyalty and number of audience members by pandering to their wants and needs and, therefore, the amount of advertising revenue paid to reach those audience members. The basic idea is that if your media organization gives the audience what it wants and needs, you will produce more audience use and, therefore, more profit.

As individuals utilize media they acquire knowledge of various kinds. One of the issues in a mass-mediated society is whether media use affects culture in terms of bringing disparate segments together, or perhaps driving them apart. The knowledge gap hypothesis was developed by Tichenor, Olien, and Donohue (1970) and supported by other work (e.g., Gaziano, 1983; Genova & Greenberg, 1979; Robinson & Levy, 1986). It proposes that as mass media are introduced into a society, those with higher knowledge and socioeconomic status will adopt it faster, thereby increasing the distance between the knowledge and technology haves from the have-nots. Also, media use tends to build skill in accessing it.

A person who has never touched a computer is not likely to be able to search sophisticated databases very quickly and may be intimidated from even trying. There is a learning curve associated with the acquisition of knowledge in the process of technological adoption. For example, to engage with the Internet, you have to have knowledge of its existence, a sense of how you may be able to use it, and you have to be able to afford a computer or at least have access to one. So a person who is not particularly oriented to mass media to begin with, and/or who does not have the disposable income necessary to acquire expensive computer equipment, is not likely to be an Internet user.

Although not all social groups may have adopted the most sophisticated technology, they have many ways of communicating information they deem important. While the knowledge gap hypothesis presumes a lack of technological expertise isolates segments of society, when a major issue arises people typically use whatever communication vehicles they possess to exchange information about it. Thus, technologically poor social groups may have substantial political clout when candidates or issues they favor are of concern. The real question in information exchange appears to be the desire or need for it on the part of the individual. We typically ignore that which we see as irrelevant, or that we cannot affect, while involving ourselves in that which we perceive as personally important or that we are empowered to change. Mayors may be elected by previously ineffective lower socioeconomic class voters who come together to exercise their power at the ballot box. Social groups emotionally involved in a cause may launch effective protest campaigns that change government policy—all with or without the most sophisticated mass media technology.

The heart of the knowledge gap hypothesis is that rather than something that brings society together, mass media may be a wedge driving social classes further apart. Media play a role in the reality construction of audience members in a wide variety of ways. But audiences are increasingly sophisticated, too, having learned about the media by living with it every day. The mass media are used to entertain, to reinforce values we already have or to change our minds, to isolate ourselves from others or to bring us together, to acquire knowledge or to escape from the concerns of the daily life. But what each person draws from media messages depends on that person.

AUDIENCE PERSPECTIVE

With the rise of modern mass communication forms came the displaced communicator physically removed from an audience. When a contemporary newspaper reporter communicates, he or she does so by punching characters on a computer terminal keyboard. The reporter is writing words on a screen. The audience is unseen, unable to respond immediately to what is being communicated, and any feedback that returns to the reporter from the audience is displaced in time and space from the sending activity of the reporter.

The same is true in television news. Many people, when given the opportunity to visit a television news studio are struck by how small and tightly confined most newscast sets are. They are constructed realities, illusions really, built for the perspective of the camera, which make them appear in ways they do not in person. When a newscaster speaks on the air, it is to a glass lens, often mounted on a robotic camera with no other human being in the room. The newscaster talks to a machine. But on the other end of the signal he or she is in a living room being watched by people who frown, smile, lose track of what's being said, or deeply concentrate on something that particularly interests them.

It is an odd thing, mass communication—a kind of interpersonal communication that is depersonalized because of the nature of the channel through which it flows. One individual sends a message that is received by another individual. But because technology allows many individuals to receive the message at the same time we think of it as communicating in mass. But it is not the same as communicating to 100,000 people in a sports stadium. It is one-on-one communication multiplied 100,000 times. Perhaps the single biggest failure of mass communication organizations, and their members, is thinking of the audience as a huge, faceless mass. It is readily apparent when someone ends a newscast by saying, "Thanks, everyone, for being with us." The newscaster doesn't understand what kind of communication is really taking place. The mass media are, in the last analysis from the audience member's perspective, a personalized experience whether you are talking about news reports, public relations information campaigns, or advertising. The next time you are home alone watching the news, and the newscaster thanks "everyone" for tuning in, look around the room and think about this fundamental problem of perception. There is no "everyone," just you.

Audience as Aggregate

One way to understand the audience with which modern media organizations interact is to consider the metaphor of a sandstone. Like sandstone, audience is an aggregate, a thing that is the product of all the little things which together create it. If you are in the American Southwest and observe a mesa, you will see a huge mountain of sandstone with cliffs perhaps 100 feet high or more, a giant thing. But if you stand right next to one part of a cliff, and look closely at it, you will see millions of tiny grains of sand, each unique in its own way. And so it is with the "mass" audience. From a distance, from the perspective of advertisers who are interested in getting as many "exposures" to their advertisements as possible, the audience target may be a huge thing, a sandstone cliff.

But from the vantage point of each grain looking out, the world is very different. Unlike sandstone, human beings are not inanimate objects. They turn off television sets, they go on vacation and stop the newspaper, they turn off the radio in the car, or play music roulette with multiple favorite stations programmed into the preselection buttons on their receiver.

There are layers of the mass audience aggregate through which any message must work its way if meaning is to be conveyed to an individual person, our metaphoric grain of sand. The first layer is the total *potential* audience to which is sent the message, for example, all the homes subscribing to the paper, or all the homes with television in a market. But not all of the potential audience will actually receive the message. Some people will be on vacation or won't have their television set on. The second layer, then, is the actual audience that *receives* the message. But just because a message gets into a person's environment doesn't mean that individual understood or cared about the message. The third layer is when a person actually *processes* a mass media message to some degree. But there is a big difference between simply recognizing a message and doing something with it. The fourth layer of mass media engagement is when the receiver is actually *influenced* by the message in some way. You can see that it can be a very long journey—sending a message to a *potential* audience, where it is actually *received* by a portion thereof, *processed* by fewer members still, to finally have a *real influence* on a person (McQuail, 1994).

Audience as Individuals

To understand the process of mass communication, you have to engage with it at both the sender and receiver end of the equation. The "mass" is not some abstract stack of numbers, a package of psychographic and demographic data over there. It is us and we are it. The failing of mass media professionals is that they do not always see things as do their audience members, nor digest their own work from a normal audience member's point of view. Typically, we are personally focused. Cassirer (1944, p. 14) pointed out that "man is always inclined to regard the small circle in which he lives as the center of the world and to make his particular, private life the standard of the universe." Perspective is a fundamental warping of reality to fit an individual's sense of reality and his or her desired ends. It is framed by cultural background, surroundings, and individual experience that cannot be discounted or ignored in the way meaning is constructed.

The mass audience is extremely complex. It is made up of unique individuals defined by their personal development who share some enculturated values but not all, who sometimes move together but often apart, and who consistently confound predictability. For example, television program producers and advertising creative directors, despite considerable audience research efforts, fail to come up with sure things. Part of the problem is that media professionals tend to think in averages—the average viewer, the average reader. But an average is a mathematical abstraction. If a very small town has two families with respective annual incomes of $50,000 and $100,000, the average annual income of families in the town would be $75,000. But no one makes that. An advertising campaign targeting consumers at the $75,000 annual income level would not address, specifically, anyone. The principle is the same in much larger collections of people. In fact, most people who make up an "average" are not average themselves but are outliers to one degree or another from the center of the distribution. So producing something for an average person in effect means producing for someone who does not exist.

PREDISPOSITION OF MEDIA TO THE CONCEPT OF MASS

Mass media, by their very definition, have to reach a lot of people—a mass. And mass media economics depend on two basic revenue forms, subscription fees charged directly to the consumer, and advertising placed in the mass media by firms hoping to influence the buying patterns of consumers. In most contemporary media organizations the largest revenue share, by a substantial margin, is provided by advertising. However, with increasingly empowered media consumers armed with channel-hopping remotes, cable and satellite services, and the rapidly expanding Internet technology, delivering a mass to any particular advertisement is problematical. As discussed earlier, from the perspective of the people in any media audience, their engagement is individual. Most of the time when we watch television it is alone or in small groups of family or friends. Radio is consumed primarily as rush hour company when we are alone in our cars on the freeway, or as background sound while we work and play. The newspaper is not usually read in a group, but individually. Indeed, the mass audience has always been a figment of the imagination. "The mass has no continuous existence except in the minds of those who want to gain the attention of and manipulate as many people as possible" (McQuail, 1987, p. 219).

Advertising as a Driving Force

But at the media organization end, customers or audiences have to be lumped together to drive the primary revenue mechanism, advertising. To decide the price of advertising, you need to estimate the number of people who will be exposed to that advertisement. Mass media audiences are estimated by circulation studies or audience ratings. "Circulation" is a newspaper industry term that indicates how many copies are purchased by regular subscribers and sold to impulse buyers through street sellers, vending machines, or other retailers. Ratings pertain to radio, television, and to magazines. Radio and television ratings estimate the size and composition of the audience of a given station at a specific time and are statistical estimates based on survey samples. See Chapter 8, "Marketing the Media Organization," for a more detailed discussion of circulation and rating research.

Advertising is usually purchased on a cost-per-thousand basis. This is simply the cost of the advertisement divided by the number of groups of 1,000 people expected to be exposed to it. For example, an advertisement cost $10,000 and is expected to reach 100,000 people. There are 100 groups of 1,000 people in the 100,000. So you just divide the cost of the ad by 100. The cost per thousand of the advertisement would be $100. Basically, the production costs are the same to prepare an advertisement to run for a relatively small audience or a large one. So it often makes the most sense to run the advertisement where it will reach the largest possible target audience. The economics of advertising, including economies of scale, predispose the media industries to thinking of the audience in terms of mass and pit them against one another to dominate their markets (Wimmer & Dominick, 1987). This is discussed further in the following chapter on media organizational decline.

The amounts of money at stake for media companies are substantial. On network television, advertisers pay $200,000 or more to air a single commercial in prime time, in addition to average production costs for national brand commercials of another $200,000 (Belch & Belch, 1995). Advertising is a huge industry, a significant factor in the United States' gross national product. Figure 11.1 shows the growth in spending on television, radio, daily newspapers, and magazines since 1984 and forecast to the turn

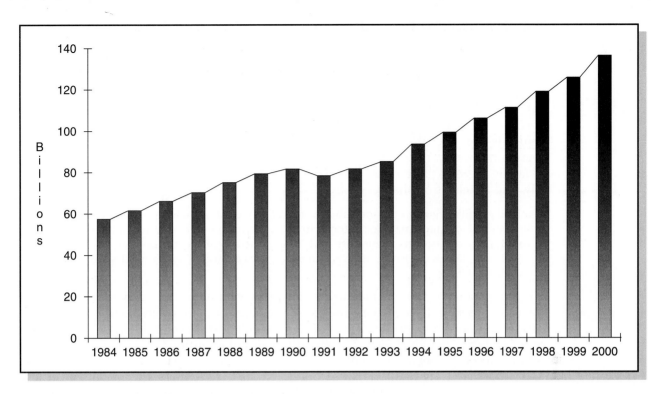

Figure 11.1 Major Media U.S. Advertising Spending, 1984–2000
(Source: Veronis, Suhler & Associates, 1996)

of the century. Note that the billions spent on the primary mass media forms do not include what are called "nonmeasured media" spending through such advertising vehicles as direct mail, the Yellow Pages telephone directories, weekly newspapers, outdoor advertising, newsletters, or other forms (Veronis, Suhler & Associates, 1996).

Audience Selectivity

Everything in advertising, which is the single biggest source of revenue for mass media organizations, is focused on aggregates of readers or viewers. Thus, the primary orientation is on audience as mass. From the beginning, mass media research used demographic categorizations, rather than more sophisticated social group memberships, to segment the audience. Demographics are the physical characteristics with which we can separate individuals and include age, sex, family size, education, ethnicity, and socioeconomic status. They are the easiest data to derive, methodologically, and are the basis of official census records. Advertising also uses psychographics, which break out audiences based on personality types and lifestyle preferences (Belch & Belch, 1995).

Because most early research was segmented by demographic characteristics, the foundation of understanding audience has been built upon divisions of audience that may not mean as much to the way people consume media as their group affiliations. Early views of the mass audience perceived it as a large collective that could be manipulated. "The prevailing idea was that the mass audience was passive, unstable, and easily influenced" (Tan, 1985, p. 68). However, contemporary theorists see media consumers as empowered by expanding media forms and choosing to "put together their particular combinations of media and their particular relationships with these media" (DeFleur & Ball-Rokeach, 1989, p. 309).

It was presumed initially, and still is by some mass media professionals, that when people attend to a mass medium they pay attention to it. However, we now know that people have a wide range of attention spans in media engagement that are in a continual state of flux. Audience members engage with media in ways that fit their wants and needs at the time. That means they are dynamic in their use of media, continually adjusting to it and the rest of their environment. Attending to a media form can mean everything from concentrating on the message being conveyed to ignoring it. Analysis of family viewing patterns demonstrates that much of the time little attention is actually paid to television that serves as

> a kind of "filler" going on continuously behind conversations and domestic events. It will be watched for quick snatches, listened to in moments of quiet and then ignored. . . . We eat dinner, knit jumpers, argue with each other, listen to music, read books, do homework, kiss, write letters and vacuum-clean the carpet [all] with the television on. (Morley, 1986, pp. 24–47)

The ratings and circulation measuring systems have a presumption that people absorb the messages sent through mass media. But research provides significant evidence that this presumption is seriously flawed. Each individual is "several different audiences at once" and can "deploy different levels and modes of attention" to a particular medium (Morley, 1986, p. 10).

The advertising industry has several methods to determine effectiveness in reaching audiences and encouraging them to buy products. One example demonstrates the issue of attention actually paid to media by audiences using them. Research was done involving "primary readers" of magazines. Individuals who purchase a magazine—primary readers—are presumed to pay more attention to its contents than "out-of-home pass-along readers." Two major techniques for determining the recall of advertisements in magazines were used, the Starch Reports and Gallup-Robinson methods. Only one-fifth of primary readers in the Starch group, and just 3.2 percent of those in the Gallup-Robinson group, recalled specific advertisements (Sissors & Bumba, 1993).

THEORETICAL "DEMASSIFICATION"

People connect with media messages for three fundamental reasons. They include information gathering to satisfy cognitive needs, entertainment and diversionary utilization of the media, and the reinforcement of personal identity by having a sense of engaging with the world at large (Blumler, 1979). From the viewpoint of audience members, the engagement is personally defined in terms of each individual's requirements. Newspapers are usually read alone, radio is typically consumed on an individual basis, and television viewing generally takes place in the quiet of the living room alone or with a few friends or family members. As the individual gazes at the flickering tube, just as in the viewing of motion pictures, "what the individual 'gets' is determined by his background *and his* [or her] *needs*" (Fearing, 1972, p. 120, emphasis in original).

From the media organization's perspective, there is a mass of viewers to which messages are sent—a mass the media organization then sells to advertisers. But from the individual audience member's perspective, the engagement is a personal one. Media organizations may perceive their audience as a mass, and advertisers can identify collections of demographic and psychographic characteristics in a faceless group called the mass audience. But those who make up that mass look back at the media organizations and the advertisers as single individuals who are relationship-dependent social beings with highly personalized meaning interpretation.

There will continue to be those instances when enormous audiences are brought together for some special reason. Examples include the Kennedy-Nixon debates in 1960, during which an estimated 85 million people watched the candidates; the 1969 Apollo moon landing, 1972 Olympics, Super Bowl football games, and other special events to which audiences of 100 million or more have tuned in. The mass media can connect us to events very rapidly and in huge aggregates. When the space shuttle *Challenger* blew up in 1986, more than two-thirds of American adults knew about the accident within a half-hour of its happening. Ultimately 82 percent of adults indicated they received most of their news about the events from television. The launch was being nationally televised when the explosion occurred (Emery & Emery, 1988). But despite those special instances, it is clear that when very large numbers of people do attend to a mass medium at the same time, they still do so as individuals. News diffusion studies have indicated that even in a major event a high proportion of people learn about it through personal contact with someone rather than primarily from a mass media source (McQuail, 1994).

The last quarter of the 20th century has experienced accelerated audience demassification—the breaking apart of what had been thought to be a single, huge audience into increasingly smaller segments. The combined forces of media deregulation and new technology have produced exponential growth in media options. The media consumer is empowered as never before, by a range of choices with which to engage, though in many cases additional channels of media are merely filled with the same kind of media products as existed before, just in more places. "Instead of the promised new diet, cable TV simple offers more of the same" (Traber, 1986, p. 1). And each person uses his or her available media options to fit individualized wants and needs. Rather than a medium constructing a so-called mass audience to deliver to advertisers, consumers are increasingly designing their own media aggregates from among a plethora of choices. That is not to say that on occasion large collections of people are not assembled by the offering of a particular medium. However, generating a single, enormous audience is increasingly challenging, as is holding the attention of the consumers within such an audience for the main event—the commercial or advertisement.

In 1933 there were only two national radio networks and both of them carried President Roosevelt's inaugural address (Head, Sterling, & Schofield, 1994). For the contemporary mass media consumer there are dozens of mass media options in print, radio, television, motion pictures, and Internet technology, most of which do not carry the president's inaugural address and can be used by people trying to escape the oratory. In the contemporary environment it is virtually impossible for the President of the United States to talk to most Americans at once. As late as 1977 that was still feasible with the cooperation of just three quasi-monopolistic television networks, which nearly all Americans watched each evening (Auletta, 1991).

We have evolved from a mass-mediated society to a society in which technology has empowered each person to set his or her own agenda of media forms with which to engage whenever he or she wishes. It is the age of the empowered media consumer whose choice is sometimes none of what is being offered. Technology, along with providing myriad sources, has also given the consumer the "clicker." Armed with the television remote control, people can simply jump through 50 or more channels, "surfing" potential programs or "zapping" out anything that provides the slightest irritation—a slow moment in a program, or a commercial that isn't creative enough to hold interest. Younger viewers tend to "zap" more frequently than older viewers, and men are more aggressive "zappers" than women (Walker & Bellamy, 1993). Most American homes also have videocassette recorders that can be used to play rented movies instead of watching television, or to shift programs to a more convenient time. In time shifting the viewer can also fast-forward, or "zip" through dull spots and commercials. Interestingly, research has demonstrated that when people record programs and then play them back, they use their remote controls to zip through more than half of the commercials in the program (Belch & Belch, 1995).

With all the technology of multiple channels, "zapping" and "zipping" to avoid anything annoying, there is a question whether the mass media experience is really any more satisfying despite its much larger number of choices. As one 41-year-old American female with a high disposable income—the ideal demographic advertisers pursue—put it, "To me, watching television is a process of elimination. I sit down and go through the channels ticking off what I don't want to watch and end up with whatever's left" (Redmond, 1991b). In a media-rich environment, the audience is hardly a mass of passive consumers who do little as their part of the communication process. Increasingly, with ever-widening ranges of mass media options, individual selectivity is clearly empowering media consumers who set their own agendas of mass media consumption. With a large number of cable television channels, a given viewer may have a set of a dozen or so regularly watched, with another 30 channels that are never tuned in. Or individuals who engage with the Internet may take that time away from what would formerly have been evening viewing of network television. At the same time, concurrent media usage occurs, whereby an individual may be "surfing" the Internet while listening to the radio, or with the television on, as the person moves almost unconsciously among a crowd of media taking bits from each all at the same time.

For media managers the important issue is whether you think of audience members as a product or as people. If it is a product aggregate, there certainly are enormous numbers of people who can be defined as an audience and segmented by demographics and psychographic divisions. But if you think of an audience from the perspective of its members, it is interfacing with media alone, or with a few others in a close group. "In practice, there is a continuum, with 'mass' at one end and 'small close-knit group' at the other, along which actual audiences can be located" (McQuail, 1987, p. 226). So, you have to understand audience both as a collective and individual experience. To the advertisers you sell space or time, the aggregate is a key factor. However, to build media products that are effective in drawing audience members, you must work at understanding the individual media consumer's perspective where media consumption is a very personalized experience.

The environment of mass communication, and the media organizations that operate within it, has undergone fundamental changes, particularly since the mid-1970s. There has been increasing deregulation of the media and of the companies that control the media, including relaxed ownership restrictions and financial incentives for a corporation to own many media outlets. Also, many new forms of media technology, including the Internet, have been introduced.

Media managers have a new audience context requiring different perspectives than those prevalent before 1975. Then, media consumers had few choices; because of that, media organizations were able to attract large audiences. In today's media world, with so many options for media consumers, it is challenging to assemble significant audience numbers. With many more competitors, the share required to be the dominant player in most markets is about the same as a third-place media organization drew two decades ago. In many cases, in terms of total audience members factored for population growth, media organizations have substantially fewer people engaging with them, and for shorter time periods.

The contemporary audience has the following characteristics, in general, across all media types.

1. It is individually engaged, with each media user setting his or her own communication agendas that are usually mixtures of personally preferred media.

2. Technology is used to remove the barriers of specific time-period use and to avoid advertising's efforts to influence consumers. It is also effective in assembling individual media engagement agendas, thus filtering out media not specific to the consumer's wants and needs.

3. The historically dominant mass media (e.g., newspapers, magazines, radio, television) are being redefined in niche market terms. Although their audiences, in most cases, are still substantial, they are experiencing continuous erosion as competition increases for media consumer attention.

4. Media organizations cannot be everything to everyone in a fragmented environment, so they are being forced to concentrate increasingly on attracting select audiences they can sell to specific advertisers. This poses significant philosophical questions about the concept of a mass media as a cultural binder. It may instead contribute to increasing social fragmentation whereby the mass media contributes more to a stratification of society based on advertiser-demanded attributes. Rather than media homogenization of society, there is a danger of media fractionalization expanding socioeconomic and knowledge-based divisions.

For a media manager to be successful in the contemporary media environment of increasing fragmentation and growing difficulty in developing consumer loyalty, the audience must be understood as individuals with hopes, fears, dreams, and shared culture. When you start thinking of an audience as an inanimate object, a sandstone cliff that is impassive and nonreactive, you are heading for serious trouble. For you will stop attempting to communicate with an audience of people and only see them as eyeballs to hand off to advertisers, pandering to the lowest common denominator in the mathematical abstraction game of averages. In the process of trying to be everything to everyone, a media organization runs a great risk of being nothing to anyone. And that is when a hollowness settles in as the audience begins to lose its sense of being a partner in the communication process.

If we accept the view that communication is an orderly way of transferring meaning, there is an interesting problem with advertiser-driven media where programming, or magazine or newspaper copy placed among the ads, is merely titillation for the real purpose of selling things with the advertisements. In the cynical view, the copy or programming among commercials is not an effort to really transfer meaning at all, but merely to hold attention until the advertisement transfers the real meaning of the contemporary mass media exercise (to get viewers or readers to buy something). Thus, much of what a mass medium provides to an audience "is liable not to be communication at all" but merely audience manipulation directed by market research studies (Elliott, 1972, p. 256). Rather than an information exchange relationship, it becomes a hand-off, and eventually the superficiality of the experience causes the audience member to disengage. Ratings drop, circulation declines, and the mass medium has a mass no more.

1. How would you describe the differences between contemporary powerful influences mass media theory, and the "magic bullet" concept for the early 20th century?

2. How are contemporary audiences different from those of the 1920s?

3. Discuss the rise of advertising and its effect on mass media.

4. Propaganda is defined as "any systematic, widespread dissemination or promotion of particular ideas, doctrines, practices, etc. to further one's own cause or to damage an opposing one" (*Webster's*, 1994, p. 1078). How would you describe contemporary media in the light of that definition?

5. What made the "fireside chat" an effective communication vehicle? Has mass media in the years since changed the way heads of state communicate?

6. What are the dangers of allowing market research to be the primary determinate of media organization content?

7. As a manager understanding how audiences engage with the media, what will you do to ensure your organization accurately serves the "wants" and "needs" of your community to increase the effective application of uses and gratification theory?

8. Media organizations consider their audience a "mass." What does that mean? Is it accurate? What's the difference between the way media organization communicators send messages and the way audience members receive them?

chapter 12

ORGANIZATIONAL DECLINE: CAUSES AND REMEDIES

DECLINE IN CONTEMPORARY MASS MEDIA

In the media industries, there are more players in the marketplace than ever before. What was formerly considered a "mass audience" is being cut up into ever smaller pieces. All contemporary media have smaller and more narrowly focused audiences than was the case when fewer media forms existed. The mass media world has evolved from large groups of people engaging with a few media options to large numbers of media options engaged by smaller groups of people. It has become a niche environment with increasing industry emphasis on more narrowly defined audiences whom advertisers want to reach (Comstock, 1989; Wimmer & Dominick, 1987).

This chapter begins with the true stories of how two great media institutions got into serious trouble and declined as media powers. It concludes with the concepts of organizational decline to help you recognize it and deal with it in the future. Decline is not merely an abstract concept floating in the ether of theory. It is an everyday occurrence that infects organizations and can bring them down. In both of the cases that begin this chapter, the onset of decline was triggered by the increase of competition through innovative forms of media entering the market with new technology. The first of the cases is the decline of daily newspapers. The second is the decline of the traditional broadcast television networks.

The Rise and Decline of Daily Newspapers

The modern newspaper was born of the economic and technological change of the industrial revolution. Before 1830 newspapers were very expensive, usually aimed at the wealthy, with relatively small circulation. But with the *New York Sun,* launched in 1833, that changed. Founder Benjamin H. Day marketed the *Sun* to ordinary people. It was the first American daily newspaper sold on a per-issue basis. The content focused on violence, human interest stories, and general happenings around town. Within six months the *Sun* was a major New York City newspaper with a circulation in the 8,000 range (Emery & Emery, 1996).

Three key factors supported the concept of a newspaper for the masses: (1) the increase of a market-based, urban society, (2) grounded in democracy, (3) with the industrial revolution's new technology making mass media possible. Steam-driven presses invented in the 1830s provided the necessary economies of scale to produce large numbers of newspapers quickly and inexpensively. Although magazines had been around since 1741, they didn't compete directly with newspapers for reporting daily events. Periodicals tended to complement daily newspaper coverage with depth and specialization. The rise of commercial radio in the 1920s provided newspapers a direct competitor to challenge them seriously for mass advertising and audience. At the same time motion pictures became the dominant American entertainment medium with 20,000 theaters open by 1930 showing films to 90 million customers a week (Emery & Emery, 1996; Head, Sterling, & Schofield, 1994).

When modern newspapers were born, they created a new industry aimed at fulfilling the information wants and needs of ordinary people. They were also the only effective way for advertisers to reach large masses of potential customers quickly. But following 1920, competition and economics caused serious problems for newspapers. First came competition in the form of new technology—radio and motion pictures—then the Great Depression—then following World War II the technology of television, several recessions, and then yet more new technology in the form of the Internet.

The economic downturns alone tended to reduce advertising revenues. But when they combined with the rise of new competition, newspapers found themselves in trouble. Newspaper circulation steadily declined compared with the nation's population while the industry consolidated into group ownership. Consider the following developments.

♦ In 1900 group owners controlled just 10 percent of total daily newspaper circulation. By 1990 they controlled 81 percent.

♦ Cities with more than one daily newspaper became rare. In 1940 there were 181 cities with competing dailies. By 1994 that number had dropped to 33.

♦ The number of general circulation dailies dropped from 1,878 in 1940 to 1,556 in 1994.

♦ The number of newspapers per household in 1930 was 1.32 but by 1994 it had declined to .043 when only six out of every ten adults were regularly reading a daily newspaper.

But perhaps the most revealing figure is comparing the change in daily newspaper circulation with the growth of the population. Total daily newspaper circulation rose during the 1930 to 1990 period from 40 million copies to just over 60 million copies, an increase of 50 percent. But during the same period the population of the United States increased 100 percent, from 122 million to nearly 250 million. Since 1990 daily newspaper circulation growth has remained flat, while the nation's population continues to grow (Emery & Emery, 1996; U.S. Census Bureau, 1997) (see Fig. 12.1).

In the mid-1800s the daily newspapers in New York competed against one another for advertising revenue. A major advertiser had a choice of papers to reach large numbers of potential customers, but that was all. Today many markets have 40 or more advertising vehicles trying to sell space or time, including multiple radio and broadcast

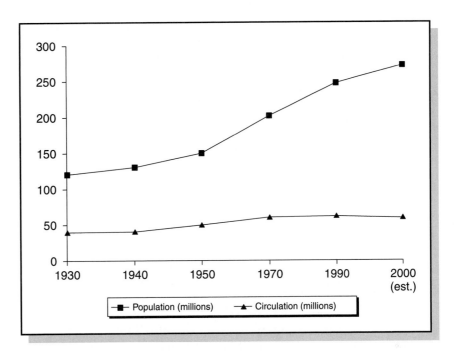

Figure 12.1 Daily Newspaper Circulation and Population Growth
(Sources: Emery & Emery, 1996; U.S. Bureau of the Census, 1997b; Veronis, Suhler & Associates, 1996)

television stations, cable television systems, billboard companies, weekly newspapers, local neighborhood shoppers, and many direct mail advertising firms. Since the mass media, in all of its forms, are paid for primarily by advertising, the competition for a piece of each advertiser's dollar is intense. It has made survival of more than one daily newspaper per market nearly impossible in an advertising-driven economic system that strongly favors the dominant player.

The first thing to understand about media economics is that, among media types within a given market, the fixed costs of production are usually about the same. In the case of competing newspapers, each will have similar expenditures for staff, office equipment, facilities, printing, and distribution. The same is true for fixed costs across radio stations in a market, television stations, or other categories of media. Since fixed costs in each media category are generally comparable, the key to making a good profit is having a larger share of the market's advertising revenue than your competitor.

The second part of the media economics equation is the cost of advertising. It is normally figured on a cost-per-thousand (CPM) basis. That means for every 1,000 people who will see an advertisement, the advertiser pays a set price negotiated with the medium to be used. If a newspaper has a price of three cents per thousand for a half-page advertisement, and a circulation of 100,000, a display ad would cost $3,000. If its competitor also charged three cents per thousand, but has a circulation of 150,000, a display ad would cost $4,500. If that were the end of it, an advertiser might buy either paper, depending on how much money he or she has. But in competitive situations, strong media outlets price themselves down to draw business away from the competition. They set their CPM rate lower but still make more money because they have more thousands to reach. If the larger paper in our preceding example, with 150,000 circulation, reduces its rate to two and one-half cents per thousand, it would cost only a *little* more for an advertiser to reach a *lot* more people. A half-page ad would cost $3,750, compared with the smaller newspaper's $3,000 price. The advertiser would only have to spend $750 more to reach 50,000 more people (an increase of 25 percent in advertising cost to reach 50 percent more potential customers). Another factor in the value of an advertising buy is the type of audience being reached, but for the sake of this example we assumed the demographics are the same for both papers.

More advertisers are attracted to the largest paper because it has more readers for their ads to reach, at a lower CPM. Many readers are advertising consumers attracted to the paper with the best ads. Grocery ads, for example, fill a real need for readers who use them to maintain household budgets as they shop for the best buys. So a circulation-advertising spiral effect takes place where the newspaper with more readers attracts more advertising, which in turn attracts more readers. For the losing paper, fewer readers attract less advertising, which in turn attracts fewer readers. The larger newspaper grows and the smaller newspaper shrinks (Lacy, Sohn, & Wicks, 1993).

An example of how circulation and advertising revenue are tied together in newspaper economics is the collapse of the Washington, D.C., market from three daily newspapers to one in the space of just ten years, 1971 to 1981. As the nation's capital, you might expect the city to be a place where several daily newspapers would do very well. Certainly there is an unending stream of news and information to cover and considerable interest in what's going on in the seat of power of the United States. And it is a major American metropolitan area with a lot of people to consume media products and millions of dollars in annual advertising expenditures.

In 1970 there were three competing dailies with press runs of 200,000 (*Washington Daily News*), 300,000 (*Washington Star*), and 500,000 (*The Washington Post*) copies. The fixed costs of all three papers were about the same, with only marginal differences due to the size and distribution of the relative press runs. The same size large advertisement would have cost $9,676 in the *News*, $12,634 in the *Star*, and $16,676 in the *Post*. On a CPM basis the cost worked out to be 4.84 cents per thousand for the *News*, 4.21 cents per thousand for the *Star*, and 3.34 cents per thousand for the *Post* (see Fig. 12.2). The *Post* was definitely the best buy for the advertiser who could afford the total cost of running an ad in the larger paper. Attracting more big advertisers with greater CPM value increased the revenues and profits for *The Washington Post* at the expense of its competitors, which continued to spiral downward. The *Washington Daily News* succumbed to organizational death in 1972. The *Washington Star* suspended operations in 1981 (Bagdikian, 1992).

The circulation-advertising spiral phenomenon is not unique to Washington, D.C. When any daily newspaper's share of a market drops below one-third, organizational death—ceasing to exist as a separate, identifiable entity either through liquidation or by

Newspaper	Circulation	Display Ad Cost	Cost Per Thousand
Washington Daily News	200,000	$9,676	$0.0484
Washington Star	300,000	$12,634	$0.0421
The Washington Post	500,000	$16,676	$0.0334

Figure 12.2 Cost per Thousand (CPM) of Washington, D.C. Newspapers in 1970 (Source: Bagdikian, 1992)

being dissolved into another organization—is highly probable. Twenty competing dailies that ceased publication from 1976 to 1985 held an average share of 32 percent in their respective markets (Picard, 1987).

Although newspapers have declined for most of the 20th century, the consolidation into group ownership, reduction of direct daily newspaper competition in most markets, and the growth of the 45-and-older population group most prone to reading newspapers appear to be stabilizing factors (Veronis, Suhler & Associates, 1996). Additionally, many newspapers are becoming more efficient and highly innovative with new section designs, sophisticated graphics, and a strong movement of newspapers into online publication for the growing population of Internet users. Where previously newspapers tended to see the rise of new competing technology as inconsequential and did not attempt to move into it with any urgency, contemporary publishers have been very aggressive establishing Internet World Wide Web sites. Virtually all the major publishers now have Internet sites, with many papers offering specially packaged Internet editions (Veronis, Suhler & Associates, 1996).

Decline has forced newspapers to redefine themselves and look beyond their traditional form. Their infrastructure provides extensive fact-gathering and information dissemination potential that can be used in many ways, including cooperative news programming with radio and television stations, and World Wide Web online newspapers and special services. For they operate in a very different world than welcomed Benjamin H. Day's *New York Sun* in September 1833.

The Rise and Decline of Broadcast Networks

The business environment of media organizations is continuously reshaped by new technology. In the 19th century that technology made mass audiences possible. In the 20th century a demassification has occurred as the former large audience has been fragmented into ever smaller, more narrowly defined niches (Comstock, 1989). As one media analyst put it, "I think most companies have finally come to the realization that they can't be single-channel operators in a multichannel world" (Mermigas, 1992).

The concept of a multichannel world has not come easily for the traditional broadcast networks and their affiliates, steeped in a tradition of quasi-monopoly that began with a four-and-a-half-hour broadcast November 15, 1926, as NBC made its debut. The concept of network broadcasting predated the Radio Act of 1927, the predecessor of the Communications Act of 1934, and the founding of the Federal Communications Commission. When CBS was born September 18, 1927, it was only seven months after the passage of the Radio Act and eleven months after NBC. The founding of ABC in 1945 was simply an ownership change of the already established NBC "Blue Network," which the FCC forced the original network to spin off (Head, Sterling, & Schofield, 1994).

From the beginning, network and affiliate broadcasting was a narrowly defined field of limited competitors of two, then three, which held enormous sway over American radio and television from corporate headquarters all within a few blocks of each other in New York City. They were, until the radical changes that began in the mid-1970s, controlled by those entrepreneurs who started them. It was a world seemingly within itself where the big three networks could be assured of making a profit, and other competitors outside the exclusive broadcasting club were fundamentally insignificant to them. Because many of their employees moved back and forth among ABC, CBS, and NBC, they were remarkably similar and formed a kind of industry corporate culture of operating patterns and beliefs. Thus, they were three different but very similar organizations.

It was a competitive but clubby world. There were enough advertising dollars to go around. Profits were assured. You lunched at the same restaurants, attended the same confabs of the National Association of Broadcasters, the National Association of Television Programming Executives, and the Association of National Advertisers, sat on the same industry boards, lobbied the same federal government. Mostly, you thought about each other. (Auletta, 1991, p. 25)

From the late 1970s to mid-1980s the economics of television dramatically changed. Up until that time the typical American viewer had a choice of only a handful of stations. In most markets the local affiliates of the three traditional networks provided the network offerings, an independent station offered alternative programs usually including former network shows and old movies, and a Public Broadcasting Service station provided programs aimed at a more cultured audience. In this environment ABC, CBS, and NBC basically carved up most of the audience among themselves.

New technology, in the form of cable television, changed everything. At first cable was merely a kind of extended antenna for network affiliates to reach beyond their normal broadcast areas. Small communities used cable systems to bring in distant, big city stations. But cable was not a significant urban television competitor. One reason was the limited amount of programming. Beginning in 1976 a kind of programming-cable expansion spiral built momentum, with cable penetration broadening as the variety of programs to be seen on cable flourished. And it all happened because of satellites (Head, Sterling, & Schofield, 1994).

Before communication satellites, all television signals had to be transmitted across the country by microwave, from tower to tower, or through fixed telephone lines, and then rebroadcast locally. Along with being technologically complex, it was expensive. But with communications satellites, programs can be sent up to a satellite and rebroadcast back down to everyone within line of sight of that satellite faster and cheaper. Home Box Office (HBO) began doing that with movies in 1975, which meant viewers could watch movies 24 hours a day if they wanted rather than waiting for the network movie of the week. And there were no irritating commercials breaking up the motion picture. But not everyone wanted to watch movies. The expansion of cable created a demand for other kinds of programming. Satellites made it possible for a small UHF station in Atlanta, Georgia, whose regular off-air signal didn't even cover the Atlanta metropolitan area, to reach the entire nation by being bounced off a satellite. Ted Turner did just that with the first superstation, WTBS in 1976. Cable-specific programming mushroomed. The cable industry set up C-SPAN in 1979 to provide noncommercial coverage of Congress and help fill cable system channels. That same year the FCC relaxed satellite dish ownership rules to make it easier for individuals to own satellite receiving dishes. Now even those who could not get cable wired into their homes could get the programming. The market was literally exploding for satellite delivered programming, and in 1980 Turner launched what would become the television news source of record, CNN. MTV began in 1981. There was something for everyone on cable, or direct to the home out of the sky, and television has never been the same (Head, Sterling, & Schofield, 1994).

The new technology of cable television and its programming companion satellite delivery turned network television upside down. No longer was the audience offered limited choices, by a handful of dominant networks with remarkably similar values and programming principles, focused on appealing to huge mass of "average" viewers. Suddenly, by the mid-1980s there were 40 or more channels available to most Americans with specialized programming, "a veritable alphabet soup of choices, including A&E, ESPN, USA, SHO, HBO, FNN, NICK, LIFE, MAX, CNN, MTV, DIS, BET, C-SPAN" (Auletta, 1991, p. 27).

If that weren't enough, millions of Americans were buying their own home videocassette recorders (VCRs) to time-shift programs on television they wanted to watch at a more convenient time, or to play rented movies (Head, Sterling, & Schofield, 1994).

In 1976, before the technology revolution provided most Americans with viewing options including videocassette recorders, cable television, and home satellite receivers, the big three networks simply divided the bulk of the national television audience among themselves. Independent stations and Public Broadcasting System affiliates were marginal competition. On a typical evening 92 percent of homes using television were tuned into one of the big three networks. By 1984 that had plummeted to 75 percent, and in 1991 it had skidded to 62 percent (Auletta, 1991).

In the midst of the technology and economic upheaval in network television, all three of the traditional broadcast networks were sold to new owners in the span of just nine months in 1986. The new owners had different attitudes about how the networks should be run. They replaced the original entrepreneurs who had controlled network broadcasting from the outset. The new ABC owner, Capital Cities Communications, had a reputation for being extremely frugal. Financier Laurence A. Tisch, a consummate investment strategist who focused on stock and financial performance reports, took over CBS. General Electric, which acquired control of NBC, was run by intensely competitive John F. "Jack" Welch, Jr., who also had a reputation for demanding top fiscal performance. The traditional networks had become fiscally cost-conscious and intensely competitive. Gone, seemingly overnight, was the old network atmosphere within which the network corporate culture was framed, which one CBS founder William Paley had described as permeated by "a sort of comfortable attitude" (Auletta, 1991, p. 25).

The sudden, radical change in top management's approach clashed with the existing network corporate culture and was nearly incomprehensible to longtime network employees like Lawrence K. Grossman, president of NBC News.

> The public owned the airwaves, Grossman believed, and it was to them that a network owed responsibility to provide news, as well as to offer occasional evenings of dramas or symphonies. If political leaders shied from issues, he believed the press had a responsibility to high-light them. This was Larry Grossman's religion, one shared by many others at the network, even those who jumped aboard when an action-adventure series, *The A-Team,* helped pull NBC out of third place. To them the thought of requiring News to earn a profit or to break even was a sacrilege. Before GE bought the network from RCA in 1986, Grant Tinker kept hands off News, respecting an invisible wall between it and business.
>
> In the GE culture, on the other hand, nothing was sacred; the thought of accepting losses as normal was sacrilege. The primary responsibility was to GE shareholders, not to some romanticized notion of a public that was abandoning the networks anyway. (Auletta, 1991, p. 20)

After the GE takeover, Grossman ended up going to Welch's office the day after a budget confrontation with the GE chairman, to try to smooth things out.

> "The first words out of Jack Welch's mouth when I walked in," recalls Grossman, were, "This is the greatest day of my life!"
>
> Grossman wondered whether one of Welch's children had just done something wonderful, whether he had become a grandfather or acquired a masterpiece.
>
> "Our stock just hit a new high," explained Welch.
>
> Grossman was stunned. "I couldn't comprehend his values," he recalls. (Auletta, 1991, p. 22)

At NBC, several years after new management brought different attitudes to the network, there continued an undercurrent of distrust and fear based on a fundamental clash of values:

> Five years after General Electric bought NBC's parent company, RCA, for $6.4 billion [in 1991], NBC is wracked not only with lowered ratings and lowered profits, but with dissension, despair and depression as well.
>
> "People either still there, or who just left, in Burbank or New York, say it's not the same company," says one former NBC executive. "It just has no soul. Nobody cares. All the people who care are gone." (Shales, 1991b, p. B1)

Such melancholy reflections by former and longtime employees are to be expected in the context of dramatic organizational change. The familiar is displaced with the unfamiliar, and uncertainty increases stress. Unless constructive efforts are made to relieve that stress, it builds upon itself in a kind of repeating cycle with accompanying self-protective tactics by employees, which then increase the difficulty of redirecting the organization. The organizational hierarchy can then be perceived by substantial numbers of organizational members as part of the problem, which may reduce their efforts to make it succeed (Guy, 1989).

Cost-cutting measures were implemented by the networks, including repeated waves of network news layoffs beginning in 1983 when 125 people lost their jobs at CBS (Stone, E., 1987). Once begun, the layoff process continued. ABC made the decision to make deep cuts, letting 2,000 people go in 1985, hoping to achieve all necessary layoffs at once. Because of the size of that layoff, ABC avoided more firings for the next four years, as audience erosion and financial pressure continued to grow. But at the other networks, reducing the employee workforce came a piece at a time, creating a climate of fear that wore on year after year. When the network layoffs began, they shocked the broadcast television industry and quickly trickled down to affiliates also anxious to cut costs in an increasingly fragmenting business environment. Virtually every television market was affected, including stations in such diverse locations as Charlotte, North Carolina, and Glendive, Montana (Redmond, 1989).

The watershed years of 1976 to 1991 in the decline of the broadcast networks saw change in every form from technology to ownership to corporate culture, and that change continues. Networks are evolving with further ownership change and adjustments in organizational focus. CBS was sold to Westinghouse, and Capital Cities/ABC was taken over by the Walt Disney Company. Meantime NBC set up a new cable service, MSNBC, in partnership with computer software giant Microsoft. All three have ongoing efforts to diversify into various mass media enterprises to broaden their economic bases with less reliance on broadcast television.

The audience for media organization products continues to fragment as more new technology evolves. An example is the Internet, which for most Americans did not exist before 1994. Within two years it had an estimated 14 million users ("What's the Internet?," 1996). New broadcast networks, including the United Paramount Network (UPN), Time Warner's WB network, and FOX, were also launched in the early 1990s. Direct broadcast satellite (DBS) services entered the market with small, less obtrusive home dishes in 1994 and within two years had more than two million subscribers. Network television, which had once controlled the industry continued to struggle. The combined broadcast network shares, including UPN, WB, and FOX, are expected to continue to erode (Veronis, Suhler & Associates, 1996) (see Fig. 12.3). Rating is the percentage of all households that possess televisions tuned into a specific program. Share is the percentage of households that have television sets turned on and tuned into a specific program.

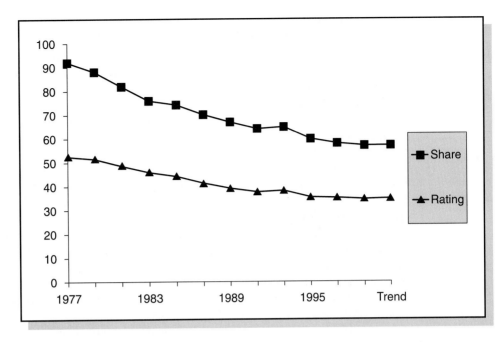

Figure 12.3 Network Audience Erosion
(Source: Veronis, Suhler, & Associates, 1996)

Yet the network evolution has provided an interesting twist. Rather than becoming irrelevant as some had forecast, and despite their continued loss of viewers, the traditional big three networks still provide the largest single television audience at any given time, which in turn attracts the bulk of television advertising. Additionally, research indicates that viewers typically sample the offerings of the traditional networks first, and then, if not satisfied, turn to independent stations or cable. Thus, although they are not as dominant as they once were, they still provide the foundation of viewing television, now as the first among many competitors, rather than the only significant competitors (Veronis, Suhler & Associates, 1996). It should be noted that the traditional broadcast networks continue to produce, or arrange for production of, television's most-watched programs. That includes most of what is seen on independent broadcast television stations and many cable networks as network programs go into syndication following their initial network runs.

THE CONCEPT OF DECLINE

Decline is a phenomenon that affects all organizations sooner or later. It is nothing more than natural evolution as an organization passes its zenith and begins to fade. But unlike the inevitability of human life, where age begins to deteriorate our resiliency in ways we cannot alter, organizational decline can often be stopped, or even reversed. The trick in doing that is to recognize the onset of decline early and avoid falling into the traps that increase its advance. It is not uncommon for managers to do the wrong thing, when faced with decline symptoms, and worsen their situation as they try to correct it. Your logic may tell you to do one thing that, on the surface, seems quite appropriate, but in fact accelerates the decline. As a media organization manager you need to be aware of the symptoms to detect the onset of decline and provide the appropriate response.

The effort to understand organizational decline as a separate phenomenon of the life cycle of organizations emerged in the last two decades of the 20th century. Decline is triggered by the failure of an organization, for whatever reason, to adapt appropriately to significant changes in its environment. Those frequently include changing markets and competition (Cameron, 1983: Harrigan, 1988). It is defined as "deterioration in an organization's adaptation to its microniche and the associated reduction of resources within the organization" (Cameron, Sutton, & Whetten, 1988, p. 9). Simply put, that means as an organization's niche flexes, due to changes in technology, competition, or whatever, the organization fails to adjust appropriately.

Decline typically happens in two stages. First, the organization fails to respond to something significant in its environment, making it less effective as a competitor. As it begins to lose ground the organization initiates actions internally to respond. But then those actions worsen the problem. For example, a media organization's sales and revenues drop because a new competitor enters the operating environment. To preserve the previous profit margin the media organization cuts its internal costs. Those cuts may include reducing product quality and/or variety, or layoffs. The net effect of the internal actions is a further reduction in competitiveness. Loss of sales results in budget cuts that cause further losses in sales as the decline becomes a vicious cycle that feeds on itself (Cameron, Sutton, & Whetten, 1988).

Decline is triggered in one of two ways (see Fig. 12.4). The first is known as type "k." The organization starts to falter because of something in its operating environment beyond the organization's control. Examples include the entry of new competitors, a major shift in technology, or a major change in the industry segment of which the organization is a part. When new competitors enter a market it's more difficult to maintain market share against increasing competition. New technology may render the organization or its products obsolete, and a major change in an organization's industry may cause a general contraction or significant realignment of the entire business sector. The second way decline begins is the type "r." The organization itself causes decline in an otherwise stable or growing operating environment. Examples include producing inferior products or engaging in inappropriate, unethical, and/or controversial activity that results in a negative customer/audience attitude toward the organization. (Cameron, Sutton, & Whetten, 1988; Harrigan, 1988).

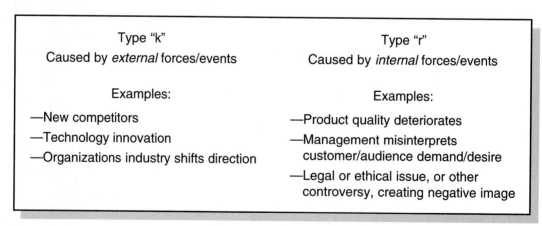

Figure 12.4 Types of Decline
(Source: Cameron, Sutton & Whetten, 1988)

One of the problems with decline is that it is often hard to identify at the beginning. What is initially believed to be just a temporary anomaly turns out to be the beginning of a serious, long-term problem. Typically, capitalist organizations do everything possible to maintain their profit margin. But when decline is setting in, that approach may speed it up. As business falls off, budgets are usually cut to maintain the profit margin just when they should be expanded to increase competitiveness. Like a dinosaur, as food begins disappearing the beast lives off whatever fat reserves it has until there is no more. If allowed to go on too long, it then starves to death. Organizations become dinosaurs when they do not adjust to changes in their energy source—their market niche or types of products—and become static in a dynamic environment. This can occur rapidly or take considerable time. It may be set in motion from external changes, internal factors, or a combination of both.

Externally Induced Decline—Type "k"

To survive, an organization must adapt to any external factors that significantly alter the context within which it operates. Changing tax laws, higher costs of raw materials such as newsprint, or other developments in the operating context beyond the control of the media organization are external factors. Occasionally, something more radical comes along and causes upheaval in the organizational environment. In some cases the external change is so dramatic the previous organizational activity is almost immediately rendered obsolete.

The invention of movable type for the printing press did just that to the book publishing industry. Book creation was previously centered in medieval monasteries where books were hand copied by monks. Books in the medieval world were extremely expensive, and only the very rich could afford to own a one. Literacy was limited both because of social class attitudes and the fact there was little written material in circulation. But after the invention of movable type, books and other printed materials became cheap and readily available. There was a reason for the average person to know how to decipher the squiggles on a printed page. The monks ended up being put out of the book-copying business, and a new commercial publishing industry arose in the midst of sweeping social, political, and religious change fostered by the printing press and the rise of literacy (Emery & Emery, 1996).

In this century the mass media have gone through several technology-driven shifts that threatened the survivability of the previous media form. Each medium, in turn, has risen to dominance, then been supplanted by a new technology and forced to redefine itself, coping with a type "k" externally induced decline. Newspapers found themselves competing with the immediacy of radio news in the early part of the 20th century. Radio reached its news, information, and entertainment programming peak in the 1940s. When broadcast television technology became widely distributed following World War II, radio was forced to adjust its focus and became primarily a music machine along with the beginnings of talk radio. FM radio emerged as the dominant radio form primarily because of its greater clarity in music transmission. Network entertainment programs were gone from radio by the mid-1950s, as consumers began spending their evenings with television. Broadcast television remained the dominant mass media technology until the 1980s, when cable and satellite programming expanded viewer options. In each of the mass medium cases, external change forced adaptation to a new marketing niche as the former industry role was supplanted by a newer technology (Head, Sterling, & Schofield, 1994).

Internally Induced Decline—Type "r"

Internal factors contributing to decline include anything an organization or industry does within itself to reduce competitiveness and cause potential customers or audience to seek other means to satisfy their wants and needs. That can include ignoring environmental changes and clinging to old technology while new forms rise, or inappropriately changing the image of the organization in its marketplace. Change is often initiated for very logical reasons, but if it is not done properly, the effort can have the effect of accelerating the decline process. (See Sidebar 12.1.)

In the Western model of the free press there is a presumption of higher purpose of the press as an exchange medium for ideas that is central to democratic government. That is why the press is the only business specifically protected by the U.S. Constitution. There is a powerful sense that although media organizations are businesses deserving of profit, they also have an underlying responsibility to serve responsibly the interests of the society as a whole.

A media organization may justify some action because of legitimate business considerations, but that action may be viewed negatively if the media organization is seen as abandoning its social contract to help advance society. Media organizations depend on their credibility with the audience. That credibility can be seriously harmed if the audience senses a loss of substance, or when there are ethical lapses resulting in public controversy.

In 1981 a highly publicized series of reports about childhood drug addiction appeared in *The Washington Post,* one of the nation's premier newspapers in a city plagued with a serious drug problem. The newspaper won a Pulitzer Prize for the series. But then it was discovered the stories were mere fiction invented by the reporter. *Washington Post* management returned the Pulitzer Prize in an aggressive move to reclaim its credibility by admitting the error, apologizing to its readers, and firing the reporter. In the record of *The Washington Post,* the 1981 incident is an isolated one. The paper is considered one of the best publications of its kind, with more than three dozen Pulitzer Prizes since the 1930s. But as the paper that aggressively pursued the Watergate controversy of the 1970s, which resulted in the resignation of President Richard Nixon, it could ill afford any taint on its reputation, which its management recognized is the very heart of any journalism organization. And so it admitted the error and took action to correct it to demonstrate that *The Washington Post* is honest even when it comes to its own failures (Emery & Emery, 1996).

Despite such cases of powerful ethics at work in media organizations, the overall public perception of journalists has deteriorated. A 1997 survey of seniors in 13 high schools across the United States was conducted by *CNN* and *Time* magazine. It found journalists ranked last in trustworthiness behind parents, teachers, doctors, clergy, police officers, lawyers, the President of the United States, and members of Congress. Part of the reason may be the increasing emphasis in journalism organizations on entertainment values, which some critics say has occurred as American mass media scrambled to preserve large audiences in the face of dramatically expanding competition ("Independence Day," 1997).

While the environment of increasing competitors would be an external factor in decline, the reaction to it—as media organizations have embraced more entertainment-oriented news product to preserve share—would be an internal factor. Thus, you can see that while the environment creates causes for decline, how an organization, or an industry, reacts internally directly affects what course that decline then takes.

Sidebar 12.1 The Mugging of FACTS

In recent years American media organizations have undergone a process of consolidation into a relatively few ownership groups. This trend of chain ownership and corporate takeovers has been well documented by Bagdikian (1992). When one company takes over another, decline can be triggered by simple greed. Consider this hypothetical case that parallels real situations in several recent media organization takeovers.

A large multimedia company, we'll call it "Megamedia Unified Group Services" or MUGS for short, takes over a well-established news organization that has shown significant growth in stature and influence. The news organization, "Federation of Accurate Coverage Technical Services," known commonly by its acronym FACTS, has built its reputation as an entrepreneurial culture focusing on no-frills coverage and spurning so-called star reporters. It has become, in a few short years, the news source of record for many people who tune in whenever something big happens because they know FACTS will be there first, with the most comprehensive coverage.

FACTS has a reputation for being fiscally "lean" with fact gathering and news presentations that emphasize coverage and not personalities. Much of its growth has come because it is so different from its major competitors that have become more entertainment oriented with "celebrity" news presenters. FACTS has developed the niche for straightforward and unencumbered news coverage to which large numbers of the news audience turn whenever anything significant happens.

Shortly after the takeover by MUGS, the new owner instituted budget cuts throughout FACTS of 5 percent. MUGS' rationale is the same as in most takeovers. It cost money to acquire FACTS. The shrewd corporate executives of MUGS pass that cost onto FACTS so the company that has been acquired underwrites its own acquisition cost. That way, MUGS maintains its high profit margin, which drives up the price of its stock and, therefore, the personal fortunes of its major investors. This is an accepted and very profitable business tactic and one MUGS has used in repeated acquisitions to become a dominant multimedia conglomerate.

FACTS has always been a "lean" news organization in the minds of its members, who have prided themselves on being economically efficient. The employees perceive the MUGS budget cuts, for which they can see no rationale other than the new owner's greed, as a kind of punishment for doing their jobs so well. FACTS morale suffers. The combination of lower morale and reduced budget for news coverage causes a significant reduction in quality and competitiveness in FACTS.

FACTS slips into type "r" decline caused by problems within itself induced by the new, greedy corporate parent. This scenario is not uncommon. Companies take over other firms all the time. And they do so to take money out of the acquired firm, not to pump money in. But there are serious consequences when the basic mission and corporate culture of the company being acquired are changed by the new owner in ways that negatively alter the essence of its competitiveness.

When a media organization makes the decision to pursue a particular demographic audience, it may set in motion a decline in total share as it repositions itself. For example, an emphasis on newspaper coverage for younger readers means less information of interest to older subscribers even though, typically, more older people read the newspaper regularly than younger people (Veronis, Suhler & Associates, 1996). You may want the younger reader your advertisers seek to reach, but great care has to be taken not to erode your total circulation in the process.

A change in a publication's image alters audience perceptions of it. If the respected financial newspaper *The Wall Street Journal* began running the kind of stories commonly found in supermarket tabloids, it would probably experience a sudden erosion of credibility among bankers, stock brokers, and financiers. Its gross circulation might very well increase in the short term, assuming more supermarket tabloid readers were drawn to *The Wall Street Journal* before the financial news audience began bailing out, but the perception of the paper would never be the same. If a radio station with a country music format suddenly changed to classical music, those interested in the Nashville sound would leave, and the station would have to promote itself to a completely different kind of listener. If a television station has a reputation for depth coverage of significant events, and switches its emphasis to so-called spot news that is less important over the long term—car wrecks, holdups, and other visually dramatic events—it may increase its total audience. But that could happen at the cost of eroding its reputation of being the station of record when a major story happens that requires insightful, depth reporting.

It's very hard, if not impossible, for any media organization in the contemporary environment to be all things to all people. So media increasingly attempt to create a niche for themselves by appealing to specific kinds of readers, listeners, and viewers considered particularly attractive to the advertisers each medium seeks. Doing that without a decrease in audience categories not within the targeted group is very difficult. A publication whose advertisements all emphasize teens and young adults clearly will not be as attractive to those whose age group is not represented, for example, senior citizens. Likewise, the newsletter of the America Association of Retired Persons (AARP) is not heavily read by the 18- to 49-year-old demographic group.

The Effects of the Onset of Decline

Decline is often tied to turbulence, which is present whenever there is significant change and tends to increase uncertainty and anxiety. When that occurs, people react in very predictable ways. They become more conservative in their approach so as not to make further errors. Decision making typically becomes more centralized and conservative in nature as the focus moves from trying to do the right thing, to avoiding doing the wrong thing. Because of increased tension, conflicts often increase among organizational members who may become more inflexible. In turbulent times organizational information flow is often reduced. That occurs because people become more sensitive about what they plan to do. If the organization is going to try something new, managers don't want the competition to find out about it. If they are planning layoffs, they don't want people to be alarmed before the final decisions are made. The organization may also grow more authoritarian and less flexible with a reduction in team or participatory approaches, eroding morale, and reducing senior management credibility among organizational members. In other words, everyone begins moving into a survival mode as they seek to minimize their risk. Just when it is important to foster innovation and creativity, the atmosphere of the organization works against it (Cameron, Kim, & Whetten, 1988) (see Fig. 12.5).

- Uncertainty and anxiety
- Turbulence
- Conservative, defensive behavior
- Centralized decision making
- Conflict
- Decreased information flow
- Authoritarianism
- Eroding morale
- Reduced creativity and innovation

Figure 12.5   Effects of Onset of Decline

CAUSES OF DECLINE

A study across a range of industries determined that organizational decline is usually set in motion by one of three things: (1) technological obsolescence, (2) sociological or demographic changes, or (3) changing fashion (see Fig. 12.6). Additionally, it was found that declining industries experience a loss of segmentation. Firms within a previously stable industry developed comfortable segments for each to dominate. But when one of the three major causes of decline occurred, those firms suddenly found themselves in an unstable environment competing with one another for a dwindling customer base (Harrigan, 1988).

Obsolete technology
Sociological or demographic [age, sex, ethnic group] changes
Changing fashion

Figure 12.6   Major Causes of Decline
(Source: Harrigan, 1988, p. 135)

Factors Triggering Organizational Decline

At various points in their life cycle, organizations are more prone to one cause of decline than another. For example, when they are young they may have greater "vulnerability" before they become well established. Then, the organization has to maintain its "legitimacy" as it grows, sometimes away from its initial reason for being. External changes in the environment may reduce its energy source, causing what is known as "environmental entropy." Finally, there may be a kind of withering away of the organization, or "organizational atrophy," as it just seems to run down (Whetten, 1988, pp. 158–162).

Early in its development the vulnerability issue comes into play when an organization struggles as a new player without the stature and business networks that time helps build. Loss of legitimacy occurs when an organization diversifies so far away from its core business it is no longer recognized as part of a given industry, or when the purpose for which it evolved has been removed. Either the organization redefines its reason to be, or it slides into decline for sheer lack of purpose or confusion within itself about the direction it should go. Loss of legitimacy is most common in public agency decline and reflects the evaporation of a constituency of support due to failure to "cultivate political acceptance" or "shifts in societal ideology." Environmental entropy "comes from the reduced capacity of the environment to support an organization." In such a case the options are simply to trim down to fit the new capacity, or to direct the organization into a new niche of activity. "Organizational atrophy" is manifested in the failure of the organization to grow or develop. It becomes stagnant and begins to, in effect, waste away. In this situation the problems may require a radical new management approach with a new vision and energy to reinvigorate the organizational culture that has become, philosophically, sedentary (Whetten, 1988, pp. 160–162).

Conceit-Caused Decline

Whenever a person or organization succeeds at something, confidence grows. With experience we learn what works and what does not, and there is a tendency to base decisions tomorrow on what worked yesterday. People and organizations develop a kind of conceit as their successes accumulate and they feel more powerful. But the world is a dynamic place, particularly in the evolving world of mass media organizations, where technology is continually being refined and new audience options rise. If not enough attention is paid to the changing environment, the successes of the past can set up a deterioration of the present and future.

When you hear the argument "we've always done it this way," that should be a red flag for you as a manager to question seriously whatever is happening. Conceit-caused decline is steeped in a lack of understanding the dynamics of change present in all organizational environments, which appear on the surface to be stable but are beset with undertows. It presumes what worked yesterday will work tomorrow, and an attitude of "we've always done it this way" is reinforced. The organization, or person, who thinks that way tends to be less sensitive to changes in the environment with a presumption of stability. "As a result, organizations that were the most successful in the past become the most vulnerable to failure in the future" (Whetten, 1988, p. 158).

When bad things happen, people rationalize them by playing down the negatives and emphasizing any positives. This may grow into a conceit of illusion when the glimmer of good news is treated like a win. In the broadcasting industry, for example, it is not uncommon for rating books to be analyzed for key demographics. When a station loses a rating point, the sales personnel usually focus on finding some good news to sell advertisers. Growth in an advertiser-sought demographic—such as the 18- to 49-year-old segment of viewers with high disposable incomes—would be a positive finding. If the overall rating for a station dropped, but the 18 to 49 demographic category went up, sales executives would emphasize the station's increasing strength in that sought after audience category and play down the total ratings picture. A media organization can so accept the mythology of success, based on growth in one area, it fails to attend to the overall slide in most areas of its activity. People in any organizational environment are very good at using whatever information is available to rationalize negative developments. But that rationalization doesn't change the reality (Weick & Daft, 1983).

A classic example of this process occurred in network television during the late 1970s and early 1980s, as discussed earlier in this chapter. Audiences for the traditional networks, ABC, CBS, and NBC, began turning to cable and home video recording (VCR) use. This process is known as audience fragmentation, as the former mass audience breaks up into many smaller niche groups. Network executives focused on positive news, ignoring the harbinger of things to come. One of those was the chief executive officer of ABC, Fred Pierce. The network was being taken over by Capitol Cities Communications, commonly referred to in the industry as Cap Cities. Pierce kept emphasizing positive aspects of network performance to his new Cap Cities bosses, despite a significant downturn in overall network revenues:

> He pressed Cap Cities to look at the brighter side—at the rising profits from ABC's 80 percent ownership of ESPN, the all sports cable channel which was inaugurated in 1979; at the steady cash flow from ABC's five owned TV stations. The drop in ad revenues was temporary, Pierce assured Murphy and Burke. He was grasping for good news. He had even secretly hired a Hollywood psychic. Beginning in 1978, Pierce placed Beverlee Dean on the payroll at $24,000 a year, consulting her in strictest confidence about what programs ABC should schedule, what scripts or actors might catch fire.
>
> While Murphy and Burke did not know of the psychic until after the merger was announced, it didn't matter. By December, Pierce had exhausted their patience. "Fred was a hostage to his experience," said Dan Burke. (Auletta, 1991, p. 114)

DETECTING DECLINE

Decline is a process in organizational life that is not always clear until it is well under way. Different sets of symptoms signal the onset of decline. There are quantitative "economic" signs of decline, and there are behavioral "subjective" clues in the way organization members act. These indicators of decline identified by Guy (1989) are reproduced in Figure 12.7.

The indicators of decline may become evident individually or in any combination. However, in most cases some of both the economic and subjective indicators are present. Generally, the presence of one or two of the indicators in each column would not indicate a serious decline already established. But if three or more in each category are present, the symptoms of long-term decline are building. The order of the factors is also important, because one tends to lead to another. For example, in the left column factors of Figure 12.7 you can see that the initial one is declining sales. That can happen at any

Economic	*Subjective*
• Declining sales	• Loss of prestige or reputation
• Declining market share	• Pessimistic tinge to corporate culture
• Declining profits	• Negativistic climate among staff
• Financial loss	• Perception that firm is in decline
• Declining resources	• Service level inadequacy
	• Unclear priorities
	• Loss of leadership, direction, or goals

Figure 12.7 Indicators of Decline
(Source: Guy, 1989, p. 3)

time, and may quickly reverse itself the following month or two if it is only an anomaly. But if declining sales continue over several months, there may also be a concurrent reduction in market share and profits signaling overall decline.

The same is true in the right column of subjective measures of decline. Just because someone says something negative about your organization does not mean it has a serious loss of prestige or reputation. However, if that perception grows, an atmosphere of pessimism and negativism among organizational members may be created. That, then, may lead to lower-quality work because of poor attitude as the organization founders emotionally.

As the decline indicators accumulate, momentum builds toward failure. The longer it continues, the more turning things around may require exceptional effort and considerable innovation. Some organizations make the decision to reduce their capabilities intentionally to reorient themselves for long-term survivability in an increasingly hostile environment. In other words, they go on a kind of diet to reduce their size and scope as a positioning tactic for future growth. This "suboptimization" strategy was used by the CBS broadcast network in its substantial downsizing process initiated in 1986. The initial wave of 600 layoffs was triggered by declining profits. The network determined change was inevitable. Rather than become a victim of a decline process it could not control, CBS orchestrated its own retrenchment (Guy, 1989).

The environmental conditions within which an organization functions have been shown to be a predictor of its tendency toward decline. For example, a study of newspapers in Ireland determined that economic and political conditions played key roles in the survivability of newly formed newspapers. Stagnant economic conditions, combined with highly volatile political situations, made success less likely (Carroll & Delacroix, 1982). Thus, any sign of operating environment instability should raise alarms about the potential for decline.

REACTIONS TO DECLINE

When decline begins, organizations react sooner or later. Even those organizations with strong cultures and a history of dominating their industry sectors eventually have to come to terms with the forces of decline. It is not uncommon, as discussed earlier, for the symptoms of decline to be treated as mere anomalies, temporary conditions that will eventually go away as the organization gets back on track. Organizational conceit, among formerly dominant companies, resists early detection, which in turn serves to worsen the situation; by the time the decline is recognized for what it is, drastic action may be required.

Coping Strategies

There are five basic strategies to cope with decline, once it's well under way, and limit the damage to the organization (see Fig. 12.8).

Reinvestment Strategy

The first strategy is to increase the organization's investment to regain its competitive position. This approach requires significant financial reserves. It's effective in organizations that are part of larger media conglomerates. A giant company like Gannett has abundant resources to pump into one of its newspapers or broadcast stations that goes

- Increase investment.
- Hold investment neutral until uncertainties are resolved.
- Reallocate investment selectively by eliminating unpromising areas while simultaneously strengthening investment in more lucrative areas.
- Harvesting or spinning off some units as quickly as possible to generate cash with little concern for what the organization will look like when the harvesting is done.
- Divesting, or getting rid of the business, as quickly but as profitably as possible.

Figure 12.8 Decline Coping Strategies
(Source: Harrigan, 1988)

into decline. This strategy, however, is not possible for a media organization without significant resources beyond the affected unit.

Neutralizing Strategy

The second strategy for coping with decline is to hold everything neutral. This approach is effective when it is not clear what is happening to the industry the organization is in, or when there are other uncertainties. This strategy means that although more resources are not pumped into the declining organization, neither are they taken out of it. Every effort is used to maintain the status quo while a complete assessment is made of all facets of organizational activity and its operating environment.

Reallocation Strategy

The third strategy is a selective decrease of poorer performing parts of the organization while increasing investment in those that are more promising. Within an individual media organization, such as a newspaper, that isn't always an option because all of the departments are essential. But in other cases some functions can be eliminated by outsourcing, or subcontracting for them to be done outside the organization. In an advertising agency coping with a decline situation, it may make sense to eliminate a video production department and hire outsiders to shoot and edit video when necessary. In large conglomerates with a number of different business units, eliminating marginal performers is a common strategy. Depending on the situation, spinning off subsidiaries that are not part of the organization's core activity makes sense. Other times the reverse is true, such as when an entire industry goes into decline. Then diversifying the company broadens its economic base so it's less vulnerable to the vagaries of one kind of business sector. The appropriate tactic, as in almost all organizational actions, depends on the situation at the time.

Harvesting Strategy

The fourth strategy for coping with decline is called "harvesting." Here the organization spins off units as quickly as possible to generate cash, with little concern for what the organization will look like when the harvesting is done. This is a fast-moving strategy in which an organization will sometimes sell its strongest asset because it will generate the most money. Harvesting is a short-term approach that serves the purpose of generating capital for what's left when the harvesting is over. The organization then redefines itself based on what it could not sell profitably. The inherent problem with harvesting is that often the best parts of the organization go first. So, at the end of harvesting, it is possible to have only the marginal units left. But cash reserves will be greater, so there will be more resources to shore up what's left to recover organizational momentum.

Divesting Strategy

The fifth strategy for coping with decline is to divest the business as advantageously as possible. In this approach the strategic decision is to shut down and move on to more lucrative types of activity. But divesting is often done carefully, and although as quickly as possible, not at the expense of getting the highest return possible from the sale of all the units. Unlike harvesting, where the aim is quick revenue generation to pump up what's left, divestiture is a complete selling off of all the assets. That means you aren't trying to preserve capital to stay in the same business, but to generate profit on the sale of everything to go into some other activity. Divesting attempts to dispose of everything, but as advantageously as possible. In divestiture a television station group owner, for example, may put the word out that the company's station in a particularly desirable market is for sale. But then the group owner may turn down several offers, and even remove the station from the market, because the company believes the station is worth more than is offered. In a harvesting mode, the group owner of five stations would sell the first 4 to the highest bidders and reinvest the money into the remaining station or other businesses.

Choosing the Right Strategy

Of the preceding five strategies for coping with decline, the most common appears to be harvesting. A study of 60 firms involved in decline situations found that 25 (41 percent) of the companies engaged in harvesting, the largest number in any of the five strategies (Harrigan, 1988).

Company managers often fail despite their best intentions, because of a static view of the environment in which they and their organizations function. Sidebar 12.2 involves a firm that made mechanical calculators. The story is particularly striking to us in the contemporary world where virtually all calculators are electronic, including even small ones attached to watchbands. And there is a parallel in the evolution of mass media, where, at each juncture of new technology, it has first been ignored or discounted in its potential effect but later becomes dominant at the expense of those who did not understand its implications.

Initiating Innovative Thinking

Decline, sooner or later, forces organizations to change. Regardless of the strategy used, organizational thinking has to break out of its previous pattern, which requires new vision. Lack of innovation, or falling into the trap of relying on past practices despite environmental change, is at the heart of the problem. Generally, dealing with decline requires adopting approaches the organization has not embraced previously and that may run counter to the instincts of organizational members.

The tendencies managers have developed as members of the organizational culture may be as much a part of the decline problem as anything else (Meyer, 1988). It is an issue of deeply rooted perspectives, of enculturated sense of rightness in the way to run an organization. When a manager grows within an organization, his or her values and

Sidebar 12.2 Miscalculating Calculators

For most of the 20th century a large company made mechanical calculators in addition to typewriter and office furnishings product lines. It was a highly successful firm. Its mechanical calculators were of high quality and priced competitively, and they dominated the market. Some electronic calculators had been designed by the company's engineers, as they tinkered with the new, infant technology. When the board of directors was asked to approve production and marketing of the new electronic calculators, it declined. The company had put a lot of money into its mechanical calculator production facilities, historically the firm's core business. Everyone in the firm understood how to make and sell mechanical calculators, and the office equipment market had always been slow to adopt new things.

This was in the mid-1960s, and within five years the company's calculator sales had skidded significantly. Previous profit margins were gone, replaced by losses as the market jumped into the electronic revolution. The company response to serious decline was to close the typewriter and office furnishings factories while concentrating on its core business for a half-century, mechanical calculators. The board of directors had initiated the third of our strategies for dealing with decline, reallocation. The problem was they reallocated in the wrong direction, clinging to the old technology and ignoring the new. Three years later, as bankruptcy appeared inevitable, the former industry leader in mechanical calculators was sold to another firm. The board of directors adopted our fifth strategy for dealing with decline, divesting. What had been for decades a major and very profitable business had become irrelevant in just a few short years (Nystrom & Starbuck, 1988).

perspectives are affected by the organization's legends and myths, which produce accepted ways of doing things and perceptions of what works in given situations. That fosters the tendency of senior managers to "misperceive events and rationalize their organizations' failures" as being caused by external forces rather than internal processes (Nystrom & Starbuck, 1988, p. 326). This is particularly acute in organizations that have had substantial success in the past. Argenti (1976) originally identified this success-breeds-failure syndrome in which previous accomplishments create a managerial overconfidence and a sense of invulnerability. "At the point of initial decline management's smugness is such that it has lost touch with internal and external factors necessary for the survival of the firm (i.e., markets, customers, employees, etc.)" (Hopkins, 1984, p. 34). Thus, innovation may be harder to initiate for those individuals who have been members of the organizational culture for a considerable length of time.

The perceptual area appears to be the most critical, as an organization confronts events. Information is filtered and interpreted. The daily flow of ordinary problems and the potential precursors of decline have to be accurately separated. The way individuals analyze and comprehend depends on their perceptual and learning structures. We absorb information from the world around us and use that information to understand and predict. Experience is the primary teacher as myths and rituals are integrated with expectations, plans, social relationships, and all the other influences swirling around us.

Thus, when confronted with new threat events in the corporate environment, for which our previous experience has not prepared us, the tendency is to postpone any radical action with a "weathering-the-storm" attitude. Cost containment, such as suspending or reducing new investments, hiring, training programs, maintenance, and the extension of credit to customers, is usually applied. At the same time, decision making may become more centralized (Nystrom & Starbuck, 1988).

THE SPIRAL OF DECLINE

The process of decline can develop into a self-fulfilling prophecy as organizational members change their behavior. As in our earlier example of the calculator company, decisions can be made that are completely wrong and that accelerate decline rather than counter it. The organization and its members go into a defensive mode rationalizing past failures and making more flawed decisions. In organizational dynamics this "downward spiral" feeds on itself (Guy, 1989).

After an organization gets past the denial stage, where the decline is misperceived as just a temporary problem, the sudden realization settles in that "we're in serious trouble here." That recognition of decline setting in increases organizational stress. A "circle the wagons" mentality is a common defense tactic in which information about the depth of the problem is limited. That can be with the best of intentions—keeping people who are not decision makers from concerning themselves with long-term strategy and thus, keeping their minds on more immediate tasks. But it produces a restricted information flow. As discussed in Chapter 6, "Communication and Power," that spurs rumors, which lead to paranoia and finger-pointing as the situation continues to erode. Collective rationalizations begin to produce myopic decisions within the organization along with a tendency toward "groupthink" (Janis, 1973). That is a group rationalization that individual members would not assert individually. The social dynamics of senior manager decision preferences produce reinforcement by lower managers for political reasons. Like dominoes, one behavior pattern may set up another until there is a downward momentum in the spiral of decline that is virtually impossible to stop (Guy, 1989) (see Fig. 12.9).

As pointed out earlier, in our discussion of advertising-circulation spirals in the decline of daily newspapers, downward momentum builds on itself. In a market with more than one daily newspaper, once the perception arises that a paper is in second or third place, financial problems increase, as advertisers and readers leave it for the number one paper, which also has the economics of advertising on its side.

> As the financial crunch hits, employees feel the pinch. They start looking elsewhere for jobs, since they fear they will lose their jobs where they are. The ones who stay devote an inordinate amount of time to gossiping among themselves about the status of the company, and wondering what will happen next while the firm continues its downward spiral. (Guy, 1989, p. 36)

MANAGING DECLINE

Regardless of the particular form of decline, one of the most difficult aspects of trying to stop, much less reverse, it is getting managers to quit rationalizing negative information symptomatic of the decline. Looking for the silver lining in an otherwise dark cloud can send an organization down the road to self-delusion, which increases its growing predicament.

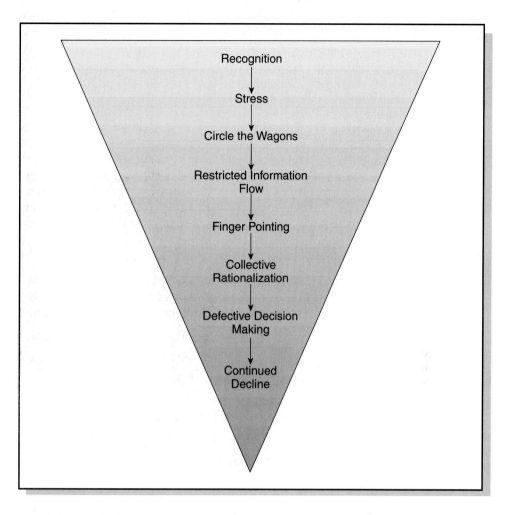

Recognition

↓

Stress

↓

Circle the Wagons

↓

Restricted Information
Flow

↓

Finger Pointing

↓

Collective
Rationalization

↓

Defective Decision
Making

Continued
Decline

Figure 12.9 Spiral of Decline
(Source: Guy, 1989, p. 37)

> In some cases business managers deliberately hide negative financial data so as not to alarm stockholders and bankers. Managers simply will not accept the implications of the negative information conveyed by doomsayers, and they juggle the accounting record until it gives what they are sure is a more accurate (and considerably more optimistic) reflection of the organization's health. (Whetten, 1988, p. 162)

Earlier in this chapter the typical ways organizations react to decline were discussed. Those include reinvestment, neutralizing, reallocation, harvesting, and divesting. But reacting to a decline situation and managing it are two different things. When managers adopt the reactive approach, their thinking tends to be linear, without considering the way decline can be a long-term environmental condition that has to be managed over time. The presumption in the reactive strategies is that decline is here and now, and once dealt with it is over. However, the organizational environment may be such that the conditions for slipping back into decline remain, and that requires a broader, more philosophical approach that fits the organization.

Decline Management Approaches

Four approaches to managing decline have been identified by Whetten (1988). They include: defending, responding, preventing, and generating (see Fig. 12.10).

- Defending
  Rather than adapting to the new situation, the organization "circles the wagons" and tries to fend off as much of the change as possible. Institutions may seek government protection of markets or industry.

- Responding
  Aggressive restructuring in a proactive effort to adapt existing systems and resources to the demands of the new environment. Sometimes crucial mistakes are made in the rush to change.

- Preventing
  A cousin of "defending," this is an aggressive effort to stop whatever is causing the change. Effort is focused on manipulating the environment by whatever means are possible.

- Generating
  Proactive restructuring and redesign of the organization to fit the new operating environment context. Underlying philosophy is that organizations and their environments are dynamic, and always changing, therefore adaptation is a never-ending process.

Figure 12.10 Decline Management Approaches
(Source: Whetten, 1988, pp. 162–166)

Defending

Defending is more common in entrenched bureaucracies or institutions that embrace a particular ideology. Rather than adapting, the organization tries to fend off change that conflicts with its entrenched beliefs. Typically, organizational members are involved because of a higher sense of purpose and will respond to what is perceived as a threat to the institution's integrity. If the decline is in an industry that is, or has been, government regulated, the circle the wagons mentality may surface. There may be a demand for the government to protect the organization as a partner in its social values.

Responding

The second decline management tactic is responding, which embodies aggressive restructuring of internal operations, staffs, production goals, and so on. In effect, the organization attempts to cure the disease by treating its symptoms. That can produce catastrophic results when the symptoms that seem obvious are not the real problems that need to be fixed. A false sense of accomplishment can occur as surface activity is changed rather than the underlying corporate culture. The responding organization may become "leaner and meaner" but still produces the same basic thing. For a time revenues may go up, because costs have gone down, but in the long term it is still the same organization that has not responded, fundamentally, to the changing environment.

A common early tactic in the responding mode, known as "decrementalism," is centered on trimming costs. It is a process of continuing reductions of staff, facilities, and any "nonessential" expenditures such as temporary help, training, expense accounts, travel, and other benefits. Decrementalization is not a radical cut, but normally a piece by piece chipping away at costs, sometimes over years. Although many organizations may have financial "fat" in them that can be trimmed, over time it is possible for such continuous cutting to erode effectiveness, not to mention the negative psychology it creates for employees who keep finding themselves having to do with less over and over again. While "decrementalization may be effective in the short-term when there is a down cycle, it is not useful in serious decline situations when the operating environment of an organization has been significantly changed" (Guy, 1989).

Another common responding approach is for senior management to misperceive the problem as manager centered, rather than organization centered. That usually results in department heads or other middle managers being changed. This is the "bring in some new blood" concept of hiring someone from outside the organization to shake things up and get it going again. However, this tactic has an inherent danger of bringing in "nonright-types, that is people who do not fit at all. Like mismatched blood, the host organism reacts to reject the foreign body" (Schneider, 1983, p. 44).

Preventing

In the preventing approach to decline, the organization does everything it can to stop whatever is causing the change external to the organization. There is little, if any, effort to adapt. The organization tries to make substantial improvement in its immediate competitive advantage. It also aggressively attempts to remove the perceived threat by changing public opinion with marketing and public relations campaigns, generating political influence, attempting to foster shifts in national policy, or whatever else is necessary. In the extreme case, that may include illegal activities such as price fixing and influence peddling. Preventing, as a decline strategy, is externally focused in the attempt to manipulate the environment to the organization's advantage, rather than the organization adapting to a changing environment (Whetten, 1988).

Generating

Finally, the generating approach to managing decline is a proactive repackaging of the organization to fit the new context. This is the theoretically ideal way of coping with changing conditions that trigger decline. The organization analyzes the changes in its environment and then alters itself to fit the new context. It generates a new self to fit the redesigned stage upon which it must function. Such ideal organizations, which appear to this point to be only theoretical, would be highly innovative, set up to respond quickly to the threat of decline through superior flexibility. In other words, generating organizations are extremely flexible without being encumbered by traditional hierarchies isolated by rigid stratification of power, position status, and transference of information up and down a vertical command-and-control organizational structure (Whetten, 1988).

The fundamental problem in any decline situation, as in most other organizational activity, is managing the people involved. And those individuals, regardless of their analytic coolness, are nonetheless governed by emotions. Decline produces effects among those involved that can have dramatic impact on organizational response. Depending on the situation, any one or all of the following may surface in the organization infected with decline:

♦ In order to avoid conflict, managers in decline conditions rely less on participative decision making than they normally would.

♦ Managers are paralyzed by a fear of failure. Hence, they become more conservative rather than more innovative.

♦ Declining profits are regarded as evidence of stagnating management rather than environmental scarcity.

♦ While the stakes for making good decisions increase, the penalties for making bad ones also increase.

(Whetten, 1988, pp. 166–168)

Frame-Breaking Change

To defeat decline in the long term, as opposed to adjusting to it in the short term, the organizational inertia often needs to be substantially changed. Particularly in large bureaucracies, such "frame-breaking change" (see Fig. 12.11) can be difficult since more is required than just small adjustments in the way things are done. Changing the strategy typically requires significant shifts in the organization's structure, processes, and people, in the following ways:

♦ Reformed Mission and Core Values—A strategy shift involves a new definition of company mission.

♦ Altered Power and Status—Frame-breaking change always alters the distribution of power. Some groups lose in the shift while others gain.

♦ Reorganization—A new strategy requires a modification in structure, systems, and procedures. New structures and revised roles deliberately break business-as-usual behavior.

Breaking away from accepted forms and processes to renovate organization according to the immediate demands of the environment, including:

• Reforming the organizational mission and core values to fit the new context.
• Altering power and status relationship—changing the sociology and hierarchy of the organization.
• Renovating systems, procedures, and roles to fit what the situation demands.
• Changing work flows, teams, and other groupings of people to put people in the right places, with the right people, to improve productivity and quality.
• New management and leader vision and philosophy if necessary to pump new life into the organization.

Figure 12.11 Frame-breaking Change
(Source: Tushman, Newman & Romanelli, 1988)

- ◆ Revised Interaction Patterns—The way people in the organization work together has to adapt during the frame-breaking change.

- ◆ New Executives—Frame-breaking change also involves new executives, usually brought in from outside the organization (or business unit) and placed in key managerial positions.

(Tushman, Newman, & Romanelli, 1988, p. 69)

All of this happens within the operating environment an organization occupies, or its niche. That niche is shaped by a number of factors, including the technology the organization utilizes, its culture, and the demand for what it produces. As the operating environment evolves, the organization has only three choices: It can (1) adapt itself within the revised niche, (2) find a new niche to justify its existence, or (3) die. An organizational niche can change slowly, or it may go through more dramatic revolution within a relatively short period of time.

In the slower niche change, an organization that begins eroding does so gradually. This "continuous decline" is a longer process of stagnation. Typically it happens more slowly, takes longer to detect, and is more time-consuming to reverse. When there is conflict in the organization, it is usually tied to the restriction of resources, which the decline or the response to it cause. Internal fights occur over who will end up with the least. There is frequently more centralization in management, in continuous decline, because it is slow. Subordinate involvement in decision making may be retained to some degree, particularly early on.

By contrast, a rapid shift in an organization's niche forces more dramatic reaction. "Discontinuous decline" usually features a sudden contraction of resources. Managers scramble to preserve the organization in a suddenly different and unexpected context. Suddenly put into a survival mode, management style typically becomes more defensive and autocratic. Conflict increases as everyone tries to react to the threat. Organizational psychology changes from a comfortable confidence presuming stability to anxiety fed by uncertainty (Cameron & Zammuto, 1988).

Regardless of whether it's slowly evolving or rapid, when decline sets in, and the organization begins to react, human relationships are affected. Consider, for a moment, how you'd feel if your job was suddenly tenuous, or your boss suddenly changed from being optimistic and coaching to moody and dictatorial. From an individual motivational perspective it is easy to see that coping with decline often results in managers and subordinates alike finding themselves back on the safety and security levels of Maslow's (1954/1970) hierarchy of needs, or Alderfer's (1972) "existence" plane, concentrating on just surviving. See Chapter 3, "Human Influences on Media Organizations," for more on the psychology of the work environment.

There is a natural resistance to change. The past is known, as is the success experienced in the past, and that is used to justify maintaining the status quo. But the natural by-product of resisting change is to hold down the innovation that is needed to cope with the new situation. More pressure to change typically creates increasing rigidity and territorialism as people go into a defending posture to hold onto what they have. Morale deteriorates and organizational harmony dissolves as people perceive themselves, in essence, pitted against one another to survive the inevitable housecleaning. To say that open communication suffers in such a situation is an understatement. Information is power, and with people throughout the organization clinging to any power and influence they have, voluntary information flows virtually cease to exist (Cameron & Zammuto, 1988).

Managerial response is highly variable, depending on whether the decline being experienced is continuous or discontinuous. The range is from relatively tame consolidation of resources to a complete revamping of everything and everyone involved with organizational activity in order to adapt to the new context. The course taken by the organization is situationally dependent upon human dynamics at work within it and the particular operating environment. Therefore, no one way of dealing with decline can be used as a model for every circumstance. Each situation is unique, requiring approaches that fit the situation (Cameron & Zammuto, 1988).

Moving from Decline to Renewal

When decline begins, it has an inertia of its own that carries it along. It is more likely to keep going. So the first issue, once decline has been identified, is stopping its momentum. Because dealing with negative situations tends to make people more defensive, any attempt to stop decline has to start with restoring clarity of purpose, a sense of positive leadership, open communication flows to build confidence and reduce rumors, and an attitude of adaptability. In other words, you have to start with the people and get them positively attacking the problem (see Fig. 12.12).

- Restore clarity of purpose, positive leadership, open communication, and an attitude of adaptability.

- Push management and technology adaptation with aggressive effort to meet the new environment and capitalize on it.

- Positively reinforce individual achievement, self-esteem, and sense of purpose.

Figure 12.12 Renewing the Organization

As decline response begins it has to be on both the external and internal levels to increase awareness of organizational members, identify critical issues, and quickly act upon them. The organizational culture must be reinforced so its basic beliefs and sense of purpose will serve as a kind of glue to hold the workforce together while changes are being made. The fear of uncertainty that can cause a "flight" response has to be dampened so that organizational members maintain a sense of confidence to solve the problem.

The most effective way to do that is through open communication where everyone is informed of as much as possible to reduce rumors and secrecy paranoia. Efforts to move administrative and technological improvement forward are important to maintain an aggressive posture toward the changing environment and capitalize on what it provides to redefine organizational activity positively. In such an environment it is particularly important for management to provide positive motivation for organizational members through recognition of individual achievements. Their self-esteem and sense of affiliation with the organization should be reinforced. An organization that retains the loyalty of members who take pride in what they do is more able to deal with the difficulty of change (Guy, 1989).

Organization decline occurs when there is failure to adapt to change in the domain or niche and the flow of resources is decreased. The general causes of decline include technological change, adjstments in the society in terms of demographics and popularity trends, and shifts in market structures that merge market segments. When faced with decline, organizations tend to initiate one of the following approaches:

1. Increase their investment.
2. Put things on hold until the uncertain environment becomes predictable.
3. Trim away declining segments of the organization to focus on the most positive niches.
4. Attempt to recover investment by dumping whatever they can spin off quickly and then trying to salvage what's left.
5. Begin divesting of the entire organization.

Decline usually occurs because the external environment shifts in a way that is incompatible to some degree with the previously successful approach. When that happens, the internal conditions of the organization change due to the stress on the organization. The combination of external and internal factors, along with the effort to respond to changes brought on by decline increase turbulence. Faltering organizational performance tends to make managers more conservative and autocratic. A circle the wagons siege mentality then may settle in, causing groupthink and other self-rationalizing that only serves to reduce organizational effectiveness in dealing with the decline.

Significant changes in an industry or organizational market niche often trigger decline. Those usually include technological obsolescence, sociological or demographic changes, or changing fashion. When decline begins, organizations are prone to defensive actions to preserve short-term goal achievement as the decline is erroneously assumed to be a short-term anomaly in the business cycle. That tends to accelerate decline rather than slow it.

Decline is encouraged by organizations when they do not understand that all operating environments are unstable and dynamic. It grows through increasingly conservative, protectionist behavior based on the successes of the past, which occurred in an entirely different operational environment. People tend to see the answer to present difficulties in the mirror of their previous experience. They then try to use yesterday's solution for today's problem, which rose out of a different context (Weick & Daft, 1983). Although historical experience is valuable, and often applicable, the successful manager of decline recognizes that the dynamics have changed to the extent new solutions have to be found.

Decline may happen quickly, or more gradually over time. Once started it's difficult to stop or reverse largely because the most common ways of dealing with the problem tend to worsen the situation. They include the following:

1. Management institutes secrecy when more openness and inclusion of organizational members may help resolve internal problems and create new ideas.
2. Extrinsic resources are diminished, so intrinsic rewards must be enhanced to keep people concerned with revitalizing the business.
3. When decline begins, organizations frequently take defensive actions to preserve short-term goals, such as quarterly profits, accelerating long-term failure.

The fact that decline has begun usually means the organization has not evolved as quickly as has its operating environment. One or more of the following steps will typically be necessary to save a declining organization from eventual death:

1. Redefining mission and core values
2. Changing power and status relationships
3. Reorganizing of structure, systems, and procedures
4. Revising interaction patterns, that is, how people work together
5. Bringing in new executives/managers

Organizational decline is a complex phenomenon for which there are no instant solutions or quick fixes. "To manage decline and subsequently resurrect an organization requires expert managerial skill, perception, and control" (Guy, 1989, p. xiv). Stress, tension, and interpersonal conflict increase as the organization is forced to get rid of well-known and comfortable past practices that are no longer relevant, replacing them with the discomforting unknown of new approaches.

Decline can be triggered by forces external to the organization, internal, or a combination of both. The fundamental problem, once it begins, is finding a new vision of where to attempt to move the organization. That is often very difficult since it can involve not just creating new products or marketing niches, but changing, fundamentally, the corporate culture itself, redefining the organizational soul.

1. Identify the kind of decline ("k" or "r") that occurred when newspapers and broadcast network television began their respective slides downward.

2. Of the three main causes of decline, which occurred first in each of the media cases discussed in this chapter, and why?

3. What is conceit-caused decline, and how would you recognize it within a media organization where you worked?

4. If you were a daily newspaper publisher today, what would you do to reinvigorate your business?

5. If you owned a broadcast network, what would be your strategy to turn the decline of ratings around?

6. Have you, after studying the material in this chapter, ever been part of a declining organization? If so, reflect on the cause, or causes, and discuss them with your classmates.

7. What can a media organization manager do to avoid decline?

section 5

LAW AND THE MEDIA MANAGER

chapter 13

FIRST AMENDMENT, LIBEL, AND PRIVACY

Shakespeare (Henry VI) wrote, "The first thing we do, let's kill all the lawyers." He didn't like lawyers, and neither do most people. For media managers, lawyers—and the law—can be troublesome. The media, and people in management positions, can be sued for a variety of harms people think they caused, which means having your lawyers defend your rights. That's expensive, certainly. But, possibly worse, it interferes with your daily operations. People have to consult with attorneys, produce materials such as notes or financial records, be deposed by opposing attorneys and, possibly, appear in court. And when not actively involved in the legal process, you worry about what impact the lawsuit may have on the public's perception of your newspaper or television station.

On the other hand, lawyers and the law protect you. They help ensure that you do not lose lawsuits that, for example, are frivolous or interfere with your First Amendment rights. And lawyers can help you by taking actions against people or companies that have wronged you, from not paying their bills to colliding with your trucks. On the journalism side of the media, lawyers help ensure access to meetings, records, and court proceedings that should be public, and they help protect reporters and editors from having to reveal sources or other confidential information.

If you are in management, then, you can't avoid lawyers. But you will need them less often if you know something about the legal areas that most commonly require legal intervention for media companies—questions involving media content; journalists' access to meetings, courts, and public records; regulations governing broadcast stations, cable systems, and other electronic media; labor law; contract law; and copyright law. This chapter and the next three will discuss these and other topics.

The goal is to make you aware of when to consult with an attorney to discuss possible problems before they arise. Then you can make decisions about what actions to take armed with knowledge, provided by the lawyer, about the potential legal ramifications. The purpose is not to have you believe you know enough about the law, based on reading these chapters, to make decisions without legal advice. When legal issues arise, you should consult an attorney.

Media managers may feel intimidated about dealing with lawyers, even their own lawyers. So they're hesitant to do what they should for fear it will turn into a legal morass. An obstinate employee can become a proverbial "tail wagging the dog" when suggesting he or she will consult a lawyer or sue. But if you have a little understanding of the basic legal issues affecting media companies, on both the business and publication sides, you'll be much more effective exercising your managerial rights and responsibilities.

For example, many managers refuse to give any information about a former employee when asked for a reference. That's because they are afraid that any honest comments based on the facts of the employee's service may bring a lawsuit. Instead, they do one of two things. They simply will confirm a person worked for them. Or they will effusively praise the former employee, if the person was at all competent. The person calling for a reference, then, simply ignores anything said by the former employer, unless the reference is a "rave." Do managers face lawsuits if they are honest about a former employee's performance? It helps you as a media manager to know the answer and to be familiar with many other aspects of the law that affect your day-to-day operations.

Again, these chapters won't make you a legal expert. Their purpose is to let you know when to call your attorney for advice.

This chapter provides background about how courts have applied the First Amendment to free speech issues. Then it deals with defamation and invasion of privacy, the lawsuits most commonly brought against the media based on content. Finally, it discusses whether the media may be held responsible for emotional and physical harms that their content allegedly causes.

THE FIRST AMENDMENT

In many respects, the media are no different before the law than other businesses—a shoe store or a pizza parlor. Businesses have a wide range of laws with which they must comply, from contract law, to tax law, to labor law, to employee health and safety law. But the media are different in one important respect: The courts have found that the First Amendment to the U.S. Constitution gives the media certain rights and protections, even beyond those of other companies or individuals.

We know little about what the framers and ratifiers of the First Amendment (and the rest of the Constitution and Bill of Rights) meant in 1791 when they drafted the language, "Congress shall make no law . . . abridging the freedom of speech, or of the press. . . ." There are no contemporaneous records of the debates that resulted in adoption of the First Amendment (Levy, 1985). Many would argue that, largely, it does not matter what the framers and ratifiers might have meant. What is important is how American courts have interpreted the language during the last 100 years. (Prior to the first decade of the 20th century, few cases arose involving the First Amendment speech and press clauses.)

The First Amendment does not refer specifically to pizza parlors or shoe stores. Not that these businesses do not have the same freedom of expression as other people in America. But it does refer to the press. And courts have extended the word *press* to include the mass media generally. It is true that not all mass media have identical rights under the First Amendment. The Supreme Court of the United States has held that the different characteristics of the various media justify not treating them identically in certain respects (*Red Lion Broadcasting Co. v. FCC*, 1969; *Joseph Burstyn, Inc. v. Wilson*, 1952). But all the media are given some protections not necessarily available to others.

The First Amendment can be seen as both a "shield" and a "sword." It acts as a shield in protecting the press from impermissible government interference and defending it against lawsuits by private individuals and companies. It is a sword when the media use it, for example, to gain entry into courtrooms when judges otherwise would keep out the press and public.

But while the First Amendment's language refers to "Congress" not interfering with expression, the Supreme Court ruled nearly 75 years ago that the amendment applies to all levels of government—federal, state, and local—and to all branches of government—administrative/executive, legislative, and judicial. And the First Amendment applies only to government actions, not to actions of private persons, companies, or groups. For example, it would be nearly impossible for a city's mayor to prevent a television station from airing a story highly critical of the mayor's administration.

However, could the television station's news director tell a reporter—for any reason—that her story about the mayor's administration will not run? Could the reporter correctly insist that, under the First Amendment, the news director can't take that action? The First Amendment simply does not apply to judgments made within a private media company, such as a television station. It protects the station from unjustified governmental interference but does not restrict the station's management from making decisions that, if ordered by the government, would not be allowed. The government censors; editors edit.

Prior Restraint

It has been suggested that if we know anything about what the First Amendment framers intended to accomplish, we know they meant to eliminate prior restraint. They wanted to allow people to print and distribute what they wished with no fear that the government would prevent publication before it took place (Levy, 1985). That is the definition of prior restraint: the government stopping dissemination of material in advance because of its message. This is not a question of "punishment" after publication, such as a libel suit or a criminal charge of distributing obscene material, but preventing people from ever receiving the information.

That is the crux of prior restraint. The government stops publication. No audience is able to assess for itself whether the material has quality or is trash. This is classic censorship—not punishment after something is published, but rather preventing publication at all. And that is why prior restraint is so antithetical to the freedom of expression to which the mass media believe they are entitled.

Prior restraints usually are attempted through a court order called an "injunction." Court orders cannot be violated until and unless they are overturned on appeal. Violation will lead to a contempt of court citation, which may result in a fine and/or jail.

In 1934 the Supreme Court of the United States decided a case involving a Minnesota law preventing distribution of publications containing "malicious, scandalous, or defamatory" material (*Near v. Minnesota*, 1934). (See Sidebar 13.1.) The Minnesota law stipulated that once a publication was banned, it could distribute again only with permission from a court. The government, then, would determine if a newspaper or magazine, for example, could communicate with the public, a decision made on the basis of content.

Sidebar 13.1 When Prior Restraints May Be Permitted

In 1934 in *Near v. Minnesota,* a landmark free speech decision, the Supreme Court sharply limited the grounds on which the government may impose a prior restraint. The case arose when the *Saturday Press,* a Minneapolis newspaper published by Jay Near and Howard Guilford, said that the Minneapolis police chief did not attempt to arrest a "Jewish gangster" who, the paper claimed, ran the gambling and illegal liquor businesses in the city. Near wrote that nearly "every vendor of vile hooch, every owner of a moonshine still, every snake-faced gangster and embryonic yegg in the Twin Cities is a JEW."

Minnesota had adopted a law in 1925 specifically to rid the state of " 'the blackmailing type of publication then prevalent' " there (Friendly, 1981, p. 21). The law made it illegal to publish "malicious, scandalous, or defamatory" material unless the publisher could prove that the stories were true and distributed for good reasons. The catch was that once a publication was found to have violated the law, it could not be circulated again without a court's permission. That meant the government—the court—prevented publication unless it approved of the contents.

The Supreme Court said this was a prior restraint—by a 5–4 vote. If one justice had voted differently, we wouldn't have the *Near* decision to rely on. And rely on it we do—to prevent the government from stopping publication before distribution unless one or more of four narrowly defined circumstances exists:

◆ *National security* would be threatened.

◆ The publication is *obscene.*

◆ The publication incites *imminent violence* or overthrow of the government.

◆ The publication includes *fighting words.*

Ironically, the *Saturday Press* likely was correct in its basic charges: "[T]he crimes it had spotlighted and for which indictments had been drawn began to move slowly through the criminal justice system. . . . There were link[s] between police and mobsters" (Friendly, 1981, pp. 55, 58). But the anti-Semitic language clouded the valid points the paper tried to make.

Fred Friendly's book *Minnesota Rag* is a wonderful recounting of Minneapolis and St. Paul of the 1920s and the Supreme Court's very important decision in the *Near* case.

The Supreme Court saw this as a prior restraint. It held that the government could impose a prior restraint only if it could show that one of four conditions existed:

1. Publishing the material would threaten national security. The Court gave such examples as revealing the location of warships at sea, or the position of troops during wartime. That this did not mean simply embarrassing the government, or the mere possibility of some future threat to national security, was shown 37 years later. The Supreme Court in 1971 refused to allow the federal government to stop *The New York Times, The Washington Post,* and other newspapers from publishing material taken from the Pentagon containing a history of the Vietnam War and America's involvement in it—the Pentagon Papers (*New York Times Co. v. United States,* 1971). A majority of the Court's justices said publishing those documents would not meet the national security standard.

2. The material is obscene. Obscenity is discussed in chapter 14. We can note here that obscenity is difficult to prove under the three-part Supreme Court test (*Miller v. California*, 1973). Nothing in the mainstream media is likely to come even close to meeting the test.

3. The material would incite people to engage in unlawful action. Decades later the Court clarified that "clear and present danger," as it is called, means that a person or mass medium intended to produce immediate lawless activity, and that it is likely the material would accomplish this (*Hess v. Indiana*, 1973). It is more likely that a speaker inciting a crowd to do something illegal would cross this line than would a mass medium. However, the government possibly could stop a radio or television station or cable system, with their more immediate impact than the print media, from airing comments by someone who intended to spur people to take the law into their own hands.

4. The material includes "fighting words." The Court once said that this is language that has the same impact as hitting someone, or that would create a danger of immediate violence (*Chaplinsky v. New Hampshire*, 1942). Later decisions indicate that only the latter definition remains (*Gooding v. Wilson*, 1972). And the Court also has held that racial epithets do not constitute "fighting words," at least under the circumstances present in those cases (see *Lewis v. New Orleans*, 1972).

In another case, the Court said that prior restraint is presumptively unconstitutional (*Bantam Books, Inc. v. Sullivan*, 1963). Essentially, the government must show that prior restraint is justified, rather than the media having to show it is not. That is a heavy burden for the government to carry, and it almost never can meet it. That is not to say, though, that it *never* can do so. The media cannot be complacent about prior restraint. For example, beginning in late 1995, a court order prevented *Business Week* magazine for months from publishing material it had obtained regarding a lawsuit between two companies (*Procter & Gamble Co. v. Bankers Trust Co.*, 1996). The order finally was overturned on appeal.

People have tried to obtain an injunction to prevent publication of material they thought would libel them. However, American courts do not recognize prior restraint as a way to deal with potentially defamatory stories. Libel suits after publication are available, but not an injunction to stop publication.

Licensing is another form of prior restraint. Obtain a license—permission—from the government, or do not publish. And the license will be granted only if the government approves of the material. This method was used in England during the 16th and 17th centuries, and for a time in the 17th and 18th centuries England imposed licensing on the American colonies. Licensing as a means of censorship hasn't existed in the United States for nearly 300 years. But today it is illegal for radio and television stations to operate without a government license. Courts have permitted this for technological reasons unique to broadcasting as a publishing medium. These reasons are discussed Chapter 15.

Taxing the media is not strictly a prior restraint, since paying the taxes allows publication to continue. But imposing high taxes on some media while not taxing others, or taxing others at a lower rate, is an effective governmental tool to effectively put out of business those not able to afford the tax. Taxing was one of the methods England used, at home and in the American colonies, to limit publication.

For more than 60 years, the Supreme Court has ruled that the government cannot impose discriminatory taxes on the media. For example, a state cannot tax newspapers with circulations of more than a certain number while not taxing other newspapers (*Grosjean v. American Press Co.,* 1936). Nor may the government impose taxes based on the amount of paper and ink a newspaper uses, since that would tax only larger publications (*Minneapolis Star & Tribune Co. v. Minnesota Commissioner of Revenue,* 1983). And a state scheme to tax general circulation magazines, but not other periodicals, also was found to violate the First Amendment (*Arkansas Writers' Project, Inc. v. Ragland,* 1987). However, the Supreme Court has allowed a state to tax cable and satellite television subscriptions, in the same way it taxed sales of many other products and services, while not taxing other media (*Leathers v. Medlock,* 1991). The Court said this was not discriminatory taxation since it was not based on media content and did not apply only to the media or to just a few speakers. In effect, you can tax the wire, if done on a nondiscriminatory basis, but not what flows through it, since the First Amendment protects the content.

Permissible Government Restrictions

Courts have held that whether the government may restrict or punish expression depends to a great extent on the government's motive. The government can act because it doesn't like the viewpoint expressed, or because it doesn't like the content, no matter which side of the issue is discussed, or for reasons that have little or nothing to do with what is being said. But rarely will courts uphold government action based on the first two motives.

If a radio station were airing a talk show host who was urging people to pick up guns—right now—and shoot all elected city officials as a way to show their displeasure with the city administration, the government likely would be able to stop the broadcast. At the same time, another talk show host advocating calm discussions with city officials to solve disagreements would be permitted to continue. While the government would be choosing sides, it would have a compelling reason to do so—if it could convince a court that there would be immediate lawless action if the first broadcast continued.

A reason for the government to be able to stop or punish expression based on content must be a compelling one. It cannot be merely because the government doesn't like the views expressed. (See Sidebar 13.2.) The government could not, for example, permit a pro-abortion magazine to continue publishing while shutting down an anti-abortion publication. Preferring one viewpoint to another is not a sufficiently "compelling" reason to abridge the latter magazine's First Amendment rights.

Similarly, the government could not stop or punish publication because it doesn't want the general topic to be discussed, regardless of the viewpoint—unless, again, it had a compelling reason to do so. It could not prevent all media discussion of health care reform, whether for or against it. It may ban all false advertising, no matter what product or service is being advertised, because courts have said not allowing the public to be deceived through fraudulent ads is a compelling purpose.

When the government regulates based on content, courts apply a "strict scrutiny" analysis. That is, they very carefully determine whether the government's purpose was a compelling one, and even if so, whether the regulation is the narrowest possible to accomplish that purpose.

However, when the government is not concerned with content, but with other matters, it needs only an "important" or "substantial" reason, a far cry from compelling, for the courts to uphold the governmental action. This is "intermediate" scrutiny. For example, the Federal Communications Commission (FCC) does not care what content is carried by "pirate" radio stations. If a station does not have a broadcasting license, it

Sidebar 13.2 Limiting Freedom of Expression

Courts have interpreted the First Amendment as limiting—but not absolutely restricting—when government may restrain freedom of expression. And they have used a variety of approaches to determine when the government crosses the line. One way to categorize expression is:

♦ Very important speech: Some expression, such as that about political matters, is considered to have high value, and is highly protected.

♦ Less important speech: Some other expression, such as commercial speech, is thought to have lower value, and is not protected as rigorously.

♦ Speech of no importance: Courts have found that certain expression has no protection, such as obscenity, deceptive advertising, and blackmail threats.

Another approach:

♦ Viewpoint-based restrictions: Courts will examine with strict scrutiny the government's attempt to limit expression based on its viewpoint (allowing pro-abortion speakers, but not anti-abortion proponents) and will permit it only if the government has a compelling reason, and the restriction is the narrowest possible to achieve the government's goal.

♦ Content-based restrictions: These restrictions (e.g., no one may discuss abortion in the city park) usually are not permitted unless the government has a compelling reason and the speech limitation is as narrow as possible. But under certain circumstances a court might permit content-based regulations, perhaps when a certain category of speech (e.g., not allowing anyone to solicit contributions) is restricted in a government-owned area (such as an airport). However, the government could not allow the Red Cross to solicit funds, while preventing Greenpeace from doing so.

♦ Content-neutral restrictions: To impose such restrictions (not to allow distribution of any leaflets in an airport, no matter what the leaflets say), the government need show only an important or substantial reason, and that the regulation does not limit much more expression than necessary to meet the government's goal.

These categories cross: Viewpoint-based restrictions are very rarely acceptable, even if it is not very important speech being limited. On the other hand, regulation forbidding any advertising that says that red meat products are not good for us—while allowing beef producers to advertise— would be found unconstitutional, even though commercial speech does not enjoy the highest level of protection.

---

cannot stay on the air. The "substantial" reason is that pirate stations can interfere with the signals of properly licensed radio broadcasters. The courts have permitted the FCC to regulate use of the broadcast spectrum through licensing.

Also, the city doesn't care whether it is KCBA-TV or KZYX-TV that wants to hold a promotional concert in the middle of the town's busiest intersection at 5 P.M. on a Friday afternoon. The city won't allow either station to do that because of the traffic problems it would cause. Courts call this a "time, place, and manner" restriction. As long as it is applied in an evenhanded way, and there is a "substantial" reason for the restriction, courts will uphold it. But, all things being equal, it won't do for the city to allow a classical music radio station to sponsor a concert in the park, but not a rock station, if both are within any noise limits the city sets for all park concerts.

When courts apply an intermediate scrutiny analysis, they are concerned about constraints on expression limiting First Amendment rights no more than necessary to accomplish the government's legitimate purpose. The city might not permit a concert at a busy intersection on Friday afternoon, but likely could not forbid concerts altogether. The intersection concert might be acceptable on Sunday at noon. And courts want assurance that there are alternatives ways for expression to take place before the government denies a request. If the intersection never is sufficiently free of traffic to allow it to be rerouted and a concert to take place at that location, there would have to be a different site available—perhaps the city park.

There are exceptions to the general approach to free speech just discussed. Courts permit the government to regulate—even ban—some forms of speech based on content, even if there is not a "compelling" reason. For example, commercial speech can be regulated more than some other kinds of expression because courts have said advertising deserves only limited protection. And obscenity can be prohibited completely. Courts have held that obscenity does not warrant being included under the First Amendment.

LIBEL

Libel is a serious problem for those media that report on news and public affairs, and sometimes even for those that do not. Libel suits remain the most common action brought against the media and can be the most disastrous. A small newspaper lost a $9 million judgment and had to be sold. A major city newspaper settled a libel suit—that had gone on for more than two decades—after losing a $34 million jury verdict. A jury told one large city television station to pay $58 million to a district attorney who had sued it for libel. The case was settled before appeal for $20 million. Another jury, which decided that an article published in *The Wall Street Journal* had defamed a company, awarded the plaintiff $222.7 million—the largest award in the history of libel litigation. Two hundred million dollars of the award was for punitive damages. The judge threw out the punitive damages judgment. However, if sustained on appeal, the remaining $22.7 million would be the largest libel award ever. Some media decide it's better to end libel suits than to fight them. NBC paid a reported $500,000 to settle a suit brought by Richard A. Jewell based on news stories about the Atlanta Olympics bombing in 1996.

Studies have shown that the media lose the great majority of libel suits that go to trial, but win most appeals of libel cases ("Reversal," 1996; Franklin, 1980). The problem is that juries both don't like the media and don't understand libel law, while more dispassionate appellate court judges generally do grasp libel's intricacies. But defending a libel action through trial and an appeal is very expensive, mostly in attorneys' fees. Libel insurance may help, but also is costly and often has a large deductible. Many large media organizations simply self-insure.

Media owners and managers cannot claim that since a reporter wrote a libelous story, he must take the blame, and owners and management are free of responsibility. The law assumes that the owners hired the managers, who hired the editors, who hired the reporters—so everyone is responsible. Even if only the reporter prepared and the news director reviewed the allegedly libelous story, and the station's general manager first saw it on the 11 P.M. news with everyone else (and the officers of the company owning the station, located 2,000 miles away, did not see it at all), the libel suit likely will name all those people as defendants (the people being sued).

What about the engineer who is operating the robot cameras and sending the signal to the transmitter? She would not be liable for the defamatory material since she had no control over it. She does not have the responsibility to black out that part of the newscast and, in fact, likely would be reprimanded or fired for doing so. People without power to control content cannot be held responsible for what is published. This would be true of those who operate newsstands or bookstores, for example, unless, under some circumstances, it can be shown that they in fact knew about the defamatory content.

Courts generally have found that when a mass medium publishes wire service stories about national and international news, the mass medium likely can disclaim responsibility for any libelous statements contained in the stories (*Medical Laboratory Consultants v. American Broadcasting Cos.,* 1996). First, it is reasonable to assume that wire services and similar organizations are reliable and accurate. Second, it would be impossible for the media to check on the accuracy of each wire service story they publish. Although not tested in the courts, this may not apply to wire service stories about local, or even statewide, matters.

Libel law's complexity grew over several hundred years as English and American courts tried to balance protecting individuals' reputations against freedom of the press. It is not easy to do that, and many attorneys would argue that the courts have made a hash of libel law by trying to achieve that balance.

Slander and Libel

Slander and libel both are "torts." A tort is the branch of civil (as opposed to criminal) law dealing with harms done by one person (or group, company, etc.) to another. Tort law is controlled by the states, rather than by federal statute. That means defamation law may vary somewhat from state to state. However, the Supreme Court has ruled that in libel law the First Amendment sets a "floor" beneath which states cannot go. That is, the First Amendment limits the states' approaches to libel.

One form of tort is "defamation," injury to reputation. And the two types of defamation are "slander" and "libel." For 300 years, slander has referred to spoken defamation—a person talking to another or to a crowd. This was thought to be less serious than written defamation—libel—because slander didn't reach as many people nor was as permanent. But what does that mean for radio, television, and motion pictures? In most, but not all, states, defamation spoken on these media usually is classified as libel.

Who Can Sue?

Although media managers may think everyone can sue them for libel, that's not quite true (see Fig. 13.1). Individuals may bring libel suits to protect their reputations. Companies, nonprofit groups, and organizations may sue for libel if their ability to operate—such as doing business, raising funds, or gaining new members—is impaired.

But the dead cannot be defamed. Courts have ruled that the dead do not have reputations to injure. Say what you like about the recently departed former mayor, and there won't be a libel suit. However, if the mayor is falsely accused of stealing public money, files a libel suit, and dies tomorrow, the mayor's family generally may continue the libel suit on the mayor's behalf.

A member of the mayor's family may not sue based on a story falsely claiming the mayor—deceased or not—stole public funds. Even though family members may believe the story reflects badly on them, it was the mayor, not the family, who was accused of illegal activities. Of course, if the story had said falsely that the mayor *and* his family were stealing, any member of the family could sue.

- The dead cannot sue (nor can their families or estates sue for them).
- There is no vicarious libel. Even if you think that what was said about someone else reflects on you, it had to have been said about you before you can sue.
- No government entity may sue for libel for what is said about its performance.
- No individual member of a large group may sue for libel based on what is said about the group or, generally, members of the group. But an individual member of a small group may sue. Courts determine whether what is said about the group may "stick to" an individual member.
- Businesses, corporations, nonprofit organizations, and groups may sue. They have reputations that can be injured. Showing an injured reputation involves proving loss of something—money, members, contributions.

Figure 13.1 Who Can Sue for Libel?

But that might depend on how large the family is. It is clear that defamatory statements about very large groups do not allow individual members of the group to sue for libel. For example, reporting that Army officers sexually harass female recruits does not allow any individual Army officer to sue for libel by claiming that he did not engage in such actions. However, a story stating that all the master sergeants at a particular Army base—if there are only, say, ten of them—harass female recruits *would* allow any one of them to sue, provided the accusation was false in that person's case.

How small does the group have to be in order for any member of it to sue based on an allegation about the group as a whole? Courts vary in their answers, although many would agree that a group of 100 or more is too large, and 25 members or fewer likely would be small enough. Between those two approximate points, courts might ask how likely it is that the charge would "stick" to any individual member of the group. To the degree it would, the court might allow any member to bring a libel suit.

The media should not depend on someone being a "libel-proof" plaintiff. (The "plaintiff" is the person, business, or group that initiates a civil lawsuit.) Few people have—according to many courts, no one has—a reputation already so badly damaged that a false story could not injure it further. Occasionally a court will rule that, say, a convicted murderer fits that category. But such decisions are quite rare.

Importantly, no unit of government in the United States is permitted to sue for defamation for comments about how it, its employees, or its elected officials are doing their jobs. Defaming the government is known as "seditious libel." The First Amendment does not permit lawsuits for seditious libel. That is not to say individual government employees and elected or appointed officials may not bring libel suits. They can, and they do.

Suing for Libel

When someone sues a mass medium for libel, the person must prove six elements. Generally, each of these must be proven or the plaintiff cannot win the lawsuit. Quite often, it is the element of "fault" that trips up plaintiffs, but libel cases may turn on any one of the six points (see Fig. 13.2). However, if a plaintiff is able to prove all six elements,

To win a libel case, if the defendant has no effective defense, a plaintiff must show:

- Publication
- Identification
- Defamation
- Fault
- Falsity
- Damages

Figure 13.2 Plaintiff's Libel Case

the mass medium must provide only one defense, out of several defenses that courts recognize, and the defendant will win the case.

Media managers need to be aware of what libel plaintiffs must prove. Only by understanding the elements in a defamation suit can managers decide whether an attorney should check a story before it runs, or whether the story comes solidly within protections for the mass media. But media managers also must realize that even if they are certain they would not lose a libel suit, ethical questions are involved in choosing to publish material that could damage someone's reputation. To successfully sue a mass medium for libel, a plaintiff must prove publication, identification, defamation, fault on the part of the media organization, and falsity. If these are proven, and the mass medium has no defense, the plaintiff may be awarded damages, if they can be proven or if the jury may, and does, assume there were damages.

Publication

To be actionable, a libelous statement must be published. Simply, that means one person—other than the person who propounds the libel and the person who is defamed—must be exposed it. Of course, plaintiffs have no trouble proving this element when the mass media are sued. But if a television station general manager were to send a memorandum to her news director falsely stating that another station's news anchor is having an affair with the mayor's daughter, there has been publication. All it took was for the news director to read the general manager's memo about the anchor. When that happens, the general manager has published a libel.

Most often the media *republish* a libelous statement—but that is enough to make them subject to a libel suit. John Jones tells a reporter that Susan Smith robbed a bank, and a magazine prints that statement. When the magazine is sued for republishing the false statement, it cannot argue that Smith can sue Jones, but not the magazine. Smith *can* sue Jones for slander. But she also can sue the magazine for republishing the defamatory statement. How was Smith harmed most, by Jones' remarks to the reporter, or by the magazine's distributing the false charges to all its readers? Journalists may believe that if they publish the "truth"—it is true that Jones said Smith is a bank robber—they can't be successfully sued for libel. But that is not the truth at issue. The question is whether Smith robbed the bank, not whether Jones said she did.

Identification

A libel plaintiff must show that the defamatory statement was "of and concerning" him. That's why the mayor's family members could not sue based on an accusation that the mayor stole public funds. The charge was against the mayor, not the family. Usually this is not a problem for a plaintiff. Her name, address, occupation, and age are given. There's no doubt who the story is about.

However, a story that the president of Second State Bank embezzled money doesn't need the president's name. There is only one Second State Bank and it has only one president. Identification is clear even without his name. An accusation that "a local bank president" embezzled funds will turn on how many bank presidents there are in the city. Quite likely not more than 25, so the group is small enough that any one of them may prove she or he was identified and sue. Courts require that a few people testify they thought the story referred to the plaintiff, and for the plaintiff to show it is reasonable that they thought so.

If a name is used, but there is not enough additional identifying information to make clear to whom the story is referring, people with that name might be able to show identification. A story stating, "Attorney Shirley Jones was found guilty of defrauding a client," may bring lawsuits from each of the Shirley Joneses who is an attorney in town but was not found guilty of fraud. It is likely that several people would reasonably say they thought the story was about Shirley Jones No. 1, and another several would reasonably testify they thought the story referred to Shirley Jones No. 2, and so on. Properly identifying the person the story is about is the best way to avoid this problem.

Real people can be identified in fictional material. If people testify that they thought a character in a story, novel, movie, or television program, for example, represented the plaintiff, and the court finds such beliefs to be reasonable, identification may be established.

On the other hand, if a novelist—or a journalist writing a news story—sufficiently disguises a person's identity, that person may not be able to prove identification.

Defamation

People sue for libel, in large part, because they believe something published about them hurts their reputations in the wider community. That's what must be proven for this part of the plaintiff's libel case: Does a significant portion of the community think less of the person by exhibiting hatred or contempt toward her, by shunning or refusing to associate with her? The question is not whether the plaintiff is embarrassed by what was published. This element does not concern someone's hurt feelings. It is about what others in the community think of the person who files the libel suit.

Defamation (the same word is used for this element of the plaintiff's case and for the legal category that includes libel and slander) can be apparent on its face. Accusing someone of a serious crime—robbing a bank, for example—is defamatory. Other common instances of defamation include charges of being unfit in a person's profession or business ("Dr. Smith consistently misdiagnoses his patients") or morally reprehensible ("Johnson sped away from the accident scene after hitting and killing the pedestrian").

Or defamation can be "written between the lines." This is defamation by implication. Take, for example, a story saying, "Mayor Bill Jones and city manager Sue Johnson went into the Midville Hotel together at noon and emerged four hours later." If the story did not go on to explain that Jones and Johnson were attending, along with 50 other people, a conference on municipal zoning regulations, it would be reasonable for people to assume they were in the hotel for a sexual encounter. The story did not say that, but without the accurate explanation, it could be found to have implied it.

Defamatory accusations can appear in a variety of ways. They can be found in photographs, cartoons, and headlines, as well as in news and feature stories. However, some courts hold that if a headline seems defamatory, but the story explains what was said in the headline, there is no defamation. For example, a headline might read "Sam Talks to Bill: Jones Brothers Discuss Public Building Sale." If Bill Jones were, say, a city council member, the headline might suggest that attorney Sam Jones is improperly trying to influence his brother Bill on behalf of one of Sam's clients. However, if the story makes clear that Sam had checked with the local real estate ethics board, and Bill with the city attorney, and both were told Sam could negotiate with Bill, then the headline is clarified. What is not clear is whether a court still would allow a libel suit based on the headline. Some might; others would not.

Fault

This is the most complex element of the plaintiff's libel case, and a relatively new one. Until 1964, when the Supreme Court decided a historic libel case brought by a Montgomery, Alabama, public official against the *New York Times,* most courts saw libel as a "strict liability" tort. If a mass medium published a defamatory statement about an identified person, the medium would lose the libel case unless it had a defense. It was strictly liable for what it published. All the plaintiff had to prove was publication, identification, and defamation.

But in the *New York Times Co. v. Sullivan* (1964) decision the Court said that if the mass media—and the public—are to engage in "robust, and wide-open" debate about the government and public officials, they had to have additional protection against losing libel suits. (See Sidebar 13.3.) The court recognized there still had to be a balance between freedom of the press and an individual's right to protect his or her reputation. But it also said that the First Amendment's purpose of allowing uninhibited debate about the country's democratic process meant that public officials had to be open to a certain level of criticism. And this could include mistaken criticism.

The Court's solution was to require public officials to prove "fault" on the mass media's part. The Court used the term "actual malice" for the level of fault public officials would have to prove. It defined the term as the media either (1) knowing the defamatory statement was false or (2) recklessly disregarding whether it was true or false. The public official could prove either to show actual malice.

The first part of actual malice requires showing the mass medium was lying, that it knew the truth but printed a false accusation, anyway. A weekly publication printed a brief item saying that "a boisterous" Carol Burnett caused an uproar in a fancy restaurant by arguing with a well-known person, "traips[ing] around the place offering everyone a bite of her dessert" and "really raised eyebrows when she accidentally knocked a glass of wine over one diner and started giggling instead of apologizing." The person who wrote the item was not at the restaurant, basing the information on "tips." A court found that there was "a high degree of probability" that at least part of the story was invented (*Burnett v. National Enquirer, Inc.,* 1981). The publication, then, could be found to have published with actual malice—with knowledge that the story was false.

It would seem that attributing words to someone that she or he did not actually say would show knowledge of falsity. The writer knew what words were said in the interview, but changed them. But the Supreme Court said, without deciding in the case before it whether words were changed, that there would be actual malice only if, by

Sidebar 13.3 *New York Times v. Sullivan*

The *New York Times Co. v. Sullivan* (1964) case involved much more than just questions of libel. Beginning in the late 1950s the civil rights movement in the southern United States attracted much national media attention. Many southern officials did not want the press looking over their shoulders and reporting to the rest of the country. One way to get rid of the northern press was to sue them out of the South. Several southern politicians brought libel suits against the media based on stories about how blacks and civil rights workers were being treated. One suit was brought by L. B. Sullivan, the Montgomery, Alabama, commissioner in charge of the police and fire departments.

A group of leading southern ministers, including Martin Luther King, had submitted to *The New York Times* a paid advertisement that was printed in the March 29, 1960, issue. The ad, titled "Heed Their Rising Voices," said that Montgomery police had padlocked the Alabama State College dining hall in order to starve students into submission and had ringed the campus. It also said students had been expelled from school for singing on the state capitol steps, and that King had been arrested seven times. Each of these statements was somewhat false. For example, the students were expelled after a demonstration at a lunch counter, King was arrested four times, and there was no evidence the dining hall was locked to starve the students. Sullivan was not mentioned in the ad, but claimed that, since he was responsible for police conduct, he was being falsely accused of wrongdoing. He sued the *Times* for libel. An Alabama jury awarded him

$500,000, and the state supreme court upheld the award.

The New York Times Co. was not then as financially strong as it is today. And $500,000 in the early 1960s was a good deal of money. In fact, by 1964 the *Times* faced eleven libel suits with plaintiffs asking for $5.6 million. Further, other media organizations even less able to pay such awards might have been scared out of the South—as some southern politicians wanted—if the *Times* lost its case. The company decided to appeal to the Supreme Court of the United States.

At the time, the Alabama courts might have been correct in their decisions. Libel could be shown by proving only publication, identification, and defamation. The *Times* did print and distribute the ad, and the ad could be read as saying there was wrongdoing by the police, although the Supreme Court said Sullivan could not show that the advertisement was about him. The *Times* had no defense—it couldn't show the ad was absoutely truthful. However, the Court—aware of the civil rights background against which the case came to it—ruled that public official plaintiffs would have to prove actual malice. The Court said that the *Times* had no reason to doubt what the ad said, and that the errors in the ad were not great enough to find that the ad generally was false. This decision essentially put a stop to the use of libel suits to rid the South of the northern press.

The story of Sullivan and the *Times*, together with insightful First Amendment history, is told very well by Anthony Lewis in his book, *Make No Law: The Sullivan Case and the First Amendment* (1991).

altering the words, the author defames the interviewee more seriously than the actual words spoken would have done (*Masson v. New Yorker Magazine Inc.,* 1991).

The second part of actual malice is more difficult to prove. Essentially the plaintiff has to prove that the mass medium didn't care whether a defamatory statement was false. This would require circumstantial evidence. It is not a question of what most journalists, for example, would have done. It is a matter of what the defendants did. Did they not interview an obvious source? Did they take at face value what an obviously biased source said? Did they fail to check pertinent public records? Did they not talk with the person defamed in the story? Were questions raised in the newsroom about whether the story was accurate? These types of factors and others could allow a finding based on the preponderance of the evidence (the civil trial standard—there is more evidence of A than of B) that the mass medium acted recklessly. Generally, courts hold that just one such factor is not sufficient to show a pattern of reckless behavior justifying a finding of actual malice.

How many factors are needed, and how serious each one is, varies among courts. In one case, involving a newspaper story quoting someone saying that a candidate for a municipal judge's position had used "dirty tricks" to try to vilify his opponent, the Supreme Court emphasized that, among other things, the paper had relied on a witness who had a criminal record and a history of treatment for mental problems, did not interview people who could have countered the story, failed to listen to an audiotape that was made available to the newspaper and contained important information pertinent to the story, paid no attention to the judicial candidate's contentions that the accusation was incorrect, and falsely stated that certain reporters were assigned to conduct interviews related to the story. The Court found this to be clear and convincing evidence of reckless disregard for the truth (*Harte-Hanks Communications, Inc. v. Connaughton,* 1989).

The Supreme Court has described reckless disregard of the truth as being a subjective judgment. Did the defendants in the libel suit have a "high degree of awareness" that the story probably was false (*Garrison v. Louisiana,* 1964) or "entertain serious doubts" about its truthfulness (*St. Amant v. Thompson,* 1968)? What were they thinking when they decided to publish the story? This requires tearing open the journalist's head and looking inside. And the Court essentially has said plaintiffs may do this (*Herbert v. Lando,* 1979). It has permitted libel plaintiffs to ask questions about how decisions were made in the newsroom. Did anyone question the story's accuracy. If so, what were the reporter's and editor's responses? Why did the editor assign this reporter instead of that reporter to the story? Were there any conversations about the story between the editor and the owner? Although the media argue that such questions interfere with their First Amendment rights to make journalistic decisions, the Court has ruled that plaintiffs may make these kinds of inquiries.

Is it sufficient, then, for a journalist to testify that he sincerely thought the story was true? A jury could consider that testimony and believe it. But courts have said that if circumstances show that it would be irrational for a person to have believed the story to be true, a statement that the defendant did think so would not necessarily be sufficient to show the story was published without actual malice.

In large part, plaintiffs have found it quite difficult to prove actual malice. It is a very high standard to reach.

Public Officials In the *New York Times* case the Supreme Court held that public officials must show actual malice on the media defendant's part to prove the fault element. Who, then, is a public official? Obviously people who are elected to office and paid by taxpayers would qualify. But courts have found that neither of those factors necessarily determines whether a libel plaintiff is a public official. Someone can be appointed, not elected, to a public office, or be a volunteer and not paid, and still be a public official. And someone can be paid out of public funds and not be a public official.

Courts have used a number of criteria to define this category. First, the person must have some connection with the government. The president of a private company will not be a public official, at least not without being more than the company president. Second, several of the important factors courts consider are whether (1) the person is in a position of public trust and responsibility, or that the public perceives that to be true, (2) the public would be interested in the person's qualifications to hold office or performance in office, (3) the person has access to the media to publicly refute any defamatory charges, and (4) the person expected to be open to media comment when taking office. A secretary in the district attorney's office, then, likely would not be a public official for purposes of proving actual malice, but the district attorney would be. However, most courts cast a wide net when identifying people connected with the government as public officials for the purpose of having to prove actual malice in a libel suit (see Fig. 13.3).

But it is not always true that every public official always must prove actual malice to win a libel case. Some courts have said that certain public officials have private sides to their lives. For example, if a member of a public parks commission is falsely accused of driving without a license, there may be an argument that the alleged crime has nothing to do with his public duties. If that were so, a discussion about whether he drove without a license would not be part of a "robust, wide-open" public debate about whether he is qualified to hold his position or properly carries out his responsibilities. It could be said that parks often have public roads through them, and drivers use those roads. Or that every public official must be law abiding. On this argument, if the charge were true, it would be relevant to his public position.

But public officials of most concern to the media—from the president of the United States to city treasurers—generally are considered not to have private sides to their lives. Nearly anything published about them—if true—would be important in assessing their qualifications for holding office and their performance of their duties. Therefore, if false, the statements could be defamatory, and the public officials would have to prove actual malice in order to win a libel suit against the mass media.

Public Figures   After deciding the *New York Times* case, the Supreme Court had an opportunity to consider whether the press should have protection to engage in "wide-open, robust debate" about people who are not public officials. The Court decided that some libel plaintiffs are "intimately involved in the resolution of important public questions" or have significant influence over shaping "events in areas of concern to society at large" (*Curtis Publishing Co. v. Butts*, 1967). The Court held that these "public figures" also would have to prove actual malice to show that there was fault on the media's part.

In a later decision, the Court identified two categories of public figures (*Gertz v. Robert Welch, Inc.*, 1974). First, there are "universal," "all-purpose," or "pervasive" public figures (courts have used all these terms to mean the same thing). These are people who, although not public officials, exercise a pervasive influence in society, are recognized as discussing a wide range of public affairs, or continually put themselves in the public eye so that the media naturally cover them concerning a variety of issues. Courts have found Johnny Carson, because of his commentaries on his long-running television program (*Carson v. Allied News Co.*, 1976), and William F. Buckley Jr., because of his opinions on diverse topics expressed on television, in print and in person (*Buckley v. Littell*, 1976), to be all-purpose public figures. Some, but not all, courts have found celebrities to be universal public figures simply because they are celebrities. This would include movie and television stars, athletes, and popular musicians, among others. But the Supreme Court has ruled that this does not include people who may be prominent in their own fields, but not necessarily known by the general public. (See Sidebar 13.4.)

To confuse things further about all-purpose public figures, some courts have found that general notoriety can be within, say, a city. It need not be on a regional or national basis, and a libel plaintiff still can be categorized as a universal public figure. One court applied the concept to an unsuccessful U.S. Senate candidate who also formerly headed the state Republican Party, wrote books about investments, and was the focus of magazine articles. He was found to be a pervasive public figure in the state (*Williams v. Pasma*, 1982). Some courts have found corporations to be universal public figures (*Stolz v. KSFM 102 FM*, 1994), while others have rejected the notion (*Blue Ridge Bank v. Veribanc., Inc.*, 1989).

By far the most common kind of public figure is a "limited purpose" public figure. The Supreme Court has defined this category as a person who voluntarily thrusts herself into a public controversy in order to influence its outcome (*Gertz v. Robert Welch, Inc.*, 1974). For example, a person who regularly writes and speaks about making abortion illegal with the intent of accomplishing that goal, is a limited purpose public figure *for the subject of abortion*. That is what "limited purpose" means. She is not a public figure for any topic other than abortion. If she sues a radio station for a false report that she once had an abortion, she would have to prove actual malice. But if she sues that station for a false report that she robbed a bank, she would not be a public figure and would not have to prove actual malice. Robbing banks has nothing to do with the abortion controversy. However, if the charge were that she robbed banks to finance her anti-abortion campaign, that would lead to a different conclusion.

The plaintiff's attempt to prove fault is a key to many libel cases. Here's the way to think about fault:

- Into which category does the plaintiff fall?
  —Public official
  —Public figure
    - Universal public figure
    - Limited purpose public figure
    - Involuntary public figure
- What level of fault does the plaintiff have to prove?
  —Actual malice (lying or reckless disregard of the truth)
    - Public official
    - Public figure
  —Negligence (mistake that a reasonable person wouldn't make)
    - Private individuals (in most states)

Figure 13.3 Fault in Libel Cases

Sidebar 13.4 The Private Individual: Elmer Gertz

Elmer Gertz is a prominent Chicago lawyer. He has published book reviews, magazine articles, and a weekly paper and has taken on civil rights cases. In 1968 he agreed to represent a family whose son was shot by a Chicago policeman while, according to the police, the boy was fleeing from a crime. The policeman was found guilty of second-degree murder, and the family brought a civil suit against the policeman in which Gertz represented them.

The John Birch Society, a politically conservative group, published a magazine, *American Opinion*. An article about the trial published in the magazine in 1969 charged that Gertz was involved in a "frame-up" against the policeman, called Gertz a "Leninist," a member of the Marxist League, and a "Communist-fronter," and said he was part of a conspiracy to undermine local police. Gertz sued for libel.

The case eventually found its way to the Supreme Court, which ruled that Gertz was a private individual, not a public figure. Why would such a visible person not be a public figure? The Court said he was not a universal public figure because, although he was "well known in some circles, he had achieved no general fame or notoriety in the community." Was he a limited purpose public figure? No, said the Court, because he did not put himself in the middle of the controversy over the policeman's shooting of the boy, except to work at his profession, as a lawyer. He didn't talk to the press about the case, or write publicly about it. That meant he was a private individual for the false statements made about him and would have to prove only negligence on the magazine's part. He was able to do that.

Gertz himself tells the story in his book *Gertz v. Robert Welch, Inc.: The Story of a Landmark Libel Case* (1992).

Courts have found that people arrested for a crime have not become limited purpose public figures simply by being arrested (*Wolston v. Readers Digest Association*, 1979). And someone who sues for divorce has not become a limited purpose public figure by virtue of using the court system (*Time Inc. v. Firestone*, 1976). Generally, owners and managers of businesses, and the companies themselves, are not limited purpose public figures simply because they do business with the public. It might be different if they deliberately thrust themselves into public controversies or are particularly assertive in how they deal with the public (*Sunshine Sportswear & Electronics Inc. v. WSOC Television, Inc.*, 1989). (See Sidebar 13.5.)

The Court also noted that there may be rare occasions when a person becomes an "involuntary" public figure. For example, a court might find that someone acting heroically in a plane crash could become a public figure without intending to. However, few courts accept this category of public figure.

Private Individuals   If a libel plaintiff is not a public official or public figure, she falls into the only other category—private individual. The Supreme Court has decided that, although defamation is a state tort and states have leeway to handle it as they choose, the First Amendment sets certain requirements when anyone sues the media for libel (*Gertz v. Robert Welch, Inc.*, 1974). Again, to balance reputational rights against freedom

Sidebar 13.5 Limited Purpose Public Figures

A doctor in residency at a public university medical school wrote an opinion piece about homosexuality for a local newspaper. She also appeared on radio programs discussing the same topic. The paper printed letters to the editor sharply critical of the opinions she expressed, saying, for example, that she had presented "lies." Based on the letters, she sued the newspaper for libel.

The court considered five factors in determining whether she was a limited purpose public figure or a private individual:

1. Did she have *access to the media* to present her views? Yes, she wrote an opinion piece for the paper and was on radio programs.

2. Did she *thrust herself into a public controversy?* Yes, by public expressions of her opinions about a controversial topic, homosexuality.

3. Did she *try to influence the outcome* of the controversy? Yes, her opinion piece purported to present evidence that very few people are born predisposed to be homosexuals.

4. Did the *controversy preexist* the defamatory publications? Yes, the controversy over homosexuality existed long before the critical letters were printed.

5. Was the plaintiff *still involved in the controversy* when the defamatory statements were made? Yes, she still was agreeing to speak publicly on the issue when the letters were printed.

Applying these factors to the plaintiff's situation, the court found her to be a limited purpose public figure for the statements made in the letters (*Faltas v. State Newspaper,* 1996). Other courts have used this test, or similar ones.

---

of the press, but this time with less concern for "robust, wide-open debate" of public issues, the court said that no one may win a libel suit against the media without showing some form of fault. Public figures and public officials under most circumstances must prove actual malice. What do private individuals have to prove?

The minimal form of fault is "negligence." Most states have adopted this level of fault for private individuals. To establish negligence, a plaintiff must show that a journalist didn't act as a reasonable person would have in the same situation, or didn't comply with accepted journalistic standards. Courts have used both the "reasonable person" and "reasonable journalist" tests. Courts do not agree which of the two tests should be used, or even if there is a difference between the two. Negligence could include a reporter copying down an incorrect name in preparing a story on a criminal trial. Or typing an incorrect name into the reporter's computer. Or not contacting an important source. A reasonable reporter would have taken more care. If a private individual plaintiff proves that such negligence led to a defamatory story, the plaintiff has shown fault.

New York has adopted a fault standard for private plaintiffs—"gross irresponsibility"—that falls between negligence and actual malice. Four other states (Alaska, Colorado, Indiana, and New Jersey) have decided that all plaintiffs—public and private alike—must prove actual malice when suing the media for libel. Courts in four states (Connecticut, Louisiana, Montana, and New Hampshire) have not yet decided which libel fault standard to apply to private plaintiffs (McCrory et al., 1996).

Falsity

At one time, the media could prove the "truth" of a story as a defense to a libel suit. However, in the series of cases establishing that public officials and public figures must show actual malice—essentially that the story was false, and that the defendant knew that or recklessly did not care—the Supreme Court made clear that such plaintiffs would have to show falsity, rather than the defendant proving truth. But that left the question of whether private individuals suing the media would have to prove the story was false.

The Court said that when truth or falsity is clear, it doesn't matter who has the burden to prove truth. But when it is unclear, and if the media have to prove truth, stories might not be reported because of fear that the media could not prove truth. Truth, after all, is an elusive concept, and showing that a story is precisely true may be an insurmountable obstacle. Therefore, the media might choose not to carry a story involving a private individual (*Philadelphia Newspapers, Inc. v. Hepps*, 1986). But, the Court said, this would inhibit the media's First Amendment rights. To prevent that, the Court ruled that even private individuals suing the media for libel would have to prove falsity.

Courts have found that stories do not have to be "true" to the last letter. It is the gist of the story that is at issue, the final idea left by the article. A story saying that "Jones stole $800 from First State Bank," when in fact Jones stole $700 from Second State Bank, likely would not be found "false." Courts ask whether the public perception of the plaintiff would be different if the precise truth were reported rather than the story that was published. Would the public think less of Jones because he was said to have stolen $100 more than he actually did and from a different bank? Of course, if the story had said "Jones stole $800 from First State Bank and shot a guard in his escape," and Jones in fact did not shoot anyone, the situation would be quite different.

Damages

Although plaintiffs sue the media for libel to clear their names, most plaintiffs also look for monetary damage awards. Concerned with the media's First Amendment rights, the Supreme Court has limited the types of damage awards certain libel plaintiffs may receive (*Gertz v. Robert Welch, Inc.*, 1974).

Any plaintiff who wins a defamation case against a mass medium is entitled to "actual" damages. These include damages for emotional suffering due to the libel. Also, any winning plaintiff may receive compensation for monetary losses directly attributable to the defamation, such as business losses or doctor's bills (called "special" damages).

However, plaintiffs often want more than compensatory damages; they want punitive damages. They want to punish the media that defamed them, and juries often want to make examples of the media so that others will not act in the same way. Punitive damages can be very large, much higher than compensatory damages. The Supreme Court generally has not found reason to overturn high punitive damage awards, although in a 1996 decision it said, without defining the term, that "grossly excessive" punitive awards would not be permitted (*BMW of North America, Inc. v. Gore*, 1996).

Again balancing plaintiffs' and the media's rights, the Court has ruled that when the media act in an egregious manner—publishing with actual malice—punitive damages may be awarded. This means any public official or public figure winning a libel case against the media could be granted punitive damages, since they have to show actual malice to get past the "fault" element. In nearly all states a private individual may win by showing a fault level less than actual malice, usually negligence. But private individuals also may attempt to prove actual malice in order to ask for punitive damages.

Additionally, juries may decide that, even if a plaintiff is unable to prove she was damaged by the libelous publication, the plaintiff deserves compensation. The jury then may award "presumed" damages—that is, presuming what damages a person normally would have suffered due to such a defamatory statement. However, the Supreme Court has limited presumed damage awards only to those plaintiffs proving actual malice.

Judges have the power to lower damage awards by juries when the damages are excessive. This allows a judge to temper a jury's passions. Appellate courts also may decrease damage awards.

Defenses Against Libel Suits

Those suing the media for libel must prove each of the plaintiff's elements, but the media need only prove one defense to win the case. Some defenses to libel actions are based on centuries of English law, as adopted in the United States. Others come from the Supreme Court's interpretation of the First Amendment. Regardless, only one of the following needs to be proven by libel defendants to win the case:

1. The statute of limitations has passed for filing the suit.

2. The plaintiff consented to publication.

3. What was said is true.

4. What was said is "privileged" against defamation suits.

5. It was "fair comment."

6. The defamatory material was protected "opinion."

7. The "neutral reportage" defense applies.

8. The "mutual interest" privilege applies.

Statute of Limitations

All states require that lawsuits be brought within a specified period of time from the event prompting the action. For libel, that period often is one year, but may be two or three or up to five years. That is, if a libelous statement is published in a newspaper on April 30, in many states a libel action would have to be filed by April 29 of the following year. If it isn't filed within the specified time period, then it can't be filed at all. This is called a "statute of limitations."

However, a lawsuit can be filed wherever the defamatory statement circulates. If the newspaper also circulated in a state with a three-year statute of limitations for libel actions, a suit could be filed in that state even if the one-year period were missed in the first state. For national publications and electronic media programs, a plaintiff may select the state with the longest statute of limitations, if she chooses to do so.

Consent

Generally, courts have held that a person cannot give an interview or agree to have a story published and then bring a libel suit based on an accurate story. Essentially, knowingly talking with a reporter is giving consent to publication of a fair piece reflecting information provided in the interview. Consent is a defense to a libel suit.

Certain people cannot give consent legally—minors, the mentally incapacitated, those too inebriated. And consent can be challenged in court. A reporter may have to prove consent was given, perhaps by providing an audiotape or videotape of the interview, or by a signed statement by the plaintiff, or by putting the reporter's word against the plaintiff's. There is no certainty a jury will believe a reporter instead of a plaintiff.

Truth

Although truth remains a defense against a charge of libel, in most cases the plaintiff must carry the burden of proving falsity. Therefore, any reason for the defendant to prove the truth of a story likely will arise to counter the plaintiff's evidence that the article was false. A few states' laws permit truth as a defense only if the publication was made with good intentions or for the public good.

Privilege

The law long has recognized that it benefits the public if the media have a privilege to publish certain defamatory material, although this privilege may be lost under certain circumstances. Usually this privilege arises when the press is reporting on statements by people with a different privilege, one that cannot be lost.

In certain situations some people have an absolute privilege against being sued successfully for libel. These individuals cannot lose the privilege as long as they are acting within its limits, regardless, for example, of why they said the defamatory statement. This right is granted because society believes that, on balance, it is better for some people to suffer injured reputations than to have individuals in certain positions not carry out their responsibilities because of a fear of being sued for libel.

First, some public officials are absolutely protected from losing libel suits if they defame someone in the course of performing their jobs. The U.S. Constitution explicitly protects U.S. senators and representatives when they speak on the floor of their chambers. Courts have extended this to official transcripts of their remarks, and to statements made when they are engaging in their official duties in any other way. For example, a senator sitting on a Senate committee who says to a witness, "I believe you are a member of organized crime," would be immune from a libel suit brought by the witness.

Many federal officials have an absolute privilege within the context of their authorized duties. A number of state public officials also do. The privilege is granted by statutes or in constitutions in some states, and by judicial rulings in others. In some states, only top-level officials have absolute privilege, while in others, as on the federal level, the privilege stretches well down the ranks. In many states, some officials on the local level, such as in cities and counties, also are absolutely privileged for comments made within the realm of their responsibilities.

Second, participants in judicial proceedings have absolute privilege as long as their remarks are part of the process. Witnesses, attorneys, parties, and judges, for example, all are free to say what they will. But the privilege ends when they step onto the steps of the courthouse. There, an accusation that "William is the murderer" will not be absolutely privileged, since in that circumstance the statement does not further the judicial process. This privilege applies to documents filed with the court and to pretrial proceedings. In most states and in federal courts, the privilege begins when the lawsuit initially is filed. In criminal matters, the privilege often begins when an arrest is made.

Third, most courts hold that participants in official governmental meetings have absolute privilege. A person appearing before the city council and accusing his neighbors of dealing drugs likely will have protection against losing a libel suit based on that charge. Some states also grant a privilege for participants in meetings of unofficial groups, such as unions or parent-teacher associations if the discussion concerns matters of public concern.

Also, records prepared by public officials in their line of responsibility are absolutely privileged, just as if the officials had said orally what the documents say on paper. This often is called "record privilege."

All this is important to the media because the press draws its "conditional privilege" or "qualified privilege" from the absolute privilege of others, or from record privilege. That is, journalists are privileged to report on absolutely privileged information—but journalists are not absolutely privileged. They can lose their conditional privilege for several reasons (see Fig. 13.4).

If a libel plaintiff proves each of the six elements in her case, she has not necessarily won. The media defendant will win the case if it can show just one of several defenses. A defense commonly used is privilege:

- Absolute privilege (not for the press, but what the press relies on)
  —Many federal and some state public officials
  —Participants during the course of judicial proceedings
  —Participants during the course of official government meetings
  —Official records
  —Possibly participants during the course of meetings of unofficial groups

- Journalist's qualified, or conditional, privilege, based on absolutely privileged material
  —Must be a fair and accurate report
  —Must be attributed to its source
  —Must not be based on ill will or other forms of malice (some courts require this)

- Fair comment

Figure 13.4 The Qualified Privilege Defense

The privilege will be lost if the story is not a fair and accurate representation of the absolutely privileged material. A biased or false account would defeat society's goal of wide dissemination of absolutely privileged statements. The story need not be precisely accurate, but significant errors of fact that distort the original material may cause the article to lose its conditional privilege.

Generally, courts also demand that material be attributed to its privileged source in order for the article to have conditional privilege. The point is for the public to know with whom the remarks originated. Thus, a reporter covering a trial may explain what was said in court, or appears in court documents, even if those things are later proved to be false. The key is attribution to the privileged source. The reporter should say,

"According to the police report . . .," or "Witness Sally Doe testified that. . . ." In other words, when a journalist reports what a witness says in court, if the reporter attributed the statements to the source, the news organization likely will not lose a libel suit if the statements turn out to be false and defamatory.

A few courts also still retain a rule that ill will, hate, or spite on the part of the press, called "common law malice," will defeat a conditional privilege.

Fair Comment

Another type of conditional privilege is called "fair comment." This protects people who publicly express their views about a wide variety of matters that invite comment. The law assumes that those who write books, perform music, operate restaurants, act, or in other ways put their work before the public should expect people to react to this creative work, sometimes harshly. It is the fair comment privilege that protects published reviews about movies, novels, plays, recordings, eating places, and so on.

This, too, is a conditional privilege. It can be lost in several ways, but most importantly by the reviewer not stating clearly the basis for his views. It is important for the public to know what the reviewer thinks, but it is equally important for members of the public to make up their own minds. They can do that only if they know why the reviewer came to his conclusions. Therefore, fair comment may not protect the bald statement, "The chef is the worst in the city—no, in the country," unless the reviewer explains why he thinks that about the chef. For example, the reviewer might say, "The chicken was dry and stringy, the sauce thick and lumpy, the asparagus cooked until limp, and the potatoes not cooked long enough." A reader might like her food prepared that way and could disagree with the reviewer's judgment about the chef's abilities. But the reviewer likely could claim fair comment because he explained the reasons for his views.

Opinion

The Supreme Court has said that "opinion" is protected by the First Amendment (*Gertz v. Robert Welch, Inc.*, 1974; but see *Milkovich v. Lorain Journal Co.*, 1990). That makes opinion a constitutionally based defense to a charge of defamation. (See Sidebar 13.6.) The problem is in determining what constitutes "opinion."

It is not sufficient simply to preface a defamatory statement with the words, "In my opinion," or "I think that." The opinion defense isn't available to defend the remark, "In my opinion, Lucille shot Ted." That is a statement of "fact." Of course, it must be "false fact" for a libel suit to be successful. If it were true, Lucille could not prove falsity, and therefore could not win a libel action. It is strange to talk of false fact, since we usually think of facts as being true. But false fact means that the statement contains a factual assertion—Lucille shot Ted. Factual assertions can't be opinion. If a statement can be proven true or false—Lucille did or did not shoot Ted—it is not a statement of opinion. But note that this does not mean that it is true that "my opinion is that Lucille shot Ted." That may be the speaker's opinion, but what is at issue is whether it is true that Lucille shot Ted.

Words without clear meanings may be opinion, depending on the circumstances. In a heated public meeting, calling someone a "blackmailer" may not be taken literally (*Greenbelt Cooperative Publishing Association v. Bresler*, 1970). It is just an epithet, a word meaning, "I'm very mad at you." Similarly, in the middle of a labor dispute, calling someone a "traitor" does not mean the person turned on her country (*National Association of Letter Carriers v. Austin*, 1974). Such words are used figuratively to show anger.

Sidebar 13.6 The Opinion Defense

In the *Gertz* case, the Supreme Court said "there is no such thing as a false idea." Courts understood this to mean that opinion is absolutely protected under the First Amendment. Later, the Supreme Court modified this a bit, but the notion still stands: Opinion is protected under the Constitution. This means the opinion defense is not conditional or qualified; it cannot be lost. The problem is determining what is a statement of *opinion,* and what is a statement of *fact.* Some are obvious: "I don't like ABC's vanilla ice cream," is a statement of opinion. But, "Sam robbed the bank," is an assertion of fact. What if Sam did not rob the bank? It's still an assertion of fact, but of "false fact." And a statement of "false fact" could be the basis of a libel suit. If you say, "In my opinion Sam robbed the bank," it still is a statement of fact—of false fact—because courts find that an accusation of committing a crime cannot be a statement of opinion, no matter what words (such as, "I believe") precede the accusation.

But many statements aren't clear. What if you wrote about a touring stage production, "It is a rip-off, a scandal, a snake-oil job"? Is that a statement of fact—maybe false fact—that the show's producers are defrauding the public, perhaps by promising or implying one thing, but presenting another? Or is it a statement of opinion that you think the show is of poor quality (*Phantom Touring Inc. v. Affiliated Publications,* 1992)? A number of courts have used a four-part test, trying to balance these factors to determine if the allegedly defamatory statement is one of fact (maybe "false fact") or opinion:

1. Do the words have a generally accepted meaning? Does the word *slumlord* have a dictionary definition? Is it one on which most people agree? The more the words can clearly be defined, the more likely it is the statement was one of fact.

2. Can the statement be verified? If it can be proven true or false, it is more likely to be a statement of fact. Opinions cannot be verified. If the word *slumlord* can be defined, it probably could be proven that the plaintiff is or is not one.

3. In what context did the statement appear? If it was part of a story on the 11 P.M. news, it is more likely to be seen as a statement of fact. If it was part of a commentary, perhaps it is more likely to be taken as opinion.

4. What was the setting of the statement? Things said during the heat of a student protest over sharply raised tuition may not be taken as statements of fact. But there would have been time to dispassionately consider something printed on a newspaper's front page, and therefore it more likely would be seen as a statement of fact (*Ollman v. Evans,* 1984).

Importantly, the Supreme Court has said that a statement of opinion that *implies* a defamatory statement—perhaps by not explaining the basis of the opinion—is not protected (*Milkovich v. Lorain Journal Co.,* 1990). "I think it might be dangerous to eat at the ABC Restaurant," seems to be a statement of opinion. However, it could be taken to mean that the food will poison you. That's an implied defamatory statement. Instead, if you explained that you meant the delicious food will cause you to return often—thus depleting your bank account—no defamatory implication could be found.

Also, where and how a statement is published may help indicate that it is opinion. A statement that "John Jones is pulling a fraud on the public by selling shares in his golf club" may be seen as a statement of fact if it appears on the front page of a newspaper. Front pages are intended to carry factual material. But if the statement were part of an editorial on the paper's editorial page, the word *fraud* might be seen as an exaggeration used for effect.

One commonly used test courts apply to determine whether a statement is one of fact (maybe false fact) or opinion is this: First, do the words at issue have clear meanings? The word *shot* is clear, while the word *pretty* is not clear. What is pretty to you may not be to someone else. The more clear the words, the more likely that the statement is one of fact. Second, can the statement be proven true or false? You can prove whether "Lucille shot Ted" is true. You can't prove that a flower is pretty.

Third, where did the statements appear? Stories in a newspaper's "world news" section are expected to be factual. However, statements on the paper's editorial page are not. Fourth, what is the broader context of the statements? If the words were printed on fliers and distributed during a labor strike, they might be taken as overstatements, as exaggerations—as opinions. But words in a flier distributed at a scientific conference are expected to be more considered.

Courts will balance these four factors and determine whether the statements are more like opinion or more like facts. But even if found to be statements of fact, they may turn out to have been false, as they would be if Lucille did not shoot Ted.

Courts will not accept an assertion that a statement is opinion if the statement suggests defamatory facts. For example, Rod writes, "I saw Mary come out of a bar at midnight last Monday. I don't think she'd make a good accountant." On one hand, it is an opinion that Rod doesn't think Mary would "make a good accountant." But why? It is quite easy to assume it is because Rod thinks Mary is a drunk. After all, it was because she came out of a bar at midnight that Rod formed his opinion. But what if Rod really meant that anyone who stays out until midnight on a work night couldn't focus on her work the next morning? If that is what Rod meant, if that was the basis of his opinion, he should have said so. By not stating the factual basis of his opinion, he allowed people to assume that he meant something defamatory—that Mary was a drunk. Rod could have said, "I saw Mary come out of a bar at midnight last Monday. I think anyone who stays out that late couldn't concentrate on her work the next day. I don't think she could tell one number from another through sleepy eyes. I don't think she would make a good accountant." Now that we know the basis for his opinion, it would not be reasonable for someone to assume Rod meant Mary was a drunk.

Also, the facts backing up an opinion must be accurate, and they must reasonably lead to the opinion. It won't do to say, "Mary is a 35-year-old accountant, and therefore I think she drinks too much." The facts do not reasonably lead to the conclusion. Being 35 years old has nothing to do with drinking too much. It is different to say, "Mary has a drink before breakfast, drinks heavily during the day and has dropped out of Alcoholics Anonymous several times. I think she drinks too much." The facts (if they are true) properly lead to an opinion.

Neutral Reportage

A few courts, but only a few, will accept "neutral reportage" as a defense (see *Edwards v. National Audubon Society, Inc.,* 1977). This may arise in a situation in which one prominent person or organization accuses another of something that is defamatory. The news media want to report the story. But if they republish the libel, they can be sued for defamation. Arguing that "We just reported that Pat said Simon is a thief" is not a defense. Publishing that statement in a newspaper, if it is false, allows Simon to sue the paper for libel—for disseminating the incorrect statement that he is a thief. But shouldn't the public know when a well-known person or group is saying false things about another?

Several courts have agreed that the First Amendment should protect such reporting if, first, the individuals or groups are prominent; second, the public should know about what is being said; and, third, the media report in a "neutral" way, that is, without expressing an opinion about what is being said. However, only a handful of courts will permit this defense.

Privilege for Mutual Interest

A privilege that relates to journalistic endeavors, but also is important for business matters, is one the courts recognize for "mutual interest." This applies in two ways. First, internal discussions about a proposed story may involve defamatory remarks being said or written within the newsroom. Because these statements are for the speaker's or writer's and receiver's mutual interest—making decisions about how the story should be investigated and written, and whether it should be published—they likely are privileged.

Second, a written or oral reference for a current or former employee may contain defamatory statements. But it probably is protected because of the mutual interest of the person requesting the reference and the person providing it.

This privilege will not pertain if defamatory statements are made to people without a direct interest in the person being discussed. And the privilege may be lost if there is common law malice (hatred, ill will, or spite toward the person defamed) or actual malice.

Avoiding Libel Suits

Understanding libel law is an important way to prevent defamation suits. Stories can be handled and published in ways that will minimize libel actions without necessarily limiting good reporting. Talk with your media attorney.

Also, people who call to complain about stories, including those who threaten libel suits, should be treated with graciousness and care (Bezanson, Cranberg, & Soloski, 1987). Media managers, not those further down the hierarchy, should talk with such callers, including inviting them in for personal discussions, if appropriate. The callers' concerns should be given courteous consideration. That may be sufficient to deflect a libel suit. Of course, it is possible to stand by a story and not admit error and still show respectful attention.

In some situations, a correction or retraction may be appropriate and can avoid a defamation action. Nearly two-thirds of the states offer some protection to media that retract a libelous statement. However, retractions may make the situation worse if not written properly. A media attorney should be consulted.

INVASION OF PRIVACY

The media may invade people's privacy in several ways. After libel, invasion of privacy suits are the most common actions against the media based on content or news gathering. The rubric "invasion of privacy" includes four different categories (see Fig. 13.5), as

- Appropriation
- Intrusion
- Embarrassing facts
- False light

Figure 13.5 The Privacy Torts

most courts divide this area. Because each is a separate cause of action, a lawsuit may include several privacy torts.

Remember that torts, which include invasion of privacy, are state matters. As with libel, states may do as they wish, except to the extent the Supreme Court has applied the First Amendment to privacy suits. Some states, in fact, have not permitted lawsuits based on certain of the privacy torts. Even where suits are allowed, courts may apply different standards to the plaintiffs' elements and to the possible defenses. Therefore, the following descriptions of privacy torts are generalizations. Attorneys should be consulted for more detailed information applicable in particular jurisdictions.

Appropriation

Courts long have recognized that a person's name, picture, or likeness cannot be used for commercial or trade purposes without permission. Simply, Doris' Restaurant cannot run an ad stating that "local auto dealer John Smith always eats here," unless John Smith has given permission.

Courts also have found that a picture of someone who looks like someone else, or a singer who sounds like someone else, cannot be used without permission. (See Sidebar 13.7.) If Woody Allen won't appear in your ad, can you hire someone who looks like Allen? Yes, but only if the ad makes quite clear that the person is not Woody Allen, or that Woody Allen is not endorsing your product or service (*Allen v. Men's World Outlet, Inc.*, 1988).

Sidebar 13.7 Lays 'n' Waits

Not all advertisers and advertising agencies took note when a jury awarded Bette Midler $400,000 in her appropriation suit against Ford Motor Co. and Young & Rubicam for using a Midler sound-alike in a radio commercial (*Midler v. Ford Motor Co.*, 1988; *Midler v. Young & Rubicam*, 1991). Frito-Lay's advertising agency, Tracy-Locke, asked Tom Waits to sing for a Doritos radio commercial. Waits refused. Instead, the ad agency hired to sing on the commercial a person who earned his living in part by impersonating Waits. Waits sued. A jury awarded him $2.5 million, including punitive damages (*Waits v. Frito-Lay, Inc.*, 1992). Advertising agencies are concerned that they may be sued by someone who claims to be a professional singer—obscure at best—whose voice sounds just like someone in a commercial. How could an ad agency know?

Bette Midler successfully sued Ford Motor Company (*Midler v. Ford Motor Co.,* 1988) and its advertising agency (*Midler v. Young & Rubicam,* 1991) for including in a radio ad a person singing a song that was a hit recording for Midler. The jury found that the singer sounded like Midler. Had the commercial made clear that the singer was not Bette Midler, it likely would not have been found to be appropriating her voice.

One court has gone a step further (*White v. Samsung Electronics America, Inc.,* 1992). A magazine advertisement showed a robot dressed in an evening gown and a long blond wig. The robot was standing in front of a game board with letters that turned. Vanna White, a hostess on the television program "Wheel of Fortune," brought a suit claiming that the ad appropriated her "identity." A federal appellate court agreed, holding that a celebrity has the right to require others to obtain her permission before exploiting her identity.

There also can be appropriation for commercial purposes without an ad being involved. The president of a soft drink company makes a public announcement that Ann Jones, star sprinter, will endorse the company's product. Newspapers print stories to the effect. But Jones has not signed a contract and changes her mind. Jones may be able to sue the company for appropriation.

Also, appropriation can occur when a person's name or picture is used for "trade" purposes, that is, not in an advertisement. For example, if a famous model's picture is made into a poster and sold without permission, there has been appropriation (*Brinkley v. Casablancas,* 1981).

Importantly, appropriation is not a tort just for the rich and famous. *No* living person's name, picture, likeness, voice, or, apparently, identity may be used for commercial or trade purposes without permission.

For most people, the right to protect their names and likenesses stops when they die. However, well-known people may be different in one respect. They already have their names and pictures widely distributed. They do not want to remain private, but want to control the publicity they receive. This right, called a "right of publicity," is recognized in nearly half the states. In some states, it, too, dies when the person does. But in some states, the right of publicity can be given to heirs just as property can be. In California, for example, the right of publicity continues for 50 years after a person dies, during which time the person's heirs control use of the person's name, likeness, and so on, just as the person herself did when she was alive.

For advertisers, the most important defense against an appropriation action is consent. Consent needs to be proven, which is why a signed contract is best. And the limits of the consent must be respected. If a singer agrees to her name being used in a commercial for a stereo system, the company cannot also use her name in ads for television sets. Consent wasn't given for that. And those who give consent must be legally capable of doing so—which excludes minors and the mentally incompetent, for example.

Courts also give a bit of leeway. If a person's picture is used very briefly in a commercial, perhaps as part of a series of faces being shown in a television ad, some courts recognize it as a "fleeting use" and not the basis for an appropriation suit.

For the news media, the defense against appropriation suits is "newsworthiness." A building is bombed and the local paper runs on its front page a picture of a bleeding, but alive, victim. Can the victim win an appropriation suit, claiming the paper is a commercial activity and no permission was given? No, the picture was newsworthy. And for appropriation, courts do not question what is "newsworthy." Nearly anything that is not in an ad or commercial, but is in the news or feature columns or on a news or "quasi-news" program, will be considered newsworthy.

Also, several courts have held that if a mass medium uses a person's name or picture in a story, and that story then is used in an advertisement for that mass medium, the ad cannot be grounds for an appropriation suit. Essentially, these courts say that the media need to advertise in order to stay in business. The First Amendment would mean little to the media if they could not support themselves. A few courts have held that even if a mass medium has not used someone's name or picture in a news or feature story, it still may be used in an ad for the medium or for a product the mass medium produces and sells (such as a book published by a magazine company).

Intrusion

Trespass has been both a crime and a tort for centuries. But intruding on someone's "space" in 21st-century America can be more subtle than walking on another person's land. Now it may include high-powered microphones, long-range camera lenses, and "bugging" devices. Many states permit lawsuits for these intrusive measures—from entering property or homes to electronic eavesdropping on conversations without permission—under the designation of "intrusion."

Courts define intrusion as a highly intrusive infringement on someone's reasonable expectation of privacy that is highly offensive to a reasonable person. For example, taking a photograph of someone in his home through a slight opening in closed curtains likely is intrusion. People expect to have privacy in their homes if their curtains are drawn to prevent others from looking in. Of course, crossing the lawn to get to the windows is both civil and criminal trespass. The photographer could face a civil suit for intrusion and trespass, and criminal charges for trespass.

However, if the curtains were open, and anyone standing on the sidewalk could look into the home and see people inside, courts likely would hold that no intrusion occurred if a photograph is taken through the window from the sidewalk. A person cannot have a reasonable expectation of privacy if an undraped window allows people to look into the house. Similarly, someone on public property, such as a park, or property open to the public, such as a grocery store, cannot expect privacy. Taking a person's picture in such places generally is not intrusion. However, one court allowed to continue a trespass suit based on a television station sending a camera crew, with lights blazing, into a restaurant unannounced (*Le Mistral, Inc. v. Columbia Broadcasting System,* 1978).

It is not only intrusive but also illegal to eavesdrop without permission on another person's telephone calls, including calls on mobile or cellular phones. Federal and state laws prohibit anyone without a court order, available only to law enforcement officials, from doing so. This also applies to eavesdropping on data transmissions via microwave, satellite, or telephone lines.

However, under federal law and the law in 40 states a person who is a participant may record a telephone or face-to-face conversation without permission of any other parties to the phone call or conversation. The only exception under federal statute is if the intent of recording is to commit a crime or a tort. Interstate calls are governed by federal law.

In ten states, all parties to a telephone conversation must consent to any recording. In some instances, civil suits may be brought against violators of these laws.

There are ethical questions about journalists secretly recording interviews, but in most states it is legal. That does not mean an intrusion suit may not result. If the recording is done in a highly intrusive way, such as by sneaking a tape recorder into someone's home, and is highly offensive to a reasonable person, perhaps secretly recording a bereaved parent, an intrusion suit might be successful.

Importantly, the Federal Communications Commission has a rule that a recorded telephone interview may be broadcast only with permission of all persons whose voices will be heard on the air. The rule does not apply to recorded in-person interviews.

The popularity of "real-life" crime programs on television has prompted questions about journalists trespassing. Journalists may be on public property, or on private property with express or implied permission. Problems arise when reporters go onto private property without consent. Most courts considering the issue have ruled that journalists may not follow public safety personnel—police, fire, ambulance—onto private property, even if public safety people give permission. In most instances, permission properly may come only from the property owner or user. Without that consent, journalists likely are trespassing on private property, whether or not they are using cameras or recorders. (See Sidebar 13.8.)

If permission is properly granted, journalists must stay within that consent. For example, they cannot go onto other parts of the property or use cameras if no permission was given for that. They also must leave when asked.

Sidebar 13.8 Following the Cops

When public safety or law enforcement personnel invite reporters and camera crews to follow them onto private property, should the journalists go? Most courts would say journalists do so only at the risk of losing a lawsuit. Although there is some dispute among courts, the consequences CBS faced typify the approach many judges take.

A U.S. Treasury agent obtained a warrant to search for evidence in a credit card fraud case. When, on his orders, other agents arrived at the suspect's apartment, the suspect was not home. But agents pushed by the suspect's wife, who was wearing only a dressing gown, and entered the apartment. More than two hours later, the lead agent came with the warrant and a CBS news crew. The suspect's wife believed the camera operator and sound technician also were federal agents, and she wasn't told differently. She objected to being videotaped, as did her son, who sat beside his mother crying.

The camera crew followed the agents through the apartment, taping while the agents searched through the family's belongings. The crew photographed personal items, letters and family pictures, and taped while agents interviewed the suspect's wife. Neither the wife nor her son was a suspect. The crew was taping for a CBS weekly program, "Street Stories," but none of the tape ever was broadcast.

The federal trial court said, "CBS had no greater right than that of a thief to be in the home, to 'capture' the scene of the search on film and to remove the photographic record" (*Ayeni v. CBS, Inc.*, 1994, at p. 368). CBS settled the lawsuit with the plaintiffs. The Treasury agent who had obtained the warrant and invited CBS to accompany him appealed the trial court decision, but the appellate court held that the plaintiffs could continue their lawsuit against him.

Embarrassing Facts

Journalists generally believe that if they stick to the "truth" they cannot be successfully sued. However, the "embarrassing facts" tort (sometimes called "private facts") is a lawsuit based on doing just that—publishing the truth. If a plaintiff can show that a story included facts about her that would be highly embarrassing to a reasonable person and that previously were private, she has grounds for an embarrassing facts suit.

Highly embarrassing facts are those that the public would think unwarranted to reveal, that are so "intimate" that they should remain private. For example, one court found that revealing that a woman had "several abortions, engaged in partner swapping, and was involved in a surrogate parenting relationship" could be grounds for an embarrassing facts lawsuit (*Winstead v. Sweeney*, 1994). And a lawsuit will not be successful if the information already is known beyond a few close family members and friends.

Consent is a defense, with the usual problems of proof and staying within the consent. The more usual defense is newsworthiness. Courts have held that even highly embarrassing facts may be published if they are "of legitimate concern to the public" (*Morgan v. Calender*, 1992). Although some courts have closely examined whether a story is newsworthy, based on part on whether it was published because it was "morbid or sensational" rather than of public concern (*Virgil v. Time Inc.*, 1975), most recognize that newsworthiness encompasses a wide range of material. And courts generally have ruled that passage of time does not diminish newsworthiness. Revealing highly embarrassing information that concerns circumstances occurring many years ago still is protected if it is of public concern.

The Supreme Court also has found a First Amendment defense to embarrassing facts suits. While not granting a sweeping protection for information obtained from public documents or official sources, the Court has ruled in several cases that the media are protected under the First Amendment when they publish such material. For example, the Court would not permit a privacy action based on a Georgia statute allowing lawsuits against the media for revealing a rape victim's name (*Cox Broadcasting Corp. v. Cohn*, 1975). A television station reporter had found a victim's name in a court clerk's documents. The Court also disallowed a suit under a similar statute in Florida based on a newspaper publishing a rape victim's name obtained from a sheriff's press release (*Florida Star v. B.J.F.*, 1989).

False Light

It is possible for the media to publish false information that does not "defame" someone. That is, people do not shun the person, nor is the person's reputation necessarily injured in the community. Nonetheless, the published material makes the person appear to be someone she is not. Writing about a person's appearance, dress, and remarks in a way to make her seem to be distraught, but not having seen or interviewed her, may make her seem to be someone she isn't. Community members are likely to embrace a person if they thought she were unhappy, not shun her. That is, there is no libel, but there may be "false light."

False light is a second cousin to libel. Like libel, it involves untrue statements that are published (but, unlike libel, false light requires widespread distribution) and that identify the plaintiff. It does not require "defamation." If there is injury to reputation, the proper lawsuit is for libel.

Courts have held that a false light plaintiff must show fault. What level of fault is the question. The Supreme Court has decided only two false light cases. In its first false light decision, the Court found that a family portrayed in a magazine story as being brutalized by escaped convicts, but who instead were treated well by their temporary captors, had to prove actual malice since the story was newsworthy (*Time Inc. v. Hill,* 1967). In its next false light decision, however, the Court was less clear (*Cantrell v. Forest City Publishing Co.,* 1974). A newspaper magazine supplement reported on the situation in a West Virginia community five months after a bridge collapse. The story described the demeanor of the widow whose husband died in the accident. However, the reporter did not see or interview the woman. The Court said that the plaintiff, clearly a private individual, had proven actual malice at trial. The Court, then, said it did not need to decide whether a private individual suing the media for false light should be required to prove actual malice or whether a lesser standard, such as negligence, would be sufficient. Nearly 25 years later, the Court has not yet decided which standard is required.

That leaves lower courts hearing false light cases without a clear direction. Some courts follow the *Time Inc. v. Hill* decision and require all false light plaintiffs—public officials, public figures, private individuals—to prove actual malice. Other courts say that since private persons need not prove actual malice in libel cases, they should not have to in false light cases. These courts have support in the *Cantrell* case, in which the Supreme Court seemed to leave the question open.

Courts in a few states have refused to allow false light lawsuits at all. They suggest that the concept does not fit into protection of privacy, and that the defamation tort sufficiently protects individuals.

HARM CAUSED BY THE MEDIA

Plaintiffs have sued arguing that the media have harmed them either physically or emotionally, or even financially. With rare exceptions, these suits have not been successful. For example, courts have not upheld actions by the family of a young girl raped with a soft drink bottle after her assailants had viewed a television drama in which a young girl was raped with a toilet plunger (*Olivia N. v. NBC,* 1981); the family of a small boy whose eye was injured when a balloon broke after he put a metal object in the balloon and spun it around, copying something he had seen on a children's program (*Walt Disney Productions, Inc. v. Shannon,* 1981); or a teenage boy who hanged himself, apparently after reading a magazine article about masturbating while hanging oneself (*Herceg v. Hustler Magazine, Inc.,* 1987). Courts find that in such instances the media did not "incite" someone in the audience to injure himself or others.

There have been lawsuits against the media for intentional infliction of emotional distress. This requires an "outrageous," deliberate action on the defendant's part that causes extreme emotional upset. Particularly assertive reporting techniques may lead to lawsuits for this tort. For example, a judge refused to dismiss a case brought against a television news organization that aired a tape showing the plaintiff soon after her husband had attacked her (*Baugh v. CBS,* 1993). The Supreme Court has held that public figures and public officials must prove actual malice to win a suit for intentional infliction of emotional distress (*Hustler Magazine, Inc. v. Falwell,* 1988).

On rare occasions a court will find that the media owed a duty, a responsibility, to a plaintiff, but breached it, causing the person emotional harm. This is "negligent" infliction of emotional distress. For example, a lawsuit might be successful if a newspaper were to publish the name and address of an assault victim if the assailant remains at large and there is evidence the assailant still could be stalking the plaintiff (*Times-Mirror Co. v. San Diego Superior Court*, 1988; *Hyde v. City of Columbia*, 1982).

Courts also have found media responsibility when advertisements or promotions are involved, in part because commercial speech has a lower degree of protection under the First Amendment (*Weirum v. RKO General, Inc.*, 1975). For example, a court found that *Soldier of Fortune* magazine was negligent in publishing an advertisement that resulted in a person employing the killer for hire who had placed the ad (*Braun v. Soldier of Fortune Magazine, Inc.*, 1992). One person was murdered and another wounded as a result. The ad used phrases such as "gun for hire" and "professional mercenary." The court held that the magazine should have been aware that there was an unreasonable risk of harm in publishing the ad.

CHAPTER SUMMARY

The First Amendment to the United States Constitution gives considerable—but certainly not absolute—protection to those working in the mass media. It usually prevents any governmental official or agency from stopping a medium from publishing based on content. However, a court may allow prior restraint if the government can carry the heavy burden of showing that national security would be endangered, the material is obscene, publication would cause imminent unlawful action, or the content includes fighting words. Similarly, the government cannot use discriminatory taxation to silence the media or to make it more expensive for the media to publish.

Under the First Amendment the government must have a compelling reason to restrict or punish expression based on the government's disagreement with the viewpoint expressed. This also is true when the government doesn't want a particular topic discussed. However, the government may be able to show a compelling reason. For example, obscene material is not protected under the First Amendment on the basis that the government has a right to protect public morals. When the government is not concerned with viewpoint or content, it need show only an "important" or "substantial" reason to limit expression, a less demanding standard than a "compelling" purpose. It can prohibit a protest march at 5 P.M. Friday down the city's busiest street in order to prevent traffic problems. But it must give the protesters a reasonable alternative time or place for their parade.

The First Amendment also often plays a role in libel litigation. A libel plaintiff must prove that the material was published, that is, seen by at least someone in addition to the plaintiff and defendant. That is easy to show when the defendant is a mass medium. A plaintiff must prove that she or he was identified in the allegedly defamatory publication. This is shown if a few people reasonably testify that they thought the publication was about the plaintiff. And a plaintiff must show injury to reputation, that a portion of the community thought less of, or shunned, the plaintiff after the publication. Most plaintiffs must show the publication was substantially false.

The plaintiff must prove fault on the defendant's part, and this is the most complex part of libel. Private plaintiffs in most states must show that the mass media defendant acted negligently, not acting as a reasonable person or reasonable journalist would have. But the Supreme Court ruled that the First Amendment requires in all states that public officials and public figures prove actual malice. Actual malice means the defendant knew the publication was false, or the defendant published with a reckless disregard for the truth.

If a libel plaintiff proves each of these elements, the defendant has an opportunity to present a defense. The defense might be that the mass medium had a qualified privilege to publish the material, or that the allegedly defamatory statements were the defendant's opinion or were protected as fair comment.

Mass media also may face suits charging they invaded plaintiffs' privacy. Most courts divide privacy into four torts: appropriation, intrusion, embarrassing facts, and false light. Not all states permit suits for each of these torts. Appropriation is the use of someone's name, picture, likeness, voice, and perhaps "identity" for commercial or trade purposes without their permission. Intrusion is violating someone's reasonable expectation of privacy by physical means, such as trespassing, or perhaps electronically, such as using a highly sensitive microphone or high-powered camera lens. Most states permit tape recording conversations if only one party to the conversation, who could be a reporter, agrees.

Embarrassing facts is the publication of highly embarrassing, private, factual material that is not newsworthy. False light is publishing untrue material that makes the plaintiff appear to be someone he or she is not. The statements usually are not defamatory, or the plaintiff would sue for libel, and even may be complimentary. Courts are divided whether all false light plaintiffs, or only public officials and public figures, must prove actual malice.

The media also may be sued, although not often successfully, for causing someone emotional or physical harm, or putting them in physical danger.

STUDY QUESTIONS

1. What is the difference between "censorship" and "editing"?

2. What does "prior restraint" mean, and when may the government impose it?

3. What elements must a plaintiff prove to win a libel case?

4. What categories of libel plaintiffs are there? What type of "fault" must each prove?

5. What types of "privilege" to defame someone are there? On which type do journalists rely as a libel defense? How may journalists lose that defense?

6. What are the invasion of privacy torts? What does a plaintiff have to prove to win a lawsuit based on each tort? What are the defenses for each tort?

chapter 14

Advertising, Obscenity, Copyright, and News Gathering

Although libel and invasion of privacy are the most troubling issues associated with media content, they are not the only ones. Courts give less protection to advertising than to most other forms of expression. They give no protection at all to obscene expression, but obscenity is difficult to define. The law does protect original material created for the media, but that also means the media generally cannot use other people's material without permission. This chapter will discuss each of these issues. Then it will turn to questions of reporters gathering information, looking at access to government records and meetings, the free press/fair trial conflict, and protecting news sources and other information when journalists are ordered to testify.

Commercial Speech

What courts call "commercial speech" is given less protection under the First Amendment than is most other expression. Although recently it hasn't been explicit about it, the Supreme Court's view is that the First Amendment is meant primarily to protect speech about matters of public concern, particularly political issues. But this only confuses matters.

First, commercial speech is advertising. Courts have tried to draw a distinction between "commercial speech" and "advertising," but not successfully. Commercial speech proposes a commercial transaction—an exchange of money, usually, for services or products—according to the courts. Some advertising does not propose a commercial transaction. An anti-abortion group might run a commercial, as might a politician or a pro-gun control organization. If these are paid messages—space or time was purchased to publish them—are they advertising? Do they deserve limited or full First Amendment protection? While courts have not made clear the basis for doing so, they continue to make a distinction between commercial speech and noncommercial speech. The former receives less First Amendment protection than the latter.

Second, courts have said that advertising can be about matters of public concern. This could be an advertisement in favor of, say, limiting driving to help clean the air. But also, the Supreme Court has said that ads listing prescription drug prices are of great importance to, among others, the "poor, the sick, and particularly the aged," for whom such information may be of more concern than "the day's most urgent political debate" (*Virginia State Board v. Virginia Citizens' Consumer Council,* 1976, p. 763). This makes it even more peculiar that commercial speech is treated differently than many other forms of communication.

But treated differently it is. Commercial speech has some protection—it isn't in the same category as blackmail and obscenity. The question is: How much? Suppose a newspaper publishes an editorial supporting a ban on liquor ads on television. Could the government stop the editorial before it ran? No, that's prior restraint, and there is no justification for it. Could the paper be punished for printing the editorial? No. Again, the First Amendment protects it. But could the federal government adopt a law banning televised liquor commercials? Does a newspaper have more speech protection than a liquor manufacturer?

The Supreme Court has established a test for deciding when and to what degree the government may regulate commercial speech (*Central Hudson Gas & Electric Corp. v. Public Service Commission,* 1980). First, courts ask whether the regulated ads are for an illegal product or service. If so, the inquiry stops here, and the government may do anything it likes. For example, it may adopt laws banning ads for crack cocaine and fine or jail people who run them.

The inquiry also stops if the ads the government wants to regulate are false or deceptive. The Federal Trade Commission (FTC) oversees the questions on the federal level, and many states also have agencies responsible for preventing such ads. The test the FTC uses to determine if an ad is deceptive is a narrow one—not many ads fall into this category. The FTC asks if a substantial number of ordinary people acting in a reasonable way would be deceived by the ad, and if so, is the deceptive part of the ad the reason the people would buy the product or service?

Lots of ads engage in "puffery": "This is the best deal in town!" People understand that this is exaggeration. No one rushes to the store believing the deal is the best available. It might be a good deal, and people might choose to purchase goods at that store. But if the ad doesn't make false or misleading claims, and reasonable people wouldn't believe the "puffed" statement as probably true or false, it isn't deceiving. However, for example, an ad stating that aspirin relieves headaches better than other forms of pain relievers was found to be deceptive (*American Home Products,* 1981). People likely could make a purchasing decision based on such a statement, one that is not supportable. When the FTC finds a deceptive or false ad, it may require the advertiser to take steps to correct the public's incorrect perception of the product or service.

Assuming that the ads to be regulated are for legal products or services, and are not false or deceptive, a court then will ask whether the government has a legitimate or important interest in controlling the ads. (See Sidebar 14.1.) For liquor ads on television, the government could argue, for example, that it needs to limit liquor use among young people and that drunk driving is a serious problem in society. These certainly are important governmental interests.

Then a court will ask whether the regulations will directly advance the government's interests. The government could say that many young people watch television and that they are influenced by advertising, and that the same is true of the general population, some of whom drink and drive. But the government must show the connection between its regulations and solving the problems it sees. The Supreme Court didn't see

Sidebar 14.1 Regulating Commercial Speech

Nearly 60 years ago, the Supreme Court ruled that commercial speech had no First Amendment protection at all (*Valentine v. Chrestensen,* 1942). Since then commercial speech has been given some protection, but it's been on a roller coaster, sometimes being more, sometimes less, under the First Amendment's wing. If the commercial speech is deceptive or fraudulent, it won't have any protection. Otherwise, the Court has ruled, regulation of commercial speech must pass each part of a test:

♦ *The government must have a substantial or important interest to justify the regulation.* It's generally easy for the government to come up with a plausible reason for the limits it wants to impose on advertising.

♦ *The regulation must directly and significantly advance the government's interest.* There must be more than speculation and guesswork on the government's part. There must be evidence to support the government's argument that the regulation will help the government achieve its goal.

♦ *There must be a "reasonable fit" between the government's interest and the regulation.* The regulation does not have to have the least possible impact on First Amendment rights while still achieving the government's goal. But the government must not choose, from among several possible approaches, a regulation that seriously limits free speech. This particularly is true if alternatives would help the government meet its goal with less of an impact on First Amendment rights.

---

the connection between the government's goal of limiting drinking and not allowing alcohol content to be listed on beer labels in one case (*Rubin v. Coors Brewing Co.,* 1995), and banning price advertising for alcoholic beverages in another case (*44 Liquormart, Inc. v. Rhode Island,* 1996).

If the government is able to prove that it has an important interest and that its ad regulations will directly further that interest, a court finally will ask whether there is a "reasonable fit" between the government's interest and the regulations (*Board of Trustees v. Fox,* 1989). The Supreme Court has said this means the government should look for ways to regulate the ads that will do less harm, rather than more harm, to the advertiser's First Amendment rights (*Cincinnati v. Discovery Network, Inc.,* 1993). The regulations do not need to be the narrowest possible, doing the absolutely least amount of harm to free speech rights. But if the government has choices of solutions, it should choose from among those that have a limited First Amendment impact.

OBSCENITY

Courts have held that certain forms of expression are outside the First Amendment's protection. Obscenity is one of these categories. There is no question about how much protection obscenity might have, as is the inquiry for commercial speech. Obscenity has no protection. The question, then, is, "What is obscene?" It is necessary to answer that question in order to know what expression *is* protected.

The Supreme Court has adopted a three-part test to determine whether material is obscene (*Miller v. California,* 1973). Each part must be met, or the material will not be found to be obscene.

1. Would a reasonable person, "applying contemporary community standards," find the material "taken as a whole, appeals to the prurient interest"?

2. Does the work show or describe sexual conduct "in a patently offensive way"?

3. Does the material, "taken as a whole," lack "serious literary, artistic, political or scientific value"? (*Miller v. California*, 1973; *Pope v. Illinois*, 1987)

Several Court terms need defining. "Contemporary community standards" means the standards that jurors believe people in their city or state have. "Prurient interest" means arousing sexual desire through particularly lewd material. "Patent offensiveness" means what in the vernacular is called "hard-core" material.

Although the Supreme Court has said that the first two parts of the test are to be determined on a local or statewide level, it has overturned one jury decision—that the movie "Carnal Knowledge" was obscene—because the Court found the material was not patently offensive (*Jenkins v. Georgia*, 1974). The third part of the test is pegged to national standards.

The Court also has found that using children in sexually oriented material, even if in poses that would be acceptable if performed by adults, means the material has no First Amendment protection (*New York v. Ferber*, 1982). This is called "child pornography." And certain sexually oriented material made available to children, which might be protected if distributed to adults, is not protected (*Ginsberg v. New York*, 1968). The term applied to this approach is "variable obscenity"—the material is obscene if directed to children, but not obscene if directed to adults.

Courts have upheld a variety of methods of restricting adult-oriented, but nonobscene, material. For example, cities have been permitted to use zoning laws to cluster adult theaters and bookstores in one area (*City of Renton v. Playtime Theatres, Inc.*, 1986; *Young v. American Mini Theatres, Inc.*, 1976), people may ask the postal service not to deliver sexually oriented material to them (*Rowan v. United States Post Office Department*, 1970), and local governments have been allowed to order stores to place adult magazines under the counter or behind racks hiding their covers (*Upper Midwest Booksellers Association v. City of Minneapolis*, 1985; *M.S. News Co. v. Casado*, 1983).

COPYRIGHT AND TRADEMARKS

Copyright law both protects the material the mass media produce and limits the material the mass media may use. The U.S. Constitution requires Congress to protect intellectual property—inventions and creative work. The very first Congress adopted a copyright law. The current law was passed in 1976, and it replaced the 1909 law. One problem is that technology advances faster than copyright laws do. Consider how the mass media changed between 1909 and 1976, and even since 1976. The copyright law can't keep up.

Copyright Protection

The law says that material that is original and "fixed in a tangible medium" is protected by copyright from the moment it is created. (See Sidebar 14.2.) It must be substantially original. You can't change three notes in a Mozart symphony and claim you have the copyright on that composition. It's not "substantially original." And the work must be in a "tangible medium"—paper, videotape or audiotape, film, computer

Sidebar 14.2 Football, Popcorn, and Copyright

You videotape the Super Bowl, which your local ABC affiliate broadcasts. It was a great game, and you invite a group of friends who were not able to see it. You know they would pay anything to watch the game, so you charge them $25 apiece to have popcorn and pizza at your house, and to watch the tape. Since you taped the game—fixed it in the tangible medium of videotape—do you own the copyright? If you don't, may you charge people to watch the tape? May you show them the tape if you don't charge them?

You don't own the copyright because you contributed nothing to make the production "original." ABC did—the announcers, the direction (which camera shots appear on the screen), the graphics, and so forth. And ABC also taped it. ABC's production, then, was substantially original and fixed in a tangible medium. In the absence of a contract, ABC would own the copyright. However, a contract between ABC and the National Football League could say the copyright belongs to the NFL, or jointly to ABC and the NFL. The federal copyright law says what happens if there is no contract.

The Supreme Court has held that people may videotape for their personal use complete programs that television stations broadcast (*Sony Corp. of America v. Universal City Studios, Inc.,* 1984). This includes showing it to friends. But once you charge friends for viewing a videotape of a broadcast program, you have used the tape for a commercial purpose. That is not permitted—it violates the copyright law—unless you have permission from the copyright owner.

What if you don't charge $25, but instead tell your friends they can't come to watch the tape unless they bring the pizza? Technically, that likely is a copyright law violation, but ABC probably won't sue you for it.

---

disk, paint on canvas, a marble statue. A broadcast of a baseball game is not "fixed" unless it is put on tape or film.

Facts and history cannot be copyrighted. A radio journalist's description of a train-school bus accident is copyrighted (if it is put on audiotape). He created the report by selecting words, and perhaps sounds, that were original with him. But the fact the accident happened cannot be protected. Even if the reporter were at the scene before other journalists, the station cannot claim a copyright on the accident itself. Others can report on it, too.

The copyright is owned by the material's creator, with two important exceptions. The U.S. government cannot have a copyright on material created for it by its employees, such as a report written by an undersecretary of labor. And "works made for hire" are controlled by the person or company who hired the creator, unless agreed otherwise. When a reporter who is regularly employed by a television station prepares a story for the 11 P.M. newscast, the story's copyright belongs to the station. However, if the station hires a freelance reporter to prepare a story, the copyright belongs to the freelancer. Either of these situations may be changed by a contract that specifies to the contrary.

Material is copyrighted from the moment it is created, and the protection lasts for the life of the creator plus 50 years. Works made for hire are protected for 100 years from the time they were created, or 75 years from the time they are published, whichever comes first.

A person who creates a copyrighted work has a "bundle of sticks," with each stick representing a right. For example, someone who writes a novel has the right to have it published in hardback, in paperback, as an excerpted piece in a magazine, made into a motion picture, made into a television drama or series, turned into a Broadway musical, and so forth. (See Sidebar 14.3.) Each of these rights is separate. The novelist may sell sticks one at a time, a few at a time, all at once, or not sell any. Once one or more sticks are sold, the work's creator no longer has those rights; they have been transferred to the purchaser, who then can sell the rights to someone else.

Sidebar 14.3 Digital Copyright

A subscription computer bulletin board contained copies of pictures taken from issues of *Playboy* magazine. The bulletin board operator said the pictures were uploaded by his subscribers, and that he did not place them on the bulletin board nor know they were there. Playboy sued for copyright infringement—the magazine's copyrighted photographs had been copied without permission. The court ruled in Playboy's favor, since copying had taken place without Playboy's permission. It did not matter whether the operator knew the pictures were on his bulletin board. Violation of the copyright law does not require intent to copy or knowledge of copying (*Playboy Enterprises, Inc. v. Frena*, 1993).

The copyright holder has the rights to public "performance" of the work. "Performance" means most methods of disseminating the work to the public. This includes, for example, retransmitting a radio station's signal into a store, restaurant, or bar. Courts have held that simply turning on a radio so that kitchen workers or a few customers may hear it is not a performance, and therefore not a copyright infringement (*Broadcast Music, Inc. v. United States Shoe Corp.*, 1982). However, using additional speakers or amplification equipment does become a performance, and then requires the copyright holder's permission.

Registration

But copyright is only the first step. If another person uses copyrighted material without permission, and if that material was produced in the United States, the creator may not sue for copyright infringement under the federal law unless the work first has been "registered." Registration requires completing a relatively simple form and sending it, together with copies of the work and a fee, to the U.S. Copyright Office. The Copyright Office does not verify that the work is original, but registration accomplishes at least two things. First, it is proof in court that the work was created no later than the day it was registered. Second, it allows the person who registered it to sue for copyright infringement.

The law no longer requires that you include a copyright notice: © Kim Jones 1998. You still will have copyright protection without the notice. However, there are strong reasons to place a notice on the material. A person found to have deliberately used another person's work can be ordered to pay to the copyright holder any gains realized by the improper use, and additional damages meant to "punish" the infringer. But if the improper use was inadvertent, if the infringer can show that it was an accidental use, the only damages will be the "ill-gotten" gains, which may be little or none. If the copyrighted material contains a notice, however, the law does not permit the infringer to claim "innocent" use, and the additional damages may be awarded.

Defenses Against Copyright Infringement Claims

If you use copyrighted material, it is not enough simply to attribute it to its creator. Reprinting a Dilbert cartoon strip and stating, "By Scott Adams," won't do. You must have the copyright holder's permission.

The exception is "fair use" of the copyrighted material. Judges have said that if absolutely no copyrighted material could be used without permission, the goal of spreading knowledge and understanding throughout American society would be frustrated. For example, would a novelist give permission to a book reviewer to reprint part of her work if she knew the review would be an unfavorable one? The fair use defense to copyright infringement, created by the courts and now part of the 1976 copyright act, gives some leeway for using copyrighted material. But it is a slippery defense, and it is difficult to know whether a court will agree the use was fair in any particular situation.

The fair use defense involves four factors, all of which are to be balanced, although not necessarily equally, in determining whether to uphold the copyright owner's rights or to allow use, without permission, to benefit society. First, a court will consider the use to which the copyrighted material was put. Was it used for educational or scientific purposes, for news reporting or comment, or as part of a review? These types of purposes tip the balance toward a fair use. That is, society is benefited by using copyrighted material in these ways and would be the poorer if the material could be used only with the creator's permission, which might not be granted. But other types of uses, such as including a portion of a copyrighted song in another composition without permission, likely will tip the balance toward a copyright infringement.

A difficult question in this part of the fair use test is parodies. A parody of a copyrighted work naturally uses the original piece as its foundation. But parodies and satires aren't always kind, and the copyright holder likely would not give permission to use his creation in a way that ridicules it. The Supreme Court has ruled that satires may be a fair use, even though the satire's purpose is not only to "comment" on the original work but also to make money for the satirist, and even though the parody uses the "heart" of the copyrighted material (*Campbell v. Acuff-Rose Music, Inc.*, 1994). However, as noted in another part of the fair use test, the satirist may have a problem if she uses too much of the original work.

The Court also has held that home videotaping of television programs for personal use is protected (*Sony Corp. of America v. Universal City Studios, Inc.*, 1984). Congress has allowed copying of recorded works, such as compact disks, for personal use. However, that is not true for copying of other protected works for your own use. For example, it is not a fair use to copy a magazine or book. This only saves you from purchasing the original work—and deprives the copyright holder of the money he would have earned if you had bought instead of copied the material.

Second, courts consider the nature and intended purpose of the copyright material. Was it meant to be used for scientific or educational purposes? Was it meant not to be distributed, such as a letter or diary? Novels are meant to earn revenue for their creators, not to be used as part of other people's works without permission.

Third, courts look at how much and what part of the copyrighted work was used. Four paragraphs from a two-page short story will be different than four paragraphs from a 500-page novel. And the four paragraphs that tell who committed the crime in a murder mystery novel will be different than four paragraphs of character development from the middle of the book.

Finally, courts consider the copying's adverse market impact on the copyrighted work. Would people be less likely to purchase the work because a portion of it was published elsewhere?

Again, this is a balancing test. All the factors are to be weighed, and a court might place more emphasis on some factors than others. For example, including several paragraphs of a novel in a review lambasting the book will not help sales. But a court likely would consider the first part of the test—using the copyrighted material for a review—more important than the last part of the test—the adverse impact on the book's market value.

Courts have held that "stealing" a competitor's work in gathering and preparing news is not fair use—from actually obtaining the prepared material and publishing it first (*Harper & Row Publishers, Inc. v. Nation Enterprises, Inc.,* 1985), to a radio station announcer reading verbatim from a newspaper without permission.

There are two other defenses available. First, if a copyright holder sues for infringement, but you can show your work is not "substantially similar" to the copyrighted work, or to look at it from the other side, that your work is "substantially original," there is no infringement. Second, showing that you had no opportunity to be exposed to the copyrighted material is a defense to infringement.

Music Licensing

Songs—the music and the lyrics—and other musical compositions are original and fixed in a tangible medium, so are copyrighted when created. But they are treated somewhat differently than other works. In part, the problem is that a song can be used by so many people in so many ways that the composer cannot possibly come to agreements with each and every person who might want to "perform" the song—even if each of those people wanted to seek permission. Instead, music publishers and composers strike an agreement with a music licensing company.

There are two major licensing organizations, ASCAP and BMI, each controlling millions of songs, but each song under the auspices of just one or the other of the groups.

The organizations grant licenses, for a fee, to people, groups, and businesses, giving them permission to use all the songs in the organization's catalog. ASCAP and BMI also check to see if businesses using copyrighted music in any way have the proper licenses. Revenues from the licenses are distributed to music publishers and composers primarily based on how often their songs are played. Since nearly all radio and television outlets play musical compositions, they must have licenses from both ASCAP and BMI.

When a composition is recorded, usually on a compact disk or audiotape, the recording company then has one and only one right: The recording cannot itself be recorded without the company's permission. Before the 1976 copyright law took effect, recording companies did not have even this right. This is not a question about the song, but about the recording itself. In fact, U.S. copyright law does not recognize any other protection for the musical performance embedded in the recording. The only exception to this right is home copying for personal use. Congress adopted a law in 1992 making this permissible.

In practice, this means that a radio station playing a recording of a song must have an ASCAP or BMI license, whichever is appropriate, but need not have permission of the recording company. However, if the station tapes the recording, while taping the program containing the recording, for example, it then must have the recording company's permission.

Additionally, if a television station uses the recording as background music for, say, a promotional piece for the station, an additional permission is required. Not only must the station have the appropriate ASCAP or BMI license, and the recording company's permission to copy the recording onto videotape, but it also must have a "synchronization" license. This allows the station to "synchronize" the music to the images on the videotape.

There is one way around all this, besides using a recording from before the mid-1970s of a composition that is in the public domain (i.e., its copyright has expired). There are companies that hire composers to write songs for the company and hire musicians to record those songs. The companies sell compact disks and tapes containing these recordings. Since the company owns the copyrights, the recording rights and the synchronization rights, it can sell a complete package. Of course, the compositions are not the best-selling recordings of well-known songs, but it may be the easier and, perhaps, less expensive way to obtain music rights. (See Sidebar 8.3, p. 207.)

Trademarks and Service Marks

Trademarks and service marks are words or symbols that identify a company's products or services. They are not copyrighted because they need not be original. But they do need to be distinctive in identifying the product or service. Trademarks and service marks must be registered with the Patent and Trademark Office in Washington, D.C., which will check to be certain no other company already is using the mark for a similar product or service. Marks are good for a ten-year period and may be renewed.

Companies must protect their marks by ensuring that the marks are not used generically for a range of brands of a product or service. The word *aspirin* used to be a mark for a particular brand of pain reliever. But when people began using it for any brand of similar pain relievers, the mark was lost to the manufacturer.

Suits may be brought for trademark and service mark infringement. However, courts generally have held that there is no infringement when marks are used in news or feature stories, or in satires.

NEWS GATHERING

Although the First Amendment protects the press and gives it rights in a number of ways, courts generally have found that it does not give journalists protection to gather news. The press and the public stand the same regarding access to private and public records and meetings. If the press has any right of access, it is not through the Constitution, but through federal and state laws, and occasionally a court decision. The problems are that statutory rights often are more restrictive than under the First Amendment, and that laws can be amended or repealed. The one exception to this is media access to criminal judicial proceedings, which the Supreme Court has found largely to be protected by the First Amendment.

Federal Freedom of Information Act

On the federal level, access to certain government records is permitted under the Freedom of Information Act (FOIA). First adopted by Congress in 1966 and amended a number of times since, the FOIA allows individuals, companies, and groups to request in writing that the federal government copy and provide records in its possession. But there are many exceptions.

The Freedom of Information Act opens for inspection the records of certain federal government agencies. But the agencies may refuse inspection if the records fall into one or more of the exemptions listed in the law:

1. National security.
2. Agency rules and practices related solely to the agency's personnel.
3. Exemptions from the FOIA that Congress has included in certain federal laws.
4. Confidential business information collected by federal agencies.
5. Internal agency memoranda.
6. Personnel, medical, and similar files.
7. Law enforcement investigatory materials.
8. Reports required of banks and other financial institutions.
9. Geological information, such as water, oil, and gas wells.

Figure 14.1 Freedom of Information Act (FOIA) Exemptions

First, the FOIA does not apply to Congress or congressional support agencies, such as the Congressional Budget Office. Nor does it apply to the president or to presidential advisers, although it does to the office of the president. Nor does it apply to the federal courts. But even after all the exceptions, the FOIA does cover a large part of the federal government, including all the cabinet departments, the many independent agencies (Federal Communications Commission, Federal Trade Commission, etc.), the Postal Service, and others.

But even for the parts of the federal government to which the FOIA does apply, not all records must be produced. The act specifies nine exemptions (see Fig. 14.1). It is important to note that these exemptions are permissive—they *permit* the government to withhold records falling into the exemptions, but do not require it. The most important of the exemptions for journalists are the first, national security and foreign policy, applying to documents classified under executive order; the second, internal agency rules and practices, primarily concerning personnel matters; the fourth, confidential business information, which includes the data that regulated business (such as broadcast stations) must submit to the federal government; the fifth, agency memorandums, which allows agencies not to reveal the deliberative processes preceding announced rules and regulations; the sixth, the "privacy" exemption, which protects personnel, medical, and "similar" files and often is used to make government-held information about individuals unavailable; and the seventh, materials related to law enforcement investigations, if revealing the information would interfere with a federal law enforcement agency's current investigations or prosecutions.

Again, the exemptions are permissive, not mandatory. Agencies are not permitted to refuse to give you a document because something in it falls within an exemption. Instead, they are to delete the exempted material (often they use an opaque marker) and provide you the document with the excisions.

Federal agencies are supposed to respond to a written request for documents within 20 days, but courts understand that the agencies are understaffed and normally cannot comply. There are provisions in the act that should allow the press to obtain search time and copying for free. If an agency does not respond in a timely manner, or charges when you think it shouldn't, the first step is an appeal within the agency itself. Each agency has someone designated to act on appeals. If that doesn't work, go to court. If you win in court, the agency can be ordered to pay your attorney's fees and court costs.

Federal Privacy Act

It would seem that the Federal Privacy Act, adopted in 1974, and the FOIA conflict. The FOIA says to provide documents, and the privacy act says not to disclose information that relates to specific individuals without permission. Although Congress and the courts have stated that the FOIA is to take precedence over the privacy act if there is a conflict, some agencies continue to hesitate providing personal information.

The privacy act also permits individuals to have access to information about them held by the federal government, and to ask for changes in those records if appropriate. But neither the FOIA nor the privacy act helped Terry Anderson, former Associated Press reporter and Middle East hostage. He sought government records about himself as a hostage and was refused (Brozan, 1994).

Federal Open Meetings Laws

The federal Sunshine Act is intended to open to the public and press meetings of the same government agencies covered by the FOIA. It, too, is filled with exemptions—most of them similar to the FOIA exemptions. But unless meetings pertain to one of the subjects covered by the exemptions, or will lead to such a meeting, they are not supposed to be held behind closed doors. Also, the act requires that agencies inform the public of impending meetings through notices in the *Federal Register*.

State Open Records and Meetings Laws

Every state has some form of open records and open meetings laws. They vary widely, some being more amenable to open government than others. And court decisions in most states interpret the statutes, again in a variety of ways. Usually the laws apply to cities and counties as well. But special agencies, such as school boards, may have different rules or may decide that the laws apply differently to them. Consult your media attorney for information about how the laws operate in your area.

Access to News Locations

When journalists enter private property without permission, they are trespassing and also may be open to intrusion suits. Is public property always open to the media? Not necessarily. Courts have held that some property used by the government is not open to the general public, and therefore not to the press. These areas include federal prisons

(*Saxbe v. Washington Post Co.,* 1974), state prisons (*Pell v. Procunier,* 1974), county jails (*Houchins v. KQED, Inc.,* 1978), and military bases (*Greer v. Spock,* 1976).

Government officials may limit public and press access to certain areas for public safety reasons. Courts rarely overturn such decisions.

Courts have said that government officials may not permit some journalists to be on government property while excluding others for capricious reasons. For example, a mayor was not permitted to hold a news conference and invite all reporters except one, barring him because the mayor did not like the stories the journalist had written about the mayor's administration (*Borreca v. Fasi,* 1974).

FREE PRESS/FAIR TRIAL

The Sixth Amendment to the U.S. Constitution guarantees a right to "a speedy and public trial, by an impartial jury" in criminal prosecutions. But is it possible to have an "impartial jury" if the media publish what some see as prejudicial stories, including revealing information that might not be admitted at trial, or, in some instances, labeling the accused as guilty before the trial even takes place? Are jury members swayed by media coverage? If so, in favor or against the defendant? To what degree? What kind of coverage is prejudicial? One problem is that we don't know the answers to these questions. Research cannot be done using real juries since no one except jury members is allowed in jury rooms. The work that has been done on jury bias is inconclusive.

A second problem is that the way to ensure that prejudicial information doesn't reach potential or sitting jurors' eyes and ears is to forbid its publication or punish media that do publish it. Essentially, that's the approach taken in such countries as England and Australia. Those countries have balanced individuals' rights to a fair trial against freedom of the press and found the former more important. In the United States, the courts have found the balance to be a closer question. Therefore, they have put in place a variety of ways to accommodate the two interests.

First, courts have not defined a "fair juror" to be someone completely ignorant of the facts of, or the people involved in, a case. What is necessary is that a juror can swear to make up her or his mind based on what is seen and heard in the courtroom.

Second, courts have a variety of ways to prevent prejudicial publicity from causing an unfair trial. They can, for example, carefully examine potential jurors to be certain the media coverage did not prejudice them (voir dire), move the trial to a different location where perhaps there has been less media coverage (change of venue), delay the trial until prejudicial publicity subsides (continuance), sequester the jury so no media coverage during the trial can affect jurors, or, in the extreme, order a new trial.

What courts cannot do, except in the rarest circumstances, is order the media not to publish information about pending or ongoing judicial proceedings. At one time, courts almost routinely issued such orders. Journalists call these "gag orders," while courts call them "restrictive orders." But these are prior restraints—the government, in the form of a court, preventing publication. When a gag order was issued in a case involving the small-town murder of a family of six, the media took it to the Supreme Court. The Court held that judges may restrict publication only if news coverage creates a clear threat to a fair trial, other methods of securing the defendant's rights will not work (continuance, change of venue, jury sequestration, etc.), and preventing publication *will* guarantee a fair trial (*Nebraska Press Association v. Stuart,* 1976). Because nearly always judges have means other than prior restraint to achieve a fair trial, gag orders very likely will be found to violate the press's First Amendment rights. However, courts have more leeway in ordering lawyers and other trial participants not to talk with the media (see Fig. 14.2).

The Supreme Court has made clear that judges have a number of steps they must consider taking before they may impose a gag order on the press or close the courthouse doors to the press and public. For example, judges could:

- Carefully question potential jurors to be certain none would be unfair (voir dire).
- Sternly warn jurors to base their decisions only on what they see and hear in court (admonish the jury).
- Prevent the jury from seeing or hearing prejudicial publicity (sequester the jury).
- Delay the trial until prejudicial publicity has lessened (continuance).
- Change the trial's location to a place where there is less prejudicial publicity (change of venue).
- Bring a group of potential jurors from somewhere outside the range of prejudicial publicity (change of venire).
- As a last resort, declare a mistral or throw out a jury's verdict based on prejudicial publicity, and have a new trial.

Figure 14.2   Instead of Gags or Closing Courts . . .

But a warning: If a judge issues a gag order against the press, the order must be appealed. Don't just assume the order is unconstitutional, so you can publish. Court orders must be obeyed and appealed. Courts are split on what happens next where gag orders are concerned. Some require waiting until an appellate court rules—even if that happens long after the story has any news value (*United States v. Dickinson*, 1972). If you publish before that, you'll likely be found in contempt of court. Some other courts will allow publication if the appellate court doesn't rule in a "reasonable" time (*Providence Journal*, 1986). In part, reasonable depends on your deadline. (But if the appellate court ultimately finds the gag order constitutional, you'll be in contempt.) Most courts haven't decided this question at all. Check with your media attorney.

In many states, statutes prevent court and other government personnel from releasing the names of defendants in juvenile proceedings. Only a few states have a restriction on publishing the names of rape or other sexual assault victims, and those laws are open to challenge. Most media choose not to print these names, but that is a question of journalistic ethics, not the law.

If courts can't limit publication of most judicial information, can they prevent the media from obtaining the information initially? One way is to close the courthouse doors, keeping the media out. Generally, this is not permitted. But if a judge can show that closure would be necessary to prevent a miscarriage of justice, no other means will accomplish that, and the courthouse is closed for no longer than necessary, an appellate court may uphold a judge's decision to keep out the press and public (*Press-Enterprise Co. v. Superior Court*, 1986). Some courts have held that the press is entitled to a hearing on the question before a court is closed to them.

The Supreme Court has said that judicial proceedings also should be open if they have been historically and if it will help the public's understanding of the judicial process (*Press-Enterprise Co. v. Superior Court*, 1986). For these reasons, jury deliberations, grand jury proceedings, and conferences in judges' chambers are not accessible to the press. Pretrial hearings, jury selection and sentencing hearings, however, presumptively are open. But while the Court has not heard cases challenging closure of civil trials, it did say that civil trials have been open throughout English and American court history. And it would seem that the public needs to know about civil as well as criminal proceedings.

Even if reporters are allowed into court, may still and television cameras follow? All but four states permit cameras in court to one degree or another. About two-thirds of the states allow cameras in trial courtrooms; several others permit cameras in appellate courts. Some states require the consent of all parties. In about one-third of the states judicial consent is not required. Cameras are banned in all federal trial courts, and nearly all federal appellate courts. (See Sidebar 14.4.)

Sidebar 14.4 Cameras in Court? Yes and No

The Supreme Court has held that having still or television cameras in a courtroom doesn't automatically mean a trial will be unfair (*Chandler v. Florida*, 1981). That left it to individual states to decide whether to allow cameras in courts—and 45 of 50 have, some having more liberal policies than others. Only Indiana, Mississippi, New York, and South Dakota do not allow them at all. In 1997 New York let its law lapse that permitted cameras in court.

But federal courts are different. Cameras never have been allowed in the Supreme Court of the United States and won't be until all justices agree (quite unlikely). And for a half-century, federal court rules have banned cameras in criminal courtrooms, trial or appellate level. However, there are no rules concerning civil trials. From 1991 to 1994 the federal judiciary conducted an experiment, permitting cameras in several trial and appellate courts dealing with civil matters. It appeared to most observers—and judges—to be a success. But at the end of the experiment, the judicial oversight group voted not to continue it.

In 1996 that same group voted to allow federal courts of appeal to decide for themselves whether to allow cameras into appellate arguments. The Second and Fourth Circuits have decided to do so. Others have decided not to or have not yet made a decision. And a few federal trial court judges in New York (part of the Second Circuit) recently have permitted cameras into civil proceedings. The federal judicial oversight group did not say trial judges couldn't do this but has urged them not to.

The end result, then, is that in nearly all states there can be still and television camera coverage of some (or many) judicial proceedings, but that is true in only a very few federal courts.

Courts generally have found that the press has access to judicial records presented in open court. Some courts hold that this is a First Amendment right. Courts are divided on whether this includes the right to copy tapes used during hearings or trials. And journalists almost certainly will be unsuccessful in asking a judge to let them see documents that are sealed by a court, or are exchanged during the pretrial discovery period but not presented in open court.

CONTEMPT OF COURT

Judges control their courtrooms through the contempt power. A contempt citation issued by a judge can lead to a fine or jail. And the "summary" contempt power allows a judge to be accuser, judge, and "executioner"—almost before the bewildered object of the judge's wrath knows what happened.

Judges use contempt to force someone to do something, such as reveal information. Called "civil" contempt, the penalty—often jail—is in force until the person complies or the court decides it no longer needs the information. Or contempt may be used to punish someone for disobeying a court order. This is "criminal" contempt and involves a finite punishment such as a specific jail term or a certain fine.

Summary contempt cannot be used if the punishment is more than six months in jail or more than a $500 fine. In those circumstances, there must be a trial on the contempt charge before a different judge.

Courts no longer may cite journalists for contempt on the basis of stories or editorials highly critical of a judge or the judicial process generally, unless it can be shown that the publication would bring about an immediate and serious miscarriage of justice (*Bridges v. California,* 1941).

Congress and most state legislatures also have the contempt tool at their disposal, and for the same purposes—to elicit information or to punish for disobeying orders.

REPORTERS' PRIVILEGE

Journalists face a difficult choice when a court orders them to produce the names of sources, other confidential information, or other materials, such as notes or outtakes. This may happen when an attorney for a party to a lawsuit or a criminal defendant, or a prosecuting attorney, or even the judge herself, seeks information from a journalist, either in court or in a deposition. If the journalist disobeys, he faces a contempt citation. But if he complies, a host of journalistic ethics questions arise: A reporter who reveals sources' names soon may have no sources; the reporter won't be trusted. Journalists contend that they don't work for lawyers, judges, or police—they work for their employers; if they found the information, so can those who want it. But what about the Sixth Amendment's guarantee that "the accused shall . . . be confronted with the witnesses against him [and be able to obtain] witnesses in his favor . . ."? If he can't find out who those witnesses are, because only the journalist knows, can there be a fair trial?

Again, courts have tried to respect both First and Sixth Amendment rights. The Supreme Court has held that journalists are like everyone else before a grand jury—answer the questions asked or be held in contempt (*Branzburg v. Hayes,* 1972). There is no protection for the press. However, many courts do recognize a qualified First Amendment privilege for reporters to withhold information at trial or pretrial hearings, or at depositions when asked by lawyers for parties to a case (see Fig. 14.3).

These courts use a balancing test to decide whether reporters have this privilege. First, they ask whether it is likely the reporter has the information being sought. This is to prevent "fishing" expeditions by lawyers, prosecutors, or judges who are just trying to find out anything the journalist might know. Sometimes the published story may make it obvious that the reporter is in possession of the information, but it may not be that evident.

Many courts have read something into a Supreme Court decision that the Court didn't say. In *Branzburg v. Hayes* (1972), the Court ruled that journalists, just like everyone else, must testify before grand juries when subpoenaed to do so. However, the four dissenting justices in that case, and one justice who agreed with the majority but wrote a separate opinion as well, took another view. They indicated that under certain circumstances journalists should have a qualified First Amendment privilege not to reveal to courts the names of sources or other confidential information, or maybe any information at all. It's a qualified privilege because judges must balance several factors before allowing journalists to remain silent. Judges should consider:

- Whether it's likely a reporter has the information being sought. Judges and attorneys are not to go on a "fishing expedition," trying to find out if a journalist might know anything pertinent.
- Whether the information is reasonably available from other sources. Reporters are not to be the first—or even among the first—source asked for the information.
- Whether the information sought is sufficiently important to override the reporter's First Amendment rights.
- The type of legal proceeding involved. Reporters are more likely to be ordered to reveal information in a criminal case, since a person's freedom—or life—may be at stake. It would be less likely in a civil proceeding, which often end in an exchange of money rather than a decision on someone's liberty.

Figure 14.3 Keeping a Reporter's Mouth Shut

Second, courts consider whether there are other reasonable ways to obtain the information. Reporters should not be the first stop. If, without an inordinate expenditure of time or money, the information may be obtained from another source, that's where it should be sought.

Third, courts ask whether the information being sought really goes to the heart of the judicial proceeding and is sufficiently important to override the incursion on the press's First Amendment rights.

Fourth, for what type of proceeding is the information wanted? Courts are less likely to find a privilege to withhold information in criminal trials. After all, people's freedom and possibly lives may be at stake. But in civil proceedings, the stakes usually are less important and courts may be more open to finding a privilege.

However, one civil proceeding may be different—when the press is a party in a libel suit. The plaintiff may need to know, for instance, the journalist's source to try to prove actual malice. If the journalist claims a privilege not to reveal her source, she may hold the result of the lawsuit in her hand and refuse to open it. Judges take umbrage at this and often order the journalist to reveal the source. Some courts go so far as to have the jury assume no source at all existed if the journalist will not reveal who the source was.

Nearly 30 states have taken another approach. They have adopted laws—called "shield laws"—that offer varying degrees of protection to the press not to reveal sources and other information in state court. (There is no national shield law to be used in federal courts.) Shield laws differ widely from state to state. There is little consistency about who is protected under the laws (generally not freelancers or book authors, for example), whether information must be confidential to be protected, the type of information protected (notes or outtakes? only if in the reporter's possession?), or whether the protection is for criminal or civil trials or both.

In an unusual but important case involving confidential information, a campaign official for a gubernatorial candidate told reporters that, if they promised to keep his name confidential, he would reveal information about the opposing candidate (*Cohen v. Cowles Media Co.*, 1991). Reporters from two newspapers promised confidentiality, and the campaign official revealed that the candidate had been convicted of shoplifting $6 worth of goods a dozen years earlier.

Editors at the two newspapers decided to reveal the campaign official's name because they thought the real story was his attempt at an "eleventh hour" attack on the opposing candidate. The campaign official sued both papers. The Supreme Court held that the First Amendment does not protect journalists who breach a promise of confidentiality. The case was returned to the state courts, and the campaign official was awarded $200,000 in damages.

Courts since then have split on the issue. But several have found that news sources may sue for breaches of promises of confidentiality. (See Sidebar 14.5.)

Sidebar 14.5 Disguised Contract

Media representatives make promises of confidentiality in many ways. For example, two rape victims and the boyfriend of one of them were asked by a television station to appear on a series of reports about rape. They agreed only if they could retain anonymity. The station promised them repeatedly that their faces and voices would be disguised. However, a number of people recognized one of the women who was shown in the first series report. When she complained to the station, she again was assured that no one would be recognized in the subsequent reports. In those broadcasts, though, each of the women was recognized, in part because apparently no attempt was made to disguise their voices. They sued, and the courts found they could maintain a lawsuit for negligent infliction of emotional distress and for breach of contract—the contract stating that they would appear on the programs if the station would disguise them, which the station promised, but seemingly failed, to do (*Doe v. American Broadcasting Companies*, 1989).

Information also may be sought from journalists through the use of search warrants. Twenty years ago, the Supreme Court ruled that if served with a properly executed warrant to search for materials, journalists can do little but stand aside and let the search take place (*Zurcher v. Stanford Daily*, 1978). Fortunately, this rarely happens. Federal law and some state statutes have limited the serving of warrants on journalists. Under the federal Privacy Protection Act, a search warrant may be used against reporters only if necessary to prevent a crime or bodily injury, if it can be shown it is likely the journalist has been directly involved in a crime, or if national security is at stake.

Reporters may believe it important to protect sources and information, but their corporate employers may not. It is most often the employers who pay legal fees to fight for a reporter's right not to reveal information. But the corporate employers may not think the fight is worth the expense or time. And they may urge journalists to pressure a source to reveal himself or herself, so the issue is diffused.

Many of these internal and legal conflicts may be avoided if newsrooms have clearly stated policies about how reporters are to handle promises of confidentiality. When is a promise to be given? Is the promise to be explicit, rather than implicit? Are editors to be notified first? Also, there will be fewer problems if media managers are certain their news staffs are thoroughly familiar with the law in their state regarding reporter's privilege.

CHAPTER SUMMARY

Commercial speech—speech proposing a commercial transaction—has less First Amendment protection than some other forms of expression. The government may regulate advertising in ways that it could not regulate a newspaper editorial or television situation comedy, for example. Advertising that is for an illegal product or service, or that is deceptive or misleading, has no protection, and the government generally may deal with it as it wishes. To regulate other commercial speech, the government first must show that it has an important interest that justifies the regulation. Then it has to prove that the advertising regulation will directly and substantially further that interest. Finally, there must be a "reasonable fit" between the regulation and the interest. That is, the government must adopt a regulation that will do less harm, rather than more harm, to the advertiser's freedom of expression, while still meeting the government's goal.

The First Amendment does not protect obscene material. Courts use a three-part test to determine if material is obscene: (1) Does the material appeal to the prurient interest, (2) is it patently offensive, and (3) taken as a whole, does it lack serious literary, artistic, political, or scientific value?

Original material that is fixed in a tangible medium is copyrighted and protected from the moment it is created. However, to sue under the Copyright Act for copyright infringement, the work must be registered with the Copyright Office. Not all uses of copyrighted works without permission are impermissible. A "fair use" defense may be available. Courts will balance four factors to determine if a use is an infringement: (1) What was the purpose of using the copyrighted material, (2) what was the nature of the copyrighted material, (3) how much and what portion of the copyrighted work was used, and (4) what is the impact on the market value of the copy-

righted work? Quoting a small portion of a novel in a book review, for example, likely would be a fair use.

Music also is protected by copyright. To use a recorded song, permission must be obtained from the composer, or a music licensing company, and from the recording company. Permission also is needed to "synchronize" a recording to film or videotape.

News gathering has little First Amendment protection. Certain records in the possession of some federal government agencies may be obtained under the Freedom of Information Act. States also have open records laws. Both the federal and state governments have open meetings laws.

The U.S. Supreme Court has found a First Amendment right for the press and public to be in courtrooms for most parts of the judicial process. The Court also has established a test for determining whether a gag order may be imposed on the press to prevent publication of material the judge considers prejudicial to a fair trial. The test is very difficult for a judge to meet, and gag orders are rarely, if ever, upheld by appellate courts. Nearly all states permit cameras in some courts under some conditions. Few federal courts allow cameras.

Judges use their contempt powers to maintain order in court. Contempt also may be used when reporters refuse to reveal the names of sources or other information when ordered by a court to do so. However, journalists often are protected in one of two ways. First, 30 states have shield laws. These are legislative declarations that reporters should not have to reveal some types of information under some circumstances. Shield laws vary widely from state to state. Second, most of the remaining states and many federal courts recognize a conditional First Amendment privilege meant to prevent courts from requiring journalists to reveal information in some instances.

1. Courts see commercial speech as having less value than some other forms of expression. How is this reflected in the way commercial speech may be regulated?

2. What limitations does copyright law place on how the media may use previously created material?

3. Generally, courts hold that news gathering is not protected by the First Amendment. What protections do journalists have for gathering information?

4. What means may judges normally not use against the media to ensure a fair trial?

Why? What tools should judges consider using instead?

5. In what ways are journalists protected from being required to reveal to courts the names of sources and other confidential information?

chapter 15

REGULATING THE ELECTRONIC MEDIA

Electronic media managers must be concerned not only with the profusion of legal issues discussed in the previous two chapters, but also with many additional laws, rules, and regulations that apply only to the electronic media. Courts have offered a variety of justifications for treating these forms of communication differently than print media under the First Amendment. Owners and managers of broadcast stations, cable systems, and newer media, and organizations that represent them, continue to rail against their "second-class" status. Adding to the travail of keeping up with the rules of the electronic media game, the regulations change, sometimes often, sometimes based on which way the political winds are blowing. All this means that it's essential to consult with your media lawyer.

RATIONALES FOR REGULATING THE ELECTRONIC MEDIA

The electronic media often have argued in courts that their First Amendment rights prohibit Congress and the FCC from limiting what they may say to their audiences or requiring them to say certain things. But the basic foundation of regulating the electronic media in ways that the First Amendment would not permit for print media has remained intact for nearly three-quarters of a century. The Supreme Court has held that different mass media may be treated differently under the First Amendment (*Joseph Burstyn, Inc. v. Wilson*, 1952), and that broadcasting (*Red Lion Broadcasting Co. v. FCC*, 1969) and cable television (*Turner Broadcasting System, Inc. v. FCC*, 1997, 1994) in particular do not have the same freedom of expression as do newspapers, magazines, pamphlets, and books.

Why Broadcasting and New Technologies Are Regulated

Radio broadcasting initially was used for ship-to-ship and ship-to-shore transmissions. After the *Titanic* disaster, in which lives might have been saved had the radio operator for a nearby ship been on duty, there were national and international calls for radio regulation. Congress adopted the Radio Act of 1912, replacing the Wireless Ship Act of 1910. But the 1912 law gave the Secretary of Commerce no power to reject radio license applications; he only could grant licenses for frequencies that, when used properly, would not interfere with other licensees. Radio transmissions, then, proliferated. Some radio operators cared little about the few rules in the law, and soon there was constant interference on the radio band.

World War I prompted the development of improved radio equipment. When the war ended, the factories manufacturing the equipment for the armed forces turned to making radio sets. But if people were to purchase radios they needed programming and assurances that they could hear it without interference. The 1912 law was hopelessly deficient for coping with the situation. Radio manufacturers and others prevailed upon Congress to adopt the Radio Act of 1924, which established the Federal Radio Commission (FRC). The FRC was supposed to clean up the mess and go out of existence. But it became clear that some agency would need to continue paying attention to commercial radio. To combine oversight of radio and interstate telephone service, Congress passed the Federal Communications Act of 1934, which gave the Federal Communications Commission (FCC) jurisdiction over use of the electromagnetic spectrum and interstate communication by wires (telephones and telegraph) (Emery & Emery, 1996; Head, Sterling, & Schofield, 1994).

But those involved in commercial radio received more than they wanted. Instead of just a "traffic cop" making certain that radio licensees did not interfere with each other's signals, the FCC took control of a number of facets of the industry. This included establishing rules governing relationships between the nascent radio networks and local radio stations. In part, the Commission believed that its responsibility was to protect "local" radio, under its charge to ensure broadcasters acted in the "public interest." The FCC argued that networks were exerting too much control over local stations, and it instituted regulations to prevent this.

The networks took the Commission to court. The Supreme Court held in the FCC's favor, stating that radio's "facilities are limited; they are not available to all who may wish to use them; the radio spectrum simply is not large enough to accommodate everybody. There is a fixed natural limitation upon the number of stations that can operate without interfering with one another" (*National Broadcasting Co. v. FCC*, 1943). The Court established the primary rationale for allowing broadcast regulation: The spectrum is a limited resource that only a few people can use; therefore, it is reasonable, even under the First Amendment, for the government to impose special conditions on these people in exchange for their right to use the spectrum.

The Court reiterated this argument in *Red Lion Broadcasting Co. v. FCC* (1969). In upholding an FCC rule requiring stations to provide free time to individuals personally attacked during a discussion of controversial matters, the Court said that the audience's First Amendment rights took precedence over the broadcaster's interests. It justified this on the basis of limited spectrum space that prevents all who want to broadcast their views to the public from doing so (see Fig. 15.1).

Although the Supreme Court has suggested it understands that new technologies may make the spectrum scarcity argument obsolete (*FCC v. League of Women Voters of California*, 1984), the rationale remains the primary one used by courts for continuing to regulate broadcasters in ways not faced by the print media.

People who own and work for radio and television stations argue that they are as entitled to full First Amendment protection as are the print media. But courts disagree. Why?

- *Spectrum scarcity.* The electromagnetic spectrum allows a limited number of radio and television stations in any geographical area. Since not everyone can own and operate a station, then, those who are given that right also can be given certain public interest obligations.
- *Broadcasting is pervasive.* You hear radio and see television everywhere. It surrounds us. Since we are exposed to it so much—often unwillingly—it can be controlled in ways not necessary for other media.
- *Impact on children.* Broadcasting—particularly television—has more of an impact on audiences than do the print media.

Figure 15.1 Why Regulate Broadcasting?

The Supreme Court also has suggested that broadcast media are pervasive, they are everywhere (*FCC v. Pacifica Foundation,* 1978). It is nearly impossible to go into a store or restaurant, or someone's home, without hearing a radio station or seeing a television set turned on, the Court said, showing broadcasting's intrusive nature. On the other hand, you have to decide to subscribe to or purchase a newspaper or magazine. That makes them different from broadcast stations, courts have argued, and again justifies treating them differently.

Some courts have said that broadcasting, especially television, has a special impact on audiences, one more powerful than the print media have (*Robinson v. American Broadcasting Co.,* 1971). Courts have applied this rationale to children, in particular. This is a third reason for imposing special regulations on radio and television.

Regulating radio and then television based on their use of the electromagnetic spectrum allowed an easy leap to regulating new communications technologies that also use the spectrum, such as direct broadcast satellites and wireless cable. The 1934 act gives the FCC jurisdiction over these media because they use the spectrum. But the Commission generally has not imposed as much regulation on them as on broadcasting, in part as a way to allow them to grow into competitors for over-the-air and cable television.

Why Cable Television Is Regulated

Cable television began as a way *not* to use the spectrum. Signals from television transmitting towers couldn't get through mountains or buildings, or stretch far enough, for some people to receive them on their television sets. Intercept the signals with a tall antenna, run them down a coaxial cable, and deliver them to people who will pay for the service, and you have cable television. It's a lot more sophisticated today, with satellite receiving dishes, optical fiber, set-top decoding boxes, and high-speed modems. But the idea is the same: Keep the signals in the cables. In fact, FCC regulations require that; cable systems can be fined if their radio frequency (RF) signals leak.

Then what justifies regulating cable? On the local level (which may mean city, county, state, or some combination), it's cable's use of public rights-of-way. Cable systems need to run their wires over (or under) public streets, alleys, parks, and other public property. The trade for receiving permission to use public rights-of-way is an agreement to be subject to some regulation by the "franchising authority." The written agreement, which essentially is a contract between the two parties, is called a "franchise."

Some cable system operators have argued that they should not be required to have a franchise in order to offer service to subscribers, that it violates cable's First Amendment rights. They say that, for example, trucks use the public streets to deliver newspapers and magazines, and no franchise is required for those media. The Supreme Court has not ruled directly on this issue, but two of its cable decisions may explain why it appears to be constitutional to require cable systems to have local franchises. In 1986 the Court said that cable does have "First Amendment interests" (*City of Los Angeles v. Preferred Communications, Inc.,* 1986). In 1994 it explained what they are (*Turner Broadcasting System, Inc. v. FCC,* 1994). If a government regulation directly concerns cable television program content, the government must show a "compelling" need to impose that rule. That is the standard used to determine whether a print media regulation is constitutional. But if a regulation is designed to serve another purpose and only incidentally affects cable content, the government must show just an "important" reason for imposing it. To the degree that a community regulates cable as it does other public utilities, the government has an "important" purpose for the regulation it imposes. For example, the city needs to oversee the use of public rights-of-way, including digging up city streets to install cable equipment, and it should ensure the widest possible availability of the cable system for the city's residents. These are goals that do not directly involve content of cable programming.

Regulation on the national level came slowly. Forty years ago the Federal Communications Commission decided that it had no jurisdiction over cable television. After all, cable does not use the electromagnetic spectrum. Shortly after that, broadcasters convinced the FCC to change its mind. Then the Supreme Court ruled that cable television has an impact on broadcasting, over which the FCC does have power (*United States v. Southwestern Cable Co.,* 1968). That allows the Commission to exercise jurisdiction over cable as "ancillary" to its control of broadcasting. Later the Court said that the FCC has expansive powers over cable, including some powers that state and local authorities do not have (*Capital Cities Cable, Inc. v. Crisp,* 1984).

Today, cable jurisdiction is split between local authorities and the FCC. A series of congressional enactments, primarily the Cable Television Acts of 1984 and 1992 and the Telecommunications Act of 1996, divide authority among the two levels and impose some limits on the extent to which local authorities may control cable.

THE FEDERAL COMMUNICATIONS COMMISSION

Since the FCC issues most of the rules and regulations affecting the electronic media, it is helpful to be familiar with the Commission's structure and how it operates. The FCC has five commissioners, one of whom is the chair. They are nominated by the president and must be approved by the Senate. They are appointed for five-year terms and may be reappointed. No more than three commissioners at any time may be members of one political party. The Commission's annual funding comes from Congress.

Much of the FCC's work is done by its approximately 2,000 staff members. They report to the heads of a series of bureaus and offices, who themselves are responsible to the commissioners. The Commission may act in several ways, including adopting regulations applicable to an entire industry, adjudicating cases involving violations of FCC rules and selecting licensees through a variety of means. Commission decisions may be appealed to the courts, most often to the federal appellate court for the District of Columbia circuit.

The FCC has several penalties it may use to enforce its rules, from letters in a licensee's file that may play a part in license renewal applications, to fines, to short-term license renewal, to license revocation. Broadcast licenses rarely are revoked, although some public interest groups have argued that they should be more often than they have been.

When the FCC is considering adopting or changing regulations, it issues a Notice of Proposed Rule Making. Members of the public—usually companies with a stake in the rules—and others, such as the U.S. Department of Justice, submit comments. Then reply comments may be submitted in response. Appropriate staff members prepare a draft of the FCC's order (or perhaps Notice of Further Proposed Rule Making, in which case comments and reply comments again may be submitted), the commissioners discuss the draft, first among themselves and then openly at a public meeting, and vote to adopt or reject the regulations. The FCC also may issue a Notice of Inquiry, usually concerning matters pertinent to the Commission but that either they do not control, such as a congressional statute, or about which they want to gather information before deciding whether to take further steps. Comments and reply comments also are submitted for Notices of Inquiry.

Complaints brought to the FCC's attention by the public or its staff may be handled by the appropriate bureau, such as the Mass Media Bureau or Compliance and Information Bureau, or be decided by an administrative law judge. These decisions can be appealed to the commissioners and then taken to court.

ELECTRONIC MEDIA CONTENT

The Communications Act of 1934 forbids the FCC from imposing censorship. The Supreme Court has found that cable television operators have First Amendment rights, and the Court never has denied that broadcasters have a certain level of protection under the First Amendment. Despite all this, both broadcasting and cable face a number of laws and rules regarding their content. Broadcasters and cable operators sometimes are told they cannot run certain material, and at other times are told they must run something. Some of this may have to do with how the political winds are blowing, and some has to do with society's assessment of what is acceptable radio and television content.

Obscenity and Indecency

Obscenity isn't a question for radio or broadcast or cable television. Obscene material—as defined by the *Miller v. California* (1973) case—is no more permissible on broadcasting and cable outlets than it is in any other mass medium. The problem is with "indecency," a concern not faced by other mass media.

The 1934 Communications Act and the U.S. Criminal Code forbid broadcasters from airing material that is "obscene, indecent or profane." The Supreme Court defined "indecency" in *FCC v. Pacifica Foundation* (1978) as words that "describe, in terms patently offensive as measured by contemporary community standards for the broadcast medium, sexual or excretory activities and organs, at times of the day where there is reasonable risk that children may be in the audience."

During the last decade, Congress has made clear that it expects the FCC to enforce the law and rid broadcasting of indecency. As a compromise between the literal words of the law and broadcasters' First Amendment rights, the Commission has channeled indecent material into time periods when children are less likely to be in the listening or viewing audience. After a series of disagreements among the FCC, Congress, and the courts, the "safe harbor" period—the times when indecent, but of course not obscene, material may be broadcast without penalty—has been set at 10 P.M. to 6 A.M. (*Action for Children's Television v. FCC,* 1995). That leaves 6 A.M. until 10 P.M. when programming may not be indecent. And the Commission enforces that. It has fined Infinity Broadcasting Corporation, syndicator of the "Howard Stern Show," $1.7 million for a series of indecency rule violations on the Stern program and has fined a number of other broadcasters thousands of dollars.

Cable television finds itself in a different position regarding indecency. Courts have held that the statutory provisions banning indecency in broadcasting do not apply to cable, since cable is invited into the home, a decision made each month when the bill is paid (*Cruz v. Ferre,* 1985). Anyone not wanting cable programming in their home simply need not take the service.

However, Congress several times has attempted to limit indecency on cable. The 1992 cable act allows cable operators to refuse programming for commercial leased access channels, discussed later in this chapter, that the operator "reasonably believes describes or depicts sexual or excretory activities or organs in a patently offensive manner as measured by contemporary community standards." The 1996 telecommunications act also lets cable operators refuse to carry programming on leased access channels "which contains obscenity, indecency, or nudity" (*Denver Area Educational Telecommunications Consortium, Inc. v. FCC,* 1996). Both these provisions are permissive: Cable operators may choose not to carry such programming and say that Congress told them they could. But they don't have to refuse.

Additionally, Congress has acted regarding public, educational, and government (PEG) channels, also discussed later in this chapter. For example, under the 1984 cable act, a franchising authority and a cable operator may agree that the system will not carry on PEG channels material that is "obscene or otherwise unprotected by the United States Constitution."

The 1996 telecommunications act instructed the FCC to develop rules regarding carriage of sexually explicit material on other cable channels. The Commission decided that systems would have to prevent "bleed" of channels primarily carrying adult programming, either by scrambling or blocking them. Bleed occurs when a channel is not completely scrambled, so that some audio or video may be discernible. If a cable system is unable to prevent these channels from "bleeding," it could carry them only during the safe harbor times of 10 P.M. to 6 A.M. The Supreme Court affirmed a lower court decision not to block enforcement of this provision of the 1996 act (*Playboy Entertainment Group, Inc. v. United States,* 1997), and the FCC now will ensure that cable systems comply with it.

Indecency on the Internet has been much in the news. In the 1996 telecommunications act, Congress prohibited sending or making available to minors any indecent material. The Supreme Court found this provision, called the Communications Decency Act (CDA), violated the First Amendment (*Reno v. ACLU,* 1997). The Court said that the Internet should be given expansive First Amendment protection.

Political Broadcasting and Cablecasting

In both the 1927 and 1934 acts, Congress made certain that broadcasters (and now cable operators) could not give preference to one candidate for public office over another.

Nothing prevents the *print* media from doing so. In general, the political broadcasting and cablecasting rules say that if one legally qualified candidate for an elective office uses a broadcast station or cable system, the station or system, if asked, must provide equal opportunity to other legally qualified candidates for the same office. This rule, which is Section 315 of the Communications Act of 1934, is in effect any time there are two legally qualified candidates for the same office, no matter how long that is before an election (see Fig. 15.2).

- When there are two or more legally qualified candidates
  —A legally qualified candidate has secured a place on the ballot or is a serious write-in candidate.
- running for the same political office
  —In a primary election, the test is whether they are running for the same nomination—the same office and the same political party.
- and one candidate uses a broadcast station or cable system
  —A use is the candidate herself or himself, the candidate's picture or likeness, or the candidate's voice (but not the candidate's name only) being on the station or system—regardless of whether the candidate discusses the election.
  —But certain appearances are not uses:
    - Regularly scheduled newscast
    - Regularly scheduled news interview program
    - On-the-spot news coverage
    - Documentary (if the candidate's appearance is not the documentary's primary focus)
- then, if asked,
  —A candidate must make a request within seven days of her or his opponent's use.
- the station or system must provide equal opportunity to the other candidate(s)
  —Equal opportunity is the opportunity to reach approximately the same audience for approximately the same amount of time.
- at a comparable price
  —For free if the first candidate did not pay for the time. For the lowest unit rate if 45 days before a primary or 60 days before a general election.
- and without any control over content of the candidate's use of the station or system.

Figure 15.2   Political Broadcasting and Cablecasting

Legally Qualified Candidates

A legally qualified candidate is one who has a place on the ballot or is a bona fide write-in candidate. A write-in candidate must have shown a definite intention to campaign, perhaps by giving speeches, having a campaign manager, opening a campaign head-quarters, or by some other means to indicate she is a serious candidate. A legally qualified candidate also must be eligible to hold the office for which he is running. For example, a 25-year-old running for the office of president of the United States is not a legally qualified candidate, since the Constitution requires the president to be at least 35 years old.

Even someone widely acknowledged as a likely candidate—the incumbent governor, for example—is not a legally qualified candidate until she is on the ballot or is a serious write-in candidate, or at least has made a formal public announcement that she is a candidate for reelection. The governor, then, can continue to give speeches and hold press conferences without triggering Section 315. On the other hand, someone with little or no chance of winning the election—a minor party candidate, for example—still is a legally qualified candidate under Section 315 and has the same right to an equal opportunity to use a broadcast station or cable system as do more prominent candidates.

Section 315 kicks in only when legally qualified candidates are running for the same office. That seems obvious, but isn't. The FCC says that in a primary election, only those candidates vying for the *same* party's nomination are running against each other. Republicans and Democrats don't run against each other in partisan primary elections. And independent candidates are not running against anyone in a primary. Neither is anyone without an opponent within his party for the same office. However, if the primary is nonpartisan (even if candidates' party affiliations are listed), then all candidates for that office are running against one another.

"Use" of a Broadcast Station or Cable System

Section 315 is triggered by an opposing candidate's "use" of a station or cable system. The FCC defines "use" as the candidate's appearance, or the candidate's picture, likeness, or voice being used. Note that simply using a candidate's name does not constitute a use. This does not have to be in a commercial. A candidate appearing on the noon cooking show has used the station, even if not a word about politics was spoken while the Moroccan chicken was being prepared. The candidate's face was seen and his voice was heard by potential voters. That's a use. What's more, the use does not have to be instigated by the candidate. If a station or cable system reruns an old cooking show on which the candidate appeared—before he even thought about being a candidate—that is a use.

Because this definition would cause news programs not to interview candidates—if you interview one, you would have to interview all, including minor party and independent candidates—and also presented other problems, Congress established four exceptions to the use rule. First, a candidate's appearance (or picture, likeness, or voice) on a regularly scheduled news program will not trigger Section 315. Second, regularly scheduled news interview programs are exempt. These must have been regularly scheduled during nonelection periods. This exception is not for programs "regularly scheduled" each Wednesday for four weeks prior to the election. Those types of programs are *not* exempted. This is meant for programs such as "Meet the Press," "Issues and Answers," and their local counterparts. But the exception also has been extended to such programs as "Entertainment Tonight" and a number of "talk" programs, both on radio and television, that are regularly scheduled outside of campaign periods.

Third, live coverage of bona fide news events is exempt. If a candidate makes a campaign appearance in your town, and you cover that live, that will not be a use. Even if you have to delay the broadcast for an hour or two because it conflicts with, say, a football game, that's OK. But you can't delay it for days and still have it considered an exception to the use rule.

Finally, there is an exemption for documentaries if the candidate's appearance is incidental to the program's topic. For example, if a candidate for governor is an expert on the environment, and you are preparing a program about cleaning up a local river, you could interview the candidate briefly, as you would any other expert on the topic. Of course, you could not run a documentary on the candidate's life as a politician and consider it exempt from Section 315 requirements.

Also, there will not be a use if the candidate's picture, likeness, or voice is used in a disparaging way. For example, in a 60-second commercial John stands in front of Jane's picture and lists all the reasons people shouldn't vote for her but should vote for him. Then he demands that the station provide him with a free minute. Jane's picture was on the station for a minute, and she didn't pay for it. No. Jane's picture was treated in a disparaging way. Jane hasn't used the station.

Requesting Equal Opportunity

Within seven days of when a candidate has used a broadcast station or cable system, other candidates for the same office may request equal opportunity. The opponents' appearances do not have to take place within seven days, but the requests must be made within that time period. If a request is not made within seven days, Section 315 does not apply.

The station or system does not have to notify other candidates of the first candidate's use. But the station or system must put in its public file information about any requests for a political use (both for commercials and other uses), and the dispositions of those requests.

Lowest Unit Rate

If a candidate uses the station or system without paying—appearing on a cooking show, for example—any other candidate for that office gets a free use. That's equal opportunity. But if the first candidate paid for commercial time, others must pay, as well. How much? This is the "lowest unit rate" rule. The station or cable system may charge no more than it would charge its best advertiser (i.e., the one purchasing the most time over the year) for that commercial time and type. Lowest unit rate is in effect for 45 days prior to primary elections, and 60 days prior to general elections. Outside those periods, candidates can be charged per the rate card. But they must be charged comparable rates; you can't charge one candidate more than another for the same office if they are purchasing approximately the same commercial time and type.

Approximately the Same Audience

Equal opportunity also means reaching approximately the same audience. If John purchases a minute at 7:58 P.M. Wednesday, Jane may purchase that time slot the following Monday. What if it already is taken? Or what if there isn't another Wednesday before the election? The station must find a time that will give Jane approximately the same audience. That cannot be 3 A.M., or even 5 P.M. But it could be 7:28 P.M. or 8:58 P.M. on a weekday. As with most questions regarding Section 315, the FCC assumes broadcasters and cable operators are acting in good faith making these decisions—unless it is shown otherwise.

Stations and Systems Cannot Edit

Stations and cable systems in no way can require changes in what candidates want to do with their time—whether that time is free or paid. If Jane has free time because John was on a cooking program, Jane need not show how to make fried chicken. She can spend her time promoting her candidacy, even though John said not a word about his. More to the point, if Jane has purchased time, she may use it as she wishes. That can include racist and homophobic remarks, for example. It also includes saying John robs banks. If that isn't true, John may sue Jane for libel. But what about suing the station for republishing the libel? Fortunately, the Supreme Court has ruled that if stations and cable systems have no control over what candidates say, they have no liability for it, either (*Farmers Educational and Cooperative Union v. WDAY, Inc.,* 1959).

When some politicians began asking to air commercials that included pictures of, or were supposed to be of, aborted fetuses, questions arose about whether stations could refuse such ads. The FCC said stations could not refuse them. But while the ads were not necessarily "indecent," they could be channeled to the safe harbor period established for indecent programming so that children would be less likely to be exposed them. A court said this would give broadcasters too much discretion and ruled that the ads had to be treated just like any other political commercials; that is, the station has no control over content (*Becker v. FCC,* 1996). (See Sidebar 15.1.)

Sidebar 15.1 Controversial Political Content

In the last decade, some politicians have included in their advertisements photographs of what were said to be aborted fetuses. Several television stations initially refused to air the ads, but the FCC told them they had no right to censor political commercials. Other stations argued that the ads were indecent and inappropriate for children. At the request of a television station owner, the FCC in 1992 considered how stations could handle such political ads. The Commission permitted stations to carry the ads only during times when fewer children would be watching, 10 P.M. to 6 A.M. But a candidate objected and appealed the Commission's order. A federal appellate court ruled that the FCC's approach would allow discrimination against certain political ads based on their content, would permit stations to censor political ads, and would not allow equal opportunity for all political candidates to reach similar broadcast audiences (*Becker v. FCC,* 1996). These ads, then, are to be dealt with just as a station would handle any other political commercial.

Federal Candidates

One way to avoid controversial political commercials might be not to allow any candidate to use your station or cable system. If the first candidate doesn't use it, other candidates can't request equal opportunity. But it won't work. The FCC essentially has said that stations need to sell (or give, if they prefer) time to candidates. Otherwise they wouldn't be acting in "the public interest." But Congress didn't leave it to chance when it came to themselves—oh, yes, and to the presidential and vice presidential candidates, too. Section 312(a)(7) of the 1934 act requires broadcast stations to provide "reasonable access" to candidates for federal offices. Courts have interpreted that to mean that when a candidate for a federal office asks to purchase advertising time, a broadcast station must sell it.

Section 312(a)(7) likely applies to cable system, as well. However, the FCC has said it will not require cable systems to comply with the "reasonable access" provision.

A Few Other Political Broadcasting and Cablecasting Matters

What if a candidate's campaign manager appears on the air saying, "Vote for Jane"? Jane isn't there, nor her likeness or voice. That, technically, isn't a use. But the FCC long ago decided that in all fairness, Jane's opponents may ask for equal opportunity for their supporters to have equal opportunity. Jane's opponents may not appear themselves, but their supporters may. This is called the "Zapple rule," named after a congressional staff attorney who asked the FCC about this situation 50 years ago.

If a station airs an editorial supporting a candidate, other candidates may ask for time (free, of course) to respond. In this case, the station must notify the other candidates.

Nothing about political broadcasting or cablecasting applies to ballot issues, referenda, constitutional amendments, or the like. Sections 315 and 312(a)(7) apply only to candidates (or their supporters, in the one instance).

The Special Case of Cable Television Systems

Cable television systems carry a number of channels, including broadcast stations, pay channels, access channels, and cable networks. (These are discussed later in this chapter.) Are system operators subject to Section 315 for the programming on all these services? Cable systems are not responsible for complying with Section 315 on broadcasting stations they carry, nor on pay channels such as HBO. System operators have no power over programming on those channels. That also is true for public, educational, and government channels, and likely for commercial leased access channels, since the law forbids cable system operators from having editorial control over these channels, except refusing to carry obscene material. All-news cable networks, such as CNN and C-SPAN, are exempt from Section 315.

Cable operators may be responsible for political advertising on other cable networks they carry. That would not be true if an operator's contract with a cable network stated the system had no control over the network's programming. And Section 315 clearly applies to programming originated by a cable operator.

Children's Programming

Congress and public interest groups on one side, and television broadcasters on the other. The issue is children and television, and the battle has raged for 50 years. Congress held hearings and slapped television networks' hands, but let broadcasters themselves regulate children's programming. In 1990 Congress lost patience and adopted the Children's Television Act. It set general programming goals for broadcast television stations to meet and limited commercial time in and around children's programs on both broadcast and cable television.

Congress and the FCC remained unhappy with broadcasters' performance under the 1990 law. In 1996 the FCC adopted standards to define the more general language of the statute. The Commission said that broadcast television stations are expected to carry three hours each week of programming specifically meant to meet children's intellectual/cognitive and social/emotional needs. These are to be at least 30 minutes in length, scheduled on a weekly basis and aired between 7 A.M. and 10 P.M. This "core programming," as the FCC calls it, will be a very important factor when a station's license is up for renewal.

If a station does not meet the "core programming" standard, it can achieve the equivalent by broadcasting public service announcements, programs of less than 30 minutes duration, and programs not scheduled on a weekly basis. All these must meet children's emotional and intellectual needs. But if a station meets neither of these goals, it will have to convince the commissioners that it has engaged in sufficient programming and nonprogramming activities for children to warrant having its license renewed.

A station's efforts to comply with these standards are to be documented, placed in a public file, and reported to the FCC annually. Noncommercial television stations need only keep appropriate records.

The 1990 act limited commercials in and around children's programming to 12 minutes per hour during weekdays and 10-1/2 minutes per hour on weekends. These are prorated so that, for example, a 30-minute children's program may have six minutes of commercials Monday through Friday. These limits apply to both broadcast and cable television.

Also, the FCC prohibits program-length commercials for children, defined as having the same cartoon or live characters in both the program and the embedded commercials. This also means that during the program characters cannot "sell" products or services. The problem the Commission is addressing is children's inability to separate in their minds programs from commercials.

Sponsorship Identification

Any message on a broadcast station or cable system must include a clear identification of what company, group, or person gave anything of value in payment for its carriage. A commercial for a product or service usually includes the brand or company name, and that is sufficient. But even a public service announcement for "keeping the river clean" must say who sponsored it.

Lotteries

The 1934 communications act permits broadcasters and cable operators to carry information about certain, but not all, lotteries. A lottery is a contest with a prize, that is won by chance rather than skill, and that requires some consideration to enter, such as purchasing a package of cereal to send in the box top or buying a lottery ticket.

You can carry information about state-run lotteries if the station or cable system is in a state that has a lottery, but not otherwise (*United States v. Edge Broadcasting*, 1993). Also, federal law permits Native American tribes to offer gaming or lotteries under certain conditions, and you can provide information about these.

If a lottery is legal in the state where it is held, and if it is sponsored by a governmental agency or nonprofit group, or by a person or company whose primary business is not sponsoring lotteries, you can carry information about it. But you cannot carry information about sports betting or gambling at casinos (although a casino could advertise its food and accommodations, for example).

The ban on broadcasters disseminating lottery information was in the 1934 act, and for more than a century previously there were limits on sending such information through the mails. But recently broadcasters have challenged the rule's constitutionality. One federal appellate court found the regulations violate broadcasters' First Amendment rights (*Valley Broadcasting Co. v. United States*, 1997). Another found to the contrary, but the Supreme Court ordered that appellate court to reconsider its decision (*Greater New Orleans Broadcasting Association, Inc. v. United States*, 1996).

Other Broadcast Content Rules

As broadcast regulation developed, and the industry expanded, additional rules were deemed necessary for broadcast licensees to meet the spirit of the 1934 communications act. Despite the deregulation of the 1980s, several areas of concern remain part of the regulatory framework.

Personal Attacks

For several decades, the FCC enforced the "fairness doctrine." This said broadcasters must present controversial issues of importance in their communities and, in doing so, carry all significant sides of the questions. (See Sidebar 15.2.) In the 1980s, courts decided that the doctrine was an FCC construct, not a congressional statute (*Telecommunications Research and Action Center v. FCC*, 1986), and that it was within the Commission's powers to rescind it (*Meredith Corp. v. FCC*, 1987), which it did in 1987 (*Syracuse Peace Council v. FCC*, 1987). However, two remnants of the doctrine remain: the political editorializing rule discussed earlier, and the personal attack rule.

The personal attack rule permits someone who has been attacked during a broadcast discussion of a controversial issue of public importance to request and receive free time on the station to reply. It also requires the station to notify the person attacked and to supply a tape or transcript. The rule does not apply to attacks on foreign governments

Sidebar 15.2 Hunting the Red Lion

The Supreme Court upheld the personal attack rule's constitutionality in *Red Lion Broadcasting Co. v. FCC* (1969). On his radio program, the Rev. Billy James Hargis said that Fred Cook, author of the book *Goldwater—Extremist on the Right,* had been fired as a reporter, worked for a Communist publication, debunked J. Edgar Hoover and the Central Intelligence Agency, and intended to destroy Republican presidential candidate Barry Goldwater. Cook asked the stations carrying Hargis' broadcast for time to respond. A station owned by Red Lion Broadcasting Company refused. Cook went to the FCC, which ordered the station to give Cook time. The station took the issue to court. The Supreme Court said that the limited electromagnetic spectrum means not everyone can have access to radio and television. Therefore, it is constitutional for the FCC to impose special obligations on those who do have access. The FCC had the right to require the station to provide Cook free time to respond, said the Court.

or public figures, or to attacks by legally qualified political candidates or their representatives. Nor does it apply to attacks made on newscasts or news interview programs, or during coverage of news events.

Miscellaneous Regulations

Aware of the communication act's limitation on the Commission censoring broadcast content, the FCC has been reluctant to interfere with news and public affairs programs. For example, the Commission will not react to charges of "slanting" the news. However, if there is clear support for a charge of distorting news, it will take action. Its concern is deliberate "faking" of news stories, rather than incidental or accidental mistakes.

The FCC has adopted a rule against hoaxes on the air. The rule forbids knowingly broadcasting false reports of crimes or catastrophes that "directly cause" foreseeable "immediate, substantial, and actual public harm." This isn't intended to discourage harmless pranks or promotions but is meant to stop those that get out of hand. For example, a radio station's news director said on the air that a show's host had been "shot in the head" (*WALE-AM*, 1992). Police officers and reporters rushed to the station—during the time the station announced that it was a dramatization. The FCC was not amused.

A spate of "payola" occurred during the 1950s and 1960s—promoters paying radio stations to play certain records. As recently as the late 1980s, the FCC again warned stations against being involved in this practice, or in "plugola," accepting money for "plugging" products outside of commercials, or using broadcast stations in any way for fraudulent purposes.

Several rules affecting broadcast programming that had been in effect for some time now are gone. For example, no longer does a broadcaster have to obtain the FCC's permission to change its format. A radio or television station needs no official permission to alter the programming, or type of programming, it carries. Also, there no longer is a prime-time access rule applicable to broadcast television. That regulation had limited broadcast television stations to three hours during prime time of first-run or repeated network programming, with certain exceptions. And as already noted, the fairness doctrine was rescinded in 1987.

Cable Television Content

Cable television operators also face a battery of laws and regulations controlling their content. As noted earlier, cable systems must comply with some of the rules imposed on broadcasters, but cable television has its own set of regulations, as well.

Must-Carry Rules and Retransmission Consent

Several times, the FCC has adopted rules generally requiring cable systems to carry local broadcast stations, and twice they were found unconstitutional by federal appellate courts (*Century Communications Corp.*, 1987; *Quincy Cable TV, Inc.*, 1985). Then Congress included this requirement, called "must-carry rules," in the 1992 cable act. By a 5-4 margin, the Supreme Court recently upheld the constitutionality of the must-carry rules (*Turner Broadcasting System v. FCC,* 1997). (See Sidebar 15.3.)

Under the current must-carry rules, cable systems must use up to one-third of their channel space to carry local stations, depending on the total number of channels the system uses. There are different standards for which commercial stations and

Sidebar 15.3 Must-Carry by a Close Vote

Much important legislation is a compromise, born partly as the result of lobbying by those who will be affected by the law and partly through discussions and trade-offs by legislators. Must-carry is no different. The FCC twice adopted rules requiring cable systems to carry local television stations, and twice the U.S. Court of Appeals for the District of Columbia threw out the regulations. After intense lobbying by broadcasters, Congress adopted must-carry as part of the 1992 cable act. The act also gave broadcasters the option of charging cable systems for carrying the stations (to be paid in money or in kind).

Cable system operators and companies distributing programming for cable systems challenged must-carry in court. In 1994 the Supreme Court found that the rules did not directly affect cable content, so the government needed only a substantial reason—not a compelling one—to adopt the regulations. But the Court said there was not enough information on the record to determine if broadcast stations would

face financial ruin if they weren't carried by cable. After 18 months of more data put on the record, the case went to a three-judge federal court. By a 2–1 vote, the court ruled that must-carry regulations did not violate the First Amendment.

Then the Supreme Court heard the case again. By a 5–4 vote, the Court agreed (*Turner Broadcasting System, Inc. v. FCC*, 1997). The majority of the justices said that there was evidence that television stations would shut down, or at least have less revenue to purchase quality programming, if cable didn't carry them. The stations would have fewer viewers, and therefore less advertising. This would limit the variety of news and information sources available for viewers who don't subscribe to cable. The decision means cable systems must devote up to one-third of their channels, depending on the system's size, to carrying local television stations. This leaves less room for cable system programming that is not from over-the-air television stations.

---

noncommercial stations can demand carriage, but even home shopping broadcast stations may qualify for must-carry.

In the 1992 act, Congress gave television broadcasters a choice. An eligible station within a cable company's service area may require the system to carry its signal. Alternatively, it could negotiate with the system for carriage. This is called "retransmission consent." The station would give its permission to have its signal retransmitted on the cable system in exchange for something—maybe a monetary payment. But many cable system operators objected to that. Instead some owners of groups of television stations asked owners of cable systems to carry new cable networks. For example, Fox permitted the television stations it owns to be carried by those cable systems that agreed to include Fox's new network, Fx, in their channel lineups. After considerable debate and threats—broadcasters to charge cable companies for carrying local broadcasters' programming, cable companies to throw local stations off their systems—the controversy ended in a draw. The cable operators need the local stations to complete their offering menu in local markets and retain local subscribers. The broadcasters need to be carried on cable to ensure the best possible signal to the largest number of potential viewers. Also, many viewers no longer use off-air antennas, and forcing them to switch back to them to receive local broadcast stations would be a serious public relations problem for broadcasters, possibly reducing total audience, and for cable systems, possibly reducing subscribers. Both sides recognized that each needs the other. Being able to carry the local broadcasters helps a cable company sign up subscribers. Being on the cable helps the broadcaster reach more homes and increase station advertising revenue. Viewers win with more choices.

Stations are to choose between must-carry and retransmission consent every three years. Some stations and cable systems chose to sign six-year contracts in 1993, the first period for choosing.

Access Channels

In the 1960s, when cable companies first began competing with one another to provide service in large cities, system owners would make many promises in hopes of being chosen. One promise was letting the public, government bodies, and educational institutions use the system without payment. This idea was written into the 1984 cable act. The act says that a franchising authority and cable system may negotiate to include public, educational, and governmental (PEG) channels on the system. Neither the 1984 act nor any other federal law requires PEG channels. The act just says the city and cable operator may agree to have them.

Most medium and larger size cable systems have PEG channels. Generally, people may use the public access channels on a first-come-first-served basis. A cable operator has no editorial control over content on PEG channels, except that it may agree with its franchising authority not to permit programming that is "obscene or otherwise unprotected by the United States Constitution."

There also is another set of access channels that is required under the 1984 act for some cable systems. Systems with 36 or more channels must have from 10 to 15 percent of their channels (depending on the system's size) devoted to commercial leased access. These are channels that may be leased for short- or long-term periods by anyone willing to pay the charge and agree to terms with the cable operator. The cable system need not have these channels sit vacant while waiting for someone to lease one. The operator may put on its own choice of programming. However, when someone does want to rent a commercial leased access channel, the operator must make a channel available.

The 1992 act required the FCC to establish charges and terms that would apply to commercial leased access channels. Some had argued that these channels generally were not being used because operators charged too much or put other onerous terms into leased access agreements.

System operators may keep off commercial leased access channels material that is "lewd, lascivious, filthy, or indecent." As explained earlier in this chapter, essentially, this means no obscene material, and no indecent programming only if the system has a set of written rules so stating. Otherwise, cable systems have no control over the content of programming on commercial leased access channels.

Blackout Rules

From early in its history, cable television carried not only local television stations but also "distant" stations, those imported from other cities. This presented problems for local broadcasters. In some instances, an imported station might be a network affiliate, and be showing the same programs, even at the same time, as the local affiliate of the same network. In others, a local independent station would have an exclusive (within the market) contract for a syndicated program, but the cable system would be importing a station carrying the same syndicated show. In either case, there could be inroads into the local station's audience, and therefore its advertising revenue.

The FCC dealt with these problems by instituting syndicated exclusivity and network nonduplication rules. Under the former regulation, a local station may notify any cable systems in its market that it wants any duplicated syndicated programs to be blacked out. It doesn't matter whether the imported station is showing the duplicating show at the same time as the local station. In fact, it doesn't matter if the local station is even running the program, as long as it has it under contract for that market. These rules have been upheld in court (*United Video Inc. v. FCC*, 1989).

The network nonduplication rules, which are similar to the syndicated exclusivity regulations, are not restricted only to affiliates of the nationwide television networks. A few stations showing a program at the same time through interconnection—such as a regional sports telecast—qualify as being a network. Each station would be able to invoke the network nonduplication rules against cable systems in the station's market. Small cable systems need not comply with requests for either type of nonduplication.

The FCC also has a rule meant to benefit local professional sports teams. A team may require any cable system in the market to black out a home game unless the game is being carried by a local television station. Owners of National Football League clubs have agreed among themselves not to ask for blackouts if a game is sold out at least 72 hours before it is to be played.

REGULATING BROADCAST STATIONS

The regulation of broadcasting stations, the rationale for which was discussed earlier in this chapter, is the responsibility of the FCC. The agency has an explicit set of criteria for who can own a station, and how licenses are to be renewed or transferred to other owners.

Licensing

The 1934 communications act requires all broadcast stations to have an FCC license. To obtain a license, a company (or an individual) must meet a set of basic criteria established by the 1934 act. First, a licensee must be an American citizen. No noncitizens are permitted to operate radio or television stations in the United States. A corporation holding a broadcast license may not be more than 20 percent foreign owned, or 25 percent if the corporation is in turn owned by another corporation.

Second, the applicant, or its principals, must be of good character. Generally, this means the Commission does not want to award licenses to those convicted of felonies or fraud or antitrust violations involving the mass media. Third, the license applicant must show that it has access to the technical expertise necessary to operate the station, and, fourth, that it has sufficient funds to run the station for the first 3 months if no revenue stream develops before that time.

Fifth, most license applicants must submit a plan for meeting the FCC's equal employment opportunity standards. This involves stating how recruiting for staff will take place, plans for training and promoting employees, and in other ways showing that the applicant intends to comply with the Commission's rules for offering employment opportunity to women and minorities.

The most complex of the Commission's basic criteria for holding a license concerns other media ownership. In keeping with its long-held belief that the public is best served by a diversity of owners, the FCC has in place certain rules limiting who can own what (see Fig. 15.3). The Commission and Congress have loosened these standards considerably in the past decade, but there still are some restrictions. The FCC is empowered, even encouraged in some instances, to waive these. Also, some ownership patterns not permitted under the rules today were acceptable before one or another set of rules was adopted. In many cases, preexisting ownership situations were grandfathered.

- National limits
  - —Radio: No limits
  - —Television: Potential to reach no more than 35 percent of households with television sets. No limit on number of stations.
- Local limits
  - —Radio
    - Communities up to 14 radio stations: Up to five stations, but no more than three Am or three FM stations, and no more than half the total number of stations.
    - Communities with 15–29 stations: Up to six stations, but no more than four AM or four FM stations.
    - Communities with 30–44 stations: Up to seven stations, but no more than four AM or four FM stations.
    - Communities with 45 or more stations: Up to eight stations, but no more than five AM or five FM stations.
  - —Television
    - One per community.
    - But FCC is considering allowing ownership of more than one if the second station is UHF.
- Cross-ownership
  - —Television and radio: Permitted in 50 largest markets; probably also in smaller markets.
  - —Cable system and television station in same market: FCC rules currently forbid this.
  - —Newspaper and broadcast station in same market: Not permitted, but rule may be waived in large markets.

Figure 15.3 Broadcast Ownership Limits

A licensee may have only one television station in any one market (the "duopoly" rule). Congress has asked the FCC to consider whether there are situations where it might be in the public interest to allow ownership of one VHF and one, or even more, UHF station in the same market. The number of radio stations one licensee may own in a single market depends on the market's size, but in no case can it be more than eight stations. There also is a limitation on the number of AM or FM stations one owner may have in a market. Also, the Antitrust Division of the U.S. Department of Justice has limited the percentage of radio advertising revenue a single owner would control if it had as many licenses as possible in one market. This may prevent one licensee from having the maximum number of licenses permitted under FCC rules.

At one time, the Commission's "one-to-a-market" regulation would not allow a single licensee to own both a commercial television station and a radio station in the same market. Under the 1996 telecommunications act, the FCC is to waive this rule in the country's 50 largest markets if it believes it is in the public interest to do so, and even may consider waiving the rule in smaller markets.

There is no limit on the number of radio stations one company may own nationwide, as long as it stays within the per-market limits. But a single owner of television stations may reach no more than 35 percent of the nation's television households, or a somewhat higher percentage if the additional stations are minority owned.

Also, FCC rules will not allow a cable system and television station in the same market to be owned by one company, although Congress eliminated the statutory restriction in 1996. And a local newspaper owner may not also control a commercial broadcast station in that same market.

If a company meets these basic criteria, and a current licensee wants to transfer its station license to the company, the FCC generally will do so. The license transfer takes place as part of selling the station. The station's assets can be sold without the Commission's permission, but the license belongs to the FCC, as the public's representative. Radio and television station licenses are granted for eight-year terms. A transferred license remains valid only for the remaining duration of the term.

Licenses must be renewed to remain valid. Under the 1996 telecommunications act, broadcast license renewal has become nearly automatic. The FCC must renew a license unless it finds the company has not operated in the public interest, regularly has violated FCC rules, or in some other way has shown a pattern of abusing the law. Consideration of these questions can include comments from the public about a station's carriage of violent programming, or other comments from the public. Only if the Commission refuses renewal can it then consider other applications for the license.

If an initial license for a station is available, or if a station license comes open for any reason, more than one applicant meeting the basic qualifications might apply for it. At one time, the Commission would hold a comparative hearing to determine which of the applicants was the best qualified. One of the FCC's comparative criteria was integration of ownership and management. Essentially, the Commission preferred it if the station owner also were managing the station. Of course, today most stations are owned by large companies that appoint general managers to run stations—general managers who are not the licensees. One of those companies challenged this criterion, and the Commission was ordered to explain to a court why it used the standard (*Bechtel v. FCC*, 1993; *Bechtel v. FCC*, 1992). The Commission has not yet chosen to do so and has not held comparative hearings since then. Instead, it has encouraged competing applicants to come to an agreement—one applicant reaching agreement with the others to withdraw their applications.

Public Files

FCC rules require broadcast stations to maintain certain information in files accessible to the public. This is part of operating in the public interest. Among materials that need to be put into public files are records of requests for political appearances, complaints about the station from members of the public, any applications made to the FCC for which local public notice is required, any petitions from the public to deny license renewal, applications for change in program service, a list of programs offering significant treatment of controversial issues aired in the past three months, and annual equal employment opportunity reports filed with the FCC. Commercial television stations also must put into public files records showing compliance with the Commission's new children's programming rules and the station's request of local cable systems of must-carry or retransmission consent.

FCC rules require keeping these records in public files for varying times. Station managers should be well aware of the Commission's public files rules—what needs to be in the files, and for how long the documents need to be retained.

Public Broadcasting

Generally, public broadcasters are subject to the same rules and regulations as commercial radio and television stations. One obvious difference is that the latter are supported by advertising, and the former are not. However, public stations still must carry the names of individuals or companies that support individual programs as part of complying with the "sponsorship identification" rules. They need not air the names of contributors to the stations' general funds.

Public stations also obtain funding from the Corporation for Public Broadcasting (CPB), which receives its moneys from Congress and other sources. CPB also helps fund the Public Broadcasting Service, providing programming for public television stations, and National Public Radio.

Congress established CPB under the Public Broadcasting Act but did not give the FCC any powers under that legislation. The Commission, then, cannot enforce the section requiring "strict adherence to objectivity and balance in all programs or series of programs of a controversial nature." And the Supreme Court has held that public stations may support political candidates and may carry editorials, despite the Public Broadcasting Act's language to the contrary (*FCC v. League of Women Voters of California,* 1984). The Court said that public broadcasting stations have "important journalistic freedoms which the First Amendment jealously protects." This also applies to noncommercial stations' selection of programming, even those stations that receive funds from governmental agencies (*Muir v. Alabama Educational Television Commission,* 1982).

Noncommercial stations also are treated differently to varying degrees under mustcarry and retransmission consent rules, public files regulations, and certain other Commission standards.

REGULATING CABLE SYSTEMS

Although cable television systems do not use the electromagnetic spectrum, they do not escape regulation. Courts have held that local (city, county, state) authorities may regulate cable systems through the franchising process, and that the FCC has jurisdiction over cable in part because of cable's impact on over-the-air broadcasters.

Cable Franchising

Cable companies are not "licensed" by the FCC in the same manner as broadcast stations. Cable systems do need to register with the Commission before they begin providing service to subscribers, listing the owner, the programming to be offered, and similar information. But under the 1984 cable act, they cannot operate without obtaining a franchise from the pertinent franchising authority. A franchise is an agreement— essentially a contract—between the cable operator and the franchising authority, which usually is the city (or county when the area is unincorporated) in which the system will offer service, or may be the state (such as in Hawaii or Connecticut), or a combination of the two (as in New York State). The 1984 and 1992 cable acts and the 1996 telecommunications act set certain franchise limitations and requirements, but much of the franchise is developed during a negotiating process between the cable operator and the franchising authority.

Franchises may contain a few or very many provisions, running from several to several hundred pages, largely depending on the size of the city (and the lawyers and consultants representing both sides). The agreements are for finite periods, often 8 to 15 years, after which they can be renewed.

Once, franchise fees were a contentious provision in franchises. The franchising authority would insist on a payment from the cable company in exchange for permission to operate in the city. Early in cable's history that amount might have been up to 35 percent of a system's gross annual revenues. The FCC put various caps on the percentage over the years, and finally the 1984 cable act set the maximum franchise fee at 5 percent of gross annual revenues. Disputes still arise over the definition of "gross annual revenues."

Franchising authorities also often have wanted control over the programming cable systems carry, requiring certain cable networks (such as CNN or C-SPAN) or forbidding others (such as The Playboy Channel or MTV). The law now limits franchising authorities to striking agreements with cable system operators for the provision of broad categories of programming. For example, a franchise might require "children's programming," but could not require carriage of Nickelodeon. But franchising authorities cannot forbid broad categories of programming, such as "adult programming."

Cable companies generally have not been known for superior customer service. Franchising authorities have tried to include service requirements in franchises. Finally, Congress took action in the 1992 cable act by ordering the FCC to establish customer service standards. However, the act permits franchising authorities to impose even stricter standards than established by the FCC. These may be written into franchises. Also, franchising authorities may change these standards at any time during the franchise period.

Franchising authorities also have wanted to put into franchises specifications for the equipment cable operators install in their communities. However, the law now says that cities have no control over cable systems' technical standards. It is in the FCC's hands to establish rules for the system's network and customer equipment that cable operators use.

Franchise Renewals

The cost of building a cable system is very high. For example, installing cables throughout a community is expensive, and much more so if they must be underground, as some franchising authorities require. Further, technology changes quickly. Franchising authorities and customers demand that more and better equipment be installed. Despite this, franchising authorities want short-duration franchises. That would make it difficult for a cable operator to amortize the cost of constructing the system over the life of the franchise. This leads to questions of renewing the franchise. If there were no likelihood the franchise would be extended, cable operators might balk at investing in the system at more than a minimal level. The 1984 act addressed this question. Although it certainly does not ensure that a franchise will be renewed, it does limit the grounds on which renewal can be denied.

A cable system and franchising authority may conduct informal talks and agree on a franchise renewal at any time before the agreement expires. Federal law does not affect that process. But the law does establish a formal procedure that can be used at the same time, giving the cable operator some protection.

The formal process begins well before the franchise expires. During the six-month period starting three years and ending two and one-half years prior to expiration, the cable operator must notify the franchising authority in writing that it wants to invoke the procedure set out in the 1984 cable act. If written notice is not given during that six-month period, the franchising authority is not required to undertake the formal process. Then, within six months after notice is given, the franchising authority must begin preparing a report assessing the cable operator's performance during the franchise period that is ending, and projecting the community's future cable-related needs. There is no deadline for finishing the report.

When the cable operator receives the city's report, it may provide in return a proposal for its plans during a new franchise period. The franchising authority may set a deadline for this plan to be submitted. When the franchising authority receives the cable operator's plan, it has four months to make a decision—renew the franchise based on the cable operator's proposal, or preliminarily refuse to renew. Refusal would be a preliminary decision because, under that circumstance, the city then would have to hold a formal hearing to make a final decision. The hearing is much like a trial—attorneys, witnesses, evidence, building a record.

In the end, the franchising authority can decline to renew only on one or more of four grounds:

1. The operator failed to comply with the terms of its franchise, or with laws applicable to the operator.

2. The cable system's overall programming offerings or customer service performance were insufficient.

3. The operator does not have the financial, technical, or legal ability to fulfill the promises in its proposal to the franchising authority.

4. The operator's proposal does not meet the city's cable-related needs spelled out in the city's report, taking into consideration the cost of what the franchising authority expects.

If the franchising authority refuses to renew the franchise, the operator can appeal the decision to the courts.

Cable Ownership

As with broadcasting stations, the ownership restrictions on cable television have been loosened considerably recently. At one time, broadcast television networks and local telephone companies could not own cable systems. That no longer is true. The ban on an owner of a television station also controlling a cable system in the same market still is an FCC rule but is under review and may be rescinded.

A cable system operator cannot own a wireless cable or satellite master antenna television (SMATV) system, both discussed later in this chapter, that operates in the same area. However, cable/wireless cable joint ownership would be acceptable if the cable system had competition from another multichannel video service in the market.

Newspaper companies may own cable systems in their areas, as may owners of other print media. Unlike broadcast stations, there are no restrictions on foreign ownership of cable systems.

A franchising authority is permitted to own a cable system, even if it goes into competition with a cable system to which it already has granted a franchise. Although the city is permitted to operate on better terms than the franchise it granted to the cable system, the 1992 cable act said that it needn't have a franchise at all, since it simply would be giving one to itself.

The 1996 telecommunications act settled long-standing disputes among telephone companies, Congress, the FCC, cable operators, and the courts over telephone companies' role, if any, in cable. Today, local telephone companies (e.g., the Bell companies—U S West, Ameritech, Bell Atlantic, etc.) may provide video programming in one of four ways: as a conduit for other video programmers, as a cable system operator, as an "open video system" provider, or as a wireless cable operator (see Fig. 15.4).

Under the Telecommunications Act of 1996, local telephone companies may offer video programming in one or more of four ways:

- As a *common carrier:* The telephone company allows its system to be used by video programmers on a first-come, first-served basis.

- As a *cable system:* The telephone company acts just like any other cable company does—and is regulated the same way.

- As an *open video system:* Congress' new creation, allowing a telephone company to use part of its systems for its own programming choices, while allowing other video programmers to use the rest of the system on a first-come, first-served basis.

- As a *wireless cable operator:* Providing video programming through microwave facilities.

Figure 15.4 Telephone Companies Offering Video

In the first case, the telephone company merely provides its system as a conduit for other companies. The telephone company provides the system, and other firms use it on a first-come-first-serve basis to send programming to subscribers. The telephone company has no control over the content. Essentially, it would be operating as it does when it provides telephone service to the public.

Second, telephone companies may be cable operators, providing video services just as any other cable system does. The one restriction is that the telephone company must offer video programming to subscribers through a separate subsidiary, not through the company that provides telephone service. The separate company would have to comply with the same rules and regulations than any other cable operator must, including having a franchise.

Third, Congress in the 1996 act invented a new animal that it called "open video system" (OVS). OVS is a hybrid between the first 2 ways a local telephone company may offer video programming. Under an OVS, a telephone company opens its system to companies that want to provide programming, and the telephone company may use part of the system to offer video services itself. If too many companies want to use the system, so that it becomes too full for the telephone company itself and other firms all to offer video programming, then the law sets a limit. The telephone company may use no more than one-third of the available channels, with the other two-thirds being used for other firms on a first-come-first-served basis. The advantage to an OVS is that the phone company may provide a certain amount of video programming without obtaining a franchise from the local community.

Finally, a telephone company may operate a "wireless cable" company. These are discussed later in this chapter.

Transferring Franchises

As with broadcast stations, cable system owners may want to sell one or more of their systems. But, like station owners, they are not entirely free to do so. Cable operators may sell their wires, trucks, and other equipment, but the franchise isn't theirs to sell. It belongs to the franchising authority, as the station license belongs to the FCC. (In both cases, the government acts for the general public.) Franchises most often require obtaining the franchising authority's permission to transfer the franchise from one company to another.

There are no restrictions on what a franchising authority may require before agreeing to transfer the franchise, including promises to upgrade the cable system, provide additional channels, install hookups in schools and other public buildings at no cost, and so forth. Usually, however, they act reasonably and agree to transfer after negotiating with the current and prospective franchise holder. If the franchising authority does not make a decision within 120 days, the 1992 cable act says it will be assumed that permission to transfer the franchise has been granted.

Rate Regulation

Disputes over rate regulation have raged almost since cable television began. Subscribers complain, prompting franchising authorities to want to limit rates, sometimes by including such provisions in franchises. In 1971, to help the then-small cable business develop, the FCC said pay-per-channel (e.g., HBO) rates could not be regulated by franchising authorities, and that the Commission itself would not do it. This also includes pay-per-program rates. But the Commission said nothing about rates for other cable services, apparently leaving them open to rate regulation. Then the 1984 cable act limited rate regulation to cable systems without "effective competition." Still wanting to foster the growth of cable as a competitor for over-the-air television networks, the Commission interpreted "effective competition" in a way that meant most cable systems did not face rate regulation. The Commission based its definition on the number of broadcast signals available in a community just by using an antenna. Most cities had more than enough for the FCC to argue that viewers there had a choice—over-the-air signals or cable, one competing with the other.

The 1992 cable law changed the definition of effective competition, and most cable systems became subject to rate regulation. Congress acted again in the 1996 telecommunications bill. It said that services most subscribers take no longer will be rate regulated as of March 31, 1999. But it may be sooner than that for some systems. As soon as a local telephone company offers multichannel video services in a cable company's area, that cable system's rates no longer will be regulated. Small cable systems' rates were deregulated when the 1996 act took effect.

Cable Programming

Cable systems carry a variety of programming. They retransmit signals of local television stations and some distant stations ("superstations," such as WGN in Chicago). They also offer PEG and leased access channels. But cable television came of age in the 1970s when it started carrying networks that offered programming to cable subscribers only, and when pay-per-channel cable networks began. Although cable customers continue to most often watch local broadcast stations affiliated with national broadcast television networks, cable networks are an important part of why people subscribe to cable.

Any technology that wants to compete with cable must develop its own programming—a very expensive and speculative thing to do, with no guarantee that viewers will like it—or be able to carry the same networks that cable does. To ensure that such media as wireless cable, SMATV, and satellites can compete with cable television—in part, as a way to hold down cable rates—Congress in the 1992 cable act required cable programming companies to offer their products to cable's competitors. The law prevents cable operators and cable programmers from entering into contracts that would give cable systems exclusive access to programming on a local or national basis (see Fig. 15.5).

Broadcasters complain about regulations limiting their First Amendment rights, but cable system operators also face many content regulations. Among them are:

- Carrying local television stations, if asked.
- Providing public, educational, governmental access channels, if their franchises require them.
- Providing commercial leased access channels if the cable system has 36 or more channels.
- Limiting the number of channels offering programming produced by companies that the cable operator wholly or partly owns.
- Blacking out syndicated programming when asked to do so by a local television station.
- Blacking out network programming when asked to do so by a local network affiliated or owned station.
- Blacking out a local sports event if asked to do so by the team owner.
- Scrambling channels that carry adult programming.
- Providing cable programming to competitors, such as satellite providers.

Figure 15.5 Cable Content Regulation

Another concern is that new cable networks have difficulty finding room on cable systems. One argument presented to Congress was that large companies own many cable systems across the country and also have investments in a number of established cable programmers. These companies, it was said, would put onto their systems programming from the firms in which they had investments. Once these systems also found room for local stations, and PEG and leased access channels, there was no more channel space for many of the new cable networks that wanted to reach an audience.

And since these large companies owned so many cable systems reaching such large numbers of subscribers, the remaining systems didn't have enough customers to support new programmers.

Under instructions from Congress in the 1992 cable act, the FCC adopted rules limiting cable systems to using no more than 40 percent of their channel capacity for programming in which the system's owner had more than a 5 percent financial interest. This applies to a system's first 75 channels, but not thereafter.

Compulsory Copyright License

As discussed in Chapter 14, U.S. and international copyright laws make clear that you cannot "perform" someone else's work without their permission, except in certain narrow circumstances. What happens when cable television retransmits a television station signal to its subscribers? There are dozens, maybe hundreds, of copyrights embedded in a broadcast station's signal—the station's newscasts and other local programming, each network or syndicated program, each commercial, the underlying music, and so forth. A single television station is able to negotiate for the rights to "perform" each of these protected works. (If it is a network affiliate, the network has obtained most of the needed permissions.) But a cable system carries many different broadcast stations. How could it negotiate with each copyright holder on each station?

When the Supreme Court first faced this issue, it decided that cable's retransmitting a television station's signal did not amount to "performing" that signal, and therefore no permissions were needed (*Teleprompter Corp. v. Columbia Broadcasting System*, 1974; *Fortnightly Corp. v. United Artists Television, Inc.*, 1968). Of course, this did not satisfy the broadcasters or television program producers. Congress decided to strike a compromise. As part of the 1976 copyright act, it developed a "compulsory copyright license." This permits cable systems to retransmit radio and television stations' signals without negotiating with the pertinent copyright holders. However, the systems must pay certain fees, calculated by a complex formula, into a pool of money. Those funds are distributed to the copyright holders through a system overseen by the U.S. Copyright Office.

Cable Customer Privacy

In the 1984 cable act, Congress expressed its concern that subscribers' privacy could be at risk with cable operators able to have access to bank- and shop-from-home records, as well as customers' programming choices. To protect subscribers, Congress limited the information cable systems could collect and distribute.

Without permission, a cable company may obtain information such as a customer's name, address, phone number, and programming taken, but only if it is needed to provide service and to be certain subscribers pay for services. And without permission, a cable company may not provide that information to others unless necessary to provide requested programming and other services, and for the cable operator's business reasons, such as giving subscriber information to a company that does the cable operator's monthly billing. Cable companies may distribute aggregate information without their subscribers' permission, if it does not identify individual customers.

On an annual basis, cable systems must provide their customers with a written notice about their privacy rights. It must say what subscriber information is being collected, what use the system makes of it, to whom it is disclosed, and for what purpose.

It also must explain how long the information will be retained, where and how subscribers may see their files, and that the customer may take legal action if the cable system does not follow the privacy rules in regard to the subscriber.

Pole Rental Agreements

Most cable systems run their wires above ground, over public rights-of-way, then to customer's homes. They need poles on which to put those wires. It is expensive to put up their own poles, and most communities wouldn't allow it, wanting to prevent further urban blight. The alternative is to rent space on poles already constructed—those owned by telephone and power companies. When cable began, some telephone companies themselves provided video service. They didn't want to rent to cable companies, or they would charge very high rental prices. Congress then adopted a law giving the FCC—or states, if they wanted—the power to regulate the rates, terms, and conditions in pole rental contracts. The Commission established a formula setting the maximum rate for the conditions present in a particular pole rental agreement.

The next concern for cable companies was that the law applied only if the telephone or power company agreed to rent space. It could refuse. The 1996 telecommunications act requires pole owners to rent to cable companies if there is room on the pole.

Also, some pole owners began charging more for pole rentals if the wires were used even in part for nonvideo services, such as providing telephone or data service. The claim was that these were not covered by the law or the FCC's rate formula. The 1996 act clarified this point. It made clear that it doesn't matter what use cable companies make of the wires attached to poles, the FCC (or a state) still has jurisdiction over a pole rental contract's rates, terms, and conditions.

REGULATING OTHER ELECTRONIC TECHNOLOGIES

The FCC has tried to foster video delivery systems that could compete with cable television as a way of having the marketplace, rather than government regulators, ensure quality cable service and increased programming offerings, and to hold down cable rates. While being conscious of demands to use the spectrum for a variety of video and nonvideo services, the Commission has allowed such technologies as satellite delivery and wireless cable to develop, as well as satellite master antenna television systems, with limited regulatory requirements. Cable companies have complained that this gives their competitors an unfair advantage.

Direct Broadcast Satellites

The FCC has not quite known what to make of direct-to-home satellite delivery of video signals. In one way, the satellite programmer is like a broadcast station. It sends signals, using the spectrum, to homes that have antennas (satellite receivers) to pick up the transmissions. A satellite operator could choose to be a broadcaster, sending its signals to anyone with a receiving dish and earning revenue from advertising time instead of subscribers. In that case, it would be regulated just like a broadcaster.

But since "broadcasting" is defined as signals meant for reception by the general public, and satellite operators do not provide signals to people not paying subscription fees, satellite operators don't act like broadcasters. The FCC, then, decided to categorize direct-to-home satellite operators as it does other subscription services, such as wireless cable and SMATV—as a point-to-multipoint nonbroadcast video service (*National Association of Better Broadcasting v. FCC*, 1988). A satellite operator also could allow others to use the satellite to offer video services. In that case, the operator would be a common carrier, like a telephone company, providing carriage on a first-come-first-served basis.

The Commission also has not been certain what to call satellite services. When it adopted rules in 1982 permitting direct-to-home satellite services, it authorized a high-power signal to be used. It called this service Direct Broadcast Satellite (DBS). But it was not high-power services, using the Ku satellite band, that developed. Instead, it was a low-power service, using the C-band, that offered video signals to those using large receiving dishes (four to eight feet in diameter). Not until recently has the high-power DBS service been offered, as well as a medium-power service, using dishes 18 to 24 inches in diameter.

Today, the generic name for satellite video services is direct-to-home (DTH). It continues to call the high-power and medium-power services DBS. And the low-power service is called "home satellite dish" (HSD), although its proper name is "fixed satellite service" (FSS).

DBS, though not HSD, operators, must comply with some rules applicable to broadcasters and cable operators. The 1992 cable act requires them to meet the political broadcasting/cablecasting rules, both Sections 315 and 312(a)(7), and the Commission's equal employment opportunity regulations. Courts have permitted direct-to-home operators to use the compulsory copyright license, as may cable operators (*NBC v. Satellite Broadcast Networks*, 1991; *National Association for Better Broadcasting v. FCC*, 1988). Satellite operators must comply with the retransmission consent provisions of the 1992 cable act, meaning that they must obtain a broadcast station's permission before carrying it. In fact, however, Congress has limited direct-to-home operators to providing broadcast station signals only to residents in areas, mostly rural, that cannot receive a quality signal from local stations by using an antenna and are not served by cable television (called "white areas").

Also, DBS operators must use 4 to 7 percent of their channel capacity for "noncommercial programming of an educational or informational nature."

The 1996 telecommunications act forbids local officials from limiting or forbidding installation of receiving antennas for DTH and wireless cable services.

Wireless Cable

Wireless cable began life as multipoint distribution service (MDS), then multichannel multipoint distribution service (MMDS). It was a set of frequencies the FCC carved out of the spectrum intended to be used primarily by businesses, for videoconferencing, for instance. But entrepreneurs discovered that video programming offered to customers at home—via a microwave signal sent to a small antenna mounted on top of a building, including houses—would be more profitable. And calling it "wireless cable" was better marketing than referring to it as MMDS.

Initially, the service could offer only a few channels because of the limited amount of spectrum available to wireless cable operators. Over the years, the FCC found additional spectrum to provide to wireless cable systems, until today 33 channels can be transmitted. With compression technology and digital transmission, that number soon will be much higher.

Although wireless cable does use the spectrum, it is not a broadcast service since it is intended only for people who pay for the service, not the general public. As with other services that are potential cable television competitors, the FCC has refrained from imposing too many regulations on wireless cable. It is subject to the retransmission consent rule, requiring it to obtain permission from any broadcast station it carries.

SMATV

Satellite master antenna television (SMATV) is a cable system for a building or a group of buildings. SMATV systems do not use public rights-of-way. If they did use them, they would be cable systems. A SMATV system uses satellite receiving dishes and antennas to collect satellite transmissions and signals of broadcast stations, just as cable does, and then sends them through wires to occupants in a building, usually an apartment house or set of condominiums.

Since SMATV systems do not use the spectrum, they are not broadcasters. Since they don't use public rights-of-way, they are not cable operators. They are subject to the retransmission consent rules and may be required to comply with the FCC's equal employment opportunity regulations, but few other Commission rules apply to them. The FCC has told local authorities they cannot regulate SMATV systems.

The Internet

The Internet is just another mass medium where the law is concerned. As already noted, the Supreme Court has held that different media may be treated in different ways under the First Amendment. This is true for the Internet (and the World Wide Web, which comes to you via the Internet), as well. Courts and Congress still are struggling with just how existing law should be applied to the Internet. There are very few court decisions to go on, so it remains anyone's guess.

Thus far, courts seem to hold that if an online Internet service provider, such as CompuServe, only provides a conduit for users, and does not attempt to edit or otherwise interfere with content sent over its system, it will not be liable for torts such as libel or invasion of privacy (*Stratton Oakmont, Inc. v. Prodigy Services Co.*, 1995; *Cubby, Inc. v. CompuServe Inc.*, 1991). In the 1996 telecommunications act, Congress said that if an online service provider interferes with content, but only in attempting to limit objectionable content on its system, that will not in itself make the provider liable for torts.

Individuals and companies can be defamed on the Internet as well as in the print media and radio and television. If a mass medium operates a web page, it must take as much care with it as with its primary outlet. (See Sidebar 15.4.)

The four invasion of privacy torts discussed in Chapter 13 apply to the Internet. For example, you can't say on Channel 4's web page "Local basketball star Cynthia Smith watches Channel 4's 11 P.M. news," unless Smith has granted permission. If you do, that's appropriation.

In 1968 Congress adopted the Electronic Communication Privacy Act. Although it was intended to restrict phone taps, it now applies to computer use. In its strictest terms, it would prohibit anyone intercepting messages you send or receive by computer, and also prohibit someone else from disclosing those messages. But there are exceptions, both for a "system operator" and more generally. Online service providers such as American Online are system operators. But if a newspaper has an internal message communication system on its computers, the newspaper becomes a system operator.

Sidebar 15.4 The Long Reach of the Law

If someone wants to sue you, it must be in a state that has "personal jurisdiction" over you. That may mean where you reside, or where you do business. If the television station you manage is in New York City, you do business in the state of New York. But if you solicit advertising from New Jersey stores, you're also doing business in that state. The New Jersey courts can "reach" into New York and require you to appear before a New Jersey judge. What if your station has a World Wide Web site? It's available in every state in the country—and in every country where the Internet is available. Does having a Web site mean you are "doing business" everywhere, and therefore you can be sued—and required to appear—anywhere?

Although the courts are not yet clearly in agreement, the trend of decisions seems to be that merely putting up a Web site—for example, with information about your station, its programs, its news reporters—likely is not enough to allow you to be sued anywhere the Web site can be received (see, e.g., *Benusan Restaurant Corp. v. King,* 1996). That is, you will not be "doing business" in each state, so there will not be "personal jurisdiction," just because you have a Web site. But if you offer commercial transactions—from selling shirts with your station's logo to explaining how to contact your advertising salespeople—that could be different (see, e.g., *Maritz Inc. v. Cybergold Inc.,* 1996). That type of information on your Web site could be seen as "doing business," and could give courts jurisdiction over your station wherever the Web site is seen (Aftab, 1997).

Among other exceptions, a system operator may intercept or disclose a message if it has the sender's or recipient's permission. If the message seems to relate to committing a crime, the system operator may disclose its contents to law enforcement authorities. And if an employee has agreed to let the system operator look at and disclose messages, the employee can't complain if the system operator does so. This would suggest that media managers should have their employees agree to interception and disclosure of messages transmitted and received by computers in their offices. The law may assume employees implicitly grant such consent by agreeing to work in a company that has internal communication through computers. But this is not clear.

Governments around the world are discussing how the Internet should be treated under copyright laws. Should new laws be written? Can present laws accommodate the Internet? Until there are definitive answers, it's best to assume the current law applies. On that basis, copying material off the Internet is the same as copying a magazine article. It's a violation of copyright unless you have explicit or implicit permission, or the copying is a fair use. The same is true of copying an e-mail message. It's just like copying a private, personal letter. The letter is protected by copyright, and so is the e-mail message, barring permission being granted or implied, or fair use.

The First Amendment permits more regulation of broadcasting than of the print media because radio and television use the electromagnetic spectrum. The spectrum is a limited natural physical property, limiting the number of stations that can broadcast in one geographical area without causing interference. Cable television, which does not use the spectrum to deliver programming to subscribers, may be regulated by state and local authorities because it uses public rights-of-way to run its wires to customers' homes. Federal authorities may regulate cable because of its impact on broadcast television. Congress established the Federal Communications Commission to oversee spectrum users and long-distance telephone providers.

Obscene material is not protected in the electronic media any more than it is in the print media. Radio and television stations also are prohibited from carrying indecent material except during the safe harbor hours between 10 P.M. and 6 A.M. Although the indecency limitation generally does not apply to cable television, cable operators may refuse to carry indecent programming on commercial leased access channels and on public, educational, or governmental channels.

Section 315 of the Communications Act establishes a system intended to achieve equal opportunities for political candidates competing for the same office to reach audiences through radio, broadcast television, and cable television appearances. Section 312(a)(7) ensures that candidates for federal offices will have reasonable access to radio and broadcast television stations.

Congress and the FCC also have adopted rules regarding children's programming on broadcast television, television program ratings, sponsorship identification, sending lottery information over broadcast stations and cable systems, and personal attacks during discussions of controversial public issues. There also are rules regulating cable system carriage of broadcast stations.

Statutes and FCC regulations control broadcast station ownership and licensing. Federal and local laws affect cable system franchising, while federal statutes and FCC rules govern other aspects of cable operations, such as rates, subscriber privacy, and pole rentals.

The FCC has adopted limited regulations for newer technologies, including direct broadcast satellites, wireless cable systems, and satellite master antenna television operations. Courts are beginning to face questions involving the Internet. The U.S. Supreme Court has ruled that the Internet has First Amendment protection more like that of the print media than the electronic media.

STUDY QUESTIONS

1. What reasons have courts given for permitting radio and broadcast television to be regulated more extensively than are the print media? For permitting cable television regulation?

2. What are the differences between obscene material and indecent material? Why is indecent material not permitted on broadcast stations except during "safe harbor" hours?

3. For purposes of Section 315, what determines if a person is a legally qualified candidate? What is a "use" of a broadcast station or cable system? What does "lowest unit rate" mean? How does Section 312(a)(7) affect candidates for federal offices?

4. What standards does the FCC apply in determining if broadcast television stations are complying with the Children's Television Act?

5. What power does a broadcast television station have in determining whether a cable system will carry that station?

6. How many radio stations may one company own in one city? Nationally? Television stations in one city? Nationally?

7. What is a cable television franchise? Who grants it? What are some common franchise provisions? How are franchises renewed?

16

Contract and Employment Law*

Media managers need to be familiar not only with First Amendment law, press law, and electronic media regulations, but also with contract and employment law. Media managers are not expected to be adroit in these specialized and complex legal fields, which are the province of experienced, expert attorneys. That is not the point of this chapter. Rather, the goal is to alert you to certain contract and employment issues that should prompt consultation with appropriate lawyers representing your media company.

The several elements of contract and employment law discussed here represent only tips of very large and deep icebergs. The intent is to prompt you, as a media manager, to seek legal advice about these matters before problems arise, as well as when you are faced with difficulties in these areas.

Contract Law

What Is a Contract?

A contract is an exchange of promises resulting in a group of agreements between two or more parties (see Fig. 16.1). Importantly, a court can enforce the agreements if a party breaches the contract—that is, if a party fails to do what it promised it would.

*Laura W. Rowland, Esq., provided assistance with this chapter.

There are three essential elements to a contract:

- Offer
- Acceptance
- Consideration

Figure 16.1 Forming a Contract

We think of contracts as written documents that the parties have signed as a way to commit their promises to paper. But an oral agreement may be a valid contract, one that a court can enforce. For example, as a television station manager you say to an independent program producer, "See if you can make a documentary about drug use in the north side of town. I'll cover expenses, and then we'll talk about running it." The producer says, "Fine. I'll do it and get back to you in two months." You say, "Good." When you get the bill for $100,000 in expenses, an amount ten times what you had in mind, do you have to pay it? Probably, yes. The agreement was that you would pay expenses. You set no limit.

And a contract may be formed by your permitting a person or company to provide services or products in a way that would allow a court to find that you had agreed to pay for them. For example, you have a two-year contract with XYZ, Inc., a computer repair company. A company representative has made visits to your newsroom every three weeks to keep your computers in good running order. The contract ends on March 20. On March 21, a computer in your newsroom goes down, and you need it fixed immediately. You call XYZ, and they come and fix the computer. Three weeks later, they come again, and then continue coming every three weeks. You don't tell them to stop, but when you get their bill, you say, "I won't pay this. We don't have a contract." A court likely would find otherwise. XYZ continued a pattern begun under a contract, and you failed to sever the relationship. A court likely would not let this go on forever, but it might for a period of time.

However, most contracts are formed through a process of negotiation. The discussion of contracts that follows may suggest a contract is permitted to contain this or that clause, or it must have a certain type of provision. In the end, the important point is that you and the other party or parties to a contract agree on what the terms and conditions are. You should not allow someone to force a contract on you.

But contracts are very complex matters. You should seek legal advice before entering into a contract.

Forming a Contract

Several provisions must be included in a contract to make it valid. The agreement must contain an offer, an acceptance, and consideration.

An Offer

A contract involves an offer and an acceptance; both must be valid for a contract to be enforceable. An offer includes the terms and conditions of the agreement and must contain certain information (see Fig. 16.2). Who are the parties to the contract: The person

Contracts often contain many provisions. Important terms to include are:

- Who are the parties to the contract?
- How long will the contract last?
- What is the consideration?
- What is each party's commitment to the other party? Goods? Services? Money?

Figure 16.2 Contract Terms

who negotiated it? The company she represents? Subsidiaries of that company? Another question is whether a party to the contract may substitute some other person or company. This is called "assigning" the contract. A contract can include a term stating that neither party can assign its obligations to someone else, or that assignments will be acceptable only with permission of the other party. If there is no provision about assigning the contract, courts generally assume it can be assigned. However, certain contracts cannot be assigned without consent, including the very types of contracts with which media managers often are involved.

For instance, you are a television station general manager, and you sign a contract with a new anchor for your 11 P.M. newscast. This is a person who raised another station's news program's ratings by 30 percent. A week before he is to do his first show, he gets a better offer in another city. He says to you, "Don't worry, I've found someone for you who will take my place." Do you have to accept his replacement? No. A personal services contract with someone who has unique abilities or a special reputation has to be fulfilled by that person, not someone else, unless the other party agrees.

Another element that must be in the offer is how long the contract will last. It is not necessarily fatal if this is missing, but courts could construe the contract as too vague to be enforced. The time provision is particularly important in employment contracts. If you want to employ a person for a certain amount of time, specify it in the contract. If you want to be able to end the contract at any time, don't specify the duration of the agreement.

A contract offer also needs clear price terms. How much will be paid for the product or service? Courts will not accept a contract stating that, for example, a columnist's salary will be "fair." That is just too vague. But you may have a contract that says the salary will be $4,000 per month if you are satisfied with the columnist's performance. You don't know if you will be satisfied, so the provision is somewhat unclear, but courts will accept it as long as the agreement states the amount to be paid if you are satisfied.

If you've made an offer, but change your mind, usually you can take back the offer and not be liable under a contract—if you revoke it before the other party has accepted it. You must let the other party know you've revoked the offer. And an offer can expire on its own terms if it isn't accepted in time: "I'll buy 100 rolls of newsprint at your quoted price if you deliver by May 1." On May 2, if the newsprint hasn't been delivered, the contract is void. But if your offer was to "buy 100 rolls of newsprint at your quoted price," and no time limit was set, the offer remains open for a "reasonable time." If you and the other party disagree on how long that is, then likely a court will decide.

You create an advertisement for a client. The ad says that television sets in your client's store are on sale starting at $150 and going up to $1,000. Has the store made an offer through the ad? If a customer points at a set and says, "I'll buy that one for $150," and the salesperson says, "Sorry, that's a floor model and we don't sell those," has the store breached a contract? Courts likely would say no; there was not an offer because there is nothing specific in the ad. What television set costs what amount? To whom—specifically—are you offering the sets? Without an offer, there could not be an acceptance. The ad would be seen as inviting a customer to make an offer to buy. The store then can accept or reject that offer.

An Acceptance

If a written contract is presented to you and you sign it, you have accepted it. If you make an oral offer to someone, and she orally agrees, she has accepted it. But some forms of responses to an offer do not constitute a valid acceptance. For example, a counteroffer is not an acceptance. You offer to purchase 100 rolls of newsprint at the quoted rate if delivered by May 1. The newsprint company says, "Great! But we'll get it there by May 15." That is not an acceptance. It really amounts to rejecting the original offer and making a new offer: The newsprint company is offering to sell you 100 rolls of paper at the quoted rate to be delivered by May 15. You now can accept the offer or not.

Also, a conditional response is not an acceptance. The paper company says, "We'll deliver by May 1 at that price if you agree to place your next order with us, too." That is a new offer from the newsprint company to you, based on your suggested terms plus the new term—you buy from that company next time you need paper. You can accept that offer or not, but the paper company has not accepted your offer. Your offer no longer is on the table (see Fig. 16.3).

If someone offers you a contract, you may:

- Accept the offer.
- Reject the offer.
- Make a counteroffer.
- Add terms (this is an acceptance if the other party agrees to the added terms).
- Change terms (this becomes a rejection).

Figure 16.3 Accepting or Rejecting a Contract

But just adding—not changing—terms is not a rejection of the offer. If the newsprint company says it agrees to all your terms, but it would like to add that you pay 10 percent of the bill upon delivery, it is accepting the contract, and then making an offer to modify it. You may reject the proposed modification, and the original contract still is in force.

Consideration

If there is a valid offer and a valid acceptance, that still isn't enough to form a legally binding contract. You also need consideration, or as courts say, "bargained-for obligations," to which both parties agree. If someone says to you, "I'd like to be the new art director for your magazine," and you say, "OK," there's no contract. The person wanting to be your art director knows what his obligations are, but you don't have any obligations in return. Specifically, you haven't agreed on a salary. Once you do, then there will be obligations on both sides. The salary is the "consideration" for the work the art director will do.

Later, the art director decides that the salary you pay him is unfair and inadequate. Even if it is—that is, it is well below the going rate for art directors on magazines with similar circulations—will that void the contract? Courts generally say no; any consideration that is a detriment to you—here, your paying money—is sufficient, and courts won't worry about whether it is fair.

Something someone already owes you—work or money, for instance—cannot act as consideration. You already pay a reporter to cover local sports. You ask her if she wants to write a column, too. She says, "Sure." Later, she changes her mind. Can you hold her to a "contract" to write a column based on the salary she already earns? No, you owe her that, anyway. There was no consideration, such as additional salary, so no "additional" contract was formed.

However, you offer to pay the reporter an extra $100 a week for a column, and she agrees. But when payday comes, she says she wants $150 each week. Even if you say, "OK," there is not a new contract. She already was under the obligation to write the column, and you had an obligation to pay her $100 more per week. Period. What if your response was, "OK, but I want two columns a week," and she says, "Fine"? Is there a new contract now? Yes, because the obligations on *both* sides changed, and you both agreed to those changes.

A contract may exist even if there is not agreement on consideration. You say to a carpenter, "Would you build a new set for the morning news program? I'll pay you well for it." She says, "Yes. When should I start?" You say, "Right now." The carpenter begins immediately and builds the set. When she asks for payment, you say, "Sorry, there wasn't a contract requiring me to pay you. We didn't set a price, so there was no consideration." Many courts would impose a doctrine called "detrimental reliance." The carpenter reasonably—and to her detriment—relied on your promise to pay her if she built the set. She fulfilled her obligation, and a court likely would require you to pay her a reasonable amount for her work and materials.

Contract Defenses

If there is a valid offer, an acceptance, and consideration, is the contract now ironclad? Not necessarily. It may be that a contract cannot be enforced for several different reasons (see Fig. 16.4).

It may appear a contract has been formed. But it may not be a valid contract if:

- One party, such as a minor, is legally incompetent to enter into a contract.
- It is an oral contract, rather than in writing, when the law requires it to be written.
- It is an unconscionable contract.
- The contract is based on a mistake made by both parties.

Figure 16.4 Invalid Contracts

The law will not allow certain people to enter into a contract. Minors—those under 18 years old—don't have the "capacity" to agree to a contract, according to the law. Neither do those who are mentally incompetent, nor those who are highly intoxicated. And it doesn't matter if the other party didn't know that the person was, for example, a minor. The contract still cannot be enforced.

Also, although the law does recognize oral contracts, it also requires certain contracts to be in writing. Contracts for the sale of goods for more than $500 must be on paper. So must contracts for services that cannot be performed within one year from the date of the agreement. This is a strange limitation. For example, if you sign a contract on May 1, 1999, to have your television studio cleaned on June 1, 2000, it must be in writing. The date the service will be performed is more than a year after the date of the agreement. But if the contract were for cleaning your studios on *or before* June 1, 2000, that task can be accomplished within a year from the agreement date. Therefore, that could be an oral contract and be enforceable. This holds true even if *in fact* the studio is not cleaned until June 1, 2000.

Another unenforceable contract is one a court finds to be "unconscionable." This is a contract that is so one-sided that it is unfair or oppressive. Courts can refuse to enforce all or part of a contract that was unconscionable when the parties entered into it. But judges rarely find a contract unconscionable if the parties are both of equal strength. That is, courts assume two multimillion dollar businesses have enough legal advice that any contract between the companies is what they wanted. It is unlikely one of them later successfully can scream "unconscionable contract." The situation more often might arise in a contract between a multimillion dollar business and a small, independent company. The large business may have imposed unfair terms on the smaller one.

Finally, some "mistakes" may make a contract unenforceable. For example, if a contract includes a term both parties reasonably interpret differently, a court could void the agreement on that basis. A contract for a "used PC" likely is not sufficiently explicit to allow both parties to agree on the exact computer, or even a narrow range of computers, to fulfill the obligation. Also, if both parties agree on the same mistake, the contract may be void. You and a feature syndication company strike a contract, both believing that a famous newspaper columnist will be part of the company's product. But at the last minute, the columnist decides to sign with another syndication company. That mutual mistake on your and the company's part may void the contract.

However, when only one party has made a mistake, most courts will not grant relief. Your newspaper bids for a printing job, but mistakenly bases the bid on a price for newsprint that is incorrect. Newsprint doubles in price unexpectedly. A court likely will not let you out of the contract if your bid is accepted. A court could void the contract, though, if the other party has not relied on your bid to its detriment. However, for example, if the other party already has entered into contracts on the basis of your bid and its agreement with you, it probably is too late for you to get relief from a court.

Contract Terms

Courts often say that a contract's terms—what you and the other parties have agreed on—is contained within "the four corners" of the contract. Although it is an overstatement to maintain that nothing outside a contract's words has any effect on interpreting what the contract means, generally it is true that the agreement's language is dispositive. That means contracts must be written very carefully, to say exactly what you believe you are committing to do. That is why contracts should be reviewed by legal counsel before you sign them. Also, you should not sign a contract that includes any words you don't understand.

The "four corners" rule means that generally any oral discussions or other documents that may relate to the contract cannot be considered in determining the contract's terms. If there is disagreement over the pact's meaning, a court will look to the words in the contract—and no further. Some contracts include a provision stating that a court will consider the contract's terms and nothing else. But even without a contract saying that, it's likely what a court will do. However, if other terms consistent with the contract were agreed upon, but were not included in the contract, some courts might accept those as part of the agreement. And if the contract is incomplete in its wording, but terms agreed upon would make the contract complete, some courts, again, might include those terms as part of the contract.

One term a contract might contain is a warranty ensuring the goods sold and purchased are as promised. This is called an "express warranty." But the law will read an "implied warranty of merchantability"—that the goods are of usable quality—into a contract even if there is not an express warranty. This is done if the goods are purchased from a "merchant," that is, a person or company normally dealing in that product. If you purchase a used PC from a company that sells used computers as a matter of course, the implied warranty will be read into the contract. If you buy a used PC from your next-door neighbor, it is unlikely a court will find an implied warranty.

Just as a contract can include an express warranty, it can include a disclaimer. If a contract clearly and conspicuously states that there is no warranty, or there is a limited warranty (and explains in what way it is limited), a court normally will accept that. But a contract cannot include both an express warranty and a disclaimer.

Complying with a Contract

If a valid contract is formed, both parties are permitted to enter into the agreement, and there is no way to void it: The parties must comply with the contract's terms. Otherwise, if a lawsuit is brought against the noncomplying party, a court can find the party in breach of contract. It can require the breaching party to comply with the contract's terms, and, if the contract includes penalties for breach, the court can enforce those, as well.

But complying with a contract may not require complete compliance. In many instances, the law wants "substantial compliance," meaning that some departure from the agreement's precise terms may be acceptable. If your agreement with a janitorial service states that your studio will be cleaned each weekday before 9 A.M., the company probably still will be in compliance if one day it doesn't finish until 10 A.M.

The company would not be in compliance, however, if the contract stated that a key element of the agreement—a "material" clause—is that cleaning be completed by 9 A.M. Perhaps the studio fills up with very busy people starting at 9 A.M. You wouldn't want a janitorial service mopping the floor at 9:30 A.M. while your employees are trying to get a noon news show on the air. In fact, the law requires "strict compliance" with a contract's *material* terms. Sometimes these are obvious and need not be stated. An agreement to deliver a four-wheel drive truck is not fulfilled by providing a rear-wheel drive car. Material terms generally include the service to be performed or product to be exchanged, the number of items to be delivered, the price, the time period of the contract, the quality of the work or product, and similar important provisions.

Also, a contract's price terms must be met strictly. An agreement to purchase a new truck for $20,000 means you will pay $20,000, not $19,000. And clearly expressed terms also must be met. A contract provision that you will buy a painting for your reception area if it is appraised at $10,000 or more means you do not have to purchase the painting if the appraisal comes in at $9,500.

Goods can't be in "approximately good condition" when delivered, unless the contract specifically allows that. Goods must be in perfect condition. What if they aren't? If the van you ordered has one bad headlight, you can decline to accept it, informing the dealer of the problem. The dealer then has until the deadline date specified in the contract to repair it or replace it with a van in perfect condition. Of course, if the dealer delivered the defective van on the deadline date, there may be no time to repair or replace—and you can void the contract.

Compliance with contract terms also might be excused by impossibility or impracticability. You contract with a retailer to supply you with a particular piece of equipment. The retailer discovers the equipment no longer is manufactured, and one cannot be found anywhere. If it is impossible for the retailer to meet its obligations, a court will excuse it from doing so. If the retailer finds the piece of equipment, but it is the last one available and will cost the retailer ten times what you agreed to pay for it, a court might find that it is "commercially impracticable" for the retailer to comply, and thereby excuse it. But courts won't let someone out of a contract simply because it turned out to be a bad bargain. Those are the risks people in business take.

Under these conditions—or for any reason—the parties can agree to modify the contract. Generally, modification requires many of the formalities necessary to forming the original contract. Or they may decide to cancel the contract.

Remedies If a Contract Is Breached

Suppose you order a shipment of videotapes. One of your camera crews takes several boxes of the tapes to cover a local fashion show. The tapes turn out to be defective. One of the fashion show's sponsors was a local department store. Because yours was the only station in town not to include tape of the show on your evening news, the department store cancels its advertising contract with your station. What can you do?

The law allows you to recover damages when a contract to which you are a party is breached. Generally, this means monetary recovery—putting you in the position you would have been in had the breach not occurred. If you have paid for the videotapes, you are due a refund. If you have not, you won't need to pay for them. (If the contract deadline has not passed, the supplier can replace all the tapes you haven't used and you will owe for those.)

But the law also expects you to "cover" your losses to the extent possible. If you found the whole shipment was bad, you could not keep using it and expect to recover damages from the supplier. You would be expected to replace it with good tape. If the replacement tape costs you more than the defective tape did, the defective tape supplier will be ordered to pay the difference.

What about the department store canceling its advertising contract (assuming the contract allowed it to do so)? You have suffered damages beyond the cost of the videotape. These are called "consequential" damages—losses caused by the contract breach. But can you recover for them? Probably not.

You would argue that your loss is provable—the amount the store did not pay you for advertising time. But many courts would not allow you to recover that loss from the tape supplier. These courts would rule that the tape supplier could not have "foreseen" that providing defective tape would cause your station to lose advertising. Therefore, the supplier would not be responsible for the consequential damages.

What if your contract with the tape supplier included a provision that if the tapes proved to be defective, the supplier would have to pay you a specified amount? This is called "liquidated damages," a provision that means the injured party—your television station—does not have to prove damages. Rather, the contract states what the damages will be if there is a breach. Liquidated damages often are found in construction contracts. If a contractor is late completing your new printing plant, and there are not "legal excuses" for it, you'll be paid $10,000 a day, or whatever the contract says. Courts generally do not like liquidated damages provisions, since they can be quite punitive to the breaching party. To uphold liquidated damages, courts will insist that when the contract was executed it was difficult to estimate what the damages would be if there were a breach, and the amount of liquidated damages is a fair forecast of the damages.

Sometimes money won't solve the problem. You sign a contract with a new editorial cartoonist. Just before she is to start, she gets a better offer from another newspaper and breaches her contract with you. Can you ask a court to require her to work for you, not for the other newspaper? This is called "specific performance"—do what the contract requires you to do. But courts won't require it. Only in highly unusual circumstances will courts impose specific performance. This is usually for unique items, such as real estate or antique goods—that is, in situations in which money, no matter how much, will not allow you to purchase a similar item, because there isn't a similar item. (Courts consider each piece of real estate to be unique.) But courts generally will not require specific performance for goods or services. The law sees monetary damages as solving most contract problems. You may not get the exact cartoonist you want, but you can hire someone else.

Uniform Commercial Code

Several decades ago, all states (except Louisiana) adopted some form of the Uniform Commercial Code (UCC). The UCC is a draft law pertaining to commercial transactions. To the extent a state has adopted part or all of the UCC, those provisions have the force of law in that state. One portion of the UCC applies to "goods." The word *goods* in the UCC applies to all products except those specifically made for the purchaser. That is, the term applies to products meant for sale generally.

Where and when applicable, the UCC governs contracts for the sale of goods. This adds a complexity to an already complex area of the law—contracts. The UCC is another reason to consult your attorney before entering into a contract.

A Reminder

It can't be emphasized enough that contracts is a very complex area of the law. The discussion here is a general one. Do not rely on it as a way to write or analyze a contract. Legal counsel should be consulted before you, as a media manager, enter into agreements. Otherwise, you may find yourself bound in ways you never expected. Obviously, from all that has been discussed about contracts, clarity is vital. Make sure you indicate exactly what you want and/or to what you agree. Be sure to give your attorney specific directions so the best language can be drafted. Courts generally interpret things that are not clear. And it is neither to your advantage, nor the other party's, for anyone to be confused. Often the simplest, most specific contract is the best.

EMPLOYMENT LAW

Many media managers hire, train, promote, and, if necessary, fire employees. Federal and state laws place requirements and restrictions on these steps. Once again, what follows will be only a quick overview of some labor law issues of importance to media managers. You should seek legal advice about employee matters when appropriate.

Employment Discrimination

From the time people began hiring and firing employees in America, they could do so "at will." They didn't have to give a reason, and their motive could be to discriminate based on any human characteristic. Not until the mid-20th century did Congress begin adopting laws, and courts make decisions, that changed this. Employment "at will"—at the employer's will—still is a basic concept in the law. In general, managers need not hire people they don't want to.

Today, management's discretion is limited by statutes and court interpretations about discrimination, union activities, and other matters. But as one court said, "No matter how medieval a firm's practices, no matter how high-handed its decisional process, no matter how mistaken the firm's managers," the company generally is free to follow its course if there is no discrimination based on race, color, national origin, sex, age, religion, disability, or citizenship (*Pollard v. Rea Magnet Wire Co.*, 1987, p. 560; *see* Player, 1992, p. 35) (see Fig. 16.5).

Laws forbid discriminating against current or prospective employees on the basis of a person's:

- Race
- Color
- National origin
- Sex
- Age
- Religion
- Disability
- Citizenship

Figure 16.5 Discrimination

Partly in reaction to employers' free hands in dealing with employees, Congress has adopted equal employment opportunity (EEO) statutes applicable to most private businesses in the United States. States also have laws requiring equal employment opportunities. And those mass media companies subject to FCC jurisdiction—radio, television, cable, direct broadcast satellites—must comply with an additional set of EEO rules established by the Commission (see Fig. 16.6).

- Title VII of the Civil Rights Act of 1964 (Title VII)
- Age Discrimination in Employment Act (ADEA)
- Americans with Disabilities Act (ADA)
- Immigration Reform and Control Act
- Civil Rights Act of 1866
- Equal Pay Act

Figure 16.6 Laws Prohibiting Employment Discrimination

Federal Laws Restricting Employment Discrimination

As a media manager, you should be familiar with the federal and state laws that apply to your interactions with prospective employees and those you hire and fire. For example, a number of federal laws protect against employment discrimination.

Title VII The most important federal statute governing employers' relations with prospective and current employees is Title VII of the Civil Rights Act of 1964. The act prohibits discrimination in hiring, firing, compensation, promotions, job duties, and other employment decisions. Discrimination may not be based on race, color, religion, sex (including pregnancy and childbirth), or national origin. Although many state statutes forbid discrimination based on marital status, Title VII does not.

> [Title VII] prohibits discrimination because of a person's racial origins in Africa or Asia, as well as discrimination against indigenous Americans such as Eskimos, Native Hawaiians, and American Indians. Whites, Europeans, or Caucasians are protected against race discrimination under the same standards as racial minorities. . . . Preferring a person based on the relative lightness of skin complexion is "color" discrimination. . . .
> "National origin" means "the country from which your forebears came. . . ." Consequently, discrimination against someone because of Italian, Latino, or Polish heritage is proscribed . . . as is favoring ethnic minorities, such as Puerto Ricans, over persons of Anglo heritage. . . . [D]iscrimination against Armenians, Cajuns, or Gypsies [for example] is "national origin" discrimination. (Player, 1992, pp. 115, 119).

Title VII prohibits employment discrimination on the basis of sex, among other characteristics. An employer may rebut a charge of sexual discrimination by showing that its employment decision, including denying promotion, was made for a "legitimate, nondiscriminatory" reason. Courts often accept this argument. Employers have argued successfully that an individual complaining of discrimination did not meet standards based on interviews or did not have the necessary professional experience or educational qualifications. Decisions based on subjective criteria have been upheld—such as an applicant not being "as well qualified" as another (Cleary, 1993, pp. 15–19).

The ban against religious discrimination includes "all aspects of religious observances and practice." That is, an employer must accommodate employees' religious practices. If an employee believes that is not happening, she or he must show that the practice is a sincerely held "religious" observance, that the employer was told of the conflict between the person's job and religious practice, and that the employer discriminated against the employee because of the practice. The employer can defend itself by showing it would cause an undue hardship on the business to accommodate the employee.

Generally, Title VII permits employers "to hire and employ" based on a person's religion, sex, or national origin if the person has a "bona fide occupational qualification" requiring such discrimination. Although this exception does not include racial discrimination, courts have found a "business necessity" defense applicable to racial classifications (Player, 1992, p. 52). These exemptions from Title VII's proscription against discrimination apply only if the employer proves "that members of the excluded class cannot safely and effectively perform *essential* job duties" (Player, 1992, p. 52). For example, a television program producer can exclude men and hire only women for roles as mothers in a show. Men could not play the roles.

Title VII is aimed at employers. The law specifies what management may not do, rather than telling employees or prospective employees what they may do. But not all employers come within the statute. Title VII applies to employers with 15 or more employees. An "employee" is someone working each business day for 20 or more weeks during a year. Part-time employees are covered by the statutes, but they are not counted in ascertaining whether a business has enough employees to be included within the law (Player, 1992, pp. 23–24). Courts disagree about whether the number of employees to be counted is in an individual business, such as a radio station, or includes a number of businesses under a corporate parent (Porto, 1997, pp. 576–586).

Title VII is enforced by the Equal Employment Opportunity Commission (EEOC), a federal agency. An individual may file suit against an employer or prospective employer, but the person "must first exhaust complicated state and federal pre-suit administrative procedures" (Player, 1992, p. 241). In effect, a private lawsuit may not be filed until the EEOC gives permission to do so.

A winning plaintiff may be awarded a range of remedies, including, as appropriate, a court order requiring the company to hire the plaintiff, back pay, "front pay" (wages until a job position opens that the plaintiff can fill), and court-ordered promotion. The Civil Rights Act of 1991 also allows winning plaintiffs under Title VII to be awarded monetary damages, such as compensation for emotional pain and suffering because of the discrimination, or punitive damages. A winning employee plaintiff likely will be awarded his or her attorney's fees. But a prevailing employer rarely will get its attorney's fees from a losing plaintiff.

Age Discrimination in Employment Act   The Age Discrimination in Employment Act of 1967 (ADEA) bars discrimination based on a person's age. The ADEA prohibits employers from taking employment-related actions based on the age of an employee or prospective employee who is at least 40 years old. There are certain exceptions, such as for police or fire fighting positions. Younger people more than 40 years old are as protected as older individuals.

The statute also prohibits any stated retirement age, unless one is justified by the business' circumstances. Any reduction in force intended to cut older workers is prohibited. However, the ADEA permits offers of early retirement if certain standards are met.

As with Title VII, the EEOC may file suit, or an individual plaintiff may sue after obtaining permission from the EEOC. There is a range of remedies available, but not monetary damages except for back wages or front pay.

Employers with 20 or more employees are affected by the ADEA. "Employee" is defined as it is for Title VII.

Americans with Disabilities Act   The Americans with Disabilities Act of 1990 (ADA) forbids employers of 15 or more employees to discriminate against persons with physical or mental disabilities who otherwise are qualified for the job. Being qualified for the job means being able to perform "essential functions" of the position with or without special accommodation. Employers, then, cannot refuse to hire people whose disabilities prevent them from performing certain nonessential—that is, secondary—tasks related to the job.

Also, the ADA requires covered employers to make "reasonable accommodations" for disabled employees. This may include providing specialized equipment or physical accommodations in the workplace. The equipment or physical situation need not be exactly what the employee requests or would prefer, nor need it be the best possible for the purpose. It need only be "reasonable" considering the employee's circumstances, and it must be provided within a reasonable time period (Koets, 1995, pp. 637–638). An employer need not accommodate a disabled employee if doing so would "impose an undue hardship"—a significant difficulty or expense—on the employer.

In addition to the types of remedies available under Title VII, a plaintiff may recover, up to a limit, compensation for nonmonetary injuries, such as emotional pain and suffering. A winning plaintiff also may collect punitive damages for an employer's malicious or reckless actions. A court may award attorney's fees to a successful plaintiff.

Immigration Reform and Control Act   The Immigration Reform and Control Act of 1986 forbids discrimination on the basis of "national origin" or "citizenship." The statute applies only to American citizens and those who are in the country legally and take certain specified actions showing an intention to become a citizen. That is, employers with four or more employees cannot choose, for example, to reject a job applicant because the person is an American citizen or an "intending citizen." A winning party in a lawsuit based on the act may be awarded attorney's fees only if the losing side's argument is "without foundation."

The statute also requires employers to refuse to hire unauthorized aliens, or to hire anyone without verifying that the individual is a U.S. citizen or otherwise legally able to work in this country. After hiring someone, if an employer later finds the person is unauthorized, the individual must be discharged. Employers can be fined and found criminally liable for knowingly violating the law.

Civil Rights Act of 1866   The Civil Rights Act of 1866 prohibits discrimination based on race in all aspects of offering or accepting a contract. This applies to employment contracts (*Johnson v. Railway Express Agency,* 1975). The 1866 law covers any employer, no matter how many employees, and bars racial discrimination, including discrimination based on ethnic origin. It does not prohibit discrimination due to sex, religion, age, or citizenship.

Title VII of the 1964 Civil Rights Act also bars racially motivated employment discrimination, but the 1866 law has greater coverage (Player, 1992, p. 18). For example, an individual may sue under the 1866 statute without first seeking permission from the EEOC. Also, the Civil Rights Act of 1866 includes contracts between a company and independent contractors (discussed in a later section) (Player, 1992, p. 36). Under the 1866 law, managers may not discriminate based on race or ethnic origin when choosing independent contractors to perform work for the company.

Equal Pay Act   The Equal Pay Act of 1963 (EPA) requires that men and women be paid equal wages for "equal work" within a company. Equal work is determined by comparing positions with "substantially equal" job requirements.

As do Title VII and the ADA, the EPA covers employees "engaged in commerce," which means producing goods and moving them in commerce. But businesses with annual sales greater than $500,000, which includes media companies of any significant size, also are included.

The EPA deals only with an employee's wages. Other forms of compensation discrimination, such as bonuses or stock options, may be dealt with under other laws. For example, if the discrimination is based on race, national origin, or religion, Title VII will apply. If age discrimination, the ADEA takes effect. And if it is discrimination based on physical or mental disability, the ADA is applicable.

The EEOC oversees disputes under this statute, but the EPA permits individuals to sue for themselves without first asking the EEOC's permission. A winning plaintiff may be awarded back pay.

The EPA allows an employer to defend against a suit by showing that the pay differential is based on a seniority system, comparative merit, or differences in the type or amount of work performed. Also, the EPA does not forbid wage discrepancies based on something other than an employee's sex.

The FCC's EEO rules

The FCC has its own EEO rules, which bar discrimination in hiring, promoting, and firing based on race, gender, religion, color, or national origin. Broadcasters and cable operators must establish procedures ensuring that employment practices do not discriminate. The stations and systems are to let employees and prospective employees know about their procedures.

The Commission's EEO rules are complex. Station and cable system managers must be familiar with the rules and should consult their attorneys to stay up-to-date about any changes in the regulations. The FCC regularly fines stations and systems that violate the EEO rules.

Broadcast stations, for example, must specify requirements for certain job categories, such as sales manager and news director. Stations must tell their employees about available jobs and the qualifications necessary to fill them. Stations also must inform groups representing minorities and women about job openings. On a regular basis, broadcasters are to review their progress in recruiting, hiring, and promoting women and minorities. They must correct any procedural problems that cause them to fall short of expectations in hiring women and minorities. Stations are to file annual EEO reports with the FCC documenting their employment practices. The reports also are put in the stations' public files, allowing community members to determine the stations' success in their equal employment efforts.

Dismissing Employees

In general, the "employment at will" approach allows an employer to discharge an employee for no reason. Employers experience problems when they discharge *for* a reason, such as an employee's race, sex, national origin, age, or union activity. These reasons, and others, are impermissible grounds for firing someone. Also, an employer cannot fire someone for refusing a manager's order to engage in illegal activities, such as committing perjury (*Petermann v. International Brotherhood of Teamsters*, 1959).

However, an employer may discharge an employee for consistently violating reasonable company rules, including, for example, consuming alcoholic products or controlled substances at work, or missing work too often. Firing people for unsatisfactorily performing their jobs also is permitted. People also may be discharged for often being insubordinate, being disruptive, or even having a bad attitude which creates an unpleasant work atmosphere. Employees can be discharged for theft of company property or funds, falsifying records, or making false statements (American Jurisprudence, 1994, §§ 2221–2284).

In all instances, it is wise to keep records of the employee's infractions, and of times management brought those infractions to the employee's attention. Also, keep records of suggestions made to the employee to improve his or her performance, and any sanctions imposed by management (American Jurisprudence, 1994, §§ 2221–2284). If a fired employee sues and wins a case for "wrongful discharge," the employee may be awarded damages that would include lost wages and other related losses. Courts may permit punitive damage awards against an employer, as well, if the firing was malicious.

An employee who is in a position to negotiate an individual contract—a news anchor or a columnist, or a member of management—may include contractual limitations on dismissal. For example, a news director's contract may state that firing may be based only on "just cause" and cannot be implemented until there have been "discussions with the station's general manager" (Player, 1992, p. 5). If an anchor's contract includes a provision stipulating the person appears on a particular newscast, and the station wants to replace that person before the contract reaches its end, the only remedy may be to pay off the rest of the anchor's contract. For that reason, many media managers are very careful about detailed assignments in employment agreements. Contracting with an anchor to read "newscasts" is very different from stipulating "anchor the 5 P.M. and 10 P.M. newscasts Monday through Friday." Increasingly, television newscast producers are also being placed on contract. The same thing applies to them. If you contract with a producer to do the 10 P.M. newscast, you can't reassign that person to do the noon newscast without negotiating a new contract. Courts will uphold these contractual provisions.

Restrictions on Sexual Harassment

Sexual harassment is equivalent to discrimination based on sex under Title VII. It is forbidden. The Supreme Court recognizes two types of sexual harassment. First, there is "quid pro quo" harassment. This occurs when an employer makes clear or implies that employment or benefits will stop unless the employee grants sexual favors or, at least, tolerates continued sexual advances (*Meritor Savings Bank v. Vinson,* 1986; see Kelly & Watt, 1996). An employer is strictly liable for this type of sexual harassment. It doesn't matter whether someone higher up in management knew that a supervisor down the line engaged in quid pro quo harassment. The company still will be responsible.

Second, there is harassment in the form of a hostile or abusive work environment. This occurs "when a co-worker or supervisor, engaging in unwelcome and inappropriate sexually based behavior, renders the workplace atmosphere intimidating, hostile, or offensive" (Roberts & Mann, 1996, p. 276). Courts "will more likely find an illegal hostile environment present when the workplace includes sexual propositions, pornography, extremely vulgar language, sexual touching, degrading comments, or embarrassing questions or jokes" (Roberts & Mann, 1996, p. 277).

The Supreme Court has found that a worker suing on this type of harassment need not prove psychological harm: "[S]o long as the environment would reasonably be perceived, and is perceived, as hostile or abusive, there is no need for it also to be psychologically injurious" (*Harris v. Forklift Systems,* 1993, p. 22). The Court identified some factors that could be considered in determining if the workplace is hostile, including how often discriminatory sexual conduct occurs, how severe that conduct is, whether the conduct is physically threatening or humiliating or mildly offensive, and whether the conduct makes it unreasonably difficult for the employee to perform the assigned work (*Harris v. Forklift Systems,* 1993, p. 22).

Employers may be found liable for creating or tolerating a hostile workplace if members of management (or supervisors) create a discriminatory environment, or if management knew or should have known sexual harassment was occurring and did not correct the situation. Courts will find that an employer knew of the hostile environment if harassment occurs openly, employees generally know it exists, or if an employee files a charge against the employer based on a hostile environment (Roberts & Mann, 1996, pp. 281–282).

For both types of harassment, the important point is that the employer's actions were "unwelcome." The Supreme Court has not defined this term, but other courts generally use the standard that a "reasonable woman" under similar circumstances would find the sexual behavior unwelcome (Kelly & Watt, 1996, p. 87). One court said that sexual behavior is unwelcome when it is "uninvited and offensive" (*Burns v. McGregor Electronic Industries,* 1993, p. 962).

It has been suggested that companies should attempt to ensure sexual harassment does not occur by, first, preparing a "comprehensive, detailed written policy on sexual harassment." The policy should be distributed to all employees, preferably by top management to show that the company takes the policy seriously. The policy should include a clear commitment to prevent sexual harassment, an explanation that sexual harassment is both quid pro quo and hostile environment, a list of possible penalties, how complaints can be filed, and an explicit statement that complaints will be kept confidential. The company also should establish procedures for handling sexual harassment complaints. In particular, the procedures should make clear that those who think they are victims will not have to deal with supervisors who may have been part of the problem or ignored the harassment. Finally, the company should enforce its policies "quickly, consistently, and aggressively" (Roberts & Mann, 1996, pp. 284–287).

Federal Laws and Collective Bargaining

Since some media employees—reporters, production workers, television program directors—may be union members, media managers should know how to interact with unions. Unions' collective bargaining activities are governed by the National Labor Relations Act (NLRA, also called the Wagner Act, adopted by Congress in 1935) and the Labor-Management Relations Act (the Taft-Hartley Act, adopted in 1947). The NLRA gives unions the right to organize workers and to bargain on their behalf with employers. The law requires employers to bargain with unions. It also lists employer labor practices that the law says are unfair. The NLRA established the National Labor Relations Board (NLRB), giving it the power to oversee management-labor relations and to interpret the NLRA.

Congress passed the Taft-Hartley Act in response to growing union strength. The statute gives employees the right not to engage in union activities. The act also limits some union actions, such as striking to convince a management to fire an employee because she or he did not join the union. The NLRB administers the Taft-Hartley Act as it does the NLRA.

The NLRA does not give a union the right to set employment terms, such as hours and wages, without management's agreement. However, if an employer can't seem to agree with any substantive union proposal, and wants to leave everything to management's discretion during the term of the union contract, a court likely will find that the employer did not bargain in good faith (see, e.g., *NLRB v. Reed & Prince Manufacturing Co.*, 1953).

While the NLRA requires "good faith" bargaining by both employer and union, it does not insist that an agreement be reached (*NLRB v. American National Insurance Co.*, 1952). In fact, the NLRB is permitted to do little in situations in which an employer simply refuses to reach an agreement.

When a union and an employer cannot reach agreement on a contract covering union members, the union's response may be to picket the business. The NLRA protects employees' rights to engage in peaceful picketing. However, the NLRA prohibits picketing under certain circumstances. Picketing to force an employer to recognize a particular union generally is forbidden. Sometimes picketing to convince employees to select a specific union to represent them may be prohibited. For example, employees vote to have one union represent them. Then another union pickets with the intent of persuading employees to substitute this union for the first one. That is not permitted under the NLRA. Also, courts occasionally have upheld states when they claim that certain public policies are violated by picketing.

Employers and Unions

The NLRA prohibits employers from interfering with employees' rights to form and join a union, and to join with other employees to bargain with management. The interference doesn't have to be effective. It is as impermissible to unsuccessfully attempt to prevent workers from engaging in union activities as it is to successfully do so. Employees are free to dissuade workers from joining a union by treating them well. But inducements meant specifically to convince employees not to join a union may be seen as unlawful interference. And management actions that do not have the intent of interfering with union activities nonetheless may be found to do so. Proof of intent is not required (American Jurisprudence, 1994, §§ 1841–1886).

The NLRA does not allow employers to discriminate on the basis of an individual's membership in a labor union. Courts have interpreted the NLRA as requiring unions to object to an employer's discriminatory actions in dealing with employees (*Local Union No. 12 v. NLRB*, 1966).

Of course, management freely may express its opinions about the good and bad points of union activity, just as employees and union representatives may. Courts and the NLRB will balance employers' free speech rights against employees' rights to organize and bargain collectively. That is, an employer's freedom of expression may at some point interfere with employees' attempts to engage in union activities. Certainly, an employer's threats against employees go beyond First Amendment protection in labor-management relations (American Jurisprudence, 1994, §§ 1841–1886).

The Media and Unions

In part, the NLRA is intended to allow employees to organize so that they may negotiate with management on a basis of equal strength. This assumes there is a distinction between management and workers. The NLRB recognizes a category of "managerial employees" that it excludes from being part of a bargaining unit when workers vote whether to form a union, which union to join, or accept a union-management contract. Supervisors also are not included within the NLRA, but the Supreme Court has said that "professional employees" are covered by the national labor acts (*NLRB v. Bell Aerospace Co.*, 1974).

There is disagreement over which newspaper and magazine editors and writers are "managerial employees," and therefore not covered by the NLRA. The distinction is based on whether a person, although not supervising other workers, is "so closely allied with management that they should be excluded from bargaining units" (Davis, 1980, p. 498). For example, one court found a newspaper's editorial writers were managerial employees because they helped establish the paper's policies (*Wichita Eagle & Beacon v. NLRB*, 1973). But the NLRB said another paper's editorial writers were not managerial employees since the editorial page editor and the publisher limited the editorial writers' discretion (*Bulletin Co.*, 1976).

Similarly, producer-directors at a television station were identified as "supervisors," and therefore not included within the NLRA, because they were responsible for news and other programs and supervised certain other employees (*KXTV*, 1971). But a court found program directors, producers, associate producers, and news assignment editors not to be supervisors because they had no power over personnel matters (*NLRB v. KDFW-TV*, 1986).

Unions are permitted to bargain to have employees paid for work performed but not needed. For example, the Supreme Court said it was not a violation of the NLRA to have union newspaper printers set type that would be eliminated because new printing processes did not require it (*American Newspaper Publishers Association v. NLRB*, 1953).

Full-Time and Part-Time Employees, and Independent Contractors

Individuals who perform services for media companies fall into several categories: full-time or part-time employees, independent contractors, agents, and volunteers. A business' legal liability in a number of areas may depend on how an individual is classified. For example, independent contractors and volunteers who perform work for a company do not come under Title VII or the ADA. A business must withhold payroll taxes and submit unemployment taxes for employees. A company is responsible for acts—such as causing a traffic accident—committed by an agent for the company, but not by an independent contractor (see Fig. 16.7).

Employees and Independent Contractors

Perhaps of most concern is whether a person is a company's employee or is acting as an independent contractor. An independent contractor is a person or business that performs work for a company but is not an employee of that company. People who are employees, and who are acting in their areas of responsibility for the business, will make the company responsible for their actions. On the other hand, a company usually is not liable for an independent contractor's actions, even when the independent contractor is performing services for the company. For example, if a newspaper employee hits another car while on his way to sell an advertisement to a business, the newspaper will be liable for the accident. In part, that is because the employee was acting within the scope of his employment when the accident happened. (If the accident happened when the employee took a long detour to pick up a new television set on the way to the advertiser's office, the station likely would not be liable.) But if an independent contractor is installing a new computer system in a television newsroom, and is involved in an auto accident while driving to the station, the television station likely will not be liable.

Federal and state statutes, as well as the rules and regulations of state and federal departments of labor and those of the Internal Revenue Service, are interpreted broadly to find that an employee-employer relationship exists. This is because of the significant social purposes of these laws, including the provision of unemployment benefits and a minimum wage for workers.

The law generally presumes a worker is an employee, requiring the employer to show otherwise. A written agreement may help show that an individual had an independent contractor, instead of an employee, relationship with a business. It always is wise to have a contract with anyone performing services for a company—and it should be prepared with the advice of an attorney. But a written agreement is not necessarily definitive. A court may look beyond the contract to the actual relationship between the business and the individual and find that it is more employee-employer than independent contractor, for example.

Assume a television station asks a carpenter to rebuild the evening news set. The process will take six weeks. The station could hire the carpenter as a full-time or part-time employee for that period. Or the carpenter could sign a contract with the station as an independent contractor. The carpenter lifts a heavy beam off a truck in the station's parking lot, and it accidentally falls on a car. Who is liable—the carpenter or the station? The answer depends largely on the relationship between the two—employer-employee or independent contractor.

People working at a media outlet may fall into several different categories. Media managers may face diverse legal liabilities depending on whether the person is:

- An employee
- An independent contractor
- An agent
- A volunteer

Figure 16.7 Who Works Here?

A court, or state or federal agency, will consider a number of factors in determining whether a person is an employee or an independent contractor. Importantly, the more control a company has over a person's activities, the more likely the individual is to be found to be an employee. Put another way, how independent is the person in performing the required tasks?

For example, does the company or the person determine the methods and manner in which the work is performed? Who sets the sequence in which the work is to be done? Does the company train the individual? Does the company set specific work hours? Is the person able to delegate tasks to others (an independent contractor is more likely to do this than is an employee)? Does the individual work full-time for the company, or does he or she also work for others? Is the person doing the same work as others employed by the company are doing? Does the individual have an office outside the company? Does the person send a bill to the company for services? Does the company or the individual provide materials used for performing the task?

Courts may see any one or several of these—and a list of other—items as most indicative of whether a person is an employee or an independent contractor. Since often there is evidence on both sides of the question, courts often balance the applicable factors. Usually, the decision turns on the question of who controls the person and the way the tasks are to be performed.

Volunteers

The problem media companies face with volunteers is that the individuals may be seen as "employees" and be able to claim compensation and benefits. A college student acting as an intern at a television station may be a "volunteer." So may a community member who helps with the public access channel at a cable system. Or a person who hosts a program at a public radio station on an unpaid basis.

Management should take care to prevent converting a volunteer into an employee. For example, regular employees should not perform tasks usually handled by volunteers. Also, management should not promise volunteers they will be considered for permanent employment at some future time. It is acceptable to offer employment to someone who once was, or still is, a volunteer when an appropriate position opens. However, no prospective promises should be made. Also, a clear distinction should be made between employees who train volunteers and the volunteers themselves.

Agents

The law sees an agent as someone acting for another person, who is called the "principal." An agent can bind the principal to a contract, or can make the principal liable for torts or other acts committed by the agent. An employee, independent contractor, or volunteer can be found to be an agent if an "agency relationship" has been established.

An "agency relationship" primarily turns on the question of how much authority the principal—a media manager, for example—has given to the agent. It does not matter if the agent is not paid. Although a person must be legally competent—that is, not drunk or mentally impaired—to be an agent, the law can find even a minor to be an agent.

If a radio station general manager clearly gives someone the authority to purchase a truck for the station, an agency relationship has been formed through the explicit authority the general manager granted. When that person signs a contract to buy a truck, the station is bound by the agreement. If that same person then buys a computer, the station likely is not bound, since that exceeded the agency relationship. The person was an agent only for the purpose of purchasing a truck for the station, and the individual, not the station, would have to pay for the truck.

If the general manager had said, "Handle matters while I'm gone for a few days," the person could buy a computer and the station would be liable for it. "Handling matters" certainly could include purchasing a computer—or firing the music director. The general manager granted implied authority to do what was necessary to run the station. Hiring someone as a newspaper's "purchasing agent" implies that person can purchase anything the newspaper usually buys—and the paper will be responsible for paying the bill.

But an agency relationship can be established even without explicit stated or written words, or implied authority. Courts recognize "apparent" authority. This means people reasonably believe a person has authority to act for a principal. A person may have been buying computers for a magazine for several years. The magazine fires that person but doesn't tell the magazine's computer supplier. Just after being fired, the person goes to the supplier and purchases a computer, saying it is for the magazine. Is the magazine responsible for paying for the computer? Probably, since the computer supplier reasonably believed the person had authority to buy a machine for the magazine. Of course, the magazine can sue the fired employee and attempt to collect the computer purchase price. But the computer supplier legally can expect the magazine to pay.

This chapter has discussed two important and complex topics of the law—contracts and employer/employee relations. When you face important questions involving either area, you should contact your attorney.

Contract Law

Media managers often enter into contracts, agreements that bind you to commitments you have made. Contract law is complex, and you should consult an attorney to be certain that you're agreeing to promises you want to make and are receiving in return the commitments you expect.

At minimum, a contract involves an offer, an acceptance, and consideration. An offer should state who is bound to fulfill the contract, the length of the contract term, and how much will be paid for the product or service. Offers can be revoked under some circumstances. An offer isn't accepted by a counteroffer or a conditional response. But agreeing to an offer, even adding additional terms, is an acceptance. If there is an offer and acceptance, when consideration is clear—how much will be paid for the product or service—a contract is formed. A court may find a contract even without clear consideration under the doctrine of "detrimental reliance."

The law does not permit certain people, such as minors and the mentally incompetent, to enter into binding contracts. While the law recognizes oral contracts, some contracts must be in writing, such as for the sale of goods for more than $500. A court might void a contract if both parties are mistaken about an important term in the agreement.

Some contract terms may be met substantially, not precisely. But an agreement's price provisions must be met strictly, and goods must be in perfect condition when delivered. A contract may be void if it is commercially impracticable to comply with its terms.

You may sue if a party doesn't meet its contract obligations. But courts expect you to cover—minimize—your losses as well as you can. If the breached contract causes you additional losses—consequential damages—courts likely will not let you recover for them unless the party who breached the contract could have foreseen the additional damages. And courts rarely require specific performance. That is, they won't order someone to provide the product or service specified in the contract. The court will award monetary damages instead.

Employment Law

Generally, hiring and firing in the United States is done "at will." Although the concept of employment at will is beginning to be eroded, employers usually need not hire or retain those they don't want to. However, federal and state antidiscrimination laws limit employers' discretion. Laws may protect employees and prospective employees from discrimination on the basis of race, color, national origin, sex, age, religion, disability, and citizenship.

Title VII of the Civil Rights Act of 1964, the Age Discrimination in Employment Act, the Americans with Disabilities Act, the Immigration Reform and Control Act, the Civil Rights Act of 1866, and the Equal Pay Act are the primary federal laws preventing employment discrimination. The Federal Communications Commission has equal employment opportunity rules applicable to the mass media under its jurisdiction.

Employers generally may dismiss employees for specific infractions, such as disobeying specific orders. It is best to keep records of employees' rules violations and other breaches. However, contracts with individual employees, or union contracts, may limit an employer's options.

Courts recognize two types of sexual harassment. Quid pro quo harassment occurs when an employer offers to exchange employment or benefits for sex. Second, a hostile or abusive workplace environment may constitute sexual harassment. For either type, courts consider whether a "reasonable woman" under similar circumstances would have found the sexual behavior unwelcome.

Federal statutes govern collective bargaining by unions. The laws set boundaries for how unions and employers may deal with each other.

Companies may use employees, independent contractors, and volunteers to perform services. Any of these people may be seen as a company's agent. A company's legal liabilities may be determined based on the category into which a person falls.

STUDY QUESTIONS

1. What terms must be in a contract for the agreement to be valid?

2. Under what circumstances may an offer be revoked so that an acceptance will not be valid?

3. Who may not enter into a contract?

4. How does a "mistake" affect a contract? How does "impracticability" affect a contract?

5. What do the terms "cover" and "consequential damages" mean in terms of suing for a breached contract?

6. If someone doesn't fulfill a contract, what will a court likely require that party to do?

7. What does "at will" employment mean?

8. What are the major federal laws preventing employment discrimination? Generally, what does each cover?

9. What two types of sexual harassment have courts found? What is the standard for determining if sexual action in the workplace is harassment?

10. Into what categories may people performing service for a company fall? Why does it matter which category a person is in?

afterword

It has been a long journey since the beginning of this book, through many facets of the art of managing media organizations. We have covered a great deal of material because of the complicated nature of the media manager's world, one that features constant change, unrelenting challenge, and always fascinating human dynamics.

As we have discussed, media organization workers tend to be creative and emotionally engaged with their work. It is a career field full of passionate people who typically feel a sense of calling about their profession. Success is often measured as much by the heart as the mind or pocketbook.

To be a successful manager in such an environment you have to remain clear-eyed, focused, and always wary, so you will catch problems—ranging from personal conflicts to legal difficulties—as early as possible. You can see that in many respects a media manager must, like a high-wire walker, maintain a critical balance to cross successfully the abyss of failure. It is a daunting challenge, but one that you are capable of meeting with the knowledge you have gained.

As you practice the art of media management, we encourage you to continue growing in an active, lifelong journey—balancing on the wire.

references

A

A. C. Nielsen. (1997). A. C. Nielsen and Nielsen Media Research home page. [Online]. Available: http://www.nielsen.com.

Abelson, R. P., & Levi, A. (1985). Decision making and decision theory. In G. Lindzey & E. Aronson (Eds.), *Handbook of social psychology* (3rd ed.) (pp. 231–309). New York: Random House.

Abrams v. United States, 250 U.S. 616 (1919).

Action for Children's Television v. FCC, 58 F.3d 654 (D.C. Cir. 1995) (en banc), *cert. denied,* 116 S. Ct. 701 (1996).

Adams, J. S. (1963). Toward an understanding of equity. *Journal of Abnormal and Social Psychology, 67,* 422–436.

Aftab, P. (1997, Jan. 27). Jurisdiction in cyberspace: Due process standards vary. *New York Law Journal,* S4.

Age Discrimination in Employment Act, 29 U.S.C. § 621 et seq.

Alderfer, C. (1972). *Existence, relatedness, and growth: Human needs in organizational settings.* New York: Free Press.

Allen v. Men's World Outlet, Inc., 679 F. Supp. 360 (S.D.N.Y. 1988).

American Home Products, 98 F.T.C. 136 (1981), *aff'd,* American Home Products Corp. v. FTC, 695 F.2d 681 (3d Cir. 1982).

American Jurisprudence Second. (1994). *Labor and labor relations.* Rochester, NY: Lawyer's Cooperative.

American Newspaper Publishers Association v. NLRB, 345 U.S. 100 (1953).

Americans with Disabilities Act, 42 U.S.C. § 12101 et seq.

Anderson, J. (Ed.). (1988). The perceptive audience. *Communication Yearbook/11.* Beverly Hills, CA: Sage.

Arbitron. (1997). Arbitron home page. [Online]. Available: http://www.arbitron.com.

Argenti, J. (1976). *Corporate collapse.* New York: Halstead.

Argyris, C. (1964). *Integrating the individual and the organization.* New York: John Wiley & Sons.

Arkansas Writers' Project, Inc. v. Ragland, 481 U.S. 221(1987).

Asami, T. (1997, January 1). New form of nationalism emerging. *The Daily Yomiuri,* p. 5.

Au, C. (1996). Rethinking organizational effectiveness: Theoretical and methodological issues in the study of organizational effectiveness for social welfare organizations. *Administration in Social Work, 20,* 1.

Audit Bureau of Circulations. (1997). *How to read a newspaper audit report.* Schaumburg, IL: Author. Available: http://www.accessabc.com/reports/howtouse.

Auletta, K. (1991). *Three blind mice: How the TV networks lost their way.* New York: Random House.

Ayeni v. CBS, Inc., 848 F. Supp. 362 (E.D.N.Y.), *aff'd,* 35 F.3d 680 (2d Cir. 1994), *cert. denied,* 514 U.S. 162 (1995).

B

Bagdikian, B. (1992). *The media monopoly* (4th ed.). Boston: Beacon Press.

Bandura, A. (1986). *Social foundations of thought and action: A social cognitive theory.* Englewood Cliffs, NJ: Prentice-Hall.

Bantam Books, Inc. v. Sullivan, 372 U.S. 58 (1963).

Barnard, C. (1938). *The functions of the executive.* Cambridge, MA: Harvard University Press.

Barnes, L. (1986, Fall). The hidden side of organizational leadership. *Sloan Management Review*, 15–25.

Barr, S. (1991). Rapid delivery. *Newsinc, 3*(5), 24–31.

Barrier, M. (1992, September). Doing well what comes naturally. *Nation's Business*, 25–26.

Basil, M. (1996). Identification as a mediator of celebrity effects. *Journal of Broadcasting & Electronic Media, 40,* 478–495.

Bates, B. (1988). The impact of deregulation on television station prices. *Journal of Media Economics, 1,* 5–22.

Baugh v. CBS, 828 F. Supp. 745 (N.D. Cal. 1993).

Beach, L. R. (1996). *Decision making in the workplace: A unified perspective*. Mahwah, NJ: Erlbaum.

Beaupre, L. K. (1995, October). The newspaper as dinosaur: Don't believe everything you read. President's address to the 62nd convention of Associated Press Managing Editors, Indianapolis, IN.

Bechmann, A. (1981). Grundlagen der Planungstheorie und Planungsmethodik [Essentials of planning theory and planning methodology]. Bern, Switzerland and Stuttgart, Germany: Haupt.

Bechtel v. FCC, 10 F.3d 875 (D.C. Cir. 1993).

Bechtel v. FCC, 957 F.2d 873 (D.C. Cir.), *cert. denied*, 506 U.S. 816 (1992).

Becker v. FCC, 95 F.3d 75 (D.C. Cir. 1996).

BehaviorScan. (1994). *When you have to be right*. Chicago: Author.

Belasco, J. (1989, November). Farmers vs. Hunters. *Executive Excellence*, 9–10.

Belch, G., & Belch, M. (1995). *Introduction to advertising and promotion: An integrated marketing communication perspective*. Chicago: Irwin.

Bennis, W. (1994). *On becoming a leader*. Reading, MA: Addison-Wesley.

Bennis, W., & Nanus, B. (1985). *Leaders: The strategies for taking charge*. New York: Harper & Row.

Benusan Restaurant Corp. v. King, 126 F.3d 25 (2d Cir. 1997).

Bergman, T., & Volkema, R. (1989). Understanding and managing interpersonal conflict at work: it's issues, interactive processes, and consequences. In M. Rahim (Ed.), *Managing conflict: An interdisciplinary approach* (pp. 7–20). New York: Praeger.

Bettelheim, A. (1992, February 5). Gillett unveils reorganization. *The Denver Post*, p. 1C.

Bezanson, R. P., Cranberg, G., & Soloski, J. (1987). *Libel law and the press: Myth and reality*. New York: Free Press.

Bissland, J. H. (1990). Accountability gap: Evaluation practices show improvement. *Public Relations Review, 16*(2), 25–34.

Blacklow, J. (1992, February 9). No news not good news: 10-second sound bites may be the undoing of real TV journalism. *The Seattle Times*, p. A19.

Blair, R., Roberts, K., & McKechnie, P. (1985). Vertical and network communication in organizations: The present and the future. In R. McPhee & P. Tompkins (Eds.), *Organizational communication: Traditional themes and new directions* (pp. 55–78). Newbury Park, CA: Sage.

Blau, G., & Boal, K. (1987). Using job involvement and organizational commitment interacively to predict turnover. *Journal of Management, 15,* 115–127.

Blue Ridge Bank v. Veribanc, Inc., 866 F.2d 681 (4th Cir. 1989).

Blumler, J. (1979). The role of uses and gratifications studies. *Communication Research, 6,* 18–20.

Blumler, J., & Spicer, C (1990). Prospects for creativity in the new television marketplace: Evidence from program-makers. *Journal of Communication, 40*(4), 78–101.

BMW of North America, Inc. v. Gore, 116 S. Ct. 1589 (1996).

Board of Trustees v. Fox, 492 U.S. 469 (1989).

Borman, W., White, L., Pulakos, E., & Oppler, S. (1991). Models of supervisory job performance ratings. *Journal of Applied Psychology, 76,* 863–872.

Bormann E. (1983). Symbolic convergence: Organizational communication and culture. In L. Putnam & M. Pacanowsky (Eds.), *Communication and organizations: An interpretative approach* (pp. 99–122). Newbury Park, CA: Sage.

Borreca v. Fasi, 369 F. Supp. 906 (D. Haw. 1974).

Borzillo, C. (1995, June 24). Promotions & syndications: Radio professionals enter the web at promax. *Billboard* [Online].

Boyer, P. (1987, January 19). Under Fowler, FCC treated TV as commerce. *The New York Times*, p. C15.

Branzburg v. Hayes, 408 U.S. 665 (1972).

Braun v. Soldier of Fortune Magazine, Inc., 968 F.2d 1110 (11th Cir. 1992), *cert. denied*, 506 U.S. 1071 (1993).

Bridges v. California, 314 U.S. 252 (1941).

Brinkley v. Casablancas, 438 N.Y.S.2d 1004 (App. Div. 1981).

Broadcast Music, Inc. v. United States Shoe Corp., 678 F.2d 816 (9th Cir. 1982).

Brocka, B., & Brocka, S. (1992). *Quality management:*

Implementing the best ideas of the masters. Burr Ridge, IL: Irwin.

Brooks, W. (1992). *Niche selling: How to find your customer in a crowded market.* Homewood, IL: Business One Irwin.

Brown, D. (1992). Why participative management won't work here. *Management Review, 81*(6), 42–46.

Brown, M. (1986, April 21). The business side: The reign of the money men. *Channels, 21.*

Brown, R. (1991, November 4). KWY-TV Election coverage: via cable systems; Philadelphia NBC affiliate will air its regular prime time lineup on election night and feed its election reports to three area cable systems without commercials. *Broadcasting, 48.*

Brozan, N. (1994, September 23). Chronicle. *The New York Times,* p. B6.

Buckley v. Littell, 539 F.2d 88 (2d Cir. 1976), *cert. denied,* 429 U.S. 1062 (1977).

Bull, R. (1997, February 13). Magazines grow to meet specific interests. *The Florida Times-Union,* p. D-1.

Bulletin Co., 1976–77 CCH NLRB ¶ 17456 (1976).

Burgi, M. (1997, February 17). TNN, CMT won't transplant eye; Westinghouse to purchase The Nashville Network and Country Music Television from Gaylord Entertainment Co. *Media Week,* p. 4.

Burke, K. (1966). *Language as symbolic action: Essays on life, literature and method.* Berkeley, CA: University of California Press.

Burnett v. National Enquirer, Inc., 7 Media L. Rep 1321 (Cal. Super. Ct. 1981), *aff'd on other grounds,* 144 Cal. App. 3d 991 (1983), *appeal dismissed,* 465 U.S. 1014 (1984).

Burns v. McGregor Electronic Industries, 989 F.2d 959 (8th Cir. 1993).

Burns, G. (1988). *Gracie: A love story.* New York: G. P. Putnam's Sons.

Burnstein, D. (Ed.). (1995). *The digital MBA.* Berkeley, CA: Osborne McGraw-Hill.

Butcher, L. (1992, January 10). Extraordinary news, recession cut area TV revenues: 62 sees growth. *Kansas City Business Journal,* p. 3.

Bütschi, G. (1997). PR-Metaplanung—Die Entwicklung einer heuristischen Entscheidungsmethode zur Bestimmung der Grundsätze einer PR-Planungskonzeption [PR-Metaplanning—The development of a heuristic model for the construction of a PR-planning concept]. Bern, Switzerland: Haupt.

C

Calamari, J., & Perillo, J. (1987). *The law of contracts* (3rd ed.). St. Paul, MN: West.

Caldwell, D. F., & O'Reilly, C. A. (1990). Measuring the person-job fit with a profile-comparison process. *Journal of Applied Psychology, 75,* 648–657.

Callinicos, A. (1988). *Making history: Agency, structure and change in social theory.* Ithaca, NY: Cornell University Press.

Cameron, K. (1983). *Organizational effectiveness: A comparison of multiple models.* New York: Academic Press.

Cameron, K., & Whetten, D. (Eds.) (1983). *Organizational effectiveness.* New York: Academic Press.

Cameron, K., & Zammuto, R. (1988). Matching managerial strategies to conditions of decline. In Kim S. Cameron, Robert I. Sutton, & David A. Whetten (Eds.), *Readings in organizational decline: Frameworks, research, and*

prescriptions (pp. 207–224). Boston: Ballinger.

Cameron, K., Kim, M., & Whetten, D. (1988). Organizational effects of decline and turbulence. In Kim S. Cameron, Robert I. Sutton, & David A. Whetten (Eds.), *Readings in organizational decline: Frameworks, research, and prescriptions* (pp. 207–224). Boston: Ballinger.

Cameron, K., Sutton, R., & Whetten, D. (Eds.) (1988). *Readings in organizational decline: Frameworks, research, and prescriptions.* Boston: Ballinger.

Campbell v. Acuff-Rose Music, Inc., 510 U.S. 569 (1994).

Campbell, J. (1996). Building an effective pyramid for leading successful organizational transformation. *Library Administration & Management, 10,* 82.

Campion, M. A., & McClelland, C. L. (1991). Interdisciplinary examination of the costs and benefits of enlarged jobs: a job design quasi-experiment. *Journal of Applied Psychology, 76,* 186–198.

Cantrell v. Forest City Publishing Co., 419 U.S. 245 (1974).

Capital Cities Cable, Inc. v. Crisp, 467 U.S. 691 (1984).

Carey, J. (1989). *Communication as culture: Essays on media and society.* Boston: Unwin Hyman.

Carman, J. (1996, February 15). Untangling TV stations' on-line webs. *The San Francisco Chronicle,* p. D1.

Carroll, G., & Delacroix, J. (1982). Organizational mortality in the newspaper industries of Argentina and Ireland: An ecological approach. *Administrative Quarterly, 27,* 169–198.

Carson v. Allied News Co., 529 F.2d 206 (7th Cir. 1976).

Cassirer, E. (1944). *An essay on man: An introduction to a philosophy of human culture.* New

Haven, CT: Yale University Press.

CBS announces fourth quarter and full year results. (1992, February 12). *PR Newswire.*

Central Hudson Gas & Electric Corp. v. Public Service Commission, 447 U.S. 557 (1980).

Century Communications Corp. v. FCC, 835 F.2d 292 (D.C. Cir. 1987), *cert. denied,* 486 U.S. 1032 (1988).

Chandler v. Florida, 449 U.S. 560 (1981).

Changing hands 1984. (1985, January 28). *Broadcasting,* 46.

Chaplinsky v. New Hampshire, 315 U.S. 568 (1942).

Chatman, J. A. (1989). Improved interactional organizational research: a model of person-organization fit. *Academy of Management Review, 11,* 333–349.

Chung, K. H. (1987). *Management: Critical success factors.* Boston: Allyn and Bacon.

Cincinnati v. Discovery Network, Inc., 507 U.S. 410 (1993).

City of Los Angeles v. Preferred Communications, Inc., 476 U.S. 488 (1986).

City of Renton v. Playtime Theatres, Inc., 475 U.S. 41 (1986).

Civil Rights Act of 1866, 42 U.S.C. § 1981.

Civil Rights Act of 1964, 42 U.S.C. § 2000e et seq.

Cleary, M. (1993). Sufficiency of defendant's nondiscriminatory reason to rebut inference of sex discrimination in promotion or demotion of employee as violation of Title VII of Civil Rights Act of 1964. *American Law Reports, Federal Series, 111,* 1–81, and 1996 supplement. Rochester, NY: Lawyer's Cooperative.

Cobb, A. (1986, July). Political diagnosis: Applications in organizational development.

Academy of Management Review, 482–496.

Cohen v. Cowles Media Co., 501 U.S. 663 (1991).

Coit, J. (1986). *John Coit: A collection from his most popular columns from the* Rocky Mountain News. Denver, CO: Denver Publishing Company.

Coleman, H. (1978). *Case studies in broadcast management: Radio and television.* New York: Hastings House.

Colford, P. (1997, February 27). Giants feast on radio/six LI stations are part of a big consolidation. A jewel called WLTW. *Newsday,* Nassau Edition, p. B48.

Company news; more technical problems for America OnLine. (1997, January 24). *The New York Times,* p. D3.

Comstock, G. (1989). *The evolution of American television.* Newbury Park, CA: Sage.

Conger, J. (1992). *Learning to lead: The art of transforming managers into leaders.* San Francisco: Jossey-Bass.

Conrad, C. (1985). Organizational power: Faces and symbolic forms. In R. McPhee & P. Tompkins (Eds.), *Organizational communication: Traditional themes and new directions* (pp. 173–194). Newbury Park, CA: Sage.

Cox Broadcasting Corp. v. Cohn, 420 U.S. 469 (1975).

Cremer, F., Keirstead, P., & Yoakam, R. (1996). *ENG television news* (3rd ed.). New York: McGraw-Hill.

Cruz v. Ferre, 755 F.2d 1415 (11th Cir. 1985).

Cubby, Inc. v. CompuServe Inc., 776 F. Supp. 135 (S.D.N.Y. 1991).

Culnan, M., & Markus, M. (1987). Information technologies. In F. Jablin, L. Putnam, K. Roberts, & L. Porter (Eds.), *Handbook of organizational communication*

(pp. 420–443). Newbury Park, CA: Sage.

Curtin, J. (1988). Putting self-esteem first. *Training and Development Journal, 42,* 41–45.

Curtis Publishing Co. v. Butts, 388 U.S. 130 (1967).

D

Dancy, J., Moravcsik, J. M., & Taylor, C. C. (Eds.). (1988). *Human agency: Language, duty, and value.* Stanford, CA: Stanford University Press.

Danziger, E. (1988, November). Minimize office gossip. *Personnel Journal,* 31–33.

Davies, J. (1963). *Human nature in politics: The dynamics of political behavior.* Westport, CT: Greenwood Press (reprinted 1978).

Davis, R. J. (1980). When are newspaper and magazine editors and writers deemed "managerial employees" excluded from coverage under National Labor Relations Act. *American Law Reports, Federal Series, 49,* 496–502, and 1996 supplement. Rochester, NY: Lawyer's Cooperative.

DeFleur, M. L., & Ball-Rokeach, S. (1989). *Theories of mass communication* (5th ed.). New York: Longman.

Demorest, M. E. (1986). Problem solving: Stages, strategies, and stumbling blocks. *Journal of the Academy of Rehabilitative Audiology, 19,* 13–26.

Denison, D., & Mishra, A. (1995). Toward a theory of organizational culture and effectiveness. *Organization Science, 6,* 204.

Denver Area Educational Telecommunications Consortium, Inc. v. FCC, 116 S. Ct. 2374 (1996).

Desai, M. (1993, November). Success through total quality

commitment. *Quality Progress,* 65–67.

Diener, E., Larsen, R., & Emmons, R. (1984). Person X situation interactions: Choice of situations and congruence response models. *Journal of Personality and social Psychology, 47,* 580–592.

Doe v. American Broadcasting Companies, 543 N.Y.S.2d 455 (App. Div.), *appeal dismissed without opinion,* 549 N.E.2d 480 (N.Y. 1989).

Downey, H. K., Hellriegel, D., & Slocum, J. W., Jr. (1975). Congruence between individual needs, organizational climate, job satisfaction and performance. *Academy of Management Journal, 18,* 149–155.

Drucker, P. (1988a, September–October). Management and the world's work. *Harvard Business Review, 39.*

Drucker, P. (1988b). Management: the problems of success. In J. Gibson, J. Ivancevich, & J. Donnelly, Jr. (Eds.), *Organizations close-up: a book of readings* (6th ed.) (pp. 4–15). Plano, TX: Business Publications.

Drucker, P. (1989). Leadership: More doing than dash. In R. Taylor & W. Rosenbach (Eds.), *Leadership: Challenges for today's manager* (pp. 109–111). New York: Nichols.

E

Eckhouse, J. (1996, March 1). The new web—you ain't seen nothing yet!—Why bother with the Internet? How do fast-action games, global radio, cheap long-distance calls, video phones and virtual reality sound for starters? *Home PC,* 64.

Edwards v. National Audubon Society, Inc., 556 F.2d 113 (2d Cir.), *cert. denied,* 434 U.S. 1002 (1977).

Einhorn, H. (1980). Overconfidence in judgement. In R. A. Shweder (Ed.), *New directions for methodology of social and behavioral science* (4th ed., pp. 1–16). San Francisco: Jossey Bass.

Elliott, P. (1972). *The making of a television series: A case study in the production of culture.* London: Constable.

Elmuti, D., & AlDiab, T. (1995). Improving quality and organizational effectiveness go hand in hand through Deming's management system. *Journal of Business Strategies, 12,* 86.

Emery, M. & Emery, E. (1996). *The press and America: An interpretive history of the mass media* (8th ed.). Boston: Allyn and Bacon.

Emery, M., & Emery, E. (1988). *The press and America: An interpretive history of the mass media* (6th ed.). Englewood Cliffs, NJ: Prentice-Hall.

Equal Pay Act of 1963, 29 U.S.C. § 206(d).

Euske, N., & Roberts, K. (1987). Evolving perspectives in organizational theory: Communication implications. In F. Jablin, L. Putnam, K. Roberts, & L. Porter (Eds.), *Handbook of organizational communication* (pp. 41–69). Newbury Park, CA: Sage.

F

Falcione, R. L., Sussman, L., & Herden, R. P. (1987). Communication climate in organizations. In F. Jablin, L. Putnam, K. Roberts, & L. Porter (Eds.), *Handbook of organizational communication* (pp. 195–227). Newbury Park, CA: Sage.

Falcione, R., Sussman, L., Herden, R. (1987). Communication climate in organizations. In R. McPhee & P. Tompkins (Eds.), *Organizational communication: Traditional themes and new directions* (pp. 195–227). Newbury Park, CA: Sage.

Faltas v. State Newspaper, 928 F. Supp. 637 (D.S.C. 1996).

Farmers Educational and Cooperative Union v. WDAY, Inc., 360 U.S. 525 (1959).

Fayol, H. (1949). *General and industrial management* (C. Storrs, Trans.). London: Sir Isaac Pitman & Sons.

FCC gains a deregulatory diplomat: New chairman Alfred Sikes moves in at 1919 M. *Broadcasting,* 29.

FCC grilled on three-year rule. (1987, June 22). *Broadcasting,* 49.

FCC v. League of Women Voters of California, 468 U.S. 364 (1984).

FCC v. Pacifica Foundation, 438 U.S. 726 (1978).

Fearing, F. (1972). Influence of the movies on attitudes and behaviour. In D. McQuail (Ed.), *Sociology of mass communication* (pp. 119–134). Hamondsworth, Great Britain: Penguin.

Feder, R. (1996, March 21). Primary coverage a winner at CLTV. *Chicago Sun-Times,* p. 45.

Fink, S. (1992). *High commitment workplaces.* New York: Quorum.

Fischer, R. (1995). Control construct design in evaluation campaigns. *Public Relations Review, 21*(1), 45–58.

Fishbein, E. (1996, March 24). Tonya yearns to get back on thin ice. *Sacramento Bee,* p. A2.

Flander, J. (1986, May). Pressure and stress in the newsroom. *RTNDA Communicator,* 14.

Florida Star v. B. J. F., 491 U.S. 524 (1989).

Fortnightly Corp. v. United Artists Television, Inc., 392 U.S. 390 (1968).

44 Liquormart, Inc. v. Rhode Island, 116 S. Ct. 1495 (1996).

Francois, W. E. (1975). *Mass media law and regulation*. Columbus, OH: Grid.

Franklin, M. (1980). Winners and losers and why: A study of defamation litigation. *American Bar Foundation Research Journal*, 455–500.

Franklin, M., & Anderson, D. (1990). *Mass media law: Cases and materials* (4th ed.). Westbury, NY: Foundation Press.

Fredin, E., & Tabaczynski, T. (1993). Media schemata, information-processing strategies, and audience assessment of the informational value of quotes and background in local news. *Journalism Quarterly, 70*(4), 801–814.

French, J., & Raven, B. (1959). The bases of social power. In D. Cartwright (Ed.), *Studies in social power* (pp. 150–167). Ann Arbor, MI: Institute for Social Research.

Friedman, S. (1985). *Leadership succession systems and corporate performance*. New York: Columbia Graduate School of Business, Center for Career Research and Human Resource Management.

Friendly, F. (1981). *Minnesota rag*. New York: Random House.

Frost, P. (1987). Power, politics, and influence. In F. Jablin, L. Putnam, K. Roberts, & L. Porter (Eds.), *Handbook of organizational communication* (pp. 503–548). Newbury Park, CA: Sage.

G

Galbraith, J., & Kanzanjian, R. (1986, Spring). Organizing to implement strategies of diversity and globalization: The role of matrix design. *Human Resource management*, 37–54.

Gannett. (1997). *Company profile* [Online]. Available: http://www.gannett.com/map/gan007.htm [1997, March 24].

Gans, H. (1980). *Deciding what's news: A study of CBS Evening News, NBC Nightly News, Newsweek and Time*. New York: Vintage Books.

Gardner, J. (1988). The tasks of leadership. In J. Gibson, J. Ivancevich, & J. Donnelly, Jr. (Eds.), *Organizations close-up: A book of readings* (6th ed.) (pp. 219–227). Plano, TX: Business Publications.

Garrison v. Louisiana, 379 U.S. 64 (1964).

Gaziano, C. (1983). The knowledge gap: An analytical review of media effects. *Communication Research, 10,* 447–486.

Gaziano, C., & Coulson, D. (1988). Effect of newsroom management styles on journalists. *Journalism Quarterly, 65,* 869–880.

Genova, B., & Greenberg, B. (1979). Interests in news and the knowledge gap. *Public Opinion Quarterly, 43,* 79–91.

Gertz v. Robert Welch, Inc., 418 U.S. 323 (1974).

Gertz, E. (1992). *Gertz v. Robert Welch, Inc.: The story of a landmark libel case*. Carbondale: Southern Illinois University Press.

Gibson, J., Ivancevich, J., & Donnelly, J., Jr. (1994). *Organizations: Behavior, structure, processes* (8th ed.). Burr Ridge, IL: Irwin.

Gibson, J., Ivancevich, J., & Donnelly, J., Jr. (1997). *Organizations: Behavior, structure, processes* (9th ed.). Chicago, IL: Irwin.

Gillooly sentenced for role in Kerrigan attack. (1994, July 14). *The Charleston Gazette*, p. P2A.

Ginsberg v. New York, 390 U.S. 629 (1968).

Goldman, K. (1990, November 21). CBS-TV to cut affiliate payments by 20% next year. *The Wall Street Journal*, p. B3.

Goldstein, N. (Ed.). (1996). *The Associated Press stylebook and libel manual* (6th trade ed.). New York: The Associated Press.

Gooding v. Wilson, 405 U.S. 518 (1972).

Graham, D. (1997, October 16). Scientists aim to forecast El Nino's worst waves; Rely on computer models of the ocean, coastline. *The San Diego Union-Tribune*, p. B1.

Grahnke, L. (1996, December 22). Broadcast blues; thanks for nothing: Few choices emerge if "Seinfeld at an end." *Chicago Sun-Times*, Show Section, p. 1.

Greater New Orleans Broadcasting Association, Inc. v. United States, 69 F.3d 1296 (5th Cir. 1995), *vacated and remanded,* 117 S. Ct. 39 (1996).

Greenbaum, T. L. (1987). *The practical handbook and guide to focus group research*. Lexington, MA: Lexington.

Greenbelt Cooperative Publishing Association v. Bresler, 398 U.S. 6 (1970).

Greer v. Spock, 424 U.S. 828 (1976).

Grimm, H. (1965). *The Reformation era 1500–1650*. New York: Macmillan.

Grosjean v. American Press Co., 297 U.S. 233 (1936).

Gross, L. (1995). *Telecommunications: An introduction to electronic media* (5th ed.). Dubuque, IA: Brown and Benchmark.

Grove, A. S. (1988). Elephants can so dance. In J. Gibson, J. Ivancevich, & J. Donnelly, Jr. (Eds.), *Organizations close-up* (pp. 418–424). Plano, TX: Business Publications.

Grunig, J. (Ed.). (1992). *Excellence in public relations and communication management*. Hillsdale, NJ: Erlbaum.

Grünig, R. (1990). Verfahren zur Ueberprüfung und Verbesserung von Planungskonzepten [Procedures for the evaluation and improvement of planning concepts]. Bern, Switzerland: Haupt.

Gunneson, A. O. (1991, June). Communicating up and down the ranks. *Chemical Engineering*, p. 135.

Guy, M. (1989). *From organizational decline to organizational renewal: The phoenix syndrome*. Westport, CT: Greenwood Press.

Guzzo, R. A. (1995). Introduction: At the intersection of team effectiveness and decision making. In R. A. Guzzo & E. Salas (Eds.), *Team effectiveness and decision making in organizations* (pp. 1–8). San Francisco: Jossey-Bass.

H

Hachten, W. (1981). *The world news prism: Changing media, clashing ideologies*. Ames, IA: Iowa State University Press.

Hakes, C. (1991). *Total quality management*. London: Chapman & Hall.

Halberstam, D. (1979). *The powers that be*. New York: Knopf.

Hannan, M., & Freeman, J. (1977). Obstacles to the comparative study of organizational effectiveness. In P. Goodman & J. Pennings (Eds.) *New perspectives on organizational effectiveness* (pp. 106–131). San Francisco: Jossey-Bass.

Harder, J. W. (1991). Equity theory versus expectancy theory: the case of major league baseball free agents. *Journal of Applied Psychology, 76*, 458–464.

Harper & Row Publishers, Inc. v. Nation Enterprises, Inc., 471 U.S. 539 (1985).

Harrigan, K. (1988). Strategies for declining industries. In Kim S. Cameron, Robert I. Sutton, &

David A. Whetten (Eds.), *Readings in organizational decline: Frameworks, research, and prescriptions* (pp. 129–149). Boston: Ballinger.

Harris v. Forklift Systems, Inc., 510 U.S. 17 (1993).

Harrison, E. F. (1975). *The managerial decision-making process*. Boston: Houghton Mifflin.

Harte-Hanks Communications, Inc. v. Connaughton, 491 U.S. 657 (1989).

Harvey, P. (Ed.). (1967). *The Oxford companion to English literature*. Oxford: Clarendon Press.

Hawkins, R. (1990, April 1). Measuring audiences in the '90s. *Cable TV Business*, 22–23.

Head, S., Sterling, C., & Schofield, L. (1994). *Broadcasting in America: A survey of electronic media* (7th ed.). Boston: Houghton Mifflin.

Heath, R. P. (1996, July). The frontier of psychographics. *American Demographics, 18*(7), 38–43.

Hentze, J., & Brose, P. (1985). Unternehmungsplanung [Corporate planning]. Bern, Switzerland and Stuttgart, Germany: Haupt.

Herbert v. Lando, 441 U.S. 153 (1979).

Herceg v. Hustler Magazine, Inc., 814 F.2d 1017 (5th Cir. 1987), *cert. denied,* 485 U.S. 959 (1988).

Hersey, P. (1984). *The situational leader*. Escondido, CA: Center for Leadership Studies.

Herzberg, F. (1966). *Work and the nature of man*. Cleveland, OH: World.

Herzberg, F., Mausner, B., & Synderman, B. (1959). *The motivation to work*. New York: John Wiley & Sons.

Hess v. Indiana, 414 U.S. 105 (1973).

Hey, J. (1982). Search for rules for search. *Journal of Economic*

Behavior and Organization, 3, 65–81.

Hirschhorn, L. (1991). *Managing in the new team environment: Skills, tools, and methods*. Reading, MA: Addison-Wesley.

History of the Internet. (1996, April 21). *The Kansas City Star*, p. K4.

Hitt, M., & Middlemist, R. (1979). A methodology to develop criteria and criteria weightings for assessing subunit effectiveness in organizations. *Academy of Management Journal, 22*, 356–374.

Hofmeister, S. (1997, April 18). Rewiring TCI; new president strives to bring the cable giant back into focus. *Los Angeles Times*, p. Business D1.

Holzinger, A. (1996, November). Business community wins some, loses some. *Nation's Business*, p. 10.

Hopkins, W. (1984). *A proposed model of environmental decline and strategic responses: An empirical investigation*. (Doctoral dissertation, University of Colorado, 1984.)

Hopkins-Doerr, M. (1989). Getting more out of MBWA. *Supervisory Management, 34*(2), 17.

Houchins v. KQED, Inc., 438 U.S. 1 (1978).

Hovland, C., Janis, I., & Kelley, H. (1953). *Communication and persuasion*. New Haven, CT: Yale University Press.

Hovland, C., Lumsdaine, A., & Sheffield, F. (1949). *Experiments on mass communication*. Princeton, NJ: Princeton University Press.

Howell, J. (1990, Summer). Substitutes for leadership: Effective alternatives to ineffective leadership. *Organizational Dynamics*, 20–38.

Hsia, H. (1988). *Mass communications research methods: A step-by-step approach*. Hillsdale, NJ: Erlbaum.

Huber, G., & Daft, R. (1987). The information environments of organizations. In F. Jablin, L. Putnam, K. Roberts, & L. Porter (Eds.), *Handbook of organizational communication* (pp. 130–164). Newbury Park, CA: Sage.

Hultman, K. (1988). The psychology of performance management. *Training & Development Journal, 42,* 34–39.

Hunter, J. (1983). A causal analysis of cognitive ability, job knowledge, job performance, and supervisor ratings. In F. Land, S. Zedeck, & J. Cleveland (Eds.), *Performance measurement and theory* (pp. 257–266). Hillsdale, NJ: Erlbaum. (Cited in Borman et al., 1991).

Huselid, M., & Day, N. (1991). Organizational commitment, job involvement, and turnover: a substantive and methodological analysis. *Journal of Applied Psychology, 76,* 380–391.

Hustler Magazine, Inc. v. Falwell, 485 U.S. 46 (1988).

Hyde v. City of Columbia 637 S.W.2d 251 (Mo. App. 1982), *cert. denied,* 459 U.S. 1226 (1983).

I

Imai, M. (1986). *Kaizen: The key to Japan's competitive success.* New York: Random House.

Immigration Reform and Control Act, 8 U.S.C. § 1324B.

Independence Day (1997, July 7). *Time, 150*(1), 93.

Ingersoll, R. (1980). Some reasons why. In E. Beck (Ed.), *Bartlett's Familiar Quotations: A collection of passages, phrases and proverbs traced to their sources in ancient and modern literature* (15th ed.). Boston: Little, Brown and Company.

Internet access: CNN and PointCast announce partnership that redefines the delivery of news over the Internet. (1996, July 15). *Edge: Work-Group Computing Report* [Online]. Available: Lexis/Nexis [1996, October 12].

Investor's Business Daily. (1996, December 18). P. A6.

IRI. (1997, January). Information Resources home page. [Online]. Available: http://www.infores.com.

Isherwood, G. (1985). Leadership effectiveness in cooperative and counteracting groups. *Journal of Educational Administration, 23,* 208–218.

J

Jacobellis v. Ohio, 378 U.S. 184, 197 (1964).

Janis, I. (1973). *Victims of groupthink: A psychological study of foreign policy decisions and fiascoes.* Boston: Houghton Mifflin.

Jawitz, W. (1996). *Understanding mass media* (5th ed.). Lincolnwood, IL: National Textbook.

Jenkins v. Georgia, 418 U.S. 153 (1974).

Jessell, H., & Rathbun E. (1996, August 19). David Smith: Striking it rich with Sinclair. *Broadcasting & Cable,* 26–32.

Jicha, T. (1996, November 3). Extensive coverage on television. (Ft. Lauderdale) *Sun-Sentinel,* p. 3H.

Job redesign on the assembly line: Farewell to blue-collar blues? (1987). In D.Organ (Ed.), *The applied psychology of work behavior: a book of readings* (pp. 150–171). Plano, TX: Business Publications. (Original work published 1973.)

Johnson v. Railway Express Agency, Inc., 421 U.S. 454 (1975).

Joseph Burstyn, Inc. v. Wilson, 343 U.S. 495 (1952).

Judge, W. (1994). Correlates of organizational effectiveness: A multilevel analysis of a multidimensional outcome. *Journal of Business Ethics, 13,* 1.

K

Kahle, L. Beatty, S., & Homer, P. (1986). Alternative measurement approaches to consumer values: The list of values (LOV) and values and lifestyles (VALS). *Journal of Consumer Research, 13,* 405–409.

Kanter, R. (1988). Change masters and the intricate architecture of corporate culture change. In J. Gibson, J. Ivancevich, & J. Donnelly, Jr. (Eds.), *Organizations close-up: A book of readings* (6th ed.) (pp. 400–417). Plano, TX: Business Publications.

Kanter, R. (1987). Power. In D. Organ (Ed.), *The applied psychology of work behavior: A book of readings* (3rd. ed.) (pp. 273–310). Plano, TX: Business Publications.

Kanter, R. (1979). Power failures in management circuits. *Harvard Business Review, 57,* 65–75.

Karasek, R. (1979). Job demands, job decision latitude, and mental strain: Implications for job redesign. *Administrative Science Quarterly, 24,* 295–308.

Katz, E., & Lazarsfeld, P. (1955). *Personal influence: The part played by people in the flow of mass communications.* Glencoe, IL: Free Press.

Keating, S. (1997, April 20). Stagnant TCI stock price distresses shareholders. *The Denver Post,* p. H1.

Keen, P. G. W. (1973). *The implications of cognitive style for individual decision making.* Unpublished doctoral dissertation, Boston.

Kelly, J. M., & Watt, B. (1996). Damages in sex harassment

cases: A comparative study of American, Canadian, and British law. *New York Law School Journal of International and Comparative Law, 16,* 79–133.

Kets de Vries, M. (1989). *Prisoners of leadership.* New York: John Wiley & Sons.

Kiechell, W. (1989). Wanted: Corporate leaders. In R. Taylor & W. Rosenbach (Eds.), *Leadership: Challenges for today's manager* (pp. 7–12). New York: Nichols.

Kirkpatrick, S., & Locke, E. (1991, May). Leadership: Do traits matter? *Academy of Management Executive,* 49.

Kirrane, D. (1990). Managing values: A systematic approach to business ethics. *Training and Development Journal, 44,* 53–60.

Klapper, J. (1960). *The effects of mass communication.* New York: Free Press.

Klein, N. (1983). Utility and decision strategies: A second look at the rational decision maker. *Organizational Behavior and Human Performance, 31,* 1–25.

Kluckhohn, C., & Murray, H. (1948). *Personality in nature, society, and culture.* New York: Alfred A. Knopf.

Kluge, P. (Ed.). (1991). *Guide to economics and business journalism.* New York: Columbia University Press.

Knox, D. (1990, July 20). Scripps to buy Vail mogul's TV station in Baltimore. *The Rocky Mountain News,* p. 59.

Koets, R. (1995). When must specialized equipment or other workplace modifications be provided to qualified disabled employee or applicant as reasonable accommodation? *American Law Reports, Federal Series,* 125, 629–646, and 1996 supplement. Rochester, NY: Lawyer's Cooperative.

Koontz, H., & O'Donnell, C. (1978). *Essentials of management* (2nd ed.). New York: McGraw-Hill.

Kosicki, G., & Becker, L. (1996). Annual survey of enrollment and degrees awarded. *Journalism & Mass Communication Educator, 51*(3), 4–14.

Kotter, J. (1988). *The leadership factor.* New York: The Free Press.

Kotter, J. (1977). Power, dependence and effective management. *Harvard Business Review, 55,* 125–136.

Krone, K., Jablin, F., & Putnam, L. (1987). Communication theory and organizational communication: Multiple perspectives. In F. Jablin, L. Putnam, K. Roberts, & L. Porter (Eds.), *Handbook of organizational communication* (pp. 18–40). Newbury Park, CA: Sage.

Kühn, R. (1985). Grundzüge eines heuristischen Verfahrens zur Erarbeitung von Planungskonzeptionen [Outline of a heuristic model for the construction of a planning concept]. *DBW, 45,* 531–543.

Kwitny, J. (1990, June). The high cost of high profits. *Washington Journalism Review,* 28.

KXTV, 1971 CCH NLRB ¶ 23453 (1971).

L

Lacy, S. Sohn, & A. Wicks, J. (1993). *Media management: A casebook approach.* Hillsdale, NJ: Erlbaum.

Lafferty, C. (1990, May). Regaining leadership. *Executive Excellence,* 17–19.

Lagerkvist, M. (1988, December). Owner makes millions, news takes a beating. *Washington Journalism Review,* 40.

Lahart, K. (1991). Corporate finance. In P. Kluge (Ed.), *Guide to economics and business*

journalism (pp. 99–107). New York: Columbia University Press.

Langer, W. (1972). Alexander the Great. In *An encyclopedia of world history.* Boston: Houghton Mifflin.

Lasswell, H. (1948). *Power and personality.* New York: W. W. Horton.

Lasswell, H. (1948). The structure and function of communication in society. In L. Bryson (Ed.), *The communication of ideas* (pp. 37–51). New York: Harper & Row.

Lavine, J., & Wackman, D. (1988). *Managing media organizations: Effective leadership of the media.* New York: Longman.

Lawrence, P., Kolodny, H., & Davis S. (1977, September). The human side of the matrix. *Organizational Dynamics,* 47.

Lazarsfeld, P., Berelson, B., & Gaudet, H. (1944). *The people's choice.* New York: Columbia University Press.

Le Mistral, Inc. v. Columbia Broadcasting System, 402 N.Y.S.2d 815 (App. Div. 1978).

Leathers v. Medlock, 499 U.S. 439 (1991).

LeNoir, R. (1987). *An analysis of adaptation in a regulated industry: responses of the domestic trunk airlines.* (Doctoral dissertation, University of Colorado, 1987.)

Leslie, D. (1991). *Labor law in a nutshell* (3d ed.). St. Paul, MN: West.

Levins, H. (1996, November 1). Newspapers may lose 14% to Internet: Research firm predicts five-year circulation decline. *Editor & Publisher Interactive* [Online]. Available: http://www.mediainfo.com [1996, November 1].

Levy, L. (1985). *Emergence of a free press.* New York: Oxford.

Lewis v. New Orleans, 408 U.S. 913 (1972).

Lewis, A. (1991). *Make no law: The Sullivan case and the First Amendment.* New York: Random House.

Liebling, A. J. (1981). *The press.* New York: Pantheon. (Original work published 1961).

Likert, R. (1961). *New patterns of management.* New York: McGraw-Hill.

Lin, C. (1992). Audience selectivity of local television newscasts. *Journalism Quarterly, 69,* 373–382.

Lippman, W. (1922). *Public opinion.* New York: Macmillan.

Livingstone, J. (1992). *The portable MBA in finance and accounting.* New York: John Wiley & Sons.

Local Union No. 12, United Rubber, Cork, Linoleum and Plastic Workers v. NLRB, 368 F.2d 12 (5th Cir. 1966), *cert. denied,* 389 U.S. 837 (1967).

Locke, E., & Kirkpatrick, S. (1991). *The essence of leadership: The four keys to leading successfully.* New York: Lexington.

Locke, E., & Latham, G. (1984). *Goal setting: A motivational technique that works.* Englewood Cliffs, NJ: Prentice-Hall.

Locke, E., & Latham, G. (1990). *A theory of goal setting and task performance.* Englewood Cliffs, NJ: Prentice-Hall.

Lombardo, M. (1989). How do leaders get to lead? In R. Taylor & W. Rosenbach (Eds.), *Leadership: Challenges for today's manager* (pp. 22–28). New York: Nichols.

Loomis, C., & Kupfer, A. (1997, January 13). High noon for John Malone; the glory days of the Bell Atlantic deal long gone, the CEO of TCI faces the fight of his life—revitalizing his cable company and salvaging his reputation. *Fortune,* 66.

Lopez, F. M., Kesselman, G. A., & Lopez, F. E. (1981). An empirical test of a trait oriented job analysis technique. *Personnel Psychology, 34,* 479–502.

Lundberg, G. (1928). The content of radio programs. *Social Forces, 7,* 58–60.

M

M. S. News Co. v. Casado, 721 F.2d 1281 (10th Cir. 1983).

Maccoby, M. (1988). *Why work: Leading the new generation.* New York: Simon and Schuster.

Macher, K. (1986, January). The politics of people. *Personnel Journal,* 50–53.

Mackenzie, K. D. (1991). *The organizational hologram: The effective management of organizational change.* Norwell, MA: Kluwer Academic Publishers Group.

Mager, R. (1989). *How to control cost for profit and performance: A practical guide to effective cost management for industrial and service organizations.* Chicago: A. G. Merrick.

Mahoney, T., & Weitzel, W. (1969). Managerial models of organizational effectiveness. *Administrative Science Quarterly, 14,* 357–365.

Makiuchi, I. (1996, December 23). New management methods will help companies globalize. *The Nikkei Weekly,* p. 23.

Marash, S. (1993). The key to TQM and world-class competitiveness—part 1. *Quality, 32*(9), 37–39.

March, J. G. (1978). Bounded rationality, ambiguity, and the engineering of choice. *The Bell Journal of Economics, 9,* 587–608.

Maritz, Inc. v. Cybergold, Inc., 947 F. Supp. 1328 & 1338 (E.D. Mo. 1996).Meredith Corp. v. FCC, 809 F.2d 863 (D.C. Cir. 1987).

Market share: Telecom markets shift across all segments. IDC releases year-end summary of telecommunications market. (1996, January 22). *Edge* [Online]. Available: Lexis/Nexis [1996, December 8].

Martin, L., Kettner, P. (1997). Performance measurement: The new accountability. *Administration in Social Work, 21*(1), 17.

Maslow, A. (1970). *Motivation and personality.* New York: Harper & Row. (Original wok published 1954).

Maslow, A. H. (1954). *Motivation and personality.* New York: Harper. (Original work published 1954).

Masson v. New Yorker Magazine Inc., 501 U.S. 496 (1991).

Mathieu, J., & Kohler, S. (1990). A test of the interactive effects of organizational commitment and job involvement on various types of absence. *Journal of Vocational Behavior, 36,* 33–44.

Mayo, E. (1946). *The human problems of an industrial civilization.* Boston: Division of Research, Graduate School of Business Administration, Harvard Union.

Mayo, E. (1953). *The human problems of an industrial civilization.* Boston: Division of Research, Graduate School of Business Administration, Harvard Union.

McAdams, M. (1995, July). Inventing an on-line newspaper. *Interpersonal computing and technology: An electronic journal for the 21st century* [Online]. Available: http://www.sentex.net/~mmcadams/invent.html.

McClelland, D. (1975). *Power: The inner experience.* New York: Irvington.

McCrory, R., et al. (1996). Constitution privilege in libel law. In J. Goodale (Ed.), *Communications law* (pp. 7–467). New York: Practicing Law Institute.

McDonnell, C. (1996, February 17). Broadcasters ask FCC for more purchasing power; some fear reduction in competition, diversity. *Broadcasting & Cable,* 20.

McElreath, M. (August, 1993). *Teaching budgeting techniques and cost-benefit analyses using case studies, class projects, and Systematic Public Relations Software (SPRS), a database management program.* Paper presented at the meeting of the Association for Education in Journalism and Mass Communication (AEJMC). Montreal, Canada.

McElwain, J. (1991, February). Succession plans designed to manage change. *HR Magazine,* 67–71.

McGregor, D. (1960). *The human side of enterprise.* New York: McGraw-Hill.

McKenney, J. L., & Keen, P. G. W. (1974). How manager's minds work. *Harvard Business Review, 52,* 79–90.

McPhee, R. (1985). Formal structure and organizational communication. In R. McPhee & P. Tompkins (Eds.), *Organizational communication: Traditional themes and new directions* (pp. 149–177). Newbury Park, CA: Sage.

McPhee, R., & Tompkins, P. (Eds.). (1985). *Organizational communication: Traditional themes and new directions.* Newbury Park, CA: Sage.

McQuail, D. (1994). *Mass communication theory: An introduction* (3rd ed.). Thousand Oaks, CA: Sage.

McQuail, D. (1987). *Mass communication theory: An introduction* (2nd ed.). London: Sage.

McQuarrie, F. (1992). Dancing on the minefield: Developing a management style in media organizations. In S. Lacy, A. Sohn, & R. Giles (Eds.), *Readings in media management*

(pp. 229–240). Columbia, SC: Media Management and Economics Division of the Association for Education in Journalism and Mass Communication.

Medical Laboratory Consultants v. American Broadcasting Cos., 931 F. Supp. 1487 (D. Ariz. 1996).

Mellman, M. (1995). *Accounting for effective decision making: A manager's guide to corporate, financial, and cost reporting.* Burr Ridge, IL: Irwin.

Merchant, K. (1989). *Rewarding results: Motivating profit center managers.* Boston: Harvard Business School Press.

Meritor Savings Bank v. Vinson, 477 U.S. 57 (1986).

Mermigas, D. (1992). Experts' outlook guarded for '92. *Electronic media, 29.*

Mermigas, D. (1991a, November 11). ABC: Cable means survival. *Electronic Media, 1.*

Mermigas, D. (1991b, December 9). TV's new breed of station owners. *Electronic Media, 1.*

Merrill Lynch. (1997). *How to read a financial report.* New Brunswick, NJ: Author.

Merton, R. (1946). *Mass persuasion.* New York: Harper.

Meyer, A. (1988). Organizational decline from an organizational perspective. In Kim S. Cameron, Robert I. Sutton, & David A. Whetten (Eds.), *Readings in organizational decline: Frameworks, research, and prescriptions* (pp. 411–416). Boston: Ballinger.

Micklethwait, J., & Wooldridge, A. (1996). *The witch doctors: Making sense of the management gurus.* New York: Times Books.

MicroVision. (1995). *MicroVision links you to your customers.* San Diego, CA: Author.

Middleton, K., Chamberlin, B., & Bunker, M. (1997). *The law of*

public communication (4th ed.). New York: Longman.

Middleton, O. (1996, August 11). Media buying frenzy not slowing; consolidation likely to continue into next century. *The Richmond Times Dispatch,* p. E1.

Midler v. Ford Motor Co., 849 F.2d 460 (9th Cir. 1988).

Midler v. Young & Rubicam, 944 F.2d 909 (9th Cir. 1991), *cert. denied,* 503 U.S. 951 (1992).

Milkovich v. Lorain Journal Co., 497 U.S. 1 (1990).

Miller v. California, 413 U.S. 15, 93 S.Ct. 2607 (1973).

Minneapolis Star & Tribune Co. v. Minnesota Commissioner of Revenue, 460 U.S. 575 (1983).

Mintzberg, H. (1989). *Mintzberg on management: Inside our strange world of organizations.* New York: The Free Press.

Mintzberg, H. (1983). *Power in and around organizations.* Englewood Cliffs, NJ: Prentice-Hall.

Mishra, J. (1990, Summer). Managing the grapevine. *Public Personnel Management,* 213–228.

Monge, P., & Eisenberg, E. (1987). Emergent communication networks. In R. McPhee & P. Tompkins (Eds.), *Organizational communication: Traditional themes and new directions* (pp. 304–342). Newbury Park, CA: Sage.

Moorman, R. H. (1991). Relationship between organizational justice and organizational citizenship behaviors: Do fairness perceptions influence employee citizenship? *Journal of Applied Psychology, 76,* 845–855.

Morgan v. Calender, 780 F. Supp. (W.D. Pa. 1992).

Morgan, M. (1986). Television and the erosion of regional diversity. *Journal of Broadcasting & Electronic Media, 30,* 135.

Morison, S., & Commager H. (1962) *The growth of the*

American republic (Vol. 2). New York: Oxford University Press.

Morley, D. (1986). *Family television: Cultural power and domestic leisure.* London: Comedia.

Moskal, B. S. (1990, December 3). World-class manufacturing. *Industry Week,* p. 54.

Muczyk, J., & Reimann, B. (1989). The case for directive leadership. In R. Taylor, & W. Rosenbach (Eds.), *Leadership: Challenges for today's manager* (pp. 89–108). New York: Nichols.

Muir v. Alabama Educational Television Commission, 688 F.2d 1033 (5th Cir. 1982) (en banc), *cert. denied,* 460 U.S. 1023 (1983).

Murphy, E. (1996). *Leadership IQ: A personal development process based on a scientific study of a new generation of leaders.* New York: John Wiley & Sons.

Must-carry wars resume. (1996, April 22). *Television Digest,* 10.

N

National Association for Better Broadcasting v. FCC, 849 F.2d 665 (1988).

National Association of Letter Carriers v. Austin, 418 U.S. 264 (1974).

National Broadcasting Co. v. FCC, 319 U.S. 190 (1943).

NBC v. Satellite Broadcast Networks, 940 F.2d 1467 (11th Cir. 1991).

Near v. Minnesota, 283 U.S. 697 (1934).

Nebraska Press Association v. Stuart, 427 U.S. 539 (1976).

New attempt to measure benefit of corporate citizenship (1997, Jan 20). *pr reporter.* 40(3), 1–2.

New York v. Ferber, 458 U.S. 747 (1982).

New York Times Co. v. Sullivan, 376 U.S. 254 (1964).

New York Times Co. v. United States, 403 U.S. 713 (1971).

Newsom, D. (1981). *The newspaper: Everything you need to know to make it in the newspaper business.* Englewood Cliffs, NJ: Prentice-Hall.

Newspapers roll with the punches: Surviving in a high-tech world. (1996, March 5). *The Record,* p. B2.

NLRB v. American National Insurance Co., 343 U.S. 395 (1952).

NLRB v. Bell Aerospace Co. Division of Textron, Inc., 416 U.S. 267 (1974).

NLRB v. KDFW-TV, Inc., 790 F.2d 1273 (5th Cir. 1986).

NLRB v. Reed & Prince Manufacturing Co., 205 F.2d 131 (1st Cir.), *cert. denied,* 346 U.S. 887 (1953).

Nossiter, B. (1985, October 26). The FCC's big giveaway. *The Nation,* 402.

Noth, D. (1996, August 23). Knight-Ridder papers flowing onto net like mercury [Online]. Available: http://www.arcfile.com/dom/col merc.html [1996, December 20].

Nystrom, P., & Starbuck, W. (1988). To avoid organizational crises, unlearn. In Kim S. Cameron, Robert I. Sutton, & David A. Whetten (Eds.), *Readings in organizational decline: Frameworks, research, and prescriptions* (pp. 323–332). Boston: Ballinger.

O

O'Brien, S. (1991, October). TV news on trial in Denver. *RTNDA Communicator,* 23–25.

O'Reilly, C. (1977). Person-job fit: Implications for individual attitudes and performance. *Organizational behavior and human performance, 18,* 36–46.

Odiorne, G. (1991). The new breed of supervisor: Leaders in self-managed work teams. *Supervision, 52*(8), 14–17.

Ogilvy, J. (1987, June). Leadership vs. management. *Marketing Communications,* 21–24.

Olivia N. v. NBC, 178 Cal. Rptr. 888 (Ct. App. 1981), *cert. denied,* 458 U.S. 1108 (1982).

Ollman v. Evans, 750 F.2d 970 (D.C. Cir. 1984), 471 U.S. 1127 (1985).

On-line services lose ground in workplace. (1996, July 22). *Electronic Buyers' News,* p. 60.

Organ, D. W. (1988). *Organizational citizenship behavior: The good soldier syndrome.* Lexington, MA: Lexington.

Ouchi, W. (1981). *Theory Z: How American business can meet the Japanese challenge.* New York: Avon.

P

Pan, Z., Ostman, R., Moy, P., & Reynolds, P. (1994). News media exposure and its learning effects during the Persian Gulf War. *Journalism Quarterly, 71*(1), 7–19.

Payne, D. (1988, Fall). Managing with style. *Executive Financial Woman,* 28–30.

Pell v. Procunier, 417 U.S. 817 (1974).

Penly, L., Alexander, E., Jernigan, E., & Henwood, C. (1991, March). Communication abilities of managers: The relationship to performance. *Journal of Management, 17,* 57–76.

Peppers, D., & Rogers, M. (1993). *The one to one future: Building relationships one customer at a time.* New York: Doubleday.

Persico, J., Jr. (1990, March). Employee motivation: Is it necessary? *Small Business Reports,* 34–37.

Petermann v. International Brotherhood of Teamsters, Local 396, 344 P.2d 25 (Cal. App. 1959).

Peters, T., & Waterman, R. (1982). *In search of excellence: Lessons* from America's best-run companies. New York: Warner.

Petrozello, D. (1996, April 8). Radio on the Internet: Study pinpoints heavy users. *Broadcasting & Cable,* 44.

Pfeffer, J. (1992). *Managing with power.* Boston: Harvard Business School Press.

Pfohl, H.-C. (1981). Planung und Kontrolle [Planning and evaluation]. Stuttgart, Germany: Kohlhammer.

Phantom Touring Inc. v. Affiliated Publications, 953 F.2d 724 (1st Cir.), *cert. denied,* 504 U.S. 974 (1992).

Philadelphia Newspapers, Inc. v. Hepps, 475 U.S. 767 (1986).

Picard, R. (1987). Evidence of a "failing newspaper" under the Newspaper Preservation Act. *Newspaper Research Journal, 9,* 73–82.

Picard, R. G. (1989). *Media economics.* Newbury Park, CA: Sage.

Pitz, G. F., & Sachs, N. J. (1984). Judgment and decision: Theory and application. *Annual Review of Psychology, 35,* 131–163.

Playboy Enterprises, Inc. v. Frena, 839 F. Supp. 1552 (M.D. Fla. 1993).

Playboy Entertainment Group, Inc. v. United States, 945 F. Supp. 772 (D. Del. 1996), *aff'd without opinion,* 117 S. Ct. 1309 (1997).

Player, M. A. (1992). *Federal law of employment discrimination in a nutshell* (3d ed.). St. Paul, MN: West.

Plunkett, L., & Fournier, R. (1991). *Participative management: Implementing empowerment.* New York: Wiley & Sons.

Pollard v. Rea Magnet Wire Co., 824 F.2d 557 (7th Cir.), *cert. denied,* 484 U.S. 977 (1987).

Pollard, G. (1995). Job satisfaction among newsworkers: The influence of professionalism, perceptions of organizational structure, and social attributes.

Journalism Quarterly, 72, 682–697.

Poole, M. S. (1985). Communication and organizational climates: Review, critique, and a new perspective. In Robert D. McPhee & Philip K. Tompkins (Eds.) (pp. 79–108), *Organizational communication: Traditional themes and new dimensions.* Newbury Park, CA: Sage.

Pope v. Illinois, 481 U.S. 497 (1987).

Porter, M. (1985). *Competitive advantage: Creating and sustaining superior performance.* New York: The Free Press.

Porto B. (1997). Who is 'employer' within meaning of age discrimination in Employment Act of 1967? *American Law Reports, Federal Series, 137,* 551–607, and 1996 supplement. Rochester, NY: Lawyer's Cooperative.

Powers, A. (1990). The changing market structure of local television news. *Journal of Media Economics, 3*(1), 37–56.

Powers, A., & Lacy, S. (1992). A model of job satisfaction in local television newsrooms. In S. Lacy, A. Sohn, and R. Giles (Eds.), *Readings in media management* (pp. 5–19). Columbia, SC: Media Management and Economics Division of the Association for Education in Journalism and Mass Communication.

Powers, R. (1977). *The newscasters.* New York: St. Martin's Press.

Presbrey, F. (1929). *The history and development of advertising.* New York: Doubleday.

Press-Enterprise Co. v. Superior Court, 478 U.S. 1 (1986).

Price, J. (1972). The study of organizational effectiveness. *Sociological Quarterly, 13,* 3–15.

Procaccini, J. (1986). *Mid-level management: Leadership as a*

performing art. New York: University Press of America.

Procter & Gamble Co. v. Bankers Trust Co., 78 F.3d 219 (6th Cir. 1996).

Providence Journal, *In re,* 820 F.2d 1342 (1st Cir. 1986), *modified,* 820 F.2d 1354 (1st Cir. 1987), *cert. dismissed,* 485 U.S. 693 (1988).

Putnam, L. (1989). Communication and conflict. In M. Rahim (Ed.), *Managing conflict: An interdisciplinary approach* (pp. 67–70. New York: Praeger.

Q

Quincy Cable TV, Inc. v. FCC, 768 F.2d 1434 (D.C. Cir. 1985), *cert. denied,* 476 U.S. 1169 (1986).

R

Rathbun, E. (1996a, July 1). The reordering of radio. *Broadcasting & Cable,* 6–7.

Rathbun, E. (1996b, October 7). Texas size: Clear channel builds a broadcast dynasty. *Broadcasting & Cable,* 56–60.

Rattner, S. (1986, Field Guide). Deals, near deals, and mega-deals. *Channels,* 12–13.

Red Lion Broadcasting Co. v. FCC, 395 U.S. 367 (1969).

Redmond, J. (1997). *Broadcasting World Wide Web sites: Public service or self service?* Paper presented at the annual convention of the Association for Education in Journalism and Mass Communication, Chicago, IL.

Redmond, J. (1993). *Network affiliate TV news directors: Becoming managers in the eye of a storm.* (Doctoral dissertation, University of Colorado, 1993).

Redmond, J. (1992). [Interviews of news directors and television consultants conducted for field research and kept on file by the researcher]. Unpublished interviews.

Redmond, J. (1991a, August). *Management in transition at the Rocky Mountain News.* Paper presented at the annual meeting of the Association for Education in Journalism and Mass Communication, Boston, MA.

Redmond, J. (1991b). Unpublished interview.

Redmond, J. (1989). *The sowing of the dragon's teeth (or how the success of American network affiliate television in the past is contributing to its current decline).* Unpublished master's thesis. Boulder, CO: University of Colorado.

Reitman, W. R. (1965). *Cognition and thought.* New York: John Wiley.

Reno v. ACLU, 117 S. Ct. (1997).

Rentsch, J. (1990). Climate and culture: Interaction and qualitative difference in organizational meanings. *Journal of Applied Psychology, 75,* 668–681.

Reversal of libel verdicts. (1996, Oct. 8). *Media Law Reporter.*

Rice, L. (1996a, November 25). NBC closes in on sweeps win: ABC, CBS in dead heat for second in households and key demos. *Broadcasting & Cable,* 12.

Rice, L. (1996b, October 21). Network TV share keeps dropping first month of 1996 prime-time season. *Broadcasting & Cable,* 13.

Ries, A., & Trout, J. (1981). *Positioning: The battle for your mind.* New York: McGraw-Hill.

Riesman, D., Glazer, N., & Denny, R. (1950). *The lonely crowd.* New Haven, CT: Yale University Press.

Roberts, B. S., & Mann, R. A. (1996). Sexual harassment in the workplace: A primer. *Akron Law Review, 29,* 269–289.

Robinson v. American Broadcasting Co., 441 F.2d 1396 (6th Cir. 1971).

Robinson, J. & Levy, M. (1986). *The main source.* Beverly Hills, CA: Sage.

Rohatyn, F. (1988, October 17). A financial house of cards. *Time,* 48–50.

Rosenberg, J. (1995, July 22). Trimmers expand newspapers' product limits: In-line machines bring variety of non-newspaper print jobs in house. *Editor & Publisher,* 26.

Rosnow, R. (1980, May). Psychology in rumor reconsidered. *Psychological Bulletin,* 578–591.

Rowan v. United States Post Office Department, 397 U.S. 728 (1970).

Rubin v. Coors Brewing Co., 514 U.S. 576 (1995).

Ryan, A., Schmit, M., & Johnson, R. (1996). Attitudes and effectiveness: Examining relations at an organizational level. *Personnel Psychology, 49*(4), 853.

S

Sandin, J., & Jessell, H. (1996, July 8). Westinghouse/CBS tops in TV: Newly merged giant reaches the most homes with its 14 stations; Tribune ranks second. *Broadcasting & Cable,* 12–20.

Saunders, D. (1996, November 5). TV "partners" improve election coverage. *Rocky Mountain News,* p. 2D.

Saxbe v. Washington Post Co., 417 U.S. 843 (1974).

Scarborough. (1997, January). Scarborough Research home page. [Online]. Available: http://www.scarborough.com.

Schachter, H. (1983). *Public agency communication.* Chicago: Nelson-Hall.

Schaeffer, F. (1976). The chief end of man. *Hymns for the family of God* (p. 364). Nashville, TN: Paragon Association.

Schein, E. (1985). *Organization culture and leadership.* San Francisco: Jossey-Bass.

Schlesinger, A. Jr. (Gen. Ed.) (1983). *The almanac of American history.* New York: Perigee.

Schmidt, W., & Finnigan, J. (1992). *The race without a finish line: America's quest for total quality.* San Francisco: Jossey-Bass.

Schneider, B. (1983). An interactionist perspective on organizational effectiveness. In K. Cameron & D. Whetten (Eds.), *Organizational effectiveness* (pp. 27–54). New York: Academic Press.

Schneider, B. (1987). The people make the place. *Personnel Psychology, 40,* 437–453.

Scholl, J. (1991). Financial documents. In P. Kluge (Ed.), *Guide to economics and business journalism* (pp. 5–12). New York: Columbia University Press.

Schramm, W. (1949). The nature of news. *Journalism Quarterly, 26,* 259–269.

Schultz, D. E., Tannenbaum, S. I., & Lauterborn, R. F. (1995). *Integrated marketing communications.* Lincolnwood, IL: NTC.

Scott, J. C., & O'Hair, D. (1989). Expanding psychographic concepts in public relations: The composite audience profile. In C. H. Botan & V. Hazelton (Eds.), *Public relations theory* (pp. 203–219). Hillsdale, NJ: Erlbaum.

Seward, D. (1986). *Napoleon's family: The notorious Bonapartes and their ascent to the thrones of Europe.* New York: Viking Penguin.

Shakespeare, W. *Henry VI,* Part II, Act IV, scene ii, line 73.

Shaklee, H., & Fischhoff, B. (1982). Strategies of information search in causal analysis. *Memory and Cognition,* 10, 520–530.

Shales, T. (1991a, April 6). CBS network eliminates 400 jobs: Latest cuts follow posting of $54.6 million loss. *The Washington Post,* p. D1.

Shales, T. (1991b, March 29). The endangered NBC peacock; GE is ravaging the once-proud network. *The Washington Post,* p. B1.

Sherman, B. (1987). *Telecommunications management.* New York: McGraw-Hill.

Simon, H. (1960). *The new science of management decision.* New York: Harper & Row.

Simon, P. (1972). The boxer. On *Simon and Garfunkel's greatest hits* [CD]. New York: Columbia Records/CBS.

Simons, J. (1996, May 6). Eye on the net. *U.S. News and World Report,* 59.

Sissors, J., & Bumba, L. (1993). *Advertising media planning* (4th ed.). Lincolnwood, IL: NTC Business Books.

Smircich, L., & Calas, M. (1987). Organizational culture: A critical assessment. In R. McPhee & P. Tompkins (Eds.), *Organizational communication: Traditional themes and new directions* (pp. 228–263). Newbury Park, CA: Sage.

Smith, C., & Becker, L. (1989). Comparison of journalistic values of television reporters and producers. *Journalism Quarterly, 66,* 793–800.

Smith, J., & Barclay, D. (1997). The effects of organizational differences and trust on the effectiveness of selling partner relationships. *The Journal of Marketing, 61*(1), 3.

Sohn, A., Ogan, C., & Polich, J. (1986). *Newspaper leadership.* Englewood Cliffs, NJ: Prentice-Hall.

Soin, S. (1992). *Total quality control essentials.* New York: McGraw-Hill.

Sony Corp. of America v. Universal City Studios, Inc., 464 U.S. 417 (1984).

Sperber, A. (1986). *Murrow: His life and times.* New York: Freundlich.

St. Amant v. Thompson, 390 U.S. 727 (1968).

Staff. (1988, July 27). *Broadcast Stats,* 3.

Staver, H. (1987, September 1987). George Gillett's private world. *Channels,* 29–34.

Steers, R. (1975). Problems in the measurement of organizational effectiveness. *Administrative Science Quarterly, 20,* 546–558.

Stempel, G., & Westley, B. (1989). *Research methods in mass communication* (2nd. ed.). Englewood Cliffs, NJ: Prentice-Hall.

Stengel, C. (1997, January 9). Waste of time. *The Tampa Tribune,* Baylife, p. 2.

Stepp, C. (1996, November). The X factor. *American Journalism Review,* 34

Stogdill, R. (1950). Leadership, membership and organization. *Psychological Bulletin, 47,* 1–14.

Stohl, C., & Redding, W. (1987). Messages and message exchange processes. In F. Jablin, L. Putnam, K. Roberts, & L. Porter (Eds.), *Handbook of organizational communication* (pp. 451–502). Newbury Park, CA: Sage.

Stolz v. KSFM 102 FM, 35 Cal. Rptr. 2d 740 (Ct. App. 1994), *cert. denied,* 116 S. Ct. 79 (1995).

Stone, E. (1987, April). The salad days are over. *RTNDA Communicator,* 14–15.

Stone, V. (1997a). [News director turnover rates]. Unpublished raw data.

Stone, V. (1997b). *Women break glass ceiling in TV news* [Online]. Available: http://www.missouri.edu/~jourvs/tvfnds.html [1997, March 4].

Stone, V. (1997c). *Minority and women in television news* [Online]. Available: http://www.missouri.edu/~jourvs/gtvminw.html [1997, March 4].

Stone, V. (1992). Women and men as news directors. *RTNDA Communicator,* pp. 143–144.

Stone, V. (1990). Newsrooms as profit centers. *RTNDA Communicator,* 13–16.

Stone, V. (1987). Changing profiles of news directors of radio and TV stations, 1972–1986. *Journalism Quarterly, 64,* 745–749.

Stone, V. (1986, June). New directors profiled. *RTNDA Communicator,* 13–16.

Stratton Oakmont, Inc. v. Prodigy Services Co., 23 Med. L. Rptr. 1794 (N.Y. Sup. Ct. 1995).

Straw, B., Sandelands, L., & Dutton, J. (1981). Threat-rigidity effects in organizational behavior: A multilevel analysis. *Administrative Science Quarterly, 26,* 501–524.

Sunshine Sportswear & Electronics Inc. v. WSOC Television Inc., 738 F. Supp. 1499 (D.S.C. 1989).

Syracuse Peace Council v. FCC, 867 F.2d 654 (D.C. Cir. 1989), *cert. denied,* 493 U.S. 1019 (1990).

T

Tan, A. (1985). *Mass communication theories and research* (2nd ed.). New York: Macmillan.

Tan, B. W., & Lo, T. W. (1991). The impact of interface customization on the effect of cognitive style on information system success. *Behavior and Information Technology, 10,* 297–310.

Taylor, C. (1994). OHBWA: Office hours by walking around. *Journal of Management education, 18*(2), 270.

Taylor, F. (1947/1967). *Scientific management.* New York: W. W. Norton & Co. (Reprint of

Scientific management, 1947, New York: Harper & Row).

Taylor, R., & Rosenbach, W. (1989). *Leadership: Challenges for today's manager.* New York: Nichols.

Technology could alter the shape of news coverage. (1993, August 15). *Chicago Tribune,* p. C9.

Telecommunications Research and Action Center v. FCC, 801 F.2d 501 (D.C. Cir. 1986), *cert. denied,* 482 U.S. 919 (1987).

Teleprompter Corp. v. Columbia Broadcasting System, 415 U.S. 394 (1974).

Terazono, E. (1996, July 19). Breaking with tradition. *Financial Times,* Japan edition, p. 6.

Terry, R. (1993). *Authentic leadership: Courage in action.* San Francisco: Jossey-Bass.

Thanepohn, S. G. (1991, August 1). The air traffic control system 10 years after PATCO. *Airline Pilot, 60,* 22.

The battle over home shopping stations. (1993, June 23). *Nightline.* New York: ABC News [Online, Lexis-Nexis].

The Bill of Rights, Amendments 1–10 of the Constitution. In *Library of Congress historical documents* [Online]. Available: http://lcweb2.loc.gov/const/bor.html [1997, March 24].

The CEO on the move. (1994, October 21). *Business Week,* 49.

The Federal Trade Commission gave an expected final approval to the merger of Time Warner Inc. and Turner Broadcasting System. (1997, February 10). *Broadcasting & Cable,* p. 76.

Thierauf, R., & Grosse, R. (1970). *Decision making through operations research.* New York: John Wiley.

Thistle, J. (1994). It's 10 P.M.; local news takes the 10 o'clock prime spots. *The Quill, 82,* 30.

Thomson. (1996). About Thomson [Online]. Available: http://www.thomcorp.com/about.html [1996, December 8].

Tichenor, P., Donohue, G., & Olien, C. (1970). Mass media flow and differential growth in knowledge. *Public Opinion Quarterly, 34,* 159–170.

Time Inc. v. Firestone, 424 U.S. 448 (1976).

Time Inc. v. Hill, 385 U.S. 374 (1967).

Time Warner Entertainment v. FCC, 93 F.3d 957 (D.C. Cir. 1996).

Times-Mirror Co. v. San Diego Superior Court, 244 Cal. Rptr. 556 (Ct. App. 1988).

Tjosvold, D. (1989). Organizational conflict: Introduction. In M. Rahim (Ed.), *Managing conflict: An interdisciplinary approach* (pp. 3–7). New York: Praeger.

Todd, J. (1995, May). Regimental news from the desk of the Sergeant Major. *The Army Lawyer,* 270.

Tompkins, P., & Cheney, G. (1983). Account analysis of organizations: Decision making and identification. In L. Putnam & M. Pacanowsky (Eds.), *Communication and organizations: An interpretative approach* (pp. 123–146). Newbury Park, CA: Sage.

Tompkins, P., & Cheney, G. (1985). Communication and unobtrusive control in contemporary organizations. In R. McPhee & P. Tompkins (Eds.), *Organizational communication: Traditional themes and new directions* (pp. 179–210). Newbury Park, CA: Sage.

Traber, M. (Ed.). (1986). *The myth of the information revolution: Social and ethical implications of communication technology.* London: Sage.

Trujillo, N. (1983). "Performing" Mintzberg's roles: The nature of managerial communication. In L. Putnam & M. Pacanowsky (Eds.), *Communication and organizations: An interpretative approach* (pp. 73–97). Newbury Park, CA: Sage.

Tunks, R. (1992). *Fast track to quality.* New York: McGraw-Hill.

Turner Broadcasting System v. FCC, 117 S. Ct. 1174 (1997).

Turner Broadcasting System, Inc. v. FCC, 512 U.S. 622 (1994).

Tushman, M., Newman, W., & Romanelli, E. (1988). Convergence and upheaval: Managing the unsteady pace of organizational evolution. In Kim S. Cameron, Robert I. Sutton, & David A. Whetten (Eds.), *Readings in organizational decline: Frameworks, research, and prescriptions* (pp. 63–74). Boston: Ballinger.

Two years of intensive deal-making. (1986, April). *Channels,* 38.

Tyrer, T., & Granger, R. (1990, December 3). Big 3 sweeps hit all-time November low. *Electronic Media,* 1.

Tzu, S. (1988). *The art of war* (T. Cleary, Trans.). Boston: Shambhala. (Original work published approximately 100 B.C.).

U

U.S. Census Bureau (1997). National monthly population estimates 1980 to 1997 [Online]. Available: http://www.census.gov/population/www/estimates/nation1.html [1997, July 29].

U.S. Census Bureau (1997a). Population: 1790–1990 [Online]. Available: http://www.census.gov/population/censusdata/table-16.pdf [1997, August 16].

Underwood, D. (1993). *When MBAs rule the newsroom.* New York: Cambridge.

United States v. Dickinson, 465 F.2d 496 (5th Cir. 1972), *cert. denied,* 414 U.S. 979 (1973).

United States v. Edge Broadcasting Co., 509 U.S. 418 (1993).

United States v. Southwestern Cable Co., 392 U.S. 157 (1968).

United Video Inc. v. FCC, 890 F.2d 1173 (D.C. Cir. 1989).

Upper Midwest Booksellers Association v. City of Minneapolis, 780 F.2d 1389 (8th Cir. 1985).

V

Valentine v. Chrestensen, 316 U.S. 52 (1942).

Valley Broadcasting Co. v. United States, 107 F.3d 1328 (9th Cir. 1997).

Van Auken, P. (1992). Control vs. development: Up-to-date or out-of-date as a supervisor? *Supervision, 53*(12), 17–19.

Van Deusen, R. (1995). *Financial management for media operations* (2nd ed.). White Plains, NY: Knowledge Industry Publications.

Veronis, Suhler & Associates (1996). *Communications industry forecast: Historical and projected expenditures for 10 industry segments* (10th ed.). New York: Author.

Virgil v. Time Inc., 527 F.2d 1122 (9th Cir. 1975), *cert. denied,* 425 U.S. 998 (1976).

Virginia State Board of Pharmacy v. Virginia Citizens' Consumer Council, 425 U.S. 748 (1976).

Vitale, J. (1987, September). The newsroom's revolving door. *Channels,* 38.

Vroom, V. (1964). *Work and motivation.* New York: John Wiley & Sons.

Vroom, V., & Jago, A. (1988). *The new leadership: Managing participation in organizations.* Englewood Cliffs, NJ: Prentice-Hall.

W

Waits v. Frito-Lay, Inc., 978 F.2d 1093 (9th Cir. 1992), *cert. denied,* 506 U.S. 1080 (1993).

WALE-AM, 7 FCC Rcd. 2345 (1992).

Walker, D. (1996, November 1). Arizona Newschannel: More news may be good news for partners. *The Arizona Republic/The Phoenix Gazette,* p. D15.

Walker, R., & Bellamy, R. (Eds.). (1993). *The remote control in the new age of television.* New York: Praeger.

Walt Disney Productions, Inc. v. Shannon, 276 S.E.2d 580 (Ga. 1981).

Walter, T. (1997, May 31). WMC-TV news updates to run on CNN. *The Commercial Appeal,* p. C1.

Walter, T. (1996, November 14). TV newsmen at stage center in safety reports. *The Commercial Appeal,* p. C1.

Walton, E. (1981, January). The comparison of measures of organization structure. *Academy of Management Review, 6,* 155–160.

Watson, K. (1982, June). An analysis of communication patterns: A method for discriminating leader and subordinate roles. *Academy of Management Journal,* 107–122.

Weatherly, K. A., & Beach, L. R. (1996). Organizational culture and decision making. In L. R. Beach (Ed.), *Decision making in the workplace: A unified perspective* (pp. 117–132). Mahwah, NJ: Erlbaum.

Webster's new world dictionary of American English (3rd college ed.) (1994). New York: Macmillan.

Weeks, D., & Whimster, S. (1985). Contexted decision making: A socio-organizational perspective. In G. Wright (Ed.), *Behavioral*

decision making (pp. 167–188). New York: Plenum.

Weick, K. (1988). Organizational culture as a source of high reliability. In J. Gibson, J. Ivancevich, & J. Donnelly, Jr. (Eds.), *Organizations close-up: A book of readings* (6th ed.) (pp. 16–33). Plano, TX: Business Publications.

Weick, K., & Daft, R. (1983). The effectiveness of interpretation systems. In Kim S. Cameron & David A. Whetten (Eds.), *Organizational effectiveness* (pp. 71–94). New York: Academic Press.

Weinstein, A. (1994). *Market segmentation: Using demographics, psychographics, and other niche marketing.* Chicago, IL: Probus.

Weirum v. RKO General, Inc., 539 P.2d 36 (1975).

Wellins, R., Byham, W., & Wilson, J (1991). *Empowerment teams.* San Francisco, CA: Jossey-Bass.

What's the Internet? (1996, July 8). *The Virginia Pilot,* p. 12.

Whetten, D. (1988). Sources, responses, and effects of organizational decline. In Kim S. Cameron, Robert I. Sutton, & David A. Whetten (Eds.), *Readings in organizational decline: Frameworks, research, and prescriptions* (pp. 151–174). Boston: Ballinger.

Whetten, D., & Cameron, K. (1995). *Developing management skills* (3rd ed.). New York: HarperCollins.

White v. Samsung Electronics America, Inc., 971 F.2d 1395 (9th Cir. 1992). *cert. denied,* 508 U.S. 951 (1993).

Wichita Eagle & Beacon Publishing Co. v. NLRB, 480 F.2d 52 (10th Cir.), *cert. denied,* 416 U.S. 982 (1973).

Williams v. Pasma, 656 P.2d 212 (Mont. 1982), *cert. denied,* 461 U.S. 945 (1983).

Williams, C. (1986, Fall). Managerial leadership for the

21st century. *Baylor Business Review*, 22–25.

Willis, J. (1988). *Surviving in the newspaper business: Newspaper management in turbulent times.* New York: Praeger.

Wilson, C., Boni, N., & Hogg, A. (1997). The effectiveness of task clarification, positive reinforcement and corrective feedback in changing courtesy among police staff. *Journal of Organizational Behavior Management, 17*(1), 65.

Wimmer, R., & Dominick, J. (1987). *Mass media research: An introduction* (2nd ed.). Belmont, CA: Wadsworth.

Winstead v. Sweeney, 517 N.W.2d 874 (Ct. App. Mich. 1994).

Wolston v. Reader's Digest Association, 443 U.S. 157 (1979).

Woodward, R. (1997, June 24). E-mail, other devices sapping efficiency? *The Commercial Appeal*, p. B-5.

Worthy, J. (1950). Organizational structure and employee morale. *American Sociological Review, 15,* 169–79.

Y

Yankelovich Partners. (1993). [Brochure]. Norwalk, CT: Author.

Yardley, J. (1992, September 2). The realities of TV journalism. *The Washington Post,* p. C3.

Young v. American Mini Theatres, Inc., 427 U.S. 50 (1976).

Yukl, G. (1989). Managerial leadership: A review of theory and research. *Journal of Management, 15,* 251–289.

Z

Zahniser, R. (1994). Design by walking around. *Operations Research/Management Science, 34*(2), 127.

Zaleznik, A. (1986). Managers and leaders: Are they different? *Harvard Business Review,* 48. (Reprinted from *Harvard Business Review,* 1977).

Zaleznik, A. (1989). *The managerial mystique.* New York: Harper & Row.

Zammuto, R. (1984, October). A comparison of multiple constituency models of organizational effectiveness. *Academy of Management Review,* 600–616.

Zammuto, R. (1982). *Assessing organizational effectiveness.* Albany, NY: State University of New York Press.

Zoglin, R. (1990, November 11). Goodbye to the mass audience. *Time,* 122.

Zurcher v. Stanford Daily, 436 U.S. 547 (1978).

credits

Excerpts on pp. 220–21, 224, 228, 229, 230–31: How to Read a Financial Report, Merrill Lynch, 1997. Printed in the U.S.A. © 1997 Merrill Lynch, Pierce, Fenner & Smith Incorporated. Member, Securities Investor Protection Corporation (SIPC).

Figure 9.1 (p. 223): How to Read a Financial Report, Merrill Lynch, 1997. Printed in the U.S.A. © 1997 Merrill Lynch, Pierce, Fenner & Smith Incorporated. Member, Securities Investor Protection Corporation (SIPC).

Figure 9.2 (p. 225): How to Read a Financial Report, Merrill Lynch, 1997. Printed in the U.S.A. © 1997 Merrill Lynch, Pierce, Fenner & Smith Incorporated. Member, Securities Investor Protection Corporation (SIPC).

Figure 9.6: R. Van Deusen. FINANCIAL MANAGEMENT FOR MEDIA OPERATIONS, 2/e. Copyright 1995. Reprinted by permission of Butterworth-Heinemann.

Figure 10.6: Reprinted by permission of the author.

Figure 11.1: Reprinted by permission of Veronis, Suhler & Associates, Inc. 350 Park Avenue, New York, NY 10022, (212) 935–4990.

Sidebar 12.2: P. Nystrom and W. Starbuck. To avoid organizational crises, unlearn. Reprinted by permission of the publisher, from

ORGANIZATIONAL DYNAMICS SPRING 1984 © 1984. American Management Association, New York. http://www.amanet.org. All rights reserved.

Figure 12.2: B. Bagdikian. THE MEDIA MONOPOLY, 4/e. Copyright 1992.

Figure 12.3: Reprinted by permission of Veronis, Suhler & Associates, Inc. 350 Park Avenue, New York, NY 10022, (212) 935–4990.

Figure 12.4: P. Nystrom and W. Starbuck. To avoid organizational crises, unlearn. Reprinted by permission of the publisher, from ORGANIZATIONAL DYNAMICS SPRING 1984 © 1984. American Management Association, New York. http://www.amanet.org. All rights reserved.

Figure 12.6: P. Nystrom and W. Starbuck. To avoid organizational crises, unlearn. Reprinted by permission of the publisher, from ORGANIZATIONAL DYNAMICS SPRING 1984 © 1984. American Management Association, New York. http://www.amanet.org. All rights reserved.

Figure 12.7: Guy, M. (1989). From organizational decline to organizational renewal: The phoenix syndrome. Westport, CT: Quorum Books, an imprint of Greenwood Publishing Group, Inc. Reprinted with permission.

Figure 12.8: P. Nystrom and W. Starbuck. To avoid organizational crises, unlearn. Reprinted by permission of the publisher, from ORGANIZATIONAL DYNAMICS SPRING 1984 © 1984. American Management Association, New York. http://www.amanet.org. All rights reserved.

Figure 12.9: Guy, M. (1989). From organizational decline to organizational renewal: The phoenix syndrome. Westport, CT: Quorum Books, an imprint of Greenwood Publishing Group, Inc. Reprinted with permission.

Figure 12.10: P. Nystrom and W. Starbuck. To avoid organizational crises, unlearn. Reprinted by permission of the publisher, from ORGANIZATIONAL DYNAMICS SPRING 1984 © 1984. American Management Association, New York. http://www.amanet.org. All rights reserved.

Figure 12.11: P. Nystrom and W. Starbuck. To avoid organizational crises, unlearn. Reprinted by permission of the publisher, from ORGANIZATIONAL DYNAMICS SPRING 1984 © 1984. American Management Association, New York. http://www.amanet.org. All rights reserved.

index

Errors, accepting responsibility for, 69

Esprit de corps, 40, 41

Ethics
journalistic, 73, 300
in organizational hologram theory, 95

Euske, N., 143

Evaluation
in communication plan, 267, 268, 270
of employees, 130–32
in Type Z organizations, 48

Exaggeration, 356

Expectancy
of audience, 118–19
and performance, 104

Expectancy theory, 90–91

Expenses
cutting, 222, 227–28, 296, 310, 313
fixed, 241–43
variable, 241–43
See also Financial management

Expert power, 150, 151–52, 154–55

Express warranty, 411

Extrinsic motivation, 75–76, 84

F

Factories, media organizations as, 14–16

Facts
embarrassing, 351
"false," 344–45

FACTS scenario, of organizational decline, 301

Fads, in management, 62–63

Fair comment, 342, 343

Fairness, perceptions of, 88–90, 91–92, 104

Fairness doctrine, 386

Fair trial, and press freedom, 366–68

Fair use, 361–62

Falcione, R., 96, 143

False facts, 344–45

Falsity, libel standards for, 339

False light, 347, 351–52, 354

Faltas v. State Newspaper, 338

Farmers Educational Cooperative Union v. WDAY, Inc., 383

Fashion changes, and organizational decline, 303

Fault, in libel cases, 332–38, 353

Favoritism, effect on productivity, 101

Fayol, Henri, 21, 40–41, 184

FCC v. League of Women Voters of California, 375, 393

FCC v. Pacifica Foundation, 376, 378

Fear, eliminating, 156

Fearing, F., 284

Fear of failure, 314

Features editor, 25

Feder, R., 121

Federal Communications Act, 375

Federal Communications Commission (FCC)
creation of, 375
equal employment rules of, 414, 418
functions of, 377–78
influence on media content, 378–90
regulation of new technologies, 400–403
requirements for broadcast stations, 390–93
role in cable television regulation, 377, 387–90, 393–400

Federal Freedom of Information Act, 364–65

Federal officials
privileged status in libel cases, 341
subject to Freedom of Information Act, 364

Federal open meetings laws, 365

Federal prisons, public access prohibited, 365–66

Federal Privacy Act, 365

Federal Radio Commission, 375

Federal Trade Commission, 356

Feedback
in fundamental communication model, 139
soliciting, 158–62, 165

Fighting words test, 324

Figure skaters, example of perceived inequity, 91

Filtering
by mass audiences, 277–78
of rumors, 144
in vertical communication, 141

Financial formulas
for current ratio, 228

for earnings per share, 230–31
for net profit, 229
for quick ratio, 228–29

Financial management
annual reports, 220–21
balance sheet, 221–24
budgeting (*see* Budgeting)
corporate income statement, 224–28
essentials of, 219–20
key business ratios for, 228–31

Financial review, 220–21

Fink, S., 58

Finnigan, J., 45, 53

Fireside chats, 276

Firing, of employees, 85, 132, 418–19

First Amendment protections, 13, 275, 321–27

Fischer, R., 268

Fischhoff, B., 251

Fishbein, E., 91

Fixed assets, 221, 223

Fixed expenses, 241–43

Flander, J., 5

Flattery, 142

Flexibility, 62, 149

Florida Star v. B.J.F., 351

Focus groups, 217

Ford Motor Company, 347, 348

Forecasting, for budgets, 240–44

Foreign ownership, of broadcast and cable stations, 390, 396

Formal power, 153, 154

Formats, for radio stations, 205

Formulas
financial, 228–31
for television news, 7–8, 59

Fortnightly Corp. v. United Artists Television, Inc., 399

44 Liquormart, Inc. v. Rhode Island, 357

Four corners rule, 411

Fournier, R., 44

Four-step managerial process, 258–59

Fowler, Mark, 19

Fragmentation, of television audience, 285, 287, 294–97, 304–5

Frame-breaking change, 314–16

Franchising, of cable systems, 377, 393–95, 397

Francios, W. E., 13
Franklin, M., 14, 327
Fredin, E., 278
Free agency dispute, 91
Freedom of Information Act
      (FOIA), 364–65
Freelancers, copyright for, 359
Freeman, J., 134
Free press
    and advertising, 9, 10
    American model of, 12–14, 275,
      321–27
    and fair trial protections,
      366–68
    influence of Reformation on,
      12–13
Free-speech movement, 275
French, J., 149, 150
Friedman, S., 180, 188
Friendly, Fred, 323
Frost, P., 141, 142, 148, 152, 153,
    163
Functional area manager, 30

G

Gag orders, 366–67
Galbraith, J., 30
Game playing, 47, 48, 49, 154
Gannett Company, Inc., 17–18, 97
Gans, H., 8, 15, 35, 196
Gardner, J., 147, 181
Garrison v. Louisiana, 334
Gates, Bill, 169
Gaudet, H., 277
Gaziano, C., 90, 124, 180, 196, 279
Gender, and employment
      discrimination, 414, 415,
      416
General Electric, 295
General managers, 25–26
Generating, as approach to
      organizational decline,
      312, 313–14
Genova, B., 279
Geological information,
      exemptions from FOIA for,
      364
Gertz, Elmer, 337
Gertz v. Robert Welch, Inc., 336,
    337, 339, 343
Gibson, J., 4, 30, 75, 107, 126, 128,
    129, 132, 145, 154, 164
Ginsberg v. New York, 358

Goal setting
    advantages of, 126–27
    commitment to, 130–34
    disadvantages of, 127–29
    implementing, 129–30, 135
    methods for, 252, 253, 254
Goldman, K., 34
Goldstein, N., 249
Good faith bargaining, 421
Gooding v. Wilson, 324
Goodwill, 121–22
Gossip, 143–45
Government
    censorship prohibited, 321–27
    ineligible for libel suits, 329
    licensing of press, 12–13
    permissible restrictions on
      media organizations,
      323–27
    See also Federal
      Communications
      Commision (FCC)
Government records, access to,
    364–65
Graham, D., 243
Grahnke, L., 72
Grand juries, 367, 370
Granger, R., 34
Grapevine, as communication
      medium, 88, 103–4,
      143–45, 158
*Greater New Orleans Broadcasting
      Association, Inc. v. United
      States,* 386
Greeley, Horace, 169
Greenbaum, T. L., 217
*Greenbelt Cooperative Publishing
      Association v. Bresler,* 343
Greenberg, B., 279
Greer v. Spock, 366
Grimm, H., 12
Grosjean v. American Press Co., 325
Gross, L., 277
Grosse, R., 200, 256
Grossman, Lawrence K., 295
Groupthink, 51–52, 310
Grove, A. S., 99
Growth, 76, 188–89
Grünig, J., 50, 260, 261, 269
Guilford, Howard, 323
Gulf War, 278
Gunneson, A. O., 98
Guy, M., 296, 305, 306, 310, 311,
    316, 317

H

Hachten, W., 13
Hakes, C., 54, 55
Halberstam, D., 276
Hannan, M., 134
Harassment, sexual, 419–20, 425
Harder, J. W., 88, 91
Hardiness, in Kets de Vries
      leadership model, 173,
      174
Harding, Tonya, 91
Harm, lawsuits for, 352–53
*Harper & Row Publishers, Inc. v.
      Nation Enterprises, Inc.,* 362
Harrigan, K., 298, 303, 307, 308
Harrison, E. F., 250
Harris v. Forklift Systems, 419, 420
Harry Fox Agency, 207, 208
*Harte-Hanks Communications, Inc. v.
      Connaughton,* 334
Harvesting strategy, 307–8
Harvey, P., 13
Hawkins, R., 59
Head, S., 18, 118, 277, 285, 290,
      293, 294, 295, 299, 375
Headlines, defamatory, 332
Heath, R. P., 211
Hellriegel, D., 79
Hentze, J., 260
Henwood, C., 98
Herbert v. Lando, 334
Herceg v. Hustler Magazine, Inc., 352
Herden, R., 96, 143
Hersey, P., 183, 195
Herzberg, F., 74, 75, 76, 77, 78
Hess v. Indiana, 324
Hey, J., 251
Hierarchy
    of communication plans, 264,
      266
    communication within, 140–41,
      157
    effect on individual power, 155
    and legitimate power, 150
    resistance to change, 180
Higher authority, invoking, 142,
      163
Hiring, and job fit criteria, 79–81
Hirschhorn, L., 123, 181
Hitler, Adolf, 174
Hitt, M., 134
Hoaxes, broadcasting prohibited,
      387
Hofmeister, S., 226

and homogenized
 programming, 8, 62
matrix organization of, 31–32
organizational structures of, 23,
 24
Media director, 28
Media factories, 14–16
Media management
 factors in, 2–3
 management science perspective
  for, 59
 parallels with other types of
  management, 38
 See also Management
Media organizations
 approaches to change, 60–61
 budgeting for (see Budgeting;
  Financial management)
 bureaucracy in, 90
 business-creative conflicts in,
  124
 changing dynamics of, 58–61
 conflicting values within, 72–73
 consolidation of, 8, 15, 17–18,
  33–35
 decision making in (see Decision
  making; Planning)
 decline of (see Organizational
  decline)
 distribution of power in, 148–56
 effectiveness of, 107–10,
  122–26, 134
 financial management of (see
  Financial management)
 First Amendment protections
  for, 12, 13, 275, 321–27
 goodwill of, 121–22
 job fit and job enlargement in,
  79–81
 as "living systems," 99–100
 management of, 56–58, 180,
  182–83, 196 (see also
  Management)
 marketing in (see Marketing)
 motivation in, 73–78 (see also
  Creativity; Motivation;
  Values)
 regulation of, 125–26, 374–77,
  378–87, 390–93
 resistance to change in, 115–16,
  180, 315
 social responsibility of, 212–14
 stock price of, 122–23

structure of
 advertising agencies, 27–29
 broadcast companies, 25–27
 conglomerates, 23, 24
 matrix organizations, 29–33
 newspapers, 23–25
 public relations agencies,
  27–29
 team building in, 181
 unique aspects of, 56–58
 See also Organizations
Media planner, 28
Media products
 analyzing costs of, 205–9
 customers for, 55
 distribution options, 204
 marketing of, 199, 209–14
 pricing, 200
 ratings services for, 213, 214–16
 on World Wide Web (see World
  Wide Web)
Medical files, exemptions from
 FOIA for, 364
Medical Laboratory Consultants v.
 American Broadcasting Cos.,
 328
Meetings, open, 365
Mellman, M., 119
Memphis Business Journal, 205
Memphis Commercial Appeal, 205
Merchant, K., 119
Meredith Corp. v. FCC, 386
Meritor Savings Bank v. Vinson, 419
Mermigas, D., 33, 34, 227, 293
Merrill Lynch, 121, 122, 221, 223,
 224, 225, 226, 228, 229,
 230, 231
Merton, R., 277
Message game, 140
Metaplanning, 259–71
Meyer, A., 308
Micklethwait, J., 62
Micro effects perspective, 278
MicroVision, address for, 212, 213
Middle manager, role of, 4
Middlemist, R., 134
Middle-range planning, 264, 265
Middleton, O., 35
Midler, Bette, 347, 348
Midler v. Ford Motor Co., 347, 348
Midler v. Young & Rubicam, 347,
 348
Military bases, public access
 prohibited, 365–66

Milkovich v. Lorain Journal Co., 343,
 344
Miller v. California, 13, 324, 357,
 358, 378
Milton, John, 12–13
Minneapolis Star & Tribune Co. v.
 Minnesota Commissioner of
 Revenue, 325
Minnesota Rag, 323
Minorities, as TV news directors, 6
Minors
 contracts with, 410
 protections in legal proceedings
  for, 367
Mintzberg, H., 56, 58, 154
Mishra, A., 108
Mishra, J., 145, 159
Mission, of organization, 267, 314
Monge, P., 143
Moorman, R. H., 92
Moravcsik, J. M., 75
Morgan, M., 7, 62
Morgan v. Calender, 351
Morley, D., 284
Morrison, S., 13
Mosaic browser, 59, 115
Moskal, B. S., 98
Motivation
 and communication, 146
 extrinsic, 84
 intrinsic, 84
 and job fit/job enlargement
  issues, 79–81
 in Kilpatrick and Locke
  leadership model, 175
 among news professionals, 10,
  58–59, 73, 124 (see also
  Creativity, managing)
 and participative management,
  45–47
 Taylor's view of, 42
 theories of, 42–44, 73–78, 81–86
Motivation-hygiene theory, 75–76
Movies
 impact on vaudeville, 114
 as mass communication tool,
  276
Moy, P., 278
M.S. News Co. v. Casado, 358
MTV, 294
Muczyk, J., 168, 186, 195
MUGS scenario, 301
Muir v. Alabama Educational
 Television Commission, 393

in Type Z organizations, 48
from within organization, 188
Promotions (marketing), managing
costs of, 120
Propaganda, 276
Property, plant, and equipment,
221, 223
Prurient interest, 358
Psychic cost, 203–4
Psychographics, 211–12
Publication, required to sue for
libel, 330, 353
Public broadcasting, regulation of,
393
Public, educational, and
government (PEG)
channels, 379, 389
Public figures, libel standards for,
336–37, 338
Public files, required of broadcast
licensees, 392–93
Public interest, in broadcast
regulations, 18–19
Public officials
libel standards for, 333, 334–36
privileged status in libel cases,
341
Public property, accessible to news
media, 365–66
Public relations
agency organizations, 27–29
decision-making example for,
252–56
as in-house department, 28–29
participative management in, 50
Public service announcements, 209
Publishers
of music, 207
of newspapers, 23, 25
Publisher's representatives, 207–8
Puffery, 356
Pulakos, E., 130, 131, 132
Punitive damages, 339–40
Puritan Roundheads, 12
Putnam, L., 139, 146

Q

Qualified privilege, 342
Quality
as goal of management, 54–55
improving, 84–86
versus price, 200
Quality circles, 46, 47
Quantity discounts, 31–32

Quarterly budget report, 238, 239
Questions
close-ended, 159, 161
open-ended, 160–61
Quick ratio, 228–29
Quid pro quo harassment, 419

R

Race, and employment
discrimination, 414, 415,
417
Radio
evolution of, 15–16, 114–15,
299
impact on newspapers, 290
impact on vaudeville, 114
influence on audience, 276–77
ratings of, 214, 282
regulation of, 375–76, 378–90
Radio Act, 18, 375
Radio advertising, 206
Radio stations
changing formats of, 118, 205
management structure of, 26
ownership limits for, 391–92
play lists, 115
revenue growth strategy, 242
sale of studio time by, 121
Rape victims, publishing names of,
351, 367
Rates, for cable television, 397
Rathbun, E., 19
Ratings, 16, 214–15, 282, 296
Rattner, S., 19, 34
Raven, B., 149, 150
Real estate, online shopping for,
199
Reality, perceptions of, 67–69
Reallocation, 307
Reasonable access provision,
383–84
Reasonable accommodations, 417
Reasonable fit test, 357
Reasonable journalist test, 338
Reasonable person test, 338
Reasoning, as communication
strategy, 142, 163
Recording Industry Sourcebook, 207
Recording rights, 207
Recordings
copyright of, 362–63
secret, 349–50
Record privilege, 342
Redding, W., 141, 144, 145, 147,
159, 165

Red Lion Broadcasting Co. v. FCC,
322, 374, 375, 386
Redmond, J., 3, 4, 99, 105, 115,
244, 286, 296
Referent power, 150, 152, 154–55
Refinancing, 227
Reformation, influence on rise of
free press, 12–13
Registration, of copyright, 360–61
Regulation
and broadcast deregulation,
18–20, 35, 195, 287
of broadcasting, 125–26,
374–77, 378–87, 390–93
of cable television, 376–77,
387–90, 393–400
of new media, 400–403
rationale for, 374–77
Reimann, B., 168, 186, 195
Reinvestment, 306–7
Reitman, W. R., 250
Relatedness needs, 76
Relationships, working, 145–46,
197
Relevance, as position power
factor, 149
Religion, employment
discrimination and, 414,
415
Remote control units, 285–86
Remuneration, in Fayol's
management principles,
41
Renewal
of cable franchises, 394–95
of organizations, 314–16, 317
Reno v. ACLU, 379
Rentsch, J., 182
Reorganization, 314
Repackaging, 120–21
Reportage, neutral, 345–46
Reporters' privilege, 369–72
Representatives, privileged status
in libel cases, 341
Research, on mass communication,
276–80
Resource network, 172
Resources, maximizing, 120–21
Responsibility for errors, 69
Restructuring, 227
RetailDirect, 216
Retained earnings, 224
Retransmission consent
for cable systems, 388–89

for direct broadcast satellite
services, 401
for wireless cable services, 402
Revenues, estimating, 241
Revision cycles, for
communication plans,
265, 266, 268, 271
Revocation of an offer, 407
Reward power, 150–51
Rewards
in expectancy theory, 90–91
managing, 92
meaningful, 83
Reynolds, P., 278
Rice, L., 439
Ries, A., 209
Right of publicity, 348
Rights fees, 206, 207–8
Risk taking, 183, 184
Roberts, B. S., 419, 420
Roberts, K., 141, 143
Robinson, J., 279
*Robinson v. American Broadcasting
Co.*, 376
Rocky Mountain News, 111–13
Rogers, M., 217
Rohatyn, F., 227
Role models, for media managers,
3
Romanelli, E., 314, 315
Roman Empire, 93–94
Roosevelt, Franklin D., 276
Rosenbach, W., 173, 176, 186
Rosenberg, J., 121
Rosnow, R., 143
Rotary boards, 209
Roth v. United States, 13
Routine decisions, 249
*Rowan v. United States Post Office
Department*, 358
Royalty-free music, 209
Rubin v. Coors Brewing Co., 357
Rule of 7s, 19
Rule of 12s, 19
Rumor mill, 88, 103–4, 143–45,
158
Ryan, A., 109

S

Sachs, N. J., 250
Safe harbor period, 379
Sales
cost of, 225, 226
projecting, 201–3

Sales manager, 26, 27
Sanctions, initiating, 142, 163
Sandelands, L., 164
Sandin, J., 19
Satellite master antenna television,
402
Satellite receiving dishes, 294,
400–401
Satellites
direct broadcast, 400–401
effect on Big Three networks,
294
Satire, and fair use, 361
Satisfaction, Taylor's view of,
41–42
Satisfiers, 75
Saunders, D., 121
Saxbe v. Washington Post Co., 366
Scantrack, 213
Scarborough Research, 216
Schachter, H., 99, 100
Schaeffer, F., 74
Schein, E., 96
Schemata theory, 278
Schlesinger, A., Jr., 275
Schmidt, W., 45, 53
Schmit, M., 109
Schneider, B., 79, 99, 103, 134, 313
Schofield, L., 18, 118, 277, 285,
290, 293, 294, 295, 299,
375
Scholl, J., 220, 224, 225
Schramm, W., 274
Schultz, D. E., 210
Scientific management, 41–42
Scott, J. C., 210
Screening, 157
Script writing, costs of, 206
Search phase, of problem solving,
251
Search warrants, use against
journalists, 371
Secretaries
and job fit criteria, 79
position power of, 149
Section 315, 380, 381, 384
Seditious libel, 329
Segmentation of markets, 211–12,
285, 287
Selective action, 70, 72
Selective attention, 69, 70, 71
Selective influence theory, 69–72,
277, 278
Selective perception, 70, 71–72

Selectivity of audience, 283–84
Self-actualization, 83
Self-confidence, 171–72, 175
Self-directed work teams, 49, 53,
55. *See also* Participative
management
Self-esteem, incentives for, 156
Self-reflective capability, 78
Self-regulatory capability, 78
Senators, privileged status in libel
cases, 341
Service marks, 363
SESAC, 207, 208
Seward, D., 168
Sex, and employment
discrimination, 414, 415,
416
Sexual harassment, 419–20, 425
Sexually oriented material, 357–58
Shadow power structure, 152, 153
Shaklee, H., 251
Shales, T., 34, 296
Share (ratings), 16, 296
Share, earnings per, 230–31
Shareholders, letter to, 220
Shareholders' equity, 223, 224
Sheffield, F., 277
Sherman, B., 62, 182
Shield laws, 370–71
Short-range planning, 264, 265
Short-term profits, emphasis on,
185, 231, 245
Sikes, Alfred, 20
Simmons Market Research Bureau,
211
Simon, H., 249, 250
Simon, P., 68
Simons, J., 115
Sinclair Broadcast Group, 19
Sissors, J., 284
Situation, effect on behavior, 82,
92–93
Sixth Amendment, 366
Slander, 328
Slocum, J. W., Jr., 79
Small-wins strategy, 113–14, 129
Smircich, L., 143
Smith, C., 196
Smith, J., 134
Smith, Kate, 277
Social cognitive theory, 77–78
Social responsibility, 212–14
Social skills, 2